A gift from NESFA.
If you enjoy this book,
visit us at www.nesfa.org.

Works of Art

Selected Short Fiction of
James Blish

edited by
James A. Mann

NESFA Press

Post Office Box 809
Framingham, MA 01701
www.nesfa.org/press
2007

© 2007 by the estate of James Blish

Dust jacket illustration copyright © 2007 by John Berkey
Dust jacket design copyright © 2007 by Kevin M. Riley
Introduction copyright © 2007 by Gregory Feeley

ALL RIGHTS RESERVED.
NO PART OF THIS BOOK MAY BE REPRODUCED IN ANY FORM OR BY ANY ELECTRONIC, MAGICAL OR MECHANICAL MEANS INCLUDING INFORMATION STORAGE AND RETRIEVAL WITHOUT PERMISSION IN WRITING FROM THE PUBLISHER, EXCEPT BY A REVIEWER, WHO MAY QUOTE BRIEF PASSAGES IN A REVIEW.

FIRST EDITION, Febuary 2008

ISBN-10: 1-886778-70-1
ISBN-13: 978-1-886778-70-2

Publication History

"A Work of Art," copyright © 1956 (as "Art Work"), by Columbia Publications, Inc., for *Science Fiction Stories*, July 1956

"Surface Tension," copyright © 1952 by Galaxy Publishing Corporation, for *Galaxy*, August 1952

"The Bridge," copyright © 1952 by Street and Smith for *Astounding Science Fiction*, February 1952

"Tomb Tapper," copyright © 1956 by Street and Smith for *Astounding Science Fiction*, July 1956

"The Box," copyright © 1949 by Standard Publications, for *Thrilling Wonder Stories*, April 1949

"The Oath," copyright © 1960 by Fantasy House Inc., for *Fantasy and Science Fiction*, October 1960

"Beep," copyright © 1954 by Galaxy Publishing Corporation, for *Galaxy*, February 1954

"FYI," copyright © 1953 by Ballantine Books, for *Star Science Fiction #2*.

"Common Time," copyright © 1953 by Columbia Publications, for *Science Fiction Quarterly*, August 1953

"There Shall Be No Darkness," copyright © 1950 by Standard Publications, for *Thrilling Wonder Stories*, April 1950

"A Dusk of Idols," copyright © 1961 by Ziff-Davis Publishing Company, for *Amazing Stories*, March 1961

"Earthman, Come Home," copyright © 1953 by Street and Smith for *Astounding Science Fiction*, November 1953

"How Beautiful with Banners," copyright © 1966 by Berkley Publishing Corporation, for *Orbit #1*

"This Earth of Hours," copyright © 1959 by Fantasy House Inc., for *Fantasy and Science Fiction*, June 1959

"Testament of Andros," copyright © 1953 by Columbia Publications, for *Future Science Fiction,* January 1953

"A Style in Treason," copyright © 1970 by Universal Publishing and Distributing Corporation, for *Galaxy,* June 1970. An earlier, shorter version appeared in the March 1966 issue of *Impulse* under the title "A Hero's Life"

"A Case of Conscience," copyright © 1953 for *If,* September 1953

"Making Waves," copyright © 1970, included in *More Issues at Hand.*

Scenario: The Edefice and *Two Brands for the Buring* copyright © 2007 by the estate of James Blish.

James Blish and the Beginning of Interpretation copyright © 2007 by Gregory Feeley

Dust jacket art, "Fire in the Hole," copyright 2007 © by John Berkey

Contents

James Blish and the Beginning of Interpretation
   by Gregory Feeley 9
A Work of Art 23
Surface Tension 39
The Bridge 101
Tomb Tapper 129
The Box 151
The Oath 171
Beep 189
FYI 225
Common Time 233
There Shall Be No Darkness 255
A Dusk of Idols 291
Earthman, Come Home 313
How Beautiful with Banners 351
This Earth of Hours 361
Testament of Andros 383
A Style in Treason 403
A Case of Conscience 435
Making Waves 493
Two Poems 517

Works of Art

Introduction:
James Blish and the Beginning of Interpretation

by Gregory Feeley

James Blish was not naturally a writer of short fiction, although he took up the form early and never abandoned it. Nor was he naturally a writer of novels, though like many of his contemporaries he concentrated his efforts at that length after it became, by the mid-1950s, both the most remunerative form of science fiction and a promising artistic frontier. An innovator by temperament and a commercial writer by necessity, Blish published short fiction, novels, and essays for thirty-five years, but he never seemed at ease with any of these forms in the way that his colleagues Damon Knight, Frederik Pohl, and Isaac Asimov respectively did. Uncomfortable almost by nature, Blish was in some ways not naturally a science fiction writer, although he wrote it all of his life and produced virtually all his best work within its compass.

Blish's best short fiction seems always in the process of becoming something else: a longer story, the seed for a novel, a statement of theme upon which he would later produce variations. The practice of developing stories into series, or expanding novellas into novels, became common in science fiction during Blish's early career (and remains so today), and Blish's habit of revisiting themes—plus his need to maximize the income from his writing—ensured that he grew adept at it. But Blish carried this practice far beyond considerations of financial expediency. Stories expanded into slightly longer stories (such as "A Hero's Life") or revised—before or after publication—into a different genre (such as *The Frozen Year* and "There Shall Be No Darkness") attest to an abiding urge to revisit earlier matchings of subject to form. Structure and dimension were important to Blish—who was at once theorist and technician—but as much as he admired the modernist ideal of a work's singular nature being realized in a unique literary form, his own SF tended to press against the boundaries of conventional fiction, producing a sense of tension rather than liberation. Short stories that comprise multiple chapters, novels that pair up to form one volume of a trilogy, or shift at their climax from prose into verse drama: Blish's fictions, however polished and assured, can seem remarkably uneasy in their skin.

One characteristic of modernism was its combination of plenitude and fragmentation: works of great scale—long novels, long poems—that are assembled out of disparate elements. Ezra Pound once claimed that a magnet could bring "order and vitality and thence beauty into a plate of iron filings," a remark Blish (who was sufficiently familiar with Pound's theoretical writings to adopt for himself the pseudonym Pound once used to write music criticism) would have known. That the individual units would not be actually touching each other, making the work seamless only in the pattern it creates (Pound's Canto 74 evokes the image of a "rose in the steel dust"), was important to the Modernists, who affirmed the unity of such works as "The Waste Land" and "Hugh Selwyn Mauberley"; that the individual units could be as mundane as an iron filing was important to Blish, who felt constantly the financial (and perhaps other) pressures that kept him from creating work from what he seemed to regard as nobler material.

Discontinuity is everywhere in Blish's work, which often comprises shards that achieve order, vitality, and beauty from their ordering and juxtaposition. The stories that begin or end with unfinished sentences (*The Night Shapes*; "We All Die Naked") are an obvious example; the stark fragmentation of "Testament of Andros" displays it at its most unremitting. Each section of *The Seedling Stars* presents a complete break with the setting and characters of the previous one; the opening and closing sentences of "A Work of Art" evoke images of radical disjuncture. "Common Time" dramatizes a "sine-curve time variation" that, while described as "a situation of continuous change," is chopped into tiny intervals marked by a timepiece's *pock*; interstellar travel, which offers a vision of transcendent communion "with all of love," proves to be possible only through the intervention of a rupture called the "pseudo-death."

What Joanna Russ calls "a concern with the conditions of being, not with particular acts or situations"[1] (which she associates with R.D. Laing's concept of "ontological insecurity") pervades Blish's fiction. Russ was writing about H. P. Lovecraft, not a writer one normally associates with Blish (although the young Blish admired Lovecraft, as does Russ).

Lovecraft's fiction is widely recognized as reflecting the distortions of a profoundly disturbed psyche, which cannot be said of Blish's. But his discomfort with form—what John Clute calls Blish's "formidable but strangely ill-at-ease range[2]" and David Ketterer the "tortured *mise en abîme*" produced by his lifelong impulse to dramatize the experience of "conceptual breakthrough"[3]—finds an echo in the insecurity of existential form, the continual undermining of continuity by gaps and fragmentation, that characterizes Blish's work.

A fragment is an unfinished something surrounded by nothing; a gap—the nothing between expanses of something—is the other aspect of discontinuity. Gaps and intermittency also appear through Blish's fiction, in overt and disguised form: "A Style in Treason" opens with a ship emerging from the "interstitium" that evidently underlies normal space, while the universe in the *Cities in Flight* novels is brought to an end by "a break or discontinuity right in the middle of the span of existence," which is named the Ginnangu-Gap. The mysterious force creating the lethal dome in "The Box" can exist only because "the intermittence [of its nature] supplies some of the necessary harmonics" and the unnatural nature of the eponymous structure in "The Bridge" owes to the fact that "it doesn't span a real gap."

To establish a connection between two somethings separated by a nothing is creative—think of the iron filings—and sometimes, in Blish's fiction, heroic; but an apparent connection that terminates in nothingness provokes tremendous anxiety. The world of Lithia in "A Case of Conscience" is an "immense structure of reason" that "does not seem to rest on anything," while its universe finally comprises "nothings moving no-place through no-time." The anguish this realization produces in the novel's two most thoughtful characters sees its apotheosis in *Black Easter*, where a physicist is destroyed by being shown "a vision and understanding of that great and ultimate Nothingness which lurks behind those signs he calls matter and energy." Signs must point to something, even if only to fragments, and structures require foundations.

Mention fragmentation in the context of Modernism, of course, and the quotation that comes to mind is Eliot's "fragments I have shored against my ruin," but Blish preferred Pound to Eliot, and Pound's declaration that "Energy creates pattern" and "Emotion is an organizer of form" is surely the apposite one. We know from Blish's own testimony that "Testament of Andros" is intended to portray "the successive stages in the disintegration of a paranoid schizophrenic," but we do not require this gloss to perceive the emotional undertow that sweeps its unnamed subject to annihilation. For all its luridness, pulp science fiction presented itself as a resolutely rationalist enterprise; yet despite Blish's apparent obedience to its strictures and the cerebral nature of his fiction (his third professionally published story was entitled "Citadel of Thought"), his work is everywhere charged with emotion. The barely repressed outbursts that seethe beneath the surface in "On the Walls of the Lodge," "Testament of Andros," "Common Time" (where repressing instinctual response is crucial to survival) and "How Beautiful with Banners" need only be contrasted with the more conventional (and coolly composed) "Earthman, Come Home" and "Beep" for confirmation of the importance Pound's dictum held for Blish: the more experimental his fiction, the more driven it is by submerged emotion.

"Submerged emotion" is present in virtually all of Blish's stories, as their titles ("Sunken Universe," "Surface Tension," *The Frozen Year*) variously suggest. In "How Beautiful with Banners," the protagonist's "good many suppressed impulses" is horrendously personified by the calamity that befalls her (Wilbur Daniel Steele's once-famous story "How Beautiful with Shoes," the source of Blish's title, also dealt with an isolated woman sundered from her emotional life who meets with a violent encounter). "Tomb Tapper" dramatizes its protagonist's shocked discovery of vivid emotions radiating from the cockpit of a wrecked rocket lodged deep within a mountain. Among other things, the story can be read as a powerful allegory of a probe attempting to penetrate the obdurate barrier of a human skull (the mountain) to communicate with the injured but still-living mind within. This strange image recurs at numerous points in Blish's fiction. "The Box" was presumably so titled because the immense dome that closes off New York City could be likened to a coffin; but the city suffering beneath the dome seems (Blish's imagery tells us) to be a human mind cut off from contact with the outside world, presumably—see the description of severed subway tunnels—through some vascular accident.

Introduction

The peculiar somatics of much of Blish's fiction has long been evident to some readers, though Blish himself seemed only fitfully aware of it. *Telecast*, an unfinished novel he worked on through the late 1940s and, evidently, in the early 1960s ("On the Walls of the Lodge" is a fragment of it edited and partly reworked by Virginia Kidd), was devised as the subjective experience of a catatonic schizophrenic, whose consciousness is "cycling helplessly through all those processes/areas of the brain where the somatic functions are represented or operated."[4] The strange topography of the published story reflects these regions of the brain, with the cloverleaf overpass in which the protagonist gets lost representing the mental analogues for the structure of the inner ear. On the other hand, Blish was not conscious of the gestation and birth imagery that runs through the early "Solar Plexus" as well as "Common Time" until Damon Knight pointed it out in a celebrated essay, and while he deliberately worked these elements into "How Beautiful with Banners," they are present in other works as well.

"A Dusk of Idols" has an unusually spare narrative; most of the story is occupied by the protagonist moving alone through a succession of strange landscapes. The story holds the reader's interest because these landscapes (most of them underground) are, like the uterine spaceship environment in "Solar Plexus" or the "twin radioceles" in "Common Time," figurative representations of an intimate system of the human body. The protagonist descends a deep vertical shaft (the esophagus) to be swept along a dark, refuse-choked river (whose intestinal nature is unmistakable) and finally be expelled into a great swirling basin. Since the planet is a pestilential death house and the protagonist intent on remaking it, the metaphor can be read as an attempt by the planet (significantly named Chandala) to digest him. More immediately, of course, it personifies the theme of unhygienic filth in the most starkly immediate manner.

If Blish's fiction offers numerous images of the mind moving through the body, the repeated ways in which Blish would represent human *nous* as a domed structure filled with dense purposeful activity (most obviously in *Cities in Flight*, but also in "The Shipwrecked Hotel," "Citadel of Thought,"[5] and "The City that Was the World") suggests a deep preoccupation with the mind in isolation. The probe in "Tomb Tapper" makes true contact with its subject just as she dies, as the probe employed in "A Style of Treason" (different in nature, but employing identical imagery) fails to reach the true mind beneath the distractions thrown over it. The image—the probe "drove directly down into his subconscious with the resistless unconcern of a spike penetrating a toy balloon"—recurs throughout Blish's work, most vividly in *The Day after Judgment*, where a discussion of angels, demons, and immortal souls considered as "unified fields" subject to laws of matter and energy leads to the declaration that a determined physical assault could "burst into such a closed system like a railroad spike going through an auto tire." One force that holds a sphere intact is, of course, surface tension, and the image of a splinter rupturing a sphere containing human intelligence appears as early as "Sunken Universe," the 1942 story that was eventually subsumed into the "Surface Tension" section of *The Seedling Stars*.

Seeds are spheroids that also get punctured—from within, and so produce life. Spherical structures—domes, bubbles, shells—are punctured from the outside over and over in Blish's fiction, usually resulting in their destruction. In "FYI," the universe is likened to a four-dimensional "pseudosphere" that may be "opened into positive curvature," saving humanity from self-destruction. This hope is no sooner expressed than it is called crucially into question, for the aliens "ready to open up our pseudospherical egg and spill us out into an inconceivably vaster universe" may be acting only on behalf of some other, unknown species. (Significantly, it is at this point that the transformation is expressed in terms of breakage.)

The hubristic account of destroying souls in *The Day after Judgment* concludes with a technocrat rapturously characterizing it as "the bliss of complete extinction," and there is no question that metaphysical annihilation held a fascination for Blish that was not entirely unattractive. Entities and systems wink in and out of existence in Blish's work—it is *The Triumph of Time*, which ends with the destruction of the universe, that contains a chapter entitled "The Nursery of Time"—and as Damon Knight noted in 1957, the conception and birth imagery that runs through "Common Time" can also be read as death imagery. When Blish set about to recapitulate this pattern in "How Beautiful with Banners," he devised a plot that, unsurprisingly, combined both.

Although Blish's style grew more allusive, elliptical, and compressed over the years, even his earliest, awkwardly jocose prose can show surprising anticipations of his later work. Crude as it is, the opening sentence of the 1941 "Citadel of Thought" ("When Dan Lothar's shattered *Ganymedian* dropped into the ammoniac mists of Neptune, turning slowly and trailing a wraith-like, ephemeral fan of incandescent gas, there was nothing to show the watching police cruiser that death was not waiting to enfold it below") unmistakably foreshadows the beautiful opening line of "A Style in Treason" ("The *Karas*, a fragile transship—she was really little more than a ferry, just barely meriting a name—came fluttering out of the interstitium into the Flos Campi system a day late in a ball of rainbows, trailing behind her two gaudy contrails of false photons, like a moth unable to free herself of her cocoon") a quarter century later. The motifs of frailty, irruption, dispersal, and entanglement combined in an image of a spaceship's passage held some significance for the young Blish to which he was not able to give adequate expression; and remained intact, like undischarged potential, for him eventually to take up once more.

Originally entitled "A Hero's Life" when it was first published in shorter form in 1966, the story is a skein of complex allusions, most immediately to Richard Strauss's tone poem *Ein Heldenleben* ("A Hero's Life"), whose structure it closely follows. Darker and more ironic even than Strauss's work, Blish's novella gives us a professional traitor for a hero and a prostitute as his lover, and the protagonist's *Friedenswerke* (works for peace) here follow defeat rather than victory on the battlefield. The *Friedenswerke* section of the tone poem contains quotations from early works by Strauss, and Blish follows that as well, as the "voices" that surge up from the protagonist's subconscious are quotations from his own oeuvre. But Strauss's sixth and final section, *Des Helden Weltflucht und Vollendung* (The Hero's Retreat from the World and Consummation) is in Blish's version much more equivocal: the protagonist has indeed created a work for peace and is now to retreat from the world, but his worldly success brings moral self-reproach and the taste of ashes. While Strauss's "consummation" is a fanfare that recalls an earlier musical triumph, Blish's bleak concluding line, "While he was waiting, perhaps he could learn to play the sareh," evokes the motif of music (otherwise absent from the novella) from a vantage of both world-weariness and ignorance.

It would be easy to declare that "A Style in Treason" is "based upon" *Ein Heldenleben* or "is" a retelling of Strauss's tone poem, just as *Ulysses* is commonly said to be based upon the *Odyssey*. In fact, Joyce's structural imitation of Homer is more formal than substantial; Harold Bloom has observed that "*Ulysses* has more to do with

Hamlet than with the *Odyssey*,"[6] and the Homeric parallels traced by early commentators have been of little interest to subsequent criticism. Blish set up a series of correspondences between his story and Strauss's, but—rather as Joyce once remarked that *Ulysses*' interior monologue was simply a bridge he constructed to march his episodes across—his actual story proves to lie somewhere else.

In its recounting of how an assured, worldly man travels to a backward planet and presents it, despite resistance, with an entree into modern civilization only to discover the limits of his own wisdom, Blish is retelling "That Share of Glory" by C.M. Kornbluth. Like his friend and colleague, Kornbluth began publishing science fiction in his teens, but took more than a decade—until the early fifties—to begin producing memorable work. His celebrated novelette is flush with the confident knowingness of mid-century science fiction (especially that published by John W. Campbell), where characters can declare, "We concern ourselves with the basic patterns of a people's behavior, not the day-to-day expression of the patterns" without a hint of irony, and a venerable text—here, Machiavelli's "The Prince"—is never consulted without its yielding useful wisdom.

Blish's retelling of this story darkens its counsel at every turn. His protagonist is old and perhaps superannuated rather than young and untested; his exemplary text—by "Lord Gro," venerated like Machiavelli but never read uncritically (he is named after the complex and tormented character in Eddison's *The Worm Ouroboros*, a calculating traitor who is nonetheless "motivated by an entirely unselfish, aesthetic sense of the nobility of failure and the inevitability of decay"[7])—emphasizes doubt and uncertainty; a passing remark about a planet possessing "a cultural pattern which overrides all local variations," which strongly echoes the assertion in Kornbluth's story, is made only to be immediately questioned.

The story's numerous overt allusions—including some to both Eliot and Pound, who are remembered in its far future as a composite figure, wittily called "Ezra-Tse"—do not extend to any science fiction writer; but Kornbluth's presence is as evident as that of Jack Vance, whose colorful exoticism can be found in passing details such as the mysterious "Green Exarch." The story's true center, however, lies not in Blish's mordant revision of Kornbluth, still less his pastiche of Strauss; but in Blish's unsparing depiction of himself. Simon de Kuyl is the first of Blish's late self-portraits: like Theron Ware in *Black*

Easter, Alex in "We All Die Naked," and John Hillary Dane in the published sections of his unfinished novel *King Log*, he recognizes his essential coldness as a profound moral disfigurement.

"How Beautiful with Banners" grimly subverts the imagery of Pound's "A Virginal" (though it is a different Pound poem, "Hugh Selwyn Mauberley," that is quoted at its end) and may seem, in its story of a "frigid" woman scientist's comeuppance, routinely sexist. But its protagonist's resemblance to Blish's other characters is indisputable, and her failure to others is, if anything, less culpable. Blish may have set about deliberately to produce the *forêt de symboles* he had unconsciously created in earlier stories, and he may have played with Pound's use of "cloak" and "sheath," but "How Beautiful With Banners," like "A Style in Treason," originated in meditation upon his own self.

The Blish protagonist is a profoundly solitary figure—this characteristic became steadily more pronounced over time—compelled by circumstances into contemplation of the relationship between the self and the universe; but he is not a solipsist. The physical world exists, and while genuine communion between other *nous* may be possible (as, briefly and uncertainly, in "Common Time"), the entity most frequently explored is the text. Records, written or broadcast, abound in Blish's fiction from 1952 on, from the engraved plates in "Surface Tension" and the apocalyptic Scripture in "Testament of Andros" to the more problematic texts of the later stories—the shriek of seemingly undifferentiated noise in "Beep" or the misread scrap of verse in "The Oath"—and the stories turn increasingly on their deciphering and comprehension.

A commercial genre whose early magazine history presented an appeal to scientifically-minded young men, and which turned increasingly after the War to imagining the astonishing transformations promised (or threatened) by technology, science fiction was markedly ingenuous toward the nature of texts. Like the tomb inscriptions and ransom letters of other genres, a written text invariably contained vital information, whose unambiguous meaning would become clear with sufficient study. Whether cited as an authoritative source within the fictional world (like Asimov's *Handbook of Robotics* or the Machiavelli of "That Share of Glory"), a hitherto unknown document whose significance must be puzzled out (as in Bester's "Star Light, Star Bright"), or a text that is produced in the course of the story's action (as in John W. Campbell's "Twilight" or Clifford D. Simak's "Huddling Place"), the texts that appear in SF stories between the mid-thirties and the mid-fifties were essentially unproblematic. Even those that are malign (such as the bleating advertisements in Pohl and Kornbluth's *The Space Merchants*) or ignorant (such as the news story filed by the narrator at the beginning of Kornbluth's "Gomez") are *fathomable*: we readily understand how, and why, their representations differ from reality. Even sophisticated genre writers—as Bester, Kornbluth, and Pohl certainly were—treated texts as artifacts that could invariably *be read*, their meaning *unequivocally established*, and this meaning prove *applicable in the real world*.

Blish knew better than this. A lifelong reader of *Finnegans Wake* (in which numerous problematic texts are argued over and dubiously interpreted) and the fragments of Kafka (where no question of interpretation regarding motives or meaning is ever satisfactorily resolved), Blish brought to his work a temperamental skepticism that increasingly called all three propositions into question. The missing plate in "Surface Tension" may be recovered and perhaps the text's mysteries dispelled (though a careful reading suggests otherwise[8]), and the competing testimonies in "Testament of Andros" may yield—to the reader, if not any of its characters—a single meaning; but Garrard of "Common Time" can only yearn to make sense of the beademungen's words, and the intercepted text of "FYI" yields only a plausible interpretation, which may be fatally compromised by the interpreters' wishfulness.

For Blish's predecessors and early contemporaries, texts were either straightforward repositories of knowledge or puzzles to be (successfully) deciphered. For Blish after 1953, exploring a text becomes a matter of *interpretation*, an undertaking that is inescapably subjective and provisional. Even the Bridge in "The Bridge" is a kind of text (note how Blish actually describes its nature in terms of a propagating wordstring), and how one responds to it—whether it seems "good" or "bad"—proves a function not of one's skills in observation, but of one's personal psychology.

This represents the first appearance of interpretation in science fiction. (Even stories that turned on a textual misreading, such as Eric Frank Russell's "Allamagoosa," left their true meaning clear to the reader.) The mordant Cyril Kornbluth wrote numerous stories in which written documents are suppressed, willfully distorted, or misunderstood—look at "The Little Black Bag" or "Theory of

Rocketry"—but their essential comprehensibility is always affirmed. The text that can only be interpreted—that compels an act which yields no final answers and denies science fiction's faith in objective inquiry—was, in genre SF, unthinkable before Blish.

"Beep," a seemingly upbeat story whose philosophical implications are profoundly disheartening—"the bitterest of all pills," as one character remarks—culminates in an image of an utterly deterministic universe, in which "the consciousness of the observer is just along for the ride through time, and can't alter the events—though it can comment, explain, invent." This qualification is important, as the speaker immediately adds, "That's fortunate, for none of us could stand going through motions which were truly free of what we think of as personal significances." That commentary and explanation are "personal significances" capable of reconciling humankind with an otherwise intolerable existence is not a sentiment one would expect of a mid-century science fiction writer, but it is entirely characteristic of James Blish, who saw the universe not as something to comprehend and categorize, but to interpret.

At once a literary modernist and a writer of genre science fiction, Blish adhered to the modernist aesthetic of a deeply personal vision achieved in singular form, as well as the narrative conventions of the pulp magazines, while straining against—in some ways subverting—both. One reason why his short fiction continues to be read nearly forty years after the last of it was published is surely this ontological flickering, which is more unsettling and perhaps intriguing than either the modernist conviction of a marred and fragmented world or the pulp SF confidence in a unified, triumphalist one. Garrard, the protagonist of "Common Time," supposes that he underwent the pseudo-death because of a trait of the human mind—its supposed inability to survive long without external stimuli—posited by psychoanalytic theorists of the 1940s. Readers may find this uncompelling today (as, interestingly, did Garrard's interlocutor, who ironically replies, "Unquote: Harry Stack Sullivan"), but the story remains deeply engaging for its depiction of what Garrard calls "the essential *I*" dissolving under relativistic stresses and then reforming in radically altered conditions; and for the characters' subsequent efforts to *interpret* these, making a provisional and subjective sense of phenomena too complex to fully comprehend. This grappling with essentials—whether cosmological or psychological—extends through every element of Blish's stories, from their theme and structural principles to the level of metaphor, and contributes significantly to their fascination.

Notes

1. In Smith, Curtis C., *Twentieth-Century Science-Fiction Writers*, second edition (Chicago: St. James Press), 1986, 463.

2. Clute, John. *Strokes: Essays and Reviews 1966-1986* (Seattle: Serconia Press), 1988, 90.

3. Ketterer, 319.

4. From a letter Blish wrote in 1970. Various accounts of the story by Blish and Kidd are quoted in David Ketterer's *Imprisoned in a Tesseract: The Life and Work of James Blish* (Kent: Kent State University Press), 1987, 140-45.

5. David Ketterer notes how the "citadel of thought" is also the protagonist's brain case. *Ibid.*, 35.

6. Bloom, Harold. *The Western Canon: The Books and School of the Ages* (New York: Harcourt Brace), 1994, 388.

7. This concise and apposite description is from the Wikipedia entry on *The Worm Ouroboros*, http://en.wikipedia.org/wiki/The_Worm_Ouroboros. Accessed June 25, 2007.

8. The second plate is recovered, but the first remains lost. See Gregory Feeley, "Cages of Conscience from Seedling Novels: The Development of Blish's Novels." *Foundation*, no 24 (February 1982): 59-68.

A Work of Art

Instantly, he remembered dying. He remembered it, however, as if at two removes—as though he were remembering a memory, rather than an actual event; as though he himself had not really been there when he died.

Yet the memory was all from his own point of view, not that of some detached and disembodied observer which might have been his soul. He had been most conscious of the rasping, unevenly drawn movements of the air in his chest. Blurring rapidly, the doctor's face had bent over him, loomed, come closer, and then had vanished as the doctor's head passed below his cone of vision, turned sideways to listen to his lungs.

It had become rapidly darker, and then, only then, had he realized that these were to be his last minutes. He had tried dutifully to say Pauline's name, but his memory contained no record of the sound—only of the rattling breath, and of the film of sootiness thickening in the air, blotting out everything for an instant.

Only an instant, and then the memory was over. The room was bright again, and the ceiling, he noticed with wonder, had turned a soft green. The doctor's head lifted again and looked down at him.

It was a different doctor. This one was a far younger man, with an ascetic face and gleaming, almost fey eyes. There was no doubt about it. One of the last conscious thoughts he had had was that of gratitude that the attending physician, there at the end, had not been the one who secretly hated him for his one-time associations with the Nazi hierarchy. The attending doctor, instead, had worn an expression amusingly proper for that of a Swiss expert called to the deathbed of an eminent man: a mixture of worry at the prospect of losing so eminent a patient, and complacency at the thought that, at the old man's age, nobody could blame this doctor if he died. At 85, pneumonia is a serious matter, with or without penicillin.

"You're all right now," the new doctor said, freeing his patient's head of a whole series of little silver rods which had been clinging to it by a sort of network cap. "Rest a minute and try to be calm. Do you know your name?"

He drew a cautious breath. There seemed to be nothing at all the matter with his lungs now; indeed, he felt positively healthy. "Certainly," he said, a little nettled. "Do you know yours?"

The doctor smiled crookedly. "You're in character, it appears," he said. "My name is Barkun Kris; I am a mind sculptor. Yours?"

"Richard Strauss."

"Very good," Dr. Kris said, and turned away. Strauss, however, had already been diverted by a new singularity. *Strauss* is a word as well as a name in German; it has many meanings—an ostrich, a bouquet; von Wolzogen had had a high old time working all the possible puns into the libretto of *Feuersnot*. And it happened to be the first German word to be spoken either by himself or by Dr. Kris since that twice-removed moment of death. The language was not French or Italian, either. It was most like English, but not the English Strauss knew; nevertheless, he was having no trouble speaking it and even thinking in it.

Well, he thought, *I'll be able to conduct* The Love of Danae *after all. It isn't every composer who can premiere his own opera posthumously.* Still, there was something queer about all this—the queerest part of all being that conviction, which would not go away, that he had actually been dead for just a short time. Of course medicine was making great strides, but . . .

"Explain all this," he said, lifting himself to one elbow. The bed was different, too, and not nearly as comfortable as the one in which he had died. As for the room, it looked more like a dynamo shed than a sickroom. Had modern medicine taken to reviving its corpses on the floor of the Siemanns-Schukert plant?

"In a moment," Dr. Kris said. He finished rolling some machine back into what Strauss impatiently supposed to be its place, and crossed to the pallet. "Now. There are many things you'll have to take for granted without attempting to understand them, Dr. Strauss. Not everything in the world today is explicable in terms of your assumptions. Please bear that in mind."

"Very well. Proceed."

"The date," Dr. Kris said, "is 2161 by your calendar— or, in other words, it is now two hundred and twelve years after your death. Naturally, you'll realize that by this time nothing remains of your body but the bones. The body you have now was volunteered for your use. Before you look into a mirror to see what it's like, remember that its physical difference from the one you were used to is all in your favor. It's in perfect health, not unpleasant for other people to look at, and its physiological age is about fifty."

A miracle? No, not in this new age, surely. It was simply a work of science. But what a science! This was Nietzsche's eternal recurrence and the immortality of the superman combined into one.

"And where is this?" the composer said.

"In Port York, part of the State of Manhattan, in the United States. You will find the country less changed in some respects than I imagine you anticipate. Other changes, of course, will seem radical to you; but it's hard for me to predict which ones will strike you that way. A certain resilience on your part will bear cultivating."

"I understand," Strauss said, sitting up. "One question, please; is it still possible for a composer to make a living in this century?"

"Indeed it is," Dr. Kris said, smiling. "As we expect you to do. It is one of the purposes for which we've—brought you back."

"I gather, then," Strauss said somewhat dryly, "that there is still a demand for my music. The critics in the old days—"

"That's not quite how it is," Dr. Kris said. "I understand some of your work is still played, but frankly I know very little about your current status. My interest is rather—"

A door opened somewhere, and another man came in. He was older and more ponderous than Kris and had a certain air of academicism; but he too was wearing the oddly tailored surgeon's gown, and looked upon Kris's patient with the glowing eyes of an artist.

"A success, Kris?" he said. "Congratulations."

"They're not in order yet," Dr. Kris said. "The final proof is what counts. Dr. Strauss, if you feel strong enough, Dr. Seirds and I would like to ask you some questions. We'd like to make sure your memory is clear."

"Certainly. Go ahead."

"According to our records," Kris said, "you once knew a man whose initials were RKL; this was while you were conducting at the Vienna *Staatsoper.*" He made the double "a" at least twice too long, as though German were a dead language he was striving to pronounce in some "classical" accent. "What was his name, and who was he?"

"That would be Kurt List—his first name was Richard, but he didn't use it. He was assistant stage manager."

The two doctors looked at each other. "Why did you offer to write a new overture to *The Woman Without a Shadow,* and give the manuscript to the City of Vienna?"

"So I wouldn't have to pay the garbage removal tax on the Maria Theresa villa they had given me."

"In the back yard of your house at Garmisch-Partenkirchen there was a tombstone. What was written on it?"

Strauss frowned. That was a question he would be happy to be unable to answer. If one is to play childish jokes upon oneself, it's best not to carve them in stone, and put the carving where you can't help seeing it every time you go out to tinker with the Mercedes. "It says," he replied wearily, *"Sacred to the memory of Guntram, Minnesinger, slain in a horrible way by his father's own symphony orchestra."*

"When was *Guntram* premiered?"

"In—let me see—1894, I believe."

"Where?"

"In Weimar."

"Who was the leading lady?"

"Pauline de Ahna."

"What happened to her afterward?"

"I married her. Is she . . ." Strauss began anxiously.

"No," Dr. Kris said. "I'm sorry, but we lack the data to reconstruct more or less ordinary people."

The composer sighed. He did not know whether to be worried or not. He had loved Pauline, to be sure; on the other hand, it would be pleasant to be able to live the new life without being forced to take off one's shoes every time one entered the house, so as not to scratch the polished hardwood floors. And also pleasant, perhaps, to have two o'clock in the afternoon come by without hearing Pauline's everlasting, *"Richard—jetzt komponiert!"*

"Next question," he said.

For reasons which Strauss did not understand, but was content to take for granted, he was separated from Drs. Kris and Seirds as soon as both were satisfied that the composer's memory was reliable and his health stable. His estate, he was given to understand, had long since been broken up—a sorry end for what had been one of the principal fortunes of Europe—but he was given sufficient money to set up lodgings and resume an active life. He was provided, too, with introductions which proved valuable.

It took longer than he had expected to adjust to the changes that had taken place in music alone. Music was, he quickly began to suspect, a dying art, which would soon have a status not much above that held by flower arranging back in what he thought of as his own century. Certainly it couldn't be denied that the trend toward fragmentation, already visible back in his own time, had proceeded almost to completion in 2161.

He paid no more attention to American popular tunes than he had bothered to pay in his previous life. Yet it was evident that their assembly-line production methods— all the ballad composers openly used a slide-rule-like device called a Hit Machine—now had their counterparts almost throughout serious music.

The conservatives these days, for instance, were the twelve-tone composers—always, in Strauss's opinions, a dryly mechanical lot, but never more so than now. Their gods—Berg, Schoenberg, von Webern—were looked upon by the concert-going public as great masters, on the abstruse side perhaps, but as worthy of reverence as any of the Three B's.

There was one wing of the conservatives, however, which had gone the twelve-tone procedure one better. These men composed what was called "stochastic music," put together by choosing each individual note by consultation with tables of random numbers. Their bible, their basic text, was a volume called *Operational Aesthetics,* which in turn derived from a discipline called information theory; and not one word of it seemed to touch upon any of the techniques and customs of composition which Strauss knew. The ideal of this group was to produce music which would be "universal"—that is, wholly devoid of any trace of the composer's individuality, wholly a musical expression of the universal Laws of Chance. The Laws of Chance seemed to have a style of their own, all right; but to Strauss it seemed the style of an idiot child being taught to hammer a flat piano, to keep him from getting into trouble.

By far the largest body of work being produced, however, fell into a category misleadingly called "science-music." The term reflected nothing but the titles of the works, which dealt with space flight, time travel, and other subjects of a romantic or an unlikely nature. There was nothing in the least scientific about the music, which consisted of a melange of cliches and imitations of natural sounds, in which Strauss was horrified to see his own time-distorted and diluted image.

The most popular form of science-music was a nine-minute composition called a concerto, though it bore no resemblance at all to the classical concerto form; it was instead a sort of free rhapsody after Rachmaninoff—long after. A typical one—"Song of Deep Space" it was called, by somebody named H. Valerion Krafft—began with a loud assault on the tam-tam, after which all the strings rushed up the scale in unison, followed at a respectful distance by the harp and one clarinet in parallel 6/4's. At the top of the scale cymbals were bashed together, *forte possibile,* and the whole orchestra launched itself into a major-minor, wailing sort of melody; the whole orchestra, that is, except for the French horns, which were plodding back down the scale again in what was evidently supposed to be a countermelody. The second phrase of the theme was picked up by a solo trumpet with a suggestion of tremolo; the orchestra died back to its roots to await the next cloudburst, and at this point—as any four-year-old could have predicted—the piano entered with the second theme.

Behind the orchestra stood a group of thirty women, ready to come in with a wordless chorus intended to suggest the eeriness of Deep Space—but at this point, too, Strauss had already learned to get up and leave. After a few such experiences he could also count upon meeting in the lobby Sindi Noniss, the agent to whom Dr. Kris had introduced him, and who was handling the reborn composer's output—what there was of it thus far. Sindi had come to expect these walkouts on the part of his client, and patiently awaited them, standing beneath a bust of Gian Carlo–Menotti; but he liked them less and less, and lately had been greeting them by turning alternately red and white like a totipotent barber pole.

"You shouldn't have done it," he burst out after the Krafft incident. "You can't just walk out on a new Krafft composition. The man's the president of the Interplanetary Society for Contemporary Music. How am I ever going to persuade them that you're a contemporary if you keep snubbing them?"

"What does it matter?" Strauss said. "They don't know me by sight."

"You're wrong; they know you very well, and they're watching every move you make. You're the first major composer the mind sculptors ever tackled, and the ISCM would be glad to turn you back with a rejection slip."

"Why?"

"Oh," said Sindi, "there are lots of reasons. The sculptors are snobs; so are the ISCM boys. Each of them wants to prove to the other that their own art is the king of them all. And then there's the competition; it would be easier to flunk you than to let you into the market. I really think you'd better go back in. I could make up some excuse—"

"No," Strauss said shortly. "I have work to do."

"But that's just the point, Richard. How are we going to get an opera produced without the ISCM? It isn't as though you wrote theremin solos, or something that didn't cost so—"

"I have work to do," he said, and left.

And he did: work which absorbed him as had no other project during the last thirty years of his former life. He had scarcely touched pen to music paper—both had been astonishingly hard to find—when he realized that nothing in his long career had provided him with touchstones by which to judge what music he should write *now*.

The old tricks came swarming back by the thousands, to be sure: the sudden, unexpected key changes at the crest of a melody; the interval stretching; the piling of divided strings, playing in the high harmonics, upon the already tottering top of a climax; the scurry and bustle as phrases were passed like lightning from one choir of the orchestra to another; the flashing runs in the brass, the chuckling in the clarinets, the snarling mixtures of colors to emphasize dramatic tension—all of them.

But none of them satisfied him now. He had been content with them for most of a lifetime, and had made them do an astonishing amount of work. But now it was time to strike out afresh. Some of the tricks, indeed, actively repelled him: where had he gotten the notion, clung to for decades, that violins screaming out in unison somewhere in the stratosphere was a sound interesting enough to be worth repeating inside a single composition, let alone in all of them?

And nobody, he reflected contentedly, ever approached such a new beginning better equipped. In addition to the past lying available in his memory, he had always had a technical armamentarium second to none; even the hostile critics had granted him that. Now that he was, in a sense, composing his first opera—his first after fifteen of them!—he had every opportunity to make it a masterpiece.

And every such intention.

* * *

There were, of course, many minor distractions. One of them was that search for old-fashioned score paper, and a pen and ink with which to write on it. Very few of the modern composers, it developed, wrote their music at all. A large bloc of them used tape, patching together snippets of tone and sound snipped from other tapes, superimposing one tape on another, and varying the results by twirling an elaborate array of knobs this way or that. Almost all the composers of 3-V scores, on the other hand, wrote on the sound track itself, rapidly scribbling jagged wiggly lines which, when passed through a photocell-audio circuit, produced a noise reasonably like an orchestra playing music, overtones and all.

The last-ditch conservatives who still wrote notes on paper, did so with the aid of a musical typewriter. The device, Strauss had to admit, seemed perfected at last; it had manuals and stops like an organ, but it was not much more than twice as large as a standard letter-writing typewriter, and produced a neat page. But he was satisfied with his own spidery, highly-legible manuscript and refused to abandon it, badly though the one pen nib he had been able to buy coarsened it. It helped to tie him to his past.

Joining the ISCM had also caused him some bad moments, even after Sindi had worked him around the political road blocks. The Society man who examined his qualifications as a member had run through the questions with no more interest than might have been shown by a veterinarian examining his four thousandth sick calf.

"Had anything published?"

"Yes, nine tone poems, about three hundred songs,"

"Not when you were alive," the examiner said, somewhat disquietingly. "I mean since the sculptors turned you out again."

"Since the sculptors—ah, I understand. Yes, a string quartet, two song cycles, a—"

"Good. Alfie, write down 'songs.' Play an instrument?"

"Piano."

"Hm." The examiner studied his fingernails. "Oh, well. Do you read music? Or do you use a Scriber, or tape clips? Or a Machine?"

"I read."

"Here." The examiner sat Strauss down in front of a viewing lectern, over the lit surface of which an endless belt of translucent paper was traveling. On the paper was an immensely magnified sound track. "Whistle me the tune of that, and name the instruments it sounds like."

"I don't read that *Musiksticheln,*" Strauss said frostily, "or write it, either. I use standard notation, on music paper."

"Alfie, write down 'Reads notes only.'" He laid a sheet of grayly printed music on the lectern above the ground glass. "Whistle me that."

"That" proved to be a popular tune called "Vangs, Snifters and Store-Credit Snooky" which had been written on a Hit Machine in 2159 by a guitar-faking politician who sang it at campaign rallies. (In some respects, Strauss reflected, the United States had indeed not changed very much.) It had become so popular that anybody could have whistled it from the title alone, whether he could read the music or not. Strauss whistled it, and to prove his bona fides added, "It's in the key of B flat."

The examiner went over to the green-painted upright piano and hit one greasy black key. The instrument was horribly out of tune—the note was much nearer to the standard 440/cps A than it was to B flat—but the examiner said, "So it is. Alfie, write down, 'Also reads flats.' All right, son, you're a member. Nice to have you with us; not many people can read that old-style notation any more. A lot of them think they're too good for it."

"Thank you," Strauss said.

"My feeling is, if it was good enough for the old masters, it's good enough for us. We don't have people like them with us these days, it seems to me. Except for Dr. Krafft, of course. They were *great* back in the old days—men like Shilkrit, Steiner, Tiomkin, and Pearl . . . and Wilder and Jannsen. Real goffin."

"*Dock gewiss,*" Strauss said politely.

But the work went forward. He was making a little income now, from small works. People seemed to feel a special interest in a composer who had come out of the mind sculptors' laboratories; and in addition the material itself, Strauss was quite certain, had merits of its own to help sell it.

It was the opera which counted, however. That grew and grew under his pen, as fresh and new as his new life, as founded in knowledge and ripeness as his long full memory. Finding a libretto had been troublesome at first. While it was possible that something existed that might have served among the current scripts for 3-V—though he doubted it—he found himself unable to tell the good from the bad through the fog cast over both by incomprehensibly technical production directions. Eventually, and for only the third time in his whole career, he had fallen back upon a play written in a language other than his own, and—for the first time—decided to set it in that language.

The play was Christopher Fry's *Venus Observed*, in all ways a perfect Strauss opera libretto, as he came gradually to realize. Though nominally a comedy, with a complex farcical plot, it was a verse play with considerable depth to it, and a number of characters who cried out to be brought by music into three dimensions, plus a strong undercurrent of autumnal tragedy, of leaf-fall and apple-fall—precisely the kind of contradictory dramatic mixture which von Hofmannsthal had supplied him with in *The Knight of the Rose*, in *Ariadne at Naxos*, and in *Arabella*.

Alas for von Hofmannsthal, but here was another long-dead playwright who seemed nearly as gifted; and the musical opportunities were immense. There was, for instance, the fire which ended act two; what a gift for a composer to whom orchestration and counterpoint were as important as air and water! Or take the moment where Perpetua shoots the apple from the Duke's hand; in that one moment a single passing reference could add Rossini's marmoreal *William Tell* to the musical texture as nothing but an ironic footnote! And the Duke's great curtain speech, beginning:

> Shall I be sorry for myself? In Mortality's name
> I'll be sorry for myself. Branches and boughs.
> Brown hills, the valleys faint with brume,
> A burnish on the lake . . .

There was a speech for a great tragic comedian, in the spirit of Falstaff; the final union of laughter and tears, punctuated by the sleepy comments of Reedbeck, to whose sonorous snore (trombones, no less than five of them, *con sordini?*) the opera would gently end. . . .

What could be better? And yet he had come upon the play only by the unlikeliest series of accidents. At first he had planned to do a straight knockabout farce, in the idiom of *The Silent Woman*, just to warm himself up. Remembering that Zweig had adapted that libretto for him, in the old days, from a play by Ben Jonson, Strauss had begun to search out English plays of the period just after Jonson's, and had promptly run aground on an awful specimen in heroic couplets called *Venice Preserv'd*, by one Thomas Otway. The Fry play had directly followed the Otway in the card catalogue, and he had looked at it out of curiosity; why should a Twentieth Century playwright be punning on a title from the Eighteenth?

After two pages of the Fry play, the minor puzzle of the pun disappeared entirely from his concern. His luck was running again; he had an opera.

Sindi worked miracles in arranging for the performance. The date of the premiere was set even before the score was finished, reminding Strauss pleasantly of those heady days when Fuerstner had been snatching the conclusion of *Elektra* off his work table a page at a time, before the ink was even dry, to rush it to the engraver before publication deadline. The situation now, however, was even more complicated, for some of the score had to be scribed, some of it taped, some of it engraved in the old way, to meet the new techniques of performance; there were moments when Sindi seemed to be turning quite gray.

But *Venus Observed* was, as usual, forthcoming complete from Strauss's pen in plenty of time. Writing the music in first draft had been hellishly hard work, much more like being reborn than had been that confused awakening in Barkun Kris's laboratory, with its overtones of being dead instead; but Strauss found that he still retained all of his old ability to score from the draft almost effortlessly, as undisturbed by Sindi's half-audible worrying in the room with him as he was by the terrifying supersonic bangs of the rockets that bulleted invisibly over the city.

When he was finished, he had two days still to spare before the beginning of rehearsals. With those, furthermore, he would have nothing to do. The techniques of performance in this age were so completely bound up with the electronic arts as to reduce his own experience—he, the master *Kapellmeister* of them all—to the hopelessly primitive.

He did not mind. The music, as written, would speak for itself. In the meantime he found it grateful to forget the months'-long preoccupation with the stage for a while. He went back to the library and browsed lazily through old poems, vaguely seeking texts for a song or two. He knew better than to bother with recent poets; they could not speak to him, and he knew it. The Americans of his own age, he thought, might give him a clue to understanding this America of 2161; and if some such poem gave birth to a song, so much the better.

The search was relaxing and he gave himself up to enjoying it. Finally he struck a tape that he liked: a tape read in a cracked old voice that twanged of Idaho as that voice had twanged in 1910, in Strauss's own ancient youth. The poet's name was Pound; he said, on the tape

> *. . . the souls of all men great*
> *At times pass through us,*
> *And we are melted into them, and are not*
> *Save reflexions of their souls.*
> *Thus I am Dante for a space and am*
> *One Francois Villon, ballad-lord and thief*
> *Or am such holy ones I may not write,*
> *Lest Blasphemy be writ against my name;*
> *This for an instant and the flame is gone.*
> *'Tis as in midmost us there glows a sphere*
> *Translucent, molten gold, that is the "I"*
> *And into this some form projects itself:*
>   *Christus, or John, or eke the Florentine;*
> *And as the clear space is not if a form's*
> *Imposed thereon,*
>   *So cease we from all being for the time,*
> *And these, the Masters of the Soul, live on.*

He smiled. That lesson had been written again and again, from Plato onward. Yet the poem was a history of his own case, a sort of theory for the metempsychosis he had undergone, and in its formal way it was moving. It would be fitting to make a little hymn of it, in honor of his own rebirth, and of the poet's insight.

A series of solemn, breathless chords framed themselves in his inner ear, against which the words might be intoned in a high, gently bending hush at the beginning . . . and then a dramatic passage in which the great names of Dante and Villon would enter ringing like challenges to Time. . . . He wrote for a while in his notebook before he returned the spool to its shelf.

These, he thought, are good auspices.

And so the night of the premiere arrived, the audience pouring into the hall, the 3-V cameras riding on no visible supports through the air, and Sindi calculating his share of his client's earnings by a complicated game he played on his fingers, the basic law of which seemed

A Work of Art   35

to be that one plus one equals ten. The hall filled to the roof with people from every class, as though what was to come would be a circus rather than an opera.

There were, surprisingly, nearly fifty of the aloof and aristocratic mind sculptors, clad in formal clothes which were exaggerated black versions of their surgeon's gowns. They had bought a block of seats near the front of the auditorium, where the gigantic 3-V figures which would shortly fill the "stage" before them (the real singers would perform on a small stage in the basement) could not but seem monstrously out of proportion; but Strauss supposed that they had taken this into account and dismissed it.

There was a tide of whispering in the audience as the sculptors began to trickle in, and with it an undercurrent of excitement the meaning of which was unknown to Strauss. He did not attempt to fathom it, however; he was coping with his own mounting tide of opening-night tension, which, despite all the years, he had never quite been able to shake.

The sourceless, gentle light in the auditorium dimmed, and Strauss mounted the podium. There was a score before him, but he doubted that he would need it. Directly before him, poking up from among the musicians, were the inevitable 3-V snouts, waiting to carry his image to the singers in the basement.

The audience was quiet now. This was the moment. His baton swept up and then decisively down, and the prelude came surging up out of the pit.

For a little while he was deeply immersed in the always tricky business of keeping the enormous orchestra together and sensitive to the flexing of the musical web beneath his hand. As his control firmed and became secure, however, the task became slightly less demanding, and he was able to pay more attention to what the whole sounded like.

There was something decidedly wrong with it. Of course there were the occasional surprises as some bit of orchestral color emerged with a different *Klang* than he had expected; that happened to every composer, even after a lifetime of experience. And there were moments when the singers, entering upon a phrase more difficult to handle than he had calculated, sounded like someone about to fall off a tightrope (although none of them actually fluffed once; they were as fine a troupe of voices as he had ever had to work with).

But these were details. It was the over-all impression that was wrong. He was losing not only the excitement of the premiere—after all, that couldn't last at the same pitch all evening—but also his very interest in what was coming from the stage and the pit. He was gradually tiring; his baton arm becoming heavier; as the second act mounted to what should have been an impassioned outpouring of shining tone, he was so bored as to wish he could go back to his desk to work on that song.

Then the act was over; only one more to go. He scarcely heard the applause. The twenty minutes' rest in his dressing room was just barely enough to give him the necessary strength.

And suddenly, in the middle of the last act, he understood.

There was nothing new about the music. It was the old Strauss all over again—but weaker, more dilute than ever. Compared with the output of composers like Krafft, it doubtless sounded like a masterpiece to this audience. But he knew.

The resolutions, the determination to abandon the old cliches and mannerisms, the decision to say something new— they had all come to nothing against the force of habit. Being brought to life again meant bringing to life as well all those deeply graven reflexes of his style. He had only to pick up his pen and they overpowered him with easy automatism, no more under his control than the jerk of a finger away from a flame.

His eyes filled; his body was young, but he was an old man, an old man. Another thirty-five years of this? Never. He had said all this before, centuries before. Nearly a half century condemned to saying it all over again, in a weaker and still weaker voice, aware that even this debased century would come to recognize in him only the burnt husk of greatness?—no; never, never.

He was aware, dully, that the opera was over. The audience was screaming its joy. He knew the sound. They had screamed that way when *Day of Peace* had been premiered, but they had been cheering the man he had been, not the man that *Day of Peace* showed with cruel clarity he had become. Here the sound was even more meaningless: cheers of ignorance, and that was all.

He turned slowly. With surprise, and with a surprising sense of relief, he saw that the cheers were not, after all, for him.

They were for Dr. Barkun Kris.

Kris was standing in the middle of the bloc of mind sculptors, bow-ing to the audience. The sculptors nearest him were shaking his hand one after the other. More grasped at it as he made his way to the aisle, and walked forward to the podium. When he mounted the rostrum and took the composer's limp hand, the cheering became delirious.

Kris lifted his arm. The cheering died instantly to an intent hush.

"Thank you," he said clearly. "Ladies and gentlemen, before we take leave of Dr. Strauss, let us again tell him what a privilege it has been for us to hear this fresh example of his mastery. I am sure no farewell could be more fitting."

The ovation lasted five minutes, and would have gone another five if Kris had not cut it off.

"Dr. Strauss," he said, "in a moment, when I speak a certain formulation to you, you will realize that your name is Jerom Bosch, born in our century and with a life in it all your own. The superimposed memories which have made you assume the mask, the *persona*, of a great composer will be gone. I tell you this so that you may understand why these people here share your applause with me."

A wave of assenting sound.

"The art of mind sculpture—the creation of artificial personalities for aesthetic enjoyment—may never reach such a pinnacle again. For you should understand that as Jerom Bosch you had no talent for music at all; indeed, we searched a long time to find a man who was utterly unable to carry even the simplest tune. Yet we were able to impose upon such unpromising material not only the personality, but the genius, of a great composer. That genius belongs entirely to you—to the *persona* that thinks of itself as Richard Strauss. None of the credit goes to the man who volunteered for the sculpture. That is your triumph, and we salute you for it."

Now the ovation could no longer be contained. Strauss, with a crooked smile, watched Dr. Kris bow. This mind sculpturing was a suitably sophisticated kind of cruelty for this age; but the impulse, of course, had always existed. It was the same impulse that had made Rembrandt and Leonardo turn cadavers into art works.

It deserved a suitably sophisticated payment under the *lex talionis:* an eye for an eye, a tooth for a tooth—and a failure for a failure.

No, he need not tell Dr. Kris that the "Strauss" he had created was as empty of genius as a hollow gourd. The joke would always be on the sculptor, who was incapable of hearing the hollowness of the music now preserved on the 3-V tapes.

But for an instant a surge of revolt poured through his blood stream. *I am I,* he thought. *I am Richard Strauss until I die, and will never be Jerom Bosch, who was utterly unable to carry even the simplest tune.* His hand, still holding the baton, came sharply up, though whether to deliver or to ward off a blow he could not tell.

He let it fall again, and instead, at last, bowed—not to the audience, but to Dr. Kris. He was sorry for nothing, as Kris turned to him to say the word that would plunge him back into oblivion, except that he would now have no chance to set that poem to music.

Surface Tension

PROLOGUE

Dr. Chatvieux took a long time over the microscope, leaving la Ventura with nothing to do but look at the dead landscape of Hydrot. Waterscape, he thought, would be a better word. From space, the new world had shown only one small, triangular continent, set amid endless ocean; and even the continent was mostly swamp.

The wreck of the seed-ship lay broken squarely across the one real spur of rock which Hydrot seemed to possess, which reared a magnificent twenty-one feet above sea-level. From this eminence, la Ventura could see forty miles to the horizon across a flat bed of mud. The red light of the star Tau Ceti, glinting upon thousands of small lakes, pools, ponds and puddles, made the watery plain look like a mosaic of onyx and ruby.

"If I were a religious man," the pilot said suddenly, "I'd call this a plain case of divine vengeance."

Chatvieux said: "Hmn?"

"It's as if we'd struck down for—is it *hubris*? Pride, arrogance?"

"*Hybris*," Chatvieux said, looking up at last. "Well, is it? I don't feel swollen with pride at the moment. Do you?"

"I'm not exactly proud of my piloting," la Ventura admitted. "But that isn't quite what I mean. I was thinking about why we came here in the first place. It takes a lot of arrogance to think that you can scatter men, or at least things very much like men, all over the face of the galaxy. It takes even more pride to do the job—to pack up all the equipment and move from planet to planet and actually make men, make them suitable for every place you touch."

"I suppose it does," Chatvieux said. "But we're only one of several hundred seed-ships in this limb of the galaxy, so I doubt that the gods picked us out as special sinners." He smiled. "If they had, maybe they'd have left us our ultraphone, so the Colonization Council could hear about our cropper. Besides, Paul, we don't make men. We adapt them—adapt them to Earthlike planets, nothing more that that. We've sense enough—or humility enough, if you like that better—to know that we can't adapt men to a planet like Jupiter, or to the surface of a sun, like Tau Ceti."

"Anyhow, we're here," la Ventura said grimly. "And we aren't going to get off. Phil tells me that we don't even have our germ-cell bank any more, so we can't seed this place in the usual way. We've been thrown onto a dead world and dared to adapt to it. What are the pantropes going to do with our recalcitrant carcasses—provide built-in waterwings?"

"No," Chatvieux said calmly. "You and I and all the rest of us are going to die, Paul. Pantropic techniques don't work on the body; that was fixed for you for life when you were conceived. To attempt to rebuild it for you would only maim you. The pantropes affect only the genes, the inheritance-carrying factors. We can't give you built-in waterwings, any more than we can give you a new set of brains. I think we'll be able to populate this world with men, but we won't live to see it."

The pilot thought about it, a lump of cold blubber collecting gradually in his stomach. "How long do you give us?" he said at last.

"Who knows? A month, perhaps."

The bulkhead leading to the wrecked section of the ship was pushed back, admitting salt, muggy air, heavy with carbon dioxide. Philip Strasvogel, the communications officer, came in, tracking mud. Like la Ventura, he was now a man without a function, and it appeared to bother him. He was not well equipped for introspection, and with his ultraphone totally smashed, unresponsive to his perpetually darting hands, he had been thrown back into his own mind, whose resources were few. Only the tasks Chatvieux had set him to had prevented him from setting like a gelling colloid into a permanent state of the sulks.

He unbuckled from around his waist a canvas belt, into the loops of which plastic vials were stuffed like cartridges. "More samples, Doc," he said. "All alike—water, very wet. I have some quicksand in one boot, too. Find anything?"

"A good deal, Phil. Thanks. Are the others around?"

Strasvogel poked his head out and hallooed. Other voices rang out over the mudflats. Minutes later, the rest of the survivors of the crash were crowding into the pantrope deck: Saltonstall, Chatvieux' senior assistant, a perpetually sanguine, perpetually youthful technician willing to try anything once, including dying; Eunice Wagner, behind whose placid face rested the brains of the expedition's only remaining ecologist; Eleftherios Venezuelos, the always-silent delegate from the Colonization Council; and Joan Heath, a midshipman whose duties, like la Ventura's and Phil's, were now without meaning, but whose bright head and tall, deceptively indolent body shone to the pilot's eyes brighter than Tau Ceti—brighter, since the crash, even than the home sun.

Five men and two women—to colonize a planet on which "standing room" meant treading water.

They came in quietly and found seats or resting places on the deck, on the edges of tables, in corners. Joan Heath went to stand beside la Ventura. They did not look at each other, but the warmth of her shoulder beside his was all that he needed. Nothing was as bad as it seemed.

Venezuelos said: "What's the verdict, Dr. Chatvieux?"

"This place isn't dead," Chatvieux said. "There's life in the sea and in the fresh water, both. On the animal side of the ledger, evolution seems to have stopped with the crustacea; the most advanced form I've found is a tiny crayfish, from one of the local rivulets, and it doesn't seem to be well distributed. The ponds and puddles are well-stocked with small metazoans of lower orders, right up to the rotifers—including a castle-building genus like Earth's *Floscularidae*. In addition, there's a wonderfully variegated protozoan population, with a dominant ciliate type much like *Paramoecium*, plus various sarcodines, the usual spread of phyto-flagellates and even a phosphorescent species I wouldn't have expected to see anywhere but in salt water. As for the plants, they run from simple blue-green algae to quite advanced thallus-producing types—though none of them, of course, can live out of the water."

"The sea is about the same," Eunice said. "I've found some of the larger simple metazoans—jellyfish and so on—and some crayfish almost as big as lobsters. But it's normal to find salt-water species running larger than fresh-water. And there's the usual plankton and nannoplankton population."

"In short," Chatvieux said, "we'll survive here—if we fight."

"Wait a minute," la Ventura said. "You've just finished telling me that we wouldn't survive. And you were talking about us, the seven of us here, not about the genus man, because we don't have our germ-cells banks any more. What's—"

"We don't have the banks. But we ourselves can contribute germ-cells, Paul. I'll get to that in a moment." Chatvieux turned to Saltonstall. "Martin, what would you think of our taking to the sea? We came out of it once, long ago; maybe we could come out of it again on Hydrot."

"No good," Saltonstall said immediately. "I like the idea, but I don't think this planet ever heard of Swinburne, or Homer, either. Looking at it as a colonization problem alone, as if we weren't involved in it ourselves, I wouldn't give you an Oc dollar for *epi oinopa ponton*. The evolutionary pressure there is too high, the competition from other species is prohibitive; seeding the sea should be the last thing we attempt, not the first. The colonists wouldn't have a chance to learn a thing before they'd be gobbled up."

"Why?" la Ventura said. Once more, the death in his stomach was becoming hard to placate.

"Eunice, do your sea-going Coelenterates include anything like the Portuguese man-of-war?"

The ecologist nodded.

"There's your answer, Paul," Saltonstall said. "The sea is out. It's got to be fresh water, where the competing creatures are less formidable and there are more places to hide."

"We can't compete with a jellyfish?" la Ventura asked, swallowing.

"No, Paul," Chatvieux said. "Not with one that dangerous. The pantropes make adaptations, not gods. They take human germ-cells—in this case, our own, since our bank was wiped out in the crash—and modify them genetically toward those of creatures who can live in any reasonable environment. The result will be manlike, and intelligent. It usually shows the donors' personality patterns, too, since the modifications are usually made mostly in the morphology, not so much in the mind, of the resulting individual.

"*But we can't transmit memory.* The adapted man is worse than a child in the new environment. He has no history, no techniques, no precedents, not even a language. In the usual colonization project, like the Tellura affair, the seeding teams more or less take him through elementary school before they leave the planet to him, but we won't survive long enough to give such instructions. We'll have to design our colonists with plenty of built-in protections and locate them in the most favorable environment possible, so that at least some of them will survive learning by experience alone."

The pilot thought about it, but nothing occurred to him which did not make the disaster seem realer and more intimate with each passing second. Joan Heath moved slightly closer to him. "One of the new creatures can have my personality pattern, but it won't be able to remember being me. Is that right?"

"That's right. In the present situation we'll probably make our colonists haploid, so that some of them, perhaps many, will have a heredity traceable to you alone. There may be just the faintest of residuums of identity—pantropy's given us some data to support the old Jungian notion of ancestral memory. But we're all going to die on the Hydrot, Paul, as self-conscious persons. There's no avoiding that. Somewhere we'll leave behind people who behave as we would, think and feel as we would, but who won't remember la Ventura, or Dr. Chatvieux, or Joan Heath—or the Earth."

The pilot said nothing more. There was a gray taste in his mouth.

"Saltonstall, what would you recommend as a form?"

The pantropist pulled reflectively at his nose. "Webbed extremities, of course, with thumbs and big toes heavy and thorn-like for defense until the creature has had a chance to learn. Smaller external ears, and the eardrum larger and closer to the outer end of the ear-canal. We're going to have to reorganize the water-conservation system, I think; the glomerular kidney is perfectly suitable for living in fresh water, but the business of living immersed, inside and out, for a creature with a salty inside means that the osmotic pressure inside is going to be higher than outside, so that the kidneys are going to have to be pumping virtually all the time. Under the circumstances we'd best step up production of urine, and that means the antidiuretic function of the pituitary gland is going to have to be abrogated, for all practical purposes."

"What about respiration?"

"Hm," Saltonstall said. "I suppose book-lungs, like some of the arachnids have. They can be supplied by intercostal spiracles. They're gradually adaptable to atmosphere-breathing, if our colonist ever decides to come out of the water. Just to provide for that possibility, I'd suggest that the nose be retained, maintaining the nasal cavity as a part of the otological system, but cutting off the cavity from the larynx with a membrane of cells that are supplied with oxygen by direct irrigation, rather than by the circulatory system. Such a membrane wouldn't survive for many generations, once the creature took to living out of the water even for part of its lifetime; it'd go through two or three generations as an amphibian, and then one day it'd suddenly find itself breathing through its larynx again."

"Ingenious," Chatvieux said.

"Also, Dr. Chatvieux, I'd suggest that we have it adopt sporulation. As an aquatic animal, our colonist is going to have an indefinite lifespan, but we'll have to give it a breeding cycle of about six weeks to keep up its numbers during the learning period; so there'll have to be a definite break of some duration in its active year. Otherwise it'll hit the population problem before it's learned enough to cope with it."

"And it'd be better if our colonists could winter over inside a good, hard shell," Eunice Wagner added in agreement. "So sporulation's the obvious answer. Many other microscopic creatures have it."

"Microscopic?" Phil said incredulously.

"Certainly," Chatvieux said, amused. "We can't very well crowd a six-foot man into a two-foot puddle. But that raises a question. We'll have tough competition from the rotifers, and some of them aren't strictly microscopic; for that matter even some of the protozoa can be seen with the naked eye, just barely, with dark-field illumination. I don't think your average colonist should run much under 250 microns, Saltonstall. Give them a chance to slug it out."

"I was thinking of making them twice that big."

"Then they'd be the biggest animals in their environment," Eunice Wagner pointed out, "and won't ever develop any skills. Besides, if you make them about rotifer size, it will give them an incentive for pushing out the castle-building rotifers, and occupying the castles themselves, as dwellings."

Chatvieux nodded. "All right, let's get started. While the pantropes are being calibrated, the rest of us can put our heads together on leaving a record for these people. We'll micro-engrave the record on a set of corrosion-proof metal leaves, of a size our colonists can handle conveniently. We can tell them, very simply, what happened, and plant a few suggestions that there's more the universe than what they find in their puddles. Some day they may puzzle it out."

"Question," Eunice Wagner said. "Are we going to tell them they're microscopic? I'm opposed to it. It may saddle their entire early history with a gods-and-demons mythology that they'd be better off without."

"Yes, we are," Chatvieux said; and la Ventura could tell by the change in the tone of his voice that he was speaking now as their senior on the expedition. "These people will be of the race of men, Eunice. We want them to win their way back into the community of men. They are not toys, to be protected from the truth forever in a fresh-water womb."

"Besides," Saltonstall observed, "they won't get the record translated at any time in their early history. They'll have to develop a written language of their own, and it will be impossible for us to leave them any sort of Rosetta Stone or other key. By the time they can decipher the truth, they should be ready for it."

"I'll make that official," Venezuelos said unexpectedly. And that was that.

And then, essentially, it was all over. They contributed the cells that the pantropes would need. Privately, la Ventura and Joan Heath went to Chatvieux and asked to contribute jointly; but the scientist said that the microscopic men were to be haploid, in order to give them a minute cellular structure, with nuclei as small as Earthly rickettsiae, and therefore each person had to give germ-cells individually—there would be no use for zygotes. So even that consolation was denied them; in death they would have no children, but be instead as alone as ever.

They helped, as far as they could, with the text of the message which was to go on the metal leaves. They had their personality patterns recorded. They went through the motions. Already they were beginning to be hungry; the sea-crayfish, the only things on Hydrot big enough to eat, lived in water too deep and cold for subsistence fishing.

After la Ventura had set his control board to rights—a useless gesture, but a habit he had been taught to respect, and which in an obscure way made things a little easier to bear—he was out of it. He sat by himself at the far end of the rock ledge, watching Tau Ceti go redly down, chucking pebbles into the nearest pond.

After a while Joan Heath came silently up behind him, and sat down too. He took her hand. The glare of the red sun was almost extinguished now, and together they watched it go, with la Ventura, at least, wondering somberly which nameless puddle was to be his Lethe.

He never found out, of course. None of them did.

CYCLE ONE

In a forgotten corner of the galaxy, the watery world of Hydrot hurtles endlessly around the red star, Tau Ceti. For many months its single small continent has been snowbound, and the many pools and lakes -which dot the continent have been locked in the grip of the ice. Now, however, the red sun swings closer and closer to the zenith in Hydrot's sky; the snow rushes in torrents toward the eternal ocean, and the ice recedes toward the shores of the lakes and ponds . . .

I

The first thing to reach the consciousness of the sleeping Lavon was a small, intermittent scratching sound. This was followed by a disquieting sensation in his body, as if the world—and Lavon with it—were being rocked back and forth. He stirred uneasily, without opening his eyes. His vastly slowed metabolism made him feel inert and queasy, and the rocking did not help. At his slight motion, however, both the sound and the motion became more insistent.

It seemed to take days for the fog over his brain to clear, but whatever was causing the disturbance would not let him rest. With a groan he forced his eyelids open and made an abrupt gesture with one webbed hand. By the waves of phosphorescence which echoed away from his fingers at the motion, he could see that the smooth amber walls of his spherical shell were unbroken. He tried to peer through them, but he could see nothing but darkness outside. Well, that was natural: the amnionic fluid inside the spore would generate light, but ordinary water did not, no matter how vigorously it was stirred.

Whatever was outside the sphere was rocking it again, with the same whispering friction against its shell. Probably some nosey diatom, Lavon thought sleepily, trying to butt its way through an object it was too stupid to go around. Or some early hunter, yearning for a taste of the morsel inside the spore. Well, let it worry itself; Lavon had no intention of breaking the shell just yet. The fluid in which he had slept for so many months had held his body processes static, and had slowed his mind. Once out into the water, he would have to start breathing and looking for food again, and he could tell by the unrelieved darkness outside that it was too early in the spring to begin thinking about that.

He flexed his fingers reflectively, in the disharmonic motion from little finger to thumb that no animal but man can copy, and watched the widening wavefronts of greenish light rebound in the larger arcs from the curved spore walls. Here he was, curled up quite comfortable in a little amber ball, where he could stay until even the depths were warm and light. At this moment there was probably still some ice on the sky, and certainly there would not be much to eat as yet. Not that there was ever much, what with the voracious rotifers coming awake too with the first gust of warm water—

The rotifers! That was it. There was a plan afoot to drive them out. Memory returned in an unwelcome rush. As if to help it, the spore rocked again. That was probably one of the Protos, trying to awaken him; nothing man-eating ever came to the Bottom this early. He had left an early call with the Paras, and now the time had come, as cold and early and dark as he had thought he wanted it.

Reluctantly, Lavon uncurled, planting his webbed toes and arching his backbone as hard as he could, pressing with his whole body against his amber prison. With small, sharp, crepitating sounds, a network of cracks raced through the translucent shell.

Then the spore wall dissolved into a thousand brittle shards, and he was shivering violently with the onslaught of the icy water. The warmer fluid of his winter cell dissipated silently, a faint glowing fog. In the brief light he saw, nor far from him, a familiar shape: a transparent, bubble-filled cylinder, a colorless slipper of jelly, spirally grooved, almost as long as he was tall. Its surface was furred with gently vibrating fine hairs, thickened at the base.

The light went out. The Proto said nothing; it waited while Lavon choked and coughed, expelling the last remnants of the spore fluid from his book-lungs and sucking in the pure, ice-cold water.

"Para?" Lavon said at last. "Already?"

"Already," the invisible cilia vibrated in even, emotionless tones. Each separate hair-like process buzzed at an independent, changing rate; the resulting sound waves spread through the water, intermodulating, reinforcing or canceling each other. The aggregate wave-front, by the time it reached human ears, was rather eerie, but nevertheless recognizable human speech. "This is the time, Lavon."

"Time and more than time," another voice said from the returned darkness. "If we are to drive Flosc from his castles."

"Who's that?" Lavon said, turning futilely toward the new voice.

"I am Para also, Lavon. We are sixteen since the awakening. If you could reproduce as rapidly as we—"

"Brains are better than numbers," Lavon said. "As the Eaters will find out soon enough."

"What shall we do, Lavon?"

The man drew up his knees and sank to the cold mud of the Bottom to think. Something wriggled under his buttocks and a tiny spirillum corkscrewed away, identifiable only by feel. He let it go; he was not hungry yet, and he had the Eaters—the rotifers—to think about. Before long they would be swarming in the upper reaches of the sky, devouring everything, even men when they could catch them, even their natural enemies the Protos now and then. And whether or not the Protos could be organized to battle them was a question still to be tested.

Brains are better than numbers; even that, as a proposition, was still to be tested. The Protos, after all, were intelligent after their fashion; and they knew their world, as the men did not. Lavon could still remember how hard it had been for him to get straight in his head the various clans of beings in this world, and to make sense of their confused names; his tutor Shar had drilled him unmercifully until it had begun to penetrate.

When you said "Man," you meant creatures that, generally speaking, looked alike. The bacteria were of three kinds, the rods and the globes and the spirals, but they were all tiny and edible, so he had learned to differentiate them quickly. When it came to the Protos, identification became a real problem. Para here was a Proto, but he certainly looked very different from Stent and his family, and the family of Didin was unlike both. Anything, as it turned out, that was not green and had a visible nucleus was a Proto, no matter how strange its shape might be. The Eaters were all different, too, and some of them were as beautiful as the fruiting crowns of water-plants; but all of them were deadly, and all had the whirling crown of cilia which could suck you into the incessantly grinding mastax in a moment. Everything which was green and had an engraved shell of glass, Shar had called a diatom, dredging the strange word as he dredged them all from some Bottom in his skull which none of the rest of them could reach, and even Shar could not explain.

Lavon arose quickly. "We need Shar," he said. "Where is his spore?"

"On a plant frond, far up near the sky."

Idiot! The old man would never think of safety. To sleep near the sky, where he might be snatched up and borne off by any Eater to chance by when he emerged, sluggish with winter's long sleep! How could a wise man be so foolish?

"We'll have to hurry. Show me the way."

"Soon; wait," one of the Paras said. "You cannot see. Noc is foraging nearby." There was a small stir in the texture of the darkness as the swift cylinder shot away.

"Why do we need Shar?" the other Para said.

"For his brains, Para. He is a thinker."

"But his thoughts are water. Since he taught the Protos man's language, he has forgotten to think of the Eaters. He thinks forever of the mastery of how man came here. It is a mystery—even the Eaters are not like man. But understanding it will not help us to live."

Lavon turned blindly toward the creature. "Para, tell me something. Why do the Protos side with us? With man, I mean? Why do you need us? The Eaters fear you."

There was a short silence. When the Para spoke again, the vibrations of its voice were more blurred than before, more even, more devoid of any understandable feeling.

"We live in this world," the Para said. "We are of it. We rule it. We came to that state long before the coming of men, in long warfare with the Eaters. But we think as the Eaters do, we do not plan, we share our knowledge and we exist. Men plan; men lead; men are different from each other; men want to remake the world. And they hate the Eaters, as we do. We will help."

"And give up your rule?"

"And give it up, if the rule of men is better. That is reason. Now we can go; Noc is coming back with light."

Lavon looked up. Sure enough, there was a brief flash of cold light far overhead, and then another. In a moment the spherical Proto had dropped into view, its body flaring regularly with blue-green pulses. Beside it darted the second Para.

"Noc brings news," the second Para said. "Para is twenty-four. The Syn are awake by thousands along the sky. Noc spoke to a Syn colony, but they will not help us; they all expect to be dead before the Eaters awake."

"Of course," said the first Para. "That always happens. And the Syn are plants; why should they help the Protos?"

"Ask Noc if he'll guide us to Shar," Lavon said impatiently.

The Noc gestured with its single short, thick tentacle. One of the Paras said, "That is what he is here for."

"Then let's go. We've waited long enough."

The mixed quartet soared away from the Bottom through the liquid darkness.

"No," Lavon snapped. "Not a second longer. The Syn are awake, and Notholca of the Eaters is due right after that. You know that as well as I do, Shar. Wake up!"

"Yes, yes," the old man said fretfully. He stretched and yawned. "You're always in such a hurry, Lavon. Where's Phil? He made his spore near mine." He pointed to a still-unbroken amber sphere sealed to a leaf of the water-plant one tier below. "Better push him off; he'll be safer on the Bottom."

"He would never reach the Bottom," Para said. "The thermocline has formed."

Shar looked surprised. "It has? Is it as late as all that? Wait while I get my records together." He began to search along the leaf in the debris and the piled shards of his spore. Lavon looked impatiently about, found a splinter of stonewort, and threw it heavy end first at the bubble of Phil's cell just below. The spore shattered promptly, and the husky young man tumbled out, blue with shock as the cold water hit him.

"Wough!" he said. "Take it easy, Lavon." He looked up. "The old man's awake? Good. He insisted on staying up here for the winter, so of course I had to stay too."

"Aha," Shar said, and lifted a thick metal plate about the length of his forearm and half as wide. "Here is one of them. Now if only I haven't misplaced the other—"

Phil kicked away a mass of bacteria. "Here it is. Better give them both to a Para, so they won't burden you. Where do we go from here, Lavon? It's dangerous up this high. I'm just glad a Dicran hasn't already shown up."

"I here," something droned just above them.

Instantly, without looking up, Lavon flung himself out and down into the open water, turning his head to look back over his shoulder only when he was already diving as fast as he could go. Shar and Phil had evidently sprung at the same instant. On the next frond above where Shar had spent his winter was the armored, trumpet-shaped body of the rotifer Dicran, contracted to leap after them.

The two Protos came curving back out of nowhere. At the same moment, the bent, shortened body of Dicran flexed in its armor plate, straightened, came plunging toward them. There was a soft *plop* and

Lavon found himself struggling in a fine net, as tangled and impassable as the matte of a lichen. A second such sound was followed by a muttered imprecation from Phil. Lavon struck out fiercely, but he was barely able to wriggle in the web of wiry, transparent stuff.

"Be still," a voice which he recognized as Para's throbbed behind him. He managed to screw his head around, and then kicked himself mentally for not having realized at once what had happened. The Paras had exploded the trichocysts which lay like tiny cartridges beneath their pellicles; each one cast forth a liquid which solidified upon contact with the water in a long slender thread. It was their standard method of defense.

Farther down, Shar and Phil drifted with the second Para in the heart of a white haze, like creatures far gone in mold. Dicran swerved to avoid it, but she was evidently unable to give up; she twisted and darted around them, her corona buzzing harshly, her few scraps of the human language forgotten. Seen from this distance, the rotation of the corona was revealed as an illusion, created by the rhythm of pulsation of the individual cilia, but as far as Lavon was concerned the point was solely technical and the distance was far too short. Through the transparent armor Lavon could see the great jaws of Dicran's mastax, grinding away mechanically at the fragments which poured into her unheeding mouth.

High above them all, Noc circled indecisively, illuminating the whole group with quick, nervous flashes of his blue light. He was a flagellate, and had no natural weapons against the rotifer; why he was hanging around drawing attention to himself Lavon could not imagine.

Then, suddenly, he saw the reason: a barrel-like creature about Noc's size, ringed with two rows of cilia and bearing a ram-like prow. "Didin!" he shouted, unnecessarily. "This way!"

The Proto swung gracefully toward them and seemed to survey them, though it was hard to tell how he could see them without eyes. The Dicran saw him at the same tune and began to back slowly away, her buzzing rising to a raw snarl. She regained the plant and crouched down.

For an instant Lavon thought she was going to give up, but experience should have told him that she lacked the sense. Suddenly the lithe, crouched body was in full spring again, this time, straight at Didin. Lavon yelled an incoherent warning.

The Proto didn't need it. The slowly cruising barrel darted to one side and then forward, with astonishing speed. If he could sink that poisoned seizing-organ into a weak point in the rotifer's armor—

Noc mounted higher to keep out of the way of the two fighters, and in the resulting weakened light Lavon could not see what was happening, though the furious churning of the water and the buzzing of the Dicran continued.

After a while the sounds seemed to be retreating; Lavon crouched in the gloom inside the Para's net, listening intently. Finally there was silence.

"What's happened?" he whispered tensely.

"Didin does not say."

More eternities went by. Then the darkness began to wane as Noc dropped cautiously toward them.

"Noc, where did they go?"

Noc signaled with his tentacle and turned on his axis toward Para. "He says he lost sight of them. Wait—I hear Didin."

Lavon could hear nothing; what the Para "heard" was some one of the semi-telepathic impulses which made up the Proto's own language.

"He says Dicran is dead."

"Good! Ask him to bring the body back here."

There was a short silence. "He says he will bring it. What good is a dead rotifer, Lavon?"

"You'll see," Lavon said. He watched anxiously until Didin glided backwards into the lighted area, his poisonous ram sunk deep into the flaccid body of the rotifer, which, after the delicately-organized fashion of its kind, was already beginning to disintegrate.

"Let me out of this net, Para."

The Proto jerked sharply for a fraction of a turn on its long axis, snapping the threads off at the base; the movement had to be made with great precision, or its pellicle would tear as well. The tangled mass rose gently with the current and drifted off over the abyss.

Lavon swam forward and, seizing one buckled edge of Dicran's armor, tore away a huge strip of it. His hands plunged into the now almost shapeless body and came out again holding two dark spheroids: eggs.

"Destroy these, Didin," he ordered. The Proto obligingly slashed them open.

"Hereafter," Lavon said, "that's to be standard procedure with every Eater you kill."

"Not the males," one of the Para pointed out.

"Para, you have no sense of humor. All right, not the males—but nobody kills the males anyhow, they're harmless." He looked down grimly at the inert mass. "Remember—destroy the eggs. Killing the beasts isn't enough. We want to wipe out the whole race."

"We never forget," Para said emotionlessly.

II

The band of over two hundred humans, with Lavon and Shar and a Para at its head, fled swiftly through the warm, light waters of the upper level. Each man gripped a wood splinter, or a fragment of lime chipped from stonewort, as a club; and two hundred pairs of eyes darted watchfully from side to side. Cruising over them was a squadron of twenty Didins, and the rotifers they encountered only glared at them from single red eye-spots, making no move to attack. Overhead, near the sky, the sunlight was filtered through a thick layer of living creatures, fighting and feeding and spawning, so that all the depths below were colored a rich green. Most of this heavily populated layer was made up of algae and diatoms, and there the Eaters fed unhindered. Sometimes a dying diatom dropped slowly past the army.

The spring was well advanced; the two hundred, Lavon thought, probably represented all of the humans who had survived the winter. At least no more could be found. The others—nobody would ever know how many—had awakened too late in the season, or had made their spores in exposed places, and the rotifers had snatched them up. Of the group, more than a third were women. That meant that in another forty days, if they were unmolested, they could double the size of their army.

If they were unmolested. Lavon grinned and pushed an agitated colony of Eudorina out of his way. The phrase reminded him of a speculation Shar had brought forth last year: if Para were left unmolested, the oldster had said, he could reproduce fast enough to fill this whole universe with a solid mass of Paras before the season was out. Nobody, of course, ever went unmolested in this world; nevertheless, Lavon meant to cut the odds for people considerably below anything that had heretofore been thought of as natural.

His hand flashed up, and down again. The darting squadrons plunged after him. The light on the sky faded rapidly, and after a while Lavon began to feel slightly chilly. He signaled again. Like dancers, the two hundred swung their bodies in mid-flight, plunging now feet first toward the Bottom. To strike the thermocline in this position would make their passage through it faster, getting them out of the upper level where every minute, despite the convoy of Protos, concentrated danger.

Lavon's feet struck a yielding surface, and with a splash he was over his head in icy water. He bobbed up again, feeling the icy division drawn across his shoulders. Other splashes began to sound all along the thermocline as the army struck it, although, since there was water above and below, Lavon could not see the actual impacts.

Now they would have to wait until their body temperatures fell. At this dividing line of the universe, the warm water ended and the temperature dropped rapidly, so that the water below was much denser and buoyed them up. The lower level of cold reached clear down to the Bottom—an area which the rotifers, who were not very clever, seldom managed to enter.

A moribund diatom drifted down beside Lavon, the greenish-yellow of its body fading to a sick orange, its beautifully-marked, oblong, pillbox-like shell swarming with greedy bacteria. It came to rest on the thermocline, and the transparent caterpillar tread of jelly which ran around it moved feebly, trying vainly to get traction on the sliding water interface. Lavon reached out a webbed hand and brushed away a clot of vibrating rods which had nearly forced its way into the shell through a costal opening.

"Thank . . ." the diatom said, in an indistinct, whispering voice. And again, "Thank . . . Die . . ." The gurgling whisper faded. The caterpillar tread shifted again, then was motionless.

"It is right," a Para said. "Why do you bother with those creatures? They are stupid. Nothing can be done for them."

Lavon did not try to explain. He felt himself sinking slowly, and the water about his trunk and legs no longer seemed cold, only gratefully cool after the stifling heat of what he was breathing. In a moment the cool still depths had closed over his head. He hovered until he was reasonably sure that all the rest of his army was safely through, and the long ordeal of search for survivors in the upper level really ended. Then he twisted and streaked for the Bottom, Phil and Para beside him, Shar puffing along with the vanguard.

A stone loomed; Lavon surveyed it in the half-light. Almost immediately he saw what he had hoped to see: the sand-built house of a caddis-worm, clinging to the mountainous slopes of the rock. He waved in his special cadre and pointed.

Cautiously the men spread out in a U around the stone, the mouth of the U facing the same way as the opening of the worm's masonry tube. A Noc came after them, drifting like a star-shell above the peak; one of the Paras approached the door of the worm's house, buzzing defiantly. Under cover of this challenge the men at the back of the U settled on the rock and began to creep forward. The house was three times as tall as they were; the slimy black sand grains of which it was composed were as big as their heads.

There was a stir inside, and after a moment the ugly head of the worm peered out, weaving uncertainly at the buzzing Para which had disturbed it. The Para drew back, and the worm, in a kind of blind hunger, followed it. A sudden lunge brought it nearly halfway out of its tube.

Lavon shouted. Instantly the worm was surrounded by a howling horde of two-legged demons, who beat and prodded it mercilessly with fists and clubs. Somehow it made a sound, a kind of bleat as unlikely as the bird-like whistle of a fish, and began to slide backwards into its home—but the rear guard had already broken in back there. It jerked forward again, lashing from side to side under the flogging.

There was only one way now for the great larva to go, and the demons around it kept it going that way. It fell toward the Bottom down the side of the rock, naked and ungainly, shaking its blind head and bleating.

Lavon sent five Didin after it. They could not kill it, for it was far too huge to die under their poison, but they could sting it hard enough to keep it traveling. Otherwise, it would be almost sure to return to the rock to start a new house.

Lavon settled on an abutment and surveyed his prize with satisfaction. It was more than big enough to hold his entire clan—a great tubular hall, easily defended once the breach in the rear wall was rebuilt, and well out of the usual haunts of the Eaters. The muck the caddis-worm had left behind would have to be cleaned up, guards posted, vents knocked out to keep the oxygen-poor water of the depths in motion inside. It was too bad that the amoebae could not be detailed to scavenge the place, but Lavon knew better than to issue such an order. The Fathers of the Protos could not be asked to do useful work; that had been made very clear.

He looked around at his army. They were standing around him

in awed silence, looking at the spoils of their attack upon the largest creature in the world. He did not think they would ever again feel as timid toward the Eaters. He stood up quickly.

"What are you gaping at?" he shouted. "It's yours, all of it. Get to work!"

Old Shar sat comfortably upon a pebble which had been hollowed out and cushioned with spirogyra straw. Lavon stood nearby at the door, looking out at the maneuvers of his legions. They numbered more than three hundred now, thanks to the month of comparative quiet which they had enjoyed in the great hall, and they handled their numbers well in the aquatic drill which Lavon had invented for them. They swooped and turned above the rock, breaking and reassembling their formations, fighting a sham battle with invisible opponents whose shape they could remember only too well.

"Noc says there's all kinds of quarreling going on among the Eaters," Shar said. "They didn't believe we'd joined with the Protos at first, and then they didn't believe we'd all worked together to capture the hall. And the mass raid we had last week scared them. They'd never tried anything of the kind before, and they *knew* it wouldn't fail. Now they're fighting with each other over why it did. Cooperation is something new to this world, Lavon; it's making history."

"History?" Lavon said, following his drilling squadrons with a technical eye. "What's that?"

"These." The old man leaned over one arm of the pebble and touched the metal plates which were always with him. Lavon turned to follow the gesture, incuriously. He knew the plates well enough—the pure un-corroded shining, graven deeply on both sides with characters no-one, not even Shar, could read. The Protos called the plates *Not-stuff*—neither wood nor flesh nor stone.

"What good is that? I can't read it. Neither can you."

"I've got a start, Lavon. I know the plates are written in our language. Look at the first word: *ha ii ss tuh oh* pr *ee*—exactly the right number of characters for 'history.' That can't be a coincidence. And the next two 'words have to be 'of the.' And going on from there, using just the characters I already know—" Shar bent and traced in the sand with a stick a new train of characters: *i/terstellar ell/e/ition.*

"What's that?"

"It's a start, Lavon. Just a start. Some day we'll have more."

Lavon shrugged. "Perhaps, when we're safer. We can't afford to worry about that kind of thing now. We've never had that kind of time, not since the First Awakening."

The old man frowned down at the characters in the sand. "The First Awakening. Why does everything seem to stop there? I can remember in the smallest detail nearly everything that happened to me since then. But what happened to our childhoods, Lavon? None of us who survived the First Awakening seems to have had one. Who were our parents? Why were we so ignorant of the world, and yet grown men and women, all of us?"

"And the answer is in the plates?"

"I hope so," Shar said. "I believe it is. But I don't know. The plates were beside me in the spore at the First Awakening. That's all I know about them, except that there's nothing else like them in the world. The rest is deduction, and I haven't gotten very far with it. Some day . . . some day."

"I hope so too," Lavon said soberly. "I don't mean to mock, Shar, or to be impatient. I've got questions, too; we all have. But we're going to have to put them off for a while. Suppose we never find the whole answer?"

"Then our children will."

"But there's the heart of the problem, Shar: we have to live to have children. And make the kind of a world in which they'll have time to study. Otherwise—"

Lavon broke off as a figure darted between the guards at the door of the hall and twisted to a halt.

"What news, Phil?"

"The same," Phil said, shrugging with his whole body. His feet touched the floor. "The Flosc's castles are going up all along the bar; they'll be finished with them soon, and then we won't dare to get near them. Do you still think you can drive them out?"

Lavon nodded.

"But why?"

"First, for effect. We've been on the defensive so far, even though we've made a good job of it. We'll have to follow that up with an attack of our own if we're going to keep the Eaters confused. Second, the castles Flosc builds are all tunnels and exits and entrances—much better than worm-houses for us. I hate to think of what would have happened if the Eaters had thought of blockading us inside this hall. And we need an outpost in enemy country, Phil, where there are Eaters to kill."

"This is enemy country," Phil said. "Stephanost is a Bottom-dweller."

"But she's only a trapper, not a hunter. Any time we want to kill her, we can find her right where we left her last. It's the leapers like Dicran and Notholca, the Swimmers like Rotar, the colony-builders like Flosc that we have to wipe out first."

"Then we'd better start now, Lavon. Once the castles are finished—"

"Yes. Get your squads together, Phil. Shar, come on. We're leaving the hall."

"To raid the castles?"

"Of course."

Shar picked up his plates.

"You'd better leave those here; they'll be in your way in the fighting."

"No," Shar said determinedly. "I don't want them out of my sight. They go along."

III

Vague forebodings, all the more disturbing because he had felt nothing quite like them ever before, passed like clouds of fine silt through Lavon's mind as the army swept away from the hall on the Bottom and climbed toward the thermocline. As far as he could see, everything seemed to be going as he had planned it. As the army moved, its numbers were swelled by Protos who darted into its ranks from all sides. Discipline was good; and every man was armed with a long, seasoned splinter, and from each belt swung a stonewort-flake hand-axe, held by a thong run through a hole Shar had taught them all how to drill. There would probably be much death before the light of today faded, but death was common enough on any day, and this *tune* it should heavily disfavor the Eaters.

But there was a chill upon the depths that Lavon did not like, and a suggestion of a current in the water which was unnatural below the thermocline. A great many days had been consumed in collecting the army, recruiting from stragglers, and in securing the hall. The intensive breeding which had followed, and the training of the new-born and the newly recruited, had taken still more time, all of it essential, but all irrevocable. If the chill and the current marked the beginning of the fall turnover . . .

If it did, nothing could be done about it. The turnover could no more be postponed than the coming of day or night. He signaled to the nearest Para.

The glistening torpedo veered toward him. Lavon pointed up. "Here comes the thermocline, Para. Are we pointed right?"

"Yes, Lavon. That way is the place where the Bottom rises toward the sky. Flosc's castles are on the other side, where she will not see us."

"The sand bar that runs out from the north. Right. It's getting warmer. Here we go."

Lavon felt his flight suddenly quicken, as if he had been shot like a seed from some invisible thumb and forefinger. He looked over his shoulder to watch the passage of the rest through the temperature barrier, and what he saw thrilled him as sharply as any awakening. Up to now he had had no clear picture of the size of his forces, or the three-dimensional beauty of their dynamic, mobile organization. Even the Protos had fitted themselves into the squads; pattern after pattern of power came soaring after Lavon from the Bottom: first a single Noc bowling along like a beacon to guide all the rest, then an advance cone of Didin to watch for individual Eaters who might flee to give the alarm, and then the men, and the Protos, who made up the main force, in tight formations as beautiful as the elementary geometry from which Shar had helped derive them.

The sand-bar loomed ahead, as vast as any mountain range. Lavon soared sharply upward, and the tumbled, raw-boned boulders of the sand grains swept by rapidly beneath him in a broad, stony flood. Far beyond the ridge, towering up to the sky through glowing green obscurity, were the befronded stems of the plant jungle which was their objective. It was too dim with distance to allow him to see the clinging castles of the Flosc yet, but he knew that the longest part of the march was over. He narrowed his eyes and cleft the sunlit waters with driving, rapid strokes of his webbed hands and feet. The invaders poured after him over the crest of the bar in an orderly torrent.

Lavon swung his arm in a circle. Silently, the following squadrons glided into a great paraboloid, its axis pointed at the jungle. The castles were visible now; until the formation of the army, they had been the only products of close cooperation that this world had ever seen. They were built of single brown tubes, narrow at the base, attached to each other in a random pattern in an ensemble as delicate as a branching coral. In the mouth of each tube was a rotifer, a Flosc, distinguished from other Eaters by the four-leaf-clover of its corona, and by the single, prehensile finger springing from the small of its back, with which it ceaselessly molded its brown spittle into hard pellets and cemented them carefully to the rim of its tube.

As usual, the castles chilled Lavon's muscles with doubt. They were perfect, and they had always been one of the major, stony flowers of summer, long before there had been any First Awakening, or any men. And there was surely something wrong with the water in the upper level; it was warm and sleepy. The heads of the Flosc hummed contentedly at the mouths of their tubes; everything was as it should be, as it had always been; the army was a fantasm, the attack a failure before it had begun—

Then they were spied.

The Flosc vanished instantly, contracting violently into their tubes. The placid humming of their continuous feeding upon everything that passed was snuffed out; spared motes drifted about the castle in the light.

Lavon found himself smiling. Not long ago, the Flosc would only have waited until the humans were close enough, and then would have sucked them down, without more than a few struggles here and there, a few pauses in the humming while the out-size morsels were enfolded and fed into the grinders. Now, instead, they hid; they were afraid.

"Go!" he shouted at the top of his voice. "Kill them! Kill them while they're down!"

The army behind him swept after him with a stunning composite shout.

Tactics vanished. A petalled corona unfolded in Lavon's face, and a buzzing whirlpool spun him toward its black heart. He slashed wildly with his edged wooden splinter.

The sharp edge sliced deeply into the ciliated lobes. The rotifer screamed like a siren and contracted into her tube, closing her wounded face. Grimly, Lavon followed.

It was pitch dark inside the castle, and the raging currents of pain which flowed past him threw him from one pebbly wall to another. He gritted his teeth and probed with the splinter. It bit into a yielding surface at once, and another scream made his ears ring, mixed with mangled bits of words in Lavon's own language, senseless and horrible with agony. He slashed at them until they stopped, and continued to slash until he could control his terror.

As soon as he was able, he groped in the torn corpse for the eggs. The point found their life and pricked it. Trembling, he pulled himself back to the mouth of the tube, and without stopping to think pushed himself off at the first Eater to pass it.

The thing was a Dicran; she doubled viciously upon him at once. Even the Eaters had learned something about cooperation. And the Dicrans fought well in open water. They were the best possible reinforcements the Flosc could have called.

The Dicran's armor turned the point of Lavon's splinter easily. He jabbed frantically, hoping to hit a joint, but the agile creature gave him no time to aim. She charged him irresistibly, and her humming corona folded down around his head, pinned his forearms to his sides—

The Eater heaved convulsively and went limp. Lavon half slashed, half tore his way free. A Didin was drawing back, pulling out its seizing-organ. The body floated downward.

"Thanks," Lavon gasped. The Proto darted off without replying; it lacked sufficient cilia to imitate human speech. Possibly it lacked the desire as well; the Didins were not sociable.

A tearing whirlpool sprang into being again around him, and he flexed his sword arm. In the next five dreamlike minutes he developed a technique for dealing with the sessile, sucking Flosc. Instead of fighting the current and swinging the splinter back and forth against it, he gave in to the vortex, rode with it, and braced the splinter between his feet, point down. The results were even better than he had hoped. The point, driven by the full force of the Flosc's own trap, pierced the soft, wormlike body half through while it gaped for the human quarry. After each encounter, Lavon doggedly went through the messy ritual of destroying the eggs.

At last he emerged from a tube to find that the battle had drifted away from him. He paused on the edge to get his breath back, clinging to the rounded, translucent bricks and watching the fighting. It was difficult to make any military sense out of the melee, but as far as he could tell the rotifers were getting the worst of it. They did not know how to meet so carefully organized an attack, and they were not in any real sense intelligent.

The Didin were ranging from one side of the fray to the other, in two tight, vicious efficient groups, englobing and destroying freeswimming rotifers in whole flocks at a time. Lavon saw no fewer than half a dozen Eaters trapped by teams of Paras, each pair dragging a struggling victim in a trichocyst met remorselessly toward the Bottom, where she would inevitably suffocate. He was astonished to see one of the few Nocs that had accompanied his army scouring a cringing Rotar with its virtually harmless tentacle; the Eater seemed too astonished to fight back, and Lavon for once knew just how she felt.

A figure swam slowly and tiredly up to him from below. It was old Shar, puffing hard. Lavon reached a hand down to him and hauled him onto the lip of the tube. The man's face wore a frightening expression, half shock, half pure grief.

"Gone, Lavon," he said. "Gone. Lost."

"What? What's gone? What's the matter?"

"The plate. You were right. I should have known." He sobbed convulsively.

"What plate? Calm down. What happened? Did you lose one of the history plates—or both of them?"

Slowly his tutor seemed to be recovering control of his breathing. "One of them," he said wretchedly. "I dropped it in the fight. I hid the other one in an empty Flosc tube. But I dropped the first one—the one I'd just begun to decipher. It went all the way down to the Bottom, and I couldn't get free to go after it—all I could do was watch it go, spinning down into the darkness. We could sift the mud forever and never find it."

He dropped his face into his hands. Perched on the edge of the brown tube in the green glow of the waters, he looked both pathetic and absurd. Lavon did not know what to say; even he realized that the loss was major and perhaps final, that the awesome blank in their memories prior to the First Awakening might now never be filled. How Shar felt about it he could comprehend only dimly.

Another human figure darted and twisted toward him. "Lavon!" Phil's voice cried. "It's working, it's working! The swimmers are running away, what's left of them. There are still some Flosc in the castles, hiding in the darkness. If we could only lure them out in the open—"

Jarred back to the present, Lavon's mind raced over the possibilities. The whole attack could still fail if the Flosc entrenched themselves successfully. After all, a big kill had not been the only object; they had started out to capture the castles.

"Shar—do these tubes connect with each other?"

"Yes," the old man said without interest. "It's a continuous system."

Lavon sprang out upon the open water. "Come on, Phil. We'll attack them from the rear." Turning, he plunged into the mouth of the tube, Phil on his heels.

It was very dark, and the water was fetid with the odor of the tube's late owner, but after a moment's groping Lavon found the opening which lead into the next tube. It was easy to tell which way was out because of the pitch of the walls; everything the Flosc built had a conical bore, differing from the next tube in size. Determinedly Lavon worked his way toward the main stem, going always down and in.

Once they passed beneath an opening beyond which the water was in furious motion, and out of which poured muffled sounds of shouting and a defiant buzz. Lavon stopped to probe through the hole with his sword. The rotifer gave a shrill, startled shriek and jerked her wounded tail upward, involuntarily releasing her toe-hold upon the walls of the tube. Lavon moved on, grinning. The men above would do the rest.

Reaching the central stem at last, Lavon and Phil went methodically from one branch to another, spearing the surprised Eaters from behind or cutting them loose so that the men outside could get at them as they drifted upward, propelled by the drag of their own coronas. The trumpet shape of the tubes prevented the Eaters from turning to fight, and from following them through the castle to surprise them from behind; each Flosc had only the one room, which she never left.

The gutting of the castles took hardly fifteen minutes. The day was just beginning to end when Lavon emerged with Phil at the mouth of a turret to look down upon the first City of Man.

He lay in darkness, his forehead pressed against his knees, as motionless as a dead man. The water was stuffy, cold, the blackness complete. Around him were the walls of a tube of Flosc's castle; above him a Para laid another sand grain upon a new domed roof. The rest of the army rested in other tubes, covered with other new stony caps, but there was no sound of movement or of voices. It was as quiet as a necropolis.

Lavon's thoughts were slow and bitter as drugged syrup. He had been right about the passage of the seasons. He had had barely enough time to bring all his people from the hall to the castles before the annual debacle of the fall overturn. Then the waters of the universe had revolved once, bringing the skies to the Bottom, and the

Bottom to the skies, and then mixing both. The thermocline was destroyed until next year's spring overturn would reform it.

And inevitably, the abrupt change in temperature and oxygen concentration had started the spore-building glands again. The spherical amber shell was going up around Lavon now, and there was nothing he could do about it. It was an involuntary process, as dissociated from his control as the beating of his heart. Soon the light-generating oil which filled the spore would come pouring out, expelling and replacing the cold, foul water, and then sleep would come . . .

And all this had happened just as they had made a real gain, had established themselves in enemy country, had come within reach of the chance to destroy the Eaters wholesale and forever. Now the eggs of the Eaters had been laid, and next year it would have to be done all over again. And there was the loss of the plate; he had hardly begun to reflect upon what that would mean for the future.

There was a soft chunk as the last sand grain fell into place on the roof. The sound did not quite bring the final wave of despair against which he had been fighting in advance. Instead, it seemed to carry with it a wave of obscure contentment, with which his consciousness began to sink more and more rapidly toward sleep. They were safe, after all. They could not be ousted from the castle. And there would be fewer Eaters next year, because of all the eggs that had been destroyed, and the layers of those eggs . . . There was one plate still left . . .

Quiet and cold; darkness and silence.

In a forgotten corner of the galaxy, the watery world of Hydrot hurtles endlessly around the red star, Tau Ceti. For many months life has swarmed in its lakes and pools, but now the sun retreats from the zenith, and the snow falls, and the ice advances from the eternal ocean. Life sinks once more toward slumber, simulating death, and the battles and lusts and ambitions and defeats of a thousand million microscopic creatures retreat into the limbo where such things matter not at all.

No, such things matter not at all when winter reigns on Hydrot; but winter is an inconstant king.

CYCLE TWO

I

Old Shar set down the thick, ragged-edged metal plate at last, and gazed instead out the window of the castle, apparently resting his eyes on the glowing green-gold obscurity of the summer waters. In the soft fluorescence which played down upon him, from the Noc dozing impassively in the groined vault of the chamber, Lavon could see that he was in fact a young man. His face was so delicately formed as to suggest that it had not been many seasons since he had first emerged from his spore.

But of course there had been no real reason to have expected an old man. All the Shars had been referred to traditionally as "old" Shar. The reason, like the reasons for everything else, had been forgotten, but the custom had persisted. The adjective at least gave weight and dignity to the office—that of the center of wisdom of all the people, as each Lavon had been the center of authority.

The present Shar belonged to the generation XVI, and hence would have to be at least two seasons younger than Lavon himself. If he was old, it was only in knowledge.

"Lavon, I'm going to have to be honest with you," Shar said at last, still looking out of the tall, irregular window. "You've come to me at your maturity for the secrets on the metal plate, just as your predecessors did to mine. I can give some of them to you—but for the most part, I don't know what they mean."

"After so many generations?" Lavon asked, surprised. "Wasn't it Shar III who made the first complete translation? That was a long time ago."

The young man turned and looked at Lavon with eyes made dark and wide by the depths into which they had been staring. "I can read what's on the plate, but most of it seems to make no sense. Worst of all, the record's incomplete. You didn't know that? It is. One of the plates was lost in a battle during the first war with the Eaters, while these castles were still in their hands."

"What am I here for, then?" Lavon said. "Isn't there anything of value on the remaining plate? Did they really contain 'the wisdom of the Creators,' or is that another myth?"

"No. No, it's true," Shar said slowly, "as far as it goes."

He paused, and both men turned and gazed at the ghostly creature which had appeared suddenly outside the window. Then Shar said gravely, "Come in, Para."

The slipper-shaped organism, nearly transparent except for the thousands of black-and-silver granules and frothy bubbles which packed its interior, glided into the chamber and hovered, with a muted whirring of cilia. For a moment it remained silent, speaking telepathically to the Noc floating in the vault, after the ceremonious fashion of all the Protos. No human had ever intercepted one of these colloquies, but there was no doubt about their reality; humans had used them for long-range communication for generations.

Then the Para's cilia vibrated once more. "We are arrived, Shar and Lavon, according to the custom."

"And welcome," said Shar. "Lavon, let's leave this matter of the plates for a while, until you hear what Para has to say; that's a part of the knowledge Lavons must have as they come into their office, and it comes before the plates. I can give you some hints of what we are. First Para has to tell you something about what we aren't."

Lavon nodded, willingly enough, and watched the Proto as it settled gently to the surface of the hewn table at which Shar had been sitting. There was in the entity such a perfection and economy of organization, such a grace and surety of movement, that he could hardly believe in his own new-won maturity. Para, like all the Protos, made him feel, not perhaps poorly thought-out, but at least unfinished.

"We know that in this universe there is logically no place for man," the gleaming, now immobile cylinder upon the table droned abruptly. "Our memory is the common property of all our races. It reaches back to a time when there were no such creatures as man here, nor any even remotely like men. It remembers also that once upon a day there were men here, suddenly, and in some numbers. Their spores littered the Bottom; we found the spores only a short time after our season's Awakening, and inside them we saw the forms of men, slumbering.

"Then men shattered their spores and emerged. At first they seemed helpless, and the Eaters devoured them by scores, as in those days they devoured everything that moved. But that soon ended. Men were intelligent, active. And they were gifted with a trait, a character, possessed by no other creature in this world. Not even the savage Eaters had it. Men organized us to exterminate the Eaters, and therein lay the difference. Men had initiative. We have the word now, which you gave us, and we apply it, but we still do not know what the thing is that it labels."

"You fought beside us," Lavon said.

"Gladly. We would never have thought of that war by ourselves, but it was good and brought good. Yet we wondered. We saw that men were poor swimmers, poor walkers, poor crawlers, poor climbers. We saw that men were formed to make and use tools, a concept we still do not understand, for so wonderful a gift is largely wasted in this universe, and there is no other. What good are tool-useful members such as the hands of men? We do not know. It seems plain that so radical a thing should lead to a much greater rulership over the world than has, in fact, proven to be possible for men."

Lavon's head was spinning. "Para, I had no notion that you people were philosophers."

"The Protos are old," Shar said. He had again turned to look out the window, his hands locked behind his back. "They aren't philosophers, Lavon, but they are remorseless logicians. Listen to Para."

"To this reasoning there could be but one outcome," the Para said. "Our strange ally, Man, was like nothing else in this universe. He was and is unfitted for it. He does not belong here; he has been—adapted. This drives us to think that there are other universes besides this one, but where these universes might be, and what their properties might be, it is impossible to imagine. We have no imagination, as men know."

Was the creature being ironic? Lavon could not tell. He said slowly. "Other universes? How could that be true?"

"We do not know," the Para's uninflected voice hummed. Lavon waited, but obviously the Proto had nothing more to say.

Shar had resumed sitting on the window sill, clasping his knees, watching the come and go of dim shapes in the lighted gulf. "It is quite true," he said. "What is written on the plate makes it plain. Let me tell you now what it says.

"*We were made,* Lavon. We were made by men who were not as we are, but men who were our ancestors all the same. They were caught in some disaster, and they made us, and put us here in our universe—so that, even though they had to die, the race of men would live."

Lavon surged up from the woven spirogyra mat upon which he had been sitting. "You must think I'm a fool," he said sharply.

"No. You're our Lavon; you have a right to know the facts. Make what you like of them." Shar swung his webbed toes back into the chamber. "What I've told you may be hard to believe, but it seems to be so; what Para says backs it up. Our unfitness to live here is self-evident. I'll give you some examples:

"The past four Shars discovered that we won't get any farther in our studies until we learn how to control heat. We've produced enough heat chemically to show that even the water around us changes when the temperature gets high enough—or low enough, that we knew from the beginning. But there we're stopped."

"Why?"

"Because heat produced in open water is carried off as rapidly as it's produced. Once we tried to enclose that heat, and we blew up a whole tube of the castle and killed everything in range; the shock was terrible. We measured the pressures that were involved in that explosion, and we discovered that no substance we know could have resisted them. Theory suggests some stronger substances—but we need heat to form them!

"Take our chemistry. We live in water. Everything seems to dissolve in water, to some extent. How do we confine a chemical test to the crucible we put it in? How do we maintain a solution at one dilution? I don't know. Every avenue leads me to the same stone door. We're thinking creatures, Lavon, but there's something drastically wrong in the way we think about this universe we live in. It just doesn't seem to lead to results."

Lavon pushed back his floating hair futilely. "Maybe you're thinking about the wrong results. We've had no trouble with warfare, or crops, or practical things like that. If we can't create much heat, well, most of us won't miss it; we don't need more than we have. What's the other universe supposed to be like, the one our ancestors lived in? Is it any better than this one?"

"I don't know," Shar admitted. "It was so different that it's hard to compare the two. The metal plate tells a story about men who were traveling from one place to another in a container that moved by itself. The only analogue I can think of is the shallops of diatom shells that our youngsters used to sled along the thermocline; but evidently what's meant is something much bigger.

"I picture a huge shallop, closed on all sides, big enough to hold many people—maybe twenty or thirty. It had to travel for generations through some kind of medium where there wasn't any water to breathe, so the people had to carry their own water and renew it constantly. There were no seasons; no ice formed on the sky, because there couldn't be any sky in a closed shallop; and so there was no spore formation.

"Then the shallop was wrecked somehow. The people in it knew they were going to die. They made us, and put us here, as if we were their children. Because they had to die, they wrote their story on the plates, to tell us what had happened. I suppose we'd understand it better if we had the plate Shar I lost during the war—but we don't."

"The whole thing sounds like a parable," Lavon said, shrugging. "Or a song. I can see why you don't understand it. What I can't see is why you bother to try."

"Because of the plate," Shar said. "You've handled it yourself now, so you know that we've nothing like it. We have crude, impure metals we've hammered out, metals that last for a while and then decay. But the plate shines on, generation after generation. It doesn't change; our hammers and our graving tools break against it; the little heat we can generate leaves it unharmed. That plate wasn't formed in our universe—and that one fact makes every word on it important to me. Someone went to a great deal of trouble to make those plates indestructible, and to give them to us. Someone to whom the word 'stars' was important enough to be worth fourteen repetitions, despite the fact that the word doesn't seem to mean anything. I'm ready to think that if our makers repeated a word even twice on a record that seems likely to last forever, then it's important for us to know what it means."

Lavon stood up once more.

"All these extra universes and huge shallops and meaningless words—I can't say that they don't exist, but I don't see what difference it makes," he said. "The Shars of a few generations ago spent their whole lives breeding better algae crops for us, and showing us how to cultivate them, instead of living haphazardly on bacteria. Farther back, the Shars devised war engines, and war plans. All that was work worth doing. The Lavons of those days evidently got along without the metal plate and its puzzles, and saw to it that the Shars did, too. Well, as far as I'm concerned, you're welcome to the plate, if you like it better than crop improvement—but I think it ought to be thrown away."

"All right," Shar said, shrugging. "If you don't want it, that ends the traditional interview. We'll go our—"

There was a rising drone from the tabletop. The Para was lifting itself, waves of motion passing over its cilia, like the waves which went silently across the fruiting stalks of the fields of delicate fungi with which the Bottom was planted. It had been so silent that Lavon had forgotten it; he could tell from Shar's startlement that Shar had, too.

"This is a great decision," the waves of sound washing from the creature throbbed. "Every Proto has heard it, and agrees with it. We have been afraid of this metal plate for a long time, afraid that men would learn to understand it and follow what it says to some secret place, leaving the Protos behind. Now we are not afraid."

"There wasn't anything to be afraid of," Lavon said indulgently.

"No Lavon before you, Lavon, had ever said so," the Para said. "We are glad. We will throw the plate away, as Lavon orders."

With that, the shining creature swooped toward the embrasure. With it, it bore away the remaining plate, which had been resting under it on the tabletop, suspended delicately in the curved tips of its supple ventral cilia. Inside its pellucid body, vacuoles swelled to increase its buoyancy and enable it to carry the heavy weight.

With a cry, Shar plunged through the water toward the window. "Stop, Para!"

But Para was already gone, so swiftly that it had not even heard the call. Shar twisted his body and brought up one shoulder against the tower wall. He said nothing. His face was enough. Lavon could not look into it for more than an instant.

The shadows of the two men began to move slowly along the uneven cobbled floor. The Noc descended toward them from the vault, its tentacle stirring the water, its internal light flaring and fading irregularly. It, too, drifted through the window after its cousin, and sank slowly away toward the Bottom. Gently its living glow dimmed, flickered in the depths, and winked out.

II

For many days, Lavon was able to avoid thinking much about the loss. There was always a great deal of work to be done. Maintenance of the castles was a never-ending task. The thousand dichotomously-branching wings tended to crumble with time, especially at their bases where they sprouted from one another, and no Shar had yet come forward with a mortar as good as the rotifer-spittle which had once held them together. In addition, the breaking through of windows and the construction of chambers in the early days had been haphazard and often unsound. The instinctive architecture of the Eaters, after all, had not been meant to meet the needs of human occupants.

And then there were the crops. Men no longer fed precariously upon passing bacteria snatched to the mouth; now there were the drifting mats of specific water-fungi and algae, and the mycelia on the Bottom, rich and nourishing, which had been bred by five generations of Shars. These had to be tended constantly to keep the strains pure, and to keep the older and less intelligent species of the Protos from grazing on them. In this latter task, to be sure, the more intricate and far-seeing Proto types cooperated, but men were needed to supervise.

There had been a time, after the war with the Eaters, when it had been customary to prey upon the slow-moving and stupid diatoms, whose exquisite and fragile glass shells were so easily burst, and who were unable to learn that a friendly voice did not necessarily mean a friend. There were still people who would crack open a diatom when no one else was looking, but they were regarded as barbarians, to the puzzlement of the Protos. The blurred and simple-minded speech of the gorgeously engraved plants had brought them into the category of community pets—a concept which the Protos were utterly unable to grasp, especially since men admitted that diatoms on the half-frustrule were delicious.

Lavon had had to agree, very early, that the distinction was tiny. After all, humans did eat the desmids, which differed from the diatoms only in three particulars: their shells were flexible, they could not move (and for that matter neither could all but a few groups of diatoms), and they did not speak. Yet to Lavon, as to most men, there did seem to be some kind of distinction, whether the Protos could see it or not, and that was that. Under the circumstances he felt that it was a part of his duty, as the hereditary leader of men, to protect the diatoms from the occasional poachers who browsed upon them, in defiance of custom, in the high levels of the sunlit sky.

Yet Lavon found it impossible to keep himself busy enough to forget that moment when the last clues to Man's origin and destination had been seized, on authority of his own careless exaggeration, and borne away into dim space.

It might be possible to ask Para for the return of the plate, explain that a mistake had been made. The Protos were creatures of implacable logic, but they respected men, were used to illogic in men, and might reverse their decision if pressed—

We are sorry. The plate was carried over the bar and released in the gulf. We will have the Bottom there searched, but . . .

With a sick feeling he could not repress, Lavon knew that that would be the answer, or something very like it. When the Protos decided something was worthless, they did not hide it in some chamber like old women. They threw it away—efficiently.

Yet despite the tormenting of his conscience, Lavon was nearly convinced that the plate was well lost. What had it ever done for

Man, except to provide Shars with useless things to think about in the late seasons of their lives? What the Shars themselves had done to benefit Man, here, in the water, in the world, in the universe, had been done by direct experimentation. No bit of useful knowledge had ever come from the plates. There had never been anything in the second plate, at least, but things best left unthought. The Protos were right.

Lavon shifted his position on the plant frond, where he had been sitting in order to overlook the harvesting of an experimental crop of blue-green, oil-rich algae drifting in a clotted mass close to the top of the sky, and scratched his back gently against the coarse bole. The Protos were seldom wrong, after all. Their lack of creativity, their inability to think an original thought, was a gift as well as a limitation. It allowed them to see and feel things at all times as they were—not as they hoped they might be, for they had no ability to hope, either.

"La-von! Laa-vah-on!"

The long halloo came floating up from the sleepy depths. Propping one hand against the top of the frond, Lavon bent and looked down. One of the harvesters was looking up at him, holding loosely the adze with which he had been splitting free from the raft the glutinous tetrads of the algae.

"I'm up here. What's the matter?"

"We have the ripened quadrant cut free. Shall we tow it away?"

"Tow it away," Lavon said, with a lazy gesture. He leaned back again. At the same instant, a brilliant reddish glory burst into being above him, and cast itself down toward the depths like mesh after mesh of the finest-drawn gold. The great light which lived above the sky during the day, brightening or dimming according to some pattern no Shar ever had fathomed, was blooming again.

Few men, caught in the warm glow of that light, could resist looking up at it—especially when the top of the sky itself wrinkled and smiled just a moment's climb or swim away. Yet, as always, Lavon's bemused upward look gave him back nothing but his own distorted, bobbling reflection, and a reflection of the plant on which he rested.

Here was the upper limit, the third of the three surfaces of the universe. The first surface was the Bottom, where the water ended.

The second surface was the thermocline, definite enough in summer to provide good sledding but easily penetrable if you knew how.

The third surface was the sky. One could no more pass through that surface than one could penetrate the Bottom, nor was there any better reason to try. There the universe ended. The light which played over it daily, waxing and waning as it chose, seemed to be one of its properties.

Toward the end of the season, the water gradually became colder and more difficult to breathe, while at the same time the light grew duller and stayed for shorter periods between darknesses. Slow currents started to move. The high waters turned chill and started to fall. The Bottom mud stirred and smoked away, carrying with it the spores of the fields of fungi. The thermocline tossed, became choppy, and melted away. The sky began to fog with particles of soft silt carried up from the Bottom, the walls, the corners of the universe. Before very long, the whole world was cold, inhospitable, flocculent with yellowing, dying creatures. The world died until the first tentative current of warm water broke the winter silence.

That was how it was when the second surface vanished. If the sky were to melt away . . .

"Lavon!"

Just after the long call, a shining bubble rose past Lavon. He reached out and poked it, but it bounded away from his sharp thumb. The gas bubbles which rose from the Bottom in late summer were almost invulnerable—and when some especially hard blow or edge did penetrate them, they broke into smaller bubbles which nothing could touch, leaving behind a remarkably bad smell.

Gas. There was no water inside a bubble. A man who got inside a bubble would have nothing to breathe.

But, of course, it was impossible to enter a bubble. The surface tension was too strong. As strong as Shar's metal plate. As strong as the top of the sky.

As strong as the top of the sky. And above that—once the bubble was broken—a world of gas instead of water? Were all worlds bubbles of water drifting in gas?

If it were so, travel between them would be out of the question, since it would be impossible to pierce the sky to begin with. Nor did the infant cosmography include any provisions for Bottoms for the worlds.

And yet some of the local creatures did burrow into the Bottom, quite deeply, seeking something in those depths which was beyond the reach of Man. Even the surface of the ooze, in high summer, crawled with tiny creatures for which mud was a natural medium. And though many of the entities with which man lived could not pass freely between the two countries of water which were divided by the thermocline, men could and did.

And if the new universe of which Shar had spoken existed at all, it had to exist beyond the sky, where the light was. Why could not the sky be passed, after all? The fact that bubbles could sometimes be broken showed that the surface skin formed between water and gas wasn't completely invulnerable. Had it ever been tried?

Lavon did not suppose that one man could butt his way through the top of the sky, any more than he could burrow into the Bottom, but there might be ways around the difficulty. Here at his back, for instance, was a plant which gave every appearance of continuing beyond the sky; its upper fronds broke off and were bent back only by a trick of reflection.

It had always been assumed that the plants died where they touched the sky. For the most part, they did, for frequently the dead extension could be seen, leached and yellow, the boxes of its component cells empty, floating imbedded in the perfect mirror. But some were simply chopped off, like the one which sheltered him now. Perhaps that was only an illusion, and instead it soared indefinitely into some other place—some place where men might once have been born, and might still live . . .

Both plates were gone. There was only one other way to find out.

Determinedly, Lavon began to climb toward the wavering mirror of the sky. His thorn-thumbed feet trampled obliviously upon the clustered sheathes of fragile stippled diatoms. The tulip-heads of Vortae, placid and murmurous cousins of Para, retracted startledly out of his way upon coiling stalks, to make silly gossip behind him.

Lavon did not hear them. He continued to climb doggedly toward the light, his fingers and toes gripping the plant-bole.

"Lavon! Where are you going? Lavon!"

He leaned out and looked down. The man with the adze, a doll-like figure, was beckoning to him from a patch of blue-green retreating over a violet abyss. Dizzily he looked away, clinging to the bole; he had never been so high before. He had, of course, nothing to fear from falling, but the fear was in his heritage. Then he began to climb again.

After a while, he touched the sky with one hand. He stopped

Surface Tension

to breathe. Curious bacteria gathered about the base of his thumb where blood from a small cut was fogging away, scattered at his gesture, and wriggled mindlessly back toward the dull red lure.

He waited until he no longer felt winded, and resumed climbing. The sky pressed down against the top of his head, against the back of his neck, against his shoulders. It seemed to give slightly, with a tough, frictionless elasticity. The water here was intensely bright, and quite colorless. He climbed another step, driving his shoulders against that enormous weight.

It was fruitless. He might as well have tried to penetrate a cliff.

Again he had to rest. While he panted, he made a curious discovery. All around the bole of the water plant, the steel surface of the sky curved upward, making a kind of sheathe. He found that he could insert his hand into it—there was almost enough space to admit his head as well. Clinging closely to the bole, he looked up into the inside of the sheathe, probing it with his injured hand. The glare was blinding.

There was a kind of soundless explosion. His whole wrist was suddenly encircled in an intense, impersonal grip, as if it were being cut in two. In blind astonishment, he lunged upward.

The ring of pain traveled smoothly down his upflung arm as he rose, was suddenly around his shoulders and chest. Another lunge and his knees were being squeezed in the circular vise. Another—

Something was horribly wrong. He clung to the bole and tried to gasp, but there was—nothing to breathe.

The water came streaming out of his body, from his mouth, his nostrils, the spiracles in his sides, spurting in tangible jets. An intense and fiery itching crawled over the surface of his body. At each spasm, long knives ran into him, and from a great distance he heard more water being expelled from his book-lungs in an obscene, frothy sputtering. Inside his head, a patch of fire began to eat away at the floor of his nasal cavity. Lavon was drowning.

With a final convulsion, he kicked himself away from the splintery bole, and fell. A hard impact shook him; and then the water, who had clung to him so tightly when he had first attempted to leave her, took him back with cold violence.

Sprawling and tumbling grotesquely, he drifted, down and down and down, toward the Bottom.

III

For many days, Lavon lay curled insensibly in his spore, as if in the winter sleep. The shock of cold which he had felt on re-entering his native universe had been taken by his body as a sign of coming winter, as it had taken the oxygen-starvation of his brief sojourn above the sky. The spore-forming glands had at once begun to function.

Had it not been for this, Lavon would surely have died. The danger of drowning disappeared even as he fell, as the air bubbled out of his lungs and readmitted the life-giving water. But for acute desiccation and third degree sunburn, the sunken universe knew no remedy. The healing amnionic fluid generated by the spore-forming glands, after the transparent amber sphere had enclosed him, offered Lavon his only chance.

The brown sphere, quiescent in the eternal winter of the Bottom, was spotted after some days by a prowling amoeba. Down there the temperature was always an even 4°, no matter what the season, but it was unheard of that a spore should be found there while the high epilimnion was still warm and rich in oxygen.

Within an hour, the spore was surrounded by scores of astonished Protos, jostling each other to bump their blunt eyeless prows against the shell. Another hour later, a squad of worried men came plunging from the castles far above to press their own noses against the transparent wall. Then swift orders were given.

Four Para grouped themselves about the amber sphere, and there was a subdued explosion as their trichocysts burst. The four Paras thrummed and lifted, tugging.

Lavon's spore swayed gently in the mud and then rose slowly, entangled in the fine web. Nearby, a Noc cast a cold pulsating glow over the operation, for the benefit of the baffled knot of men. The sleeping figure of Lavon, head bowed, knees drawn up into its chest, revolved with an absurd solemnity inside the shell as it was removed.

"Take him to Shar, Para."

The young Shar justified, by minding his own business, the traditional wisdom with which his hereditary office had invested him. He observed at once that there was nothing he could do for the encysted Lavon which would not be classifiable as simple meddling.

He had the sphere deposited in a high tower room of his castle, where there was plenty of light and the water was warm, which should suggest to the estivating form that spring was again on the way. Beyond that, he simply sat and watched, and kept his speculations to himself.

Inside the spore, Lavon's body seemed to be rapidly shedding its skin, in long strips and patches. Gradually, his curious shrunkenness disappeared. His withered arms and legs and sunken abdomen filled out again.

The days went by while Shar watched. Finally he could discern no more changes, and, on a hunch, had the spore taken up to the topmost battlements of the tower, into the direct daylight.

An hour later, Lavon moved in his amber prison.

He uncurled and stretched, turned blank eyes up toward the light. His expression was that of a man who had not yet awakened from a ferocious nightmare. His whole body shone with a strange pink newness.

Shar knocked gently on the walls of the spore. Lavon turned his blind face toward the sound, life coming into his eyes. He smiled tentatively and braced his hands and feet against the inner wall of the shell.

The whole sphere fell abruptly to pieces with a sharp crackling. The amniotic fluid dissipated around him and Shar, carrying away with it the suggestive odor of a bitter struggle against death.

Lavon stood among the shards and looked at Shar silently. At last he said:

"Shar—I've been above the sky."

"I know," Shar said gently.

Again Lavon was silent. Shar said, "Don't be humble, Lavon. You've done an epoch-making thing. It nearly cost you your life. You must tell me the rest—all of it."

"The rest?"

"You taught me a lot while you slept. Or are you still opposed to 'useless' knowledge?"

Lavon could say nothing. He no longer could tell what he knew from what he wanted to know. He had only one question left, but he could not utter it. He could only look dumbly into Shar's delicate face.

"You have answered me," Shar said, even more gently than before. "Come, my friend; join me at my table. We will plan our journey to the stars."

There were five of them around Shar's big table: Shar himself, Lavon, and the three assistants assigned by custom to the Shars from the families Than, Tanol, and Stravol. The duties of these three men—or, sometimes, women—under many previous Shars had been simple and onerous: to put into effect in the field the genetic changes in the food crops which the Shar himself had worked out in little, in laboratory tanks and flats. Under other Shars more interested in metal-working or in chemistry, they had been smudged men—diggers, rock-splitters, fashioners and cleaners of apparatus.

Under Shar XVI, however, the three assistants had been more envied than usual among the rest of Lavon's people, for they seemed to do very little work of any kind. They spent long hours of every day talking with Shar in his chambers, poring over records, making minuscule scratch-marks on slate, or just looking intently at simple things about which there was no obvious mystery. Sometimes they actually worked with Shar in his laboratory, but mostly they just sat.

Shar XVI had, as a matter of fact, discovered certain rudimentary rules of inquiry which, as he explained it to Lavon, he had recognized as tools of enormous power. He had become more interested in passing these on to future workers than in the seductions of any specific experiment, the journey to the stars perhaps excepted. The Than, Tanol, and Stravol of his generation were having scientific method pounded into their heads, a procedure they maintained was sometimes more painful than heaving a thousand rocks.

That they were the first of Lavon's people to be taxed with the problem of constructing a spaceship was, therefore, inevitable. The results lay on the table: three models, made of diatom-glass, strands of algae, flexible bits of cellulose, flakes of stonewort, slivers of wood, and organic glues collected from the secretions of a score of different plants and animals.

Lavon picked up the nearest one, a fragile spherical construction inside which little beads of dark-brown lava—actually bricks of rotifer-spittle painfully chipped free from the wall of an unused castle—moved freely back and forth in a kind of ball-bearing race. "Now whose is this one?" he said, turning the sphere curiously to and fro.

"That's mine," Tanol said. "Frankly, I don't think it comes anywhere near meeting all the requirements. It's just the only design I could arrive at that I think we could build with the materials and knowledge we have to hand now."

"But how does it work?"

"Hand it here a moment, Lavon. This bladder you see inside at the center, with the hollow spirogyra straws leading out from it to the skin of the ship, is a buoyancy tank. The idea is that we trap ourselves a big gas-bubble as it rises from the Bottom and install it in the tank. Probably we'll have to do that piecemeal. Then the ship rises to the sky on the buoyancy of the bubble. The little paddles, here along these two bands on the outside, rotate when the crew—that's these bricks you hear shaking around inside—walks a treadmill that runs around the inside of the hull; they paddle us over to the edge of the sky. I stole that trick from the way Didin gets about. Then we pull the paddles in—they fold over into slots, like this—and, still by weight-transfer from the inside, we roll ourselves up the slope until we're out in space. When we hit another world and enter the water again, we let the gas out of the tank gradually through the exhaust tubes represented by these straws, and sink down to a landing at a controlled rate."

"Very ingenious," Shar said thoughtfully. "But I can foresee some difficulties. For one thing, the design lacks stability."

"Yes, it does," Tanol agreed. "And keeping it in motion is going to require a lot of footwork. But if we were to sling a freely-moving weight from the center of gravity of the machine, we could stabilize it at least partly. And the biggest expenditure of energy involved in the whole trip is going to be getting the machine up to the sky in the first place, and with this design that's taken care of—as a matter of fact, once the bubble's installed, we'll have to keep the ship tied down until we're ready to take off."

"How about letting the gas out?" Lavon said. "Will it go out through those little tubes when we want it to? Won't it just cling to the walls of the tubes instead? The skin between water and gas is pretty difficult to deform—to that I can testify."

Tanol frowned. "That I don't know. Don't forget that the tubes will be large in the real ship, not just straws as they are in the model."

"Bigger than a man's body?" Than said.

"No, hardly. Maybe as big though as a man's head, at the most."

"Won't work," Than said tersely. "I tried it. You can't lead a bubble through a pipe that small. As Lavon says, it clings to the inside of the tube and won't be budged unless you put pressure behind it—lots of pressure. If we build this ship, we'll just have to abandon it once we hit our new world; we won't be able to set it down anywhere."

"That's out of the question," Lavon said at once. "Putting aside for the moment the waste involved, we may have to use the ship again in a hurry. Who knows what the new world will be like? We're going to have to be able to leave it again if it turns out to be impossible to live in."

"Which is your model, Than?" Shar said.

"This one. With this design, we do the trip the hard way—crawl along the Bottom until it meets the sky, crawl until we hit the next world, and crawl wherever we're going when we get there. No aquabatics. She's treadmill-powered, like Tanol's, but not necessarily man-powered; I've been thinking a bit about using motile diatoms. She steers by varying the power on one side or the other. For fine steering we can also hitch a pair of thongs to opposite ends of the rear axle and swivel her that way."

Shar looked closely at the tube-shaped model and pushed it experimentally along the table a little way. "I like that," he said presently. "It sits still when you want it to. With Than's spherical ship, we'd be at the mercy of any stray current at home or in the new world—and for all I know there may be currents of some sort in space, too, gas currents perhaps. Lavon, what do you think?"

"How would we build it?" Lavon said. "It's round in cross-section. That's all very well for a model, but how do you make a really big tube of that shape that won't fall in on itself?"

"Look inside, through the front window," Than said. "You'll see beams that cross at the center, at right angles to the long axis. They hold the walls braced."

"That consumes a lot of space," Stravol objected. By far the quietest and most introspective of the three assistants, he had not spoken until now since the beginning of the conference. "You've got to have free passage back and forth inside the ship. How are we going to keep everything operating if we have to be crawling around beams all the time?"

"All right, come up with something better," Than said, shrugging.

"That's easy. We bend hoops."

"Hoops!" Tanol said. "On *that* scale? You'd have to soak your wood in mud for a year before it would be flexible enough, and then it wouldn't have the strength you'd need."

"No, you wouldn't," Stravol said. "I didn't build a ship model, I just made drawings, and my ship isn't as good as Than's by a long distance. But my design for the ship is also tubular, so I did build a model of a hoop-bending machine—that's it on the table. You lock one end of your beam down in a heavy vise, like so, leaving the butt striking out on the other side. Then you tie up the other end with a heavy line, around this notch. Then you run your line around a windlass, and five or six men wind up the windlass, like so. That pulls the free end of the beam down until the notch engages with this key-slot, which you've pre-cut at the other end. Then you unlock the vise, and there's your hoop; for safety you might drive a peg through the joint to keep the thing from springing open unexpectedly."

"Wouldn't the beam you were using break after it had bent a certain distance?" Lavon asked.

"Stock timber certainly would," Stravol said. "But for this trick you use *green* wood, not seasoned. Otherwise you'd have to soften your beam to uselessness, as Tanol says. But live wood will flex enough to make a good, strong, single-unit hoop—or if it doesn't, Shar, the little rituals with numbers that you've been teaching us don't mean anything after all!"

Shar smiled. "You can easily make a mistake in using numbers," he said.

"I checked everything."

"I'm sure of it. And I think it's well worth a trial. Anything else to offer?"

"Well," Stravol said, "I've got a kind of live ventilating system I think should be useful. Otherwise, as I said, Than's ship strikes me as the type we should build; my own's hopelessly cumbersome."

"I have to agree," Tanol said regretfully. "But I'd like to try putting together a lighter-than-water ship sometime, maybe just for local travel. If the new world is bigger than ours, it might not be possible to swim everywhere you might want to go."

"That never occurred to me," Lavon exclaimed. "Suppose the new world *is* twice, three times, eight times as big as ours? Shar, is there any reason why that couldn't be?"

"None that I know of. The history plate certainly seems to take all kinds of enormous distances practically for granted. All right, let's make up a composite design from what we have here. Tanol, you're the best draftsman among us, suppose you draw it up. Lavon, what about labor?"

"I've a plan ready," Lavon said. "As I see it, the people who work on the ship are going to have to be on the job full time. Building the vessel isn't going to be an overnight task, or even one that we can finish in a single season, so we can't count on using a rotating force.

Besides, this is technical work; once a man learns how to do a particular task, it would be wasteful to send him back to tending fungi just because somebody else has some time on his hands.

"So I've set up a basic force involving the two or three most intelligent hand-workers from each of the various trades. Those people I can withdraw from their regular work without upsetting the way we run our usual concerns, or noticeably increasing the burden on the others in a given trade. They will do the skilled labor, and stick with the ship until it's done. Some of them will make up the crew, too. For heavy, unskilled jobs, we can call on the various seasonal pools of unskilled people without disrupting our ordinary life."

"Good," Shar said. He leaned forward and rested linked hands on the edge of the table—although, because of the webbing between his fingers, he could link no more than the fingertips. "We've really made remarkable progress. I didn't expect that we'd have matters advanced a tenth as far as this by the end of this meeting. But maybe I've overlooked something important. Has anybody any more suggestions, or any questions?"

"I've got a question," Stravol said quietly.

"All right, let's hear it."

"Where are we going?"

There was quite a long silence. Finally Shar said: "Stravol, I can't answer that yet. I could say that we're going to the stars, but since we still have no idea what a star is, that answer wouldn't do you much good. We're going to make this trip because we've found that some of the fantastic things that the history plate says are really so. We know now that the sky can be passed, and that beyond the sky there's a region where there's no water to breathe, the region our ancients called 'space.' Both of these ideas always seemed to be against common sense, but nevertheless we've found that they're true.

"The history plate also says that there are other worlds than ours, and actually that's an easier idea to accept, once you've found out that the other two are so. As for the stars—well, we just don't know yet, we haven't any information at all that would allow us to read the history plate on that subject with new eyes, and there's no point in making wild guesses unless we can test the guesses. The stars are in space, and presumably, once we're out in space, we'll see them and the meaning of the word will become clear. At least we can confidently expect to see some clues—look at all the information we got from Lavon's trip a few seconds above the sky!

"But in the meantime, there's no point in our speculating in a bubble. We think there are other worlds somewhere, and we're devising means to make the trip. The other questions, the pendant ones, just have to be put aside for now. We'll answer them eventually— there's no doubt in my mind about that. But it may take a long time."

Stravol grinned ruefully. "I expected no more. In a way, I think the whole project is crazy. But I'm in it right out to the end, all the same."

Shar and Lavon grinned back. All of them had the fever, and Lavon suspected that their whole enclosed universe would share it with them before long. He said:

"Then let's not waste a minute. There's still a huge mass of detail to be worked out, and after that, all the hard work will just have begun. Let's get moving!"

The five men arose and looked at each other. Their expressions varied, but in all their eyes there was in addition the same mixture of awe and ambition: the composite face of the shipwright and of the astronaut.

Then they went out, severally, to begin their voyages.

It was two winter sleeps after Lavon's disastrous climb beyond the sky that all work on the spaceship stopped. By then, Lavon knew that he had hardened and weathered into that temporarily ageless state a man enters after he has just reached his prime; and he knew also that there were wrinkles engraved on his brow, to stay and to deepen.

"Old" Shar, too, had changed, his features losing some of their delicacy as he came into his maturity. Though the wedge-shaped bony structure of his face would give him a withdrawn and poetic look for as long as he lived, participation in the plan had given his expression a kind of executive overlay, which at best made it assume a mask-like rigidity, and at worst coarsened it somehow.

Yet despite the bleeding away of the years, the spaceship was still only a hulk. It lay upon a platform built above the tumbled boulders of the sandbar which stretched out from one wall of the world. It was an immense hull of pegged wood, broken by regularly spaced gaps through which the raw beams of its skeleton could be seen.

Work upon it had progressed fairly rapidly at first, for it was not hard to visualize what kind of vehicle would be needed to crawl through empty space without losing its water; Than and his colleagues had done that job well. It had been recognized, too, that the sheer size of the machine would enforce a long period of construction, perhaps as long as two full seasons; but neither Shar and his assistants or Lavon had anticipated any serious snag.

For that matter, part of the vehicle's apparent incompleteness was an illusion. About a third of its fittings were to consist of living creatures, which could not be expected to install themselves in the vessel much before the actual takeoff.

Yet time and time again, work on the ship had to be halted for long periods. Several times whole sections needed to be ripped out, as it became more and more evident that hardly a single normal, understandable concept could be applied to the problem of space travel.

The lack of the history plate, which the Para steadfastly refused to deliver up, was a double handicap. Immediately upon its loss, Shar had set himself to reproduce it from memory; but unlike the more religious of his ancestors, he had never regarded it as holy writ, and hence had never set himself to memorizing it word by word. Even before the theft, he had accumulated a set of variant translations of passages presenting specific experimental problems, which were stored in his library, carved in wood. Most of these translations, however, tended to contradict each other, and none of them related to spaceship construction, upon which the original had been vague in any case.

No duplicates of the cryptic characters of the original had ever been made, for the simple reason that there was nothing in the sunken universe capable of destroying the originals, nor of duplicating their apparently changeless permanence. Shar remarked too late that through simple caution they should have made a number of verbatim temporary records—but after generations of green-gold peace, simple caution no longer covers preparation against catastrophe. (Nor, for that matter, does a culture which has to dig each letter of its simple alphabet into pulpy water-logged wood with a flake of stonewort encourage the keeping of records in triplicate.)

As a result, Shar's imperfect memory of the contents of the history plate, plus the constant and millennial doubt as to the accuracy of the various translations, proved finally to be the worst obstacle to progress on the spaceship itself.

"Men must paddle before they can swim," Lavon observed belatedly, and Shar was forced to agree with him.

Obviously, whatever the ancients had known about the spaceship construction, very little of that knowledge was usable to a people still trying to build its first spaceship from scratch. In retrospect, it was not surprising that the great hulk rested incomplete upon its platform above the sand boulders, exuding a musty odor of wood steadily losing its strength, two generations after its flat bottom had been laid down.

The fat-faced young man who headed the strike delegation to Shar's chambers was Phil XX, a man two generations younger than Shar, four younger than Lavon. There were crow's-feet at the corners of his eyes, which made him look both like a querulous old man and like an infant spoiled in the spore.

"We're calling a halt to this crazy project," he said bluntly. "We've slaved away our youth on it, but now that we're our own masters, it's over, that's all. It's over."

"Nobody's compelled you," Lavon said angrily.

"Society does; our parents do," a gaunt member of the delegation said. "But now we're going to start living in the real world. Everybody these days knows that there's no other world but this one. You oldsters can hang on to your superstitions if you like. We don't intend to."

Baffled, Lavon looked over at Shar. The scientist smiled and said, "Let them go, Lavon. We have no use for the fainthearted."

The fat-faced young man flushed. "You can't insult us into going back to work. We're through. Build your own ship to no place!"

"All right," Lavon said evenly. "Go on, beat it. Don't stand around here orating about it. You've made your decisions and we're not interested in your self-justifications. Goodbye."

The fat-faced young man evidently still had quite a bit of heroism to dramatize which Lavon's dismissal had short-circuited. An examination of Lavon's stony face, however, seemed to convince him that he had to take his victory as he found it. He and the delegation trailed ingloriously out the archway.

"Now what?" Lavon asked when they had gone. "I must admit, Shar, that I would have tried to persuade them. We do need the workers, after all."

"Not as much as they need us," Shar said tranquilly. "I know all those young men. I think they'll be astonished at the runty crops their fields will produce next season, after they have to breed them without my advice. Now, how many volunteers have you got for the crew of the ship?"

"Hundreds. Every youngster of the generation after Phil's wants to go along. Phil's wrong about the segment of the populace, at least. The project catches the imagination of the very young."

"Did you give them any encouragement?"

"Sure," Lavon said. "I told them we'd call on them if they were chosen. But you can't take that seriously! We'd do badly to displace our picked group of specialists with youths who have enthusiasm and nothing else."

"That's not what I had in mind, Lavon. Didn't I see a Noc in these chambers somewhere? Oh, there he is, asleep in the dome. Noc!"

The creature stirred its tentacle lazily.

"Noc, I've a message," Shar called. "The Protos are to tell all men that those who wish to go to the next world with the spaceship must come to the staging area right away. Say that we can't promise to take everyone, but that only those who help us to build the ship will be considered at all."

The Noc curled its tentacle again, and appeared to go back to sleep.

IV

Lavon turned from the arrangement of speaking-tube megaphones which was his control board and looked at Para. "One last try," he said. "Will you give us back the history plate?"

"No, Lavon. We have never denied you anything before. But this we must."

"You're going with us, though, Para. Unless you give us back the knowledge we need, you'll lose your life if we lose ours."

"What is one Para?" the creature said. "We are all alike. This cell will die; but the Protos need to know how you fare on this journey. We believe you should make it without the plate, for in no other way can we assess the real importance of the plate."

"Then you admit you still have it. What if you can't communicate with your fellows once we're out in space? How do you know that water isn't essential to your telepathy?"

The Proto was silent. Lavon stared at it a moment, then turned deliberately back to the speaking tubes. "Everyone hang on," he said. He felt shaky. "We're about to start. Stravol, is the ship sealed?"

"As far as I can tell, Lavon."

Lavon shifted to another megaphone. He took a deep breath. Already the water seemed stifling, although the ship hadn't moved.

"Ready with one-quarter power. . . . One, two, three, *go*."

The whole ship jerked and settled back into place again. The raphe diatoms along the under hull settled into their niches, their jelly treads turning against broad endless belts of crude caddis-worm leather. Wooden gears creaked, stepping up the slow power of the creatures, transmitting it to the sixteen axles of the ship's wheels.

The ship rocked and began to roll slowly along the sand bar. Lavon looked tensely through the mica port. The world flowed painfully past him. The ship canted and began to climb the slope. Behind him, he could feel the electric silence of Shar, Para, and the two alternate pilots, Than and Stravol, as if their gaze were stabbing directly through his body and on out the port. The world looked different, now that he was leaving it. How had he missed all this beauty before

The slapping of the endless belts and the squeaking and groaning of the gears and axles grew louder as the slope steepened. The ship continued to climb, lurching. Around it, squadrons of men and Protos dipped and wheeled, escorting it toward the sky.

Gradually the sky lowered and pressed down toward the top of the ship.

"A little more work from your diatoms, Tanol," Lavon said. "Boulder ahead." The ship swung ponderously. "All right, slow them up again. Give us a shove from your side, Tol—no, that's too much—there, that's it. Back to normal; you're still turning us! Tanol, give us one burst to line up again. Good. All right, steady drive on all sides. It shouldn't be long now."

"How can you think in webs like that?" the Para wondered behind him.

"I just do, that's all. It's the way men think. Overseers, a little more thrust now; the grade's getting steeper."

The gears groaned. The ship nosed up. The sky brightened in Lavon's face. Despite himself, he began to be frightened. His lungs seemed to burn, and in his mind he felt his long fall through nothingness toward the chill slap of the water as if he were experiencing it for the first time. His skin itched and burned. Could he go up there again? Up there into the burning void, the great gasping agony where no life should go?

The sand bar began to level out and the going became a little easier. Up here, the sky was so close that the lumbering motion of the huge ship disturbed it. Shadows of wavelets ran across the sand.

Silently, the thick-barreled bands of blue-green algae drank in the light and converted it to oxygen, writhing in their slow mindless dance just under the long mica skylight which ran along the spine of the ship. In the hold, beneath the latticed corridor and cabin floors, whirring Vortae kept the ship's water in motion, fueling themselves upon drifting organic particles.

One by one, the figures wheeling outside about the ship waved arms of cilia and fell back, coasting down the slope of the sand bar toward the familiar world, dwindling and disappearing. There was at last only one single Euglena, half-plant cousin of the Protos, forging along beside the spaceship into the marshes of the shallows. It loved the light, but finally it, too, was driven away into deeper, cooler waters, its single whiplike tentacle undulating placidly as it went. It was not very bright, but Lavon felt deserted when it left.

Where they were going, though, none could follow.

Now the sky was nothing but a thin, resistant skin of water coating the top of the ship. The vessel slowed, and when Lavon called for more power, it began to dig itself in among the sandgrains and boulders.

"That's not going to work," Shar said tensely. "I think, we'd better step down the gear-ratio, Lavon, so you can apply stress more slowly."

"All right," Lavon agreed. "Full stop, everybody. Shar, will you supervise gear-changing, please?"

Insane brilliance of empty space looked Lavon full in the face just beyond his big mica bull's-eye. It was maddening to be forced to stop here upon the threshold of infinity; and it was dangerous, too. Lavon could feel building in him the old fear of the outside. A few moments more of inaction, he knew with a gathering coldness in his belly, and he would be unable to go through with it.

Surely, he thought, there must be a better way to change gear-ratios than the traditional one, which involved dismantling almost the entire gear-box. Why couldn't a number of gears of different sizes be carried on the same shaft, not necessarily all in action at once, but awaiting use simply by shoving the axle back and forth longitudinally in its sockets? It would still be clumsy, but it could be worked on orders from the bridge and would not involve shutting down the entire machine—and throwing the new pilot into a blue-green funk.

Shar came lunging up through the trap and swam himself to a stop.

"All set," he said. "The bid reduction gears aren't taking the strain too well, though."

"Splintering?"

"Yes. I'd go it slow at first."

Lavon nodded mutely. Without allowing himself to stop, even for a moment, to consider the consequences of his words, he called: "Half power."

The ship hunched itself down again and began to move, very slowly indeed, but more smoothly than before. Overhead, the sky thinned to complete transparency. The great light came blasting in. Behind Lavon there was an uneasy stir. The whiteness grew at the front ports.

Again the ship slowed, straining against the blinding barrier. Lavon swallowed and called for more power. The ship groaned like something about to die. It was now almost at a standstill.

"More power," Lavon ground out.

Once more, with infinite slowness, the ship began to move. Gently, it tilted upward.

Then it lunged forward and every board and beam in it began to squall.

"Lavon! Lavon!"

Lavon started sharply at the shout. The voice was coming at him from one of the megaphones, the one marked for the port at the rear of the ship.

"Lavon!"

"What is it? Stop your damn yelling."

"I can see the top of the sky! From the *other* side, from the top side! It's like a big flat sheet of metal. We're going away from it. We're above the sky, Lavon, we're above the sky!"

Another violent start swung Lavon around toward the forward port. On the outside of the mica, the water was evaporating with shocking swiftness, taking with it strange distortions and patterns made of rainbows. Lavon saw space.

It was at first like a deserted and cruelly dry version of the Bottom. There were enormous boulders, great cliffs, tumbled, split, riven, jagged rocks going up and away in all directions, as if scattered at random by some giant.

But it had a sky of its own—a deep blue dome so far away that he could not believe in, let alone estimate, what its distance might be. And in this dome was a ball of reddish-white fire that seared his eyeballs.

The wilderness of rock was still a long way away from the ship, which now seemed to be resting upon a level, glistening plain. Beneath the surface-shine, the plain seemed to be made of sand, nothing but familiar sand, the same substance which had heaped up to form a bar in Lavon's universe, the bar along which the ship had climbed. But the glassy, colorful skin over it—

Suddenly Lavon became conscious of another shout from the megaphone banks. He shook his head savagely and said, "What is it now?"

"Lavon, this is Tol. What have you gotten us into? The belts are locked. The diatoms can't move them. They aren't faking, either; we've rapped them hard enough to make them think we were trying to break their shells, but they still can't give us more power."

"Leave them alone," Lavon snapped. "They can't fake; they haven't enough intelligence. If they say they can't give you more power, they can't."

"Well, then, you get us out of it."

Shar came forward to Lavon's elbow. "We're on a spacewater interface, where the surface tension is very high," he said softly. "If you order the wheels pulled up now, I think we'll make better progress for a while on the belly tread."

"Good enough," Lavon said with relief. "Hello below—haul up the wheels."

"For a long while," Shar said, "I couldn't understand the reference of the history plate to 'retractable landing gear,' but it finally occurred to me that the tension along a space-mud interface would hold any large object pretty tightly. That's why I insisted on our building the ship so that we could lift the wheels."

"Evidently the ancients knew their business after all, Shar."

Quite a few minutes later—for shifting power to the belly treads involved another setting of the gear box— the ship was crawling along the shore toward the tumbled rock. Anxiously, Lavon scanned the jagged, threatening wall for a break. There was a sort of rivulet off toward the left which might offer a route, though a dubious one, to the next world. After some thought, Lavon ordered his ship turned toward it.

"Do you suppose that thing in the sky is a 'star'?" he asked. "But there were supposed to be lots of them. Only one is up there—and one's plenty for my taste."

"I don't know," Shar admitted. "But I'm beginning to get a picture of the way the universe is made, I think. Evidently our world is a sort of cup in the Bottom of this huge one. This one has a sky of its own; perhaps it, too, is only a cup in the Bottom of a still huger world, and so on and on without end. It's a hard concept to grasp, I'll admit. Maybe it would be more sensible to assume that all the worlds are cups in this one common surface, and that the great light shines on them all impartially."

"Then what makes it go out every night, and dim even in the day during winter?" Lavon demanded.

"Perhaps it travels in circles, over first one world, then another. How could I know yet?"

"Well, if you're right, it means that all we have to do is crawl along here for a while, until we hit the top of the sky of another world," Lavon said. "Then we dive in. Somehow it seems too simple, after all our preparations."

Shar chuckled, but the sound did not suggest that he had discovered anything funny. "Simple? Have you noticed the temperature yet?"

Lavon had noticed it, just beneath the surface of awareness, but at Shar's remark he realized that he was gradually being stifled. The oxygen content of the water, luckily, had not dropped, but the temperature suggested the shallows in the last and worst part of autumn. It was like trying to breathe soup.

"Than, give us more action from the Vortae," Lavon said. "This is going to be unbearable unless we get more circulation."

There was a reply from Than, but it came to Lavon's ears only as a mumble. It was all he could do now to keep his attention on the business of steering the ship.

The cut or defile in the scattered razor-edged rocks was a little closer, but there still seemed to be many miles of rough desert to cross. After a while, the ship settled into a steady, painfully slow crawling, with less pitching and jerking than before, but also with less progress. Under it, there was now a sliding, grinding sound, rasping against the hull of the ship itself, as if it were treadmilling over some coarse lubricant the particles of which were each as big as a man's head.

Finally Shar said, "Lavon, we'll have to stop again. The sand this far up is dry, and we're wasting energy using the tread."

"Are you sure we can take it?" Lavon asked, gasping for breath. "At least we are moving. If we stop to lower the wheels and change gears again, we'll boil."

"We'll boil if we don't," Shar said calmly. "Some of our algae are dead already and the rest are withering. That's a pretty good sign that we can't take much more. I don't think we'll make it into the shadows, unless we do change over and put on some speed."

There was a gulping sound from one of the mechanics. "We ought to turn back," he said raggedly. "We were never meant to be out here in the first place. We were made for the water, not for this hell."

"We'll stop," Lavon said, "but we're not turning back. That's final."

The words made a brave sound, but the man had upset Lavon more than he dared to admit, even to himself. "Shar," he said, "make it fast, will you?"

The scientist nodded and dived below.

The minutes stretched out. The great red-gold globe in the sky blazed and blazed. It had moved down the sky, far down, so that the light was pouring into the ship directly in Lavon's face, illuminating every floating particle, its rays like long milky streamers. The currents of water passing Lavon's cheek were almost hot.

How could they dare go directly forward into that inferno? The land directly under the "star" must be even hotter than it was here.

"Lavon! Look at Para!"

Lavon forced himself to turn and look at his Proto ally. The great slipper had settled to the deck where it was lying with only a feeble pulsation of its cilia. Inside, its vacuoles were beginning to swell, to become bloated, pear-shaped bubbles, crowding the granulated cytoplasm, pressing upon the dark nuclei.

"Is . . . is he dying?"

"This cell is dying," Para said, as coldly as always. "But go on—go on. There is much to learn, and you may live, even though we do not. Go on."

"You're—for us now?" Lavon whispered.

"We have always been for you. Push your folly to the uttermost. We will benefit in the end, and so will Man."

The whisper died away. Lavon called the creature again, but it did not respond.

There was a wooden clashing from below, and then Shar's voice came tinnily from one of the megaphones. "Lavon, go ahead! The diatoms are dying, too, and then we'll be without power. Make it as quickly and directly as you can."

Grimly, Lavon leaned forward. "The 'star' is directly over the land we're approaching."

"It is? It may go lower still and the shadows will get longer. That may be our only hope."

Lavon had not thought of that. He rasped into the banked megaphones. Once more, the ship began to move, a little faster now, but seemingly still at a crawl. The thirty-two wheels rumbled.

It got hotter.

Steadily, with a perceptible motion, the "star" sank in Lavon's face. Suddenly a new terror struck him. Suppose it should continue to go down until it was gone entirely? Blasting though it was now, it was the only source of heat. Would not space become bitter cold on the instant—and the ship an expanding, bursting block of ice?

The shadows lengthened menacingly, stretching across the desert toward the forward-rolling vessel. There was no talking in the cabin, just the sound of ragged breathing and the creaking of the machinery.

Then the jagged horizon seemed to rush upon them. Stony teeth cut into the lower run of the ball of fire, devoured it swiftly. It was gone.

They were in the lee of the cliffs. Lavon ordered the ship turned to parallel the rock-line; it responded heavily, sluggishly. Far above, the sky deepened steadily, from blue to indigo.

Shar came silently up through the trap and stood beside Lavon, studying that deepening color and the lengthening of the shadows down the beach toward their own world. He said nothing, but Lavon was sure that the same chilling thought was in his mind.

"Lavon."

Lavon jumped. Shar's voice had iron in it. "Yes?"

"We'll have to keep moving. We must make the next world, wherever it is, very shortly."

"How can we dare move when we can't see where we're going? Why not sleep it over—if the cold will let us?"

"It will let us," Shar said. "It can't get dangerously cold up here. If it did, the sky—or what we used to think of as the sky—would have frozen over every night, even in summer. But what I'm thinking about is the water. The plants will go to sleep now. In our world that wouldn't matter; the supply of oxygen there is enough to last through the night. But in this confined space, with so many creatures in it and no supply of fresh water, we will probably smother."

Shar seemed hardly to be involved at all, but spoke rather with the voice of implacable physical laws.

"Furthermore," he said, staring unseeingly out at the raw landscape, "the diatoms are plants, too. In other words, we must stay on the move for as long as we have oxygen and power—and pray that we make it."

"Shar, we had quite a few Protos on board this ship once. And Para there isn't quite dead yet. If he were, the cabin would be intolerable. The ship is nearly sterile of bacteria, because all the Protos have been eating them as a matter of course and there's no outside supply of them, either. But still and all there would have been some decay."

Shar bent and tested the pellicle of the motionless Para with a probing finger. "You're right, he's still alive. What does that prove?"

"The Vortae are also alive; I can feel the water circulating. Which proves that it wasn't the heat that hurt Para. It *was the light*. Remember how badly my skin was affected after I climbed beyond the sky? Undiluted starlight is deadly. We should add that to the information from the plate."

"I still don't get the point."

"It's this: We've got three or four Noc down below. They were shielded from the light, and so must be still alive. If we concentrate them in the diatom galleys, the dumb diatoms will think it's still daylight and will go on working. Or we can concentrate them up along the spine of the ship, and keep the algae putting out oxygen. So the question is: Which do we need more, oxygen or power? Or can we split the difference?"

Shar actually grinned. "A brilliant piece of thinking. We may make a Shar out of you some day, Lavon. No, I'd say that we can't split the difference. Noc's light isn't intense enough to keep the plants making oxygen; I tried it once, and the oxygen production was too tiny to matter. Evidently the plants use the light for energy. So we'll have to settle for the diatoms for motive power."

"All right. Set it up that way, Shar."

Lavon brought the vessel away from the rocky lee of the cliff, out onto the smoother sand. All trace of direct light was now gone, although there was still a soft, general glow on the sky.

"Now then," Shar said thoughtfully, "I would guess that there's water over there in the canyon, if we can reach it. I'll go below again and arrange—"

Lavon gasped.

"What's the matter?"

Silently, Lavon pointed, his heart pounding.

The entire dome of indigo above them was spangled with tiny, incredible brilliant lights. There were hundreds of them, and more and more were becoming visible as the darkness deepened. And far away, over the ultimate edge of the rocks, was a dim red globe, crescented with ghostly silver. Near the zenith was another such body, much smaller, and silvered all over . . .

Under the two moons of Hydrot, and under the eternal stars, the two-inch wooden spaceship and its microscopic cargo toiled down the slope toward the drying little rivulet.

V

The ship rested on the Bottom of the canyon for the rest of the night. The great square doors were unsealed and thrown open to admit the raw, irradiated, life-giving water from outside—and the wriggling bacteria which were fresh food.

No other creatures approached them, either out of curiosity or for hunting, while they slept, although Lavon had posted guards at the doors just in case. Evidently, even up here on the very floor of space, highly organized creatures were quiescent at night.

But when the first flush of light filtered through the water, trouble threatened.

First of all, there was the bug-eyed monster. The thing was green and had two snapping claws, either one of which could have broken the ship in two like a spiro-gyra strand. Its eyes were black and globular, on the ends of short columns, and its long feelers were thicker through than a plant bole. It passed in a kicking fury of motion, however, never noticing the ship at all.

"Is that—a sample of the kind of life they have here?" Lavon whispered. "Does it all run as big as that?" Nobody answered, for the very good reason that nobody knew.

After a while, Lavon risked moving the ship forward against the current, which was slow but heavy. Enormous writhing worms whipped past them. One struck the hull a heavy blow, then thrashed on obliviously.

"They don't notice us," Shar said. "We're too small. Lavon, the ancients warned us of the immensity of space, but even when you see it, it's impossible to grasp. And all those stars—can they mean what I think they mean? It's beyond thought, beyond belief!"

"The Bottom's sloping," Lavon said, looking ahead intently. "The walls of the canyon are retreating, and the water's becoming rather silty. Let the stars wait, Shar; we're coming toward the entrance of our new world."

Shar subsided moodily. His vision of space apparently had disturbed him, perhaps seriously. He took little notice of the great thing that was happening, but instead huddled worriedly over his own expanding speculations. Lavon felt the old gap between their minds widening once more.

Now the Bottom was tilting upward again. Lavon had no experience with delta-formation, for no rivulets left his own world, and the phenomenon worried him. But his worries were swept away in wonder as the ship topped the rise and nosed over.

Ahead, the Bottom sloped away again, indefinitely, into glimmering depths. A proper sky was over them once more, and Lavon could see small rafts of plankton floating placidly beneath it. Almost at once, too, he saw several of the smaller kinds of Protos, a few of which were already approaching the ship—

Then the girl came darting out of the depths, her features blurred and distorted with distance and terror. At first she did not seem to see the ship at all. She came twisting and turning lithely through the water, obviously hoping only to throw herself over the mound of the delta and into the savage streamlet beyond.

Lavon was stunned. Not that there were men here—he had hoped for that, had even known somehow that men were everywhere in the universe—but at the girl's single-minded flight toward suicide.

"What—"

Then a dim buzzing began to grow in his ears, and he understood.

"Shar! Than! Stravol!" he bawled. "Break out crossbows and spears! Knock out all the windows!" He lifted a foot and kicked through the port in front of him. Someone thrust a crossbow into his hand.

"What?" Shar blurted. "What's the matter? What's happening?"

"*Eaters!*"

The cry went through the ship like a galvanic shock. The rotifers back in Lavon's own world were virtually extinct, but everyone knew thoroughly the grim history of the long battle man and Proto had waged against them.

The girl spotted the ship suddenly and paused, obviously stricken with despair at the sight of this new monster. She drifted with her own momentum, her eyes alternately fixed upon the ship and jerking back over her shoulder, toward where the buzzing snarled louder and louder in the dimness.

"Don't stop!" Lavon shouted. "This way, this way! We're friends! We'll help!"

Three great semi-transparent trumpets of smooth flesh bored over the rise, the many thick cilia of their coronas whirring greedily. Dicrans, arrogant in their flexible armor, quarreling thickly among themselves as they moved, with the few blurred, pre-symbolic noises which made up their own language.

Carefully, Lavon wound the crossbow, brought it to his shoulder, and fired. The bolt sang away through the water. It lost momentum rapidly, and was caught by a stray current which brought it closer to the girl than to the Eater at which Lavon had aimed.

He bit his lip, lowered the weapon, wound it up again. It did not pay to underestimate the range; he would have to wait. Another bolt, cutting through the water from a side port, made him issue orders to cease firing "until," he added, "you can see their eyespots."

The irruption of the rotifers decided the girl. The motionless wooden monster was of course strange' to her, but it had not yet menaced her—and she must have known what it would be like to have three Dicrans over her, each trying to grab from the others the largest share. She threw herself toward the bull's-eye port. The three Eaters screamed with fury and greed and bored in after her.

She probably would have not made it, had not the dull vision of the lead Dicran made out the wooden shape of the ship at the last instant. The Dicran backed off, buzzing, and the other two sheered away to avoid colliding with her. After that they had another argument, though they could hardly have formulated what it was that they were fighting about; they were incapable of exchanging any thought much more complicated than the equivalent of "Yaah," "Drop dead," and "You're another."

While they were still snarling at each other, Lavon pierced the nearest one all the way through with an arablast bolt. The surviving two were at once involved in a lethal battle over the remains.

"Than, take a party out and spear me those two Eaters while they're still fighting," Lavon ordered. "Don't forget to destroy their eggs, too. I can see that this world needs a little taming."

The girl shot through the port and brought up against the far wall of the cabin, flailing in terror. Lavon tried to approach her, but from somewhere she produced a flake of stonewort chipped to a nasty point. Since she was naked, it was hard to tell where she had been hiding it, but she obviously knew how to use it, and meant to. Lavon retreated and sat down on the stool before his control board, waiting while she took in the cabin, Lavon, Shar, the other pilots, the senescent Para.

At last she said: "Are—you—the gods—from beyond the sky?"

"We're from beyond the sky, all right," Lavon said. "But we're not gods. We're human beings, just like you. Are there many humans here?"

The girl seemed to assess the situation very rapidly, savage though she was. Lavon had the odd and impossible impression that he should recognize her: a tall, deceptively relaxed, tawny woman, not after all quite like this one . . . a woman from another world, to be sure, but still . . .

She tucked the knife back into her bright, matted hair—aha, Lavon thought confusedly, there's a trick I may need to remember—and shook her head.

"We are few. The Eaters are everywhere. Soon they will have the last of us."

Her fatalism was so complete that she actually did not seem to care.

"And you've never cooperated against them? Or asked the Protos to help?"

"The Protos?" She shrugged. "They are as helpless as we are against the Eaters, most of them. We have no weapons that kill at a distance, like yours. And it's too late now for such weapons to do any good. We are too few, the Eaters too many."

Lavon shook his head emphatically. "You've had one weapon that counts, all along. Against it, numbers mean nothing. We'll show you how we've used it. You may be able to use it even better than we did, once you've given it a try."

The girl shrugged again. "We dreamed of such a weapon, but never found it. Are you telling the truth? What is the weapon?"

"Brains, of course," Lavon said. "Not just one brain, but a lot of them. Working together. Cooperation."

"Lavon speaks the truth," a weak voice said from the deck.

The Para stirred feebly. The girl watched it with wide eyes. The sound of the Para using human speech seemed to impress her more than the ship itself, or anything else that it contained.

"The Eaters can be conquered," the thin, burring voice said. "The

Protos will help, as they helped in the world from which we came. The Protos fought this flight through space, and deprived Man of his records; but Man made the trip without the records. The Protos will never oppose Man again. We have already spoken to the Protos of this world, and have told them that what Man can dream, Man can do. Whether the Protos will it or not.

"Shar—your metal record is with you. It was hidden in the ship. My brothers will lead you to it.

"This organism dies now. It dies in confidence of knowledge, as an intelligent creature dies. Man has taught us this. There is nothing. That knowledge. Cannot do. With it . . . men . . . have crossed . . . have crossed space . . ."

The voice whispered away. The shining slipper did not change, but something about it was gone. Lavon looked at the girl; their eyes met. He felt an unaccountable warmth.

"We have crossed space," Lavon repeated softly.

Shar's voice came to him across a great distance. The young-old man was whispering: "But—have we?"

Lavon was looking at the girl. He had no answer for Shar's question. It did not seem to be important.

The Bridge

A screeching tornado was rocking the Bridge when the alarm sounded; it was making the whole structure shudder and sway. This was normal and Robert Helmuth barely noticed it. There was always a tornado shaking the Bridge. The whole planet was enswathed in tornadoes, and worse.

The scanner on the foreman's board had given 114 as the sector of the trouble. That was at the northwestern end of the Bridge, where it broke off, leaving nothing but the raging clouds of ammonia crystals and methane, and a sheer drop thirty miles to the invisible surface. There were no ultraphone "eyes" at that end which gave a general view of the area—in so far as any general view was possible—because both ends of the Bridge were incomplete.

With a sigh Helmuth put the beetle into motion. The little car, as flat-bottomed and thin through as a bedbug, got slowly under way on ball-bearing races, guided and held firmly to the surface of the Bridge by ten close-set flanged rails. Even so, the hydrogen gales made a terrific siren-like shrieking between the edge of the vehicle and the deck, and the impact of the falling drops of ammonia upon the curved roof was as heavy and deafening as a rain of cannon balls. As a matter of fact, they weighed almost as much as cannon balls here, though they were not much bigger than ordinary raindrops. Every so often, too, there was a blast, accompanied by a dull orange glare, which made the car, the deck, and the Bridge itself buck savagely.

These blasts were below, however, on the surface. While they shook the structure of the Bridge heavily, they almost never interfered with its functioning, and could not, in the very nature of things, do Helmuth any harm.

Had any real damage ever been done, it would never have been repaired. There was no one on Jupiter to repair it.

The Bridge, actually, was building itself. Massive, alone, and lifeless, it grew in the black deeps of Jupiter.

The Bridge had been well-planned. From Helmuth's point of view almost nothing could be seen of it, for the beetle tracks ran down the center of the deck, and in the darkness and perpetual storm even ultrawave-assisted vision could not penetrate more than a few hundred yards at the most. The width of the Bridge was eleven miles; its height, thirty miles; its length, deliberately unspecified in the plans, fifty-four miles at the moment—a squat, colossal structure, built with engineering principles, methods, materials, and tools never touched before—

For the very good reason that they would have been impossible anywhere else. Most of the Bridge, for instance, was made of ice: a marvelous structural material under a pressure of a million atmospheres, at a temperature of $-94°C$. Under such conditions, the best structural steel is a friable, talc-like powder, and aluminum becomes a peculiar, transparent substance that splits at a tap.

Back home, Helmuth remembered, there had been talk of starting another Bridge on Saturn, and perhaps still later, on Uranus, too. But that had been politicians' talk. The Bridge was almost five thousand miles below the visible surface of Jupiter's atmosphere, and its mechanisms were just barely manageable. The bottom of Saturn's atmosphere had been sounded at sixteen thousand eight hundred and seventy-eight miles, and the temperature there was below $-150°C$. There even pressure-ice would be immovable, and could not be worked with anything except itself. And as for Uranus . . .

As far as Helmuth was concerned, Jupiter was quite bad enough.

The beetle crept within sight of the end of the Bridge and stopped automatically. Helmuth set the vehicle's eyes for highest penetration, and examined the nearby beams.

The great bars were as close-set as screening. They had to be, in order to support even their own weight, let alone the weight of the components of the Bridge, the whole webwork was flexing and fluctuating to the harpist-fingered gale, but it had been designed to do that. Helmuth could never help being alarmed by the movement, but habit assured him that he had nothing to fear from it.

He took the automatics out of the circuit and inched the beetle forward manually. This was only Sector 113, and the Bridge's own Wheatstone-bridge scanning system—there was no electronic device anywhere on the Bridge, since it was impossible to maintain a vacuum on Jupiter—said that the trouble was in Sector 114. The boundary of Sector 114 was still fully fifty feet away.

It was a bad sign. Helmuth scratched nervously in his red beard. Evidently there was really cause for alarm—real alarm, not just the deep, grinding depression which he always felt while working on the Bridge. Any damage serious enough to halt the beetle a full sector short of the trouble area was bound to be major.

It might even turn out to be the disaster which he had felt lurking ahead of him ever since he had been made foreman of the Bridge—that disaster which the Bridge itself could not repair, sending man reeling home from Jupiter in defeat.

The secondaries cut in and the beetle stopped again. Grimly, Helmuth opened the switch and sent the beetle creeping across the invisible danger line. Almost at once, the car tilted just perceptibly to the left, and the screaming of the winds between its edges and the deck shot up the scale, sirening in and out of the soundless-dogwhistle range with an eeriness that set Helmuth's teeth on edge. The beetle itself fluttered and chattered like an alarm-clock hammer between the surface of the deck and the flanges of the tracks.

Ahead there was still nothing to be seen but the horizontal driving of the clouds and the hail, roaring along the length of the Bridge, out of the blackness into the beetle's fanlights, and onward into blackness again towards the horizon no eye would ever see.

Thirty miles below, the fusillade of hydrogen explosions continued. Evidently something really wild was going on on the surface. Helmuth could not remember having heard so much activity in years.

There was a flat, especially heavy crash, and a long line of fuming orange fire came pouring down the seething atmosphere into the depths, feathering horizontally like the mane of a Lipizzan horse, directly in front of Helmuth. Instinctively, he winced and drew back from the board, although that stream of flame actually was only a little less cold than the rest of the streaming gases, far too cold to injure the Bridge.

In the momentary glare, however, he saw something—an upward twisting of shadows, patterned but obviously unfinished, fluttering in silhouette against the hydrogen cataract's lurid light.

The end of the Bridge.

Wrecked.

Helmuth grunted involuntarily and backed the beetle away. The flare dimmed; the light poured down the sky and fell away into the raging sea below. The scanner clucked with satisfaction as the beetle recrossed the line into Zone 113.

He turned the body of the vehicle 180°, presenting its back to the dying torrent. There was nothing further that he could do at the moment on the Bridge. He scanned his control board—a ghost image of which was cast across the scene on the Bridge—for the blue button marked *Garage,* punched it savagely, and tore off his helmet.

Obediently, the Bridge vanished.

II

Dillon was looking at him.

"Well?" the civil engineer said. "What's the matter, Bob? Is it bad— ?"

Helmuth did not reply for a moment. The abrupt transition from the storm-ravaged deck of the Bridge to the quiet, placid air of the control shack on Jupiter V was always a shock. He had never been able to anticipate it, let alone become accustomed to it; it was worse each time, not better.

He put the helmet down carefully in front of him and got up, moving carefully upon shaky legs; feeling implicit in his own body the enormous pressures and weights his guiding intelligence had just quitted. The fact that the gravity on the foreman's deck was as weak as that of most of the habitable asteroids only made the contrast greater, and his need for caution in walking more extreme.

He went to the big porthole and looked out. The unworn, tumbled, monotonous surface of airless Jupiter V looked almost homey after the perpetual holocaust of Jupiter itself. But there was an overpowering reminder of that holocaust—for through the thick quartz, the face of the giant planet stared at him, across only one hundred and twelve thousand and six hundred miles: a sphere-section occupying almost all of the sky except the near horizon. It was crawling with color, striped and blotched with the eternal, frigid, poisonous storming of its atmosphere, spotted with the deep planet-sized shadows of farther moons.

Somewhere down there, six thousand miles below the clouds that boiled in his face, was the Bridge. The Bridge was thirty miles high and eleven miles wide and fifty-four miles long—but it was only a sliver, an intricate and fragile arrangement of ice-crystals beneath the bulging, racing tornadoes.

On Earth, even in the West, the Bridge would have been the mightiest engineering achievement of all history, could the Earth

The Bridge

have borne its weight at all. But on Jupiter, the Bridge was as precarious and perishable as a snowflake.

"Bob?" Dillon's voice asked. "You seem more upset than usual. Is it serious?" Helmuth turned. His superior's worn young face, lantern-jawed and crowned by black hair already beginning to grey at the temples, was alight both with love for the Bridge and the consuming ardor of the responsibility he had to bear. As always, it touched Helmuth, and reminded him that the implacable universe had, after all, provided one warm corner in which human beings might huddle together.

"Serious enough," he said, forming the words with difficulty against the frozen inarticulateness Jupiter forced upon him. "But not fatal, as far as I could see. There's a lot of hydrogen vulcanism on the surface, especially at the northwest end, and it looks like there must have been a big blast under the cliffs. I saw what looked like the last of a series of fireballs."

Dillon's face relaxed while Helmuth was talking, slowly, line by engraved line. "Oh. Just a flying chunk, then."

"I'm almost sure that's what it was. The cross-drafts are heavy now. The Spot and the STD are due to pass each other some time next week, aren't they? I haven't checked, but I can feel the difference in the storms."

"So the chunk got picked up and thrown through the end of the Bridge. A big piece?"

Helmuth shrugged. "That end is all twisted away to the left, and the deck is burst to flinders. The scaffolding is all gone, too, of course. A pretty big piece, all right, Charity—two miles through at a minimum."

Dillon sighed. He, too, went to the window, and looked out. Helmuth did not need to be a mind reader to know what he was looking at. Out there, across the stony waste of Jupiter V plus one hundred and twelve thousand and six hundred miles of space, the South Tropical Disturbance was streaming towards the great Red Spot, and would soon overtake it. When the whirling funnel of the STD—more than big enough to suck three Earths into deep-freeze—passed the planetary island of sodium-tainted ice which was the Red Spot, the Spot would follow it for a few thousand miles, at the same time rising closer to the surface of the atmosphere.

Then the Spot would sink again, drifting back towards the incredible jet of stress-fluid which kept it in being —a jet fed by no one knew what forces at Jupiter's hot, rocky, twenty-two-thousand-mile core, under sixteen thousand miles of eternal ice. During the entire passage, the storms all over Jupiter became especially violent; and the Bridge had been forced to locate in anything but the calmest spot on the planet, thanks to the uneven distribution of the few permanent landmasses.

Helmuth watched Dillon with a certain compassion, tempered with mild envy. Charity Dillon's unfortunate given name betrayed him as the son of a hangover, the only male child of a Witness family which dated back to the great Witness Revival of 2003. He was one of the hundreds of government-drafted experts who had planned the Bridge, and he was as obsessed by the Bridge as Helmuth was—but for different reasons.

Helmuth moved back to the port, dropping his hand gently upon Dillon's shoulder. Together they looked at the screaming straw yellows, brick reds, pinks, oranges, browns, even blues and greens that Jupiter threw across the ruined stone of its innermost satellite. On Jupiter V, even the shadows had color.

Dillon did not move. He said at last: "Are you pleased, Bob?"

"Pleased?" Helmuth said in astonishment, "No. It scares me white; you know that. I'm just glad that the whole Bridge didn't go."

"You're quite sure?" Dillon said quietly.

Helmuth took his hand from Dillon's shoulder and returned to his seat at the central desk. "You've no right to needle me for something I can't help," he said, his voice even lower than Dillon's. "I work on Jupiter four hours a day—not actually, because we can't keep a man alive for more than a split second down there—but my eyes and my ears and my mind are there, on the Bridge, four hours a day. Jupiter is not a nice place. I don't like it. I won't pretend I do.

"Spending four hours a day in an environment like that over a period of years—well, the human mind instinctively tries to adapt, even to the unthinkable. Sometimes I wonder how I'll behave when I'm put back in Chicago again. Sometimes I can't remember anything about Chicago except vague generalities, sometimes I can't even believe there is such a place as Earth—how could there be, when the rest of the universe is like Jupiter, or worse?"

"I know," Dillon said. "I've tried several times to show you that isn't a very reasonable frame of mind."

"I know it isn't. But I can't help how I feel. No, I don't think the

Bridge will last. It can't last; it's all wrong. But I don't *want* to see it go. I've just got sense enough to know that one of these days Jupiter is going to sweep it away."

He wiped an open palm across the control boards, snapping all the toggles "Off" with a sound like the fall of a double-handful of marbles on a pane of glass. "Like that, Charity! And I work four hours a day, every day, on the Bridge. One of these days, Jupiter is going to destroy the Bridge. It'll go flying away in little flinders into the storms. My mind will be there, supervising some puny job, and my mind will go flying away along with my mechanical eyes and ears—still trying to adapt to the unthinkable, tumbling away into the winds and the flames and the rains and the darkness and the pressure and the cold."

"Bob, you're deliberately running away with yourself. Cut it out. Cut it out, I say!"

Helmuth shrugged, putting a trembling hand on the edge of the board to steady himself. "All right. I'm all right, Charity. I'm here, aren't I? Right here on Jupiter V, in no danger, in no danger at all. The bridge is one hundred and twelve thousand and six hundred miles away from here. But when the day comes that the Bridge is swept away—

"Charity, sometimes I imagine you ferrying my body back to the cosy nook it came from, while my soul goes tumbling and tumbling through millions of cubic miles of poison. All right, Charity, I'll be good. I won't think about it out loud; but you can't expect me to forget it. It's on my mind; I can't help it, and you should know that."

"I do," Dillon said, with a kind of eagerness. "I do, Bob. I'm only trying to help, to make you see the problem as it is. The Bridge isn't really that awful, it isn't worth a single nightmare."

"Oh, it isn't the Bridge that makes me yell out when I'm sleeping," Helmuth said, smiling bitterly. "I'm not that ridden by it yet. It's while I'm awake that I'm afraid the Bridge will be swept away. What I sleep with is a fear of myself."

"That's a sane fear. You're as sane as any of us," Dillon insisted, fiercely solemn. "Look, Bob. The Bridge isn't a monster. It's a way we've developed for studying the behavior of materials under specific conditions of temperament, pressure, and gravity. Jupiter isn't Hell, either; it's a set of conditions. The Bridge is the laboratory we set up to work with those conditions."

"It isn't going anywhere. It's a bridge to no place."

"There aren't many places on Jupiter," Dillon said, missing

Helmuth's meaning entirely. "We put the bridge on an island in the local sea because we needed solid ice we could sink the caissons in. Otherwise, it wouldn't have mattered where we put it. We could have floated it on the sea itself, if we hadn't wanted to fix it in order to measure storm velocities and such things."

"I know that," Helmuth said.

"But, Bob, you don't show any signs of understanding it. Why, for instance, should the Bridge *go* any place? It isn't even, properly speaking, a bridge at all. We only call it that because we used some bridge engineering principles in building it. Actually, it's much more like a traveling crane—an extremely heavy-duty overhead rail line. It isn't going anywhere because it hasn't any place interesting to go, that's all. We're extending it to cover as much territory as possible, and to increase its stability, not to span the distance between places. There's no point to reproaching it because it doesn't span a real gap—between, say, Dover and Calais. It's a bridge to knowledge, and that's far more important. Why can't you see that?"

"I can see that; that's what I was talking about," Helmuth said, trying to control his impatience. "I have as much common sense as the average child. What I was trying to point out is that meeting colossalness with colossalness—out here—is a mug's game. It's a game Jupiter will always win, without the slightest effort. What if the engineers who built the Dover-Calais bridge had been limited to broomstraws for their structural members? They could have got the bridge up somehow, sure, and made it strong enough to carry light traffic on a fair day. But what would you have had left of it after the first winter storm came down the Channel from the North Sea? The whole approach is idiotic!"

"All right," Dillon said reasonably. "You have a point. Now you're being reasonable. What better approach have you to suggest? Should we abandon Jupiter entirely because it's too big for us?"

"No," Helmuth said. "Or maybe, yes. I don't know. I don't have any easy answer. I just know that this one is no answer at all—it's just a cumbersome evasion."

Dillon smiled. "You're depressed, and no wonder. Sleep it off, Bob, if you can—you might even come up with that answer. In the meantime—well, when you stop to think about it, the surface of Jupiter isn't any more hostile, inherently, than the surface of Jupiter V, except in degree. If you stepped out of this building naked, you'd die just as fast as you would on Jupiter. Try to look at it that way."

Helmuth, looking forward into another night of dreams, said: "That's the way I look at it now."

III

There were three yellow "Critical" signals lit on the long gang board when Helmuth passed through the gang deck on the way back to duty. All of them, as usual, were concentrated on Panel 9, where Eva Chavez worked.

Eva, despite her Latin name—such once-valid tickets no longer meant anything among Earth's uniformly mixed-race population—was a big girl, vaguely blonde, who cherished a passion for the Bridge. Unfortunately, she was apt to become enthralled by the sheer Cosmicness of it all, precisely at the moments when cold analysis and split-second decisions were most crucial.

Helmuth reached over her shoulder, cut her out of the circuit except as an observer, and donned the co-operator's helmet. The incomplete new shoals caisson sprang into being around him. Breakers of boiling hydrogen seethed seven hundred feet up along its slanted sides—breakers that never subsided, but simply were torn away into flying spray.

There was a spot of dull orange near the top of the north face of the caisson, crawling slowly towards the pediment of the nearest truss. Catalysis—

Or cancer, as Helmuth could not help but think of it. On this bitter, violent monster of a planet, even the tiny specks of calcium carbide were deadly. At these wind velocities, such specks imbedded themselves in everything; and at fifteen million pounds per square inch pressure, ice catalyzed by sodium took up ammonia and carbon dioxide, building protein-like compounds in a rapid, deadly chain of decay:

For a second, Helmuth watched it grow. It was, after all, one of the incredible possibilities the Bridge had been built to study. On Earth, such a compound, had it occurred at all, might have grown porous, bony, and quite strong. Here, under nearly eight times the gravity, the molecules were forced to assemble in strict aliphatic order, but in cross section their arrangement was hexagonal, as if the stuff would become an aromatic compound if it only could. Even here it was moderately strong in cross section—but along the long axis it smeared like graphite, the calcium atoms readily surrendering their valence hold on one carbon atom to grab hopefully for the next one in line—

No stuff to hold up the piers of humanity's greatest engineering project. Perhaps it was suitable for the ribs of some Jovian jellyfish, but in a Bridge-caisson, it was cancer.

There was a scraper mechanism working on the edge of the lesion, flaking away the shearing aminos and laying down new ice. In the meantime, the decay of the caisson-face was working deeper. The scraper could not possibly get at the core of the trouble—which was not the calcium carbide dust, with which the atmosphere was charged beyond redemption, but was instead one imbedded sodium speck which was taking no part in the reaction—fast enough to extirpate it. It could barely keep pace with the surface spread of the disease.

And laying new ice over the surface of the wound was worthless. At this rate, the whole caisson would slough away and melt like butter, within an hour, under the weight of the Bridge above it.

Helmuth sent the futile scraper aloft. Drill for it? No—too deep already, and location unknown.

Quickly he called two borers up from the shoals below, where constant blasting was taking the foundation of the caisson deeper and deeper into Jupiter's dubious "soil." He drove both blind, firesnouted machines down into the lesion.

The bottom of that sore turned out to be a hundred feet within the immense block. Helmuth pushed the red button all the same.

The borers blew up, with a heavy, quite invisible blast, as they had been designed to do. A pit appeared on the face of the caisson.

The nearest truss bent upward in the wind. It fluttered for a moment, trying to resist. It bent farther.

Deprived of its major attachment, it tore free suddenly, and went whirling away into the blackness. A sudden flash of lightning picked it out for a moment, and Helmuth saw it dwindling like a bat with torn wings being borne away by a cyclone.

The scraper scuttled down into the pit and began to fill it with ice from the bottom. Helmuth ordered down a new truss and a squad of scaffolders. Damage of this order took time to repair. He watched the tornado tearing ragged chunks from the edges of the pit until he was sure that the catalysis had stopped. Then, suddenly, prematurely, dismally tired, he took off the helmet.

He was astounded by the white fury that masked Eva's big-boned, mildly pretty face.

"You'll blow the Bridge up yet, won't you?" she said, evenly, without preamble. "Any pretext will do!"

Baffled, Helmuth turned his head helplessly away; that was no better. The suffused face of Jupiter peered swollenly through the picture-port, just as it did the foreman's desk.

He and Eva and Charity and the gang and the whole of satellite V were falling forward towards Jupiter; their uneventful cooped-up lives on Jupiter V were utterly unreal compared to the four hours of each changeless day spent on Jupiter's ever-changing surface. Every new day brought their minds, like ships out of control, closer and closer to that gaudy inferno.

There was no other way for a man—or a woman—on Jupiter V to look at the giant planet. It was simple experience, shared by all of them, that planets do not occupy four-fifths of the whole sky, unless the observer is himself up there in that planet's sky, falling, falling faster and faster—

"I have no intention," he said tiredly, "of blowing up the Bridge. I wish you could get it through your head that I want the Bridge to stay up—even though I'm not starry-eyed to the point of incompetence about the project. Did you think that rotten spot was going to go away by itself when you'd painted it over? Didn't you know that—"

Several helmeted, masked heads nearby turned blindly towards the sound of his voice. Helmuth shut up. Any distracting conversation or activity was taboo, down here in the gang room. He motioned Eva back to duty.

The girl donned her helmet obediently enough, but it was plain from the way her normally full lips were thinned that she thought Helmuth had ended the argument only in order to have the last word.

Helmuth strode to the thick pillar which ran down the central axis of the shack, and mounted the spiraling cleats towards his own foreman's cubicle. Already he felt in anticipation the weight of the helmet upon his own head.

Charity Dillon, however, was already wearing the helmet; he was sitting in Helmuth's chair.

Charity was characteristically oblivious of Helmuth's entrance. The Bridge operator must learn to ignore, to be utterly unconscious of anything happening around his body except the inhuman sounds of signals; must learn to heed only those senses which report something going on thousands of miles away.

Helmuth knew better than to interrupt him. Instead, he watched Dillon's white, blade-like fingers roving with blind sureness over the controls.

Dillon, evidently, was making a complete tour of the Bridge—not only from end to end, but up and down, too. The tally board showed that he had already activated nearly two-thirds of the ultraphone eyes. That meant that he had been up all night at the job; had begun it immediately after last talking to Helmuth.

Why?

With a thrill of unfocused apprehension, Helmuth looked at the foreman's jack, which allowed the operator here in the cubicle to communicate with the gang when necessary, and which kept him aware of anything said or done at gang boards.

It was plugged in.

Dillon sighed suddenly, took the helmet off, and turned.

"Hello, Bob," he said. "Funny about this job. You can't see, you can't hear, but when somebody's watching you, you feel a sort of pressure on the back of your neck. ESP, maybe. Ever felt it?"

"Pretty often, lately. Why the grand tour, Charity?"

"There's to be an inspection," Dillon said. His eyes met Helmuth's. They were frank and transparent. "A mob of Western officials, coming to see that their eight billion dollars isn't being wasted. Naturally, I'm a little anxious to see that they find everything in order."

"I see," Helmuth said. "First time in five years, isn't it?"

"Just about. What was that dust-up down below just now. Somebody—you, I'm sure, from the drastic handiwork involved—bailed Eva out of a mess, and then I heard her talk about your wanting to blow up the Bridge. I checked the area when I heard the fracas start, and it did seem as if she had let things go rather far, but— What was it all about?"

Dillon ordinarily hadn't the guile for cat-and-mouse games, and he had never looked less guileful than now. Helmuth said carefully, "Eva was upset, I suppose. On the subject of Jupiter we're all of us cracked by now, in our different ways. The way she was dealing with the catalysis didn't look to me to be suitable—a difference of opinion, resolved in my favor because I had the authority, Eva didn't. That's all."

"Kind of an expensive difference, Bob. I'm not niggling by nature, you know that. But an incident like that while the commission is here—"

"The point is," Helmuth said, "are we to spend an extra ten thousand, or whatever it costs to replace a truss and reinforce a caisson, or are we to lose the whole caisson—and as much as a third of the whole Bridge along with it?"

"Yes, you're right there, of course. That could be explained, even to a pack of senators. But—it would be difficult to have to explain it very often. Well, the board's yours, Bob. You could continue my spot-check, if you've time."

Dillon got up. Then he added suddenly, as if it were forced out of him:

"Bob, I'm trying to understand your state of mind. From what Eva said, I gather that you've made it fairly public. I . . . I don't think it's a good idea to infect your fellow workers with your own pessimism. It leads to sloppy work. I know that regardless of your own feelings you won't countenance sloppy work, but one foreman can do only so much. And you're making extra work for yourself—not for me, but for yourself—by being openly gloomy about the Bridge.

"You're the best man on the Bridge, Bob, for all your grousing about the job, and your assorted misgivings. I'd hate to see you replaced."

"A threat, Charity?" Helmuth said softly.

"No. I wouldn't replace you unless you actually went nuts, and I firmly believe that your fears in that respect are groundless. It's a commonplace that only sane men suspect their own sanity, isn't it?"

"It's a common misconception. Most psychopathic obsessions begin with a mild worry."

Dillon made as if to brush that subject away. "Anyhow, I'm not threatening; I'd fight to keep you here. But my say-so only covers Jupiter V; there are people higher up on Ganymede, and people higher yet back in Washington—and in this inspecting commission.

"Why don't you try to look on the bright side for a change? Obviously the Bridge isn't ever going to inspire you. But you might at least try thinking about all those dollars piling up in your account every hour you're on this job, and about the bridges and ships and who knows what-all that you'll be building, at any fee you ask, when you get back down to Earth. All under the magic words, 'One of the men who built the Bridge on Jupiter'!"

Charity was bright red with embarrassment and enthusiasm. Helmuth smiled.

"I'll try to bear it in mind, Charity," he said. "When is this gaggle of senators due to arrive?"

"They're on Ganymede now, taking a breather. They came directly from Washington without any routing. I suppose they'll make a stop at Callisto before they come here. They've something new on their ship, I'm told, that lets them flit about more freely than the usual uphill transport can."

An icy lizard suddenly was nesting in Helmuth's stomach, coiling and coiling but never settling itself. The room blurred. The persistent nightmare was suddenly almost upon him—already.

"Something . . . new?" he echoed his voice as flat and noncommittal as he could make it. "Do you know what it is?"

"Well, yes. But I think I'd better keep quiet about it until—"

"Charity, nobody on this deserted rock-heap could possibly be a Soviet spy. The whole habit of 'security' is idiotic out here. Tell me now and save me the trouble of dealing with senators; or tell me at least that you know I know. *They have antigravity!* Isn't that it?"

One word from Dillon, and the nightmare would be real.

"Yes," Dillon said. "How did you know? Of course, it couldn't be a complete gravity screen by any means. But it seems to be a good long step towards it. We've waited a long time to see that dream come true— But you're the last man in the world to take pride in the achievement, so there's no sense exulting about it to you. I'll let you know when I get a definite arrival date. In the meantime, will you think about what I said before?"

"Yes, I will." Helmuth took the seat before the board.

"Good, With you, I have to be grateful for small victories. Good trick, Bob."

"Good trick, Charity."

IV

Instead of sleeping—for now he knew that he was really afraid—he sat up in the reading chair in his cabin. The illuminated microfilm

The Bridge

pages of a book flipped by across the surface of the wall opposite him, timed precisely to the reading rate most comfortable for him, and he had several weeks' worry-conserved alcohol and smoke rations for ready consumption.

But Helmuth let his mix go flat, and did not notice the book, which had turned itself on, at the page where he had abandoned it last, when he had fitted himself into the chair. Instead, he listened to the radio.

There was always a great deal of ham radio activity in the Jovian system. The conditions were good for it, since there was plenty of power available, few impeding atmosphere layers, and those thin, no Heaviside layers, and few official and no commercial channels with which the hams could interfere.

And there were plenty of people scattered about the satellites who needed the sound of a voice.

". . . anybody know whether the senators are coming here? Doc Earth put in a report a while back on a fossil plant he found here, at least he thinks it was a plant. Maybe they'd like a look at it."

"They're supposed to hit the Bridge team next." A strong voice, and the impression of a strong transmitter wavering in and out; that would be Sweeney, on Ganymede. "Sorry to throw the wet blanket, boys, but I don't think the senators are interested in our rock-balls for their own lumpy selves. We could only hold them here three days."

Helmuth thought greyly: *Then they've already left Callisto.*

"Is that you, Sweeney? Where's the Bridge tonight?"

"Dillon's on duty," a very distant transmitter said. "Try to raise Helmuth, Sweeney."

"Helmuth, Helmuth, you gloomy beetle-gooser! Come in, Helmuth!"

"Sure, Bob, come in and dampen us."

Sluggishly, Helmuth reached out to take the mike, where it lay clipped to one arm of the chair. But the door to his room opened before he had completed the gesture.

Eva came in.

She said, "Bob, I want to tell you something."

"His voice is changing!" the voice of the Callisto operator said. "Ask him what he's drinking, Sweeney!"

Helmuth cut the radio out. The girl was freshly dressed—in so far as anybody dressed in anything on Jupiter V—and Helmuth wondered why she was prowling the decks at this hour, halfway between her sleep period and her trick. Her hair was hazy against the light from the corridor, and she looked less mannish than usual. She reminded him a little of the way she had looked when they first met.

"All right," he said. "I owe you a mix, I guess. Citric, sugar and the other stuff is in the locker . . . you know where it is. Shot-cans are there, too."

The girl shut the door and sat down on the bunk, with a free litheness that was almost grace, but with a determination which Helmuth knew meant that she had just decided to do something silly for all the right reasons.

"I don't need a drink," she said. "As a matter of fact, lately I've been turning my lux-R's back to the common pool. I suppose you did that for me—by showing me what a mind looked like that is hiding from itself."

"Eva, stop sounding like a tract. Obviously, you've advanced to a higher, more Jovian plane of existence, but won't you still need your metabolism? Or have you decided that vitamins are all-in-the-mind?"

"Now you're being superior. Anyhow, alcohol isn't a vitamin. And I didn't come to talk about that. I came to tell you something I think you ought to know."

"Which is?"

She said, "Bob, I mean to have a child here."

A bark of laughter, part sheer hysteria and part exasperation, jack-knifed Helmuth into a sitting position. A red arrow bloomed on the far wall, obediently marking the paragraph which, supposedly, he had reached in his reading, and the page vanished.

"*Women!*" he said, when he could get his breath back. "Really, Evita, you make me feel much better. No environment can change a human being much, after all."

"Why should it?" she said suspiciously. "I don't see the joke. Shouldn't a woman want to have a child?"

"Of course she should," he said, settling back. The flipping pages began again. "It's quite ordinary. All women want to have children. All women dream of the day they can turn a child out to play in an airless rock-garden, to pluck fossils and get quaintly star-burned. How cosy to tuck the little blue body back into its corner that night, promptly at the sound of the trick-change bell! Why, it's as natural as Jupiter-light—as Earthian as vacuum-frozen apple pie."

He turned his head casually away. "As for me, though, Eva, I'd much prefer that you take your ghostly little pretext out of here."

Eva surged to her feet in one furious motion. Her fingers grasped him by the beard and jerked his head painfully around again.

"You reedy male platitude!" she said, in a low grinding voice. "How you could see almost the whole point and make so little of it—*Women,* is it? So you think I came creeping in here, full of humbleness, to settle our technical differences."

He closed his hand on her wrist and twisted it away. "What else?" he demanded, trying to imagine how it would feel to stay reasonable for five minutes at a time with these Bridge-robots. "None of us need bother with games and excuses. We're here, we're isolated, we were all chosen because, among other things, we were judged incapable of forming permanent emotional attachments, and capable of such alliances as we found attractive without going unbalanced when the attraction diminished and the alliance came unstuck. None of us have to pretend that our living arrangements would keep us out of jail in Boston, or that they have to involve any Earth-normal excuses."

She said nothing. After a while he asked, gently, "Isn't that so?"

"Of course it's so. Also it has nothing to do with the matter."

"It doesn't? How stupid do you think I am? *I* don't care whether or not you've decided to have a child here, if you really mean what you say."

She was trembling with rage. "You really don't, too. The decision means nothing to you."

"Well, if I liked children, I'd be sorry for the child. But as it happens, I can't stand children. In short, Eva, as far as I'm concerned you can have as many as you want, and to me you'll *still* be the worst operator on the Bridge."

"I'll bear that in mind," she said. At this moment she seemed to have been cut from pressure-ice. "I'll leave you something to charge your mind with, too, Robert Helmuth. I'll leave you sprawled here under your precious book . . . what is Madame Bovary to you, anyhow, you unadventurous turtle? . . . to think about a man who believes that children must always be born into warm cradles—a man who thinks that men have to huddle on warm worlds, or they won't survive. A man with no ears, no eyes, scarcely any head. A man in terror, a man crying Mamma! *Mamma!* all the stellar days and nights long!"

"Parlor diagnosis!"

"Parlor labeling. Good trick, Bob. Draw your warm wooly blanket in tight about your brains, or some little sneeze of sense might creep in, and impair your—efficiency!"

The door closed sharply after her.

A million pounds of fatigue crashed down without warning on Helmuth's brain, and he fell back into the reading chair with a gasp. The roots of his beard ached, and Jupiters bloomed and wavered away before his closed eyes.

He struggled once, and fell asleep.

Instantly he was in the grip of the dream.

It started, as always, with commonplaces, almost realistic enough to be a documentary film-strip—except for the appalling sense of pressure, and the distorted emotional significance with which the least word, the smallest movement was invested.

It was the sinking of the first caisson of the Bridge. The actual event had been bad enough. The job demanded enough exactness of placement to require that manned ships enter Jupiter's atmosphere itself: a squadron of twenty of the most powerful ships ever built, with the five-million-ton asteroid, trimmed and shaped in space, slung beneath them in an immense cat's cradle.

Four times that squadron had disappeared beneath the clouds; four times the tense voices of pilots and engineers had muttered in Helmuth's ears; four times there were shouts and futile orders and the snapping of cables and someone screaming endlessly against the eternal howl of the Jovian sky.

It had cost, altogether, nine ships and two hundred and thirty-one men, to get one of five laboriously shaped asteroids planted in the shifting slush that was Jupiter's face. Helmuth had helped to supervise all five operations, counting the successful one, from his desk on Jupiter V; but in the dream he was not in the control shack, but instead on shipboard, in one of the ships that was never to come back—

Then, without transition, but without any sense of discontinuity either, he was on the Bridge itself. Not *in absentia,* as the remote guiding intelligence of a beetle, but in person, in an ovular, tank-like suit the details of which would never come clear. The high brass had discovered antigravity, and had asked for volunteers to man the Bridge. Helmuth had volunteered.

Looking back on it in the dream, he did not understand why he had volunteered. It had simply seemed expected of him, and he had not been able to help it, even though he had known what it would be like. He belonged on the Bridge, though he hated it—he had been doomed to go there, from the first.

And there was . . . something wrong . . . with the antigravity. The high brass had asked for its volunteers before the scientific work had been completed. The present antigravity fields were weak, and there was some basic flaw in the theory. Generators broke down after only short periods of use, burned out, unpredictably, sometimes only moments after testing up without a flaw—like vacuum tubes in waking life.

That was what Helmuth's set was about to do. He crouched inside his personal womb, above the boiling sea, the clouds raging about him, lit by a plume of hydrogen flame, and waited to feel his weight suddenly become eight times greater than normal. He knew what would happen to him then. It happened.

Helmuth greeted morning on Jupiter V with his customary scream.

V

The ship that landed as he was going on duty did nothing to lighten the load on his heart. In shape it was not distinguishable from any of the long-range cruisers which ran the legs of the Moon-Mars-Belt-Ganymede trip. But it grounded its huge bulk with less visible expenditures of power than one of the little intersatellary boats.

That landing told Helmuth that his dream was well on its way to coming true. If the high brass had had a real antigravity, there would have been no reason why the main jets should have been necessary at all. Obviously, what had been discovered was some sort of partial screen, which allowed a ship to operate with far less jet action than was normal, but which still left it subject to a sizeable fraction of the universal stress of space.

Nothing less than complete and completely controllable antigravity would do on Jupiter.

He worked mechanically, noting that Charity was not in evidence. Probably he was conferring with the senators, receiving what would be for him the glad news.

Helmuth realized suddenly that there was nothing left for him to do now but to cut and run.

There could certainly be no reason why he should have to reenact the entire dream, helplessly, event for event, like an actor committed to a play. He was awake now, in full control of his own senses, and still at least partially sane. The man in the dream had volunteered— but that man would not be Robert Helmuth. Not any longer.

While the senators were here, he would turn in his resignation. Direct, over Charity's head.

"Wake up, Helmuth," a voice from the gang deck snapped suddenly. "If it hadn't been for me, you'd have run yourself off the end of the Bridge. You had all the automatic stops on that beetle cut out."

Helmuth reached guiltily and more than a little too late for the controls. Eva had already run his beetle back beyond the danger line.

"Sorry," he mumbled. "Thanks, Eva."

"Don't thank me. If you'd actually been in it, I'd have let it go. Less reading and more sleep is what I recommend for you, Helmuth."

"Keep your recommendations to yourself," he snapped.

The incident started a new and even more disturbing chain of thought. If he were to resign now, it would be nearly a year before he could get back to Chicago. Antigravity or no antigravity, the senators' ship would have no room for unexpected passengers. Shipping a man back home had to be arranged far in advance. Space had to be provided, and a cargo equivalent of the weight and space requirements he would take up on the return trip had to be deadheaded out to Jupiter.

A year of living in the station on Jupiter V without any function—as a man whose drain on the station's supplies no longer could be justified in terms of what he did. A year of living under the eyes of Eva Chavez and Charity Dillon and the other men and women who still remained Bridge operators, men and women who would not hesitate to let him know what they thought of his quitting.

A year of living as a bystander in the feverish excitement of direct, personal exploration of Jupiter. A year of watching and hearing the inevitable deaths—while he alone stood aloof, privileged and useless. A year during which Robert Helmuth would become the most hated living entity in the Jovian system.

And, when he got back to Chicago and went looking for a job—for his resignation from the Bridge gang would automatically take him out of government service—he would be asked why he left the Bridge at the moment when work on the Bridge was just reaching its culmination.

He began to understand why the man in the dream had volunteered.

When the trick-change bell rang, he was still determined to resign, but he had already concluded bitterly that there were, after all, other kinds of hells besides the one on Jupiter.

The Bridge

He was returning the board to neutral as Charity came up the cleats. Charity's eyes were snapping like a skyful of comets. Helmuth had known that they would be.

"Senator Wagoner wants to speak to you, if you're not too tired, Bob," he said. "Go ahead; I'll finish up there."

"He does?" Helmuth frowned. The dream surged back upon him. *NO.* They would not rush him any faster than he wanted to go. "What about, Charity? Am I suspected of unWestern activities? I suppose you've told them how I feel."

"I have," Dillon said, unruffled. "But we're agreed that you may not feel the same after you've talked to Wagoner. He's in the ship, of course. I've put out a suit for you at the lock."

Charity put the helmet over his head, effectively cutting himself off from further conversation, or from any further consciousness of Helmuth at all.

Helmuth stood looking at him a moment. Then, with a convulsive shrug, he went down the cleats.

Three minutes later, he was plodding in a spacesuit across the surface of Jupiter V, with the vivid bulk of Jupiter splashing his shoulders with color.

A courteous Marine let him through the ship's air lock and deftly peeled him out of the suit. Despite a grim determination to be uninterested in the new anti-gravity and any possible consequence of it, he looked curiously about as he was conducted up towards the bow.

But the ship was like the ones that had brought him from Chicago to Jupiter V—it was like any spaceship: there was nothing in it to see but corridor walls and stairwells, until you arrived at the cabin where you were needed.

Senator Wagoner was a surprise. He was a young man, no more than sixty-five at most, not at all portly, and he had the keenest pair of blue eyes that Helmuth had ever seen. He received Helmuth alone, in his own cabin—a comfortable cabin as spaceship accommodations go, but neither roomy nor luxurious. He was hard to match up with the stories Helmuth had been hearing about the current Senate, which had been involved in scandal after scandal of more than Roman proportions.

Helmuth looked around. "I thought there were several of you," he said.

"There are, but I didn't want to give you the idea that you were facing a panel," Wagoner said, smiling. "I've been forced to sit in on most of these endless loyalty investigations back home, but I can't see any point in exporting such religious ceremonies to deep space. Do sit down, Mr. Helmuth. There are drinks coming. We have a lot to talk about."

Stiffly, Helmuth sat down.

"Dillon tells me," Wagoner said, leaning back comfortably In his own chair, "that your usefulness to the Bridge is about at an end. In a way, I'm sorry to hear that, for you've been one of the best men we've had on any of our planetary projects. But, in another way, I'm glad. It makes you available for something much bigger, where we need you much more."

"What do you mean by that?"

"I'll explain in a moment. First, I'd like to talk a little about the Bridge. Please don't feel that I'm quizzing you, by the way. You're at perfect liberty to say that any given question is none of my business, and I'll take no offense and hold no grudge. Also, 'I hereby disavow the authenticity of any tape or other tapping of which this statement may be a part.' In short, our conversation is unofficial, highly so."

"Thank you."

"It's to my interest; I'm hoping that you'll talk freely to me. Of course my disavowal means nothing, since such formal statements can always be exercised from a tape; but later on I'm going to tell you some things you're not supposed to know, and you'll be able to judge by what I say then that anything you say to me is privileged. Okay?"

A steward came in silently with drinks, and left again. Helmuth tasted his. As far as he could tell, it was exactly like many he had mixed for himself back in the control shack, from standard space rations. The only difference was that it was cold, which Helmuth found startling, but not unpleasant after the first sip. He tried to relax. "I'll do my best," he said.

"Good enough. Now: Dillon says that you regard the Bridge as a monster. I've examined your dossier pretty closely, and I think perhaps Dillon hasn't quite the gist of your meaning. I'd like to hear it straight from you."

"I don't think the Bridge is a monster," Helmuth said slowly. "You see, Charity is on the defensive. He takes the Bridge to be conclusive evidence that no possible set of adverse conditions ever will stop man for long, and there I'm in agreement with him. But he also thinks of it as Progress, personified. He can't admit—you asked me to speak my mind, senator—that the West is a decadent and dying culture. All the other evidence that's available shows that it is. Charity likes to think of the Bridge as giving the lie to that evidence."

"The West hasn't many more years," Wagoner agreed, astonishingly. "Still and all, the West has been responsible for some really towering achievements in its time. Perhaps the Bridge could be considered as the last and the mightiest of them all."

"Not by me," Helmuth said. "The building of gigantic projects for ritual purposes—doing a thing for the sake of doing it—is the last act of an already dead culture, Look at the pyramids in Egypt for an example. Or an even more idiotic and more enormous example, bigger than anything human beings have accomplished yet, the laying out of the 'Diagram of Power' over the whole face of Mars. If the Martians had put all that energy into survival instead, they'd probably be alive yet."

"Agreed," Wagoner said.

"All right. Then maybe you'll also agree that the essence of a vital culture is its ability to defend itself. The West has beaten off the Soviets for a century now—but as far as I can see, the Bridge is the West's 'Diagram of Power,' its pyramids, or what have you. All the money and the resources that went into the Bridge are going to be badly needed, *and won't be there,* when the next Soviet attack comes."

"Which will be very shortly, I'm told," Wagoner said, with complete calm. "Furthermore, it will be successful, and in part it will be successful for the very reasons you've outlined. For a man who's been cut off from the Earth for years, Helmuth, you seem to know more about what's going on down there than most of the general populace does."

"Nothing promotes an interest in Earth like being off it," Helmuth said. "And there's plenty of time to read out here." Either the drink was stronger than he had expected, or the senator's calm concurrence in the collapse of Helmuth's entire world had given him another shove towards nothingness; his head was spinning. Wagoner saw it. He leaned forward suddenly, catching Helmuth flat-footed. *"However,"* he said, "it's difficult for me to agree that the Bridge serves, or ever did serve, a ritual purpose. The Bridge served a huge practical purpose which is now fulfilled—the Bridge, as such, is now a defunct project."

"Defunct?" Helmuth repeated faintly.

"Quite. Of course we'll continue to operate it for a while, simply because you can't stop a process of that size on a dime, and that's just as well for people like Dillon who are emotionally tied up in it. You're the one person with any authority in the whole station who has already lost enough interest in the Bridge to make it safe for me to tell you that it's being abandoned."

"But why?"

"Because," Wagoner went on quietly, "the Bridge has now given us confirmation of a theory of stupendous importance—so important, in my opinion, that the imminent fall of the West seems like a puny event in comparison. A confirmation, incidentally, which contains in it the seeds of ultimate destruction for the Soviets, whatever they may win for themselves in the next fifty years or so."

"I suppose," Helmuth said, puzzled, "that you mean antigravity?"

For the first time, it was Wagoner's turn to be taken aback. "Man," he said at last, "do you know *everything* I want to tell you? I hope not, or my conclusions will be mighty suspicious. Surely Charity didn't tell you we had antigravity; I strictly enjoined him not to mention it."

"No, the subject's been on my mind," Helmuth said. "But I certainly don't see why it should be so world-shaking, any more than I see how the Bridge helped to bring it about. I thought it had been developed independently, for the further exploitation of the Bridge, and would step up Bridge operation, not discontinue it."

"Not at all. Of course, the Bridge has given us information in thousands of different categories, much of it valuable indeed. But the one job that *only* the Bridge could do was that of confirming, or throwing out, the Blackett-Dirac equations."

"Which are—?"

"A relationship between magnetism and the spinning of a massive body—that much is the Dirac part of it. The Blackett Equation seemed to show that the same formula also applied to gravity. If the figures we collected on the magnetic field strength of Jupiter forced to retire the Dirac equations, then none of the rest of the information we've gotten from the Bridge would have been worth the money we spent to get it. On the other hand, Jupiter was the only body in the solar system available to us which was big enough in all relevant respects to make it possible for us to test those equations at all. They involve quantities of enormous orders of magnitudes.

"And the figures show that Dirac was right. *They also show that Blackett was right.* Both magnetism *and* gravity are phenomena of rotation.

"I won't bother to trace the succeeding steps, because I think you can work them out for yourself. It's enough to say that there's a drive-generator on board this ship which is the complete and final justification of all the hell you people on the Bridge gang have been put through. The gadget has a long technical name, but the technies who tend it have already nicknamed it the spindizzy, because of what it does to the magnetic moment of any atom—*any* atom—within its field.

"While it's in operation, it absolutely refuses to notice any atom outside its own influence. Furthermore, it will notice no other strain or influence which holds good beyond the borders of that field. It's so snooty that it has to be stopped down to almost nothing when it's brought close to a planet, or it won't let you land. But in deep space . . . well, it's impervious to meteors and such trash, of course; it's impervious to gravity; and—it hasn't the faintest interest in any legislation about top speed limits."

"You're kidding," Helmuth said.

"Am I, now? The ship came to Ganymede directly from Earth. It did it in a little under two hours, counting maneuvering time."

Helmuth took a defiant pull at his drink. "This thing really has no top speed at all?" he said. "How can you be sure of that?"

"Well, we can't," Wagoner admitted. "After all, one of the unfortunate things about general mathematical formulas is that they don't contain cut-off points to warn you of areas where they don't apply. Even quantum mechanics is somewhat subject to that criticism. However, we expect to know pretty soon just how fast the spindizzy can drive an object, if there is any limit. We expect you to tell us."

"I?"

"Yes, Helmuth, you. The coming debacle on Earth makes it absolutely imperative for us—the West—to get interstellar expeditions started at once. Richardson Observatory, on the Moon, has two likely-looking systems picked out already—one at Wolf 359, another at 61 Cygni—and there are sure to be hundreds of others where Earth-like planets are highly probable. We want to scatter adventurous people, people with a thoroughly indoctrinated love of being free, all over this part of the galaxy, if it can be done.

"Once they're out there, they'll be free to flourish, with no interference from Earth. The Soviets haven't the spindizzy yet, and even after they steal it from us, they won't dare allow it to be used. It's too good and too final an escape route.

"What we want you to do . . . now I'm getting to the point, you see . . . is to direct this exodus. You've the intelligence and the cast of mind for it. Your analysis of the situation on Earth confirms that, if any more confirmation were needed. And—there's no future for you on Earth now."

"You'll have to excuse me," Helmuth said, firmly. "I'm in no condition to be reasonable now; it's been more than I could digest in a few moments. And the decision doesn't entirely rest with me, either. If I could give you an answer in . . . let me see . . . about three hours. Will that be soon enough?"

"That'll be fine," the senator said.

"And so, that's the story," Helmuth said.

Eva remained silent in her chair for a long time.

"One thing I don't understand," she said at last. "Why did you come to me? I'd have thought that you'd find the whole thing terrifying."

"Oh, it's terrifying, all right," Helmuth said, with quiet exultation. "But terror and fright are two different things, as I've just discovered. We were both wrong, Evita. I was wrong in thinking that the Bridge was a dead end. You were wrong in thinking of it as an end in itself."

"I don't understand you."

"All right, let's put it this way: The work the Bridge was doing was worthwhile, as I know now—so I was wrong in being frightened of it, in calling it a bridge to nowhere.

"But you no more saw where it was going than I, and you made the Bridge the be-all and end-all of your existence.

"Now, there's a place to go to; in fact there are places—hundreds of places. They'll be Earth-like places. Since the Soviets are about to win Earth, those places will be more Earth-like than Earth itself, for the next century or so at least!"

She said, "Why are you telling me this? Just to make peace between us?"

"I'm going to take on this job, Evita, if you'll go along?"

She turned swiftly, rising out of the chair with a marvelous fluidity of motion. At the same instant, all the alarm bells in the station went off at once, filling every metal cranny with a jangle of pure horror.

"Posts!" the speaker above Eva's bed roared, in a distorted, gigantic

version of Charity Dillon's voice. *"Peak storm overload! The STD is now passing the Spot. Wind velocity has already topped all previous records, and part of the land mass has begun to settle. This is an A-1 overload emergency."*

Behind Charity's bellow, the winds of Jupiter made a spectrum of continuous, insane shrieking. The Bridge was responding with monstrous groans of agony. There was another sound, too, an almost musical cacophony of sharp, percussive tones, such as a dinosaur might make pushing its way through a forest of huge steel tuning-forks. Helmuth had never heard that sound before, but he knew what it was.

The deck of the Bridge was splitting up the middle.

After a moment more, the uproar dimmed, and the speaker said, in Charity's normal voice, "Eva, you too, please. Acknowledge, please. This is it—unless everybody comes on duty at once, the Bridge may go down within the next hour."

"Let it," Eva responded quietly.

There was a brief, startled silence, and then a ghost of a human sound. The voice was Senator Wagoner's, and the sound just might have been a chuckle.

Charity's circuit clicked out.

The mighty death of the Bridge continued to resound in the little room.

After a while, the man and the woman went to the window and looked past the discarded bulk of Jupiter at the near horizon, where there had always been visible a few stars.

Tomb Tapper

The distant glare of the atomic explosion had already faded from the sky as McDonough's car whirred away from the blacked-out town of Port Jervis and turned north. He was making fifty m.p.h. on U.S. Route 209 using no lights but his parkers, and if a deer should bolt across the road ahead of him he would never see it until the impact. It was hard enough to see the road.

But he was thinking, not for the first time, of the old joke about the man who tapped train wheels.

He had been doing it, so the story ran, for thirty years. On every working day he would go up and down both sides of every locomotive that pulled into the yards and hit the wheels with a hammer; first the drivers, then the trucks. Each time, he would cock his head, as though listening for something in the sound. On the day of his retirement, he was given a magnificent dinner, as befitted a man with long seniority in the Brotherhood of Railway Trainmen—and somebody stopped to ask him what he had been tapping for all those years.

He had cocked his head as though listening for something, but evidently nothing came. "I don't know," he said.

That's me, McDonough thought. I tap tombs, not trains. But what am I listening for?

The odometer said he was close to the turnoff for the airport, and he pulled the dimmers on. There it was. There was at first nothing to be seen, as the headlights swept along the dirt road, but a wall of darkness deep as all night, faintly edged at the east by the low domed hills of the Neversink Valley. Then another pair of lights snapped on behind him, on the main highway, and came jolting after McDonough's car, clear and sharp in the dust clouds he had raised.

He swung the car to a stop beside the airport fence and killed the lights; the other car followed. In the renewed blackness the faint traces of dawn on the hills were wiped out, as though the whole universe had been set back an hour. Then the yellow eye of a flashlight opened in the window of the other car and stared into his face.

He opened the door. "Martinson?" he said tentatively.

"Right here," the adjutant's voice said. The flashlight's oval spoor swung to the ground. "Anybody else with you?"

"No. You?"

"No. Go ahead and get your equipment out. I'll open up the shack."

The oval spot of light bobbed across the parking area and came to uneasy rest on the combination padlock which held the door of the operations shack secure. McDonough flipped the dome light of his car on long enough to locate the canvas sling which held the components of his electroencephalograph, and eased the sling out on to the sand.

He had just slammed the car door and taken up the burden when little chinks of light sprang into being in the blind windows of the shack. At the same time, cars came droning out on to the field from the opposite side, four of them, each with its wide-spaced unblinking slits of paired parking lights, and ranked themselves on either side of the landing strip. It would be dawn before long, but if the planes were ready to go before dawn, the cars could light the strip with their brights.

We're fast, McDonough thought, with brief pride. Even the Air Force thinks the Civil Air Patrol is just a bunch of amateurs, but we can put a mission in the air ahead of any other C.A.P. squadron in this county. We can scramble.

He was getting his night vision back now, and a quick glance showed him that the windsock was flowing straight out above the black, silent hangar against the pearly false dawn. Aloft, the stars were paling without any cloud-dimming, or even much twinkling. The wind was steady north up the valley; ideal flying weather.

Small lumpy figures were running across the field from the parked cars towards the shack. The squadron was scrambling.

"Mac!" Martinson shouted from inside the shack. "Where are you? Get your junk in here and get started!"

McDonough slipped inside the door, and swung his EEG components on to the chart table. Light was pouring into the briefing room from the tiny office, dazzling after the long darkness. In the briefing room the radio blinked a tiny red eye, but the squadron's communications officer hadn't yet arrived to answer it. In the office, Martinson's voice rumbled softly, urgently, and the phone gave him back thin unintelligible noises, like an unteachable parakeet.

Then, suddenly, the adjutant appeared at the office door and peered at McDonough. "What are you waiting for?" he said. "Get that mind reader of yours into the Cub on the double."

"What's wrong with the Aeronca? It's faster."

"Water in the gas; she ices up. We'll have to drain the tank. This is a hell of a time to argue." Martinson jerked open the squealing door which opened into the hangar, his hand groping for the light switch. McDonough followed him, supporting his sling with both hands, his elbows together. Nothing is quite so concentratedly heavy as an electronics chassis with a transformer mounted on it, and four of them make a back-wrenching load.

The adjutant was already hauling the servicing platform across the concrete floor to the cowling of the Piper Cub. "Get your stuff set," he said. "I'll fuel her up and check the oil."

"All right. Doesn't look like she needs much gas."

"Don't you ever stop talkin'? Let's move!"

McDonough lowered his load to the cold floor beside the plane's cabin, feeling a brief flash of resentment. In daily life, Martinson was a job printer who couldn't, and didn't, give orders to anybody, not even his wife. Well, those were usually the boys who let rank go to their heads, even in a volunteer outfit. He got to work.

Voices sounded from the shack, and then Andy Persons, the commanding officer, came bounding over the sill, followed by two sleepy-eyed cadets. "What's up?" he shouted. "That you, Martinson?"

"It's me. One of you cadets, pass me up that can. Andy, get the doors open, hey? There's a Russki bomber down north of us, somewhere near Howells. Part of a flight that was making a run on Schenectady."

"Did they get it?"

"No, they overshot, *way* over—took out Kingston instead. Stewart Field hit them just as they turned to regroup, and knocked this baby down on the first pass. We're supposed to—"

The rest of the adjutant's reply was lost in a growing, echoing roar, as though they were all standing underneath a vast trestle over which all the railroad trains in the world were crossing at once. The 64-foot organ reeds of jets were being blown in the night zenith above the field—another hunting pack, come from Stewart Field to avenge the hydrogen agony that had been Kingston.

His head still inside the plane's greenhouse, McDonough listened transfixed. Like most C.A.P. officers, he was too old to be a jet pilot, his reflexes too slow, his eyesight too far over the line, his belly muscles too soft to take the five-gravity turns; but now and then he thought about what it might be like to ride one of those flying blowtorches, cruising at six hundred miles an hour before a thin black wake of kerosene fumes, or being followed along the ground at top speed by the double wave-front of the "supersonic bang." It was a noble notion, almost as fine as that of piloting the one-man Niagara of power that was a rocket fighter.

The noise grew until it seemed certain that the invisible jets were going to bullet directly through the hangar, and then dimmed gradually.

"The usual orders?" Persons shouted up from under the declining roar. "Find the plane, pump the live survivors, pick the corpses' brains? Who else is up?"

"Nobody," Martinson said, coming down from the ladder and hauling it clear of the plane. "Middletown squadron's deactivated; Montgomery hasn't got a plane; Newburgh hasn't got a field."

"Warwick has Group's L-16—"

"They snapped the undercarriage off it last week," Martinson said with gloomy satisfaction. "It's our baby, as usual. Mac, you got your ghoul-tools all set in there?"

"In a minute," McDonough said. He was already wearing the Walter goggles, pushed back up on his helmet, and the detector, amplifier and power pack of the EEG were secure in their frames on the platform behind the Cub's rear seat. The "hair net" —the flexible network of electrodes which he would jam on the head of any dead man whose head had survived the bomber crash—was connected to them and hung in its clips under the seat, the leads strung to avoid fouling the plane's exposed control cables. Nothing remained to do now but to secure the frequency analyzer, which was the heaviest of the units and had to be bolted down just forward of the rear joystick so that its weight would not shift in flight. If the apparatus didn't have to be collimated after every flight, it could be left in the plane—but it did, and that was that.

"O.K.," he said, pulling his head out of the greenhouse. He was trembling slightly. These tomb-tapping expeditions were hard on the nerves. No matter how much training in the art of reading a dead mind you may have had, the actual experience is different, and cannot be duplicated from the long-stored corpses of the laboratory. The newly dead brain is an inferno, almost by definition.

"Good," Persons said. "Martinson, you'll pilot. Mac, keep on the air; we're going to refuel the Airoknocker and get it up by ten o'clock if we can. In any case we'll feed you any spottings we get from the Air Force as fast as they come in. Martinson, refuel at Montgomery if you have to; don't waste time coming back here. Got it?"

"Roger," Martinson said, scrambling into the front seat and buckling his safety belt. McDonough put his foot hastily into the stirrup and swung into the back seat.

"Cadets!" Persons said. "Pull chocks! Roll 'er!"

Characteristically, Persons himself did the heavy work of lifting and swinging the tail. The Cub bumped off the apron and out on the grass into the brightening morning.

"Switch off!" the cadet at the nose called. "Gas! Brakes!"

"Switch off, brakes," Martinson called back. "Mac, where to? Got any ideas?"

While McDonough thought about it, the cadet pulled the prop backwards through four turns. "Brakes! Contact!"

"Let's try up around the Otisville tunnel. If they were knocked down over Howells, they stood a good chance to wind up on the side of that mountain."

Martinson nodded and reached a gloved hand over his head. "Contact!" he shouted, and turned the switch. The cadet swung the prop, and the engine barked and roared; at McDonough's left, the duplicate throttle slid forward slightly as the pilot "caught" the engine. McDonough buttoned up the cabin, and then the plane began to roll towards the far, dim edge of the grassy field.

The sky got brighter. They were off again, to tap on another man's tomb, and ask of the dim voice inside it what memories it had left unspoken when it had died.

The Civil Air Patrol is, and has been since 1941, an auxiliary of the United States Air Force, active in coastal patrol and in air-sea rescue work. By 1954—when its ranks totalled more than eighty thousand men and women, about fifteen thousand of them licensed pilots—the Air Force had nerved itself up to designating C.A.P. as its Air Intelligence arm, with the job of locating downed enemy planes and radioing back information of military importance.

Aerial search is primarily the task of planes which can fly low and slow. Air Intelligence requires speed, since the kind of tactical information an enemy wreck may offer can grow cold within a few hours. The C.A.P.'s planes, most of them single-engine, private-flying models, had already been proven ideal aerial search instruments; the C.A.P.'s radio net, with its more than seventy-five hundred fixed, mobile and airborne stations, was more than fast enough to get information to wherever it was needed while it was still hot.

But the expected enemy, after all, was Russia; and how many civilians, even those who know how to fly, navigate or operate a radio transmitter, could ask anyone an intelligent question in Russian, let alone understand the answer?

It was the astonishingly rapid development of electrical methods for probing the brain which provided the answer—in particular the development, in the late fifties, of flicker-stimulus aimed at the visual memory. Abruptly, EEG technicians no longer needed to use language at all to probe the brain for visual images, and read them; they did not even need to know how their apparatus worked, let alone the brain. A few moments of flicker into the subject's eyes, on a frequency chosen from a table, and the images would come swarming into the operator's toposcope goggles—the frequency chosen without the slightest basic knowledge of electrophysiology, as a woman choosing an ingredient from a cookbook is ignorant of—and indifferent to—the chemistry involved in the choice.

It was that engineering discovery which put tomb-tappers into the back seats of the C.A.P.'s putt-putts when the war finally began—for the images in the toposcope goggles did not stop when the brain died.

The world at dawn, as McDonough saw it from three thousand feet, was a world of long sculptured shadows, almost as motionless and three-dimensional as a lunar landscape near the daylight terminator. The air was very quiet, and the Cub droned as gently through the blue haze as any bee, gaining altitude above the field in a series of wide climbing turns. At the last turn the plane wheeled south over a farm owned by someone Martinson knew, a man already turning his acres from the seat of his tractor, and Martinson waggled the plane's wings at him and got back a wave like the quivering of an insect's antenna. It was all deceptively normal.

Then the horizon dipped below the Cub's nose again and Martinson was climbing out of the valley. A lake passed below them, spotted with islands, and with the brown barracks of Camp Cejwin, once a children's summer camp but now full of sleeping soldiers. Martinson continued south, skirting Port Jervis, until McDonough was able to pick up the main line of the Erie Railroad, going northeast towards

Otisville and Howells. The mountain through which the Otisville tunnel ran was already visible as a smoky hulk to the far left of the dawn.

McDonough turned on the radio, which responded with a rhythmical sputtering; the Cub's engine was not adequately shielded. In the background, the C.O.'s voice was calling them: "Huguenot to L-4. Huguenot to L-4."

"L-4 here. We read you, Andy. We're heading towards Otisville. Smooth as glass up here. Nothing to report yet."

"We read you weak but clear. We're dumping the gas in the Airoknocker *crackle* ground. We'll follow as fast as possible. No new AF spottings yet. If *crackle,* call us right away. Over."

"L-4 to Huguenot. Lost the last sentence, Andy. Cylinder static. Lost the last sentence. Please read it back."

"All right, Mac. If you see the bomber, *crackle* right away. Got it? If you see *crackle,* call us right away. Got it? Over."

"Got it, Andy. L-4 to Huguenot, over and out."

"Over and out."

The railroad embankment below them went around a wide arc and separated deceptively into two. One of the lines had been pulled up years back, but the marks of the long-ago stacked and burned ties still striped the gravel bed, and it would have been impossible for a stranger to tell from the air whether or not there were any rails running over those marks; terrain from the air can be deceptive unless you know what it is supposed to look like, rather than what it does look like. Martinson, however, knew as well as McDonough which of the two rail spurs was the discontinued one, and banked the Cub in a gentle climbing turn towards the mountain.

The rectangular acres wheeled slowly and solemnly below them, brindled with tiny cows as motionless as toys. After a while the deceptive spur-line turned sharply east into a woolly green woods and never came out again. The mountain got larger, the morning ground haze rising up its nearer side, as though the whole forest were smoldering sullenly there.

Martinson turned his head and leaned it back to look out of the corner of one eye at the back seat, but McDonough shook his head. There was no chance at all that the crashed bomber could be on this side of that heavy-shouldered mass of rock.

Martinson shrugged and eased the stick back. The plane bored up into the sky, past 4,000 feet, past 4,500. Lake Hawthorne passed under the Cub's fat little tires, an irregular sapphire set in the pommel of the mountain. The altimeter crept slowly past 5,000 feet; Martinson was taking no chances on being caught in the downdraft on the other side of the hill. At 6,000, he edged the throttle back and leveled out, peering back through the plexiglas.

But there was no sign of any wreck on that side of the mountain, either.

Puzzled, McDonough forced up the top cabin flap on the right side, buttoned it into place against the buffeting slipstream, and thrust his head out into the tearing gale. There was nothing to see on the ground. Straight down, the knife-edge brow of the cliff from which the railroad tracks emerged again drifted slowly away from the Cub's tail; just an inch farther on was the matchbox which was the Otisville siding shack. A sort of shaking pepper around the matchbox meant people, a small crowd of them—though there was no train due until the Erie's No. 6, which didn't stop at Otisville anyhow.

He thumped Martinson on the shoulder. The adjutant tilted his head back and shouted, "What?"

"Bank right. Something going on around the Otisville station. Go down a bit."

The adjutant jerked out the carburetor-heat toggle and pulled back the throttle. The plane, idling, went into a long, whistling glide along the railroad right of way.

"Can't go too low here," he said. "If we get caught in the downdraft, we'll get slammed right into the mountain."

"I know that. Go on about four miles and make an airline approach back. Then you can climb into the draft. I want to see what's going on down there."

Martinson shrugged and opened the throttle again. The Cub clawed for altitude, then made a half-turn over Howells for the bogus landing run.

The plane went into normal glide and McDonough craned his neck. In a few moments he was able to see what had happened down below. The mountain from this side was steep and sharp; a wounded bomber couldn't possibly have hoped to clear it. At night, on the other hand, the mouth of the railroad tunnel was marked on all three sides, by the lights of the station on the left, the neon sign of the tavern which stood on the brow of the cliff in Otisville ("Pop. 3,000—High and Healthy"), and on the right by the Erie's own signal standard. Radar would have shown the rest: the long regular path of the embankment leading directly into that cul-de-sac of lights, the beetling mass of contours which was the mountain. All these signs would mean "tunnel" in any language.

And the bomber pilot had taken the longest of all possible chances: to come down gliding along the right of way, in the hope of shooting his fuselage cleanly into that tunnel, leaving behind his wings with their dangerous engines and fuel tanks. It was absolutely insane, but that was what he had done.

And, miracle of miracles, he had made it. McDonough could see the wings now, buttered into two-dimensional profiles over the two pilasters of the tunnel. They had hit with such force that the fuel in them must have been vaporized instantly; at least, there was no sign of a fire. And no sign of a fuselage, either.

The bomber's body was inside the mountain, probably half-way or more down the tunnel's one-mile length. It was inconceivable that there could be anything intelligible left of it; but where one miracle has happened, two are possible.

No wonder the little Otisville station was peppered over with the specks of wondering people.

"L-4 to Huguenot. L-4 to Huguenot. Andy, are you there?"

"We read you, Mac. Go ahead."

"We've found your bomber. It's in the Otisville tunnel. Over."

"*Crackle* to L-4. You've lost your mind."

"That's where it is, all the same. We're going to try to make a landing. Send us a team as soon as you can. Out."

"Huguenot to L-4. Don't be a *crackle* idiot, Mac, you can't land there."

"Out," McDonough said. He pounded Martinson's shoulder and gestured urgently downwards.

"You want to land?" Martinson said. "Why didn't you say so? We'll never get down on a shallow glide like this." He cleared the engine with a brief burp on the throttle, pulled the Cub up into a sharp stall, and slid off on one wing. The whole world began to spin giddily.

Martinson was losing altitude. McDonough closed his eyes and hung on to his back teeth.

Martinson's drastic piloting got them down to a rough landing, on the wheels, on the road leading to the Otisville station, slightly under a mile away from the mountain. They taxied the rest of the way. The crowd left the mouth of the tunnel to cluster around the airplane the moment it had come to a stop, but a few moments' questioning convinced McDonough that the Otisvilleans knew very little. Some of them had heard "a turrible noise" in the early morning, and with the first light had discovered the bright metal coating the sides of the tunnel. No, there hadn't been any smoke. No, nobody heard any sounds in the tunnel. You couldn't see the other end of it, though. Something was blocking it.

"The signal's red on this side," McDonough said thoughtfully while he helped the adjutant tie the plane down. "You used to run the PBX board for the Erie in Port, didn't you, Marty? If you were to phone the station master there, maybe we could get him to throw a block on the other end of the tunnel."

"If there's wreckage in there, the block will be on automatically."

"Sure. But we've got to go in there. I don't want the Number Six piling in after us."

Martinson nodded, and went inside the railroad station. McDonough looked around. There was, as usual, a motorized handtruck parked off the tracks on the other side of the embankment. Many willing hands helped him set it on the right of way, and several huskies got the one-lung engine started for him. Getting his own apparatus out of the plane and on to the truck, however, was a job for which he refused all aid. The stuff was just too delicate, for all its weight, to be allowed in the hands of laymen—and never mind that McDonough himself was almost as much of a layman in neurophysiology as they were; he at least knew the collimating tables and the cookbook.

"O.K.," Martinson said, rejoining them. "Tunnel's blocked at both ends. I talked to Ralph at the dispatcher's; he was steaming—says he's lost four trains already, and another due in from Buffalo in forty-four minutes. We cried a little about it. Do we go now?"

"Right now."

Martinson drew his automatic and squatted down on the front of the truck. The little car growled and crawled towards the tunnel. The spectators murmured and shook their heads knowingly.

Inside the tunnel it was as dark as always, and cold, with a damp chill which struck through McDonough's flight jacket and dungarees. The air was still, and in addition to its musty smell it had a peculiar metallic stench. Thus far, however, there was none of the smell of fuel or of combustion products which McDonough had expected.

He found suddenly that he was trembling again, although he did not really believe that the EEG would be needed.

"Did you notice those wings?" Martinson said suddenly, just loud enough to be heard above the popping of the motor. The echoes distorted his voice almost beyond recognition.

"Notice them? What about them?"

"Too short to be bomber wings. Also, no engines."

McDonough swore silently. To have failed to notice a detail as gross as that was a sure sign that he was even more frightened than he had thought. "Anything else?"

"Well, I don't think they were aluminium; too tough. Titanium, maybe, or stainless steel. What have we got in here, anyhow? You *know* the Russkies couldn't get a fighter this far."

There was no arguing that. There was no answering the question, either—not yet.

McDonough unhooked the torch from his belt. Behind them, the white aperture of the tunnel's mouth looked no bigger than a nickel, and the twin bright lines of the rails looked forty miles long. Ahead, the flashlight revealed nothing but the slimy walls of the tunnel, coated with soot.

And then there was a fugitive bluish gleam. McDonough set the motor back down as far as it would go. The truck crawled painfully through the stifling blackness. The thudding of the engine was painful, as though his own heart were trying to move the heavy platform.

The gleam came closer. Nothing moved around it. It was metal, reflecting the light from his torch. Martinson lit his own and brought it into play.

The truck stopped, and there was absolute silence except for the ticking of water on the floor of the tunnel.

"It's a rocket," Martinson whispered. His torch roved over the ridiculously inadequate tail empennage facing them. It was badly crumpled. "In fair shape, considering. At the clip he was going, he must have slammed back and forth like an alarm clapper."

Cautiously they got off the truck and prowled around the gleaming, badly dented spindle. There were clean shears where the wings had been, but the stubs still remained, as though the metal itself had given to the impact before the joints could. That meant welded construction throughout, McDonough remembered vaguely. The vessel rested now roughly in the center of the tunnel, and the railroad tracks had spraddled under its weight. The fuselage bore no identifying marks, except for a red star at the nose; or rather, a red asterisk.

Martinson's torch lingered over the star for a moment, but the adjutant offered no comment. He went around the nose, McDonough trailing.

On the other side of the ship was the death wound: a small, ragged tear in the metal, not far forward of the tail. Some of the raw curls of metal were partially melted. Martinson touched one.

"Flak," he muttered. "Cut his fuel lines. Lucky he didn't blow up."

"How do we get in?" McDonough said nervously. "The cabin didn't even crack. And we can't crawl through that hole."

Martinson thought about it. Then he bent to the lesion in the ship's skin, took a deep breath, and bellowed at the top of his voice:

"*Hey* in there! Open up!"

It took a long time for the echoes to die away. McDonough was paralyzed with pure fright. Any one of those distorted, ominous rebounding voices could have been an answer. Finally, however, the silence came back.

"So he's dead," Martinson said practically. "I'll bet even his foot bones are broken, every one of 'em. Mac, stick your hair net in there and see if you can pick up anything."

"N-not a chance. I can't get anything unless the electrodes are actually t-touching the skull."

"Try it anyhow, and then we can get out of here and let the experts take over. I've about made up my mind it's a missile, anyhow. With this little damage, it could still go off."

McDonough had been repressing that notion since his first sight of the spindle. The attempt to save the fuselage intact, the piloting skill involved, and the obvious cabin windshield all argued against it; but even the bare possibility was somehow twice as terrifying, here under a mountain, as it would have been in the open. With so enormous a mass of rock pressing down on him, and the ravening energies of a sun perhaps waiting to break loose by his side—

No, no; it was a fighter, and the pilot might somehow still be alive. He almost ran to get the electrode net off the truck. He dangled it on its cable inside the flak tear, pulled the goggles over his eyes, and flicked the switch with his thumb.

The Walter goggles made the world inside the tunnel no darker than it actually was, but knowing that he would now be unable to see any gleam of light in the tunnel, should one appear from somewhere—say, in the ultimate glare of hydrogen fusion—increased the pressure of blackness on his brain. Back on the truck the frequency-analyzer began its regular, meaningless peeping, scanning the possible cortical output bands in order of likelihood: First the 0.5 to 3.5 cycles/second band, the delta wave, the last activity of the brain detectable before death; then the four to seven c.p.s. theta channel, the pleasure-scanning waves which went on even during sleep; the alpha rhythm, the visual scanner at eight to thirteen c.p.s.; the beta rhythms at fourteen to thirty c.p.s. which mirror the tensions of conscious computation, not far below the level of real thought; the gamma band, where—

The goggles lit.

. . . And still the dazzling sky-blue sheep are grazing in the red field under the rainbow-billed and pea-green birds . . .

McDonough snatched the goggles up with a gasp, and stared frantically into the blackness, now swimming with residual images in contrasting colors, melting gradually as the rods and cones in his retina gave up the energy they had absorbed from the scene in the goggles. Curiously, he knew at once where the voice had come from; it had been his mother's, reading to him, on Christmas Eve, a story called "A Child's Christmas in Wales." He had not thought of it in well over two decades, but the scene in the toposcope goggles had called it forth irresistibly.

"What's the matter?" Martinson's voice said. "Get anything? Are you sick?"

"No," McDonough muttered. "Nothing."

"Then let's beat it. Do you make a noise like that over nothing every day? My Uncle Crosby did, but then, *he* had asthma."

Tentatively, McDonough lowered the goggles again. The scene came back, still in the same impossible colors, and almost completely without motion. Now that he was able to look at it again, however, he saw that the blue animals were not sheep; they were too large, and they had faces rather like those of kittens. Nor were the enormously slow-moving birds actually birds at all, except that they did seem to be flying—in unlikely straight lines, with slow, mathematically even flappings of unwinglike wings; there was something vegetable about them. The red field was only a dazzling blur, hazing the feet of the blue animals with the huge, innocent kitten's faces. As for the sky, it hardly seemed to be there at all; it was as white as paper.

"Come on," Martinson muttered, his voice edged with irritation. "What's the sense of staying in this hole any more? You bucking for pneumonia?"

"There's . . . something alive in there."

"Not a chance," Martinson said. His voice was noticeably more ragged. "You're dreaming. You said yourself you couldn't pick up—"

"I know what I'm doing," McDonough insisted, watching the scene in the goggles. "There's a live brain in there. Something nobody's ever hit before. It's powerful—no mind in the books ever put out a broadcast like this. It isn't human."

"All the more reason to call in the AF and quit. We can't get in there anyhow. What do you mean, it isn't human? It's a Red, that's all."

"No it isn't," McDonough said evenly. Now that he thought he knew what they had found, he had stopped trembling. He was still terrified, but it was a different kind of terror: the fright of a man who has at last gotten a clear idea of what it is he is up against. "Human beings just don't broadcast like this. Especially not when they're near dying. And they don't remember huge blue sheep with cat's heads on them, or red grass, or a white sky. Not even if they come from the USSR. Whoever it is in there comes from some place else."

"You read too much. What about the star on the nose?"

McDonough drew a deep breath. "What about it?" he said steadily. "It isn't the insignia of the Red Air Force. I saw that it stopped you, too. No air force I ever heard of flies a red asterisk. It isn't a *cocarde* at all. It's just what it is."

"An asterisk?" Martinson said angrily.

"No, Marty, I think it's a star. A symbol for a *real* star. The AF's gone and knocked us down a spaceship." He pushed the goggles up and carefully withdrew the electrode net from the hole in the battered fuselage.

"And," he said carefully, "the pilot, whatever he is, is still alive—and thinking about home, wherever *that* is."

In the ensuing silence, McDonough realized belatedly that Martinson was as frightened as he was.

Though the Air Force had been duly notified by the radio net of McDonough's preposterous discovery, it took its own time about getting a technical crew over to Otisville. It had to, regardless of how much stock it took in the theory. The nearest source of advanced Air

Force EEG equipment was just outside Newburgh, at Stewart Field, and it would have to be driven to Otisville by truck; no AF plane slow enough to duplicate Martinson's landing on the road could have handled the necessary payload.

For several hours, therefore, McDonough could do pretty much as he liked with his prize. After only a little urging, Martinson got the Erie dispatcher to send an oxyacetylene torch to the Port Jervis side of the tunnel, on board a Diesel camelback. Persons, who had subsequently arrived in the Aeronca, was all for trying it immediately in the tunnel, but McDonough was restrained by some dim memory of high-school experiments with magnesium, a metal which looked very much like this. He persuaded the C.O. to try the torch on the smeared wings first.

The wings didn't burn. They carried the torch into the tunnel, and Persons got to work with it, enlarging the flak hole.

"Is that what-is-it still alive?" Persons asked, cutting steadily.

"I think so," McDonough said, his eyes averted from the tiny sun of the torch. "I've been sticking the electrodes in there about once every five minutes. I get essentially the same picture. But it's getting steadily weaker."

"D'you think we'll reach it before it dies?"

"I don't know. I'm not even sure I want to."

Persons thought that over, lifting the torch from the metal. Then he said, "You've got something there. Maybe I better try that gadget and see what I think."

"No," McDonough said. "It isn't tuned to you."

"Orders, Mac. Let me give it a try. Hand it over."

"It isn't that, Andy. I wouldn't buck you, you know that; you made this squadron. But it's dangerous. Do you want to have an epileptic fit? The chances are nine to five that you would."

"Oh," Persons said. "All right. It's your show." He resumed cutting.

After a while McDonough said, in a remote, emotionless voice: "That's enough. I think I can get through there now, as soon as it cools."

"Suppose there's no passage between the tail and the nose?" Martinson said. "More likely there's a firewall, and we'd never be able to cut through that."

"Probably," McDonough agreed. "We couldn't run the torch near the fuel tanks, anyhow, that's for sure."

"Then what good—"

"If these people think anything like we do, there's bound to be some kind of escape mechanism—something that blows the pilot's capsule free of the ship. I ought to be able to reach it."

"And fire it in *here?*" Persons said. "You'll smash the cabin against the tunnel roof. That'll kill the pilot for sure."

"Not if I disarm it. If I can get the charge out of it, all firing it will do is open the locking devices; then we can take the windshield off and get in. I'll pass the charge out back to you; handle it gently. Let me have your flashlight, Marty, mine's almost dead."

Silently, Martinson handed him the light. He hesitated a moment, listening to the water dripping in the background. Then, with a deep breath, he said, "Well. Here goes nothin'."

He clambered into the narrow opening.

The jungle of pipes, wires and pumps before him was utterly unfamiliar in detail, but familiar in principle. Human beings, given the job of setting up a rocket motor, set it up in this general way. McDonough probed with the light beam, looking for a passage large enough for him to wiggle through.

There didn't seem to be any such passage, but he squirmed his way forward regardless, forcing himself into any opening that presented itself, no matter how small and contorted it seemed. The feeling of entrapment was terrible. If he were to wind up in a cul-de-sac, he would never be able to worm himself backwards out of this jungle of piping. . .

He hit his head a sharp crack on a metal roof, and the metal resounded hollowly. A tank of some kind, empty, or nearly empty. Oxygen? No, unless the stuff had evaporated long ago; the skin of the tank was no colder than any of the other surfaces he had encountered. Propellant, perhaps, or compressed nitrogen—something like that.

Between the tank and what he took to be the inside of the hull, there was a low freeway, just high enough for him to squeeze through if he turned his head sideways. There were occasional supports and ganglions of wiring to be writhed around, but the going was a little better than it had been, back in the engine compartment. Then his head lifted into a slightly larger space, made of walls that curved gently against each other: the front of the tank, he guessed, opposed to the floor of the pilot's capsule and the belly of the hull. Between the capsule and the hull, up rather high, was the outside curve of a tube, large in diameter but very short; it was encrusted with motors, small pumps, and wiring.

An air lock? It certainly looked like one. If so, the trick with the escape mechanism might not have to be worked at all—if indeed the escape device existed.

Finding that he could raise his shoulders enough to rest on his elbows, he studied the wiring. The thickest of the cables emerged from the pilot's capsule; that should be the power line, ready to activate the whole business when the pilot hit the switch. If so, it could be shorted out—provided that there was still any juice in the batteries.

He managed to get the big nippers free of his belt, and dragged forward into a position where he could use them, with considerable straining. He closed their needlelike teeth around the cable and squeezed with all his might. The jaws closed slowly, and the cusps bit in.

There was a deep, surging hum, and all the pumps and motors began to whirr and throb. From back the way he had come, he heard a very muffled distant shout of astonishment.

He hooked the nippers back into his belt and inched forward, raising his back until he was almost curled into a ball. By careful, small movements, as though he were being born, he managed to somersault painfully in the cramped, curved space, and get his head and shoulders back under the tank again, face up this time. He had to trail the flashlight, so that his progress backwards through the utter darkness was as blind as a mole's; but he made it, at long last.

The tunnel, once he had tumbled out into it again, seemed miraculously spacious—almost like flying.

"The damn door opened right up, all by itself," Martinson was chattering. "Scared me green. What'd you do—say 'Open sesame' or something?"

"Yeah," McDonough said. He rescued his electrode net from the hand truck and went forward to the gaping air lock. The door had blocked most of the rest of the tunnel, but it was open wide enough.

It wasn't much of an air lock. As he had seen from inside, it was too short to hold a man; probably it had only been intended to moderate the pressure-drop between inside and outside, not prevent such a drop absolutely. Only the outer door had the proper bank-vault heaviness of a true air lock. The inner one, open, was now nothing but a narrow ring of serrated blades, machined to a Johannson block finish so fine that they were air-tight by virtue of molecular cohesion alone—a highly perfected iris diaphragm. McDonough wondered vaguely how the pinpoint hole in the centre of the diaphragm was plugged when the iris was fully closed, but his layman's knowledge of engineering failed him entirely there; he could come up with nothing better than a vision of the pilot plugging that hole with a wad of well-chewed bubblegum.

He sniffed the damp, cold, still air. Nothing. If the pilot had breathed anything alien to Earth-normal air, it had already dissipated without trace in the organ pipe of the tunnel. He flashed his light inside the cabin.

The instruments were smashed beyond hope, except for a few at the sides of the capsule. The pilot had smashed them—or rather, his environment had.

Before him in the light of the torch was a heavy, transparent tank of iridescent greenish brown fluid, with a small figure floating inside it. It had been the tank, which had broken free of its moorings, which had smashed up the rest of the compartment. The pilot was completely enclosed in what looked like an ordinary G-suit, inside the oil; flexible hoses connected to bottles on the ceiling fed him his atmosphere, whatever it was. The hoses hadn't broken, but something inside the G-suit had; a line of tiny bubbles was rising from somewhere near the pilot's neck.

He pressed the EEG electrode net against the tank and looked into the Walter goggles. The sheep with the kitten's faces were still there, somewhat changed in position; but almost all of the color had washed out of the scene. McDonough grunted involuntarily. There was now an atmosphere about the picture which hit him like a blow, a feeling of intense oppression, of intense distress. . .

"Marty," he said hoarsely. "Let's see if we can't cut into that tank from the bottom somehow." He backed down into the tunnel.

"Why? If he's got internal injuries—"

"The suit's been breached. It's filling with that oil from the bottom. If we don't drain the tank, he'll drown first."

"All right. Still think he's a man-from-Mars, Mac?"

"I don't know. It's too small to be a man, you can see that. And the memories aren't like human memories. That's all I know. Can we drill the tank some place?"

"Don't need to," Person's echo-distorted voice said from inside the air lock. The reflections of his flashlight shifted in the opening like ghosts. "I just found a drain petcock. Roll up your trouser cuffs, gents."

But the oil didn't drain out of the ship. Evidently it went into storage somewhere inside the hull, to be pumped back into the pilot's cocoon when it was needed again.

It took a long time. The silence came flooding back into the tunnel.

"That oil-suspension trick is neat," Martinson whispered edgily. "Cushions him like a fish. He's got inertia still, but no mass—like a man in free fall."

McDonough fidgeted, but said nothing. He was trying to imagine what the multi-colored vision of the pilot could mean. Something about it was nagging at him. It was wrong. Why would a still-conscious and gravely injured pilot be solely preoccupied with remembering the fields of home? Why wasn't he trying to save himself instead—as ingeniously as he had tried to save the ship? He still had electrical power, and in that litter of smashed apparatus which he alone could recognize, there must surely be expedients which still awaited his trial. But he had already given up, as though he knew he was dying.

Or did he? The emotional aura suggested a knowledge of things desperately wrong, yet there was no real desperation, no frenzy, hardly any fear—almost as though the pilot did not know what death was, or, knowing it, was confident that it could not happen to him. The immensely powerful, dying mind inside the G-suit seemed curiously uncaring and passive, as though it awaited rescue with supreme confidence—so supreme that it could afford to drift, in an oil-suspended floating dream of home, nostalgic and unhappy, but not really afraid.

And yet it was dying!

"Almost empty," Andy Person's quiet, garbled voice said into the tunnel.

Clenching his teeth, McDonough hitched himself into the air lock again and tried to tap the fading thoughts on a higher frequency. But there was simply nothing to hear or see, though with a brain so strong, there should have been, at as short a range as this. And it was peculiar, too, that the visual dream never changed. The flow of thoughts in a powerful human mind is bewilderingly rapid; it takes weeks of analysis by specialists before its essential pattern emerges.

This mind, on the other hand, had been holding tenaciously to this one thought—complicated though it was—for a minimum of two hours. A truly sub-idiot performance—being broadcast with all the drive of a super genius.

Nothing in the cookbook provided McDonough with any precedent for it.

The suited figure was now slumped against the side of the empty tank, and the shapes inside the toposcope goggles suddenly began to be distorted with regular, wrenching blurs: pain waves. A test at the level of the theta waves confirmed it; the unknown brain was responding to the pain with terrible knots of rage, real blasts of it, so strong and uncontrolled that McDonough could not endure them for more than a second. His hand was shaking so hard that he could hardly tune back to the gamma level again.

"We should have left the oil there," he whispered. "We've moved him too much. The internal injuries are going to kill him in a few minutes."

"We couldn't let him drown, you said so yourself," Persons said practically. "Look, there's a seam on this tank that looks like a torsion seal. If we break it, it ought to open up like a tired clam. Then we can get him out of here."

As he spoke, the empty tank parted into two shell-like halves. The pilot lay slumped and twisted at the bottom, like a doll, his suit glistening in the light of the C.O.'s torch.

"Help me. By the shoulders, real easy. That's it; lift. Easy, now."

Numbly, McDonough helped. It was true that the oil would have drowned the fragile, pitiful figure, but this was no help, either. The thing came up out of the cabin like a marionette with all its strings cut. Martinson cut the last of them: the flexible tubes which kept it connected to the ship. The three of them put it down, sprawling bonelessly.

. . . AND STILL THE DAZZLING SKY-BLUE SHEEP ARE GRAZING IN THE RED . . .

Just like that, McDonough saw it.

A coloring book!

That was what the scene was. That was why the colors were wrong, and the size referents. Of course the sheeplike animals did not look much like sheep, which the pilot could never have seen except in pictures. Of course the sheep's heads looked like the heads of kittens; everyone has seen kittens. Of course the brain was powerful out of all proportion to its survival drive and its knowledge of death; it was the brain of a genius, but a genius without experience. And of course, *this* way, the USSR could get a rocket fighter to the United States on a one-way trip.

The helmet fell off the body, and rolled off into the gutter which carried away the water condensing on the wall of the tunnel. Martinson gasped, and then began to swear in a low, grinding monotone. Andy Persons said nothing, but his light, as he played it on the pilot's head, shook with fury.

McDonough, his fantasy of spaceships exploded, went back to the handtruck and kicked his tomb-tapping apparatus into small shards and bent pieces. His whole heart was a fuming cauldron of pity and grief. He would never knock upon another tomb again.

The blond head on the floor of the tunnel, dreaming its waning dream of a colored paper field, was that of a little girl, barely eight years old.

The Box

When Meister got out of bed that Tuesday morning, he thought it was before dawn. He rarely needed an alarm clock these days—a little light in his eyes was enough to awaken him and sometimes his dreams brought him upright long before the sun came up.

It had seemed a reasonably dreamless might, but probably he had just forgotten the dreams. Anyhow, here he was, awake early. He padded over to the window, shut it, pulled up the blind and looked out.

The street lights were not off yet, but the sky was already a smooth, dark gray. Meister had never before seen such a sky. Even the dullest overcast before a snowfall shows some variation in brightness. The sky here—what he could see of it between the apartment houses—was like the inside of a lead helmet.

He shrugged and turned away, picking up the clock from the table to turn off the alarm. Some day, he promised himself, he would sleep long enough to hear it ring. That would be a good day; it would mean that the dreams were gone. In Concentration Camp Dora, one had awakened the moment the tunnel lights were put on; otherwise one might be beaten awake, or dead. Meister was deaf in the left ear on that account. For the first three days at Dora he had had to be awakened.

He became aware suddenly that he was staring fixedly at the face of the clock, his subconscious ringing alarm bells of its own. *Nine o'clock!* No, it was not possible. It was obviously close to sunrise. He shook the clock stupidly, although it was ticking and had been since he first noticed it. Tentatively he touched the keys at the back.

The alarm had run down.

This was obviously ridiculous. The clock was wrong. He put it back on the table and turned on the little radio. After a moment it responded with a terrific thrumming, as if a vacuum cleaner were imprisoned in its workings.

"B-flat," Meister thought automatically. He had only one good ear, but he still had perfect pitch—a necessity for a resonance engineer. He shifted the setting. The hum got louder. Hastily he reversed the dial. Around 830 kc, where WNYC came in, the hum was almost gone, but of course it was too early yet for the city station to be on the air—

". . . in your homes," a voice struck in clearly above the humming. "We are awaiting a report from Army headquarters. In the meantime, any crowding at the boundaries of the barrier will interrupt the work of the Mayor's inquiry commission . . . Here's a word just in from the Port Authority: all ferry service has been suspended until further notice. Subways and tubes are running outbound trains only; however, local service remains normal so far."

Barrier? Meister went to the window again and looked out. The radio voice continued:

"NBC at Radio City disclaims all knowledge of the persistent signal which has blotted out radio programs from nine hundred kilocycles on up since midnight last night. This completes the roster of broadcasting stations in the city proper. It is believed that the tone is associated with the current wall around Manhattan and most of the other boroughs. Some outside stations are still getting through, but at less than a fiftieth of their normal input." The voice went on:

"At Columbia University, the dean of the Physics Department estimates that about the same proportion of sunlight is also getting through. We do not yet have any report about the passage of air through the barrier. The flow of water in the portions of the East and Hudson Rivers which lie under the screen is said to be normal, and no abnormalities are evident at the Whitehall Street tidal station."

There was a pause; the humming went on unabated. Then there was a sharp *beep!* and the voice said, "At the signal— 9 A.M., Eastern Daylight Savings Time."

Meister left the radio on while he dressed. The alarming pronouncements kept on, but he was not yet thoroughly disturbed, except for Ellen. She might be frightened; but probably nothing more serious would happen. Right now, he should be at the labs. If the Team had put this thing up overnight, they would tease him unmercifully for sleeping through the great event.

The radio continued to reel off special notices, warnings, new bulletins. The announcer sounded as if he were on the thin edge of hysteria; evidently he had not yet been told what it was all about. Meister was tying his left shoe when he realized that the reports were beginning to sound much worse.

"From LaGuardia Field we have just been notified that an experimental plane has been flown through the barrier at a point over the jammed Triboro Bridge. It has not appeared over the city and is presumed lost. On the *Miss New York* disaster early this morning we still have no complete report. Authorities on Staten Island say the ferry ordinarily carried less than two hundred passengers at that hour, but thus far only eleven have been picked up. One of these survivors was brought in to a Manhattan slip by the tub *Marjorie Q*; he is still in a state of extreme shock and Bellevue Hospital says no statement can be expected from him until tomorrow. It appears, however, that he swam *under* the barrier."

His voice carried the tension he evidently felt. "Outside the screen a heavy fog still prevails—the same fog which hid the barrier from the ferry captain until his ship was destroyed almost to the midpoint. The Police Department has again requested that all New Yorkers stay—"

Alarmed at last, Meister switched off the machine and left the apartment, locking it carefully. Unless those idiots turned off their screen, there would be panic and looting before the day was out.

Downstairs in the little grocery there was a mob arguing in low, terrified voices, their faces as gray as the ominous sky. He pushed through them to the phone.

The grocer was sitting behind it. "Phone service is tied up, Mr. Meister," he said hoarsely.

"I can get through, I think. What has happened?"

"Some foreign enemy, is *my* guess. There's a big dome of somethin' all around the city. Nobody can get in or out. You stick your hand in, you draw back a bloody stump. Stuff put through on the other side don't come through." He picked up the phone with a trembling hand and passed it over. "Good luck."

Meister dialed Ellen first. He needed to know if she were badly frightened, and to reassure her if she were. Nothing happened for a while; then an operator said, "I'm sorry, sir, but there will be no private calls for the duration of the emergency, unless you have a priority."

"Give me Emergency Code B-Nineteen, then," Meister said.

"Your group, sir?"

"Screen Team."

There was a faint sound at the outer end of the line, as if the girl had taken a quick breath. "Yes, sir," she said. "Right away." There was an angry crackle, and then the droning when the number was being rung.

"Screen Team," a voice said.

"Resonance section, please," Meister said, and when he was connected and had identified himself, a voice growled:

"Hello, Jake, this is Frank Schafer. Where the deuce are you? I sent you a telegram—but I suppose you didn't get it, the boards are jammed. Get on down here, quick!"

"No, I haven't any telegram," Meister said. "Whom do I congratulate?"

"Nobody, you fool! *We* didn't do this. We don't even know how it's been done!"

Meister felt the hairs on the back of his neck stirring. It was as if he were back in the tunnels of Concentration Camp Dora again. He swallowed and said, "But it is the antibomb screen?"

"The very thing." Schafer's tinny voice said bitterly. "Only somebody else has beat us to it—and we're trapped under it."

"It's really bombproof—you're sure of that?"

"It's anything-proof! Nothing can pass it! *And we can't get out of it, either!*"

It took quite a while to get the story straight. Project B-19, the meaningless label borne by the top-secret, billion-dollar Atomic Defense Project, was in turmoil. Much of its laboratory staff had been in the field or in Washington when the thing happened, and the jam in phone service had made it difficult to get the men who were still in the city back to the central offices.

"It's like this," Frank Schafer said, kneading a chunk of art gum rapidly. "This dome went up last night. It lets in a little light and a few of the strongest outside radio stations near by. But that's all—or anyhow, all that we've been able to establish so far. It's a perfect dome, over the whole island and parts of the other boroughs and New Jersey. It doesn't penetrate the ground or the water, but the only really big water frontage is way out in the harbor, so that lets out much chance of everybody swimming under it like that man from the *Miss New York.*"

"The subways are running, I heard," Meister said.

"Sure; we can evacuate the city if we have to, but not fast enough." The mobile fingers crumbled bits off the sides of the art gum. "It won't take long to breathe up the air here, and if any fires start it'll be worse. Also there's a layer of ozone about twenty feet deep all along the inside of the barrier—but don't ask me why! Even if we don't have any big blazes, we're losing oxygen at a terrific rate by ozone-fixing and surface oxidization of the ionized area."

"Ionized?" Meister frowned. "Is there much?"

"Plenty!" Schafer said. "We haven't let it out, but in another twenty hours you won't be able to hear anything on the radio but a noise like a tractor climbing a pile of cornflakes. There's been an increase already. Whatever we're using for ether these days is building up tension fast."

A runner came in from the private wires and dropped a flimsy on Frank's desk. The physicist looked at it quickly, then passed it to Meister.

"That's what I figured. You can see the spot we're in."

The message reported that oxygen was diffusing inward through the barrier at about the same rate as might be accounted for by osmosis. The figures on loss of CO_2 were less easy to establish, but it appeared that the rate here was also of an osmotic order of magnitude. It was signed by a top-notch university chemist.

"Impossible!" Meister said.

"No, it's so. And New York is entirely too big a cell to live, Jake. If we're getting oxygen only osmotically, we'll be suffocated in a week. And did you ever hear of semipermeable membrane passing a lump of coal, or a tomato? Air, heat, food—all cut off."

"What does the Army say?"

"What they usually say: 'Do something, on the double!' We're lucky we're civilians, or we'd be court-martialed for dying!" Schafer laughed angrily and pitched the art gum away. "It's a very pretty problem, in a way," he said. "We have our antibomb screen. Now we have to find how to make ourselves *vulnerable* to the bomb—or cash in our chips. And in six days—"

The phone jangled and Schafer snatched at it. "Yeah, this is Dr. Schafer . . . I'm sorry, Colonel, but we have every available man called in now except those on the Mayor's commission . . . No, I don't know. Nobody knows, yet. We're tracing that radio signal now. If it has anything to do with the barrier, we'll be able to locate the generator and destroy it."

The physicist slammed the phone into its cradle and glared at Meister. "I've been taking this phone stuff all morning! I wish you'd showed up earlier. Here's the picture, briefly: The city is dying. Telephone and telegraph lines give us some communication with the outside, and we will be able to use radio inside the dome for a little while longer. There are teams outside trying to hack the barrier, but all the significant phenomena are taking place inside. Out there it just looks like a big black dome—no radiation effects, no ionization, no radio tone, no nothin'!

"We are evacuating now," he went on, "but if the dome stays up, over three quarters of the trapped people will die. If there's any fire or violence, almost all of us will die."

"You talk," Meister said, "as if you want me to kill the screen all by myself."

Schafer grinned nastily. "Sure, Jake! This barrier obviously doesn't act specifically on nuclear reactions; it stops almost everything. Almost everyone here is a nuclear man, as useless for this problem as a set of cooky-cutters. Every fact we've gotten so far shows this thing to be an immense and infinitely complicated form of cavity-resonance—and you're the only resonance engineer inside."

The grin disappeared. Schafer said, "We can give you all the electronics technicians you need, plenty of official backing, and general theoretical help. It's not much but it's all we've got. We estimate about eleven million people inside this box—eleven million corpses unless you can get the lid off it."

Meister nodded. Somehow, the problem did not weigh as heavily upon him as it might have. He was remembering Dora, the wasted bodies jammed under the stairs, in storerooms, fed into the bake-oven five at a time. One could survive almost anything if one had had practice in surviving. There was only Ellen—

Ellen was probably in The Box—the dome. That meant something, while eleven million was only a number.

"Entdecken," he murmured.

Schafer looked up at him, his blue eyes snapping sparks. Schafer certainly didn't look like one of the world's best nuclear physicists. Schafer was a sandy-haired runt—with the bomb hung over his head by a horsehair.

"What's that?" he said.

"A German word," Meister answered. "It means, to discover—literally, to take the roof off. That is the first step, it seems. To take the roof off, we must discover that transmitter."

"I've got men out with loop antennae. The geometrical center of the dome is right at the tip of the Empire State Building, but WNBT says there's nothing up there but their television transmitters."

"What they mean," Meister said, "is that there was nothing else up there two weeks ago. There *must* be a radiator at a radiant point no matter how well it is disguised."

"I'll send a team." Schafer got up, fumbling for the art gum he had thrown away. "I'll go myself, I guess. I'm jittery here."

"With your teeth? I would not advise it. You would die slain, as the Italians say!"

"Teeth?" Schafer said. He giggled nervously. "What's that got to—"

"You have metal in your mouth. If the mast is actually radiating this effect, your jawbones might be burnt out of your head. Get a group with perfect teeth, or porcelain fillings at best. And wear nothing with metal in it, not even shoes."

"Oh," Schafer said. "I knew we needed you, Jake." He rubbed the back of his hand over his forehead and reached into his shirt pocket for a cigarette.

Meister struck it out of his hand. "Six days' oxygen remaining," he said.

Schafer lunged up out of his chair, aimed a punch at Meister's head, and fainted across the desk.

The dim city stank of ozone. The street lights were still on. Despite radioed warnings to stay indoors surging mobs struggled senselessly toward the barrier. Counterwaves surged back, coughing, from the unbreathable stuff pouring out from it. More piled up in subway stations; people screamed and trampled one another. Curiously, the city's take that day was enormous. Not even disaster could break the deeply entrenched habit of putting a token in the turnstile.

The New York Central and Long Island Railroads, whose tracks were above ground where the screen cut across them, were shut down, as were the underground lines which came to the surface inside The Box. Special trains were running every three minutes from Pennsylvania Station, with passengers jamming the aisles and platforms.

In the Hudson Tubes the situation was worse. So great was the crush of fleeing humans there, they could hardly operate at all. The screen drew a lethal line between Hoboken and Newark, so that Tube trains had to make the longer of the two trips to get their passengers out of the Box. A brief power interruption stopped one train in complete darkness for ten minutes beneath the Hudson River, and terror and madness swept through it.

Queens and Brooklyn subways siphoned off a little pressure, but only a little. In a major disaster the normal human impulse is to go north, on the map-fostered myth that north is "up."

Navy launches were readied to ferry as many as cared to make the try out to where The Box lay over the harbor and the rivers, but thus far there were no such swimmers. Very few people can swim twenty feet under water, and to come up for air short of that twenty feet would be disastrous. That would be as fatal as coming up in the barrier itself; ozone is lung-rot in high concentrations. That alone kept most of the foolhardy from trying to run through the wall—that, and the gas-masked police cordon.

From Governor's Island, about half of which was in The Box, little Army ferries shipped over several cases of small arms which were distributed to subway and railroad guards. Two detachments of infantry also came along, relieving a little of the strain on the police.

Meister, hovering with two technicians and the helicopter pilot over a building on the edge of the screen, peered downward in puzzlement. It was hard to make any sense of the geometry of shadows below him.

"Give me the phone," he said.

The senior technician passed him the mike. A comparatively long-wave channel had been cleared by a major station for the use of emergency teams and prowl cars, since nothing could be heard on short-wave above that eternal humming.

"Frank, are you on?" Meister called. "Any word from Ellen yet?"

"No, but her landlady says she went to Jersey to visit yesterday," came over the air waves. There was an unspoken understanding between them that the hysterical attack of an hour ago would not be mentioned. "You'll have to crack The Box to get more news, I guess, Jake. See anything yet?"

"Nothing but more trouble. Have you thought yet about heat conservation? I am reminded that it is summer; we will soon have an oven here."

"I thought of that, but it isn't so," Frank Schafer's voice said. "It seems hotter only because there's no wind. Actually, the Weather Bureau says we're *losing* heat pretty rapidly; they expect the drop to level at fifteen to twenty above."

Meister whistled. "So low! Yet there is a steady supply of calories in the water—"

"Water's a poor conductor. What worries me is this accursed

ozone. It's diffusing through the city—already smells like the inside of a transformer around here!"

"What about the Empire State Building?"

"Not a thing. We ran soap bubbles along the power leads to see if something was tapping some of WNBT's power, but there isn't a break in them anywhere. Maybe you'd better go over there when you're through at the barrier. There are some things we can't make sense of."

"I shall," Meister said. "I will leave here as soon as I start a fire."

Schafer began to sputter. Meister smiled gently and handed the phone back to the technician.

"Break out the masks," he said. "We can go down now."

A rooftop beside the barrier was like some hell dreamed up in the violent ward of a hospital. Every movement accumulated a small static charge on the surface of the body, which discharged stingingly and repeatedly from the fingertips and even the tip of the nose if it approached a grounded object too closely.

Only a few yards away was the unguessable wall itself, smooth, deep gray, featureless, yet somehow quivering with a pseudo-life of its own—a shimmering haze just too dense to penetrate. It had no definite boundary. Instead, the tarpaper over which it lay here began to dim, and within a foot faded into the general mystery.

Meister looked at the barrier. The absence of anything upon which the eye could fasten was dizzying. The mind made up patterns and flashes of lurid color and projected them into the grayness. Sometimes it seemed that the fog extended for miles. A masked policeman stepped over from the inside parapet and touched him on the elbow.

"Wouldn't look at her too long, sir," he said. "We've had ambulances below carting away sightseers who forgot to look away. Pretty soon your eyes sort of get fixed."

Meister nodded. The thing was hypnotic all right. And yet the eye was drawn to it because it was the only source of light here. The ionization was so intense that it bled off power from the lines, so that street lamps had gone off all around the edge. From the helicopter, the city had looked as if its rim was inked out in a vast ring. Meister could feel the individual hairs all over his body stirring; it made him feel infested. Well, there'd been no shortage of lice at Dora!

Behind him the technicians were unloading the apparatus from the 'copter. Meister beckoned. "Get a reading on field strength first of all," he said gloomily. "Whoever is doing this has plenty of power. Ionized gas, a difficult achievement—"

He stopped suddenly. Not so difficult. The city was enclosed; it was, in effect, a giant Geissler tube. Of course the concentration of rare gases was not high enough to produce a visible glow, but—

"Plenty high," the technician with the loop said, "Between forty-five and fifty thousand. Seems to be rising a little, too."

"Between—" Meister stepped quickly to the instrument. Sure enough, the black needle was wavering, so rapidly as to be only a fan-shaped blur between the two figures. "This is ridiculous! Is that instrument reliable?"

"I just took the underwriters' seal off it," the technician said. "Did you figure this much ozone could be fixed out without any alteration?"

"Yes, I had presupposed the equivalent of UV bombardment. This changes things. No wonder there is light leaking through that screen! Sergeant—"

"Yes sir?" the policeman mumbled through his mask.

"How much of the area below can you clear?"

"As much as you need."

"Good." Meister reached into his jacket pocket and produced the map of the city the pilot had given him. "We are here, yes? Make a cordon, then, from here to here." His soft pencil scrawled a black line around four buildings. "Then get as much fire-fighting equipment outside the line as you can muster."

"You're expecting a bad fire?"

"No, *a good* one. But hurry!"

The cop scratched his head in puzzlement, but he went below. Meister smiled. Members of the Screen Team were the Mister Bigs in this city now. Twenty hours ago nobody'd ever heard of the Screen Team.

The technician, working with nervous quickness, was trying an oscilloscope into the loop circuit. Meister nodded approvingly. If there was a pulse to this phenomenon, it would be just as well to know its form. He snapped his fingers.

"What's wrong, doctor?"

"My memory. I have put my head on backwards when I got up this morning, I think. We will have to photograph the waveform; it will be too complex to analyze here."

"How do you know?" the technician asked.

"By that radio tone," Meister said. "You Americans work by sight. There are almost no resonance electronics men in this country. But in Germany we worked as much by ear as by eye. Where you convert a wave into a visible pattern, we turned it into an audible one. We had a saying that resonance engineers were disappointed musicians."

The face of the tube suddenly produced a green wiggle. It was the kind of wiggle a crazy man might make. The technician looked at it in dismay. "That," he said, "doesn't exist. I won't work in a science where it *could* exist!"

Meister grinned. "That is what I meant. The radio sound was a fundamental B-flat, but with hundreds of harmonics and overtones. You don't have it all in the field yet."

"I don't?" He looked. "So I don't! But when I reduce it that much, you can't see the shape of the modulations."

"We will have to photograph it by sections."

Bringing over the camera, the other man set it up. They worked rapidly, oppressed by the unnatural pearly glimmer, the masks, the stink of ozone which crept in at the sides of the treated cloth, the electrical prickling, above all by the silent terror of any trapped animal.

While they worked, the cop came back and stood by silently, watching. The gas mask gave no indication of his expression, but Meister could feel the pressure of faith radiating from the man. Doubtless these bits of equipment were meaningless to him—but bits of equipment like these had put up The Box, beyond the powers of policemen or presidents to take down again. Men who knew about such things were as good as gods now.

Unless they failed.

"That does it," the technician said.

The cop stepped forward. "I've got the area you marked roped off," he said diffidently. "We've searched the apartments and there's nobody in them. If there's any fire here, we'll be able to control it."

"Excellent!" Meister said. "Remember that this gas will feed the flames, however. You will need every possible man."

"Yes, sir. Anything else?"

"Just get out of the district yourself."

Meister climbed into the plane and stood by the open hatch, looking at his wrist watch. He gave the cop ten minutes to leave the tenement and get out to the fire lines. Then he struck a match and pitched it out onto the roof.

"Up!" he shouted.

The rotors roared. The pitch on the roof began to smolder. A tongue of flame shot up. In three seconds the whole side of the roof nearest the gray screen was blazing.

The helicopter lurched and clawed for altitude.

Behind the plane arose a brilliant and terrifying yellow glare. Meister didn't bother to watch it. He squatted with his back to the fire and waved pieces of paper over the neck of a bottle.

The ammonia fumes were invisible and couldn't be smelled through the mask, but on the dry-plates wiggly lines were appearing. Meister studied them, nibbling gently at his lower lip. With luck, the lines would answer one question at least: they would tell what The Box was. With luck, they might even tell how it was produced.

They would *not* tell where it came from.

The motion of the 'copter changed suddenly, and Meister's stomach stirred uneasily under his belt. He stowed the plates and looked up. The foreshortened spire of the Empire State Building pointed up at him through the transparent deck; another 'copter hovered at its tip. The television antennae were hidden now in what seemed to be a globe of some dark substance.

Meister picked up the radio-phone. "Schafer?" he called—this to the Empire State Building.

"No, this is Talliafero," came back an answer. "Schafer's back at the labs. We're about ready to leave. Need any help?"

"I don't think so," Meister said. "Is that foil you have around the tower mast?"

"Yes, but it's only a precaution. The whole tower's radiating. The foil radiates, too, now that we've got it up. See you later."

The other 'copter stirred and swooped away.

Meister twisted the dial up into the short-wave region. The humming surged in; he valved down the volume and listened intently. The sound was different somehow. After a moment his mind placed it. The fundamental B-flat was still there, but some of the overtones were gone; that meant that hundreds of them, which the little amplifier could not reproduce, were also gone. He was listening on an FM set; his little table set at the apartment was AM. So the wave was modulated along both axes, and probably pulse-modulated as well. But why should it simplify as one approached its source?

Resonance, of course. The upper harmonics were echoes. Yet a simple primary tone in a well-known frequency range couldn't produce The Box by itself. It was the harmonics that made the difference,

The Box   163

and the harmonics couldn't appear without the existence of some chamber like The Box. Along this line of reasoning, The Box was a precondition of its own existence. Meister felt his head swimming.

"Hey," the pilot said. "It's started to snow!"

Meister turned off the set and looked out. "All right, let's go home now."

Despite its depleted staff, the Screen Team was quiet with the intense hush of concentration that was its equivalent of roaring activity. Frank Schafer's door was closed, but Meister didn't bother to knock. He was on the edge of an idea and there was no time to be lost in formalities.

There were a number of uniformed men in the office with Frank. There was also a big man in expensive clothes, and a smaller man who looked as if he needed sleep. The smaller man had dark circles under his eyes, but despite his haggardness Meister knew him. The mayor. The big man did not look familiar—nor pleasant.

As for the high brass, nothing in a uniform looked pleasant to Meister. He pushed forward and put the dry-plates down on Schafer's desk. "The resonance products," he said. "If we can duplicate the fundamental in the lab—"

There came a roar from the big man. "Dr. Schafer, is this the man we've been waiting for?"

Schafer made a tired gesture. "Jake, this is Roland Dean," he said. "You know the mayor, I think. These others are security officers. They seem to think you made The Box."

Meister stiffened. "I? That's idiotic!"

"Any noncitizen is automatically under suspicion," one of the Army men said. "However, Dr. Schafer exaggerates. We just want to ask a few questions."

The mayor coughed. He was obviously tired, and the taint of ozone did not make breathing very comfortable.

"I'm afraid there's more to it than that, Dr. Meister," he added. "Mr. Dean here has insisted upon an arrest. I'd like to say for myself that I think it all quite stupid."

"Thank you," Meister said. "What is Mr. Dean's interest in this?"

"Mr. Dean," Schafer growled, "is the owner of that block of tenements you're burning out up north. The fire's spreading, by the way. When I told him I didn't know why you lit it, he blew his top."

"Why not?" Dean said, glaring at Meister. "I fail to see why this emergency should be made an excuse for irresponsible destruction of property. Have you any reason for burning my buildings, Meister?"

"Are you having any trouble with breathing, Mr. Dean?" Meister asked.

"Certainly! Who isn't? Do you think you can make it easier for us by filling The Box with smoke?"

Meister nodded. "I gather that you have no knowledge of elementary chemistry, Mr. Dean. The Box is rapidly converting our oxygen into an unbreathable form. A good hot fire will consume some of it, but it will also break up the ozone molecules. The ratio is about two atoms of oxygen consumed for every one set free—out of three which in the form of ozone could not have been breathed at all."

Schafer sighed gustily. "I should have guessed. A neat scheme, Jake. But what about the ratio between reduction of ozone and overall oxygen consumption?"

"Large enough to maintain five of the six days' grace with which we started. Had we let the ozone-fixing process continue unabated, we should not have lasted forty hours longer."

"Mumbo jumbo!" Dean said stonily, turning to Schafer. "A halfway measure. The problem is to get us out of this mess, not to stretch our sufferings out by three days by invading property rights. This man is a German, probably a Nazi! By your own admission, he's the only man in your whole section who's seemed to know what to do. And nothing he's done so far has shown any result, except to destroy some of my buildings!"

"Dr. Meister, just what *has* been accomplished thus far?" a colonel of Intelligence said.

"Only a few tentative observations," Meister said. "We have most of the secondary phenomena charted."

"Charts!" Dean snorted.

"Can you offer any assurance that The Box will be down in time?" the colonel asked.

"That," Meister said, "would be very foolish of me. The possibility exists, that is all. Certainly it will take time—we have barely scratched the surface."

"In that case, I'm afraid you'll have to consider yourself under arrest—"

"See here, Colonel!" Schafer surged to his feet, his face flushed. "Don't you know that he's the only man in The Box who can crack it? That fire was good common sense. If you arrest my men for *not* doing anything, we'll never get anything done!"

"I am not exactly stupid, Dr. Shafer," the colonel said harshly. "I have no interest in Mr. Dean's tenements, and if the mayor is forced to jail Dr. Meister we will spring him at once. All I'm interested in is the chance that Dr. Meister may be *maintaining* The Box instead of trying to *crack it."*

"Explain, please," Meister said mildly.

Pulling himself up to military straightness, the colonel cleared his throat and said:

"You're inside The Box. If you put it up, you have a way out of it, and know where the generator is. You may go where you please, but from now on we'll have a guard with you. . . . Satisfied, Dr. Schafer?"

"It doesn't satisfy me!" Dean rumbled. "What about my property? Are you going to let this madman burn buildings with a guard to help?"

The colonel looked at the landlord. "Mr. Dean," he said quietly, "you seem to think The Box was created to annoy you personally. The Army hasn't the technical knowledge to destroy it, but it has sense enough to realize that more than just New York is under attack here. The enemy, whoever he may be, thinks his screen uncrackable, otherwise he wouldn't have given us this chance to work on it by boxing in one city alone. If The Box is not down in, say, eight days, he'll know that New York failed and died—and every city in the country will be bombed to slag the next morning."

Schafer sat down again, looking surly. "Why?" he asked the army man. "Why would they waste the bombs when they could just box in the cities?"

"Inefficient. America's too big to occupy except slowly, piecemeal. They'd have no reason to care if large parts of it were uninhabitable for a while. The important thing is to knock us out as a military force, as a power in world affairs."

"If they boxed in all the cities at once—"

The colonel shook his head. "We have rocket emplacements of our own, and they *aren't* in large cities. Neither Box nor bomb would catch more than a few of them. No. They have to know that The Box is uncrackable, so they can screen their own cities against our bombs until our whole country is knocked out. With The Box, that would take more than a week, and their cities would suffer along with ours.

With bombs, a day would be enough. So they've allowed us this test. If New York comes out of this, there'll be no attack, at least until they've gotten a better screen. The Box seems good enough so far!"

"Politics," Schafer said, shaking his head disgustedly. "It's much too devious for me! Doesn't The Box constitute an attack?"

"Certainly—but who's doing the attacking?" the colonel demanded. "We can guess, but we don't know. And I doubt very much that the enemy has left any traces."

Meister stiffened suddenly, a thrill of astonishment shooting up his backbone. Schafer stared at him.

"Traces!" Meister said. "Of course! That is what has been stopping us all along. Naturally there would be no traces. We have been wasting time looking for them. Frank, the generator is not in the Empire State Building. *It is not even in The Box!*"

"But, Jake, it's got to be," Schafer said. "It's physically impossible for it to be outside!"

"A trick," Dean rumbled.

Meister waved his hands excitedly. "No, no! This is the reasoning which has made our work so fruitless. Observe. As the colonel says, the enemy would not dare leave traces. Now, workmanship is traceable, particularly if the device is revolutionary, as this one is. Find that generator and you know at once which country has made it. You observe the principle, and you say to yourself, 'Ah, yes, there were reports, rumors, whispers of shadows of rumors of such a principle, but I discounted them as fantasy; they came out of Country X.' Do you follow?"

"Yes, but—"

"But no country would leave such a fingerprint where it could be found. This we can count upon. Whereas we know as yet next to nothing about the physics of The Box. Therefore, if it is physically impossible for the generator to be outside The Box, this does not mean that we must continue to search for it inside. It means that we must find a physical principle which makes it possible to be outside!"

Frank Schafer threw up his hands. "Revise basic physics in a week! Well, let's try. I suppose Meister's allowed lab work, Colonel?"

"Certainly, as long as my guards aren't barred from the laboratory."

Thirty hours later the snow stopped falling, leaving a layer a little over three inches deep. The battling mobs were no longer on the streets. Hopeless masses were jammed body to body in railroad stations and subways. The advancing ozone had driven the people in upon themselves, and into the houses and basements where rooms could be sealed against the searing stench.

Thousands had already died along the periphery. The New Jersey and Brooklyn shores were charnel heaps of those who had fought to get back across the river to Manhattan and cleaner air. The tenements along the West Side of the island still blazed—twenty linear blocks of them—but the fire had failed to jump Ninth Avenue and was dying for want of fuel. Elsewhere it was very cold. The city was dying.

Over it, The Box was invisible. It was the third night.

In the big lab at the Team Office, Meister, Schafer, and the two technicians suddenly disappeared under a little Box of their own, leaving behind four frantic soldiers. Meister sighed gustily and looked at the black screen a few feet from his head.

"Now we know," he said. "Frank, you can turn on the light now."

The desk lamp clicked on. In the shaded glow Meister saw that tears were trickling down Schafer's cheeks.

"No, no, don't weep yet, the job is not quite done!" Meister cried. "But see—so simple, so beautiful!" He gestured at the lump of metal in the exact center of the Boxed area. "Here we are—four men, a bit of metallic trash, an empty desk, a lamp, a cup of foil. Where is the screen generator? Outside!"

Schafer swallowed. "But it isn't," he said hoarsely. "Oh, you were right, Jake—the key projector *is* outside. But it doesn't generate the screen; it just excites the iron there, and that does the job." He looked at the scattered graphs on the desk top. "I'd never have dreamed such a jam of fields was possible! Look at those waves—catching each other, heterodyning, slowing each other up as the tension increases. No wonder the whole structure of space gives way when they finally get in phase!"

One of the technicians looked nervously at the little Box and cleared his throat. "I still don't see why it should leak light, oxygen, and so forth, even the little that it does. The jam has to be radiated away, and the screen should be the subspatial equivalent of a perfect radiator, a black body. But it's gray."

"No, it's black," Schafer said. "But it isn't turned on all the time. If it were, the catalyst radiation couldn't get through. It's a perfect electromagnetic push-me-pull-you. The apparatus outside projects the catalyst fields in. The lump of iron—in this case the Empire State Building—is excited and throws off the screen fields. The screen goes up. The screen cuts off the catalyst radiation. The screen goes down. In comes the primary beam again. And so on. The kicker is that without the off-again-on-again, you wouldn't get anything—the screen couldn't exist because the intermittence supplies some of the necessary harmonics."

He grinned ruefully. "Here I am explaining it as if I understood it. You're a good teacher, Jake!"

"Once one realizes that the screen has to *be* up before it can *go* up," Meister said, grinning back, "one has the rest—or most of it. Introducing a rhythmic interruption of the very first pulses is a simple trick. The hardest thing about it is timing—to know just when the screen goes up for the first time, so that the blinker can be cut out at precisely that moment."

"So how do we get out?"

"Feedback," Meister said. "There must be an enormous back EMF in the incoming beam. And whether it is converted and put back into the system again at the source, or just efficiently wasted, we can burn it out." He consulted a chalk line which ran along the floor from the edge of the little Box to the lump of iron, then picked up the cup of foil and pointed it along the mark away from the lump. "The trick," he said soberly, "is not to nullify, but to amplify—"

The glare of the overheads burst in upon them. The lab was jammed with soldiers, all with rifles at the ready and all the rifles pointing in at them. The smell of burned insulation curled from an apparatus at the other end of the chalk line.

"Oh," said Schafer. "We forgot the most important thing! Which way does our chalk line run from the Empire State Building, I wonder?"

"It could be anywhere above the horizon," Meister said. "Try pointing your reflector straight up, first."

Schafer swore. "Any time you want a diploma for unscrewing the inscrutable, Jake," he said, "I'll write you one with my nose!"

It was cold and quiet now in the city. The fires on the West Side, where one of the country's worst slums had been burned out, smoldered and flickered.

The air was a slow, cumulative poison. It was very dark.

On top of the Empire State Building a great, shining bowl swung in a certain direction, stopped, waited. Fifty miles above it, in a region where neither *cold* nor *air* have any human meaning, a clumsy torpedo began to warm slightly. Inside it, delicate things glowed, fused—melted. There was no other difference; the torpedo kept on, traveled at its assigned twenty-one and eight-tenths miles per minute. It would always do so.

The Box vanished. The morning sunlight glared in. There was a torrent of rain as cold air hit hot July. Within minutes the city was as gray as before, but with roiling thunderheads. People poured out of the buildings into the downpour, hysterical faces turned to the free air, shouting amid the thunder, embracing each other, dancing in the lightning flares.

The storm passed almost at once, but the dancing went on quite a while.

"Traces!" Meister said to Frank Schafer. "Where else could you hide them? An orbital missile was the only answer."

"That sunlight," Schafer said, "sure looks good! You'd better go home to bed, Jake, before the official hero-worshipers catch up with you."

But Meister was already dreamlessly asleep.

The Oath

Remembering conscientiously to use the hand brake as well as the foot, Dr. Frank Tucci began to slow down toward the middle of the bridge, examining the toll booths ahead with a cold eye.

He despised everything about scouting by motor scooter, though he agreed, when forced to it, that a man on a scooter made the smallest possible target consistent with getting anywhere—and besides, it conserved gas, of which there was very little left. Most of all he despised crossing bridges. It made him feel even more exposed than usual, and toll booths made natural ambushes.

These, however, were as deserted as they looked. The glass had been broken and the tills rifled. Without question the man who had taken the money had not lived long enough afterward to discover that it was worthless. Still, the looting of money was unusual, for there had been little time for it. Most people outside target areas had died during the first two days; the 38-hour dose in the open had averaged 9100 roentgens.

Naturally the small town ahead would be thoroughly looted of food and other valuables, but that was different. There was a physician in the area—that was the man Dr. Tucci had come all this way to see—and as usual, people would have drifted in again to settle around him. People meant looting, necessarily. For one thing, they were accustomed to getting 70 percent of their calcium from milk, and the only milk that was drinkable out here was canned stuff from before the Day.

There might still be a cow or two outside the Vaults, but her milk would be lethal.

There would be no more dairy products of any kind for the lifetime of anyone now living, once the lootables were gone. There was too much strontium-90 in the soil. The Nutrition Board had worked out some way around the calcium supply problem, Tucci had heard, but he knew nothing about it; that wasn't his province.

His province was in the valley ahead, in the large reddish frame house where, all the reports assured him, he would find another doctor—or somebody who was passing for one. The house, he noted professionally, was fairly well situated. There was a broad creek running rapidly over a stone bed not far away, and the land was arable and in cultivation: truck crops for the most part, a good acre of them, enough to supply a small family by today's starvation standards. The family was there, that was evident: two children in the four-to-seven age bracket—hence survivors, both of them—were playing a stalking game in the rows of corn to which the other acre was planted.

Tucci wondered if the owner knew the Indian trick of planting pumpkins, beans, and a fish from the stream in the same hill with the corn. If he didn't, he wasn't getting more than half as much from the acre as he might.

The position was not optimum for defense. Though the centrally located house did offer clear shots all around, anyone could put it under siege almost indefinitely from the high ground which surrounded it. But presumably a doctor did not need to conduct a lonely defense against the rare roving band, since his neighbors would help him. A "neighbor" in that sense would include anyone within a hundred miles who could pick up a weapon and get to the scene fast enough.

Even a mob might pause before it could come to that. Its first sight of the house would be from here, looking down into the valley; and on the roof of the house, over green paint much streaked by repeated antifallout hosings, was painted a large red cross.

That would hardly have protected the owner during the first six months after the Day, but that was more than a year ago. Things had settled somewhat since then. Initially a good deal of venom had expressed itself against doctors when the dying had discovered that they could not be saved. That was why, now, rumors of the existence of a physician could bring Dr. Tucci two hundred bumpy miles on a rusty Lambretta whose side panels had fallen off, carrying a conspicuous five-gallon can of the liquid gold that was gasoline on his luggage rack, sweating inside a bullet-proof suit in whose efficacy he thoroughly disbelieved.

He gunned the motor three times in neutral before putting the scooter back in gear and starting it slowly down the hill. The last thing he wanted was to seem to be sneaking up on anybody. Sure enough, as he clambered down from his perch onto the road in front of the house and lurched the scooter up onto its kickstand, he saw someone watching him from a ground floor window.

He knew that he was an odd sight. Short dumpy men look particularly short and dumpy on motor scooters, and he doubted that his green crash helmet and dark goggles made him look any less bizarre. But those, at least, he could take off. There was nothing he could do right now about the putatively bullet-proof coverall.

He was met at the door by a woman. She was a tall, muscular blonde wearing shorts and a halter, a cloth tying up her hair in the back. He approved of her on sight. She was rather pretty in her own heroic fashion, but more than that, she was obviously strong and active. That was what counted these days, although animal cunning was also very helpful.

"Good morning," he said. He produced from his pocket the ritual gift of canned beans without which it was almost impossible to open negotiations with a stranger. "My name is Frank Tucci, from up north. I'm looking for someone named Gottlieb, Nathan Gottlieb; I think—"

"Thank you, this is where he lives," the woman said, with unusual graciousness. Obviously she was not afraid or suspicious. "I'm Sigrid Gottlieb. You'll have to wait a while, I'm afraid. He's seeing another patient now, and there are several others waiting."

"Patient?" Tucci said, without attempting to look surprised. He knew that he would overdo it. Just speaking slowly should be sufficient for an unsuspicious audience. "But it's—of course everything's different now, but the Gottlieb I'm looking for is a poet."

Another pause. He added, "Er . . . was a poet."

"Is a poet," Sigrid said. "Well, come in please, Mr. Tucci. He'll be astonished. At least, *I'm* astonished—hardly anybody knew his name, even Back Then."

Score one, thanks to the Appalachian Vaults' monstrous library. Out of a personal crotchet, Tucci checked with the library each name that rumor brought him, and this time it had paid off. It never had before.

From here on out, it ought to be easy.

Nathan Gottlieb listened with such intensity that he reduced every other listener in Tucci's memory to little better than a catatonic. His regard made Tucci acutely aware of the several small lies upon which his story rested; and of the fact that Gottlieb was turning over and over in his hands the ritual can of beans Tucci had given Sigrid. In a while, perhaps Gottlieb would see that it had been made *after* the Day, and would draw the appropriate conclusions. Well, there was no help for it. Onward and upward.

Physically, Gottlieb was small and gaunt, nearly a foot shorter than his wife, and rather swarthy. He looked as though, nude, you might be able to count all his bones. His somatotype suggested that he had not looked much plumper Back Then. But the body hardly mattered. What overwhelmed Tucci was the total, balanced alertness which informed its every muscle. Somehow, he kept talking.

". . .Then when the word was brought in that there was not only a settlement here, but that a man named Nathan Gottlieb was some sort of key figure in it, it rang a bell. Sheer accident, since the name was common enough, and I'd never been much of a reader, either; but right away a line came to me and I couldn't get rid of it."

"A line?"

"Yes. It goes: 'And the duned gold clean drifted over the forelock of time.' It had haunted me for years, and when I saw your name in the report, it came back, full force."

"As a last line, it's a smasher," Gottlieb said thoughtfully. "Too bad the rest of the poem wasn't up to it. The trouble was, the minute I thought of it, I knew it was a last line, and I waited around for two years for a poem to come along to go with it. None ever did, so finally I constructed one synthetically, with the predictable bad results."

"Nobody would ever know if you didn't tell them," Tucci said with genuine warmth. He had, as a matter of fact, particularly admired that poem for the two whole days *since* he had first read it. "In any event, I was sufficiently curious to don my parachute-silk underwear and come jolting down here to see if you were the same man as the one who wrote *The Coming-Forth*. I'm delighted to find that you are, but I'm overwhelmed to find you practicing medicine as well! We're terribly short of physicians, and that happens to be my particular department. So all in all it's an incredible coincidence."

"That's for true," Gottlieb said, turning the can around in his hands. "And there's still a part of it that I don't understand. Who is this 'we' you mention?"

"Well. We just call it the Corporation now, since it's the last there is. Originally it was the Bryan Moving and Warehouse Corporation. If you lived in this area Back Then, you may remember our radio commercials on WASM-FM, for our Appalachian Mountain Vaults. 'Businessmen, what would happen to your records if some (unnamed) disaster struck? Put them in our mountain vaults, and die happy.' That was the general pitch."

"I remember. I didn't think you meant it."

"We did. Oddly enough, a good many corporation executives took us at face value, too. When the Day came, of course, it was obvious that those papers were going to be no good to anybody. We threw them out and moved in ourselves, instead. We had thought that would be the most likely outcome and had been planning on it."

Gottlieb nodded, and set the can on the floor between his feet, as though the question it had posed him was now answered. "A sane procedure, that's for sure. Go on."

"Well, since the Reds saturated Washington and the ten 'hard' SAC sites out West, we appear to be the only such major survival project that came through. We've had better than a year to hear differently, and haven't heard a whisper. We know that there were several other industrial projects, but they were conducted in such secrecy that the enemy evidently concluded they were really military. We advertised ours on the radio, and like you, they didn't believe that we could be serious; or so we conclude.

"Now we're out and doing. We're trying to organize a—well, not a government exactly, since we don't want to make laws and we don't want to give orders—but at least the service functions of government, to help bring things into some kind of shape. Doing for people, in short, what they can't do for themselves, especially with things in their present shambles."

"I see. And how do you profit?"

"Profit? In a great many ways, all intangible, but quite real. We attract specialists, which we need. This indebts the community to us and helps us manage it better. It's a large community now, about as big as New York and Pennsylvania combined, though it's shaped rather more like Texas. How many people are included I can't say; we may try to run a census in a year or so. Every specialist we recruit is, so to speak, an argument for reviving the institution of government."

He paused, counted to ten, and added: "I hope you are persuaded. Now that I've found you out, I'd be most reluctant to let you off the hook."

Gottlieb said, "I'm flattered, but I think you're making a mistake. I'm still only a poet, and as such, quite useless. I'm the world's worst medical man, even in these times."

"Ah. Now that's something I've been burning to ask you. How *did* you get into this profession?"

"Deliberately. When Sigrid and I got alarmed by all those Berlin crises, and then the summit fiasco, and decided to start on a basement shelter out here, I had to start thinking of what I might be able to do if we did survive. There wasn't any way to make a living as a poet Back Then, either, but I'd always been able to turn a marginal dollar as a flack—you know, advertising copy, the trade papers, popular articles, ghosting speeches, all those dodges. But obviously there wasn't going to be anything doing in those lines in a primitive world."

"So you chose medicine instead?" Tucci said. "But why? Surely you had some training in it?"

"Some," Gottlieb said. "I was a medical laboratory technician for four years in World War II—the Army's idea of what to do with a poet, I suppose. I did urinalyses, hematology, blood chemistry, bacteriology, serology and so on; it involved some ward collecting too, so I got to see the patients, not just their body fluids. At first I did it all by the cookbook, but after a while I began to understand parts of it, and by God I seemed to have a feeling for it. I think most literary people might, if they'd just have been able to get rid of their notion that the humanities were superior to the sciences. You know, the pride of the professor of medieval Latin, really a desperately complicated language, is the fact that he couldn't 'do' simple arithmetic. Hell, *anybody* can do arithmetic; my oldest daughter could 'do' algebra at the age of nine, and I think she's a little retarded. Anyhow, that's why I chose medicine. Nowadays I understand why the real medicos had the interne system Back Then, though. There's nothing that turns you into a doctor like actually working at it, accumulating patient-hours and diagnostic experience."

Tucci nodded abstractedly. "What did you do for equipment, materia medica, and so on?"

"I don't have any equipment to speak of. I don't do even simple surgery; I have to be hyperconservative out of sheer ignorance—lancing a boil and installing a tube drain is as far in that line as I dare to go. And of course I've no electricity. I've been reading up on building a dam across my creek and winding a simple generator, but so far the proposition's been too much for me. I'm not at all handy, though I've been forced to try.

"As for supplies, that was easy—just a matter of knowing in advance what I hoped to do. I simply looted the local drugstore the moment I came out of the hole, while everybody else who'd survived that long was busy loading up on canned goods and clothing and hardware. I was lucky that the whole dodge hadn't occurred to the pharmacist himself before the Day came, but it didn't. He hadn't even thought to dig himself a hole.

"I figured that anything I missed in the line of consumer goods would come my way later, if the doctor business paid off. And you'd be surprised how much of my medical knowledge comes from the package inserts the manufacturers used to include with the drugs. By believing a hundred percent of the cautions and contraindications, and maybe thirty percent of the claims, I hardly ever poison a patient."

"Hmmm," Tucci said, suppressing a smile only by a heroic effort. "How long will your supplies hold out?"

"Quite a while yet, I think. I'm being conservative there, too. In infectious cases, for instance, if I have a choice between an antibiotic and synthetic—such as a sulfa drug—I use the antibiotic, since it has an expiration date and the sulfa drug doesn't. In another year I'm going to have to start doubling my antibiotic doses, but there's no use worrying about that—and I'll still have an ample stock of the synthetics."

Tucci thought about it, conscientiously. It was a strange case, and he was not sure he liked it. Most of the few "doctors" he had tracked down in the field were simple quacks, practicing folk medicine or outright fakery to fill a gap left by the wholesale slaughter of specialists of all kinds, bar none—doctors, plumbers, farmers, you name it, it was almost extinct. Occasionally he had hit a survivor who had been a real physician Back Then; those had been great discoveries, and instantly recruited.

Gottlieb was neither one nor the other. He had no right to practice, by the old educational, lodge-brother or government standards. Yet obviously he was trying to do an honest job from a limited but real base of knowledge. The Vaults could use him, that was certain; but would they offer him the incentives they still reserved for the genuine, 24-carat, pre-Day M.D.?

Tucci decided that they would have to. This was the first case of its kind, but it would not be the last. Sooner or later they would have to face up to it.

"I think we can solve at least some of your problems," he said slowly. "So far as shelf-life of antibiotics is concerned, we keep them in cold storage and have enough to last a good fifty years. We have electricity, and we can give you the use of a great deal of equipment, as you learn how to use it: for example, X-rays, fluoroscopes, ECGs, EEGs. I think we need you, Mr. Gottlieb; and it's self-evident that you need us."

Gottlieb shook his head, slowly, but not at all hesitantly. It took Tucci several seconds to register that that was what he was doing.

"No," he said. "You're very kind. But I'm afraid it doesn't attract me."

The refusal was stunning, but Tucci was well accustomed to shocks. He drew a deep breath and came back fighting.

"For heaven's sake, why not? I don't like to be importunate, but you ought at least to think of what the other advantages might be. You could give up this marginal farming; we have a large enough community so we can leave that to experienced farmers. We use specialists in their specialties. You and your family could live in the Vaults, and breathe filtered air; that alone should run your children's life expectancy up by a decade or more. You know very well that the roentgen level in the open is still far above any trustable level, and if you came out of your hole in anything under three months—as I'm sure you did—you and your family have had your lifetime dose already. And above all, you'd be able to practice medicine in a way that's quite impossible here, and help many more people than you're helping now."

Gottlieb stood up. "I don't doubt a word of that," he said. "The answer is still no. I could explain, but it would be faster in the long run if you first took a look at the kind of medicine I'm actually practicing now. After that the explanations can be shorter, and probably more convincing."

"Well . . . of course. It's your decision. I'll play it your way."

"Good. I've still got three patients out there. I'm aware that you yourself are a bona-fide physician, Dr. Tucci; you disguise it well, but not well enough. And you may not want me so badly when we're through."

The first patient was a burly, bearded, twisted man with heavily calloused hands who might always have been a farmer; in any event, everybody in the field was some kind of farmer now. He stank mightily, and part of the stench seemed to Tucci to be alcohol. His troubles, which he explained surlily, were intimate.

"Before we go on, there's something we have to get clear, Mr. Herwood," Gottlieb told him, in what subsequently proved to be a set speech for new patients. "I'm not a real doctor and I can't promise to help you. I know something about medicine and I'll do the best I can, as I see it. If it doesn't work, you don't pay me. Okay?"

"I don't give a damn," the patient said. *"You* do what you can, that's okay with me."

"Good." Gottlieb took a smear and rang a little hand bell on his desk. His 15-year-old daughter popped her head in through the swinging door that led to the kitchen, and Gottlieb handed her the slide.

"Check this for gram-positive diplococci," he told her. She nodded and disappeared. Gottlieb filled in the time discussing payment with the patient. Herwood had, it turned out, a small case of anchovy fillets which he had liberated in the first days, when people were grabbing up anything, but nobody in his surviving family would eat them. Only tourists ate such stuff, not people.

The teenager pushed open the swinging door again. "Positive," she reported.

"Thanks, honey. Now, Mr. Herwood, who's your contact?"

"Don't follow you."

"Who'd you get this from?"

"I don't have to tell you that."

"Of course you don't," Gottlieb said. "I don't have to treat you, either."

Herwood squirmed in his straight-backed chair. He was obviously in considerable physical discomfort.

"You got no right to blackjack me," he growled. "I thought you was here to help people, not t'make trouble."

"That's right. But I already told you. I'm not a real doctor. I never took the Hippocratic Oath and I'm not *bound* to help anybody. I make up my own mind about that. In this case, I want to see that woman, and if I don't get to see her, I don't treat you."

"Well. . ." Herwood shifted again in the chair. "All right, damn you. You got me over a barrel and you know it. I'll tell her to come in."

"That's only a start," Gottlieb said patiently. "That leaves it up to her. Not good enough. I want to know her name, so if she doesn't show up for treatment here herself, I can do something about it."

"You got no right."

"I said so. But that's how it's going to be."

The argument continued for several minutes more but it was clear from the beginning that Gottlieb had won it. He gave the man an injection with matter-of-fact skill.

"That should start clearing up the trouble, but don't jump to conclusions when you begin to feel better. It'll be temporary. These things are stubborn. I'll need to see you three more times, at least.

So don't forget to tell Gertie that I want to see her—and that I know who she is."

Herwood left, muttering blackly. Gottlieb turned to his observer.

"I see a lot of that kind of thing, of course. I'm doing my best to stamp it out—which I might even be able to do in a population as small and isolated as this," he said. "I don't have any moral strictures on the subject, incidentally. The old codes are gone, and good riddance. In fact, without widespread promiscuity I can't see how we'll ever repopulate the world before we become extinct. But the diseases involved cost us an enormous sum in man-hours; and some of them have long latent periods that store up hell for the next generations. In *this* generation it's actually possible to wipe them out for good and all—and if it can be done, it should be done."

"True," Tucci said noncommittally. Thus far, he was baffled. Gottlieb had done nothing that he would not have done himself.

The next patient was also a man, shockingly plump, though as workworn as his predecessor. Gottlieb greeted him with obvious affection. His symptoms made up an odd constellation, obviously meaningless to the patient himself; and after a while Tucci began to suspect that they meant very little to Gottlieb, either.

"How did that toe clear up?" Gottlieb was saying.

"All right, fine, Nat. It's just that I keep getting these boils and all every time I hit a splinter, looks like. And lately I'm always thirsty, I can't seem to get enough water; and the more I drink the more it cuts into my sleep, so I'm tired all the time too. The same with food. People are talking, they say I eat like a pig, and it's true, and it shows. But I can't help it. A bad name to have, these days, and me with a family."

"I know what you mean. But it's pretty indefinite now, Hal. We'll just have to wait and see what develops." Gottlieb paused, and quite surreptitiously drew a deep, sad breath. "Try to cut down a little on the intake, I'll give you some pills that will help you there, and some sleeping tablets. Don't hit the sleepy pills too hard, though."

Payment was arranged. It was only nominal this time.

"Are you aware," Tucci said when they were alone again, "that you've just committed manslaughter—at the very least?"

"Sure I am," Gottlieb said in a low voice. "I told you you wouldn't like what you saw. The man's a new diabetic. There's nothing I can do for him, that's all."

"Surely that's not so. I'm aware that you can't store insulin without any refrigeration, but surely there were some of the oral hypoglycemic agents in the stock you found at the drugstore—tolbutamide, carbutamide, chlorpropamide? If you don't recognize them by their old trade names, I can help you. In the meantime—well, at least you could have put the man on a rational diet."

"I threw all those pills out," Gottlieb said flatly. "I don't treat diabetics. Period. You heard what I told Herwood: I never took the Hippocratic Oath, and I don't subscribe to it. In the present instance, we're having a hard enough time with all the new antisurvival mutations that have cropped up. I am not going to have any hand in preserving any of the old ones. If I ever hit a hemophiliac, the first thing I'll do is puncture him for a test—and forget to put a patch over the hole. Do you remember, Dr. Tucci, that just before the Day there was a national society soliciting funds to look for a cure for hemophilia? When the Oath takes you that far, into saving lethal genes, either it's crazy or you are!"

"What would you have done with LaGuardia? Or Edison?" Tucci said evenly.

"Were they hemophiliacs?" Gottlieb said in astonishment.

"No. But they were diabetics. It's the same thing, in your universe."

After a long time, Gottlieb said, almost to himself:

"I can't say. It isn't easy. Am I to save every lethal gene because I suspect that the man who carries it is a genius? That may have been worth while in the old days, when there were millions of diabetics. But now? The odds are all against it. I make harder decisions than that every day, Dr. Tucci. Hal is no genius, but he's a friend of mine."

"And so you've killed him."

"Yes," Gottlieb said stonily. "He wasn't the first, and he won't be the last. There are not many people left in the world. We cannot tolerate lethal genes. The doctor who does may save one adult life—but he will kill hundreds of children. I won't do that. I never swore to preserve every life that was put in my hands, regardless of consequences. That's my curse . . . and my lever on the world."

"In short, you have set yourself up to play God."

"To *play* God?" Gottlieb said. "Now you're talking nonsense. In this village, I *am* God . . . the only god that's left."

The last patient was relatively commonplace. She had frequent, incapacitating headaches—and had earned them, for she had five children, two survivors and three new ones. While Gottlieb doled out aspirin to her (for which he charged a price so stiff—after all, there had been 15,670,944,200 aspirin tablets, approximately, in storage in the United States alone on the Day—that Tucci suspected it was intended to discourage a further visit), Tucci studied her fasciae and certain revealing tics, tremors, and failures of coordination which were more eloquent to him than anything she had said.

"There, that does it for today," Gottlieb said. "And with no more telephones, I'm almost never called out at night—never for anything trivial. I'll clean up and then we can talk further. You'll eat with us, of course. I have a canned Polish ham I've been saving for our first guest after the Day, and you've earned the right to be that guest."

"I'd be honored," Tucci said. "But first, one question. Have you a diagnosis for the last patient?"

"Oh, migraine, I suppose, though that's about as good as no diagnosis at all. Possibly menopausal—or maybe just copelessness. That's a disease I invented, but I see a lot of it. Why?"

"It's not copelessness. It's glioblastoma multiforme—a runaway malignant tumor of the brain. At the moment, that's only a provisional opinion, but I think exploration would confirm it. Aspirin won't last her long—and in the end, neither will morphine."

"Well. . . I'm sorry. Annie's a warm and useful woman. But if you're right, that's that."

"No. We have a treatment. We give the patient a boric acid injection—"

"Great God," Gottlieb said. "The side effects must be fierce."

"Yes, but if the patient is doomed anyhow? . . . After all, it's a little late in the day for gentleness."

"Sorry. Go ahead. Why boric acid?"

"Boron won't ordinarily cross the blood-brain barrier," Tucci explained. "But it will concentrate in the tumor. Then we irradiate the whole brain with slow neutrons. The boron atoms split, emitting two quanta of gamma radiation per atom, and the tumor is destroyed. The fission fragments are nontoxic, and the neutrons don't harm the normal brain tissue. As for the secondary gammas, they can't get through more than a layer of tissue a single cell thick, so they never leave the tumor at all. It works very well—one of our inheritances from Back Then; a man named Lee Parr invented it."

"Fantastic! If only poor Annie could have—" Gottlieb's mouth shut with the suddenness of a rabbit-trap, and his eyes began to narrow.

"Wait a minute," he said. "I'm being a little slow today. You said,

'We *have* a treatment,' not 'We *had*.' What you mean me to understand is that you also have an atomic pile. That's the only possible source of slow neutrons."

"Yes, we have one. It generates our electricity. It's clumsy and inefficient—but we've got it."

"All right," Gottlieb said slowly. "I'll go and change, and then we'll talk. But the purpose of my demonstration, Dr. Tucci, is what I mean *you* to understand; and I wish you'd think about it a while, while I'm gone."

The dinner was enormously pleasant; remarkably good even by the standards of the Vaults, and almost a unique experience in the field. Sigrid Gottlieb proved to be a witty table companion as well as an imaginative cook. Some of her shafts had barbs on them, for it was plain that she had overheard enough to divine Tucci's mission and had chosen to resent it. But these were not frequent enough or jagged enough to make Tucci believe that she was trying to make up her husband's mind for him. All well and good.

As for the children—the one prospect of the meal to which Tucci had not been looking forward, for as a bachelor he was categorically frightened of children—they were not even in evidence. They were fed in the kitchen by the eldest, the same girl who served as her father's laboratory technician.

There was no medical talk until dinner was over. Instead, Gottlieb talked of poetry, with a curious mixture of intensity and wistfulness. This kept his guest a little on guard. Tucci knew more than most surviving Americans about the subject, he was sure, but far less than he had pretended to know.

Afterward however, Gottlieb got directly to the point.

"Any conclusions?" he said.

"A few," Tucci said, refusing to be rushed. "I'm still quite convinced that you'd be better off with us. I'm not terribly alarmed by your odd brand of medicine—and I don't know whether you were afraid I would be or whether you meant me to be. In the Vaults, we sometimes have to short-circuit the Oath too, for similar reasons."

"Yes. I don't doubt that you do. The Oath was full of traps even Back Then," Gottlieb said. "But I hoped you'd see that there's more to my refusal to join you than that. To begin with, Dr. Tucci, *I don't like medicine*; so I don't care whether I could do it better in the Vaults, or not."

"Oh? Well, then, you're quite right. I have somehow missed the point."

"It's this. You say you are so well organized that you can use specialists as specialists, rather than requiring them to do their own subsistence farming, policing, and so on. But—could you use me *as a poet?* No, of course not. I'd have to practice medicine in the Vaults.

"But to what end? I really hate medicine. No, I shouldn't say that, but I'm certainly no fonder of it than I am of farming. I picked it as a profession because I knew it would be in demand after the Day—and that's all.

"In your Vaults I'd be an apprentice, to a trade I don't much like. After all, you're sure to have real M.D.s there, beginning with yourself. All of a sudden, I'd be nobody. And more than that, I'd lose control over policy—over the kind of medicine *I* think suitable for the world we live in now—which is the only aspect of my practice that does interest me. I don't want to save diabetics at your behest. I want to let them die, at mine. Call it playing God if you like, but nothing else make sense to me now. Do you follow me?"

"I'm afraid I do. But go on anyhow."

"There isn't much farther to go. I'm satisfied where I am—that's the essence of it. My patients may not be as well served by me as they think they are, but all the same they swear by me and come back for more. And I'm the only one of my kind in these parts. I don't have to farm my place to the last square inch because most of my fees are in kind—which is lucky, because I have a brown thumb. Sigrid is a little better with plants, but not much. I don't have to fortify it, or keep a twenty-four-hour watch, because my patients wouldn't dare let anything happen to me. I don't need the medical facilities, the laboratories and equipment and so on that you're offering me, because I wouldn't know how to use them.

"So of course I'll keep on the way I've been going. What else could I do?"

"I'm sure," Tucci said quietly, "that you'd find plenty of time in the Vaults to practice poetry as well—and many people who value it. I doubt that you find either here."

"What of it? Poetry has been a private art for a century, anyhow," Gottlieb said bitterly. "Certainly it's no art for a captive audience, which wants to pat the poet on the head because it thinks he's really valuable for something quite different, like writing advertising copy or practicing medicine. I'm no longer interested in being tolerated. I wrote that off the day before the Day, and I'm not going back to it."

"But surely if—"

"Listen to me, Dr. Tucci," Gottlieb said. "If you are really running a sort of Institute for Advanced Study, and can promise me *all* my time to perfect myself as a poet, I'll go with you."

"Obviously, I can't make such a promise."

"Then I'll stay here. If I *have* to practice medicine, I may as well do so under conditions that I myself have laid down. Otherwise it would be too unrewarding for me to even tolerate. I wasn't really called to the vocation in the beginning, and there are times even now when it makes me quite sick. I can't help it; that's the way I am."

"So we have nothing more to say to each other, it seems," Tucci said. "I'm truly sorry that it worked out this way. I had no idea that the question would even arise. But, in a way, I'm on your side. And besides, were you to come with us, you'd leave your own people without a doctor—and though many of them would doubtless follow you into our community, there must be almost as many who wouldn't be able to do so."

"That's true," Gottlieb said, but he said it with a sort of convulsive shrug, as of a man who would dismiss the question and finds that it is not so easy as that. "Thank you anyhow for the offer. I must say that I feel a little like a boy getting a diploma; all this fakery, and now . . . well; and it's run so late that you will have to spend the night with us. I don't want the Vaults to lose you on my account."

"I'm grateful for all your thoughtfulness—yours, and your wife's as well."

"Come back when you can," Gottlieb said, "and we'll talk poetry some more."

"Thank you," Tucci said inadequately. And that was all. He was guided up to bed, in the wake of a hurricane lamp.

Or was it all? In the insect-strident night, so full of reminders of how many birds had died after the Day, and how loaded with insensible latent death was the black air he breathed as he lay tense in the big cool bed, Tucci was visited by a whole procession of phantoms. Mostly they were images of himself. Some of them were dismissible as nightmares, surfacing during brief shallow naps from which he was awakened by convulsive starts that made his whole body leap against the sheets, as though his muscles were crazily trying to relax in a single bound the moment sleep freed them from the tensions of his cortex. He was used to that. It had been going on for years, and he had come to take it as a sign that though he was not yet deeply asleep, he would be shortly. In the meantime, the nightmares were fantastic and entertaining, not at all like the smothering, dread-loaded replays of the Day which woke him groaning and drenched with sweat many mornings just after dawn.

This time the starts did not presage deep sleep; instead, they left him wide awake and considering images of himself more disquieting than any he could remember having seen in dreams. One of the shallow nightmares was a fantasy of what might be going on in the Gottlieb's bedroom—evidently Sigrid had marked Tucci's celibate psyche more profoundly than he had realized—but from this he awoke suddenly to find himself staring at the invisible ceiling and straining to visualize, not the passages of love between the poet and his wife about which he had been dreaming, but what they might be saying about Dr. Frank Tucci and his errand.

That errand hadn't looked hard to begin with. By all the rules of this kind of operation, Sigrid should now be bringing all possible feminine pressures to bear against Gottlieb's stand, and furthermore, she should be winning. After all, she would think first of her children, an argument of almost absolute potency compared with Gottlieb's abstract and selfish reasons for refusing to go to the Vaults. That was generally how it went.

But Gottlieb was not typical. He was, in fact, decidedly hard upon Tucci's image of himself. He was a quack, by his own admission, but he was not a charlatan—a distinction without a difference before the Day, but presently one of the highest importance, now that Tucci was forced to think about it. And in this cool darkness after the preliminary, complacent nightmares, Tucci was beginning to see himself with horror as a flipped coin. Not a quack, no. He was an authentic doctor with a pre-Day degree, nobody could take that away from him. But he *was* a charlatan, or at the very least a shill. When, after all, had Tucci last practiced medicine? Not since the Day. Ever since, he had been scooting about the empty menacingly quiet countryside on recruiting errands—practicing trickery, not medicine.

Outside, a cloud rolled off the moon, and somewhere nearby a chorus of spring peepers began to sing: *Here we are, here we are, here we are. . .* They had been tadpoles in the mud when the hot water had come down toward the rivers in the spring floods; they might be bearing heavy radiation loads, but that was not something they were equipped to think about. They were celebrating only the eternal *now* in which they had become inch-long frogs, each with a St. Andrew's cross upon its back... *Here we are, we made it...*

Here we are. We made it. Some are quacks, and nevertheless practice medicine as best they can. Some are flacks, for all their qualifications, and do nothing but shill . . . and burden the practitioners with hard decisions the Tuccis have become adroit at ducking. The Tuccis can always say that they were specialists before the Day—Tucci himself had been an electrophysiologisist and most of the machines that he needed to continue down the road were still unavailable in the Vaults—but every doctor begins as a general practitioner. Was there any excuse, now, for shilling instead of practicing?

The phantoms marched whitely across the ceiling. Their answer was *No*, and again. *No*.

In this world, in fact, Gottlieb was a doctor, and Dr. Frank Tucci was not. That was the last nightmare of all

He was ruminatively strapping his gear onto the baggage rack of the scooter, very early the next morning when he heard the screen door bang and looked up to see Gottlieb coming down the front walk toward him. There were, he saw for the first time, tall lilacs and lilies of the valley blooming all around the sides of the house. It was hard to believe that the world had ended, even here in Gottlieb's hollow. He straightened painfully in the bullet-proof suit and hoisted his bubble goggles.

"Nice of you," he said. "But you really needn't have seen me off. Keeping doctor's hours, you need all the sleep you can store up."

"Oh sure," Gottlieb said abstractedly. He leaned on the sagging gate. "But I wanted to talk to you. I had some trouble sleeping—I was thinking—I woke up this morning on the floor, and that hasn't happened to me since just before my final exams. If you've got a minute—"

"Of course. Certainly. But I'd like to get on the road before too long, to skip some of the heat of the day. This helmet absolutely fries my brains when the sun is high."

"Sure. I only wanted to say—I've changed my mind."

"Well. *That* was worth waiting for." Tucci took the helmet off and dropped the goggles carefully into it. "I hope you won't mind if I'm in a hurry, or rather, if we're in a hurry. We'll have trucks down here for you in about a week at the latest; it takes a while to get a convoy organized. We'll also send a bus, since I think you'll find that about half your patients will want to follow you, once you've explained the proposition to them."

"That'll cost a lot of gasoline," Gottlieb said. He seemed embarrassed and disturbed.

Tucci waited a moment, and then said, very gently: "If you don't mind, Mr. Gottlieb, would you tell me why you reversed yourself? I'd about given up."

"It's my own fault," Gottlieb broke out, in a transport of anger. "I must have given that speech about the Hippocratic Oath two thousand times in the last year or so. I never took the Oath, that's a fact, and I don't believe in it. But . . . you said I'd be able to treat more patients, and treat them better, if I went to work for you. That's been on my mind all night. And I can't get away from it. It began to look to me as though a man can't be just half a doctor, whether that's all he wants or not. And I did go into this doctor business by my own choice."

He scuffed at the foot of the gate with one broganed toe, as though he might kick it if no one were watching him.

"So there I am. I have to go with you—and never mind that I'm giving up everything I've won so far—and a lot more that I hoped for. I may stop hating you five or ten years from now. But I could have spared myself, if I hadn't been so superior about Hippocrates all this time and just minded my own business."

"The oath that you don't take," Tucci agreed, resuming his goggles and helmet, "is often more binding than the one you do."

He stamped on the kick starter. Miraculously, the battered old Lambretta spat and began to snarl on the first try. Gottlieb stepped back, with a gesture of farewell. At the last moment, however, something else seemed to occur to him.

"Dr. Tucci!" he shouted above the noise of the one-lung engine.

"Yes? Better make it loud, Mr. Gottlieb—I'm almost deaf aboard this thing."

"It's not 'the forelock of time,' you know," Gottlieb said. He did not seem to be yelling, but Tucci could hear him quite plainly. "The word in the poem is 'forepaws.'"

Tucci nodded gravely, glad that the helmet and goggles could be counted on to mask his expression, and put the scooter in gear. As he tooled off up the hill, his methodical mind began to chew slowly, gently, inexorably upon the question of who had been manipulating whom.

He knew that it would be a good many years before he had an answer.

Beep

Josef Faber lowered his newspaper slightly. Finding the girl on the park bench looking his way, he smiled the agonizingly embarrassed smile of the thoroughly married nobody caught bird-watching, and ducked back into the paper again.

He was reasonably certain that he looked the part of a middle-aged, steadily employed, harmless citizen enjoying a Sunday break in the bookkeeping and family routines. He was also quite certain, despite his official instructions, that it wouldn't make the slightest bit of difference if he didn't. These boy-meets-girl assignments always came off. Jo had never tackled a single one that had required him.

As a matter of fact, the newspaper, which he was supposed to be using only as a blind, interested him a good deal more than his job did. He had only barely begun to suspect the obvious ten years ago when the Service had snapped him up; now, after a decade as an agent, he was still fascinated to see how smoothly the really important situations came off. The *dangerous* situations—not boy-meets-girl.

This affair of the Black Horse Nebula, for instance. Some days ago the papers and the commentators had begun to mention reports of disturbances in that area, and Jo's practiced eye had picked up the mention. Something big was cooking.

Today it had boiled over—the Black Horse Nebula had suddenly spewed ships by the hundreds, a massed armada that must have taken more than a century of effort on the part of a whole star cluster, a production drive conducted in the strictest and most fanatical kind of secrecy....

And, of course, the Service had been on the spot in plenty of time. With three times as many ships, disposed with mathematical precision so as to enfilade the entire armada the moment it broke from the nebula. The battle had been a massacre, the attack smashed before the average citizen could even begin to figure out what it had been aimed at—and good had triumphed over evil once more.

Of course.

Furtive scuffings on the gravel drew his attention briefly. He looked at his watch, which said 14:58:03. That was the time, according to his instructions, when boy had to meet girl.

He had been given the strictest kind of orders to let nothing interfere with this meeting—the orders always issued on boy-meets-girl assignments. But, as usual, he had nothing to do but observe. The meeting was coming off on the dot, without any prodding from Jo. They always did.

Of course.

With a sigh, he folded his newspaper, smiling again at the couple—yes, it was the right man, too—and moved away, as if reluctantly. He wondered what would happen were he to pull away the false mustache, pitch the newspaper on the grass, and bound away with a joyous whoop. He suspected that the course of history would not be deflected by even a second of arc, but he was not minded to try the experiment.

The park was pleasant. The twin suns warmed the path and the greenery without any of the blasting heat which they would bring to bear later in the summer. Randolph was altogether the most comfortable planet he had visited in years. A little backward, perhaps, but restful, too.

It was also slightly over a hundred light-years away from Earth. It would be interesting to know how Service headquarters on Earth could have known in advance that boy would meet girl at a certain spot on Randolph, precisely at 14:58:03.

Or how Service headquarters could have ambushed with micrometric precision a major interstellar fleet, with no more preparation than a few days' buildup in the newspapers and video could evidence.

The press was free, on Randolph as everywhere. It reported the news it got. Any emergency concentration of Service ships in the Black Horse area, or anywhere else, would have been noticed and reported on. The Service did not forbid such reports for "security" reasons or for any other reasons. Yet there had been nothing to report but that (a) an armada of staggering size had erupted with no real warning from the Black Horse Nebula, and that (b) the Service had been ready.

By now, it was a commonplace that the Service was always ready. It had not had a defect or a failure in well over two centuries. It had not even had a fiasco, the alarming-sounding technical word by which it referred to the possibility that a boy-meets-girl assignment might not come off.

Jo hailed a hopper. Once inside he stripped himself of the mustache, the bald spot, the forehead creases—all the makeup which had given him his mask of friendly innocuousness.

The hoppy watched the whole process in the rear-view mirror. Jo glanced up and met his eyes.

"Pardon me, mister, but I figured you didn't care if I saw you. You must be a Service man."

"That's right. Take me to Service HQ, will you?"

"Sure enough." The hoppy gunned his machine. It rose smoothly to the express level. "First time I ever got close to a Service man. Didn't hardly believe it at first when I saw you taking your face off. You sure looked different."

"Have to, sometimes," Jo said, preoccupied.

"I'll bet. No wonder you know all about everything before it breaks. You must have a thousand faces each, your own mother wouldn't know you, eh? Don't you care if I know about your snooping around in disguise?"

Jo grinned. The grin created a tiny pulling sensation across one curve of his cheek, just next to his nose. He stripped away the overlooked bit of tissue and examined it critically.

"Of course not. Disguise is an elementary part of Service work. Anyone could guess that. We don't use it often, as a matter of fact—only on very simple assignments."

"Oh." The hoppy sounded slightly disappointed, as melodrama faded. He drove silently for about a minute. Then, speculatively: "Sometimes I think the Service must have time-travel, the things they pull. . . . Well, here you are. Good luck, mister."

"Thanks."

Jo went directly to Krasna's office. Krasna was a Randolpher. Earth-trained, and answerable to the Earth office, but otherwise pretty much on his own. His heavy, muscular face wore the same expression of serene confidence that was characteristic of Service officials everywhere—even some that, technically speaking, had no faces to wear it.

"Boy meets girl," Jo said briefly. "On the nose and on the spot."

"Good work, Jo. Cigarette?" Krasna pushed the box across his desk.

"Nope, not now. Like to talk to you, if you've got time."

Krasna pushed a button, and a toadstoollike chair rose out of the floor behind Jo. "What's on your mind?"

"Well," Jo said carefully. "I'm wondering why you patted me on the back just now for not doing a job."

"You did a job."

"I did not," Jo said flatly. "Boy would have met girl, whether I'd been here on Randolph or back on Earth. The course of true love always runs smooth. It has in all my boy-meets-girl cases, and it has in the boy-meets-girl cases of every other agent with whom I've compared notes."

"Well, good," Krasna said, smiling. "That's the way we like to have it run. And that's the way we expect it to run. But, Jo, we like to have somebody on the spot, somebody with a reputation for resourcefulness, just in case there's a snag. There almost never is, as you've observed. But—if there were?"

Jo snorted. "If what you're trying to do is to establish preconditions for the future, any interference by a Service agent would throw the eventual result farther *off* the track. I know that much about probability."

"And what makes you think that we're trying to set up the future?"

"It's obvious even to the hoppies on your own planet; the one that brought me here told me he thought the Service had time-travel. It's especially obvious to all the individuals and governments and entire populations that the Service has bailed out of serious messes for centuries, with never a single failure." Jo shrugged. "A man can be asked to safeguard only a small number of boy-meets-girl cases before he realizes, as an agent, that what the Service is safeguarding is the future children of those meetings. Ergo—the Service *knows* what those children are to be like, and has reason to want their future existence guaranteed. What other conclusion is possible?"

Krasna took out a cigarette and lit it deliberately; it was obvious that he was using the maneuver to cloak his response.

"None," he admitted at last. "We have some foreknowledge, of course. We couldn't have made our reputation with espionage alone. But we have obvious other advantages: genetics, for instance, and operations research, the theory of games, the Dirac transmitter—it's quite an arsenal, and of course there's a good deal of prediction involved in all those things."

"I see that," Jo said. He shifted in his chair, formulating all he wanted to say. He changed his mind about the cigarette and helped himself to one. "But these things don't add up to infallibility—and that's a qualitative difference, Kras. Take this affair of the Black Horse armada. The moment the armada appeared, we'll assume, Earth heard about it by Dirac, and started to assemble a counterarmada. But it takes *finite time* to bring together a concentration of ships and men, even if your message system is instantaneous.

"The Service's counterarmada was *already on hand*. It had been building there for so long and with so little fuss that nobody even noticed it concentrating until a day or so before the battle. Then planets in the area began to sit up and take notice, and be uneasy about what was going to break. But not very uneasy; the Service always wins—that's been a statistical fact for centuries. *Centuries*, Kras. Good Lord, it takes almost as long as that, in straight preparation, to pull some of the tricks we've pulled! The Dirac gives us an advantage of ten to twenty-five years in really extreme cases out on the rim of the Galaxy, but no more than that."

He realized that he had been fuming away on the cigarette until the roof of his mouth was scorched, and snubbed it out angrily. "That's a very different thing," he said, "than knowing in a general way how an enemy is likely to behave, or what kind of children the Mendelian laws say a given couple should have. It means that we've some way of reading the future in minute detail. That's in flat contradiction to everything I've been taught about probability, but I have to believe what I see."

Krasna laughed. "That's a very able presentation," he said. He seemed genuinely pleased. "I think you'll remember that you were first impressed into the Service when you began to wonder why the news was always good. Fewer and fewer people wonder about that nowadays; it's become a part of their expected environment." He stood up and ran a hand through his hair. "Now you've carried yourself through the next stage. Congratulations, Jo. You've just been promoted!"

"I have?" Jo said incredulously. "I came in here with the notion that I might get myself fired."

"No. Come around to this side of the desk, Jo, and I'll play you a little history." Krasna unfolded the desktop to expose a small visor screen. Obediently Jo rose and went around the desk to where he could see the blank surface. "I had a standard indoctrination tape sent up to me a week ago, in the expectation that you'd be ready to see it. Watch."

Krasna touched the board. A small dot of light appeared in the center of the screen and went out again. At the same time, there was a small *beep* of sound. Then the tape began to unroll and a picture clarified on the screen.

"As you suspected," Krasna said conversationally, "the Service is infallible. How it got that way is a story that started several centuries back."

II

Dana Lje—her father had been a Hollander, her mother born in the Celebes—sat down in the chair which Captain Robin Weinbaum had indicated, crossed her legs, and waited, her blue-black hair shining under the lights.

Weinbaum eyed her quizzically. The conqueror Resident who had given the girl her entirely European name had been paid in kind, for his daughter's beauty had nothing fair and Dutch about it. To the eye of the beholder, Dana Lje seemed a particularly delicate virgin of Bali, despite her Western name, clothing and assurance. The combination had already proven piquant for the millions who watched her television column, and Weinbaum found it no less charming at first hand.

"As one of your most recent victims," he said, "I'm not sure that I'm honored, Miss Lje. A few of my wounds are still bleeding. But I am a good deal puzzled as to why you're visiting me now. Aren't you afraid that I'll bite back?"

"I had no intention of attacking you personally, and I don't think I did," the video columnist said seriously. "It was just pretty plain that our intelligence had slipped badly in the Erskine affair. It was my job to say so. Obviously you were going to get hurt, since you're head of the bureau—but there was no malice in it."

"Cold comfort," Weinbaum said dryly. "But thank you, nevertheless."

The Eurasian girl shrugged. "That isn't what I came here about, anyway. Tell me, Captain Weinbaum—have you ever heard of an outfit calling itself Interstellar Information?"

Weinbaum shook his head. "Sounds like a skip-tracing firm. Not an easy business, these days."

"That's just what I thought when I first saw their letterhead," Dana said. "But the letter under it wasn't one that a private-eye outfit would write. Let me read part of it to you."

Her slim fingers burrowed in her inside jacket pocket and emerged again with a single sheet of paper. It was plain typewriter bond, Weinbaum noted automatically: she had brought only a copy with her, and had left the original of the letter at home. The copy, then, would be incomplete—probably seriously.

"It goes like this: 'Dear Miss Lje: As a syndicated video commentator with a wide audience and heavy responsibilities, you need the best sources of information available. We would like you to test our service, free of charge, in the hope of proving to you that it is superior to any other source of news on Earth. Therefore, we offer below several predictions concerning events to come in the Hercules and the so-called "Three Ghosts" areas. If these predictions are fulfilled 100 percent—no less—we ask that you take us on as your correspondents for those areas, at rates to be agreed upon later. If the predictions are wrong in *any* respect, you need not consider us further.'"

"H'm," Weinbaum said slowly. "They're confident cusses—and that's an odd juxtaposition. The Three Ghosts make up only a little solar system, while the Hercules area could include the entire star cluster—or maybe even the whole constellation, which is a hell of a lot of sky. This outfit seems to be trying to tell you that it has thousands of field correspondents of its own, maybe as many as the government itself. If so, I'll guarantee that they're bragging."

"That may well be so. But before you make up your mind, let me read you one of the two predictions." The letter rustled in Dana Lje's hand. "'At 03:16:10, on Year Day, 2090, the Hess-type interstellar liner *Brindisi* will be attacked in the neighborhood of the Three Ghosts system by four—'"

Weinbaum sat bolt upright in his swivel chair. "Let me see that letter!" he said, his voice harsh with repressed alarm.

"In a moment," the girl said, adjusting her skirt composedly. "Evidently I was right in riding my hunch. Let me go on reading: '—by four heavily armed vessels flying the lights of the navy of Hammersmith II. The position of the liner at that time will be at coded co-ordinates 88-A-theta-88-aleph-D and-per-se-and. It will—'"

"Miss Lje," Weinbaum said. "I'm sorry to interrupt you again, but what you've said already would justify me jailing you at once, no matter how loudly your sponsor might scream. I don't know about this Interstellar Information outfit, or whether or not you did receive any such letter as the one you pretend to be quoting. But I can tell you that you've shown yourself to be in possession of information that only yours truly and four other men are supposed to know. It's already too late to tell you that everything you say may be held against you; all I can say now is, it's high time you clammed up!"

"I thought so," she said, apparently not disturbed in the least. "Then that liner *is* scheduled to hit those co-ordinates, and the coded time co-ordinate corresponds with the predicted Universal Time. Is it also true that the *Brindisi* will be carrying a top-secret communication device?"

"Are you deliberately trying to make me imprison you?" Weinbaum said, gritting his teeth. "Or is this just a stunt, designed to show me that my own bureau is full of leaks?"

"It could turn into that," Dana admitted. "But it hasn't, yet. Robin, I've been as honest with you as I'm able to be. You've had nothing but square deals from me up to now. I wouldn't yellow-screen you, and you know it. If this unknown outfit has this information, it might easily have gotten it from where it hints that it got it: from the field."

"Impossible."

"Why?"

"Because the information in question hasn't even reached my *own* agents in the field yet—it couldn't possibly have leaked as far as Hammersmith II or anywhere else, let alone to the Three Ghosts system! Letters have to be carried on ships, you know that. If I were to send orders by ultrawave to my Three Ghosts agent, he'd have to wait three hundred and twenty-four years to get them. By ship, he can get them in a little over two months. These particular orders have only been under way to him five days. Even if somebody has read them on board the ship that's carrying them, they couldn't possibly be sent on to the Three Ghosts any faster than they're traveling now."

Dana nodded her dark head. "All right. Then what are we left with but a leak in your headquarters here?"

"What, indeed," Weinbaum said grimly. "You'd better tell me who signed this letter of yours."

"The signature is J. Shelby Stevens."

Weinbaum switched on the intercom. "Margaret, look in the business register for an outfit called Interstellar Information and find out who owns it."

Dana Lje said, "Aren't you interested in the rest of the prediction?"

"You bet I am. Does it tell you the name of this communications device?"

"Yes," Dana said.

"What is it?"

"The Dirac communicator."

Weinbaum groaned and turned on the intercom again, "Margaret, send in Dr. Wald. Tell him to drop everything and gallop. Any luck with the other thing?"

"Yes, sir," the intercom said. "It's a one-man outfit, wholly owned by a J. Shelby Stevens, in Rico City. It was first registered this year."

"Arrest him, on suspicion of espionage."

The door swung open and Dr. Wald came in, all six and a half feet of him. He was extremely blond, and looked awkward, gentle, and not very intelligent.

"Thor, this young lady is our press nemesis, Dana Lje. Dana, Dr. Wald is the inventor of the Dirac communicator, about which you have so damnably much information."

"It's out *already?*" Dr. Wald said, scanning the girl with grave deliberation.

"It is, and lots more—*lots* more. Dana, you're a good girl at heart, and for some reason I trust you, stupid though it is to trust anybody in this job. I should detain you until Year Day, videocasts or no videocasts. Instead, I'm just going to ask you to sit on what you've got, and I'm going to explain why."

"Shoot."

"I've already mentioned how slow communication is between star and star. We have to carry all our letters on ships, just as we did locally before the invention of the telegraph. The overdrive lets us beat the speed of light, but not by much of a margin over really long distances. Do you understand that?"

"Certainly," Dana said. She appeared a bit nettled, and Weinbaum decided to give her the full dose at a more rapid pace. After all, she could be assumed to be better informed than the average layman.

"What we've needed for a long time, then," he said, "is some virtually instantaneous method of getting a message from somewhere to anywhere. Any time lag, no matter how small it seems at first, has a way of becoming major as longer and longer distances are involved. Sooner or later we must have this instantaneous method, or we won't be able to get messages from one system to another fast enough to hold our jurisdiction over outlying regions of space."

"Wait a minute," Dana said. "I'd always understood that ultrawave is faster than light."

"Effectively it is; physically it isn't. You don't understand that?"

She shook her dark head.

"In a nutshell," Weinbaum said, "ultrawave is radiation, and all radiation in free space is limited to the speed of light. The way we hype up ultrawave is to use an old application of wave-guide theory, whereby the real transmission of energy is at light speed, but an imaginary thing called 'phase velocity' is going faster. But the gain in speed of transmission isn't large—by ultrawave, for instance, we get a message to Alpha Centauri in one year instead of nearly four. Over long distances, that's not nearly enough extra speed."

"Can't it be speeded further?" she said, frowning.

"No. Think of the ultrawave beam between here and Centaurus III as a caterpillar. The caterpillar himself is moving quite slowly, just at the speed of light. But the pulses which pass along his body are going forward faster than he is—and if you've ever watched a caterpillar, you'll know that that's true. But there's a physical limit to the number of pulses you can travel along that caterpillar, and we've already reached that limit. We've taken phase velocity as far as it will go.

"That's why we need something faster. For a long time our relativity theories discouraged hope of anything faster—even the high-phase velocity of a guided wave didn't contradict those theories; it just found a limited, mathematically imaginary loophole in them. But when Thor here began looking into the question of the velocity of propagation of a Dirac pulse, he found the answer. The communicator he developed does seem to act over long distances, *any* distance, instantaneously—and it may wind up knocking relativity into a cocked hat."

The girl's face was a study in stunned realization. "I'm not sure I've taken in all the technical angles," she said. "But if I'd had any notion of the political dynamite in this thing—"

"—you'd have kept out of my office," Weinbaum said grimly. "A good thing you didn't. The *Brindisi* is carrying a model of the Dirac communicator out to the periphery for a final test; the ship is supposed to get in touch with me from out there at a given Earth time, which we've calculated very elaborately to account for the residual Lorentz and Milne transformations involved in overdrive flight, and for a lot of other time phenomena that wouldn't mean anything at all to you.

"If that signal arrives here at the given Earth time, then—aside from the havoc it will create among the theoretical physicists whom we decide to let in on it—we will really have our instant communicator, and can include all of occupied space in the same time zone. And we'll have a terrific advantage over any lawbreaker who has to resort to ultrawave locally and to letters carried by ships over the long haul."

"Not," Dr. Wald said sourly, "if it's already leaked out."

"It remains to be seen how much of it has leaked," Weinbaum said. "The principle is rather esoteric, Thor, and the name of the thing alone wouldn't mean much even to a trained scientist. I gather that Dana's mysterious informant didn't go into technical details . . . or did he?"

"No," Dana said.

"Tell the truth, Dana. I know that you're suppressing some of that letter."

The girl started slightly. "All right—yes, I am. But nothing technical. There's another part of the prediction that lists the number and class of ships you will send to protect the *Brindisi*—the prediction says they'll be sufficient, by the way—and I'm keeping that to myself, to see whether or not it comes true along with the rest. If it does, I think I've hired myself a correspondent."

"If it does," Weinbaum said, "you've hired yourself a jailbird. Let's see how much mind reading J. Whatsit Stevens can do from the subcellar of Fort Yaphank."

III

Weinbaum let himself into Stevens's cell, locking the door behind him and passing the keys out to the guard. He sat down heavily on the nearest stool.

Stevens smiled the weak benevolent smile of the very old, and laid his book aside on the bunk. The book, Weinbaum knew—since his office had cleared it—was only a volume of pleasant, harmless lyrics by a New Dynasty poet named Nims.

"Were our predictions correct, Captain?" Stevens said. His voice was high and musical, rather like that of a boy soprano.

Weinbaum nodded. "You still won't tell us how you did it?"

"But I already have," Stevens protested. "Our intelligence network is the best in the Universe, Captain. It is superior even to your own excellent organization, as events have shown."

"Its results are superior, that I'll grant," Weinbaum said glumly. "If Dana Lje had thrown your letter down her disposal chute, we would have lost the *Brindisi* and our Dirac transmitter both. Incidentally, did your original letter predict accurately the number of ships we would send?"

Stevens nodded pleasantly, his neatly trimmed white beard thrusting forward slightly as he smiled.

"I was afraid so," Weinbaum leaned forward. "Do you have the Dirac transmitter, Stevens?"

"Of course, Captain. How else could my correspondents report to me with the efficiency you have observed?"

"Then why don't our receivers pick up the broadcasts of your agents? Dr. Wald says it's inherent in the principle that Dirac 'casts are picked up by *all* instruments tuned to receive them, bar none. And at this stage of the game there are so few such broadcasts being made that we'd be almost certain to detect any that weren't coming from our own operatives."

"I decline to answer that question, if you'll excuse the impoliteness," Stevens said, his voice quavering slightly. "I am an old man, Captain, and this intelligence agency is my sole source of income. If I told you how we operated, we would no longer have any advantage over your own service, except for the limited freedom from secrecy which we have. I have been assured by competent lawyers that I have every right to operate a private investigation bureau, properly licensed, upon any scale that I may choose; and that I have the right to keep my methods secret, as the so-called 'intellectual assets' of my firm. If you wish to use our services, well and good. We will provide them, with absolute guarantees on all information we furnish you, for an appropriate fee. But our methods are our own property."

Robin Weinbaum smiled twistedly. "I'm not a naive man, Mr. Stevens," he said. "My service is hard on naiveté. You know as well as I do that the government can't allow you to operate on a free-lance basis, supplying top-secret information to anyone who can pay the price, or even free of charge to video columnists on a 'test' basis, even though you arrive at every jot of that information independently of espionage—which I still haven't entirely ruled out, by the way. If you can duplicate this *Brindisi* performance at will, we will have to have your services exclusively. In short, you become a hired civilian arm of my own bureau."

"Quite," Stevens said, returning the smile in a fatherly way. "We anticipated that, of course. However, we have contracts with other governments to consider; Erskine, in particular. If we are to work exclusively for Earth, necessarily our price will include compensation for renouncing our other accounts."

"Why should it? Patriotic public servants work for their government at a loss, if they can't work for it any other way."

"I am quite aware of that. I am quite prepared to renounce my other interests. But I do require to be paid."

"How much?" Weinbaum said, suddenly aware that his fists were clenched so tightly that they hurt.

Stevens appeared to consider, nodding his flowery white poll in senile deliberation. "My associates would have to be consulted. Tentatively, however, a sum equal to the present appropriation of your bureau would do, pending further negotiations."

Weinbaum shot to his feet, eyes wide. "You old buccaneer! You know damned well that I can't spend my entire appropriation on a single civilian service! Did it ever occur to you that most of the civilian outfits working for us are on cost-plus contracts, and that our civilian executives are being paid just a credit a year, by their own choice? You're demanding nearly two thousand credits an hour from your own government, and claiming the legal protection that the government affords you at the same time, in order to let those fanatics on Erskine run up a higher bid!"

"The price is not unreasonable," Stevens said. "The service is worth the price."

"That's where you're wrong! We have the discoverer of the machine working for us. For less than half the sum you're asking, we can find the application of the device that you're trading on—of that you can be damned sure."

"A dangerous gamble, Captain."

"Perhaps. We'll soon see!" Weinbaum glared at the placid face. "I'm forced to tell you that you're a free man, Mr. Stevens. We've been unable to show that you came by your information by any illegal method. You had classified facts in your possession, but no classified documents, and it's your privilege as a citizen to make guesses, no matter how educated.

"But we'll catch up with you sooner or later. Had you been reasonable, you might have found yourself in a very good position with us, your income as assured as any political income can be, and your person respected to the hilt. Now, however, you're subject to censorship—you have no idea how humiliating that can be, but I'm going to see to it that you find out. There'll be no more newsbeats for Dana

Lje, or for anyone else. I want to see every word of copy that you file with any client outside the bureau. Every word that is of use to me will be used, and you'll be paid the statutory one cent a word for it—the same rate that the FBI pays for anonymous gossip. Everything I don't find useful will be killed without clearance. Eventually we'll have the modification of the Dirac that you're using, and when that happens, you'll be so flat broke that a pancake with a harelip could spit right over you."

Weinbaum paused for a moment, astonished at his own fury.

Stevens's clarinetlike voice began to sound in the windowless cavity. "Captain, I have no doubt that you can do this to me, at least incompletely. But it will prove fruitless. I will give you a prediction, at no charge. It is guaranteed, as are all our predictions. It is this: *You will never find that modification.* Eventually, I will give it to you, on my own terms, but you will never find it for yourself, nor will you force it out of me. In the meantime, not a word of copy will be filed with you; for, despite the fact that you are an arm of the government, I can well afford to wait you out."

"Bluster," Weinbaum said.

"Fact. Yours is the bluster—loud talk based on nothing more than a hope. I, however, *know* whereof I speak. . . . But let us conclude this discussion. It serves no purpose; you will need to see my points made the hard way. Thank you for giving me my freedom. We will talk again under different circumstances on—let me see; ah, yes, on June 9 of the year 2091. That year is, I believe, almost upon us."

Stevens picked up his book again, nodding at Weinbaum, his expression harmless and kindly, his hands showing the marked tremor of *paralysis agitans*. Weinbaum moved helplessly to the door and flagged the turnkey. As the bars closed behind him, Stevens's voice called out: "Oh, yes; and a Happy New Year, Captain."

Weinbaum blasted his way back into his own office, at least twice as mad as the proverbial nest of hornets, and at the same time rather dismally aware of his own probable future. If Stevens's second prediction turned out to be as phenomenally accurate as his first had been, Capt. Robin Weinbaum would soon be peddling a natty set of secondhand uniforms.

He glared down at Margaret Soames, his receptionist. She glared right back; she had known him too long to be intimidated.

"Anything?" he said.

"Dr. Wald's waiting for you in your office. There are some field reports, and a couple of Diracs on your private tape. Any luck with the old codger?"

"That," he said crushingly, "is Top Secret."

"Poof. That means that nobody still knows the answer but J. Shelby Stevens."

He collapsed suddenly. "You're so right. That's just what it does mean. But we'll bust him wide open sooner or later. We've *got* to."

"You'll do it," Margaret said. "Anything else for me?"

"No. Tip off the clerical staff that there's a half holiday today, then go take in a stereo or a steak or something yourself. Dr. Wald and I have a few private wires to pull . . . and unless I'm sadly mistaken, a private bottle of aquavit to empty."

"Right," the receptionist said. "Tie one on for me, Chief. I understand that beer is the best chaser for aquavit—I'll have some sent up."

"If you should return after I am suitably squiffed," Weinbaum said, feeling a little better already, "I will kiss you for your thoughtfulness. *That* should keep you at your stereo at least twice through the third feature."

As he went on through the door of his own office, she said demurely behind him, "It certainly should."

As soon as the door closed, however, his mood became abruptly almost as black as before. Despite his comparative youth—he was now only fifty-five—he had been in the service a long time, and he needed no one to tell him the possible consequences which might flow from possession by a private citizen of the Dirac communicator. If there was ever to be a Federation of Man in the Galaxy, it was within the power of J. Shelby Stevens to ruin it before it had fairly gotten started. And there seemed to be nothing at all that could be done about it.

"Hello, Thor," he said glumly. "Pass the bottle."

"Hello, Robin. I gather things went badly. Tell me about it."

Briefly, Weinbaum told him. "And the worst of it," he finished, "is that Stevens himself predicts that we won't find the application of the Dirac that he's using, and that eventually we'll have to buy it at his price. Somehow I believe him—but I can't see how it's possible. If I were to tell Congress that I was going to spend my entire appropriation for a single civilian service, I'd be out on my ear within the next three sessions."

"Perhaps that isn't his real price," the scientist suggested. "If he wants to barter, he'd naturally begin with a demand miles above what he actually wants."

"Sure, sure . . . but frankly, Thor, I'd hate to give the old reprobate even a single credit if I could get out of it." Weinbaum sighed. "Well, let's see what's come in from the field."

Thor Wald moved silently away from Weinbaum's desk while the officer unfolded it and set up the Dirac screen. Stacked neatly next to the ultraphone—a device Weinbaum had been thinking of, only a few days ago, as permanently outmoded—were the tapes Margaret had mentioned. He fed the first one into the Dirac and turned the main toggle to the position labeled START.

Immediately the whole screen went pure white and the audio speakers emitted an almost instantly end-stopped blare of sound—a *beep* which, as Weinbaum already knew, made up a continuous spectrum from about 30 cycles per second to well above 18,000 cps. Then both the light and the noise were gone as if they had never been, and were replaced by the familiar face and voice of Weinbaum's local ops chief in Rico City.

"There's nothing unusual in the way of transmitters in Stevens's offices here," the operative said without preamble. "And there isn't any local Interstellar Information staff, except for one stenographer, and she's as dumb as they come. About all we could get from her is that Stevens is 'such a sweet old man.' No possibility that she's faking it; she's genuinely stupid, the kind that thinks Betelgeuse is something Indians use to darken their skins. We looked for some sort of list or code table that would give us a line on Stevens's field staff, but that was another dead end. Now we're maintaining a twenty-four-hour Dinwiddie watch on the place from a joint across the street. Orders?"

Weinbaum dictated to the blank stretch of tape which followed: "Margaret, next time you send any Dirac tapes in here, cut that damnable *beep* off them first. Tell the boys in Rico City that Stevens has been released, and that I'm proceeding for an Order In Security to tap his ultraphone and his local lines—this is one case where I'm sure we can persuade the court that tapping's necessary. Also—and be damned sure you code this—tell them to proceed with the tap immediately and to maintain it regardless of whether or not the court O.K.s it. I'll thumbprint a Full Responsibility Confession for them. We can't afford to play pat-a-cake with Stevens—the potential is just too damned big. And oh, yes, Margaret, send the message by carrier, and send out general orders to everybody concerned not to use the Dirac again except when distance and time rule every other medium out. Stevens has already admitted that he can receive Dirac 'casts."

He put down the mike and stared morosely for a moment at the beautiful Eridanean scrollwood of his desktop. Wald coughed inquiringly and retrieved the aquavit.

"Excuse me, Robin," he said, "but I should think that would work both ways."

"So should I. And yet the fact is that we've never picked up so much as a whisper from either Stevens or his agents. I can't think of any way that could be pulled, but evidently it can."

"Well, let's rethink the problem, and see what we get," Wald said. "I didn't want to say so in front of the young lady, for obvious reasons—I mean Miss Lje, of course, not Margaret—but the truth is that the Dirac is essentially a simple mechanism in principle. I seriously doubt that there's any way to transmit a message from it which can't be detected—and an examination of the theory with that proviso in mind might give us something new."

"What proviso?" Weinbaum said. Thor Wald left him behind rather often these days.

"Why, that a Dirac transmission doesn't *necessarily* go to all communicators capable of receiving it. If that's true, then the reasons why it is true should emerge from the theory."

"I see. O.K., proceed on that line. I've been looking at Stevens's dossier while you were talking, and it's an absolute desert. Prior to the opening of the office in Rico City, there's no dope whatever on J. Shelby Stevens. The man as good as rubbed my nose in the fact that he's using a pseud when I first talked to him. I asked him what the 'J' in his name stood for, and he said, 'Oh, let's make it Jerome.' But who the man behind the pseud *is* . . ."

"Is it possible that he's using his own initials?"

"No," Weinbaum said. "Only the dumbest ever do that, or transpose syllables, or retain any connection at all with their real names. Those are the people who are in serious emotional trouble, people who drive themselves into anonymity, but leave clues strewn all around the landscape—those clues are really a cry for help, for discovery. Of course we're working on that angle—we can't neglect anything—but J. Shelby Stevens isn't that kind of case, I'm sure." Weinbaum stood up abruptly. "O.K., Thor—what's first on your technical program?"

"Well . . . I suppose we'll have to start with checking the frequencies we use. We're going on Dirac's assumption—and it works very well, and always has—that a positron in motion through a crystal lattice is accompanied by de Broglie waves which are transforms of the waves of an electron in motion somewhere else in the Universe. Thus if we control the frequency and path of the positron, we control the placement of the electron—we cause it to appear, so to speak, in the circuits of a communicator somewhere else. After that, reception is just a matter of amplifying the bursts and reading the signal."

Wald scowled and shook his blond head. "If Stevens is getting out messages which we don't pick up, my first assumption would be that he's worked out a fine-tuning circuit that's more delicate than ours, and is more or less sneaking his messages under ours. The only way that could be done, as far as I can see at the moment, is by something really fantastic in the way of exact frequency control of his positron gun. If so, the logical step for us is to go back to the beginning of our tests and rerun our diffractions to see if we can refine our measurements of positron frequencies."

The scientist looked so inexpressibly gloomy as he offered this conclusion that a pall of hopelessness settled over Weinbaum in sheer sympathy. "You don't look as if you expected that to uncover anything new."

"I don't. You see, Robin, things are different in physics now than they used to be in the twentieth century. In those days, it was always presupposed that physics was limitless—the classic statement was made by Weyl, who said that 'It is the nature of a real thing to be inexhaustible in content.' We know now that that's not so, except in a remote, associational sort of way. Nowadays, physics is a defined and self-limited science; its scope is still prodigious, but we can no longer think of it as endless.

"This is better established in particle physics than in any other branch of the science. Half of the trouble physicists of the last century had with Euclidean geometry—and hence the reason why they evolved so many recomplicated theories of relativity—is that it's a geometry of lines, and thus can be subdivided infinitely. When Cantor proved that there really is an infinity, at least mathematically speaking, that seemed to clinch the case for the possibility of a really infinite physical universe, too."

Wald's eyes grew vague, and he paused to gulp down a slug of the licorice-flavored aquavit which would have made Weinbaum's every hair stand on end.

"I remember," Wald said, "the man who taught me theory of sets at Princeton, many years ago. He used to say: 'Cantor teaches us that there are many kinds of infinities. *There* was a crazy old man!'"

Weinbaum rescued the bottle hastily. "So go on, Thor."

"Oh." Wald blinked. "Yes. Well, what we know now is that the geometry which applies to ultimate particles, like the positron, isn't Euclidean at all. It's Pythagorean—a geometry of points, not lines. Once you've measured one of those points, and it doesn't matter what kind of quantity you're measuring, you're down as far as you can go. At that point, the Universe becomes discontinuous, and no further refinement is possible.

"And I'd say that our positron-frequency measurements have already gotten that far down. There isn't another element in the Universe denser than plutonium, yet we get the same frequency values by diffraction through plutonium crystals that we get through osmium crystals—there's not the slightest difference. If J. Shelby Stevens is operating in terms of fractions of those values, then he's doing what an organist would call 'playing in the cracks'—which is certainly something you can *think* about doing, but something that's in actuality impossible to do. Hoop."

"Hoop?" Weinbaum said.

"Sorry. A hiccup only."

"Oh. Well, maybe Stevens has rebuilt the organ?"

"If he has rebuilt the metrical frame of the Universe to accommodate a private skip-tracing firm," Wald said firmly, "I for one see no reason why we can't countercheck him—*hoop*—by declaring the whole cosmos null and void."

"All right, all right," Weinbaum said, grinning. "I didn't mean to push your analogy right over the edge—I was just asking. But let's get to work on it anyhow. We can't just sit here and let Stevens get away with it. If this frequency angle turns out to be as hopeless as it seems, we'll try something else."

Wald eyed the aquavit bottle owlishly. "It's a very pretty problem," he said. "Have I ever sung you the song we have in Sweden called 'Nat-og-Dag?'"

"*Hoop,*" Weinbaum said, to his own surprise, in a high falsetto. "Excuse me. No. Let's hear it."

The computer occupied an entire floor of the Security building, its seemingly identical banks laid out side by side on the floor along an advanced pathological state of Peano's "space-filling curve." At the current business end of the line was a master control board with a large television screen at its center, at which Dr. Wald was stationed, with Weinbaum looking, silently but anxiously, over his shoulder.

The screen itself showed a pattern which, except that it was drawn in green light against a dark gray background, strongly resembled the grain in a piece of highly polished mahogany. Photographs of similar patterns were stacked on a small table to Dr. Wald's right; several had spilled over onto the floor.

"Well, there it is," Wald sighed at length. "And I won't struggle to keep myself from saying 'I told you so.' What you've had me do here, Robin, is to reconfirm about half the basic postulates of particle physics—which is why it took so long, even though it was the first project we started." He snapped off the screen. "There are no cracks for J. Shelby to play in. That's definite."

"If you'd said 'That's flat,' you would have made a joke," Weinbaum said sourly. "Look . . . isn't there still a chance of error? If not on your part, Thor, then in the computer? After all, it's set up to work only with the unit charges of modern physics; mightn't we have to disconnect the banks that contain that bias before the machine will follow the fractional-charge instructions we give it?"

"'Disconnect,' he says," Wald groaned, mopping his brow reflectively. "The bias exists everywhere in the machine, my friend, because it functions everywhere on those same unit charges. It wasn't a matter of subtracting banks; we had to add one with a bias all its own, to countercorrect the corrections the computer would otherwise apply to the instructions. The technicians thought I was crazy. Now, five months later, I've proved it."

Weinbaum grinned in spite of himself. "What about the other projects?"

"All done—some time back, as a matter of fact. The staff and I checked every single Dirac tape we've received since you released J. Shelby from Yaphank, for any sign of inter-modulation, marginal signals, or anything else of the kind. There's nothing, Robin, absolutely nothing. That's our net result, all around."

"Which leaves us just where we started," Weinbaum said. "All the monitoring projects came to the same dead end; I strongly suspect that Stevens hasn't risked any further calls from his home office to his field staff, even though he seemed confident that we'd never intercept such calls—as we haven't. Even our local wire tapping hasn't turned up anything but calls by Stevens's secretary, making appointments for him with various clients, actual and potential. Any information he's selling these days he's passing on in person—and not in his office, either, because we've got bugs planted all over that and haven't heard a thing."

"That must limit his range of operation enormously," Wald objected.

Weinbaum nodded. "Without a doubt—but he shows no signs of being bothered by it. He can't have sent any tips to Erskine recently, for instance, because our last tangle with that crew came out very well for us, even though we had to use the Dirac to send the orders to our squadron out there. If he overheard us, he didn't even try to pass the word. Just as he said, he's sweating us out—" Weinbaum paused. "Wait a minute, here comes Margaret. And by the length of her stride, I'd say she's got something particularly nasty on her mind."

"You bet I do," Margaret Soames said vindictively. "And it'll blow plenty of lids around here, or I miss my guess. The I. D. squad has finally pinned down J. Shelby Stevens. They did it with the voice-comparator alone."

"How does that work?" Wald said interestedly.

"Blink microphone," Weinbaum said impatiently. "Isolates inflections on single, normally stressed syllables and matches them. Standard I. D. searching technique, on a case of this kind, but it takes so long that we usually get the quarry by other means before it pays off. Well, don't stand there like a dummy, Margaret. Who is he?"

"'He,'" Margaret said, "is your sweetheart of the video waves, Miss Dana Lje."

"They're crazy!" Wald said, staring at her.

Weinbaum came slowly out of his first shock of stunned disbelief. "No, Thor," he said finally. "No, it figures. If a woman is going to go in for disguises, there are always two she can assume outside her own sex: a young boy, and a very old man. And Dana's an actress; that's no news to us."

"But—but why did she do it, Robin?"

"That's what we're going to find out right now. So we wouldn't get the Dirac modification by ourselves, eh! Well, there are other ways of getting answers besides particle physics. Margaret, do you have a pick-up order out for that girl?"

"No," the receptionist said. "This is one chestnut I wanted to see you pull out for yourself. You give me the authority, and I send the order—not before."

"Spiteful child. Send it, then, and glory in my gritted teeth. Come on, Thor—let's put the nutcracker on this chestnut."

As they were leaving the computer floor, Weinbaum stopped suddenly in his tracks and began to mutter in an almost inaudible voice.

Wald said, "What's the matter, Robin?"

"Nothing. I keep being brought up short by those predictions. What's the date?"

"M'm . . . June 9. Why?"

"It's the exact date that 'Stevens' predicted we'd meet again, damn it! Something tells me that this isn't going to be as simple as it looks."

If Dana Lje had any idea of what she was in for—and considering the fact that she was 'J. Shelby Stevens' it had to be assumed that she did—the knowledge seemed not to make her at all fearful. She sat as composedly as ever before Weinbaum's desk, smoking her eternal cigarette, and waited, one dimpled knee pointed directly at the bridge of the officer's nose.

"Dana," Weinbaum said, "this time we're going to get all the answers, and we're not going to be gentle about it. Just in case you're not aware of the fact, there are certain laws relating to giving false information to a security officer, under which we could heave you in prison for a minimum of fifteen years. By application of the statutes on using communications to defraud, plus various local laws against transvestism, pseudonymity and so on, we could probably pile up enough additional short sentences to keep you in Yaphank until you really *do* grow a beard. So I'd advise you to open up."

"I have every intention of opening up," Dana said. "I know, practically word for word, how this interview is going to proceed, what information I'm going to give you, just when I'm going to give it to you—and what you're going to pay me for it. I knew all that many months ago. So there would be no point in my holding out on you."

"What you're saying, Miss Lje," Thor Wald said in a resigned voice, "is that the future is fixed, and that you can read it, in every essential detail."

"Quite right, Dr. Wald. Both those things are true."

There was a brief silence.

"All right," Weinbaum said grimly. "Talk."

"All right, Captain Weinbaum, pay me," Dana said calmly.

Weinbaum snorted.

"But I'm quite serious," she said. "You still don't know what I know about the Dirac communicator. I won't be forced to tell it, by threat of prison or by any other threat. You see, I know for a fact that you aren't going to send me to prison, or give me drugs, or do anything else of that kind. I know for a fact, instead, that you are going to pay me—so I'd be very foolish to say a word until you do. After all, it's quite a secret you're buying. Once I tell you what it is, you and the entire service will be able to read the future as I do, and then the information will be valueless to me."

Weinbaum was completely speechless for a moment. Finally he said, "Dana, you have a heart of purest brass, as well as a knee with an invisible gunsight on it. I say that I'm *not* going to give you my appropriation, regardless of what the future may or may not say about it. I'm not going to give it to you because the way my government—and yours—runs things makes such a price impossible. Or is that really your price?"

"It's my real price . . . but it's also an alternative. Call it my second choice. My first choice, which means the price I'd settle for, comes in two parts: (a) to be taken into your service as a responsible officer; and, (b) to be married to Captain Robin Weinbaum."

Weinbaum sailed up out of his chair. He felt as though copper-colored flames a foot long were shooting out of each of his ears.

"Of all the—" he began. There his voice failed completely.

From behind him, where Wald was standing, came something like a large, Scandinavian-model guffaw being choked into insensibility.

Dana herself seemed to be smiling a little.

"You see," she said, "I don't point my best and most accurate knee at every man I meet."

Weinbaum sat down again, slowly and carefully. "Walk, do not run, to nearest exit," he said. "Women and childlike security officers first. Miss Lje, are you trying to sell me the notion that you went through this elaborate hanky-panky—beard and all—out of a burning passion for my dumpy and underpaid person?"

"Not entirely," Dana Lje said. "I want to be in the bureau, too, as I said. Let me confront you, though, Captain, with a fact of life that doesn't seem to have occurred to you at all. Do you accept as a fact that I can read the future in detail, and that that, to be possible at all, means that the future is fixed?"

"Since Thor seems able to accept it, I suppose I can too—provisionally."

"There's nothing provisional about it," Dana said firmly. "Now, when I first came upon this—uh, this gimmick—quite a while back, one of the first things that I found out was that I was going to go through the 'J. Shelby Stevens' masquerade, force myself onto the staff of the bureau, and marry you, Robin. At the time, I was both astonished and completely rebellious. I didn't want to be on the bureau staff; I liked my free-lance life as a video commentator. I didn't want to marry you, though I wouldn't have been averse to living with you for a while—say a month or so. And above all, the masquerade struck me as ridiculous.

"But the facts kept staring me in the face. I *was* going to do all those things. There were no alternatives, no fanciful 'branches of time,' no decision-points that might be altered to make the future change. My future, like yours, Dr. Wald's, and everyone else's, was fixed. It didn't matter a snap whether or not I had a decent motive for what I was going to do; I was going to do it anyhow. Cause and effect, as I could see for myself, just don't exist. One event follows another because events are just as indestructible in space-time as matter and energy are.

"It was the bitterest of all pills. It will take me many years to swallow it completely, and you too. Dr. Wald will come around a little sooner, I think. At any rate, once I was intellectually convinced that all this was so, I had to protect my own sanity. I knew that I couldn't alter what I was going to do, but the least I could do to protect myself was to supply myself with motives. Or, in other words, just plain rationalizations. That much, it seems, we're free to do; the consciousness of the observer is just along for the ride through time, and can't alter events—but it can comment, explain, invent. That's fortunate, for none of us could stand going through motions which were truly free of what we think of as personal significances.

"So I supplied myself with the obvious motives. Since I was going to be married to you and couldn't get out of it, I set out to convince myself that I loved you. Now I do. Since I was going to join the bureau staff, I thought over all the advantages that it might have over video commentating, and found that they made a respectable list. Those are my motives.

"But I had no such motives at the beginning. Actually, there are never motives behind actions. All actions are fixed. What we called motives evidently are rationalizations by the helpless observing consciousness, which is intelligent enough to smell an event coming—and, since it cannot avert the event, instead cooks up reasons for wanting it to happen."

"Wow," Dr. Wald said, inelegantly but with considerable force.

"Either 'wow' or 'balderdash' seems to be called for—I can't quite decide which," Weinbaum agreed. "We know that Dana is an actress, Thor, so let's not fall off the apple tree quite yet. Dana, I've been saving the *really* hard question for the last. That question is: *How?* How did you arrive at this modification of the Dirac transmitter? Remember, we know your background, where we didn't know that of 'J. Shelby Stevens.' You're not a scientist. There were some fairly high-powered intellects among your distant relatives, but that's as close as you come."

"I'm going to give you several answers to that question," Dana Lje said. "Pick the one you like best. They're all true, but they tend to contradict each other here and there.

"To begin with, you're right about my relatives, of course. If you'll check your dossier again, though, you'll discover that those so-called 'distant' relatives were the last surviving members of my family besides myself. When they died, second and fourth and ninth cousins though they were, their estates reverted to me, and among their effects I found a sketch of a possible instantaneous communicator based on de Broglie-wave inversion. The material was in very rough form, and mostly beyond my comprehension, because I am, as you say, no scientist myself. But I was interested; I could see, dimly, what such a thing might be worth—and not only in money.

"My interest was fanned by two coincidences—the kind of coincidences that cause-and-effect just can't allow, but which seem to happen all the same in the world of unchangeable events. For most of my adult life, I've been in communications industries of one kind or another, mostly branches of video. I had communications equipment around me constantly, and I had coffee and doughnuts with communications engineers every day. First I picked up the jargon; then, some of the procedures; and eventually a little real knowledge. Some of the things I learned can't be gotten any other way. Some other things are ordinarily available only to highly educated people like Dr. Wald here, and came to me by accident, in horseplay, between kisses, and a hundred other ways—all natural to the environment of a video network."

Weinbaum found, to his own astonishment, that the "between kisses" clause did not sit very well in his chest. He said, with unintentional brusqueness: "What's the other coincidence?"

"A leak in your own staff."

"Dana, you ought to have that set to music."

"Suit yourself."

"I can't suit myself," Weinbaum said petulantly. "I work for the government. Was this leak direct to you?"

"Not at first. That was why I kept insisting to you in person that there might be such a leak, and why I finally began to hint about it in public, on my program. I was hoping that you'd be able to seal it up inside the bureau before my first rather tenuous contact with it got lost. When I didn't succeed in provoking you into protecting yourself, I took the risk of making direct contact with the leak myself—and the first piece of secret information that came to me through it was the final point I needed to put my Dirac communicator together. When it was all assembled, it did more than just communicate. It predicted. And I can tell you why."

Weinbaum said thoughtfully, "I don't find this very hard to accept, so far. Pruned of the philosophy, it even makes some sense of the 'J. Shelby Stevens' affair. I assume that by letting the old gentleman become known as somebody who knew more about the Dirac transmitter than I did, and who wasn't averse to negotiating with anybody who had money, you kept the leak working through you—rather than transmitting data directly to unfriendly governments."

"It did work out that way," Dana said. "But that wasn't the genesis or the purpose of the Stevens masquerade. I've already given you the whole explanation of how that came about."

"Well, you'd better name me that leak, before the man gets away."

"When the price is paid, not before. It's too late to prevent a getaway, anyhow. In the meantime, Robin, I want to go on and tell you the other answer to your question about how I was able to find this particular Dirac secret, and you didn't. What answers I've given you up to now have been cause-and-effect answers, with which we're all more comfortable. But I want to impress on you that all apparent cause-and-effect relationships are accidents. There is no such thing as a cause, and no such thing as an effect. I found the secret because I found it; that event was fixed; that certain circumstances seem to explain why I found it, in the old cause-and-effect terms, is irrelevant. Similarly, with all your superior equipment and brains, you didn't find it for one reason, and one reason alone: because you didn't find it. The history of the future says you didn't."

"I pays my money and I takes no choice, eh?" Weinbaum said ruefully.

"I'm afraid so—and I don't like it any better than you do."

"Thor, what's your opinion of all this?"

"It's just faintly flabbergasting," Wald said soberly. "However, it hangs together. The deterministic universe which Miss Lje paints was a common feature of the old relativity theories, and as sheer speculation has an even longer history. I would say that, in the long run, how much credence we place in the story as a whole will rest upon her method of, as she calls it, reading the future. If it is demonstrable beyond any doubt, then the rest becomes perfectly credible—philosophy and all. If it doesn't, then what remains is an admirable job of acting, plus some metaphysics which, while self-consistent, is not original with Miss Lje."

"That sums up the case as well as if I'd coached you, Dr. Wald," Dana said. "I'd like to point out one more thing. If I can read the future, then 'J. Shelby Stevens' never had any need for a staff of field operatives, and he never needed to send a single Dirac message which you might intercept. All he needed to do was to make predictions from his readings, which he knew to be infallible; no private espionage network had to be involved."

"I see that," Weinbaum said dryly. "All right, Dana, let's put the proposition this way: *I do not believe you.* Much of what you say is probably true, but in totality I believe it to be false. On the other hand, if you're telling the whole truth, you certainly deserve a place on the bureau staff—it would be dangerous as hell not to have you with us—and the marriage is a more or less minor matter, except to you and me. You can have that with no strings attached; I don't want to be bought, any more than you would.

"So: if you will tell me where the leak is, we will consider that part of the question closed. I make that condition not as a price, but because I don't want to get myself engaged to somebody who might be shot as a spy within a month."

"Fair enough," Dana said. "Robin, your leak is Margaret Soames. She is an Erskine operative, and nobody's bubble-brain. She's a highly trained technician."

"Well, I'll be damned," Weinbaum said in astonishment. "Then she's already flown the coop—she was the one who first told me we'd identified you. She must have taken on that job in order to hold up delivery long enough to stage an exit."

"That's right. But you'll catch her, day after tomorrow. And you are now a hooked fish, Robin."

There was another suppressed burble from Thor Wald.

"I accept the fate happily," Weinbaum said, eying the gunsight knee. "Now, if you will tell me how you work your swami trick, and if it backs up everything you've said to the letter, as you claim, I'll see to it that you're also taken into the bureau and that all charges against you are quashed. Otherwise, I'll probably have to kiss the bride between the bars of a cell."

Dana smiled. "The secret is very simple. It's in the beep."

Weinbaum's jaw dropped. "The beep? The Dirac noise?"

"That's right. You didn't find it out because you considered the beep to be just a nuisance, and ordered Miss Soames to cut it off all tapes before sending them in to you. Miss Soames, who had some inkling of what the beep meant, was more than happy to do so, leaving the reading of the beep exclusively to 'J. Shelby Stevens'—who she thought was going to take on Erskine as a client."

"Explain," Thor Wald said, looking intense.

"Just as you assumed, every Dirac message that is sent is picked up by every receiver that is capable of detecting it. *Every* receiver—including the first one ever built, which is yours, Dr. Wald, through the hundreds of thousands of them which will exist throughout the Galaxy in the twenty-fourth century, to the untold millions which will exist in the thirtieth century, and so on. The Dirac beep is the simultaneous reception of *every one of the Dirac messages which have ever been sent, or ever will be sent.* Incidentally, the cardinal number of the total of those messages is a relatively small and of course finite number; it's far below really large finite numbers such as the number of electrons in the universe, even when you break each and every message down into individual 'bits' and count those."

"Of course," Dr. Wald said softly. "Of course! But, Miss Lje . . . how do you tune for an individual message? We tried fractional positron frequencies, and got nowhere."

"I didn't even know fractional positron frequencies existed," Dana confessed. "No, it's simple—so simple that a lucky layman like me could arrive at it. You tune individual messages out of the beep by time lag, nothing more. All the messages arrive at the same instant, in the smallest fraction of time that exists, something called a 'chronon.'"

"Yes," Wald said. "The time it takes one electron to move from one quantum-level to another. That's the Pythagorean point of time measurement."

"Thank you. Obviously no gross physical receiver can respond to a message that brief, or at least that's what I thought at first. But because there are relay and switching delays, various forms of feedback and so on, in the apparatus itself, the beep arrives at the output end as a complex pulse which has been 'splattered' along the time axis for a full second or more. That's an effect which you can exaggerate by recording the 'splattered' beep on a high-speed tape, the same way you would record any event that you wanted to study in slow motion. Then you tune up the various failure-points in your receiver, to exaggerate one failure, minimize all the others, and use noise-suppressing techniques to cut out the background."

Thor Wald frowned. "You'd still have a considerable garble when you were through. You'd have to sample the messages—"

"Which is just what I did; Robin's little lecture to me about the ultrawave gave me that hint. I set myself to find out how the ultrawave channel carries so many messages at once, and I discovered that you people sample the incoming pulses every thousandth of a second and pass on one pip only when the wave deviates in a certain way from the mean. I didn't really believe it would work on the Dirac beep, but it turned out just as well: 90 percent as intelligible as the original transmission after it came through the smearing device. I'd already got enough from the beep to put my plan in motion, of course—but now every voice message in it was available, and crystal-clear: If you select three pips every thousandth of second, you can even pick up an intelligible transmission of music—a little razzy, but good enough to identify the instruments that are playing—and that's a very close test of any communications device."

"There's a question of detail here that doesn't quite follow," said Weinbaum, for whom the technical talk was becoming a little too thick to fight through. "Dana, you say that you knew the course this conversation was going to take—yet it isn't being Dirac-recorded, nor can I see any reason why any summary of it would be sent out on the Dirac afterwards."

"That's true, Robin. However, when I leave here, I will make such a transcast myself, on my own Dirac. Obviously I will—because I've *already* picked it up, from the beep."

"In other words, you're going to call yourself up—months ago."

"That's it," Dana said. "It's not as useful a technique as you might think at first, because it's dangerous to make such broadcasts while a situation is still developing. You can safely 'phone back' details only after the given situation has gone to completion, as a chemist might put it. Once you know, however, that when you use the Dirac you're dealing with time, you can coax some very strange things out of the instrument."

She paused and smiled. "I have heard," she said conversationally, "the voice of the President of our Galaxy, in 3480, announcing the federation of the Milky Way and the Magellanic Clouds. I've heard the commander of a world-line cruiser, traveling from 8873 to 8704 along the world line of the planet Hathshepa, which circles a star on the rim of NGC 4725, calling for help across eleven million light-years—but what kind of help he was calling for, or will be calling for, is beyond my comprehension. And many other things. When you check on me, you'll hear these things too—and you'll wonder what many of them mean.

"And you'll listen to them even more closely than I did, in the hope of finding out whether or not anyone was able to understand in time to help."

Weinbaum and Wald looked dazed.

Her voice became a little more somber. "Most of the voices in the Dirac beep are like that—they're cries for help, which you can overhear decades or centuries before the senders get into trouble. You'll feel obligated to answer every one, to try to supply the help that's needed. And you'll listen to the succeeding messages and say: 'Did we—will we get there in time? Did we understand in time?'

"And in most cases you won't be sure. You'll know the future, but not what most of it means. The farther into the future you travel with the machine, the more incomprehensible the messages become, and so you're reduced to telling yourself that time will, after all, have to pass by at its own pace, before enough of the surrounding events can emerge to make those remote messages clear.

"The long-run effect, as far as I can think it through, is not going to be that of omniscience—of our consciousness being extracted entirely from the time stream and allowed to view its whole sweep from one side. Instead, the Dirac in effect simply slides the bead of consciousness forward from the present a certain distance. Whether it's five hundred of five thousand years still remains to be seen. At that point the law of diminishing returns sets in—or the noise factor begins to overbalance the information, take your choice—and the observer is reduced to traveling in time at the same old speed. He's just a bit ahead of himself."

"You've thought a great deal about this," Wald said slowly. "I dislike to think of what might have happened had some less conscientious person stumbled on the beep."

"That wasn't in the cards," Dana said.

In the ensuing quiet, Weinbaum felt a faint, irrational sense of letdown, of something which had promised more than had been delivered—rather like the taste of fresh bread as compared to its smell, or the discovery that Thor Wald's Swedish "folk song" Nat-og-Dag was only Cole Porter's *Night and Day* in another language. He recognized the feeling: it was the usual emotion of the hunter when the hunt is over, the born detective's professional version of the *post coitum tristre*. After looking at the smiling, supple Dana Lje a moment more, however, he was almost content.

"There's one more thing," he said. "I don't want to be insufferably skeptical about this—but I want to see it work. Thor, can we set up a sampling and smearing device such as Dana describes and run a test?"

"In fifteen minutes," Dr. Wald said. "We have most of the unit in already assembled form on our big ultrawave receiver, and it shouldn't take any effort to add a high-speed tape unit to it. I'll do it right now."

He went out. Weinbaum and Dana looked at each other for a moment, rather like strange cats. Then the security officer got up, with what he knew to be an air of somewhat grim determination, and seized his fiancée's hands, anticipating a struggle.

That first kiss was, by intention at least, mostly *pro forma*. But by the time Wald padded back into the office, the letter had been pretty thoroughly superseded by the spirit. The scientist harrumphed and set his burden on the desk. "This is all there is to it," he said, "but I had to hunt all through the library to find a Dirac record with a beep still on it. Just a moment more while I make connections. . . ."

Weinbaum used the time to bring his mind back to the matter at hand, although not quite completely. Then two tape spindles began to whir like so many bees, and the end-stopped sound of the Dirac beep filled the room. Wald stopped the apparatus, reset it, and started the smearing tape very slowly in the opposite direction.

A distant babble of voices came from the speaker. As Weinbaum leaned forward tensely, one voice said clearly and loudly above the rest:

"Hello, Earth bureau. Lt. T. L. Matthews at Hercules Station NGC 6341, transmission date 13-22-2091. We have the last point on the orbit curve of your dope-runners plotted, and the curve itself points to a small system about twenty-five light-years from the base here; the place hasn't even got a name on our charts. Scouts show the home planet at least twice as heavily fortified as we anticipated, so we'll need another cruiser. We have a 'can-do' from you in the beep for us, but we're waiting as ordered to get it in the present. NGC 6341 Matthews out."

After the first instant of stunned amazement—for no amount of intellectual willingness to accept could have prepared him for the overwhelming fact itself—Weinbaum had grabbed a pencil and begun to write at top speed. As the voice signed out he threw the pencil down and looked excitedly at Dr. Wald.

"Seven months ahead," he said, aware that he was grinning like an idiot. "Thor, you know the trouble we've had with that needle in the Hercules haystack! This orbit-curve trick must be something Matthews has yet to dream up—at least he hasn't come to me with it yet, and there's nothing in the situation as it stands now that would indicate a closing time of six months for the case. The computers said it would take three more years."

"It's new data," Dr. Wald agreed solemnly.

"Well, don't stop there, in God's name! Let's hear some more!"

Dr. Wald went through the ritual, much faster this time. The speaker said:

"Nausentampen. Eddettompic. Berobsilom. Aimkaksetchoc. Sanbetogmow. Datdectamset. Domatrosmin. Out."

"My word," Wald said. "What's all that?"

"That's what I was talking about," Dana Lje said. "At least half of what you get from the beep is just as incomprehensible. I suppose it's whatever has happened to the English language, thousands of years from now."

"No, it isn't," Weinbaum said. He had resumed writing, and was still at it, despite the comparative briefness of the transmission. "Not this sample, anyhow. That, ladies and gentlemen, is code—no language consists exclusively of four-syllable words, of that you can be sure. What's more, it's a version of our code. I can't break it down very far— it takes a full-time expert to read this stuff—but I get the date and some of the sense. It's March 12, 3022, and there's some kind of a mass evacuation taking place. The message seems to be a routing order."

"But why will we be using code?" Dr. Wald wanted to know. "It implies that we think somebody might overhear us—somebody else with a Dirac. That could be very messy."

"It could indeed," Weinbaum said. "But we'll find out, I imagine. Give her another spin, Thor."

"Shall I try for a picture this time?"

Weinbaum nodded. A moment later, he was looking squarely into the green-skinned face of something that looked like an animated traffic signal with a helmet on it. Though the creature had no mouth, the Dirac speaker was saying quite clearly, "Hello, Chief. This is Thammos NGC 2287, transmission date Gor 60, 302 by my calendar, July 2, 2973 by yours. This is a lousy little planet. Everything stinks of oxygen, just like Earth. But the natives accept us and that's the important thing. We've got your genius safely born. Detailed report coming later by paw. NGC 2287 Thammos out."

"I wish I knew my New General Catalogue better," Weinbaum said. "Isn't that M 41 in Canis Major, the one with the red star in the middle? And we'll be using non-humanoids there! What *was* that creature, anyhow? Never mind, spin her again."

Dr. Wald spun her again. Weinbaum, already feeling a little dizzy, had given up taking notes. That could come later, all that could come later. Now he wanted only scenes and voices, more and more scenes and voices from the future. They were better than aquavit, even with a beer chaser.

IV

The indoctrination tape ended, and Krasna touched a button. The Dirac screen darkened, and folded silently back into the desk.

"They didn't see their way through to us, not by a long shot," he said. "They didn't see, for instance, that when one section of the government becomes nearly all-knowing—no matter how small it was to begin with—it necessarily becomes all of the government that there is. Thus the bureau turned into the Service and pushed everyone else out.

"On the other hand, those people did come to be afraid that a government with an all-knowing arm might become a rigid dictatorship. That couldn't happen and didn't happen, because the more you know, the wider your field of possible operation becomes and the more fluid and dynamic a society you need. How could a rigid society expand to other star systems, let alone other galaxies? It couldn't be done."

"I should think it could," Jo said slowly. "After all, if you know in advance what everybody is going to do . . ."

"But we don't, Jo. That's just a popular fiction—or, if you like, a red herring. Not all of the business of the cosmos is carried on over the Dirac, after all. The only events we can ever overhear are those which are transmitted as a message. Do you order your lunch over the Dirac? Of course you don't. Up to now, you've never said a word over the Dirac in your life.

"And there's much more to it than that. All dictatorships are based on the proposition that government can somehow control a man's thoughts. We know now that the consciousness of the observer is the only free thing in the Universe. Wouldn't we look foolish trying to control that, when our entire physics shows that it's impossible to do so? That's why the Service is in no sense a thought police. We're interested only in acts. We're an Event Police."

"But why?" Jo said. "If all history is fixed, why do we bother with these boy-meets-girl assignments, for instance? The meetings will happen anyhow."

"Of course they will," Krasna agreed immediately. "But look, Jo. Our interests as a government depend upon the future. We operate *as if* the future is as real as the past, and so far we haven't been disappointed: the Service is 100 percent successful. But that very success isn't without its warnings. What would happen if we *stopped* supervising events? We don't know, and we don't dare take the chance. Despite the evidence that the future is fixed, we have to take on the role of the caretaker of inevitability. We believe that nothing can possibly go wrong . . . but we have to act on the philosophy that history helps only those who help themselves.

"That's why we safeguard huge numbers of courtships right through to contract, and even beyond it. We have to see to it that *every single person who is mentioned in any Dirac 'cast gets born*. Our obligation as Event Police is to make the events of the future possible, because those events are crucial to our society—even the smallest of them. It's an enormous task, believe me, and it gets bigger and bigger every day. Apparently it always will."

"Always?" Jo said. "What about the public? Isn't it going to smell this out sooner or later? The evidence is piling up at a terrific rate."

"Yes and no," Krasna said. "Lots of people are smelling it out right now, just as you did. But the number of new people we need in the Service grows faster—it's always ahead of the number of laymen who follow the clues to the truth."

Jo look a deep breath. "You take all this as if it were as commonplace as boiling an egg, Kras," he said. "Don't you ever wonder about some of the things you get from the beep. That 'cast Dana Lje picked up from Canes Venatici, for instance, the one from the ship that was traveling backward in time? How is that possible? What could be the purpose? Is it—"

"*Pace, pace,*" Krasna said. "I don't know and I don't care. Neither should you. That event is too far in the future for us to worry about. We can't possibly know its context yet, so there's no sense in trying to understand it. If an Englishman of around 1600 had found out about the American Revolution, he would have thought it a tragedy; an Englishman of 1950 would have a very different view of it. We're in the same spot. The messages we get from the really far future have no contexts as yet."

"I think I see," Jo said. "I'll get used to it in time, I suppose, after I use the Dirac for a while. Or does my new rank authorize me to do that?"

"Yes, it does. But, Jo, first I want to pass on to you a rule of Service etiquette that must never be broken. You won't be allowed anywhere near a Dirac mike until you have it I burned into your memory beyond any forgetfulness."

"I'm listening, Kras, believe me."

"Good. This is the rule: *The date of a Serviceman's death must never be mentioned in a Dirac 'cast.*"

Jo blinked, feeling a little chilly. The reason behind the rule was decidedly tough-minded, but its ultimate kindness was plain. He said, "I won't forget that. I'll want that protection myself. Many thanks, Kras. What's my new assignment?"

"To begin with," Krasna said, grinning, "as simple a job as I've ever given you, right here on Randolph. Skin out of here and find me that cab driver—the one who mentioned time-travel to you. He's uncomfortably close to the truth; closer than you were in one category.

"Find him, and bring him to me. The Service is about to take in a new raw recruit!"

FYI

"I've got definite proof that we've been granted a reprieve," Lord Rogge was insisting to thin air. "Perfectly definite proof."

We had been listening, either tensely or with resignation, according to the man, to the evening news roundup in the bar of the Orchid Club. With the world tottering on the brink, you might have thought that an announcement like that would have elicited at least some interest. Had Rogge said the same thing in public, the reporters would have spread it to the antipodes in half an hour.

Which only goes to show that the world knew less than it should about poor old George. Once the Orchid Club got to know him intimately, it had become impossible to believe in him any longer as one of the world's wise men. Oh, he is one of the great mathematicians of all time, to be sure, but on any other subject he can be counted on to make a complete ass of himself. Most of us already knew, in a general way, what he meant by a "reprieve," and how well his proof would stand up—supported, as usual, by a pillar of ectoplasm.

"What is it now, George?" I said. Somebody has to draw him off, or he'll continue to clamor for attention through the news bulletins. It was now my turn.

"It's proof," he said, sitting down beside me at once. "I've found a marvelous woman in Soho—oh, a perfect illiterate, she has no idea of the magnitude of the thing she's got hold of. But Charles, she has a pipeline to the gods, as clear and direct a contact as any human being ever had. I've written proof of it."

"And the gods tell her that truth and light will prevail? George, don't you ever listen to the wireless? Don't you know that these are almost surely our last days? Don't you know that your medium is never going to have another child, that the earth's last generation has already been born, that the final war is upon us right at this instant?"

"Bother," Rogge said, exactly as he might have spoken had he found soda instead of water in his whisky. "You can't see beyond the end of your nose, Charles. Here you are, a speck in a finite universe in finite time, full of angst because there may not be any more specks. What does that matter? You're a member of a finite class. If you ever thought about it all, you knew from the beginning that the class was doomed to be finite. What do you care about its ultimate cardinality?"

". . . has accused India of deliberately attempting to wreck the conference," the wireless was saying. "Meanwhile, the new government of Kashmir which seized power last week has signed a treaty of 'everlasting friendship and assistance' with the Peiping government. The latest reports still do not reveal . . ."

Well, I'd be briefed later; that was part of the agreement. I said, "I thought you were the one who cared about cardinality. Wouldn't you like to see the number of the class of human beings get up some day into your precious transfinite realm? How can we do that if we kill each other off this very month?"

"We can't do it in any case, not in the physical sense," Rogge said, settling back into his chair. "No matter how long the race lives or how fruitful it is, it will always be denumerable—each member of the race can be put in one-to-one relationship with the integers. If we all lived forever and produced descendants at a great rate, we might wind up as a denumerably infinite class—in infinite time. But we haven't got infinite time; and in any case, the very first transfinite number is the cardinal number of all such classes. No, my boy, we'll never make it."

I was, to say the least, irritated. How the man could be so smug in the face of the red ruin staring us all in the face . . .

"So the reprieve you were talking about is no reprieve for us."

"It may well be, but that's the smallest part of the implications. . . . Have you another of those panatelas, Charles? . . . There now. No, what I was talking about was a reprieve for the universe. It's been given a chance to live up to man."

"You really ought to listen to the BBC for a few minutes," I said. "Just to get some idea of what man is. Not much for the universe to live up to."

"But it's a two-penny universe to begin with," Rogge said, from behind a cloud of newborn smoke. "There's no scope to it. It's certainly no more than ten billion years old at the outside, and already it's dying. The space-time bubble may or may not continue to expand forever, but before long there won't be anything in it worth noticing. It's ridiculously finite."

"So is man."

"Granted, Charles, but man has already made that heritage look stupid. We've thought of things that utterly transcend the universe we live in."

"Numbers, I suppose."

"Numbers indeed," Rogge said, unruffled. "Transfinite numbers. Numbers larger than infinity. And we live in a universe where they don't appear to stand for anything. A piece of primer-work, like confining a grown man in a pram."

I looked back at the wireless. "We don't sound so grown-up to me."

"Oh, you're not grown-up, Charles, and that holds true for most people. But a few men have shown what the race could do. Look at Cantor. He thought his way right out of the universe he lived in. He created a realm of numbers which evolve logically out of the numbers the universe runs on—and then found no provision had been made for them in the universe as it stands. Which would seem to indicate that Whoever created this universe knew less math than Cantor did! Isn't that silly?"

"I've no opinion," I said. "But you're a religious man, George. Aren't you skirting blasphemy?"

"Don't talk nonsense. Obviously there was a mathematician involved somewhere, and there are no bad mathematicians. If this one was as good as His handiwork indicates, of course He knew about the transfinites; the limitation was purposeful. And I think I've found out the purpose."

Now, of course, the great revelation was due. Promptly on schedule, Rogge fussed inside his jacket pocket. I sat back and waited. He finally produced a grubby piece of paper, a fragment of a kraft bag.

"You're going to need a little background here," he said, drawing the paper out of reach as I leaned forward again. "Transfinite numbers don't work like finite ones. They don't add, subtract, multiply, or divide in any normal sense. As a matter of fact, the only way to change one is to involute it—to raise it to its own power."

"I'm bored already," I said.

"No doubt, but you'll listen because you have to." He grinned at me through the cigar smoke, and I began to feel rather uncomfortable. Could the old boy have been tipped off to our rotating system of running interference with him? "But I'll try to make it clear. Suppose that all the ordinary numbers you know were to change their behavior, so that zero to the zero power, instead of making zero, made one? Then one to the first power would make two; two squared would equal three; three cubed would be four, and so on. Any other operation would leave you just where you were: two times three, for instance, would equal three, and ten times 63 would equal 63. If your ordinary numbers behaved that way, you'd probably be considerably confused at first, but you'd get used to it.

"Well, that's the way the transfinite numbers work. The first one is Aleph-null, which as I said before is the cardinal number of all denumerably infinite classes. If you multiply it by itself, you get Aleph-one. Aleph-one to the Aleph-first equals Aleph-two. Do you follow me?"

"Reluctantly. Now let me crack your brains for a minute. What do these numbers number?"

Rogge smiled more gently. "Numbers," he said. "You'll have to try harder than that, Charles."

"You said Aleph-null was the cardinal number of—of all the countably infinite classes, isn't that right? All right, then what is Aleph-one the cardinal number of?"

"Of the class of all real numbers. It's sometimes called C, or the power of the continuum. Unhappily, the continuum as we know it seems to have no use for it."

"And Aleph-two?"

"Is the cardinal number of the class of all one-valued functions."

"Very good." I had been watching this process with considerable secret glee. Rogge is sometimes pitifully easy to trap, I had been told, if you've read his works and know his preoccupations; and I'd taken the trouble to do so. "It seems to me that you've blasted your own argument. First you say that these transfinite numbers don't stand for anything in the real universe. Then you proceed to tell me, one by one, what they stand for."

Rogge looked stunned for an instant, and I got ready to go back to listening to the wireless. But I had misinterpreted his expression. I hadn't stumped him; he had simply underestimated my ignorance, one of his more ingratiating failings.

"But Charles," he said, "to be sure the transfinite numbers stand for numbers. The point is that they stand for nothing else. We can apply a finite number, such as seven, to the universe; we can, perhaps, point to seven apples. But there aren't Aleph-one apples in the universe; there aren't Aleph-one atoms in the universe; there is no distance in the universe as great as Aleph-one miles; and the universe won't last for Aleph-one years. The number Aleph-one applies only to concepts of number, which are things existing solely in the minds of men. Why, Charles, we don't even know if there is such a thing as infinity in nature. Or we didn't know until now. At this present moment, not even infinity exists."

Impossibly enough, Rogge was actually beginning to make me feel a little bit circumscribed, a little bit offended that the universe was so paltry. I looked around. Cyril Weaver was sitting closest to the broadcaster, and there were tears running down his craggy face onto his medals. John Boyd was pacing, slamming his fist repeatedly and mechanically into his left palm. Off in the corner next to the fire, Sir Leslie Crawford was well along into one of his ghastly silent drunks, which wind up in a fixed, cataleptic glare at some inconsequential object, such as a tuft in the carpet or the space where a waiter once stood; he was Her Majesty's Undersecretary for Air, but at such moments no event or appeal can reach him.

Evidently nothing that had come through on the wireless had redeemed our expectations in the slightest. Of them all, I was the only one—not counting Lord Rogge, of course—who had failed to hear the news, and so would still be listening for a word of hope during tomorrow's broadcast.

"Almost thou persuadest me, George," I said. "But I warn you, none of this affects my opinion of mediums and spiritualism in the least. So your cause is lost in advance."

"My boy, I'm not going to ask you to believe anything but what I'm going to put before your own eyes. This charwoman, as I said, is utterly uneducated. She happens to have a great gift, but not the slightest idea of how to use it. She stages seances for ignorant folk like herself, and gives out written messages which purport to be from her clientele's departed relatives. The usual thing."

"Not at all impressive as a start."

"No, but wait," Rogge said. "I'm interested in such things, as you know, and I got wind of her through the Psychical Research Society. It seems that some of the woman's patrons had been complaining: They couldn't understand the spirit messages. 'Uncle Bill, 'e wasn't never no one to talk like that.' That sort of complaint. I wouldn't have bothered at all, if I hadn't seen one of the 'messages,' and after that I couldn't wait to see her.

"She was terrified, as such people are of anybody who speaks reasonable English and asks questions. I won't rehearse the details, but eventually she admitted that she's been practicing a fraud on her trade."

"Remarkable."

"I agree," Rogge said, somewhat mockingly, it seemed to me. "It appears that the voices she hears during her trances are not the voices of the relatives of her neighbors. As a matter of fact, she isn't even sure that they're spirit voices, or human voices. And she doesn't herself understand what it is that they say. She just writes it down, and then, once she's conscious again, tries to twist what she's written enough to make it apply to the particular client."

I expect I had begun to look a little sour. Rogge held up a hand as if to forestall an interruption. "After I got her calmed down sufficiently, I had her do the trick for me. Believe me, I'm not easily fooled after all these years. That trance was genuine enough, and the writing was fully automatic. I performed several tests to make sure. And this is what she wrote."

Without any attempt at a dramatic pause, he passed the scrap of brown paper over to me. The block printing on it was coarse, sprawling, and badly formed; it had evidently been written with a soft pencil, and there were smudge marks to show where the heel of a hand had rested. The text read:

FYI WER XTENDIN THE FIE NIGHT CONTIN YOU UMBRELLAS OF THIS CROWN ON TO OMEGA AHED OF SHEDYULE DO TO CHRIST IS IN HEAVEN ROOSHIAN OF CHILDREN OPEN SUDO SPEAR TO POSITIV CURVACHER AND BEGIN TRANSFORMATION TO COZ MOST OF MACRO SCOPICK NUMBER

I handed the paper back to Rogge, astonished to find that my heart had sunk. I hadn't realized that it had attained any altitude from which to sink. Had I really been expecting some sort of heavenly pardon through this absurd channel? But I suppose that, in this last agony of the world, anyone might have grasped at the same straw.

"On to omega, indeed," I said. "But don't forget your bumbershoot. How did she manage to spell 'transformation' right?"

"She wears one," Rogge said. "And that's the key to the whole thing. Obviously she didn't understand more than a few words of what she—well, what she overheard. So she tried to convert it into familiar terms, letting a lot of umbrellas and Russians into it in the process. If you read the message phonetically, though, you can spot the interpolations easily—and converted back into its own terms, it's perhaps the most important message anybody on earth ever got."

"If anybody told me that message was from Uncle Bill, I wouldn't just guess it was a fraud. Go ahead, translate."

"First of all, it's obviously a memorandum of some sort. FYI—for your information. The rest says: 'We are extending the finite continuum as of this chronon to omega ahead of schedule due to crisis in evolution of children. Open pseudosphere to positive curvature and begin transformation to cosmos of macroscopic number.'"

"Well," I said, "it's certainly more resonant that way. But just as empty."

"By no means. Consider, Charles. Omega is the cardinal number of infinity. The finite continuum is our universe. A chronon can be nothing but a unit of time, probably the basic Pythagorean time-point. The pseudosphere is the shape our universe maintains in four-dimensional space-time. To open it to a positive curvature would, in effect, change it from finite to infinite."

I took time out to relight my cigar and try to apply the glossary to the message. To my consternation, it worked. I got the cheroot back into action only a second before my hands began to shake.

"My word, George," I said, carefully. "Some creature with a spiral nebula for a head has taken up reading your books."

He said nothing, he simply looked at me. At last I had to ask him the preposterous question which I could not drive from me in any other way.

"George," I said, "George, are we the children?"

"I don't know," Rogge said frankly. "I came here convinced that we are. But while talking to you I began to wonder again. Whatever powers sent and received this message evidently regard some race in this universe as their children, to be educated gradually into their world—a world where transfinite numbers are everyday facts of arithmetic, and finite numbers are just infinitesimal curiosities. Those powers are graduating that race to an infinite universe as the first step in the change.

"The human race has learned about transfinite numbers, which would seem to be a crucial stage in such an education. And we're certainly in the midst of a crisis in our evolution. We seem to qualify. But . . . Well, there are quite a few planets in this universe, Charles.

We may be the children of whom they speak. Or they may not even know that we exist!"

He got up, his face troubled. "The gods," he said quietly. "They're out there, somewhere in a realm beyond infinity, getting ready to open up our pseudospherical egg and spill as out into an inconceivably vaster universe. But is it for our benefit or for—someone else's? And how will we detect it when it happens? On what time-scale do they plan to do it—tomorrow for us, or tomorrow for them, billions of years too late for us?"

"Or," I said, "the whole thing may be a phantom."

"It may be," he said. He knew, I think, that I had said that for the record, but he gave no sign of it. "Well, in the meantime you're relieved of duty, Charles. I shan't keep you any longer. I had to tell someone, and I have. Think about it."

He went out, his chin ducked reflectively, dribbling cigar ashes onto his vest.

I thought about it. It was, of course, the sheerest nonsense. The woman's scrawled "message" was gibberish. Where Lord Rogge had read into it the mathematical terms with which he was most familiar, someone else might read into it the jargon of some other specialty. How else could a charwoman speak the language of relativity and transfinite numbers? Of course, she might have been picking some expert's brains by telepathy, maybe even Rogge's own—but that explanation just substituted one miracle for another. If I was going to believe in telepathy, I might as well admit that I'd just read an interoffice memo from Olympus.

The Third Programme had gone back to music now, but there was another sound in the bar. It was not very loud, but steady and pervasive. It could be felt in the floor, even through the thick-piled carpet, and it shook the air slightly. Sir Leslie's gaze stirred from the vase upon which it had finally become fixed, and rose slowly, slowly toward the dark oak ceiling. There was a preliminary flicker from the lights.

Children of the gods—

We would know soon now. The bombers were coming.

Common Time

"... the days went slowly round and round, endless and uneventful as cycles in space. Time, and timepieces! How many centuries did my hammock tell, as pendulum-like it swung to the ship's dull roll, and ticked the hours and ages."

—Herman Melville, in *Mardi*

Don't move.

It was the first thought that came in Garrard's mind when he awoke, and perhaps it saved his life. He lay where he was, strapped against the padding, listening to the round hum of the engines. That in itself was wrong; he should be unable to hear the overdrive at all.

He thought to himself: *Has it begun already?*

Otherwise everything seemed normal. The DFC-3 had crossed over into interstellar velocity, and he was still alive, and the ship was still functioning. The ship should at this moment be traveling at 22.4 times the speed of light—a neat 4,157,000 miles per second.

Somehow Garrard did not doubt that it was. On both previous tries, the ships had whiffed away toward Alpha Centauri at the proper moment when the overdrive should have cut in; and the split second of residual image after they had vanished, subjected to spectroscopy, showed a Doppler shift which tallied with the acceleration predicted for that moment by Haertel.

The trouble was not that Brown and Cellini hadn't gotten away in good order. It was simply that neither of them had ever been heard from again.

Very slowly, he opened his eyes. His eyelids felt terrifically heavy. As far as he could judge from the pressure of the couch against his skin, the gravity was normal; nevertheless, moving his eyelids seemed almost an impossible job.

After long concentration, he got them fully open. The instrument chassis was directly before him, extended over his diaphragm on its elbow joint. Still without moving anything but his eyes—and those only with the utmost patience—he checked each of the meters. Velocity: 22.4 c. Operating temperature: normal. Ship temperature: 37° C. Air pressure: 778 mm. Fuel: No.1 tank full, No.2 tank full, No.3 tank full, No.4 tank nine-tenths full. Gravity: 1 g. Calendar: stopped.

He looked at it closely, though his eyes seemed to focus very slowly, too. It was, of course, something more than a calendar—it was an all-purpose clock, designed to show him the passage of seconds, as well as of the ten months his trip was supposed to take to the double star. But there was no doubt about it: the second hand was motionless.

That was the second abnormality. Garrard felt an impulse to get up and see if he could start the clock again. Perhaps the trouble had been temporary and safely in the past. Immediately there sounded in his head the injunction he had drilled into himself for a full month before the trip had begun—

Don't move!

Don't move until you know the situation as far as it can be known without moving. Whatever it was that had snatched Brown and Cellini irretrievably beyond human ken was potent, and totally beyond anticipation. They had both been excellent men, intelligent, resourceful, trained to the point of diminishing returns and not a micron beyond that point—the best men in the Project. Preparations for every knowable kind of trouble had been built into their ships, as they had been built into the DFC-3. Therefore, if there was something wrong nevertheless, it would be something that might strike from some commonplace quarter—and strike only once.

He listened to the humming. It was even and placid, and not very loud, but it disturbed him deeply. The overdrive was supposed to be inaudible, and the tapes from the first unmanned test vehicles had recorded no such hum. The noise did not appear to interfere with the overdrive's operation, or to indicate any failure in it. It was just an irrelevancy for which he could find no reason.

But the reason existed. Garrard did not intend to do so much as draw another breath until he found out what it was.

Incredibly, he realized for the first time that he had not in fact drawn one single breath since he had first come to. Though he felt not the slightest discomfort, the discovery called up so overwhelming a flash of panic that he very nearly sat bolt upright on the couch.

Luckily—or so it seemed, after the panic had begun to ebb—the curious lethargy which had affected his eyelids appeared to involve his whole body, for the impulse was gone before he could summon the energy to answer it. And the panic, poignant though it had been for an instant, turned out to be wholly intellectual. In a moment, he was observing that his failure to breathe in no way discommoded him as far as he could tell—it was just there, waiting to be explained...

Or to kill him. But it hadn't, yet.

Engines humming; eyelids heavy; breathing absent; calendar stopped. The four facts added up to nothing. The temptation to move something—even if it were only a big toe—was strong, but Garrard fought it back. He had been awake only a short while—half an hour at most—and already had noticed four abnormalities. There were bound to be more, anomalies more subtle than these four; but available to close examination before he had to move. Nor was there anything in particular that he had to do, aside from caring for his own wants; the Project, on the chance that Brown's and Cellini's failure to return had resulted from some tampering with the overdrive, had made everything in the DFC-3 subject only to the computer. In a very real sense, Garrard was just along for the ride. Only when the overdrive was off could he adjust—

Pock.

It was a soft, low-pitched noise, rather like a cork coming out of a wine bottle. It seemed to have come just from the right of the control chassis. He halted a sudden jerk of his head on the cushions toward it with a flat fiat of will. Slowly, he moved his eyes in that direction.

He could see nothing that might have caused the sound. The ship's temperature dial showed no change, which ruled out a heat noise from differential contraction or expansion—the only possible explanation he could bring to mind.

He closed his eyes—a process which turned out to be just as difficult as opening them had been—and tried to visualize what the calendar had looked like when he had first come out of anesthesia. After he got a clear and—he was almost sure—accurate picture, Garrard opened his eyes again.

The sound had been the calendar, advancing one second. It was now motionless again, apparently stopped.

He did not know how long it took the second hand to make that jump, normally; the question had never come up. Certainly the jump, when it came at the end of each second, had been too fast for the eye to follow.

Belatedly, he realized what all this cogitation was costing him in terms of essential information. The calendar had moved. Above all and before anything else, he *must* know exactly how long it took it to move again...

He began to count, allowing an arbitrary five seconds lost. *One-and-a-six, one-and-a-seven, one-and-an eight –*

Garrard had gotten only that far when he found himself plunged into hell.

First, and utterly without reason, a sickening fear flooded swiftly through his veins, becoming more and more intense. His bowels began to knot, with infinite slowness. His whole body became a field of small, slow pulses—not so much shaking him as putting his limbs into contrary joggling motions, and making his skin ripple gently under his clothing. Against the hum another sound became audible, a nearly subsonic thunder which seemed to be inside his head. Still the fear mounted, and with it came the pain, and the tenesmus—a board-like stiffening of his muscles, particularly across his abdomen and his shoulders, but affecting his forearms almost as grievously. He felt himself beginning, very gradually, to double at the middle, a motion about which he could do precisely nothing—a terrifying kind of dynamic paralysis . . .

It lasted for hours. At the height of it, Garrard's mind, even his very personality, was washed out utterly; he was only a vessel of horror. When some few trickles of reason began to return over that burning desert of reasonless emotion, he found that he was sitting up on the cushions, and that with one arm he had thrust the control chassis back on its elbow so that it no longer jutted over his body. His clothing was wet with perspiration, which stubbornly refused to evaporate or to cool him. And his lungs ached a little, although he could still detect no breathing.

What under God had happened? Was it this that had killed Brown and Cellini? For it would kill Garrard, too—of that he was sure, if it happened often. It would kill him even if it happened only twice more, if the next two such things followed the first one closely. At the very best it would make a slobbering idiot of him; and though the computer might bring Garrard and the ship back to Earth, it would not be able to tell the Project about this tornado of senseless fear.

The calendar said that the eternity in hell had taken three seconds. As he looked at it in academic indignation, it said *pock* and condescended to make the total seizure four seconds long. With grim determination, Garrard began to count again.

He took care to establish the counting as an absolutely even, automatic process which would not stop at the back of his mind no matter what other problem he tackled along with it, or what emotional typhoons should interrupt him. Really compulsive counting can not be stopped by anything—not the transports of love nor the agonies of empires. Garrard knew the dangers in deliberately setting up such a mechanism in his mind, but he also knew how desperately he needed to time that clock tick. He was beginning to understand what had happened to him—but he needed exact measurement before he could put that understanding to use.

Of course there had been plenty of speculation on the possible effect of the overdrive on the subjective time of the pilot, but none of it had come to much. At any speed below the velocity of light, subjective and objective time were exactly the same as far as the pilot was concerned. For an observer on Earth, time aboard the ship would appear to be vastly slowed at near-light speeds; but for the pilot himself there would be no apparent change.

Since flight beyond the speed of light was impossible—although for slightly differing reasons—by both the current theories of relativity, neither theory had offered any clue as to what would happen on board a translight ship. They would not allow that any such ship could even exist. The Haertel transformation, on which, in effect, the DFC-3 flew was nonrelativistic: it showed that the apparent elapsed time of a translight journey should be identical in ship-time, and in the time of observers at both ends of the trip.

But since ship and pilot were part of the same system, both covered by the same expression in Haertel's equation, it had never occurred to anyone that the pilot and the ship might keep different times. The notion was ridiculous.

One - and - a - sevenhundredone, one - and - a - sevenhundredtwo, one - and - a - sevenhundredthree, one and- a - sevenhundredfour . . .

The ship was keeping ship-time, which was identical with observer-time. It would arrive at the Alpha Centauri system in ten months. But the pilot was keeping Garrard-time, and it was beginning to look as though he wasn't going to arrive at all.

It was impossible, but there it was. Something—almost certainly an unsuspected physiological side effect of the overdrive field on human metabolism, an effect which naturally could not have been detected in the preliminary, robot-piloted tests of the overdrive—had speeded up Garrard's subjective apprehension of time, and had done a thorough job of it.

The second hand began a slow, preliminary quivering as the calendar's innards began to apply power to it. *Seventy-hundred-forty-one, seventy-hundred- forty-two, seventy-hundred-forty-three . . .*

At the count of 7,058 the second hand began the jump to the next graduation. It took it several apparent minutes to get across the tiny distance, and several more to come completely to rest. Later still, the sound came to him:

Pock.

In a fever of thought, but without any real physical agitation, his mind began to manipulate the figures. Since it took him longer to count an individual number as the number became larger, the interval between the two calendar ticks probably was closer to 7,200 seconds than to 7,058. Figuring backward brought him quickly to the equivalence he wanted:

One second in ship-time was two hours in Garrard-time.

Had he really been counting for what was, for him, two whole hours? There seemed to be no doubt about it. It looked like a long trip ahead.

Just how long it was going to be struck him with stunning force. Time had been slowed for him by a factor of 7200. He would get to Alpha Centauri in just 72,000 months.

Which was—

Six thousand years!

2

Garrard sat motionless for a long time after that, the Nessus-shirt of warm sweat swathing him persistently, refusing even to cool. There was, after all, no hurry.

Six thousand years. There would be food and water and air for all that time, or for sixty or six hundred thousand years; the ship would synthesize his needs, as a matter of course, for as long as the fuel lasted, and the fuel bred itself. Even if Garrard ate a meal every three seconds of objective, or ship, time (which, he realized suddenly, he wouldn't be able to do, for it took the ship several seconds of objective time to prepare and serve up a meal once it was ordered; he'd be lucky if he ate once a day, Garrard-time), there would be no reason to fear any shortage of supplies. That had been one of the earliest of the possibilities for disaster that the Project engineers had ruled out in the design of the DFC-3.

But nobody had thought to provide a mechanism which would indefinitely refurbish Garrard. After six thousand years, there would be nothing left of him but a faint film of dust on the DFC-3's dully gleaming horizontal surfaces. His corpse might outlast him a while, since the ship itself was sterile—but eventually he would be consumed by the bacteria which he carried in his own digestive tract. He needed those bacteria to synthesize part of his B-vitamin needs while he lived, but they would consume him without compunction once he had ceased to be as complicated and delicately balanced a thing as a pilot—or as any other kind of life.

Garrard was, in short, to die before the DFC-3 had gotten fairly away from Sol; and when, after 12,000 apparent years, the DFC-3 returned to Earth, not even his mummy would be still aboard.

The chill that went through him at that seemed almost unrelated to the way he thought he felt about the discovery; it lasted an enormously long time, and insofar as he could characterize it at all, it seemed to be a chill of urgency and excitement—not at all the kind of chill he should be feeling at a virtual death sentence. Luckily it was not as intolerably violent as the last such emotional convulsion; and when it was over, two clock ticks later, it left behind a residuum of doubt.

Suppose that this effect of time-stretching was only mental? The rest of his bodily processes might still be keeping ship-time; Garrard had no immediate reason to believe otherwise. If so, he would be able to move about only on ship-time, too; it would take many apparent months to complete the simplest task.

But he would live, if that were the case. His mind would arrive at Alpha Centauri six thousand years older, and perhaps madder, than his body, but he would live.

If, on the other hand, his bodily movements were going to be as fast as his mental processes, he would have to be enormously careful. He would have to move slowly and exert as little force as possible. The normal human hand movement, in such a task as lifting a pencil, took the pencil from a state of rest to another state of rest by imparting to it an acceleration of about two feet per second per second—and, of course, decelerated it by the same amount. If Garrard were to attempt to impart to a two-pound weight, which was keeping ship-time, an acceleration of 14,440 ft/sec^2 in his time, he'd have to exert a force of 900 pounds on it.

The point was not that it couldn't be done—but that it would take as much effort as pushing a stalled jeep. He'd never be able to lift that pencil with his forearm muscles alone; he'd have to put his back into the task.

And the human body wasn't engineered to maintain stresses of that magnitude indefinitely. Not even the most powerful professional weight-lifter is forced to show his prowess throughout every minute of every day.

Pock.

That was the calendar again; another second had gone by. Or another two hours. It had certainly seemed longer than a second, but less than two hours, too. Evidently subjective time was an intensively recomplicated measure. Even in this world of micro-time—in which Garrard's mind, at least, seemed to be operating—he could make the lapses between calendar ticks seem a little shorter by becoming actively interested in some problem or other. That would help, during the waking hours, but it would help only if the rest of his body were *not* keeping the same time as his mind. If it were not, then he would lead an incredibly active, but perhaps not intolerable, mental life during the many centuries of his awake-time, and would be mercifully asleep for nearly as long.

Both problems—that of how much force he could exert with his body, and how long he could hope to be asleep in his mind—emerged simultaneously into the forefront of his consciousness while he still sat inertly on the hammock, their terms still much muddled together. After the single tick of the calendar, the ship—or the part of it that Garrard could see from here—settled back into complete rigidity. The sound of the engines, too, did not seem to vary in frequency or amplitude, at least as far as his ears could tell. He was still not breathing. Nothing moved, nothing changed.

It was the fact that he could still detect no motion of his diaphragm or his rib cage that decided him at last. His body had to be keeping ship-time, otherwise he would have blacked out from oxygen starvation long before now. That assumption explained, too, those two incredibly prolonged, seemingly sourceless saturnalias of emotion through which he had suffered: they had been nothing more nor less than the response of his endocrine glands to the purely intellectual reactions he had experienced earlier. He had discovered that he was not breathing, had felt a flash of panic and had tried to sit up. Long after his mind had forgotten those two impulses, they had inched their way from his brain down his nerves to the glands and muscles involved, and actual, *physical* panic had supervened. When that was over, he actually *was* sitting up, though the flood of adrenalin had prevented his noticing the motion as he had made it. The later chill—less violent, and apparently associated with the discovery that he might die long before the trip was completed—actually had been his body's response to a much earlier mental command—the abstract fever of interest he had felt while computing the time differential had been responsible for it.

Obviously, he was going to have to be very careful with apparently cold and intellectual impulses of any kind—or he would pay for them later with a prolonged and agonizing glandular reaction. Nevertheless, the discovery gave him considerable satisfaction, and Garrard allowed it free play; it certainly could not hurt him to feel pleased for a few hours, and the glandular pleasure might even prove helpful if it caught him at a moment of mental depression. Six thousand years, after all, provided a considerable number of opportunities for feeling down in the mouth; so it would be best to encourage all pleasure moments, and let the after-reaction last as long as it might. It would be the instants of panic, of fear, of gloom, which he would have to regulate sternly the moment they came into his mind; it would be those which would otherwise plunge him into four, five, six, perhaps even ten, Garrard-hours of emotional inferno.

Pock.

There now, that was very good: there had been two Garrard-hours which he had passed with virtually no difficulty of any kind, and without being especially conscious of their passage. If he could really settle down and become used to this kind of scheduling, the trip might not be as bad as he had at first feared. Sleep would take immense bites out of it; and during the waking periods he could put in one hell of a lot of creative thinking. During a single day of ship-time, Garrard could get in more thinking than any philosopher of Earth could have managed during an entire lifetime. Garrard could, if he disciplined himself sufficiently, devote his mind for a century to running down the consequences of a single thought, down to the last detail, and still have millennia left to go on to the next thought.

What panoplies of pure reason could he not have assembled by the time 6,000 years had gone by? With sufficient concentration, he might come up with the solution to the Problem of Evil between breakfast and dinner of a single ship's day, and in a ship's month might put his finger on the First Cause!

Pock.

Not that Garrard was sanguine enough to expect that he would remain logical or even sane throughout the trip. The vista was still grim, in much of its detail. But the opportunities, too, were there. He felt a momentary regret that it hadn't been Haertel, rather than himself, who had been given such an opportunity—

Pock.

—for the old man could certainly have made better use of it than Garrard could. The situation demanded someone trained in the highest rigors of mathematics to be put to the best conceivable use. Still and all Garrard began to feel—

Pock.

—that he would give a good account of himself, and it tickled him to realize that (as long as he held onto his essential sanity) he would return—

Pock.

—to Earth after ten Earth months with knowledge centuries advanced beyond anything—

Pock.

—that Haertel knew, or that anyone could know—

Pock.

—who had to work within a normal lifetime. *Pck.* The whole prospect tickled him. *Pck.* Even the clock tick seemed more cheerful. *Pck.* He felt fairly safe now *Pck* in disregarding his drilled-in command *Pck* against moving *Pck,* since in any *Pck* event he *Pck* had already *Pck* moved *Pck* without *Pck* being *Pck* harmed *Pck* Pck Pck Pck Pck *pckpckpckpckpckpckpck.* . . .

He yawned, stretched, and got up. It wouldn't do to be too pleased, after all. There were certainly many problems that still needed coping with, such as how to keep the impulse toward getting a ship-time task performed going, while his higher centers were following the ramifications of some purely philosophical point. And besides. . .

And besides, he had just moved.

More than that; he had just performed a complicated maneuver with his body *in normal time!*

Before Garrard looked at the calendar itself, the message it had been ticking away at him had penetrated. While he had been enjoying the protracted, glandular backwash of his earlier feeling of satisfaction, he had failed to notice, at least consciously, that the calendar was accelerating.

Good-bye, vast ethical systems which would dwarf the Greeks. Good-bye, calculuses aeons advanced beyond the spinor calculus of Dirac. Good-bye, cosmologies by Garrard which would allot the Almighty a job as third-assistant-waterboy in an n-dimensional backfield.

Good-bye, also, to a project he had once tried to undertake in college—to describe and count the positions of love, of which, according to under-the-counter myth, there were supposed to be at least forty-eight. Garrard had never been able to carry his tally beyond twenty, and he had just lost what was probably his last opportunity to try again.

The micro-time in which he had been living had worn off, only a few objective minutes after the ship had gone into overdrive and he had come out of the anesthetic. The long intellectual agony, with its glandular counterpoint, had come to nothing. Garrard was now keeping ship-time.

Garrard sat back down on the hammock, uncertain whether to be bitter or relieved. Neither emotion satisfied him in the end; he simply felt unsatisfied. Micro-time had been bad enough while it lasted; but now it was gone, and everything seemed normal. How could so transient a thing have killed Brown and Cellini? They were stable men, more stable, by his own private estimation, than Garrard himself. Yet he had come through it. Was there more to it than this?

And if there was—what, conceivably, could it be?

There was no answer. At his elbow, on the control chassis which he had thrust aside during that first moment of infinitely protracted panic, the calendar continued to tick. The engine noise was gone. His breath came and went in natural rhythm. He felt light and strong. The ship was quiet, calm, unchanging.

The calendar ticked, faster and faster. It reached and passed the first hour, ship-time, of flight in overdrive.

Pock . . .

Garrard looked up in surprise. The familiar noise, this time, had been the hour-hand jumping one unit. The minute-hand was already sweeping past the past half-hour. The second-hand was whirling like a propeller-and while he watched it, it speeded up to complete invisibility

Pock.

Another hour. The half-hour already passed. *Pock.* Another hour. *Pock.* Another. *Pock. Pock. Pock, Pock, Pock, Pock, pck-pck-pck-pck-pckpckpckpck.* . . .

The hands of the calendar swirled toward invisibility as time ran away with Garrard. Yet the ship did not change. It stayed there, rigid, inviolate, invulnerable. When the date tumblers reached a speed at which Garrard could no longer read them, he discovered that once more he could not move—and that, although his whole body seemed to be aflutter like that of a hummingbird, nothing coherent was coming to him through his senses. The room was dimming, becoming redder; or no, it was . . .

But he never saw the end of the process, never was allowed to look from the pinnacle of macro-time toward which the Haertel overdrive was taking him.

Pseudo-death took him first.

3

That Garrard did not die completely, and within a comparatively short time after the DFC-3 had gone into overdrive, was due to the purest of accidents; but Garrard did not know that. In fact, he knew nothing at all for an indefinite period, sitting rigid and staring, his metabolism slowed down to next to nothing, his mind almost utterly inactive. From time, to time, a single wave of low-level metabolic activity passed through him—what an electrician might have termed a "maintenance turnover"—in response to the urgings of some occult survival urge; but these were of so basic a nature as to reach his consciousness not at all. This was the pseudo-death.

When the observer actually arrived, however, Garrard woke. He could make very little sense out of what he saw or felt even now; but one fact was clear: the overdrive was off—and with it the crazy alterations in time rates—and there was strong light coming through one of the ports. The first leg of the trip was over. It had been these two changes in his environment which had restored him to life.

The thing (or things) which had restored him to consciousness, however, was—it was what? It made no sense. It was a construction, a rather fragile one, which completely surrounded his hammock. No, it wasn't a construction, but evidently something alive—a living being, organized horizontally, that had arranged itself in a circle about him. No, it was a number of beings. Or a combination of all these things.

How it had gotten into the ship was a mystery, but there it was. Or there they were.

"How do you hear?" the creature said abruptly. Its voice, or their voices, came at equal volume from every point in the circle, but not from any particular point in it. Garrard could think of no reason why that should be unusual.

"I—" he said. "Or we—we hear with our ears. Here."

His answer, with its unintentionally long chain of open vowel sounds, rang ridiculously. He wondered why he was speaking such an odd language.

"We-they wooed to pitch you-yours thiswise," the creature said. With a thump, a book from the DFC-3's ample library fell to the deck beside the hammock. "We wooed there and there and there for a many. You are the being-Garrard. We-they are the clinesterton beademung, with all of love."

"With all of love," Garrard echoed. The beademung's use of the language they both were speaking was odd; but again Garrard could find no logical reason why the beademung's usage should be considered wrong.

"Are—are you-they from Alpha Centauri?" he said hesitantly.

"Yes, we hear the twin radioceles, that show there beyond the gift-orifices. We-they pitched that the being-Garrard with most adoration these twins and had mind to them, soft and loud alike. How do you hear?"

This time the being-Garrard understood the question. "I hear Earth," he said. "But that is very soft, and does not show."

"Yes," said the beademung. "It is a harmony, not a first, as ours. The All-Devouring listens to lovers there, not on the radioceles. Let me-mine pitch you-yours so to have mind of the rodalent beademung and other brothers and lovers, along the channel which is fragrant to the being-Garrard."

Garrard found that he understood the speech without difficulty. The thought occurred to him that to understand a language on its own terms—without having to put it back into English in one's own mind—is an ability that is won only with difficulty and long practice.

Yet, instantly his mind said, "But it *is* English," which of course it was. The offer the clinesterton beademung had just made was enormously hearted, and he in turn was much minded and of love, to his own delighting as well as to the beademungen; that almost went without saying.

There were many matings of ships after that, and the being-Garrard pitched the harmonies of the beademungen, leaving his ship with the many gift orifices in harmonic for the All-Devouring to love, while the beademungen made show of they-theirs.

He tried, also, to tell how he was out of love with the overdrive, which wooed only spaces and times, and made featurelings. The rodalent beademung wooed the overdrive, but it did not pitch he-them.

Then the being-Garrard knew that all the time was devoured, and he must hear Earth again.

"I pitch you-them to fullest love," he told the beademungen. "I shall adore the radioceles of Alpha and Proxima Centauri, 'on Earth as it is in Heaven.' Now the overdrive my-other must woo and win me, and make me adore a featureling much like silence."

"But you will be pitched again," the clinesterton beademung said. "After you have adored Earth. You are much loved by Time, the All-Devouring. We-they shall wait for this othering."

Privately Garrard did not faith as much, but he said, "Yes, we-they will make a new wooing of the beademungen at some other radiant. With all of love."

On this the beademungen made and pitched adorations, and in the midst the overdrive cut in. The ship with the many gift orifices and the being-Garrard him-other saw the twin radioceles sundered away.

Then, once more, came the pseudo-death.

4

When the small candle lit in the endless cavern of Garrard's pseudo-dead mind, the DFC-3 was well inside the orbit of Uranus. Since the sun was still very small and distant, it made no spectacular display through the nearby port; and nothing called him from the post-death sleep for nearly two days.

The computers waited patiently for him. They were no longer immune to his control; he could now tool the ship back to Earth himself if he so desired. But the computers were also designed to take into account the fact that he might be truly dead by the time the DFC-3 got back. After giving him a solid week, during which time he did nothing but sleep, they took over again. Radio signals began to go out, tuned to a special channel.

An hour later, a very weak signal came back. It was only a directional signal, and it made no sound inside the DFC-3—but it was sufficient to put the big ship in motion again.

It was that which woke Garrard. His conscious mind was still glazed over with the icy spume of the pseudo-death; and as far as he could see the interior of the cabin had not changed one whit, except for the book on the deck—

The book. The clinesterton beademung had dropped it there. But what under God was a clinesterton beademung? And what was he, Garrard, crying about? It didn't make sense. He remembered dimly some kind of experience out there by the Centauri twins—

—*the twin radioceles*—

There was another one of those words. It seemed to have Greek roots, but he knew no Greek—and besides, why would Centaurians speak Greek?

He leaned forward and actuated the switch which would roll the shutter off the front port, actually a telescope with a translucent viewing screen. It showed a few stars, and a faint nimbus off on one edge which might be the Sun. At about one o'clock on the screen, was a planet about the size of a pea which had tiny projections, like teacup handles, on each side. The DFC-3 hadn't passed Saturn on its way out; at that time it had been on the other side of the Sun from the route the starship had had to follow. But the planet was certainly difficult to mistake.

Garrard was on his way home—and he was still alive and sane. Or was he still sane? These fantasies about Centaurians—which still seemed to have such a profound emotional effect upon him—did not argue very well for the stability of his mind.

But they were fading rapidly. When he discovered, clutching at the handiest fragments of the "memories," that the plural of *beademung* was *beademungen,* he stopped taking the problem seriously. Obviously a race of Centaurians who spoke Greek wouldn't also be forming weak German plurals. The whole business had obviously been thrown up by his unconscious.

But what *had* he found by the Centaurus stars?

There was no answer to that question but that incomprehensible garble about love, the All-Devouring, and beademungen. Possibly, he had never seen the Centaurus stars at all, but had been lying here, cold as a mackerel, for the entire twenty months.

Or had it been 12,000 years? After the tricks the overdrive had played with time, there was no way to tell what the objective date actually was. Frantically, Garrard put the telescope into action. Where was the Earth? After 12,000 years—

The Earth was there. Which, he realized swiftly, proved nothing. The Earth had lasted for many millions of years; 12,000 years was nothing to a planet. The Moon was there, too; both were plainly visible, on the far side of the Sun—but not too far to pick them out clearly, with the telescope at highest power. Garrard could even see a clear sun-highlight on the Atlantic Ocean, not far east of Greenland; evidently the computers were bringing the DFC-3 in on the Earth from about 23° north of the plane of the ecliptic.

The Moon, too, had not changed. He could even see on its face the huge splash of white, mimicking the sun-highlight on Earth's ocean, which was the magnesium hydroxide landing beacon, which had been dusted over the Mare Vaporum in the earliest days of space flight, with a dark spot on its southern edge which could only be the crater Monilius.

But that again proved nothing. The Moon never changed. A film of dust laid down by modern man on its face would last for millennia—what, after all, existed on the Moon to blow it away? The Mare Vaporum beacon covered more than 4,000 square miles; age would not dim it, nor could man himself undo it—either accidentally, or on purpose—in anything under a century. When you dust an area that large on a world without atmosphere, it stays dusted.

He checked the stars against his charts. They hadn't moved; why should they have, in only 12,000 years? The pointer stars in the Dipper still pointed to Polaris. Draco, like a fantastic bit of tape, wound between the two Bears, and Cepheus and Cassiopeia, as it always had done. These constellations told him only that it was spring in the northern hemisphere of Earth.

But spring of what year?

Then, suddenly, it occurred to Garrard that he had a method of finding the answer. The Moon causes tides in the Earth, and action and reaction are always equal and opposite. The Moon cannot move things on Earth without itself being affected—and that effect shows up in the moon's angular momentum. The Moon's distance from the Earth increases steadily by 0.6 inches every year. At the end of 12,000 years, it should be 600 feet farther away from the Earth.

Was it possible to measure? Garrard doubted it, but he got out his ephemeris and his dividers anyhow, and took pictures. While he worked, the Earth grew nearer. By the time he had finished his first calculation—which was indecisive, because it allowed a margin for error greater than the distances he was trying to check—Earth and Moon were close enough in the telescope to permit much more accurate measurements.

Which were, he realized wryly, quite unnecessary. The computer had brought the DFC-3 back, not to an observed sun or planet, but simply to a calculated point. That Earth and Moon would not be near that point when the DFC-3 returned was not an assumption that the computer could make. That the Earth was visible from here was already good and sufficient proof that no more time had elapsed than had been calculated for from the beginning.

This was hardly new to Garrard; it had simply been retired to the back of his mind. Actually he had been doing all this figuring for one reason, and one reason only: because deep in his brain, set to work by himself, there was a mechanism that demanded counting. Long ago, while he was still trying to time the ship's calendar, he had initiated compulsive counting—and it appeared that he had been counting ever since. That had been one of the known dangers of deliberately starting such a mental mechanism; and now it was bearing fruit in these perfectly useless astronomical exercises.

The insight was healing. He finished the figures roughly, and that unheard moron deep inside his brain stopped counting at last. It had been pawing its abacus for twenty months now, and Garrard imagined that it was as glad to be retired as he was to feel it go.

His radio squawked, and said anxiously, "DFC-3, DFC-3. Garrard, do you hear me? Are you still alive? Everybody's going wild down here. Garrard, if you hear me, call us!"'

It was Haertel's voice. Garrard closed the dividers so convulsively that one of the points nipped into the heel of his hand. "Haertel, I'm here. DFC-3 to the Project. This is Garrard." And then, without knowing quite why, he added: "With all of love."

Haertel, after all the hoopla was over, was more than interested in the time effects. "It certainly enlarges the manifold in which I was working," he said. "But I think we can account for it in the transformation. Perhaps even factor it out, which would eliminate it as far as the pilot is concerned. We'll see, anyhow."

Garrard swirled his highball reflectively. In Haertel's cramped old office, in the Project's administration shack, he felt both strange and as old, as compressed, constricted. He said, "I don't think I'd do that, Adolph. I think it saved my life."

"How?"

"I told you that I seemed to die after a while. Since I got home, I've been reading; and I've discovered that the psychologists take far less stock in the individuality of the human psyche than you and I do. You and I are physical scientists, so we think about the world as being all outside our skins—something which is to be observed, but which doesn't alter the essential *I*. But evidently, that old solipsistic position isn't quite true. Our very personalities, really, depend in large part upon *all* the things in our environment, large and small, that exist outside our skins. If by some means you could cut a human being off from every sense impression that comes to him from outside, he would cease to exist as a personality within two or three minutes. Probably he would die."

"Unquote: Harry Stack Sullivan," Haertel said; dryly. "So?"

"So," Garrard said, "think of what a monotonous environment the inside of a spaceship is. It's perfectly rigid, still, unchanging, lifeless. In ordinary interplanetary flight, in such an environment, even the most hardened spaceman may go off his rocker now and then. You know the typical spaceman's psychosis as well as I do, I suppose. The man's personality goes rigid, just like his surroundings. Usually he recovers as soon as he makes port, and makes contact with a more-or-less normal world again.

"But in the DFC-3, I was cut off from the world around me much more severely. I couldn't look outside the ports—I was in overdrive, and there was nothing to see. I couldn't communicate with home, because I was going faster than light. And then I found I couldn't move either, for an enormous long while; and that even the instruments that are in constant change for the usual spaceman wouldn't be in motion for me. Even those were fixed.

"After the time rate began to pick up, I found myself in an even more impossible box. The instruments moved, all right, but then they moved too *fast* for me to read them. The whole situation was now utterly rigid—and, in effect, I died. I froze as solid as the ship around me, and stayed that way as long as the overdrive was on."

"By that showing," Haertel said dryly, "the time effects were hardly your friends."

"But they were, Adolph. Look. Your engines act on subjective time; they keep it varying along continuous curves—from far-too-slow to far-too-fast—and, I suppose back down again. Now, this is a *situation of continuous change.* It wasn't marked enough, in the long run, to keep me out of pseudo-death; but it was sufficient to protect me from being obliterated altogether, which I think is what happened to Brown and Cellini. Those men knew that they could shut down the overdrive if they could just get to it, and they killed themselves trying. But I knew that I just had to sit and take it—and, by my great good luck, your sine-curve time variation made it possible for me to survive."

"Ah, ah," Haertel said. "A point worth considering—though I doubt that it will make interstellar travel very popular!"

He dropped back into silence, his thin mouth pursed. Garrard took a grateful pull at his drink.

At last Haertel said: "Why are you in trouble over these Centaurians? It seems to me that you have done a good job. It was nothing that you were a hero—any fool can be brave—but I see also that you *thought,* where Brown and Cellini evidently only reacted. Is there some secret about what you found when you reached those two stars?"

Garrard said, "Yes, there is. But I've already told you what it is. When I came out of the pseudo-death, I was just a sort of plastic palimpsest upon which anybody could have made a mark. My own environment, my ordinary Earth environment, was a hell of a long way off. My present surroundings were nearly as rigid as they had ever been. When I met the Centaurians—if I did, and I'm not at all sure of *that*—*they* became the most important thing in my world, and my personality changed to accommodate and understand them. That was a change about which I couldn't do a thing.

"Possibly I did understand them. But the man who understood them wasn't the same man you're talking to now, Adolph. Now that I'm back on Earth, I don't understand that man. He even spoke English in a way that's gibberish to me. If I can't understand myself during that period—and I can't; I don't even believe that that man was the Garrard I know—what hope have I of telling you or the Project about the Centaurians? They found me in a controlled environment, and they altered me by entering it. Now that they're gone, nothing comes through; I don't even understand why I think they spoke English!"

"Did they have a name for themselves?"

"Sure," Garrard said. "They were the beademungen."

"What did they look like?"

"I never saw them."

Haertel leaned forward. "Then . . ."

"I heard them. I think." Garrard shrugged, and tasted his Scotch again. He was home, and on the whole he was pleased.

But in his malleable mind he heard someone say, *On Earth, as it is in Heaven;* and then, in another voice, which might also have been his own (why had he thought "him-other"?), *It is later than you think.*

"Adolph," he said, "is this all there is to it? Or are we going to go on with it from here? How long will it take to make a better starship, a DFC-4?"

"Many years," Haertel said, smiling kindly. "Don't be anxious, Garrard. You've come back, which is more than the others managed to do, and nobody will ask you to go out again. 1 really think that it's hardly likely that we'll get another ship built during your lifetime; and even if we do, we'll be slow to launch it. We really have very little information about what kind of playground you found out there."

"I'll go," Garrard said. "I'm not afraid to go back—I'd like to go. Now that I know how the DFC-3 behaves, I could take it out again, bring you back proper maps, tapes, photos."

"Do you really think," Haertel said, his face suddenly serious, "that we could let the DFC-3 go out again? Garrard, we're going to take that ship apart practically molecule by molecule; that's preliminary to the building of any DFC-4. And no more can we let you go. I don't mean to be cruel, but has it occurred to you that this desire to go back may be the result of some kind of post-hypnotic suggestion? If so, the more badly you want to go back, the more dangerous to us all you may be. We are going to have to examine you just as thoroughly as we do the ship. If these beademungen wanted you to come back, they must have had a reason—and we have to know that reason."

Garrard nodded, but he knew that Haertel could see the slight movement of his eyebrows and the wrinkles forming in his forehead, the contractions of the small muscles which stop the flow of tears only to make grief patent on the rest of the face.

"In short," he said, *"don't move."*

Haertel looked politely puzzled. Garrard, however, could say nothing more. He had returned to humanity's common time, and would never leave it again.

Not even, for all his dimly remembered promise; with all there was left in him of love.

There Shall Be No Darkness

It was about 10:00 P.M. when Paul Foote decided that there was a monster at Newcliffe's houseparty.

Foote was tight at the time—tighter than he liked to be ever. He sprawled in a too-easy chair in the front room on the end of his spine, his arms resting on the high arms of the chair. A half-empty glass depended laxly his right hand. A darker spot on one gray trouser-leg showed where some of the drink had gone.

Through half-shut eyes he watched Jarmoskowski at the piano.

The pianist was playing, finally, the Scriabin sonata for which the rest of the gathering had been waiting but for Foote, who was a painter with a tin ear, it wasn't music at all. It was a cantrap, whose implications were secret and horrible.

The room was stuffy and was only half as large as it had been during the afternoon and Foote was afraid that he was the only living man in it except for Jan Jarmoskowski. The rest were wax figures, pretending to be humans in an aesthetic trance.

Of Jarmoskowski's vitality there could be no question. He was not handsome but there was in him a pure brute force that had its own beauty—that and the beauty of precision with which the force was controlled. When his big hairy hands came down it seemed that the piano should fall into flinders. But the impact of fingers on keys was calculated to the single dyne.

It was odd to see such delicacy behind such a face. Jarmoskowski's hair grew too low on his rounded head despite the fact that he had avoided carefully any suggestion of Musician's Haircut. His brows were straight, rectangular, so shaggy that they seemed to meet.

From where Foote sat he noticed for the first time the odd way the Pole's ears were placed—tilted forward as if in animal attention, so that the vestigial "point" really was in the uppermost position.

They were cocked directly toward the keyboard, reminding Foote irresistibly of the dog on the His Master's Voice trademark.

Where had he seen that head before? In Matthias Gruenwald,

perhaps—in that panel on the Isenheim Altar that showed the Temptation of St. Anthony. Or was it one of the illustrations in the *Red Grimoire*, those odd old woodcuts that Chris Lundgren called "Rorschak tests of the mediaeval mind" ?

Jarmoskowski finished the Scriabin, paused, touched his hands together reflectively, began a work of his own, the *Galliard Fantasque*.

The wax figures did not stir, but a soft eerie sigh of recognition came from their frozen lips. There was another person in the room but Foote could not tell who it was. When he turned his unfocused eyes to count, his mind went back on him and he never managed to reach a total. But somehow there was the impression of another presence that had not been of the party before.

Jarmoskowski was not the presence. He had been there before. But he had something to do with it. There was an eighth presence now and it had something to do with Jarmoskowski.

What was it?

For it was there—there was no doubt about that. The energy which the rest of Foote's senses ordinarily would have consumed was flowing into his instincts now because his senses were numbed. Acutely, poignantly, his instincts told him of the Monster. It hovered around the piano, sat next to Jarmoskowski as he caressed the musical beast's teeth, blended with the long body and the serpentine fingers.

Foote had never had the horrors from drinking before and he knew he did not have them now. A part of his mind which was not drunk had recognized real horror somewhere in this room. And the whole of his mind, its skeptical barriers down, believed and trembled within itself.

The batlike circling of the frantic notes was stilled abruptly. Foote blinked, startled. "Already?" he said stupidly.

"Already?" Jarmoskowski echoed. "But that's a long piece, Paul. Your fascination speaks well for my writing."

His eyes flashed redly as he looked directly at the painter. Foote tried frantically to remember whether or not his eyes had been red during the afternoon. Or whether it was possible for any man's eyes to be as red at any time as this man's were now.

"The writing?" he said, condensing the far-flung diffusion of his brain. Newcliffe's highballs were damn strong. "Hardly the writing, Jan. Such fingers as those could put fascination into *Three Blind Mice*."

He laughed inside at the parade of emotions which marched across

Jarmoskowski's face. Startlement at a compliment from Foote—for there had been an inexplicable antagonism between the two since the pianist had first arrived—then puzzled reflection—then finally veiled anger as the hidden slur bared its fangs in his mind. Nevertheless the man could laugh at it.

"They are long, aren't they?" he said to the rest of the group, unrolling them like the party noisemakers which turn from snail to snake when blown through. "But it's a mistake to suppose that they assist my playing, I assure you. Mostly they stumble over each other. Especially over this one."

He held up his hands for inspection. Suddenly Foote was trembling. On both hands, the index fingers and the middle fingers were exactly the same length.

"I suppose Lundgren would call me a mutation. It's a nuisance at the piano."

Doris Gilmore, once a student of Jarmoskowski in Prague, and still obviously, painfully, in love with him, shook coppery hair back from her shoulders and held up her own hands.

"My fingers are so stubby," she said ruefully. "Hardly pianist's hands at all."

"The hands of a master pianist," Jarmoskowski said. He smiled, scratching his palms abstractedly, and Foote found himself in a universe of brilliant perfectly-even teeth. No, not perfectly even. The polished rows were bounded almost mathematically by slightly longer cuspids. They reminded him of that idiotic Poe story—was it "Berenice"? Obviously Jarmoskowski would not die a natural death. He would be killed by a dentist for possession of those teeth.

"Three fourths of the greatest pianists I know have hands like truck drivers," Jarmoskowski was saying. "Surgeons too, as Lundgren will tell you. Long fingers tend to be clumsy."

"You seem to manage to make tremendous music, all the same," Newcliffe said, getting up.

"Thank you, Tom." Jarmoskowski seemed to take his host's rising as a signal that he was not going to be required to play any more. He lifted his feet from the pedals and swung them around to the end of the bench. Several of the others rose also. Foote struggled up to numb feet from the infernal depths of the armchair. He set his glass cautiously on the side-table and picked his way over to Christian Lundgren.

"I read your paper, the one you read to the Stockholm Congress," he said, controlling his tongue with difficulty. "Jarmoskowski's hands are—"

"Yes," the psychiatrist said looking at Foote with sharp, troubled eyes. Suddenly Foote was aware of Lundgren's chain of thought. The gray, chubby little man was assessing his drunkenness, and wondering whether or not Foote would have forgotten the whole business in the morning.

Lundgren made a gesture of dismissal. "I saw them, he said, his tone flat. "A mutation probably, as he himself suggests. This is the twentieth century. I'm going to bed and forget it. Which you may take for advice as well as information."

He stalked out of the room, leaving Foote standing alone, wondering whether to be reassured or more alarmed than before. Lundgren should know. Still, if Jarmoskowski was what he seemed—

The party appeared to be surviving quite nicely without Foote. Conversations were starting up about the big room. Jarmoskowski and Doris shared the piano bench and were talking in low tones, punctuated now and then by brilliant arpeggios as the Pole showed her easier ways of handling the work she played before dinner.

James and Bennington, the American critic, were dissecting James' most recent novel for a fascinated Newcliffe. Blandly innocent Caroline Newcliffe was talking to the air about nothing at all. Nobody missed Lundgren and it seemed unlikely that Foote would be missed.

He walked with wobbly nonchalance into the dining room, where the butler was still clearing the table.

"Scuse me," he said. "Little experiment. Return in the morning." He snatched a knife from the table, looked for the door which led from the dining room into the foyer, propelled himself through it. The hallway was dim but intelligible.

As he closed the door to his room he paused for a moment to listen to Jarmoskowski's technical exhibition on the keys. It might be that at midnight Jarmoskowski would give another sort of exhibition. If he did Foote would be glad to have the knife. He shrugged uneasily, closed the door all the way and walked over to his bedroom window.

At 11:30, Jarmoskowski stood alone on the terrace of Newcliffe's country house. Although there was no wind the night was frozen with a piercing cold—but he did not seem to notice it. He stood motionless, like a black statue, with only the long streamers of his breathing, like twin jets of steam from the nostrils of a dragon, to show that he was alive.

Through the haze of lace that curtained Foote's window Jarmoskowski was an heroic pillar of black stone—but a pillar above a fumarole.

The front of the house was entirely dark and the moonlight gleamed dully on the snow. In the dim light the heavy tower which was the central structure was like some ancient donjon-keep. Thin slits of embrasures watched the landscape with a dark vacuity and each of the crowning merlons wore a helmet of snow.

The house huddled against the malice of the white night. A sense of age invested it. The curtains smelt of dust and antiquity. It seemed impossible that anyone but Foote and Jarmoskowski could be alive in it. After a long moment Foote moved the curtain very slightly and drew it back.

His face was drenched in moonlight and he drew back into the dark again, leaving the curtains parted.

If Jarmoskowski saw the furtive motion he gave no sign. He remained engrossed in the acerb beauty of the night. Almost the whole of Newcliffe's estate was visible from where he stood. Even the black border of the forest, beyond the golf course to the right, could be seen through the dry frigid air. A few isolated trees stood nearer the house, casting grotesque shadows on the snow, shadows that flowed and changed shape with infinite slowness as the moon moved.

Jarmoskowski sighed and scratched his left palm. His lips moved soundlessly.

A wandering cloud floated idly toward the moon, its shadow preceding it, gliding in a rush of darkness toward the house. The gentle ripples of the snowbanks contorted in the vast umbra, assumed demon shapes, twisted bodies half-rising from the earth, sinking back, rising again, whirling closer. A damp frigid wind rose briefly, whipping crystalline showers of snow from the terrace flagstones.

The wind died as the shadow engulfed the house. For a long instant the darkness and silence persisted. Then, from somewhere among the stables behind the house, a dog raised his voice in a faint sustained throbbing howl. Others joined him.

Jarmoskowski's teeth gleamed dimly in the occluded moonlight. He stood a moment longer—then his head turned with startling quickness and his eyes flashed a feral scarlet at the dark window where Foote hovered. Foote released the curtains hastily. Even through them he could see the pianist's grim phosphorescent smile. Jarmoskowski went back into the house.

There was a single small light burning in the corridor. Jarmoskowski's room was at the end of the hail next to Foote's. As he walked reflectively toward it the door of the room across from Foote's swung open and Doris Gilmore came out, clad in a housecoat, a towel over her arm and a toothbrush in her hand.

"Oh!" she said. Jarmoskowski turned toward her. Foote slipped behind his back and into Jarmoskowski's room. He did not propose to have Doris a witness to the thing he expected from Jarmoskowski.

In a quieter voice Doris said, "Oh, it's you, Jan. You startled me."

"So I see," Jarmoskowski's voice said. Foote canted one eye around the edge of the door. "It appears that we are the night-owls of the party."

"The rest are tight. Especially that horrible painter. I've been reading the magazines Tom left by my bed and I finally decided to go to sleep too. What have you been doing?"

"Oh, I was just out on the terrace, getting a breath of air. I like the winter night—it bites."

"The dogs are restless, too," she said. "Did you hear them?"

"Yes," Jarmoskowski said and smiled. "Why does a full moon make a dog feel so sorry for himself?"

"Maybe there's a banshee about."

"I doubt it," Jarmoskowski said. "This house isn't old enough to have any family psychopomps. As far as I know none of Tom's or Caroline's relatives have had the privilege of dying in it."

"You talk as if you almost believed it." There was a shiver in her voice. She wrapped the housecoat more tightly about her slim waist.

"I come from a country where belief in such things is common. In Poland most of the skeptics are imported."

"I wish you'd pretend to be an exception," she said. "You give me the creeps."

He nodded seriously. They looked at each other. Then he stepped forward and took her hands in his.

Foote felt a belated flicker of embarrassment. If he were wrong he'd speedily find himself in a position for which no apology would be possible.

The girl was looking up at Jarmoskowski, smiling uncertainly. "Jan," she said.

"No," Jarmoskowski said. "Wait. It has been a long time since Prague."

"I see," she said. She tried to release her hands.

Jarmoskowski said sharply, "You don't see. I was eighteen then. You were—what was it?—eleven, I think. In those days I was proud of your schoolgirl crush but of course infinitely too old for you: I am not so old any more and you are so lovely—no, no, hear me out, please! Doris, I love you now, as I can see you love me, but—"

In the brief pause Foote could hear the sharp indrawn breaths that Doris Gilmore was trying to control. He writhed with shame for himself. He had no business being—

"But we must wait, Doris—until I warn you of something neither of us could have dreamed in the old days."

"Warn me?"

"Yes," Jarmoskowski paused again. Then he said, "You will find it hard to believe. But if you do we may yet be happy. Doris, I cannot be a skeptic. I am—"

He stopped. He had looked down abstractedly at her hands as if searching for precisely the right words. Then, slowly, he turned her hands over until they rested palms up upon his. An expression of inexpressible shock crossed his face and Foote saw his grip tighten spasmodically.

In that silent moment, Foote knew that he had been right about Jarmoskowski and despite his pleasure he was frightened.

For an instant Jarmoskowski shut his eyes. The muscles along his jaw stood out with the violence with which he was clenching his teeth. Then, deliberately, he folded Doris' hands together and his curious fingers made a fist about them. When his eyes opened again they were red as flame in the weak light.

Doris jerked her hands free and crossed them over her breasts. "Jan—what is it? What's the matter?"

His face, that should have been flying into flinders under the force of the thing behind it, came under control muscle by muscle.

"Nothing," he said. "There's really no point in what I was going to say. Nice to have seen you again, Doris. Goodnight."

He brushed past her, walked the rest of the way down the corridor, wrenched back the doorknob of his own room. Foote barely managed to get out of his way.

Behind the house a dog howled and was silent again.

II

In Jarmoskowski's room the moonlight played in through the open window upon a carefully turned-down bed and the cold air had penetrated every cranny. He shut the door and went directly across the room to the table beside his bed. As he crossed the path of silvery light of his shadow oddly foreshortened, so that it looked as if it were walking on all fours. There was a lamp on the side table and he reached for it.

Then he stopped dead still, his hand halfway to the switch. He seemed to be listening. Finally, he turned and looked back across the room, directly at the spot behind the door where Foote was standing.

It was the blackest spot of all, for it had its back to the moon. But Jarmoskowski said immediately, "Hello, Paul. Aren't you up rather late?"

Foote did not reply for a while. His senses were still a little alcohol-numbed and he was overwhelmed by the thing he knew to be. He stood silently in the darkness, watching the Pole's barely-visible figure beside the fresh bed, and the sound of his own breathing was loud in his ears. The broad flat streamer of moonlight lay between them like a metallic river.

"I'm going to bed shortly," he said at last. His voice sounded flat and dead and faraway, as if belonging to someone else entirely. "I just came to issue a little warning."

"Well, well," said Jarmoskowski pleasantly. "Warnings seem to be all the vogue this evening. Do you customarily pay your social calls with a knife in your hand?"

"That's the warning, Jarmoskowski. The knife is a—*silver* knife."

"You must be drunker than ever," said the pianist. "Why don't you just go to bed? We can talk about it in the morning."

"Don't give me that," Foote snapped savagely. "You can't fool me. I know you for what you are."

"All right. I'll bite, as Bennington would say."

"Yes, you'd bite," Foote said and his voice shook a little despite himself. "Shall I give it a name, Jarmoskowski? In Poland they called you *Vrolok*, didn't they? And in France it was *loup-garou*, In the Carpathians it was *stregoica* or *strega* or *Vikoslak*."

"Your command of languages is greater than your common sense. But you interest me strangely. Isn't it a little out of season for such things? The aconites do not bloom in the dead of winter. And perhaps the thing you call so many fluent names is also out of the season in nineteen sixty-two."

"The dogs hate you," Foote said softly. "That was a fine display Brucey put on when Tom brought him in from his run and he found you here. Walked sidewise through the room, growling, watching you with every step until Tom dragged him out. He's howling now. And that shock you got from the table silver at dinner—I heard your excuse about rubber-soled shoes."

"I looked under the table, if you recall, and your shoes turned out to be leather-soled. But was a pretty feeble excuse anyhow, for anybody knows that you can't get an electric shock from an ungrounded piece of tableware, no matter how long you've been scuffing rubber. It was the silver that hurt you the first time you touched it. Silver's deadly, isn't it?

"And those fingers—the index fingers as long as the middle ones—you were clever about those. You were careful to call everybody's attention to them. It's supposed to be the obvious that everybody misses. But Jarmoskowski, that 'Purloined Letter' gag has been worked too often in detective stories. It didn't fool Lundgren and it didn't fool me."

"Ah," Jarmoskowski said. "Quite a catalogue."

"There's more. How does it happen that your eyes were gray all afternoon and turned red as soon as the moon rose? And the palms of your hands—there was some hair growing there, but you shaved it off, didn't you, Jarmoskowski? I've been watching you scratch them. Everything about you, the way you look, the way you act—everything you say screams your nature in a dozen languages to anyone who knows the signs."

After a long silence Jarmoskowski said, "I see. You've been most attentive, Paul—I see you are what people call the suspicious drunk. But I appreciate your warning, Paul. Let us suppose that what you say of me is true. Have you thought that, knowing that you know, I would have no choice any more? That the first word you said to me about it all might brand your palm with the pentagram?"

Foote had not thought about it. He had spent too much time trying to convince himself that it was all a pipe dream. A shock of blinding terror convulsed him. The silver knife clattered to the floor. He snatched up his hands and stared frantically at them, straining his eyes through the blackness. The full horror implicit in Jarmoskowski's suggestion struck him all at once with paralyzing force.

From the other side of his moonlit room, Jarmoskowski's voice came mockingly. "So—you hadn't thought. *Better never* than late, Paul!"

The dim figure of Jarmoskowski began to writhe and ripple in the reflected moonlight. It foreshortened, twisting obscenely, sinking toward the floor, flesh and clothing alike *changing* into something not yet describable.

A cry ripped from Foote's throat and he willed his legs to move with frantic, nightmarish urgency. His clutching hand grasped the doorknob. Tearing his eyes from the hypnotic fascination of the thing that was going on across from him he leaped from his corner and out into the corridor.

A bare second after he had slammed the door, something struck it a frightful blow from the inside. The paneling split. He held it shut with all the strength in his body.

A dim white shape drifted down upon him through the dark corridor and a fresh spasm of fear sent rivers of sweat down on his back, his sides, into his eyes. But it was only the girl.

"Paul! What on earth! What's the *matter*!"

"Quick!" he choked out. "Get something silver—something heavy made out of silver—quick, *quick*!"

Despite her astonishment the frantic urgency in his voice was enough. She darted back into her room.

To Foote it seemed eternity before she returned—an eternity while he listened with abnormally sensitized ears for a sound inside the room. Once he thought he heard a low growl but he was not sure. The sealike hissing and sighing of his blood, rushing through the channels of the inner ear, seemed very loud to him. He couldn't imagine why it was not arousing the whole countryside. He clung to the doorknob and panted.

Then the girl was back, bearing a silver candlestick nearly three feet in length—a weapon that was almost too good, for his fright-weakened muscles had some difficulty in lifting it. He shifted his grip on the knob to his left hand, hefted the candlestick awkwardly.

"All right," he said, in what he hoped was a grim voice. "Now let him come."

"What in heaven's name is this all about?" Doris said. "You're waking everybody in the house with this racket. Look—even one of the dogs is in to see—"

"*The dog!*"

There Shall Be No Darkness

He swung around, releasing the doorknob. Not ten paces from them, an enormous coal-black animal, nearly five feet in length, grinned at them with polished fangs. As soon as it saw Foote move it snarled. Its eyes gleamed red in the single bulb.

It sprang.

Foote lifted the candlestick high and brought it down—but the animal was not there. Somehow the leap was never completed. There was a brief flash of movement at the open end of the corridor, then darkness and silence.

"He saw the candlestick," Foote panted. "Must have jumped out the window and come around through the front door. Saw the silver and beat it."

"Paul!" Doris cried. "What—how did you know that thing would jump? It was so big! Silver—"

He chuckled, surprising even himself. He had a mental picture of what the truth would sound like to Doris. "That," he said, "was a wolf and a whopping one. Even the usual kind of wolf isn't very friendly and—"

Footsteps sounded on the floor above and the voice of Newcliffe, grumbling loudly, came down the stairs. Newcliffe liked his evenings noisy and his nights quiet. The whole house seemed to have heard the commotion, for in a moment a number of half-clad figures were elbowing out into the corridor, wanting to know what was up.

Abruptly the lights went on, revealing blinking faces and pajama-clad forms struggling into robes. Newcliffe came down the stairs. Caroline was with him, impeccable even in disarray, her face openly and honestly ignorant and unashamedly beautiful. She made an excellent foil for Tom. She was no lion-hunter but she loved parties. Evidently she was pleased that the party was starting again.

"What's all this?" Newcliffe demanded in a gravelly voice. "Foote, are you the center of this whirlpool? Why all the noise?"

"Werewolf," said Foote, suddenly very conscious of how meaningless the word would be here. "We've got a werewolf here. And somebody's marked out for him."

How else could you put it? Let it stand.

There was a chorus of "What's" as the group jostled about him. "Eh? What was that? . . . Werewolf, I thought he said . . . What's this all about? . . . Somebody's been a wolf . . . Is that new? What an uproar!"

"Paul," Lundgren's voice cut through. "Details, please."

"Jarmoskowski's a werewolf," Foote said grimly, making his tone as emotionless and factual as he could. "I suspected it earlier tonight and went into his room and accused him of it. He changed shape, right on the spot while I was watching."

The sweat started out afresh at the recollection of that horrible, half-seen mutation. "He came around into the hall and went for us and I scared him off with a silver candlestick for a club." He realized suddenly that he still held the candlestick, brandished it as proof. "Doris saw the wolf—she'll vouch for that."

"I saw a big doglike thing, all right," Doris admitted. "And it did jump at us. It was black and had huge teeth. But—Paul, was that supposed to be Jan? Why, that's ridiculous!"

"It certainly is," Newcliffe said feelingly. "Getting us all up for a practical joke. Probably one of the dogs is loose."

"Do you have any coal-black dogs five feet long?" Foote demanded desperately. "And where's Jarmoskowski now. Why isn't he here? Answer me that!"

Bennington gave a skeptical grunt from the background and opened Jarmoskowski's door. The party tried to jam itself into the room. Foote forced his way through the jam.

"See? He isn't here, either. And the bed's not been slept in. Doris, you saw him go in there. Did you see him come out?"

The girl looked startled. "No, but I was in my room—"

"All right. Here. Look at this." Foote led the way over to the window and pointed. "See? The prints on the snow?"

One by one the others leaned out. There was no arguing it. A set of animal prints, like large dogtracks, led away from a spot just beneath Jarmoskowski's window—a spot where the disturbed snow indicated the landing of some heavy body.

"Follow them around," Foote said. "They lead around to the front door, and in."

"Have you traced them?" James asked.

"I don't have to. I saw the thing, James."

"Maybe he just went for a walk," Caroline suggested.

"Barefoot? There are his shoes."

Bennington vaulted over the windowsill with an agility astonishing for so round a man and plowed away with slippered feet along the line of tracks. A little while later he entered the room behind their backs.

"Paul's right," he said, above the hub-bub of excited conversation.

"The tracks go around to the front door, then come out again and go away around the side of the house toward the golf course." He rolled up his wet pajama-cuffs awkwardly.

"This is crazy," Newcliffe declared angrily. "This is the twentieth century. We're like a lot of little children, panicked by darkness. There's no such thing as a werewolf."

"I wouldn't place any wagers on that," James said. "Millions of people have thought so for hundreds of years. That's a lot of people."

Newcliffe turned sharply to Lundgren. "Chris, I can depend upon you at least to have your wits about you."

The psychiatrist smiled wanly. "You didn't read my Stockholm paper, did you, Tom? I mean my paper on mental diseases. Most of it dealt with lycanthropy— werewolfism."

"You mean—you believe this idiot story?"

"I spotted Jarmoskowski early in the evening," Lundgren said. "He must have shaved the hair on his palms but he has all the other signs—eyes bloodshot with moonrise, first and second fingers of equal length, pointed ears, domed prefrontal bones, elongated upper cuspids or fangs—in short, the typical hyperpineal type—a lycanthrope."

'Why didn't you say something?"

"I have a natural horror of being laughed at," Lundgren said dryly.

"And *I didn't want to draw Jarmoskowski's attention to me.* These endocrine-imbalance cases have a way of making enemies very easily."

Foote grinned ruefully. If he had thought of that part of it before accusing Jarmoskowski he would have kept his big mouth shut.

"Lycanthropy is quite common," Lundgren droned, "but seldom mentioned. It is the little-known aberration of a little-known ductless gland. It appears to enable the victim to control his body."

"I'm still leery of this whole business," Bennington growled, from somewhere deep in his pigeon's chest. "I've known Jan for years. Nice fella—did a lot for me once. And I think there's enough discord in this house so that I won't add to it much if I say I wouldn't trust Paul Foote as far as I could throw him. By heaven, Paul, if this does turn out to be some practical joke of yours—"

"Ask Lundgren," Foote said.

There was dead silence, broken only by heavy breathing. Lundgren was known to every one of them as the world's ultimate authority on hormone-created insanity. Nobody seemed to want to ask him.

"Paul's right," Lundgren said at last. "Take it or leave it. Jarmoskowski is a lycanthrope. A hyper-pineal. No other gland could affect the blood-vessels of the eyes like that or make such a reorganization of the cells possible. Jarmoskowski is inarguably a werewolf."

Bennington sagged, the light of righteous incredulity dying from his eyes. "I'll be damned!" he muttered.

"We've got to get him tonight," Foote said. "He's seen the pentagram on somebody's palm—somebody in the party."

"What's that?" asked James.

"Common illusion of lycanthropic seizures," Lundgren said. "Hallucination, I should say. A five-pointed star inscribed in a circle—you find it in all the old mystical books, right back to the so-called fourth and fifth Books of Moses. The werewolf sees it on the palm of his next victim."

There was a gasping little scream from Doris. "So that's it!" she cried. "Dear God, I'm the one! He saw something on my hand tonight while we were talking in the hall. He was awfully startled and went away without another word. He said he was going to warn me about something and then he—"

"Steady," Bennington said in a soft voice that had all the penetrating power of a thunderclap. "There's safety in numbers. We're all here." Nevertheless, he could not keep himself from glancing surreptitiously over his shoulder.

"Well, that settles it," James said in earnest squeaky tones. "We've got to trail the—the beast and kill him. It should be easy to follow his trail in the snow. We must kill him before he kills Doris or somebody else. Even if he misses us it would be just as bad to have him roaming the countryside."

"What are you going to kill him with?" asked Lundgren matter-of-factly.

"Eh?"

"I said, what are you going to kill him with? With that pineal hormone in his blood he can laugh at any ordinary bullet. And since there are no chapels dedicated to St. Hubert around here you can't scare him to death with a church-blessed bullet."

"Silver will do," Foote said.

"Yes, silver will do. It poisons the pinearin-catalysis. But are you going out to hunt a full-grown wolf, a giant wolf, armed with table silver and candlesticks? Or is somebody here metallurgist enough to cast a decent silver bullet?"

Foote sighed. With the burden of proof lifted from him, completely sobered up by shock, he felt a little more like his old self, despite the pall of horror which hung over them.

"Like I always tell my friends," he said, "there's never a dull moment at a Newcliffe houseparty."

III

The clock struck one-thirty. Foote picked up one of Newcliffe's rifles and hefted it. It felt—useless. He said, "How are you coming?"

The group by the kitchen stove shook their heads in comical unison. One of the gas burners had been jury-rigged as a giant Bunsen burner and they were trying to melt down some soft unalloyed silver articles, mostly of Mexican manufacture.

They were using a small earthenware bowl also Mexican, for a crucible. It was lidded with the bottom of a flower pot, the hole in which had been plugged with a mixture of garden clay and rock wool yanked forcibly out of the insulation in the attic. The awkward flame leapt uncertainly and sent fantastic shadows flickering over their intent faces.

"We've got it melted, all right," Bennington said, lifting the lid cautiously with a pair of kitchen tongs and peering in. "But what do we do now? Drop it from the top of the tower?"

"You can't kill a wolf with buckshot," Newcliffe pointed out. Now that the problem had been reduced temporarily from a hypernatural one to ordinary hunting he was in his element. "And I haven't got a decent shotgun here anyhow. But we ought to be able to whack together a mold. The bullet should be soft enough so that it won't ruin the rifling of my guns."

He opened the door to the cellar stairs and disappeared, carrying several ordinary cartridges in one hand. Faintly the dogs renewed their howling and Doris began to tremble. Foote put his arm around her.

"It's all right," he said. "We'll get him. You're safe enough."

She swallowed. "I know," she agreed in a small voice. "But every time I think of the way he looked at my hands and how red his eyes were—You don't suppose he's prowling around the house? That that's what the dogs are howling about?"

"I don't know," Foote said carefully. "But dogs are funny that way. They can sense things at great distances. I suppose a man with pinearin in his blood would have a strong odor to them. But he probably knows that we're after his scalp, so he won't be hanging around if he's smart."

She managed a tremulous smile. "All right," she said. "I'll try not to be frightened." He gave her an awkward reassuring pat, feeling a little absurd.

"Do you suppose we can use the dogs?" James wanted to know.

"Certainly," said Lundgren. "Dogs have always been our greatest allies against the abnormal. You saw what a rage Jarmoskowski's very presence put Brucey in this afternoon. He must have smelled the incipient seizure. Ah, Tom—what did you manage?"

Newcliffe set a wooden box on the table. "I pried the slug out of one shell for each gun," he said, "and made impressions in clay. The cold has made the stuff pretty hard, so it's a passable mold. Bring the silver over here."

Bennington lifted his improvised crucible from the burner, which immediately shot up a tall blue flame. James carefully turned it off.

"All right, pour," Newcliffe said. "Lundgren, you don't suppose it might help to chant a blessing or something?"

"Not unless Jarmoskowski overheard it—probably not even then since we haven't a priest among us."

"Okay. Pour, Bennington, before the goo hardens." Bennington decanted sluggishly molten silver into each depression in the clay and Newcliffe cleaned away the oozy residue from the casts before it had time to thicken. At any other time the whole scene would have been funny—now it was grimly grotesque. Newcliffe picked up the box and carried it back down to the cellar, where the emasculated cartridges awaited their new slugs.

"Who's going to carry these things, now?" Foote asked. "There are five rifles. James, how about you?"

"I couldn't hit an elephant's rump at three paces. Tom's an expert shot. So is Bennington here, with a shotgun anyhow."

"I can use a rifle," Bennington said diffidently.

"I've done some shooting," Foote said. "During the Battle of the Bulge I even hit something."

"I," Lundgren said, "am an honorary member of the Swiss Militia."

Nobody laughed. Most of them were aware that Lundgren in his own obscure way was bragging, that he had something to brag about. Newcliffe appeared abruptly from the cellar.

"I pried 'em loose, cooled 'em with snow and rolled 'em out with a file. They're probably badly crystallized but we needn't let that worry us."

There Shall Be No Darkness

He put one cartridge in the chamber of each rifle and shot the bolts home. "There's no sense in loading these any more thoroughly; ordinary bullets are no good anyhow, Chris says. Just make your first shots count. Who's elected?"

Foote, Lundgren and Bennington each took a rifle. Newcliffe took the fourth and handed the last one to his wife.

"I say, wait a minute," James objected. "Do you think that's wise, Tom? I mean, taking Caroline along?"

"Why certainly," Newcliffe said, looking surprised. "She shoots like a fiend—she's snatched prizes away from me a couple of times. I thought everybody was going along."

"That isn't right," Foote said. "Especially not Doris, since the wolf—that is, I don't think she ought to go."

Are you going to leave her here by herself?"

"Oh no!" Doris cried. "Not here! I've got to go! I don't want to wait all alone in this house. He might come back, and there'd be nobody here. I couldn't stand it!"

"We're *all* going," Newcliffe concluded. "We can't leave Doris here unprotected and we need Caroline's marksmanship. Let's get going. It's two now."

He put on his heavy coat and, with the heavy eyed butler, went out to get the dogs. The rest of the company got out their own heavy clothes. Doris and Caroline climbed into ski-suits. They assembled one by one in the living room. Lundgren's eyes swung on a vase of iris-like flowers.

"Hello, what's this?" he said.

"Monkshood," Caroline informed him. "We grow it in the greenhouse. It's pretty, isn't it? Though the gardener says it's poisonous."

"Chris," Foote said. "That isn't wolfbane, is it?"

The psychiatrist shook his head. "I'm no botanist. I can't tell one aconite from the other. But it hardly matters. Hyperpineals are allergic to the whole group. The pollen, you see. As in hay fever, your hyperpineal breathes the pollen, anaphylaxis sets in and—"

"The last twist of the knife," James murmured.

A clamoring of dogs outside announced that Newcliffe was ready. With somber faces the party filed out through the front door. For some reason all of them avoided stepping on the wolf's prints in the snow. Their mien was that of condemned prisoners on the way to the tumbrels. Lundgren took one of the sprigs of flowers from the vase.

The moon had passed its zenith and was almost halfway down the sky, projecting the Bastillle-like shadow of the house before it. But there was still plenty of light and the house itself was glowing from basement to tower room. Lundgren located Brucey in the milling yapping pack and abruptly thrust the sprig of flowers under his muzzle. The animal sniffed once, then crouched back and snarled softly.

"Wolfbane," Lundgren said. "Dogs don't react to the other aconites—basis of the legend, no doubt. Better fire your gardener, Caroline, In the end he's to blame for all this in the dead of winter. Lycanthropy normally is an autumn affliction."

James said,

"Even a man who says his prayers
Before he sleeps each night
May turn to a wolf when the wolfbane blooms
And the moon is high and bright."

"Stop it, you give me the horrors," Foote snapped angrily.

"Well, the dog knows now," said Newcliffe. "Good. It would have been hard for them to pick up the spoor from cold snow but Brucey can lead them. Let's go."

The tracks of the wolf were clear and sharp in the snow. It had formed a hard crust from which fine, powdery showers of tiny ice-crystals were shipped by a fitful wind. The tracks led around the side of the house and out across the golf course. The little group plodded grimly along beside them. The spoor was cold for the dogs but every so often they would pick up a faint trace and go bounding ahead, yanking their master after them. For the most part however the party had to depend upon its eyes.

A heavy mass of clouds had gathered in the west. The moon dipped lower. Foote's shadow, grotesquely lengthened, marched on before him and the crusted snow crunched and crackled beneath his feet. There was a watchful unnaturally-still atmosphere to the night and they all moved in tense silence except for a few subdued growls and barks from the dogs.

Once the marks of the werewolf doubled back a short distance, then doubled again as if the monster had turned for a moment to look back at the house before continuing his prowling. For the most part however the trail led directly toward the dark boundary of the woods.

As the brush began to rise about them they stopped by mutual consent and peered warily ahead, rifles held ready for instant action. Far out across the countryside behind them, the great cloud-shadow once more began its sailing. The brilliantly-lit house stood out fantastically in the gloom.

"Should have turned those out," Newcliffe muttered, looking back. "Outlines us."

The dogs strained at their leashes, In the black west was an inaudible muttering as of winter thunder. Brucey pointed a quivering nose at the woods and growled.

"He's in there, all right."

"We'd better step on it," Bennington said, whispering. "Going to be plenty dark in about five minutes. Storm."

Still they hesitated, regarding the menacing darkness of the forest. Then Newcliffe waved his gun hand in the conventional deploy-as-skirmishers signal and plowed forward. The rest spread out in a loosely-spaced line and followed and Foote's finger trembled over his trigger.

The forest in the shrouded darkness was a place of clutching brittle claws, contorted bodies, and the briefly-glimpsed demon-faces of ambushed horrors. It was Dante's jungle, the woods of Purgatory, where each tree was a body frozen in agony and branches were gnarled arms and fingers which groaned in the wind or gave sharp tiny tinkling screams as they were broken off.

The underbrush grasped at Foote's legs. His feet broke jarringly through the crust of snow or were supported by it when he least expected support. His shoulders struck unseen tree-trunks. Imagined things sniffed frightfully at his heels or slunk about him just beyond his range of vision. The touch of a hand was enough to make him jump and smother an involuntary outcry. The dogs strained and panted, weaving, no longer snarling, silent with a vicious intentness.

"They've picked up something, all right," Bennington whispered. "Turn 'em loose, Tom?"

Newcliffe bent and snapped the leashes free. Without a sound the animals shot ahead and disappeared.

Over the forest the oncoming storm-clouds crawled across the moon. Total blackness engulfed them. The beam of a powerful flashlight lanced from Newcliffe's free hand, picking out a path of tracks on the brush-littered snow. The rest of the night drew in closer about the blue-white ray.

"Hate to do this," Newcliffe said. "It gives us away. But he knows we're— Hello, it's snowing."

"Let's go then," Foote said. "The tracks will be blotted out shortly."

A terrible clamorous baying rolled suddenly through the woods. "That's *it*!" Newcliffe shouted. "Listen to them! Go get him, Brucey!"

They crashed ahead. Foote's heart was beating wildly, his nerves at an impossible pitch. The bellowing cry of the dogs echoed all around him, filling the universe with noise.

"They must have sighted him," he panted. "What a racket! They'll raise the whole countryside."

They plowed blindly through the snow-filled woods. Then, without any interval, they stumbled into a small clearing. Snowflakes flocculated the air. Something dashed between Foote's legs, snapping savagely, and he tripped and fell into a drift.

A voice shouted something indistinguishable. Foote's mouth was full of snow. He jerked his head up—and looked straight into the red rage-glowing eyes of the wolf.

It was standing on the other side of the clearing, facing him, the dogs leaping about it, snapping furiously at its legs. It made no sound at all but crouched tiger-fashion, its lips drawn back in a grinning travesty of Jarmoskowski's smile. It lashed at the dogs as they came closer. One of the dogs already lay writhing on the ground, a dark pool spreading from it, staining the snow.

"Shoot, for heaven's sake!" somebody screamed.

Newcliffe clapped his rifle to his shoulder, then lowered it indecisively. "I can't," he said. "The dogs are in the way."

"The heck with the dogs!" James shouted. "This is no fox-hunt! Shoot, Tom, you're the only one of us that's clear."

It was Foote who fired first. The rifle's flat crack echoed through the woods and snow pulled up in a little explosion by the wolf's left hind pad. A concerted groan arose from the party and Newcliffe's voice thundered above it, ordering his dogs back. Bennington aimed with inexorable care.

The werewolf did not wait. With a screaming snarl he burst through the ring of dogs and charged.

Foote jumped in front of Doris, throwing one arm across his throat. The world dissolved into rolling, twisting pandemonium, filled with screaming and shouting and the frantic hatred of dogs. The snow flew thick. Newcliffe's flashlight rolled away and lay on the snow, regarding the tree-tops with an idiot stare.

Then there was the sound of a heavy body moving swiftly away. The shouting died gradually.

"Anybody hurt?" James' voice asked. There was a general chorus of no's. Newcliffe retrieved his flashlight and played it about but the snowfall had reached blizzard proportions and the light showed nothing but shadows and cold confetti.

"He got away," Bennington said. "And the snow will cover his tracks. Better call your dogs back, Tom."

"They're back," Newcliffe said. "When I call them off they come off."

He bent over the body of the injured animal, which was still twitching feebly. "So—so," he said softly. "So— Brucey. Easy—easy. So, Brucey—so."

Still murmuring, he brought his rifle into position with one arm. The dog's tail beat feebly against the snow.

"So, Brucey."

The rifle crashed.

Newcliffe arose, and looked away. "It looks as if we lose round one," he said tonelessly.

IV

It seemed to become daylight very quickly. The butler went phlegmatically around the house, snapping off the lights. If he knew what was going on he gave no sign of it.

"Cappy?" Newcliffe said into the phone. "Listen and get this straight—it's important. Send a cable to Consolidated Warfare Service—no, no, not the Zurich office, they've offices in London—and place an order for a case of .44 calibre rifle cartridges.

"Listen to me, dammit, I'm not through yet—with silver slugs. Yes, that's right—silver—and it had better be the pure stuff, too. No, not sterling, that's too hard. Tell them I want them flown over, and that they've got to arrive here tomorrow. Yes, I know it's impossible but if you offer them enough—yes, of course I'll cover it. Got that?"

"Garlic," Lundgren said to Caroline. She wrote it dutifully on her marketing list. "How many windows does this place have? All right, make it one clove for each and get half a dozen boxes of rosemary, too."

He turned to Foote. "We must cover every angle," he said somberly. "As soon as Tom gets off the phone I'll try to raise the local priest and get him out here with a truckload of silver crucifixes. Understand, Paul, there is a strong physiological basis behind all the mediaeval mumbo-jumbo.

'The herbs are anti-spasmodics—they act rather as ephedrine does in hay fever to reduce the violence of the seizure. It's possible that Jan may not be able to maintain the wolf shape if he gets a good enough sniff. As for the religious trappings, that's all psychological.

"If Jan happens to be a skeptic in such matters they won't bother him but I suspect he's—" Lundgren's English abruptly gave out. The word he wanted obviously was not in his vocabulary. "*Aberglaeubig*," he said. "*Criandre*."

"Superstitious?" Foote suggested, smiling grimly.

"Yes. Yes, certainly. Who has better reason, may I ask?"

"But how does he maintain the wolf shape at all?"

"Oh, that's the easiest part. You know how water takes the shape of a vessel it sits in? Well, protoplasm is a liquid. This pineal hormone lowers the surface tension of the cells and at the same time short-circuits the sympathetic nervous system directly to the cerebral cortex.

"Result, a plastic, malleable body within limits. A wolf is easiest because the skeletons are similar—not much pinearin can do with bone, you see. An ape would be easier, but apes don't eat people."

"And vampires? Are they just advanced cases of the same thing?"

"Vampires," said Lundgren pontifically, "are people we put in padded cells. It's impossible to change the bony structure that much. They just think they're bats. But yes, it's advanced hyperpinealism, In the last stages it is quite something to see.

"The surface tension is lowered so much that the cells begin to boil a way. Pretty soon there is just a mess. The process is arrested when the vascular system can no longer circulate the hormone but of course the victim is dead long before that."

"No cure?"

"None yet. Someday perhaps, but until then— We will be doing Jan a favor."

"Also," Newcliffe was saying, "drive over and pick me up six Browning automatic rifles. Never mind the bipods, just the rifles themselves. What? Well, you might call it a siege. All right, Cappy. No, I won't be in today. Pay everybody off and send them home until further notice."

"It's a good thing," Foote said, "that Newcliffe has money."

"It's a good thing," said Lundgren, "that he has me—and you. We'll see how twentieth century methods can cope with this Dark-Age disease."

Newcliffe hung up and Lundgren took possession of the phone. "As soon as my man gets back from the village I'm going to set out traps. He may be able to detect hidden metal. I've known dogs that could do it by smell in wet weather but it's worth a try."

"What's to prevent his just going away?" Doris asked. Somehow the shadows of exhaustion and fear around her eyes made her lovelier than ever.

"As I understand it he thinks he's bound by the pentagram," Foote said. At the telephone, where Lundgren evidently was listening to a different conversation with each ear, there was an energetic nod.

"In the old books, the figure is supposed to be a sure trap for demons and such if you can lure them into it. And the werewolf feels compelled to go only for the person whom he thinks is marked with it."

Lundgren said, "Excuse me," and put his hand over the mouthpiece. "Only lasts seven days," he said.

"The compulsion? Then we'll have to get him before then."

"Well, maybe we'll sleep tonight anyhow," Doris said dubiously.

Lundgren hung up and rejoined them. "I didn't have much difficulty selling the good Father the idea," he said. "But he only has crucifixes enough for our ground floor windows. By the way, he wants a picture of Jan in case he should turn up in the village."

"There are no existing photographs of Jarmoskowski," Newcliffe said positively. "He never allowed any to be taken. It was a headache to his concert manager."

"That's understandable," Lundgren said. "With his cell radiogens under constant stimulation any picture of him would turn out overexposed anyhow—probably a total blank. And that in turn would expose Jan."

"Well, that's too bad but it's not irreparable," Foote said. He was glad to be of some use again. He opened Newcliffe's desk and took out a sheet of stationery and a pencil. In ten minutes he had produced a head of Jarmoskowski in three quarter profile as he had seen him at the piano that last night so many centuries ago.

Lundgren studied it. "To the life," he said. "I'll send this over by messenger. You draw well, Paul."

Bennington laughed. "You're not telling him anything he doesn't know," he said. Nevertheless, Foote thought, there was considerably less animosity in the critic's manner.

"What now?" James asked.

"We wait," Newcliffe said. "Bennington's gun was ruined by that one handmade slug. We can't afford to have our weapons taken out of action. If I know Consolidated they'll have the machine-made jobs here tomorrow. Then we'll have some hope of getting him. Right now he's shown us he's more than a match for us in open country."

The group looked at each other. Some little understanding of what it would mean to wait through nervous days and fear-stalked nights, helpless and inactive, already showed on their faces. But there were necessities before which the demands of merely human feelings were forced to yield.

The conference broke up in silence.

For Foote, as for the rest, that night was instilled with dread, pregnant every instant with terror of the outcry that the next moment might bring. The waning moon, greenish and sickly, reeled over the house through a sky troubled with fulgurous clouds. An insistent wind made distant wolf-howls, shook from the trees soft sounds like the padding of stealthy paws, rattled windows with the scrape of claws trying for a hold.

The atmosphere of the house, hot and stuffy because of the closed windows and reeking of garlic, was stretched to an impossible tautness with waiting. In the empty room next to Foote there was the imagined coming and going of thin ghosts and the crouched expectancy of a turned-down bed—awaiting an occupant who might depress the sheets in a shocking pattern, perhaps regardless of the tiny pitiful glint of the crucifix upon the pillow. Above him, other sleepers turned restlessly, or groaned and started up from chilling nightmares.

The boundary between the real and the unreal had been let down in his mind and in the flickering shadows of the moon and the dark errands of the ghosts there was no way of making any selection. He had entered the cobwebby blackness of the borderland between the human and the demon, where nothing is ever more than half true—or half untruth.

After awhile, on the threshold of this darkness, the blasphemous voices of the hidden evil things beyond it began to seep through. The wind, abandoning the trees and gables, whispered and echoed the voices, counting the victims slowly as death stalked through the house.

One.

Two.

Three—closer now!

Four—the fourth sleeper struggled a little. Foote could hear a muffled creak of springs over his head.

Five.

Six—who was Six? Who is next? When?

Seven—Oh Lord, I'm next . . . I'm next . . . I'm next.

He curled into a ball, trembling. The wind died away and there was silence, tremendous silence. After a long while he uncurled, swearing at himself but not aloud-because he was afraid to hear his own voice. Cut that out, now. Foote, you bloody fool. You're like a kid hiding from the goblins. You're perfectly safe. Lundgren says so.

Mamma says so.

How the heck does Lundgren know?

He's an expert. He wrote a paper. Go ahead, be a kid. Remember your childhood faith in the printed word? All right then. Go to sleep, will you?

There goes that damned counting again.

But after awhile his worn-down nerves would be denied no longer. He slept a little but fitfully, falling in his dreams through such deep pits of evil that he awoke fighting the covers and gasping for the vitiated garlic-heavy air. There was a fetid foulness in his mouth and his heart pounded. He threw off the covers and sat up, lighting a cigarette with trembling hands and trying not to see the shadows the flame threw.

He was no longer waiting for the night to end. He had forgotten that there ever was such a thing as daylight, was waiting only for the inevitable growl that would herald the last horror. Thus it was a shock almost beyond bearing to look out the window and see the brightening of dawn over the forest.

After staring incredulously at it for a moment he snubbed out his cigarette in the candlestick—which he had been carrying around the house as if it had grown to him—and collapsed. With a sigh he was instantly in deep and dreamless sleep.

When he finally came to consciousness he was being shaken and Bennington's voice was in his ear. "Get up, man, the critic was saying. "No, you needn't reach for the candlestick everything's okay thus far."

Foote grinned. "It's a pleasure to see a friendly expression on your face, Bennington," he said with a faint glow of general relief.

Bennington looked a little abashed. "I misjudged you," he admitted. "I guess it takes a crisis to bring out what's really in a man so that blunt brains like mine can see it. You don't mind if I continue to dislike your latest abstractions, I trust?"

"That's your function," Foote said cheerfully. "To be a gadfly. Now what's happened?"

"Newcliffe got up early and made the rounds of the traps. We got a good-sized rabbit out of one of them and made a stew—very good—you'll see. The other one was empty but there was blood on it and on the snow. Lundgren isn't up yet but we've saved scrapings for him."

James poked his head around the door jamb, then came in. "Hope it cripples him," he said, dextrously snaffling a cigarette from Foote's shirt pocket. "Pardon me. All the servants have deserted us but the butler, and nobody will bring cigarettes up from the village."

"My, my," said Foote. "Everyone feels so chipper. Boy, I never thought I'd be as glad to see any sunrise as I was today's."

"If you—"

There was a sound outside. It sounded like the world's biggest teakettle. Something flitted through the sky, wheeled and came back.

"Gripes," Foote said, shading his eyes. "A big jet job. What's he doing here?"

The plane circled silently, jets cut. It lost flying speed and glided in over the golf course, struck and rolled at breakneck speed straight for the forest. At the last minute the pilot spun to a stop expertly.

"By heaven, I'll bet that's Newcliffe's bullets."

They pounded downstairs. By the time they reached the front room the pilot was coming in with Newcliffe. A heavy case was slung between them.

Newcliffe pried the case open. Then he sighed. "Look at 'em," he said. "Nice, shiny brass cartridges, and dull-silver heads machined for perfect accuracy—yum, yum. I could just stand here and pet them. Where are you from?"

"Croydon," said the pilot. "If you don't mind, Mr. Newcliffe, the company said I was to collect from you. That's a hundred pounds for the cartridges and five hundred for me."

"Cheap enough. Hold on. I'll write you a check."

Foote whistled. He didn't know whether to be more awed by the trans-Atlantic express service or the vast sum it had cost.

The pilot took the check and shortly thereafter the tea-kettle began to whistle again. From another huge wooden crate Newcliffe was handing out brand-new Brownings.

"Now let him come," he said grimly. "Don't worry about wasting shots—there's a full case of clips. As soon as you see him, blaze away like mad. Use it like a hose if you have to."

"Somebody go wake Chris," Bennington said. "He should have lessons too. Doris, go knock on his door like a good girl."

Doris nodded and went upstairs. "Now this stud here," Newcliffe said, "is the fire-control button. You put it in this position and the gun will fire one shot and reload. Put it here and you have to reload it yourself like any rifle. Put it here and it goes into automatic operation, firing every shell in the clip, one after the other."

"*Thunder!*" James said admiringly. "We could stand off an army."

"Wait a minute—there seem to be two missing."

"Those are all you unpacked," Bennington said.

"Yes but there were two older models of my own. I never used 'em because it didn't seem right to hunt with such a cannon. But I got 'em out last night on account of this trouble."

"Oh," Bennington said with an air of sudden enlightenment. "I thought that thing I had looked odd. I slept with one last night. I think Lundgren has another."

"Where is Lundgren? Doris should have had him up by now. Go see, Bennington, and get that gun."

"Isn't there a lot of recoil?" Foote asked.

"Sure. These are really meant to operate from bipods. Hold the gun at your hip, not your shoulder— what's *that?*"

"Bennington's voice," Foote said, suddenly tense. "Something must be wrong with Doris." The four of them clattered for the stairs.

They found Doris at Bennington's feet in front of Lundgren's open door. Evidently she had fainted without a sound. The critic was in the process of being very sick. On Lundgren's bed lay a crimson horror.

The throat was ripped out and the face and all the soft parts of the body had been eaten away. The right leg had been gnawed in one place all the way to the bone, which gleamed white and polished in the reassuring sunlight.

V

Foote stood in the living room by the piano in the full glare of all the electric lights. He hefted the B. A. R. and surveyed the remainder of his companions, who were standing in a puzzled group before him.

"No," he said, "I don't like that. I don't want you all bunched together. String out in a line, in front of me, so I can see everybody."

He grinned briefly. "Got the drop on you, didn't I? Not a rifle in sight. Of course, there's the big candlestick behind you, Newcliffe, but I can shoot quicker than you can club me." His voice grew ugly. "And I will, if you make it necessary. So I would advise everybody—including the women—not to make any sudden moves."

"What is this all about, Paul?" Bennington demanded angrily. "As if things aren't bad enough!"

"You'll see directly. Now line up the way I told you. Quick!" He moved the gun suggestively. "And remember what I said about sudden moves. It may be dark outside but I didn't turn on all the lights for nothing."

Quietly the line formed and the eyes that looked at Foote were narrowed with suspicion of madness—or worse.

"Good. Now we can talk comfortably. You see, after what happened to Chris I'm not taking any chances. That was partly his fault and partly mine. But the gods allow no one to err twice in matters like this. He paid a ghastly price for his second error—a price I don't intend to pay or to see anyone else here pay."

"Would you honor us with an explanation of this error?" Newcliffe said icily.

"Yes. I don't blame you for being angry, Tom, since I'm your guest. But you see I'm forced to treat you all alike for the moment. I was fond of Lundgren."

There was silence for a moment, then a thin in-drawing of breath from Bennington. "You were fond—my Lord!" he whispered raggedly. "What do you mean?"

"I mean that Lundgren was not killed by Jarmoskowski," Foote said coldly and deliberately. "He was killed by someone else. Another werewolf. *One who is standing before me at this moment.*"

A concerted gasp went up.

"Surprised? But it's true. The error for which Chris paid so dearly, which I made too, was this—we forgot to examine everybody for injuries after the encounter with Jan. We forgot one of the cardinal laws of lycanthropy.

"A man who survives being bitten by a werewolf himself becomes a werewolf. That's how the disease is passed on. The pinearin in the saliva gets in the bloodstream, stimulates the victim's own pineal gland and—"

"But nobody was bitten, Paul," Doris said in a reasonable voice.

"Somebody was, lightly. None of you but Chris and myself could know about the bite-infection. Evidently somebody got a few small scratches, didn't think them worth mentioning, put iodine on them and forgot them—until it was too late."

There were slow movements in the line—heads turning surreptitiously, eyes glancing nervously at persons to left and right.

"Once the attack occurred," Foote said relentlessly, "Chris was the logical first victim. The expert, hence the most dangerous enemy. I wish I had thought of this before lunch. I might have seen which one of you was uninterested in his lunch. In any event Chris' safeguards against letting Jarmoskowski in also keep you from getting out. You won't leave this room ever again."

He gritted his teeth and brought himself back into control. "All right," he said. "This is the showdown. Everybody hold up both hands in plain view."

Almost instantly there was a ravening wolf in the room.

Only Foote, who could see at a glance the order of the people in the line, knew who it was. The frightful tragedy of it struck him such a blow that the gun dropped nervelessly from his hands. He wept convulsively. The monster lunged for his throat like a reddish projectile.

Newcliffe's hand darted back, grasped the candlestick. He leapt forward in a swift, catlike motion and brought it down across the werewolf's side. Ribs burst with a horrible splintering sound. The beast spun, snarling with agony. Newcliffe hit it again across the backbone. It fell, screaming, fangs slashing the air.

Three times, with concentrated viciousness, Newcliffe struck at its head. Then it cried out once in an almost familiar voice—and died.

Slowly the cells of its body groped back toward their natural positions. The awful crawling metamorphosis was never completed. But the hairy-haunched thing with the crushed skull which sprawled at Newcliffe's feet was recognizable.

It had been Caroline Newcliffe.

There was a frozen tableau of wax figures in the yellow lamplight. Tears coursed along Foote's palms, dropped from under them, fell silently to the carpet. After awhile he dropped his hands. Bennington's face was gray with illness but rigidly expressionless like a granite statue. James' back was against the wall. He watched the anomalous corpse as if waiting for some new movement.

As for Newcliffe he had no expression at all. He merely stood where he was, the bloody candlestick held loosely in a limp hand.

His eyes were quite empty.

After a moment Doris walked over to Newcliffe and touched his shoulder compassionately. The contact seemed to let something out of him. He shrank visibly into himself, shoulders slumping, his whole body withering visibly into a dry husk.

The candlestick thumped against the floor, rocked wildly on its base, toppled across the body. As it struck, Foote's cigarette butt, which had somehow remained in it all day, tumbled out and rolled crazily along the carpet.

"Tom," Doris said softly. "Come away now. There's nothing you can do."

"Blood," he said emptily. "She had a cut. On her hand. Handled the scrapings from the trap—my trap. I did it. Just a bread knife cut from making canapes. I did it."

"No, you didn't, Tom. Let's get some rest." She took his hand. He followed her obediently, stumbling a little as his blood-spattered shoes scuffed over the thick rug, his breath expelling from his lungs with a soft whisper. The two disappeared up the stairs.

Bennington bolted for the kitchen sink.

Foote sat down on the piano bench, his worn face taut with dried tears, and picked at the dusty keys. The lightly-struck notes aroused James. He crossed the room and looked down at Foote.

"You did well," the novelist said shakily. "Don't condemn yourself, Paul."

Foote nodded. He felt—nothing. Nothing at all.

"The body?"

"Yes. I suppose so." He got up from the bench. Together they carried the tragic corpse out through the house to the greenhouse.

"We should leave her here," Foote said with a faint return of his old irony. "Here's where the wolfbane bloomed and started the whole business."

"Poetic justice, I suppose," James said. "But I don't think it's wise. Tom has a tool shed at the other end that isn't steam heated. It should be cold enough."

Gently they placed the body on the cement floor, laying some gunny-sacks under it, "In the morning," Foote said, "we can have someone come for her."

"How about legal trouble?" James said frowning. "Here's a woman whose skull has been crushed with a blunt instrument."

"I think I can get Lundgren's priest to help us there," Foote said somberly. "They have some authority to make death certificates in this state. Besides, James—is that a woman? Inarguably it isn't Caroline."

James looked sidewise at the hairy, contorted haunches. "Yes. It's—legally it's nothing. I see your point."

Together they went back into the house. "Jarmoskowski?" James said.

"Not tonight. We're all too tired and sick. And we do seem to be safe enough in here. Chris saw to that."

Whatever James had to say in reply was lost in the roar of an automatic rifle somewhere over their heads, exhausting its shots in a quick stream. After a moment there was another burst of ten. Footsteps echoed. Then Bennington came bouncing down the stairs.

"Watch out tonight," he panted. "He's around. I saw him come out of the woods in wolf form. I emptied the clip but missed and he went back again. I sprayed another ten rounds around where I saw him go in but I don't think I hit him."

"Where were you shooting from?"

"The top of the tower." His face was very grim. "Went up for a last look around and there he was. I hope he comes tonight, I want to be the one who kills him."

"How is Tom?"

"Bad. Doesn't seem to know where he is or what he's doing. Well, goodnight. Keep your eyes peeled."

James nodded and followed him upstairs. Foote remained in the empty room a few minutes longer, looking thoughtfully at the splotch of blood on the priceless Persian carpet. Then he felt of his face and throat, looked at his hands, arms and legs, inside his shirt. Not so much as a scratch—Tom had seen to that.

So hard not to hate these afflicted people, so impossible to remember that lycanthropy was a disease like any other! Caroline, like the man in *The Red Laugh*, had been noble-hearted and gentle and had wished no one evil. Yet—

Maybe God is on the side of the werewolves.

The blasphemy of an exhausted mind. Yet he could not put it from him. Suppose Jarmoskowski should conquer his compulsion and lie out of sight until the seven days were over. Then he could disappear. It was a big country. It would not be necessary for him to kill all his victims—just those he actually needed for food. But he could nip a good many. Every other one, say.

And from wherever he lived the circle of lycanthropy would grow and widen and engulf—Maybe God had decided that proper humans had made a mess of running the world, had decided to give the *nosferatu*, the undead, a chance at it. Perhaps the human race was on the threshold of that darkness into which he had looked throughout last night.

He ground his teeth and made an exasperated noise. Shock and exhaustion would drive him as crazy as Newcliffe if he kept this up.

He went around the room, making sure that all the windows were tightly closed and the crucifixes in place, turning out the lights as he went. The garlic was getting rancid—it smelled like mercaptan—but he was too tired to replace it. He clicked out the last light, picked up the candlestick and went out into the hall.

As he passed Doris' room, he noticed that the door was ajar. Inside two voices murmured. Remembering what he had heard before he stopped to eavesdrop.

It was years later that Foote found out exactly what had happened at the very beginning. Doris, physically exhausted by the hideous events of the day, emotionally drained by tending the childlike Newcliffe, feeding him from a spoon and seeing him into bed, had fallen asleep almost immediately.

It was a sleep dreamless except for a vague, dull undercurrent of despair. When the light tapping against the window-panes finally reached her consciousness she had no idea how long she had slumbered.

She struggled to a sitting position and forced her eyelids up. Across the room the moonlight, gleaming in patches against the rotting snow outside, glared through the window. Silhouetted against it was a tall human figure. She could not see its face but there was no mistaking the red glint of the eyes. She clutched for the rifle and brought it awkwardly into position.

Jarmoskowski did not dodge. He moved his arms out a little way away from his body, palms forward in a gesture that looked almost supplicating, and waited. Indecisively she lowered the gun again. Was he inviting death?

As she lowered the weapon she saw that the stud was in the continuous-fire position and carefully she shifted it to *repeat*. She was afraid of the recoil Newcliffe had mentioned, felt surer of her target if she could throw one shot at a time at it.

Jarmoskowski tapped again and motioned with his finger. Reasoning that he would come in if he were able, she took time out to get into her housecoat. Then, holding her finger against the trigger, she went to the window. It was closed tightly and a crucifix, suspended from a silk thread, hung exactly in the center of it. She checked it, and then opened one of the small panes directly above Jarmoskowski's head.

"Hello, Doris," he said softly.

"Hello." She was more uncertain than afraid. Was this actually happening or just the recurrent nightmare? "What do you want? I should shoot you. Can you tell me why I shouldn't?"

"Yes I can. Otherwise I wouldn't have risked exposing myself. That's a nasty-looking weapon."

"There are ten silver bullets in it."

"I know it. I've seen Brownings before. I would be a good target for you too, so I have no hope of escape—my nostrils are full of rosemary." He smiled ruefully. "And Lundgren and Caroline are dead and I am responsible. I deserve to die. That is why I am here."

"You'll get your wish, Jan," she said. "You have some other reason, I know. I will back my wits against yours. I want to ask you questions."

"Ask."

"You have your evening clothes on. Paul said they changed with you. How is that possible?"

"But a wolf has clothes," Jarmoskowski said. "He is not naked like a man. And surely Chris must have spoken of the effect of the pineal upon the cell radiogens. These little bodies act upon any organic matter, including wool or cotton. When I change my clothes change with me. I can hardly say how, for it is in the blood, like musicianship. Either you can or you can't. But they change."

His voice took on a darkly somber tone. "Lundgren was right throughout. This werewolfery is now nothing but a disease. It is not pro-survival. Long ago there must have been a number of mutations which brought the pineal gland into use.

"None of them survived but the werewolves and these are dying. Someday the pineal will come into better use and all men will be able to modify their forms without this terrible madness as a penalty. For us, the lycanthropes, the failures, nothing is left.

"It is not good for a man to wander from country to country, knowing that he is a monster to his fellow-men and cursed eternally by his God—if he can claim a God. I went through Europe, playing the piano and giving pleasure, meeting people, making friends—and always, sooner or later, there were whisperings, and strange looks and dawning horror.

"And whether I was hunted down for the beast I was or whether there was merely a vague gradually-growing revulsion, they drove me out. Hatred, silver bullets, crucifixes—they are all the same in the end.

"Sometimes, I could spend several months without incident in some one place and my life would take on a veneer of normality. I could attend to my music and have people about me that I liked and be—human. Then the wolfbane bloomed and the pollen freighted the air and when the moon shone down on that flower my blood surged with the thing I have within me.

"And then I made apologies to my friends and went north to Sweden, where Lundgren was and where spring was much later. I loved him and I think he missed the truth about me until night before last. I was careful.

"Once or twice I did *not* go North and then the people who had been my friends would be hammering silver behind my back and waiting for me in dark corners. After years of this few places in Europe would have me. With my reputation as a musician spread darker rumors.

"Towns I had never visited closed their gates to me without a word. Concert halls were booked up too many months in advance for me to use them, inns and hotels were filled indefinitely, people were too busy to talk to me, to listen to my playing, to write me any letters.

"I have been in love. That—I cannot describe.

"And then I came to this country. Here no one believes in the werewolf. I sought scientific help—not from Lundgren, because I was afraid I should do him some harm. But here I thought someone would know enough to deal with what I had become.

"It was not so. The primitive hatred of my kind lies at the heart of the human as it lies at the heart of the dog. There was no help for me.

"I am here to ask for an end to it."

Slow tears rolled over Doris' cheeks. The voice faded away indefinitely. It did not seem to end at all but rather to retreat into some limbo where men could not hear it. Jarmoskowski stood silently in the moonlight, his eyes burning bloodily, a somber sullen scarlet.

Doris said, "Jan—Jan, I am sorry, I am so sorry. What can I do?"

"Shoot."

"I—can't!"

"Please, Doris."

The girl was crying uncontrollably. "Jan, don't. I can't. You know I can't. Go away, please go away."

Jarmoskowski said, "Then come with me, Doris. Open the window and come with me."

"Where?"

"Does it matter? You have denied me the death I ask. Would you deny me this last desperate love, would you deny your own love, your own last and deepest desire? It is too late now, too late for you to pretend revulsion. Come with me."

He held out his hands.

"Say goodbye," he said. "Goodbye to these self-righteous humans. I will give you of my blood and we will range the world, wild and uncontrollable, the last of our race. They will remember us, I promise you."

"I am here. Come now."

Like a somnambulist she swung the panes out. Jarmoskowski did not move but looked first at her, then at the crucifix. She lifted one end of the thread and let the little thing tinkle to the floor.

"After us there shall be no darkness comparable to our darkness," Jarmoskowski said. "Let them rest—let the world rest."

He sprang into the room with so sudden, so feral a motion that he seemed hardly to have moved at all. From the doorway the automatic rifle yammered with demoniac ferocity. The impact of the slugs hurled Jarmoskowski back against the wall. Foote lowered the smoking muzzle and took one step into the room.

"Too late, Jan," he said stonily.

Doris wailed like a little girl awakened from a dream. Jarmoskowski's lips moved but there was not enough left of his lungs. The effort to speak brought a bloody froth to his mouth. He stood for an instant, stretched out a hand toward the girl. Then the fingers clenched convulsively and the long body folded.

He smiled, put aside that last of all his purposes and died.

A Dusk of Idols

I can tell you now what happened to Naysmith. He hit Chandala.

Quite by coincidence—he was on his way home at the time—but it caught him. It was in all respects a most peculiar accident. The chances were against it, including that I should have heard anything about it.

Almost everyone in Arm II knows that Chandala is, pre-eminently among civilized planets, a world in mortal agony—and a world about which, essentially, nothing can be done. Naysmith didn't know it. He had had no experience of Arm II and was returning along it from his first contact with the Heart stars when his ship (and mine) touched Chandala briefly. He was on his way back to Earth (which technically is an Arm II planet, but so far out in the hinterlands that no Earthman ever thinks of it as such) when this happened, and since it happened during ship's night, he would never have known the difference if it hadn't been for an attack of simple indigestion which awakened him—and me.

It's very hard to explain the loss of so eminent a surgeon as Naysmith without maligning his character, but as his only confidant, more or less, I don't seem to have much of a choice. The fact is that he should have been the last person in the Galaxy to care about Chandala's agony. He had used his gifts to become exclusively a rich man's surgeon; as far as I know, he had never done any time in a clinic after his residency days. He had gone to the Heart stars only to sterilize, for a very large fortune in fees, the sibling of the Bbiben of Bbenaf—for the fees, and for the additional fortune the honor would bring him later. Bbenaf law requires that the operation be performed by an off-worlder, but Naysmith was the first Earthman to be invited to do it.

But if during the trip there or back some fellow passenger had come down with a simple appendicitis, Naysmith wouldn't have touched him. He would have said, with remote impartiality, that that was the job of the ship's surgeon (me). If for some reason I had been too late to help, Naysmith still would not have lifted a finger.

There are not supposed to be any doctors like that, but there are. Nobody should assume that I think they are in the majority—they are in fact very rare—but I see no point in pretending that they don't exist. They do; and the eminent Naysmith was one of them. He was in fact almost the Platonic ideal of such a doctor. And you do not have to be in the Heart stars to begin to think of the Hippocratic Oath as being quaint, ancient, and remote. You can become isolated from it just as easily on Earth, by the interposition of unclimbable mountains of money, if you share Naysmith's temperament.

His temperament, to put it very simply, was that of a pathologically depressed man carrying a terrible load of anxiety. In him, it showed up by making him a hypochondriac, and I don't think he would ever have gone into medicine at all had it not been for an urgent concern about his own health which set in while he was still in college. I had known him slightly then, and was repelled by him. He was always thinking about his own innards. Nothing pleased him, nothing took him out of himself, he had no eye for any of the elegance and the beauty of the universe outside his own skin. Though he was as brilliant a man as I ever knew, he was a bore, the kind of bore who replies to "How are you?" by telling you how he is, in clinical detail. He was forever certain that his liver or his stomach or some other major organ had just quit on him and was going to have to be removed—probably too suddenly for help to be summoned in time.

It seems inarguable to me, though I am not a psychologist, that he took up medicine primarily in the hope (unrecognized in his own mind) of being able to assess his own troubles better, and treat them himself when he couldn't get another doctor to take them as seriously as he did. Of course this did not work. It is an old proverb in medicine that the man who treats himself has a fool for a physician, which is only a crude way of saying that the doctor-patient relationship absolutely requires that there be two people involved. A man can no more be his own doctor than he can be his own wife, no matter how much he knows about marriage or medicine.

The result was that even after becoming the kind of surgeon who gets called across 50,000 light-years to operate on the sibling of the Bbiben of Bbenaf, he was still a hypochondriac. In fact, he was worse off than ever, because he now had the most elaborate and sophisticated knowledge of all the obscure things that might be wrong with him. He had a lifelong case of interne's syndrome, the cast of mind which makes beginners in medicine sure that they are suffering from everything they have just read about in the textbook. He knew this; he was, as I have said, a brilliant man; though he had reached his ostensible goal, he was now in a position where he did not dare to treat himself, even for the hiccups.

And this was why he called me at midnight, ship's time, to look him over. There was nothing curable the matter with him. He had eaten something on Bbenaf—though he was a big, burly, bearded man, immoderate eating had made him unpleasantly soft—that was having trouble accommodating itself to his Terrestrial protein complement. I judged that tomorrow he would have a slight rash, and thereafter the episode would be over. I told him so.

"Um. Yes. Daresay you're right. Still rather a shock though, to be brought bolt upright like that in the middle of the night."

"Of course. However I'm sure it's nothing more than a slight food allergy—the commonest of all tourist complaints," I added, a little maliciously. "The tablets are antihistaminic, of course. They ought to head off any serious sequelae, and make you a little sleepy to boot. You could use the relaxation, I think."

He nodded absently, without taking any apparent notice of my mean little dig. He did not recognize me, I was quite sure. It had been a long time since college.

"Where are we?" he said. He was wide awake, though his alarm reaction seemed to be wearing off, and he didn't seem to want to take my hint that he use the pills as sleepy drugs; he wanted company, at least for a little while. Well, I was curious, too. He was an eminent man in my own profession, and I had an advantage over him: I knew more about him than he thought I did. If he wanted to talk, I was delighted to let him.

"Chandala, I believe. A real running sore of a planet, but we won't be here long; it's just a message stop."

"Oh? What's the matter with the place? Barbaric?"

"No, not in the usual sense. It's classified as a civilized planet. It's just sick, that's all. Most of the population is being killed off."

"A pandemic?" Naysmith said slowly. "That doesn't sound like a civilized planet."

"It's hard to explain," I said. "It's not just one plague. There are scores of them going. I suppose the simple way to put it is to say that the culture of Chandala doesn't believe in sanitation—but that's not really true either. They believe in it, thoroughly, but they don't practice it very much. In fact a large part of the time they practice it in reverse."

"In reverse? That doesn't make any sense."

"I warned you it was hard to explain. I mean that public health there is a privilege. The ruling classes make it unavailable to the people they govern, as a means of keeping them in line."

"But that's insane!" Naysmith exclaimed.

"I suppose it is, by our ideas. It's obviously very hard to keep under control, anyhow; the rulers often suffer as much as the ruled. But all governments are based on the monopoly of the right to use violence—only the weapons vary from planet to planet. This one is Chandala's. And the Heart stars have decided not to interfere."

He fell silent. I probably had not needed to remind him that what the federation we call the Heart stars decided to do, or not to do, was often very difficult to riddle. Its records reach back about a million years, which however cover only its period of stability. Probably it is as much as twice that old. No Arm II planet belonged to the group yet. Earth could be expected to be allowed to join in about forty-five thousand years—and that was what remained of half our originally allotted trial period; the cut was awarded us after our treaty with the star-dwelling race of Angels. In the meantime, we could expect no help . . . nor could Chandala. Earth was fortunate to be allowed any intercourse whatsoever with the Heart stars; there again, we could thank the Angels—who live forever—for vouching for us.

"Dr. Rosenbaum," Naysmith said slowly, "do you think that's right and proper?"

So he had recognized me after all. He would never have bothered to look up my name on the roster.

"Well, no, I suppose not. But the rule is that every planet is to be allowed to go to hell in its own handbasket. It isn't my rule, or the Earth's rule; but there it is. The Heart stars just won't be bothered with any world that can't achieve stability by itself. They have seen too many of them come and go."

"I think there's more to it than that. Some of the planets that failed to get into the federation failed because they got into planet-wide wars—or into wars with each other."

"Sure," I said, puzzled. "That's just the kind of thing the Heart stars have no use for."

"So they didn't interfere to stop the wars."

"No." Now I was beginning to see what he was driving at, but he bore down on me relentlessly all the same.

"So there is in fact no Heart-star rule that we can't help Chandala if we want to. In fact, doing so may not even prejudice our case with the federation. We just don't know."

"I suppose that's true, but—"

"And, in fact, it might help us? We don't know that either?"

"No, we don't," I admitted, but my patience was beginning to run out. It had been a long night. "All we do know is that the Heart stars follow certain rules of their own. Common sense suggests that our chances would be best if we followed them, too."

"Common sense for our remotely imaginable great-great-greatest of grandchildren, maybe. But by then conditions will have changed beyond our remotest imaginings. Half a millennium!"

"They don't change in the Heart stars. That's the whole point—stability. And above all, I'd avoid picking up a stick of TDX like Chandala. It's obviously just the kind of nonsurvival planet the Heart stars *mean* to exclude by their rules. There'd be nothing you could do with it but blow yourself up. And there's obviously nothing we could do *for* it, anyhow!"

"Gently now, Doctor. Are you sure of that? Sanitation isn't the only public-health technique there is."

"I don't follow you," I said. The fact is that by now I wasn't trying very hard.

"Well," Naysmith said, "consider that there was once a thing called the Roman Empire. It owned all the known world and lasted many centuries. But fifty men with modern weapons could have conquered it, even when it was at its most powerful."

"But the Heart stars—"

"I am not talking about the Heart stars. I'm talking about Chandala. Two physicians with modern field kits could have wiped out almost all the diseases that raddled the Roman Empire. For instance, you and I."

I swallowed and looked at my watch. We were still a good two hours away from takeoff time.

"No, Doctor, you'll have to answer me. Shall we try it?" I could still stall, though I was not hopeful that it would help me much. "I don't understand your motives, Dr. Naysmith. What do you want to try it *for*? The Chandalese are satisfied with their system. They won't thank you for trying to upset it. And where's the profit? I can't see any."

"What kind of profit are you talking about?" Naysmith said, almost abstractedly.

"Well . . . I don't know; that's what I'm asking you. It seems to me you shouldn't lack for money by now. And as for honor, you're up to your eyebrows in that already, and after Bbenaf you'll have much more. And yet you seem to be proposing to throw all that away for a moribund world you never heard of until tonight. And your life, too. They would kill you instantly down there if they knew what you had in mind."

"I don't plan to tell the ruling class, whatever that is, what I have in mind," Naysmith said. "I have that much sense. As for my motives . . . they're properly my own. But I can satisfy your curiosity a little. I know what you see when you look at me: a society doctor. It's not an unusual opinion. My record supports it. Isn't that true?"

I didn't nod, but my silence must have given my assent.

"Yes, it's true, of course. And if I had excuses, I wouldn't give a damn for your opinion—or for Chandala. But you see, I don't. I not only know what the opinion of me is, *but I share it myself.* Now I see a chance to change that opinion of me; not yours, but mine. Does that help you any?"

It did. Every man has his own Holy Grail. Naysmith had just identified his.

"I wish you luck."

"But you won't go along?"

"No," I said, miserable, yet defiantly sure that there were no good reasons why I should join Naysmith's quest—not even the reason that it could not succeed without me and my field kit. It could not succeed with me, either; and my duty lay with the ship, until the day when I might sight my own Grail, whatever that might be. All the same, that one word made me feel like an assassin.

But it did not surprise Naysmith. He had had the good sense to expect nothing else. Whatever the practical notions that had sprung into his head in the last hour or so, and I suppose they were many, he must have known all his life—as we all do—that Grail-hunting is essentially the loneliest of hobbies.

He made himself wholly unpopular on the bridge, which up to now had barely known he was aboard, wangling a ship's gig and a twenty-four-hour delay during which he could be force-fed the language of the nearest city-state by a heuristics expert, and then disembarked. The arrangement was that we were to pick him up on our next cruise, a year from now.

If he had to get off the planet before then, he could go into orbit and wait; he had supplies enough. He also had his full field medical kit, including a space suit. Since it is of the nature of Chandalese political geography to shift without notice, he agreed to base himself on the edge of a volcanic region which we could easily identify from space, yet small enough so that we wouldn't have to map it to find the gig.

Then he left. Everything went without incident (he told me later) until he entered the city-state of Gandu, whose language he had and where our embassy was. He had of course been told that the Chandalese, though humanoid, are three times as tall as Earthmen, but it was a little unnerving all the same to walk among them. Their size suited their world, which was a good twelve thousand miles in diameter. Surprisingly, it was not very dense, a fact nobody had been able to explain, since it was obviously an Earthlike planet; hence there was no gravitational impediment to growing its natives very large, and grow large they did. He would have to do much of his doctoring here on a stepladder, apparently.

The chargé d'affaires at the embassy, like those of us on ship, did his best to dissuade Naysmith.

"I don't say that you can't do something about the situation here," he said. "Very likely you can. But you'll be meddling with their social structure. Public health here is politics, and vice versa. The Heart stars—"

"Bother the Heart stars," Naysmith said, thereby giving the chargé d'affaires the worst fright he had had in years. "If it can be done, it ought to be done. And the best way to do it is to go right to the worst trouble spot."

"That would be Iridu, down the river some fifteen miles," the chargé d'affaires said. "Dying out very rapidly. But it's proscribed, as all those places are."

"Criminal. What about language?"

"Oh, same as here. It's one of three cities that spoke the same tongue. The third one is dead."

"Where do I go to see the head man?"

"To the sewer. He'll be there."

Naysmith stared.

"Well, I'm sorry, but that's the way things are. When you came through the main plaza here, did you see two tall totem poles?"

"Yes."

"The city totems always mark the local entrance to the Grand Sewer of Chandala, and the big stone building behind them is always where the priest-chief lives. And I'm warning you, Dr. Naysmith, he won't give you the time of day."

Naysmith did not bother to argue any more. It seemed to him that no matter how thoroughly a chieftain may subscribe to a political system, he becomes a rebel when it is turned against him—especially if as a consequence he sees his people dying all around him. He left, and went downriver, on a vessel rather like a felucca.

He had enough acumen to realize very early that he was being trailed. One of the two Chandalese following him looked very like a man who had been on duty at the embassy. He did not let it bother him, and in any event, they did not seem to follow him past the gates of Iridu.

He found the central plaza easily enough—that is to say, he was never lost; the physical act of getting through the streets was anything but easy, though he was towing his gear on an antigrav unit. They were heaped with refuse and bodies. Those who still lived made no attempt to clear away the dead or help the dying, but simply sat in the doorways and moaned. The composite sound thrummed through the whole city. Now and then he saw small groups scavenging for food amid all the garbage; and quite frequently he saw individuals drinking from puddles. This last fact perplexed him particularly, for the chargé d'affaires had told him plainly that Chandala boasted excellent water-supply systems.

The reception of the chief-priest was hostile enough, more so than Naysmith had hoped, yet less than the chargé d'affaires had predicted—at least at first. He was obviously sick himself, and seemingly had not bathed in a long time, nor had any of his attendants; but as long as all Naysmith wanted was information, he was grudgingly willing to give it.

"What you observe are the Articles of the Law and their consequences," he said. "Because of high failures before the gods, Iridu and all its people have been abased to the lowest caste; and since it is not meet that people of this caste speak the same tongue as the Exalted, the city is proscribed."

"I can understand that," Naysmith said, guardedly. "But why should that prevent you from taking any care of yourselves? Drinking from puddles—"

"These are the rules for our caste," the priest-chief said. "Not to wash; not to eat aught less than three days old; not to aid the sick or bury the dead. Drinking from puddles is graciously allowed us."

There was no apparent ironic intention in the last sentence. Naysmith said, "Graciously?"

"The water in the city's plumbing now comes directly from the Grand Sewer. The only other alternative is the urine of the anah, but that is for holy men doing penance for the people."

This was a setback. Without decent water he would be sadly handicapped, and obviously what came out of the faucets was not under the control of the doomed city.

"Well, we'll manage somehow. Rain barrels should serve for the time being; I can chlorinate them for you. But it's urgent to start cleaning things up; otherwise, I'll never be able to keep up with all the new cases. Will you help me?"

The priest-chief looked blank. "We can help no one any more, little one."

"You could be a big help. I can probably stop this plague for you, with a few willing hands."

The priest-chief stood up, shakily, but part of his shakiness was black rage. "To break the rules of caste is the highest of failures before the gods," he said. "We are damned to listen to such counsels! Kill him!"

Naysmith was fool enough to pause to protest. Only the fact that most of the gigantic soldiers in the chamber were clumsy with disease, and unused to dealing with so small an object as he, got him out of the building alive. He was pursued to the farther gate of Iridu by a shambling and horrible mob, all the more frightening because there was hardly a healthy creature in its rank.

Outside, he was confronted by a seemingly trackless jungle. He plunged in at hazard, and kept going blindly until he could no longer hear the noise of the pack; evidently they had stopped at the gate. He could thank the proscription of the city-nation for that.

On the other hand, he was lost.

Of course, he had his compass, which might help a little. He did not want to go westward, which would take him back to the river, but also into the vicinity of Iridu again. Besides, his two trackers from Gandu might still be lurking at the west gate, and this time their hostility might be a good deal more active. Striking north-northwest toward Gandu itself was open to the same objection. There seemed to be nothing for it but to go north-northeast, in the hope of arriving at the field of fumaroles and hot springs where his ship was, there to take thought.

He was still utterly determined to try again; shaken though he was, he was convinced that this first failure was only a matter of tactics. But he did have to get back to the ship.

He pushed forward through the wiry tangle. It made it impossible for him to follow a straight compass course; he lost hours climbing and skirting and hacking, and began to worry about the possibility of spending the night in this wilderness, With the thought, there was a sodden thump behind him, and he was stopped as though he had run into a wall. Then there was a diminishing crackle and bumping over his head.

What was holding him back, he realized after a moment, was the tow to his gear. He backtracked. The gear was lying on the moist ground. Some incredibly tough vine had cut the antigrav unit free of it; the other sound he heard had been the unit fighting its way skyward.

Now what? He could not possibly drag all this weight. It occurred to him that he might put on the space suit; that would slow him a good deal, but it would also protect him from the underbrush, which had already slashed him pretty painfully. The rest of the load—a pack and two oxygen bottles—would still be heavy, but maybe not impossibly so.

He got the suit on, though it was difficult without help, and lumbered forward again. It was exhausting, even with the suit's air conditioning to help, but there was nothing he could do about that. At least, if he had to sleep in the jungle, the suit might also keep out vermin, and some larger entities. . .

For some reason, however, the Chandalese forest seemed peculiarly free of large animals. Occasional scamperings and brief glimpses told of creatures which might have been a little like antelope, or like rabbits, but even these were scarce; and there were no cries of predators. This might have been because Chandalese predators were voiceless, but Naysmith doubted this on grounds of simple biology; it seemed more likely that most of the more highly organized wildlife of Chandala had long since been decimated by the plagues the owners of the planet cultivated as though they were ornamental gardens.

* * *

Late in the afternoon, the fates awarded him two lucky breaks. The first of these was a carcass, or rather, a shell. It was the greenish-brown carapace of some creature which, from its size, he first took to be the Chandalese equivalent of a huge land turtle, but on closer examination seemed actually to have been a good deal more like a tick. Well, if any planet had ticks as big as rowboats, it would be Chandala, that much was already plain even to Naysmith. In any event, the shell made an excellent skid for his gear, riding on its back through the undergrowth almost as though it had been designed for the task.

The second boon was the road. He did not recognize it as such at first, for it was much broken and overgrown, but on reflection he decided that this was all to the good; a road that had not been in use for a long time would be a road on which he would be unlikely to meet anybody. It would also not be likely to take him to any populated place, but it seemed to be headed more or less in the direction he wanted to go; and if it meandered a little, it could hardly impose upon him more detours than the jungle did.

He took off the space suit and loaded it into the skid, feeling almost cheerful.

It was dusk when he rounded the bend and saw the dead city. In the gathering gloom, it looked to be almost twice the size of Gandu, despite the fact that much of it had crumbled and fallen.

At its open gates stood the two Chandalese who had followed him downriver, leaning on broad-bladed spears as tall as they were.

Naysmith had a gun, and he did not hesitate.

Had he not recognized the face of the Chandalese from the chargé d'affaires' office, he might have assumed that the two guards were members of some savage tribe. Again, it seemed to him, he had been lucky.

It might be the last such stroke of luck. The presence of the guards testified, almost in letters of fire, that the Chandalese could predict his route with good accuracy—and the spears testified that they did not mean to let him complete it.

Again, it seemed to him that his best chance led through the dead city, protected while he was there by its proscription. He could only hope that the firelands lay within some reachable distance of the city's other side.

The ancient gate towered over him like the Lion Gate of Mycenae as remembered from some nightmare—fully as frowning as that narrow, heavy, tragedy-ridden breach, but more than five times as high. He studied it with sober respect, and perhaps even a little dread, before he could bring himself to step over the bodies of the guards and pass through it. When he did, he was carrying with him one of the broad-bladed fifteen-foot spears, because, he told himself, you never could tell when such a lever might come in handy . . . and because, instinctively, he believed (though he later denied it) that no stranger could pass under that ancient arch without one.

The Atridae, it is very clear, still mutter in their sleep not far below the surface of our waking minds, for all that we no longer allow old Freud to cram our lives back into the straitjackets of those old religious plays. Perhaps one of the changes in us that the Heart stars await is the extirpation of these last shadows of Oedipus, Elektra, Agamemnon, and all those other dark and bloody figures, from the way we think.

Or maybe not. There are still some forty thousand years to go. If after that they tell us that that was one of the things they were waiting for, we probably won't understand what they're talking about.

Carrying the spear awkwardly and towing his belongings behind him in the tick shell, Naysmith plodded toward the center of the dead city. There was nothing left in the streets but an occasional large bone; one that he stumbled over fell promptly to shivers and dust. The scraping noise of his awkward sledge echoed off the fronts of the leaning buildings; otherwise, there was no sound but the end-stopped thuds of his footfalls, and an occasional bluster of evening wind around the tottering, flaking cornices far above his bent head.

In this wise he came draggingly at last into the central plaza, and sat down on a drum of a fallen stone pillar to catch his breath. It was now almost full dark, so dark that nothing cast a shadow any more; instead, the night seemed to be soaking into the ground all around him. There would be, he knew already, no stars; the atmosphere of Chandala was too misty for that. He had perhaps fifteen minutes more to decide what he was going to do.

As he mopped his brow and tried to think, something rustled behind him. Freezing, he looked carefully over his shoulder, back toward the way he had come. Of course he saw nothing; but in this dead silence a sound like that was easy to interpret.

They were still following him. For him, this dead city was not a proscripted sanctuary. Or if it ever had been, it was no longer, since he had killed the two guards.

He stood up, as soundlessly as he could. All his muscles were aching; he felt as soft and helpless as an overripe melon. The shuffling noise stopped at once.

They were already close enough to see him!

He knew that he could vanish quickly enough into any of the tomblike buildings around him, and evade them for a while as deftly as any rat. They probably knew this labyrinth little better than he did, and the sound of their shuffling did not suggest that there were many of them—surely not a large enough force to search a whole city for a man only a third as big as a Chandalese. And they would have to respect taboos that he could scamper past out of simple ignorance.

But if he took that way, he would have to abandon his gear. He could carry his medical kit easily enough, but that was less important to him now than the space suit and its ancillary oxygen bottles—both heavy and clumsy, and both, furthermore, painted white. As long as he could drag them with him in the tick shell, their whiteness would be masked to some extent; but if he had to run with them, he would surely be brought down.

In the last remains of the evening, he stood cautiously forward and inched the sledge toward the center of the plaza, clenching the spear precariously against his side under one armpit, his gun in his other hand. Behind him, something went, *scuffle . . . rustle. . .*

As he had seen on arrival, the broad-mouthed well in the center of the plaza, before the house of the dead and damned priest-chief, was not flanked by the totems he had been taught to expect. Where they should be jutted only two grey and splintered stumps, as though the poles had been pushed over by brute force and toppled into the abyss. On the other side of the well, a stone beast—an anah?—stared forever downward with blind eyes, ready to rend any soul who might try to clamber up again from Hell.

As it might try to do; for a narrow, rail-less stone stairway, slimy and worn, spiralled around the well into the depths.

Around the mouth of the well, almost impossible to see, let alone interpret, in the last glimmers, was a series of bas-reliefs, crudely and hastily cut; he could detect the rawness of the sculpturing even under the weathering of the stone and the moss.

He went cautiously down the steps a little way to look at them.

With no experience whatsoever of Chandalese graphic conventions, he knew that he had little chance of understanding them even had he seen them in full daylight. Nevertheless, it was clear that they told a history . . . and, it seemed to him, a judgment. This city had been condemned, and its totems toppled, because it had been carrying on some kind of congress with the Abyss.

He climbed back to the surface of the plaza, pulling his nose thoughtfully. They were still following him, that was sure. But would they follow him down there? It might be a way to get to the other side of the dead city which would promise him immunity—or at least, a temporary sanctuary of an inverted kind.

He did not delude himself that he could live down there for long. He would have to wear the space suit again, and breathe nothing but the oxygen in the white bottles. He could still keep by him the field medical kit with which he had been planning to re-enrich his opinion of himself, and save a planet; but even with this protection he could not for long breathe the air and drink the water of the pit. As for food, that hardly mattered, because his air and water would run out much sooner.

Let it be said that Naysmith was courageous. He donned the space suit again, and began the descent, lowering his tick-shell coracle before him on a short, taut tether. Bump, bump, bump went the shell down the steps ahead of him, teetering on its back ridge, threatening to slip sidewise and fall into the well at every irregularity in the slimy old platforms. Then he would stop in the blackness and wait until he could no longer hear it rocking. Then down again: bump, bump, bump; step, step, step. Behind him, the butt of the spear scraped against the wall; and once the point lodged abruptly in some chink and nearly threw him.

He had his chest torch going, but it was not much help; the slimy walls of the well seemed to soak up the light, except for an occasional delusive reflection where a rill of seepage oozed down amid the nitre. Down, down, down.

After some centuries, he no longer expected to reach the bottom. There was nothing left in his future but this painful descent. He was still not frightened; only numb, exhausted, beyond caring about himself, beyond believing in the rest of the universe.

Then the steps stopped, sending him staggering in the suit. He touched the wall with a glove—he imagined that he could feel its coldness, though of course he could not—and stood still. His belt radios brought him in nothing but a sort of generalized echo, like running water.

Of course. He flashed the chest light around, and saw the Grand Sewer of Chandala.

He was standing on what appeared to be a wharf made of black basalt, over the edge of which rushed the black waters of an oily river, topped with spinning masses of soapy froth. He could not see the other side, nor the roof of the tunnel it ran in—only the sullen and ceaseless flood, like a cataract of ink. The wharf itself had evidently been awash not long since, for there were still pools standing sullenly wherever the black rock had been worn down; but now the surface of the river was perhaps a foot below the level of the dock.

He looked up. Far aloft, he saw a spot of blue-black sky about the size of a pea, and gleaming in it, one reddish star. Though he was no better judge of distance than any other surgeon or any other man who spends his life doing close work, he thought he was at least a mile beneath the surface. To clamber back up there would be utterly beyond him.

But why a wharf? Who would be embarking on this sunless river, and why? It suggested that the river might go toward some other inhabited place . . . or some place that had once been inhabited. Maybe the Chandalese had been right in condemning the city to death for congress with the pit—and if that Other Place were inhabited even now, it was probably itself underground, and populated by whatever kind of thing might enjoy and prosper by living in total darkness by the side of a sewer—

There was an ear-splitting explosion to Naysmith's right, and something struck his suit just under his armpit. He jerked his light toward the sound, just in time to see fragments of rock scampering away across the wet wharf, skidding and splashing. A heavier piece rolled eccentrically to the edge of the dock and dropped off into the river. Then everything was motionless again.

He bent and picked up the nearest piece. It was part of one of the stones of the staircase.

There was no sanctuary, even here; they were following him down. In a few moments it might occur to them to stone him on purpose; the suit could stand that, but the helmet could not. And above all, he had to keep his air pure.

He had to go on. But there was no longer any walkway; only the wharf and the sewer. Well, then, that way. Grimly he unloaded the tick shell and lowered it into the black water, hitching its tether to a basalt post. Then, carefully, he ballasted it with the pack and the oxygen bottles. It rocked gently in the current, but the ridge along its back served as a rudimentary keel; it would be stable, more or less.

He sat down on the edge of the wharf and dangled his feet into his boat while he probed for the bottom of the river with the point of the spear. The point caught on something after he had thrust nearly twelve feet of the shaft beneath the surface; and steadying himself with this, he transferred his weight into the coracle and sat down.

Smash! Another paving stone broke on the dock. A splinter, evidently a large one, went whooshing past his helmet and dropped into the sewer. Hastily, he jerked the loop of the tether off the basalt post, and poled himself hard out into the middle of the torrent.

The wharf vanished. The shell began to turn round and round. After several minutes, during which he became deathly seasick, Naysmith managed to work out how to use the blade of the spear as a kind of steering oar; if he held it hard against one side of the shell at the back, and shifted the shaft with the vagaries of the current, he could at least keep his frail machine pointed forward.

There was no particular point in steering it any better than that, since he did not know where he was going.

The chest light showed him nothing except an occasional glimpse of a swiftly passing tunnel wall, and after a while he shut it off to conserve power, trusting his sense of balance to keep his shell headed forward and in the middle of the current. Then he struck some obstacle which almost upset him; and though he fought himself back into balance again, the shell seemed sluggish afterwards. He put on the light and discovered that he had shipped so much of the slimy water that the shell was riding only a few inches above the roiling river.

He ripped the flap of his pack open and found a cup to bail with. Thereafter, he kept the light on.

After a while, the noise of the water took on a sort of hissing edge. He hardly noticed it at first; but soon it became sharp, like the squeak of a wet finger on the edge of a glass, and then took on deeper tones until it made the waters boil like the noise of a steam whistle. Turning the belt radio down did him very little good; it dropped the volume of the sound, but not its penetrating quality.

Then the coracle went skidding around a long bend and light burst over him.

He was hurtling past a city, fronted by black basalt docks like the one he had just quitted, but four or five times more extensive. Beyond these were ruins, as far as he could see, tumbled and razed, stark in the unwavering flare of five tall, smokeless plumes of gas flames which towered amid the tumbled stones. It was these five fountains of blue-white fire, as tall as sequoias, which poured out the vast organ-diapason of noise he had heard in the tunnel.

They were probably natural, though he had never seen anything like them before. The ruins, much more obviously, were not; and for them there was no explanation. Broken and aged though they were, the great carved stones still preserved the shapes of geometrical solids which could not possibly have been reassembled into any building Naysmith could imagine, though as a master surgeon he had traded all his life on structural visualization. The size of the pieces did not bother him, for he had come to terms with the fact that the Chandalese were three times as tall as men, but their shapes were as irrational as the solid geometry of a dream.

And the crazy way in which the city had been dumped over, as though something vast and stupid had sat down in the middle of it and lashed a long heavy tail, did not suggest that its destroyers had been Chandalese either.

Then it was gone. He clung to his oar, keeping the coracle pointed forward. He did not relish the thought of going on to a possible meeting with the creatures who had razed that city; but obviously there had been no hope for him in its ruins. It dwindled and dimmed, and then he went wobbling around a bend and even its glow vanished from the sides of the tunnel.

As he turned that corner, something behind him shrieked, cutting through the general roar of noise like a god in torture. He shrank down into the bottom of the boat, almost losing his hold on the spear. The awful yell must have gone on for two or three minutes, utterly overpowering every echo. Then, gradually, it began to die, at first into a sort of hopeless howl, then into a series of raw, hoarse wails, and at last into a choked mixture of weeping and giggling . . . oh! oooh! . . . wheel . . . oh, oh, oh . . . wheel . . . which made Naysmith's every hair stand on end. It was, obviously, only one of the high-pressure gas jets fluting over a rock lip.

Obviously.

After that he was glad to be back in the darkness, however little it promised. The boat bobbed and slithered in the midst of the flood.

On turns it was washed against the walls and Naysmith poled it back into the center of the current as best he could with his break-bone spear, which kept knocking him about the helmet and ribs every time he tried to use it for anything but steering. Some of those collisions were inexplicably soft; he did not try to see why, because he was saving the chest light for bailing, and in any event he was swept by them too fast to look back.

Just under him gurgled the Grand Sewer of Chandala, a torrent of filth and pestilence. He floated down it inside his suit, Naysmith, master surgeon, a bubble of precarious life in a universe of corruption, skimming the entropy gradient clinging to the edges of a tick's carapace . . . and clinging to incorruption to the last.

Again, after a while, he saw light ahead, sullenly red at first, but becoming more and more orange as the boat swept on. For the first time he saw the limits of the tunnel, outlined ahead of him in the form of a broad arch. Could he possibly be approaching the surface? It did not seem possible; it was night up there—and besides, Chandalese daylight was nothing like this.

Then the tunnel mouth was behind him, and he was coasting on an enormous infernal sea.

The light was now a brilliant tangerine color, but he could not see where it came from; billowing clouds of mist rising from the surface of the sewage limited visibility to perhaps fifty feet. The current from the river was quickly dissipated, and the coracle began to drift sidewise; probing with the spear without much hope, he was surprised to touch bottom, and began to pole himself forward with the aid of his compass—though he had almost forgotten why it was that he had wanted to go in that direction.

The bottom was mucky, as was, of course, to be expected; pulling the spear out of it was tiring work. Far overhead in the mists, he twice heard an odd fluttering sound, rather like that of a tightly wound rubber band suddenly released, and once a measured flapping which seemed to pass quite low over his head; he saw nothing, however.

After half an hour he stopped poling to give himself five minutes' rest. Again he began to drift sidewise. Insofar as he could tell, the whole of this infernal deep seemed to be eddying in a slow circle.

Then a tall, slender shadow loomed ahead of him. He drove the spear into the bottom and anchored himself, watching intently, but the shadow remained fixed. Finally he pushed the shell cautiously toward it.

It was a totem pole, obviously very old; almost all its paint was gone, and the exposed wood was grey. There were others ahead; within a few moments he was in what was almost a forest of them, their many mute faces grinning and grimacing at him or staring hopelessly off into the mists. Some of them were canted alarmingly and seemed to be on the verge of falling into the ordure, but even with these he found it hard to set aside the impression that they were watching him.

There was, he realized slowly, a reason for this absurd, frightening feeling. The totems testified to something more than the deaths of uncountable thousands of Chandalese. They were witness also to the fact that this gulf was known and visited, at least by the priest-chief caste; obviously the driving of the poles in this abyss was the final ritual act of condemnation of a city-state. He was not safe from pursuit yet.

And what, he found himself wondering despite his desperation, could it possibly be all about—this completely deliberate, systematic slaughter of whole nations of one's fellow beings by pestilence contrived and abetted? It was certainly not a form of warfare; that he might have understood. It was more like the extermination of the rabbits of Australia by infecting them with a plague. He remembered very dimly that the first settlers of North America had tried, unsuccessfully, to spread smallpox among the Indians for the same reason; but the memory seemed to be no help in understanding Chandala.

Again he heard that rhythmic sound, now much closer, and something large and peculiarly rubbery went by him, almost on a level with his shoulders. At his sudden movement, it rose and perched briefly on one of the totems, just too far ahead in the mist to be clearly visible.

He had not the slightest desire to get any closer to it, but the current was carrying him that way. As he approached, dragging the blade of the spear fruitlessly, the thing seemed to fall off the pole, and with a sudden flap of wings—he could just make out their spread, which seemed to be about four feet—disappeared into the murk.

He touched his gun. It did not reassure him much. It occurred to him that since this sea was visited, anything that lived here might hesitate to attack him, but he knew he could not count on that. The Chandalese might well have truces with such creatures which would not protect Naysmith for an instant. It was imperative to keep going, and if possible, to get out.

The totem poles were beginning to thin out. He could see high-water marks on the remaining ones, which meant that the underground ocean was large enough to show tides, but he had no idea what size that indicated; for one thing, he knew neither the mass nor the distance of Chandala's moon. He did remember, however, that he had seen no tide marks as he had entered the forest of idols, which meant that it was ebbing now; and it seemed to him that the current was distinctly faster than before.

He poled forward vigorously. Several times he heard the flapping noise and the fluttering sounds again, and not these alone. There were other noises. Some of them were impossible to interpret, and some of them so suggestive that he could only pray that he was wrong about them. For a while he tried shutting the radio off, but he found the silence inside the helmet even less possible to endure, as well as cutting him off from possible cues to pursuit.

But the current continued to pick up, and shortly he noticed that he was casting a shadow into the shell before him. If the source of the light, whatever it was, was over the center of the sea, it was either relatively near the water or he had come a long distance; perhaps both.

Then there was a wall looming to his left side. Five more long thrusts with the spear, and there was another on his right. The light dimmed; the water ran faster.

He was back on a river again. By the time the blackness closed down the current was rushing, and once more he was forced to sit down and use the spear as a steering oar. Again ahead of him he heard the scream of gas jets.

Mixed with that sound was another noise, a prolonged roaring which at first completely baffled him. Then, suddenly, he recognized it; it was the sound of a great cataract.

Frantically, he flashed his light about. There was a ledge of sorts beside the torrent, but he was going so fast now that to make a leap for it would risk smashing his helmet. All the same, he had no choice. He thrust the skidding coracle toward the wall and jumped.

He struck fair, on his feet. He secured his balance in time to see the shell swept away, with his pack and spare oxygen bottles.

For a reason he cannot now explain, this amused him.

* * *

This, as Naysmith chooses to tell it, is the end of the meaningful part of the story, though by no means the end of his travails; these he dismisses as "scenery." As his historian, I can't be quite so offhand about them, but he has supplied me with few details to go by.

He found the cataract, not very far ahead; evidently, he had jumped none too soon. As its sound had suggested, it was a monster, leaping over an underground cliff which he guesses must have been four or five miles high, into a cavern which might have been the Great Gulf itself. He says, and I think he is right, that we now have an explanation for the low density of Chandala: If the rest of it has as much underground area as the part he saw, its crust must be extremely porous. By this reckoning, the Chandalese underworld must have almost the surface area of Mars.

It must have seemed a world to itself indeed to Naysmith, standing on the rim of that gulf and looking down at its fire-filled floor. Where the cataract struck, steam rose in huge billows and plumes, and with a scream which forced him to shut off the radio at once. Occasionally the ground shook faintly under his feet.

Face to face with Hell, Naysmith found reason to hope. This inferno, it seemed to him, might well underlie the region of hot springs, geysers, and fumaroles toward which he had been heading from the beginning; and if so, there should be dead volcanic funnels through which he might escape to the surface. This proved to be the case; but first he had to pick his way around the edge of the abyss to search for one, starting occasional rockslides, the heat blasting through his helmet, and all in the most profound and unnatural silence. If this is scenery, I prefer not to be offered any more scenic vacations.

"But on the way, I figured it out," Naysmith told me. "Rituals don't grow without a reason—especially not rituals involving a whole culture. This one has a reason that I should have been the first to see—or any physician should. You, too."

"Thanks. But I don't see it. If the Heart stars do, they aren't telling."

"They must think it's obvious," Naysmith said. "It's eugenics. Most planets select for better genes by controlling breeding. The Chandalese do it by genocide. They force their lower castes to kill themselves off."

"Ugh. Are you sure? Is it scientific? I don't see how it could be, under the circumstances."

"Well, I don't have all the data. But I think a really thorough study of Chandalese history, with a statistician to help, would show that it is. It's also an enormously dangerous method, and it may wind up with the whole planet dead; that's the chance they're taking, and I assume they're aware of it."

"Well," I said, "assuming that it does work, I wouldn't admit a planet that 'survived' by that method into any federation I ran."

"No," Naysmith said soberly. "Neither would I. And there's the rub, you see, because the Heart stars *will*. That's what shook me. I may have been a lousy doctor—and don't waste your breath denying it, you know what I mean—but I've been giving at least lip service to all our standard humanitarian assumptions all my life, without ever examining them. What the Chandalese face up to, and we don't, is that death is now and has always been *the* drive wheel of evolution. They not only face up to it, they *use* it.

"When I was down there in the middle of that sewer, I was in the middle of my own *Goetzendaemmerung*—the twilight of the idols that Nietzsche speaks of. I could see all the totems of my own world, of my own life, falling into the muck . . . shooting like logs over the brink into Hell. And it was then that I knew I couldn't be a surgeon any more."

Come now," I said. "You'll get over it. After all, it's just another planet with strange customs. There are millions of them."

"You weren't there," Naysmith said, looking over my shoulder at nothing. "For you, that's all it is. For me . . . 'No other taste shall change this.' Don't you see? All planets are Chandalas. It's not just that Hell is real. The laws that run it are the laws of life everywhere."

His gaze returned to me. It made me horribly uneasy. "What was it Mephistopheles said? 'Why, this is Hell, nor am I out of it.' The totems are falling all around us as we sit here. One by one, Rosenbaum; one by one."

And that is how we lost Naysmith. It would have been easy enough to say simply that he had a desperate experience on a savage planet and that it damaged his sanity, and let it go at that. But it would not be true. I would dismiss it that way myself if I could.

But I cannot bring myself to forget that the Heart stars classify Chandala as a civilized world.

EARTHMAN, COME HOME

The city hovered, then settled silently through the early morning darkness toward the broad expanse of heath which the planet's Proctors had designated as its landing place. At this hour, the edge of the misty acres of diamonds which were the Greater Magellanic Cloud was just beginning to touch the western horizon; the whole cloud covered nearly 35° of the sky. The cloud would set at 5:12 a.m.; at 6:00 the near edge of the home galaxy would rise, but during the summer the sun rose earlier and would blot it out.

All of which was quite all right with Mayor Amalfi. The fact that no significant amount of the home galaxy would begin to show in the night sky for months was one of the reasons why he had chosen this planet to settle on. The situation confronting the city posed problems enough without its being complicated by an unsatisfiable homesickness.

The city grounded, and the last residual hum of the spindizzies stopped. From below there came a rapidly rising and more erratic hum of human activity, and the clank and roar of heavy equipment getting under way. The geology team was losing no time, as usual.

Amalfi, however, felt no disposition to go down at once. He remained on the balcony of City Hall looking at the thickly-set night sky. The star-density here in the Greater Magellanic was very high, even outside the clusters—at most, the distances between stars were matters of light-months rather than light-years. Even should it prove impossible to move the city itself again—which was inevitable, considering that the Sixtieth Street spindizzy had just followed the Twenty-third Street machine into the junkpit—it should be possible to set interstellar commerce going here by cargoship. The city's remaining drivers, ripped out and remounted on a one-per-hull basis, would provide the nucleus of quite a respectable little fleet.

It would not be much like cruising among the far-scattered, various civilizations of the Milky Way had been, but it would be commerce of a sort, and commerce was the Okies' oxygen.

He looked down. The brilliant starlight showed that the blasted heath extended all the way to the horizon in the west; in the east it stopped about a kilo away and gave place to land regularly divided into tiny squares. Whether each of these minuscule fields represented an individual farm he could not tell, but he had his suspicions. The language the Proctors had used in giving the city permission to land had had decidedly feudal overtones.

While he watched, the black skeleton of some tall structure erected itself swiftly nearby, between the city and the eastern stretch of the heath. The geology team already had its derrick in place. The phone at the balcony's rim buzzed and Amalfi picked it up.

"Boss, we're going to drill now," the voice of Mark Hazleton, the city manager, said. "Coming down?"

"Yes. What do the soundings show?"

"Nothing very hopeful, but we'll know for sure shortly. This does look like oil land, I must say."

"We've been fooled before," Amalfi grunted. "Start boring; I'll be right down."

He had barely hung up the phone when the burring roar of the molar drill violated the still summer night, echoing calamitously among the buildings of the city. It was almost certainly the first time any planet in the Greater Magellanic had heard the protest of collapsing molecules, though the technique had been a century out of date back in the Milky Way.

Amalfi was delayed by one demand and another all the way to the field, so that it was already dawn when he arrived. The test bore had been sunk and the drill was being pulled up again; the team had put up a second derrick, from the top of which Hazleton waved to him. Amalfi waved back and went up in the lift.

There was a strong, warm wind blowing at the top, which had completely tangled Hazleton's hair under the earphone clips. To Amalfi, who was bald, it could make no such difference, but after years of the city's precise air-conditioning it did obscure things to his emotions.

"Anything yet, Mark?"

"You're just in time. Here she comes."

The first derrick rocked as the long core sprang from the earth and slammed into its side girders. There was no answering black fountain. Amalfi leaned over the rail and watched the sampling crew rope in the cartridge and guide it back down to the ground. The winch rattled and choked off, its motor panting.

"No soap," Hazleton said disgustedly. "I knew we shouldn't have trusted the Proctors."

"There's oil under here somewhere all the same," Amalfi said. "We'll get it out. Let's go down."

On the ground, the senior geologist had split the cartridge and was telling his way down the boring with a mass-pencil. He shot Amalfi a quick reptilian glance as the mayor's blocky shadow fell across the table.

"No dome," he said succinctly.

Amalfi thought about it. Now that the city was permanently cut off from the home galaxy, no work that it could do for money would mean a great deal to it. What was needed first of all was oil, so that the city could eat. Work that would yield good returns in the local currency would have to come much later. Right now the city would have to work for payment in drilling permits.

At the first contact that had seemed to be easy enough. This planet's natives had never been able to get below the biggest and most obvious oil domes, so there should be plenty of oil left for the city. In turn, the city could throw up enough low-grade molybdenum and tungsten as a by-product of drilling to satisfy the terms of the Proctors. But if there was no oil to crack for food—

"Sink two more shafts," Amalfi said. "You've got an oil-bearing till down there, anyhow. We'll pressure jellied gasoline into it and split it. Ride along a Number Eleven gravel to hold the seam open. If there's no dome, we'll boil the oil out."

"Steak yesterday and steak tomorrow," Hazleton murmured. "But never steak today."

Amalfi swung upon the city manager, feeling the blood charging upward through his thick neck. "Do you think you'll get fed any other way?" he growled. "This planet is going to be home for us from now on. Would you rather take up farming, like the natives? I thought you outgrew *that* notion after the raid on Gort."

"That isn't what I meant," Hazleton said quietly. His heavily space-tanned face could not pale, but it blued a little under the taut, weathered bronze. "I know just as well as you do that we're here for good. It just seemed funny to me that settling down on a planet for good should begin just like any other job."

"I'm sorry," Amalfi said, mollified. "I shouldn't be so jumpy. Well, we don't know yet how well off we are. The natives never have mined this planet to anything like pay-dirt depth, and they refine stuff by throwing it into a stew pot. If we can get past this food problem, we've still got a good chance of turning this whole Cloud into a tidy corporation."

He turned his back abruptly on the derricks and began to walk slowly eastward away from the city. "I feel like a walk," he said. "Like to come along, Mark?"

"A walk?" Hazleton looked puzzled. "Why—sure. O.K., boss."

For a while they trudged in silence over the heath. The going was rough; the soil was clayey, and heavily gullied, particularly deceptive in the early morning light. Very little seemed to grow on it: only an occasional bit of low, starved shrubbery, a patch of tough, nettlelike stalks, a few clinging weeds like crabgrass.

"This doesn't strike me as good farming land," Hazleton said. "Not that I know a thing about it."

"There's better land farther out, as you saw from the city," Amalfi said. "But I agree about the heath. It's blasted land. I wouldn't even believe it was radiologically safe until I saw the instrument readings with my own eyes."

"A war?"

"Long ago, maybe. But I think geology did most of the damage. The land was let alone too long; the topsoil's all gone. It's odd, considering how intensively the rest of the planet seems to be farmed."

They half-slid into a deep arroyo and scrambled up the other side. "Boss, straighten me out on something," Hazleton said. "Why did we adopt this planet, even after we found that it had people of its own? We passed several others that would have done as well. Are we going to push the local population out? We're not too well set up for that, even if it were legal or just."

"Do you think there are Earth cops in the Greater Magellanic, Mark?"

"No," Hazleton said, "but there are Okies now, and if I wanted justice I'd go to Okies, not to cops. What's the answer, Amalfi?"

"We may have to do a little judicious pushing," Amalfi said, squinting ahead. The double suns were glaring directly in their faces. "It's all in knowing where to push, Mark. You heard the character some of the outlying planets gave this place, when we spoke to them on the way in."

"They hate the smell of it," Hazleton said, carefully removing a burr from his ankle. "It's my guess that the Proctors made some early expeditions unwelcome. Still—"

Amalfi topped a rise and held out one hand. The city manager fell silent almost automatically, and clambered up beside him.

The cultivated land began, only a few meters away. Watching them were two—creatures.

One, plainly, was a man; a naked man, the color of chocolate, with matted blue-black hair. He was standing at the handle of a single-bladed plow, which looked to be made of the bones of some large animal. The furrow that he had been opening stretched behind him beside its fellows, and farther back in the field there was a low hut. The man was standing, shading his eyes, evidently looking across the dusky heath toward the Okie city. His shoulders were enormously broad and muscular, but bowed even when he stood erect, as now.

The figure leaning into the stiff leather straps which drew the plow also was human; a woman. Her head hung down, as did her arms, and her hair, as black as the man's but somewhat longer, fell forward and hid her face.

As Hazleton froze, the man lowered his head until he was looking directly at the Okies. His eyes were blue and unexpectedly piercing. "Are you the gods from the city?" he said.

Hazleton's lips moved. The serf could hear nothing; Hazleton was speaking into his throat-mike, audible only to the receiver imbedded in Amalfi's right mastoid bone.

"English, by the gods of all stars! The Proctors speak Interlingua. What's this, boss? Was the Cloud colonized *that* far back?"

Amalfi shook his head. "We're from the city," the mayor said aloud, in the same tongue. "What's your name, young fella?"

"Karst, lord."

"Don't call me 'lord.' I'm not one of your Proctors. Is this your land?"

"No, lord. Excuse . . . I have no other word—"

"My name is Amalfi."

"This is the Proctors' land, Amalfi. I work this land. Are you of Earth?"

Amalfi shot a swift sidelong glance at Hazleton. The city manager's face was expressionless.

"Yes," Amalfi said. "How did you know?"

"By the wonder," Karst said. "It is a great wonder, to raise a city in a single night. IMT itself took nine men of hands of thumbs of suns to build, the singers say. To raise a second city on the Barrens overnight—such a thing is beyond words."

He stepped away from the plow, walking with painful, hesitant steps, as if all his massive muscles hurt him. The woman raised her head from the traces and pulled the hair back from her face. The eyes that looked forth at the Okies were dull, but there were phosphorescent stirrings of alarm behind them. She reached out and grasped Karst by the elbow.

"It . . . is nothing," she said.

He shook her off. "You have built a city over one of night," he I repeated. "You speak the Engh tongue, as we do on feast days. You speak to such as me, with words, not with the whips with the little tags. You have fine woven clothes, with patches of color of finewoven cloth."

It was beyond doubt the longest speech he had ever made in his life. The clay on his forehead was beginning to streak with the effort.

"You are right," Amalfi said. "We are from Earth, though we left it long ago. I will tell you something else, Karst. You, too, are of Earth."

"That is not so," Karst said, retreating a step. "I was born here, and all my people. None claim Earth blood—"

"I understand," Amalfi said. "You are of this planet. But you are an Earthman. And I will tell you something else. I do not think the Proctors are Earthmen. I think they lost the right to call themselves Earthmen long ago, on another planet, a planet named Thor V."

Karst wiped his calloused palms against his thighs. "I want to understand," he said. "Teach me."

"Karst!" the woman said pleadingly. "It is nothing. Wonders pass. We are late with the planting."

"Teach me," Karst said doggedly. "All our lives we furrow the fields, and on the holidays they tell us of Earth. Now there is a marvel here, a city raised by the hands of Earthmen, there are Earthmen in it who speak to us—" He stopped. He seemed to have something in his throat.

"Go on," Amalfi said gently.

"Teach me. Now that Earth has built a city on the Barrens, the Proctors cannot hold knowledge for their own any longer. Even when you go, we will learn from your empty city, before it is ruin by wind and rain. Lord Amalfi, if we are Earthmen, teach us as Earthmen are teached."

"Karst," said the woman, "it is not for us. It is a magic of the Proctors. All magics are of the Proctors. They mean to take us from our children. They mean us to die on the Barrens. They tempt us."

The serf turned to her. There was something indefinably gentle in the motion of his brutalized, crackle-skinned, thick-muscled body.

"You need not go," he said, in a slurred Interlingua patois which was obviously his usual tongue. "Go on with the plowing, does it please you. But this is no thing of the Proctors. They would not stoop to tempt slaves as mean as we are. We have obeyed the laws, given our tithes, observed the holidays. This is of Earth."

The woman clenched her horny hands under her chin and shivered. "It is forbidden to speak of Earth except on holidays. But I will finish the plowing. Otherwise our children will die."

"Come, then," Amalfi said. "There is much to learn."

To his complete consternation, the serf went down on both knees. A second later, while Amalfi was still wondering what to do next, Karst was up again, and climbing up onto the Barrens toward them. Hazleton offered him a hand, and was nearly hurled like a flat stone through the air when Karst took it; the serf was as solid and strong as a pile driver, and as sure on his stony feet.

"Karst, will you return before night?" the woman cried.

Karst did not answer. Amalfi began to lead the way back toward the city. Hazleton started down the far side of the rise after them, but something moved him to look back again at the little scrap of farm. The woman's head had fallen forward again, the wind stirring the tangled curtain of her hair. She was leaning heavily into the galling traces, and the plow was again beginning to cut its way painfully through the stony soil. There was now, of course, nobody to guide it.

"Boss," Hazleton said into the throat-mike, "are you listening?"

"I'm listening."

"I don't think I want to snitch a planet from these people."

Amalfi didn't answer; he knew well enough that there was no answer. The Okie city would never go aloft again. This planet was home. There was no place else to go.

The voice of the woman, crooning as she plowed, dwindled behind them. Her song droned monotonously over unseen and starving children: a lullaby. Hazleton and Amalfi had fallen from the sky to rob her of everything but the stony and now unharvestable soil. It was Amalfi's hope to return her something far more valuable.

It had been the spindizzy, of course, which had scooped up the cities of Earth—and later, of many other planets—and hurled them into space. Two other social factors, however, had made possible the roving, nomadic culture of the Okies, a culture which had lasted more than three thousand years, and which probably would take another five hundred to disintegrate completely.

One of these was personal immortality. The conquest of so-called "natural" death had been virtually complete by the time the technicians on the Jovian Bridge had confirmed the spindizzy principle, and the two went together like hand in spacemitt. Despite the fact that the spindizzy would drive a ship—or a city—at speeds enormously faster than that of light, interstellar flight still consumed finite time. The vastness of the galaxy was sufficient to make long flights consume lifetimes even at top spindizzy speed.

But when death yielded to the antiathapic drugs, there was no longer any such thing as a "lifetime" in the old sense.

The other factor was economic: the rise of the metal germanium as the jinni of electronics. Long before flight in deep space became a fact, the metal had assumed a fantastic value on Earth. The opening of the interstellar frontier drove its price down to a manageable level, and gradually it emerged as the basic, stable monetary standard of space trade. Coinage in conductor metals, whose value had always been largely a matter of pressure politics, became extinct; it became impossible to maintain, for instance, the fiction that silver was precious, when it lay about in such flagrant profusion in the rocks of every newly-discovered Earthlike planet. The semiconductor germanium became the coin of the starman's realm.

And after three thousand years, personal immortality and the germanium standard joined forces to destroy the Okies.

It had always been inevitable that the germanium standard would not last. The time was bound to come when the metal would be synthesized cheaply, or a substance even more versatile would be found, or some temporary center of trade would corner a significant fraction of the money in circulation. It was not even necessary to predict specifically how the crisis would occur, to be able to predict what it would do to the economy of the galaxy. Had it happened a little earlier, before the economies of thousands of star-systems had become grounded in the standard, the effect probably would have been only temporary.

But when the germanium standard finally collapsed, it took with it the substrate in which the Okies had been imbedded. The semiconductor base was relegated to the same limbo which had claimed the conductor-metal base. The most valuable nonconductors in the galaxy were the antiathapic drugs; the next currency was based on a drug standard.

As a standard it was excellent, passing all the tests that a coinage is supposed to meet. The drugs could be indefinitely diluted for small change; they had never been synthesized, and any other form of counterfeiting could be detected easily by bio-assay and other simple tests; they were very rare; they were universally needed; their sources of supply were few enough in number to be readily monitored.

Unfortunately, the star-cruising Okies needed the drugs *as drugs.* They could not afford to use them as money.

From that moment on, the Okies were no longer the collective citizens of a nomadic culture. They were just interstellar bums. There was no place for them in the galaxy any more.

Outside the galaxy, of course, the Okie commerce lanes had never penetrated—

The city was old—unlike the men and women who manned it, who had merely lived a long time, which is quite a different thing. And like any old intelligence, its past sins lay very near the surface, ready for review either in nostalgia or in self-accusation at the slightest cue. It was difficult these days to get any kind of information out of the City Fathers without having to submit to a lecture, couched in as high a moral tone as was possible to machines whose highest morality was survival.

Amalfi knew well enough what he was letting himself in for when he asked the City Fathers for a review of the Violations Docket. He got it, and in bells—big bells. The City Fathers gave him everything, right down to the day a dozen centuries ago when they had discovered that nobody had dusted the city's ancient subways since the city had first gone into space. That had been the first time the Okies had heard that the city had ever had any subways.

But Amalfi stuck to the job, though his right ear ached with the pressure of the earphone. Out of the welter of minor complaints and wistful recollections of missed opportunities, certain things came through clearly and urgently.

The city had never been officially cleared of its failure to observe the "Vacate" order the cops had served on it during the reduction of Utopia. Later, during the same affair, the city had been hung with a charge of technical treason—not as serious as it sounded, but subject to inconvenient penalties—while on the neighboring planet of Hrunta, and had left the scene with the charge still on the docket. There had been a small trick pulled there, too, which the cops could hardly have forgotten: while it had not been illegal, it had created laughter at the expense of the cops in every Okie wardroom in the galaxy, and cops seldom like to be laughed at.

Then there was the moving of He. The city had fulfilled its contract with that planet to the letter, but unfortunately that could never be proven; He was now well on its way across the intergalactic gap toward Andromeda, and could not testify on the city's behalf. As far as the cops knew, the city had destroyed He, a notion the cops would be no less likely to accept simply because it was ridiculous.

Worst of all, however, was the city's participation in the March on Earth. The March had been a tragedy from beginning to end, and few of the several hundred Okie cities which had taken part in it had survived it. It had been a product of the galaxy-wide depression which had followed the collapse of the germanium standard. Amalfi's city—already accused of several crimes in the star-system where the March had started, crimes which as a matter of fact the city had actually been forced to commit—had gone along because it had had no better choice, and had done what it could to change the March from a mutual massacre to a collective bargaining session; but the massacre had occurred all the same. No one city, not even Amalfi's, could have made its voice heard above the long roar of galactic collapse.

There was the redeeming fact that the city, during the March, had found and extirpated one of the last residues of the Vegan tyranny. But it could never be proven: like the affair on He, the city had done so thorough a job that even the evidence was gone irrevocably.

Amalfi sighed. In the end, it appeared that the Earth cops would remember Amalfi's city for two things only. *One:* The city had a long Violations Docket, and still existed to be brought to book on it. *Two:* The city had gone out toward the Greater Magellanic, just as a far older and blacker city had done centuries before—the city which had perpetrated the massacre on Thor V, the city whose memory still stank in the nostrils of cops and surviving Okies alike.

Amalfi shut off the City Fathers in mid-reminiscence and removed the phone from his aching ear. The control boards of the city stretched before him, still largely useful, but dead forever in one crucial bloc—the bank that had once flown the city from star to new star. The city was grounded; it had no choice now but to accept, and then win, this one poor planet for its own.

If the cops would let it. The Magellanic Clouds were moving steadily and with increasing velocity away from the home galaxy; the gap was already so large that the city had had to cross it by using a dirigible planet as a booster-stage. It would take the cops time to decide that they should make that enormously long flight in pursuit of one miserable Okie. But in the end they would make that decision. The cleaner the home galaxy became of Okies—and there was no doubt but that the cops had by now broken up the majority of the space-faring cities—the greater the urge would become to track down the last few stragglers.

Amalfi had no faith in the ability of a satellite starcloud to outrun human technology. By the time the cops were ready to cross from the home lens to the Greater Magellanic, they would have the techniques with which to do it, and techniques far less clumsy than those Amalfi's city had used. If the cops wanted to chase the Greater Magellanic, they would find ways to catch it. If—

Amalfi took up the earphone again. "Question," he said. "Will the need to catch us be urgent enough to produce the necessary techniques in time?"

The City Fathers hummed, drawn momentarily from their eternal mulling over the past. At last they said:

"YES, MAYOR AMALFI. BEAR IN MIND THAT WE ARE NOT ALONE IN THIS CLOUD. REMEMBER THOR V."

There it was: the ancient slogan that had made Okies hated even on planets that had never seen an Okie city, and could never expect to. There was only the smallest chance that the city which had wrought the Thor V atrocity had made good its escape to this Cloud; it had all happened a long time ago. But even the narrow chance, if the City Fathers were right, would bring the cops here sooner or later, to destroy Amalfi's own city in expiation of that still-burning crime.

Remember Thor V. No city would be safe until that raped and murdered world could be forgotten. Not even out here, in the virgin satellites of the home lens.

"Boss? Sorry, we didn't know you were busy. But we've got an operating schedule set up, as soon as you're ready to look at it."

"I'm ready right now, Mark," Amalfi said, turning away from the boards. "Hello, Dee. How do you like your planet?"

The former Utopian girl smiled. "It's beautiful," she said simply.

"For the most part, anyway," Hazleton agreed. "This heath is an ugly place, but the rest of the land seems to be excellent—much better than you'd think it from the way it's being farmed. The tiny little fields they break it up into here just don't do it justice, and even I know better cultivation methods than these serfs do."

"I'm not surprised," Amalfi said. "It's my theory that the Proctors maintain their power partly by preventing the spread of any knowledge about farming beyond the most rudimentary kind. That's also the most rudimentary kind of politics, as I don't need to tell you."

"On the politics," Hazleton said evenly, "we're in disagreement. While that's ironing itself out, the business of running the city has to go on."

"All right," Amalfi said. "What's on the docket?"

"I'm having a small plot on the heath, next to the city, turned over and conditioned for some experimental plantings, and extensive soil tests have already been made. That's purely a stopgap, of course. Eventually we'll have to expand onto good land. I've drawn up a tentative contract of lease between the city and the Proctors, which provides for us to rotate ownership geographically so as to keep displacement of the serfs at a minimum, and at the same time opens a complete spectrum of seasonal plantings to us—essentially it's the old Limited Colony contract, but heavily weighted in the direction of the Proctors' prejudices. There's no doubt in my mind but that they'll sign it. Then—"

"They won't sign it," Amalfi said. "They can't even be shown it. Furthermore, I want everything you've put into your experimental plot here on the heath yanked out."

Hazleton put a hand to his forehead in frank exasperation. "Boss," he said, "don't tell me that we're *still* not at the end of the old squirrel-cage routine—intrigue, intrigue, and then more intrigue. I'm sick of it, I'll tell you that directly. Isn't two thousand years enough for you? I thought we had come to this planet to settle down!"

"We did. We will. But as you reminded me yourself yesterday, there are other people in possession of this planet at the moment—people we can't legally push out. As matters stand right now, we can't give them the faintest sign that we mean to settle here; they're already intensely suspicious of that very thing, and they're watching us for evidence of it every minute."

"Oh, no," Dee said. She came forward swiftly and put a hand on Amalfi's shoulder. "John, you promised us after the March was over that we were going to make a home here. Not necessarily on this planet, but somewhere in the Cloud. You promised, John."

The mayor looked up at her. It was no secret to her, or to Hazleton either, that he loved her; they both knew, as well, the cruelly just Okie law that forbade the mayor of an Okie city any permanent alliance with a woman—and the vein of iron loyalty in Amalfi that would have compelled him to act by that law even had it never existed. Until the sudden crisis far back in the Acolyte cluster which had forced Amalfi to reveal to Hazleton the existence of that love, neither of the two youngsters had suspected it over a period of nearly nine decades.

But Dee was comparatively new to Okie mores, and was in addition a woman. Only to know that she was loved had been unable to content her long. She was already beginning to put the knowledge to work.

"Of course I promised," Amalfi said. "I've delivered on my promises for nearly two thousand years, and I'll continue to do so. The blunt fact is that the City Fathers would have me shot if I didn't—as they nearly had Mark shot on more than one occasion. This planet will be our home, if you'll give me just the minimum of help in winning it. It's the best of all the planets we passed on the way in, for a great many reasons—including a couple that won't begin to show until you see the winter constellations here, plus a few more that won't become evident for a century yet. But there's one thing I certainly can't give you, and that's immediate delivery."

"All right," Dee said. She smiled. "I trust you, John, you know that. But it's hard to be patient."

"Is it?" Amalfi said, surprised. "Come to think of it, I remember once during the tipping of He when the same thought occurred to me. In retrospect the problem doesn't seem large."

"Boss, you'd better give us some substitute courses of action," the city manager's voice cut in, a little coldly. "With the possible exception of yourself, every man and woman and alley cat in the city is ready to spread out all over the surface of this planet the moment the starting gun is fired. You've given us every reason to think that that would be the way it would happen. If there's going to be a delay, you have a good many idle hands to put to work."

"Use straight work-contract procedure, all the way down the line," Amalfi said. "No exploiting of the planet that we wouldn't normally do during the usual stopover for a job. That means no truck-gardens or any other form of local agriculture; just refilling the oil tanks, re-breeding the Chlorella strains from local sources for heterosis, and so on."

"That won't work," Hazleton said. "It may fool the Proctors, Amalfi, but how can you fool our own people? What are you going to do with the perimeter police, for instance? Sergeant Paterson's whole crew knows that it won't ever again have to make up a boarding squad or defend the city or take up any other military duty. Nine tenths of them are itching to throw off their harness for good and start dirt-farming. What am I to do with them?"

"Send 'em out to your experimental potato patch on the heath," Amalfi said. "On police detail. Tell 'em to pick up everything that grows."

Hazleton started to turn toward the lift-shaft, holding out his hand to Dee. Then he turned back.

"But why, boss?" he said plaintively. "What makes you think that the Proctors suspect us of squatting? And what could they do about it if they did?"

"The Proctors have asked for the standard work-contract," Amalfi said. "They know what it is, and they insist upon its observation, to the letter, *including* the provision that the city must be off this planet by the date of termination. As you know, that's impossible; we can't leave this planet, either inside or outside the contract period. But we'll have to pretend that we're going to leave, up to the last possible minute."

Hazleton looked stunned. Dee took his hand reassuringly, but it didn't seem to register.

"As for what the Proctors themselves can do about it," Amalfi said, picking up the earphone again, "I don't yet know. I'm trying to find out. But this much I do know:

"The Proctors have *already* called the cops."

II

Under the gray, hazy light in the schoolroom, voices and visions came thronging even into the conscious and prepared mind of the visitor, pouring from the memory cells of the City Fathers. Amalfi could feel their pressure, just below the surface of his mind; it was vaguely unpleasant, partly because he already knew what they sought to impart, so that the redoubled impressions tended to shoulder forward into the immediate attention, nearly with the vividness of immediate experience.

Superimposed upon the indefinite outlines of the schoolroom, cities soared across Amalfi's vision, cities aloft, in flight, looking for work, cracking their food from oil, burrowing for ores the colonial planets could not reach without help, and leaving again to search for work; sometimes welcomed grudgingly, sometimes driven out, usually underpaid, often potential brigands, always watched jealously by the police of hegemon Earth; spreading, ready to mow any lawn, toward the limits of the galaxy—

He waved a hand annoyedly before his eyes and looked for a monitor, found one standing at his elbow, and wondered how long he had been there—or, conversely, how long Amalfi himself had been lulled into the learning trance.

"Where's Karst?" he said brusquely. "The first serf we brought in? I need him."

"Yes, sir. He's in a chair toward the front of the room." The monitor—whose function combined the duties of classroom supervisor and nurse—turned away briefly to a nearby wall server, which opened and floated out to him a tall metal tumbler. The monitor took it and led the way through the room, threading his way among the scattered couches. Usually most of these were unoccupied, since it took less than five hundred hours to bring the average child through tensor calculus and hence to the limits of what he could be taught by passive inculcation alone. Now, however, every couch was occupied, and few of them by children.

One of the counterpointing, subaudible voices was murmuring: "Some of the cities which turned bindlestiff did not pursue the usual policy of piracy and raiding, but settled instead upon faraway worlds and established tyrannical rules. Most of these were overthrown by the Earth police; the cities were not efficient fighting machines. Those which withstood the first assault sometimes were allowed to remain in power for various reasons of policy, but such planets were invariably barred from commerce. Some of these involuntary empires may still remain on the fringes of Earth's jurisdiction. Most notorious of these recrudescences of imperialism was the reduction of Thor V, the work of one of the earliest of the Okies, a heavily militarized city which had already earned itself the popular nickname of 'the Mad Dogs.' The epithet, current among other Okies as well as planetary populations, of course referred primarily—"

"Here's your man," the monitor said in a low voice. Amalfi looked down at Karst. The serf already had undergone a considerable change. He was no longer a distorted and worn caricature of a man, chocolate-colored with sun, wind and ground-in dirt, so brutalized as to be almost beyond pity. He was, instead, rather like a foetus as he lay curled on the couch, innocent and still perfectable, as yet unmarked by any experience which counted. His past—and there could hardly have been much of it, for although he had said that his present wife, Eedit, had been his fifth, he was obviously scarcely twenty years old—had been so completely monotonous and implacable that, given the chance, he had sloughed it off as easily and totally as one throws away a single garment. He was, Amalfi realized, much more essentially a child than any Okie infant could ever be.

The monitor touched Karst's shoulder and the serf stirred uneasily, then sat up, instantly awake, his intense blue eyes questioning Amalfi. The monitor handed him the metal tumbler, now beaded with cold, and Karst drank from it. The pungent liquid made him sneeze, quickly and without seeming to notice that he had sneezed, like a cat.

"How's it coming through, Karst?" Amalfi said.

"It is very hard," the serf said. He took another pull at the tumbler. "But once grasped, it seems to bring everything into flower at once. Lord Amalfi, the Proctors claim that IMT came from the sky on a cloud. Yesterday I only believed that. Today I think I understand it."

"I think you do," Amalfi said. "And you're not alone. We have serfs by scores in the city now, learning—just look around you and you'll see. And they're learning more than just simple physics or cultural morphology. They're learning freedom, beginning with the first one—freedom to hate."

"I know that lesson," Karst said, with a profound and glacial calm. "But you awakened me for something."

"I did," the mayor agreed grimly. "We've got a visitor we think you'll be able to identify: a Proctor. And he's up to something that smells funny to me and Hazleton both, but we can't pin down what it is. Come give us a hand, will you?"

"You'd better give him some time to rest, Mr. Mayor," the monitor said disapprovingly. "Being dumped out of hypnopaedic trance is a considerable shock; he'll need at least an hour."

Amalfi stared at the monitor incredulously. He was about to note that neither Karst nor the city had the hour to spare, when it occurred to him that to say so would take ten words where one was plenty. "Vanish," he said.

The monitor did his best.

Karst looked intently at the judas. The man on the screen had his back turned; he was looking into the big operations tank in the city manager's office. The indirect light gleamed on his shaven and oiled head. Amalfi watched over Karst's left shoulder, his teeth sunk firmly in a new hydroponic cigar.

"Why, the man's as bald as I am," the mayor said. "And he can't be much past his adolescence, judging by his skull; he's forty-five at the most. Recognize him, Karst?"

"Not yet," Karst said. "All the Proctors shave their heads. If he would only turn around . . . ah. Yes. That's Heldon. I have seen him myself only once, but he is easy to recognize. He is young, as the Proctors go. He is the stormy petrel of the Great Nine—some think him a friend of the serfs. At least he is less quick with the whip than the others."

"What would he be wanting here?"

"Perhaps he will tell us." Karst's eyes remained fixed upon the Proctor's image.

"Your request puzzles me," Hazleton's voice said, issuing smoothly from the speaker above the judas. The city manager could not be seen, but his expression seemed to modulate the sound of his voice almost specifically: the tiger mind masked behind a pussy-cat purr as behind a pussy-cat smile. "We're glad to hear of new services we can render to a client, of course. But we certainly never suspected that antigravity mechanisms even existed in IMT."

"Don't think me stupid, Mr. Hazleton," Heldon said. "You and I know that IMT was once a wanderer, as your city is now. We also know that your city, like all Okie cities, would like a world of its own. Will you allow me this much intelligence, please?"

"For discussion, yes," Hazleton's voice said.

"Then let me say that it's quite evident to me that you're nurturing an uprising. You have been careful to stay within the letter of the contract, simply because you dare not breach it, any more than we; the Earth police protect us from each other to that extent. Your Mayor Amalfi was told that it was illegal for the serfs to speak to your people, but unfortunately it is illegal only for the serfs, not for your citizens. If we cannot keep the serfs out of your city, you are under no obligation to do it for us."

"A point you have saved me the trouble of making," Hazleton said.

"Quite so. I'll add also that when this revolution of yours comes, I have no doubt but that you'll win it. I don't know what weapons you can put into the hands of our serfs, but I assume that they are better than anything we can muster. We haven't your technology. My fellows disagree with me, but I am a realist."

"An interesting theory," Hazleton's voice said. There was a brief pause. In the silence, a soft pattering sound became evident. Hazleton's fingertips, Amalfi guessed, drumming on the desk top, as if with amused impatience. Heldon's face remained impassive.

"The Proctors believe that they can hold what is theirs," Heldon said at last. "If you overstay your contract, they will go to war against you. They will be justified, but unfortunately Earth justice is a long way away from here. You will win. My interest is to see that we have a way of escape."

"Via spindizzy?"

"Precisely." Heldon permitted a stony smile to stir the corners of his mouth. "I'll be honest with you, Mr. Hazleton. If it comes to war, I will fight as hard as any other Proctor to hold this world of ours. I come to you only because you can repair the spindizzies of IMT. You needn't expect me to enter into any extensive treason on that account."

Hazleton, it appeared, was being obdurately stupid. "I fail to see why I should lift a finger for you," he said.

"Observe, please. The Proctors will fight, because they believe that they must. It will probably be a hopeless fight, but it will do your city some damage all the same. As a matter of fact, it will cripple your city beyond repair, unless your luck is phenomenal. Now then: none of the Proctors except one other man and myself know that the spindizzies of IMT are still able to function. That means that they won't try to escape with them, they'll try to knock you out instead. But with the machines in repair, and one knowledgeable hand at the controls—"

"I see," Hazleton said. "You propose to put IMT into flight while you can still get off the planet with a reasonably whole city. In return you offer us the planet, and the chance that our own damages will be minimal. Hm-m-m. It's interesting, anyhow. Suppose we take a look at your spindizzies, and see if they're in operable condition. It's been a good many years, without doubt, and untended machinery has a way of gumming up. If they can still be operated at all, we'll talk about a deal. All right?"

"It will have to do," Heldon grumbled. Amalfi saw in the Proctor's eyes a gleam of cold satisfaction which he recognized at once, from having himself looked out through it often—though never in such a poor state of concealment. He shut off the screen.

"Well?" the mayor said. "What's he up to?"

"Trouble," Karst said slowly. "It would be very foolish to give or trade him any advantage. His stated reasons are not his real ones."

"Of course not," Amalfi said. "Whose are? Oh, hello, Mark. What do you make of our friend?"

Hazleton stepped out of the lift shaft, bouncing lightly once on the resilient concrete of the control-room floor. "He's stupid," the city manager said, "but he's dangerous. He knows that there's something he doesn't know. He also knows that we don't know what he's driving at, and he's on his home grounds. It's a combination I don't care for."

"I don't like it myself," Amalfi said. "When the enemy starts giving away information, look out! Do you think the majority of the Proctors really don't know that IMT has operable spindizzies?"

"I am sure they do not," Karst offered tentatively. Both men turned to him. "The Proctors do not even believe that you are here to capture the planet. At least, they do not believe that that is what you intend, and I'm sure they don't care, one way or the other."

"Why not?" Hazleton said. "I would."

"You have never *owned* several million serfs," Karst said, without rancor. "You have serfs working for you, and you are paying them wages. That in itself is a disaster for the Proctors. And they cannot stop it. They know that the money you are paying is legal, with the power of the Earth behind it. They cannot stop us from earning it. To do so would cause an uprising at once."

Amalfi looked at Hazleton. The money the city was handing out was the Oc Dollar. It was legal here—but back in the galaxy it was just so much paper. It was only germanium-backed. Could the Proctors be that naive? Or was IMT simply too old to possess the instantaneous Dirac transmitters which would have told it of the economic collapse of the home lens?

"And the spindizzies?" Amalfi said. "Who else would know of them among the Great Nine?"

"Asor, for one," Karst said. "He is the presiding officer, and the religious fanatic of the group. It is said that he still practices daily the full thirty yogas of the Semantic Rigor, even to chinning himself upon every rung of the Abstraction Ladder. The prophet Maalvin banned the flight of men forever, so Asor would not be likely to allow IMT to fly at this late date."

"He has his reasons," Hazleton said reflectively. "Religions rarely exist in a vacuum. They have effects on the societies they reflect. He's probably afraid of the spindizzies, in the last analysis. With such a weapon it takes only a few hundred men to make a revolution—more than enough to overthrow a feudal set-up like this. IMT didn't dare keep its spindizzies working."

"Go on, Karst," Amalfi said, raising his hand impatiently at Hazleton. "How about the other Proctors?"

"There is Bemajdi, but he hardly counts," Karst said. "Let me think. Remember I have never seen most of these men. The only one who matters, it seems to me, is Larre. He is a dour-faced old man with a potbelly. He is usually on Heldon's side, but seldom travels with Heldon all the way. He will worry less about the money the serfs are earning than will the rest. He will contrive a way to tax it away from us—perhaps by declaring a holiday, in honor of the visit of Earthmen to our planet. The collection of tithes is a duty of his."

"Would he allow Heldon to put IMT's spindizzies in shape?"

"No, probably not," Karst said. "I believe Heldon was telling the truth when he said that he would have to do that in secret."

"I don't know," Amalfi said. "I don't like it. On the surface, it looks as though the Proctors hope to scare us off the planet as soon as the contract expires, and then collect all the money we've paid the serfs—with the cops to back them up. But when you look closely at it, it's crazy. Once the cops find out the identity of IMT—and it won't take them long—they'll break up both cities, and be glad of the chance."

Karst said: "Is this because IMT was the Okie city that did . . . what was done . . . on Thor V?"

Amalfi suddenly found that he was having difficulty in keeping his

Adam's apple where it belonged. "Let that pass, Karst," he growled. "We're not going to import that story into the Cloud. That should have been cut from your learning tape."

"I know it now," Karst said calmly. "And I am not surprised. The Proctors never change."

"Forget it. Forget it, do you hear? Forget everything. Karst, can you go back to being a dumb serf for a night?"

"Go back to my land?" Karst said. "It would be awkward. My wife must have a new man by now—"

"No, not back to your land. I want to go with Heldon and look at his spindizzies, as soon as he says the word. I'll need to take some heavy equipment, and I'll need some help. Will you come along?"

Hazleton raised his eyebrows. "You won't fool Heldon, boss."

"I think I will. Of course he knows that we've educated some of the serfs, but that's not a thing he can actually see when he looks at it; his whole background is against it. He just isn't accustomed to thinking of serfs as intelligent. He knows we have thousands of them here, and yet he isn't really afraid of that idea. He thinks we may arm them, make a mob of them. He can't begin to imagine that a serf can learn something better than how to handle a sidearm—something better, and far more dangerous."

"How can you be sure?" Hazleton said.

"By analogue. Remember the planet of Thetis Alpha called Fitzgerald, where they used a big beast called a horse for everything—from pulling carts to racing? All right: suppose you visited a place where you had been told that a few horses had been taught to talk. While you're working there, somebody comes to give you a hand, dragging a spavined old plug with a straw hat pulled down over its ears and a pack on its back. (Excuse me, Karst, but business is business.) You aren't going to think of that horse as one of the talking ones. You aren't accustomed to thinking of horses as being able to talk at all."

"All right," Hazleton said, grinning at Karst's evident discomfiture. "What's the main strategy from here on out, boss? I gather that you've got it set up. Are you ready to give it a name yet?"

"Not quite," the mayor said. "Unless you like long titles. It's still just another problem in political pseudomorphism."

Amalfi caught sight of Karst's deliberately incurious face and his own grin broadened. "Or," he said, "the fine art of tricking your opponent into throwing his head at you."

III

IMT was a squat city, long rooted in the stony soil, and as changeless as a forest of cenotaphs. Its quietness, too, was like the quietness of a cemetery, and the Proctors, carrying the fanlike wands of their office, the pierced fans with the jagged tops and the little jingling tags, were much like friars moving among the dead.

The quiet, of course, could be accounted for very simply. The serfs were not allowed to speak within the walls of IMT unless spoken to, and there were comparatively few Proctors in the city to speak to them. For Amalfi there was also the imposed silence of the slaughtered millions of Thor V blanketing the air. He wondered if the Proctors could still hear that raw silence.

The naked brown figure of a passing serf glanced furtively at the party, saw Heldon, and raised a finger to its lips in the established gesture of respect. Heldon barely nodded. Amalfi, necessarily, took no overt notice at all, but he thought: *Shh, is it? I don't wonder. But it's too late, Heldon. The secret is out.*

Karst trudged behind them, shooting an occasional wary glance at Heldon from under his tangled eyebrows. His caution was wasted on the Proctor. They passed through a decaying public square, in the center of which was an almost-obliterated statuary group, so weatherworn as to have lost any integrity it might ever have had; integrity, Amalfi mused, is not a characteristic of monuments. Except to a sharp eye, the mass of stone on the old pedestal might have been nothing but a moderately large meteorite, riddled with the twisting pits characteristic of siderites.

Amalfi could see, however, that the spaces sculpted out of the interior of that block of stone, after the fashion of an ancient sculptor named Moore, had once had meaning. Inside that stone there had once stood a powerful human figure, with its foot resting upon the neck of a slighter. Once, evidently, IMT had actually been *proud* of the memory of Thor V—

"Ahead is the Temple," Heldon said suddenly. "The machinery is beneath it. There should be no one of interest in it at this hour, but I had best make sure. Wait here."

"Suppose somebody notices us?" Amalfi said.

"This square is usually avoided. Also, I have men posted around it to divert any chance traffic. If you don't wander away, you'll be safe."

The Proctor strode away toward the big domed building and disappeared abruptly down an alleyway. Behind Amalfi, Karst began to sing, in an exceedingly scratchy voice, but very softly: a folk-tune of some kind, obviously. The melody, which once had had to do with a town named Kazan, was too many thousands of years old for Amalfi to recognize it, even had he not been tune-deaf. Nevertheless, the mayor abruptly found himself listening to Karst, with the intensity of a hooded owl sonar-tracking a field mouse, Karst chanted:

> "Wild on the wind rose the righteous wrath of Maalvin,
> Borne like a brand to the burning of the Barrens.
> Arms of hands of rebels perished then,
> Stars nor moons bedecked that midnight,
> IMT made the sky
> Fall!"

Seeing that Amalfi was listening to him, Karst stopped with an apologetic gesture. "Go ahead, Karst," Amalfi said at once. "How does the rest go?"

"There isn't time. There are hundreds of verses; every singer adds at least one of his own to the song. It is always supposed to end with this one:

> "Black with their blood was the brick of that barrow.
> Toppled the tall towers, crushed to the clay.
> None might live who flouted Maalvin,
> Earth their souls spurned spaceward, wailing,
> IMT made the sky
> Fall!"

"That's great," Amalfi said grimly. "We really are in the soup—just about in the bottom of the bowl, I'd say. I wish I'd heard that song a week ago."

"What does it tell you?" Karst said, wonderingly. "It is only an old legend."

"It tells me why Heldon wants his spindizzies fixed. I knew he wasn't telling me the straight goods, but that old Laputa gag never occurred to me—more recent cities aren't strong enough in the keel to risk it. But with all the mass this burg packs, it can squash us flat —and we'll just have to sit still for it!"

"I don't understand—"

"It's simple enough. Your prophet Maalvin used IMT like a nutcracker. He picked it up, flew it over the opposition, and let it down again. The trick was dreamed up away before spaceflight, as I recall. Karst, stick close to me; I may have to get a message to you under Heldon's eye, so watch for—*Sst,* here he comes."

The Proctor had been uttered by the alleyway like an untranslatable word. He came rapidly toward them across the crumbling flagstones.

"I think," Heldon said, "that we are now ready for your valuable aid, Mayor Amalfi."

Heldon put his foot on a jutting pyramidal stone and pressed down. Amalfi watched carefully, but nothing happened. He swept his flash around the featureless stone walls of the underground chamber, then back again to the floor. Impatiently, Heldon kicked the little pyramid.

This time, there was a protesting rumble. Very slowly, and with a great deal of scraping, a block of stone perhaps five feet long by two feet wide began to rise, as if pivoted or hinged at the far end. The beam of the mayor's flash darted into the opening, picking out a narrow flight of steps.

"I'm disappointed," Amalfi said. "I expected to see Jonathan Swift come out from under it. All right, Heldon, lead on."

The Proctor went cautiously down the steps, holding his skirts up against the dampness. Karst came last, bent low under the heavy pack, his arms hanging laxly. The steps felt cold and slimy through the thin soles of the mayor's sandals, and little trickles of moisture ran down the close-pressing walls. Amalfi felt a nearly intolerable urge to light a cigar; he could almost taste the powerful aromatic odor cutting through the humidity. But he needed his hands free.

He was almost ready to hope that the spindizzies had been ruined by all this moisture, but he discarded the idea even as it was forming in the back of his mind. That would be the easy way out, and in the end it would be disastrous. If the Okies were ever to call this planet their own, IMT had to be made to fly again.

How to keep it off his own city's back, once IMT was aloft, he still was unable to figure. He was piloting, as he invariably wound up doing in the pinches, by the seat of his pants.

The steps ended abruptly in a small chamber, so small, chilly and damp that it was little more than a cave. The flashlight's eye roved, came to rest on an oval doorway sealed off with dull metal—almost certainly lead. So IMT's spindizzies ran "hot"? That was already bad news; it backdated them far beyond the year to which Amalfi had tentatively assigned them.

"That it?" he said.

"That is the way," Heldon agreed. He twisted an inconspicuous handle.

Ancient fluorescents flickered into bluish life as the valve drew back, and glinted upon the humped backs of machines. The air was quite dry here—evidently the big chamber was kept sealed—and Amalfi could not repress a fugitive pang of disappointment. He scanned the huge machines, looking for control panels or homologues thereof.

"Well?" Heldon said harshly. He seemed to be under considerable strain. It occurred to Amalfi that Heldon's strategy might well be a personal flier, not an official policy of the Great Nine; in which case it might go hard with Heldon if his colleagues found him in this particular place of all places with an Okie. "Aren't you going to make any tests?"

"Certainly," Amalfi said. "I was a little taken aback at their size, that's all."

"They are old, as you know," said the Proctor. "Doubtless they are built much larger nowadays."

That, of course, wasn't so. Modern spindizzies ran less than a tenth the size of these. The comment cast new doubt upon Heldon's exact status. Amalfi had assumed that the Proctor would not let him touch the spindizzies except to inspect; that there would be plenty of men in IMT capable of making repairs from detailed instructions; that Heldon himself, and any Proctor, would know enough physics to comprehend whatever explanations Amalfi might proffer. Now he was not so sure—and on this question hung the amount of tinkering Amalfi would be able to do without being detected.

The mayor mounted a metal stair to a catwalk which ran along the tops of the generators, then stopped and looked down at Karst. "Well, stupid, don't just stand there," he said. "Come on up, and bring the stuff."

Obediently Karst shambled up the metal steps, Heldon at his heels. Amalfi ignored them to search for an inspection port in the casing, found one, and opened it. Beneath was what appeared to be a massive rectifying circuit, plus the amplifier for some kind of monitor—probably a digital computer. The amplifier involved more vacuum tubes than Amalfi had ever before seen gathered into one circuit, and there was a separate power supply to deliver D.C. to their heaters. Two of the tubes were each as big as his fist.

Karst bent over and slung the pack to the deck. Amalfi drew out of it a length of slender black cable and thrust its double prongs into a nearby socket. A tiny bulb on the other end glowed neon-red.

"Your computer's still running," he reported. "Whether it's still sane or not is another matter. May I turn the main banks on, Heldon?"

"I'll turn them on," the Proctor said. He went down the stairs again and across the chamber.

Instantly Amalfi was murmuring through motionless lips into the inspection port. The result to Karst's ears must have been rather weird. The technique of speaking without moving one's lips is simply a matter of substituting consonants which do not involve lip movement, such as "y," for those which do, such as "w." If the resulting sound is picked up from inside the resonating chamber, as it is with a throat-mike, it is not too different from ordinary speech, only a bit more blurred. Heard from outside the speaker's nasopharyngeal cavity, however, it has a tendency to sound like Japanese Pidgin.

"Yatch Heldon, Karst. See yhich syitch he kulls, an' nenorize its location. Got it? Good."

The tubes lit. Karst nodded once, very slightly. The Proctor watched from below while Amalfi inspected the lines.

"Will they work?" he called. His voice was muffled, as though he were afraid to raise it as high as he thought necessary.

"I think so. One of these tubes is gassing, and there may have been some failures here and there. Better check the whole lot before you try anything ambitious. You do have facilities for testing tubes, don't you?"

Relief spread visibly over Heldon's face, despite his obvious effort to betray nothing. Probably he could have fooled any of his own people without effort, but for Amalfi, who like any Okie mayor could follow the parataxic "speech" of muscle interplay and posture as readily as he could spoken dialogue, Heldon's expression was as clear as a signed confession.

"Certainly," the Proctor said. "Is that all?"

"By no means. I think you ought to rip out about half of these circuits, and install transistors wherever they can be used; we can sell you the necessary germanium at the legal rate. You've got two or three hundred tubes to a unit here, by my estimate, and if you have a tube failure in flight . . . well, the only word that fits what would happen then is *blooey!*"

"Will you be able to show us how?"

"Probably," the mayor said. "If you'll allow me to inspect the whole system, I can give you an exact answer."

"All right," Heldon said. "But don't delay. I can't count on more than another half-day at most."

This was better than Amalfi had expected—miles better. Given that much time, he could trace at least enough of the leads to locate the master control. That Heldon's expression failed totally to match the content of his speech disturbed Amalfi profoundly, but there was nothing that he could do that would alter that now. He pulled paper and stylus out of Karst's pack and began to make rapid sketches of the wiring before him.

After he had a fairly clear idea of the first generator's set-up, it was easier to block in the main features of the second. It took time, but Heldon did not seem to tire.

The third spindizzy completed the picture, leaving Amalfi wondering what the fourth one was for. It turned out to be a booster, designed to compensate for the losses of the others wherever the main curve of their output failed to conform to the specs laid down for it by the crude, over-all regenerative circuit. The booster was located on the backside of the feedback loop, behind the computer rather than ahead of it, so that all the computer's corrections had to pass through it; the result, Amalfi was sure, would be a small but serious "base surge" every time any correction was applied. The spindizzies of IMT seemed to have been wired together by Cro-Magnon Man.

But they would fly the city. That was what counted.

Amalfi finished his examination of the booster generator and straightened up, painfully, stretching the muscles of his back. He had no idea how many hours he had consumed. It seemed as though months had passed. Heldon was still watching him, deep blue circles under his eyes, but still wide awake and watchful.

And Amalfi had found no point anywhere in the underground chamber from which the spindizzies of IMT could be controlled. The control point was somewhere else; the main control cable ran into a pipe which shot straight up through the top of the cavern.

. . . *IMT made the sky / Fall . . .*

Amalfi yawned ostentatiously and bent back to fasten the plate over the booster's observation port. Karst squatted near him, frankly asleep, as relaxed and comfortable as a cat drowsing on a high ledge. Heldon watched.

"I'm going to have to do the job for you," Amalfi said. "It's really major; might take weeks."

"I thought you would say so," Heldon said. "And I was glad to give you the time to find out. But I do not think we will make any such replacements."

"You need 'em."

"Possibly. But obviously there is a big factor of safety in the apparatus, or our ancestors would never have flown the city at all. You will understand, Mayor Amalfi, that we cannot risk your doing something to the machines which we cannot do ourselves, on the unlikely assumption that you are increasing their efficiency. If they will run as they are, that will have to be good enough."

"Oh, they'll run," Amalfi said. He began, methodically, to pack up his equipment. "For a while. I'll tell you flatly that they're not safe to operate, all the same."

Heldon shrugged and went down the spiral metal stairs to the floor of the chamber. Amalfi rummaged in the pack a moment more. Then he ostentatiously kicked Karst awake—and kicked hard, for he knew better than to play-act with a born overseer for an audience—and motioned the serf to pick up the bundle. They went down after Heldon.

The Proctor was smiling, and it was not a nice smile. "Not safe?" he said. "No, I never supposed that they were. But I think now that the dangers are mostly political."

"Why?" Amalfi demanded, trying to moderate his breathing. He was suddenly almost exhausted; it had taken—how many hours? He had no idea.

"Are you aware of the time, Mayor Amalfi?"

"About morning, I'd judge," Amalfi said dully, jerking the pack more firmly onto Karst's drooping left shoulder. "Late, anyhow."

"Very late," Heldon said. He was not disguising his expression now. He was openly crowing. "The contract between your city and mine expired at noon today. It is now nearly an hour after noon; we have been here all night and morning. And your city is still on our soil, in violation of the contract, Mayor Amalfi."

"An oversight—"

"No; a victory." Heldon drew a tiny silver tube from the folds of his robe and blew into it. "Mayor Amalfi, you may consider yourself a prisoner of war."

The little silver tube had made no audible sound, but there were already ten men in the room. The mesotron rifles they carried were of an ancient design, probably pre-Kammerman, like the spindizzies of IMT.

But, like the spindizzies, they looked as though they would work.

IV

Karst froze; Amalfi unfroze him by jabbing him surreptitiously in the ribs with a finger, and began to unload the contents of his own small pack into Karst's.

"You've called the Earth police, I suppose?" he said.

"Long ago. That way of escape will be cut by now. Let me say, Mayor Amalfi, that if you expected to find down here any controls that you might disable—and I was quite prepared to allow you to search for them—you expected too much stupidity from me."

Amalfi said nothing. He went on methodically repacking the equipment.

"You are making too many motions, Mayor Amalfi. Put your hands up in the air and turn around very slowly."

Amalfi put up his hands and turned. In each hand he held a small black object about the size and shape of an egg.

"I expected only as much stupidity as I got," he said conversationally. "You can see what I'm holding up there. I can and will drop one or both of them if I'm shot. I may drop them anyhow. I'm tired of your back-cluster ghost town."

Heldon snorted. "Explosives? Gas? Ridiculous; nothing so small could contain enough energy to destroy the city; and you have no masks. Do you take me for a fool?"

"Events prove you one," Amalfi said steadily. "The possibility was quite large that you would try to ambush me, once you had me in the city. I could have forestalled that by bringing a guard with me. You haven't met my perimeter police; they're tough boys, and they've been off duty so long that they'd love the chance to tangle with your palace crew. Didn't it occur to you that I left my city without a bodyguard only because I had less cumbersome ways of protecting myself?"

"Eggs," Heldon said scornfully.

"As a matter of fact, they *are* eggs; the black color is an aniline stain, put on the shells as a warning. They contain chick embryos inoculated with a two-hour alveolytic mutated Terrestrial rickettsialpox—a new air-borne strain developed in our own BW lab. Free space makes a wonderful laboratory for that kind of trick; an Okie town specializing in agronomy taught us the techniques a couple of centuries back. Just a couple of eggs—but if I were to drop them, you would have to crawl on your belly behind me all the way back to my city to get the antibiotic shot that's specific for the disease; we developed that ourselves, too."

There was a brief silence, made all the more empty by the hoarse breathing of the Proctor. The armed men eyed the black eggs uneasily, and the muzzles of their rifles wavered out of line. Amalfi had chosen his weapon with great care; static feudal societies classically are terrified by the threat of plague—they have seen so much of it.

"Impasse," Heldon said at last. "All right, Mayor Amalfi. You and your slave have safe-conduct from this chamber—"

"From the building. If I hear the slightest sound of pursuit up the stairs, I'll chuck these down on you. They burst hard, by the way—the virus generates a lot of gas in chick-embryo medium."

"Very well," Heldon said, through his teeth. "From the building, then. But you have won nothing, Mayor Amalfi. If you can get back to your city, you'll be just in time to be an eyewitness of the victory of IMT—the victory you helped make possible. I think you'll be surprised at how thorough we can be."

"No, I won't," Amalfi said, in a flat, cold, and quite merciless voice. "I know all about IMT, Heldon. This is the end of the line for the Mad Dogs. When you die, you and your whole crew of Interstellar Master Traders, *remember Thor V.*"

Heldon turned the color of unsized paper, and so, surprisingly, did at least four of his riflemen. Then the blood began to rise in the Proctor's plump, fungoid cheeks. "Get out," he croaked, almost inaudibly. Then, suddenly, at the top of his voice: "Get out! *Get out!*"

Juggling the eggs casually, Amalfi walked toward the lead radiation-lock. Karst shambled after him, cringing as he passed Heldon. Amalfi thought that the serf might be overdoing it, but Heldon did not notice; Karst might as well have been—a horse.

The lead plug swung to, blocking out Heldon's furious, frightened face and the glint of the fluorescents on the ancient spindizzies. Amalfi plunged one hand into Karst's pack, depositing one egg in the silicone-foam nest from which he had taken it, and withdrew the hand again grasping an ugly Schmeisser acceleration-pistol. This he thrust into the waistband of his breeches.

"Up the stairs, Karst. Fast. I had to shave it pretty fine. Go on, I'm right behind you. Where would the controls for those machines be, by your guess? The control lead went up through the roof of that cavern."

"On the top of the Temple," Karst said. He was mounting the narrow steps in huge bounds, but it did not seem to cost him the slightest effort. "Up there is Star Chamber, where the Great Nine meets. There isn't any way to get to it that I know."

They burst up into the cold stone antechamber. Amalfi's flash roved over the floor, found the jutting pyramid; Amalfi kicked it. With a prolonged groan, the tilted slab settled down over the flight of steps and became just another block in the floor. There was certainly some way to raise it again from below, but Heldon would hesitate before he used it; the slab was noisy in motion, noisy enough to tell Amalfi that he was being followed. At the first such squawk, Amalfi would lay a black egg, and Heldon knew it.

"I want you to get out of the city, and take every serf that you can find with you," Amalfi said. "But it's going to take timing. Somebody's got to pull that switch down below that I asked you to memorize, and I can't do it; I've got to get into Star Chamber. Heldon will guess that I'm going up there, and he'll follow me. After he's gone by, Karst, you have to go down there and open that switch."

Here was the low door through which Heldon had first admitted them to the Temple. More stairs ran up from it. Strong daylight poured under it.

Amalfi inched the old door open and peered out. Despite the brightness of the afternoon, the close-set, chunky buildings of IMT turned the alleyway outside into a confusing multitude of colored shadows. Half a dozen leaden-eyed serfs were going by, with a Proctor walking behind them, half asleep.

"Can you find your way back into that crypt?" Amalfi whispered.

"There's only one way to go."

"Good. Go back then. Dump the pack outside the door here; we don't need it any more. As soon as Heldon's crew goes on up these stairs, get back down there and pull that switch. Then get out of the city; you'll have about four minutes of accumulated warm-up time from all those tube stages; don't waste a second of it. Got it?"

"Yes. But—"

Something went over the Temple like an avalanche of gravel and dwindled into some distance. Amalfi closed one eye and screwed the other one skyward. "Rockets," he said. "Sometimes I don't know why I insisted on a planet as primitive as this. But maybe I'll learn to love it. Good luck, Karst."

He turned toward the stairs.

"They'll trap you up there," Karst said.

"No, they won't. Not Amalfi. But me no buts, Karst. Git."

Another rocket went over, and far away there was a heavy explosion. Amalfi charged like a bull up the new flight of stairs toward Star Chamber.

The staircase was long and widely curving, as well as narrow, and both its risers and its treads were infuriatingly small. Amalfi remembered that the Proctors did not themselves climb stairs; they were carried up them on the forearms of serfs. Such pussy-ant steps made for sure footing, but not for fast transit.

As far as Amalfi was able to compute, the steps rose gently along the outside curvature of the Temple's dome, following a one-and-a-half helix to the summit. Why? Presumably, the Proctors didn't require themselves to climb long flights of stairs for nothing, even with serfs to carry them. Why couldn't Star Chamber be under the dome with the spindizzies, for instance, instead of atop it?

Amalfi was not far past the first half-turn before one good reason became evident. There was a rustle of voices jostling its way through the chinks in the dome from below; a congregation, evidently, was gathering. As Amalfi continued to mount the flat spiral, the murmuring became more and more discrete, until individual voices could almost be separated out from it. Up there at what mathematically would be the bottom of the bowl, where the floor of Star Chamber was, the architect of the Temple evidently had contrived a whispering-gallery—a vault to which a Proctor might put his ear, and hear the thinnest syllable of conspiracy in the crowd of suppliants below.

It was ingenious, Amalfi had to admit. Conspirators on church-bearing planets generally tend to think of churches as safe places for quiet plotting. In Amalfi's universe—for he had never seen Earth—any planet which sponsored churches probably had a revolt coming to it.

Blowing like a porpoise, he scrambled up the last arc of the long Greek-spiral staircase. A solidly-closed double door, worked all over with phony Byzantine scrolls, stood looking down at him. He didn't bother to stop to admire it; he hit it squarely under the paired, patently synthetic sapphires just above its center, and hit it hard. It burst.

Disappointment stopped him for a moment. The chamber was an ellipse of low eccentricity, monastically bare and furnished only with a heavy wooden table and nine chairs, now drawn back against the wall. There were no controls here, nor any place where they could be concealed. The chamber was windowless.

The lack of windows told him what he wanted to know. The other, the compelling reason why Star Chamber was on top of the Temple dome was that it harbored, somewhere, the pilot's cabin of IMT. And that, in as old a city as IMT, meant that visibility would be all-important—requiring a situation atop the tallest structure in the city, and as close to 360° visibility as could be managed. Obviously, Amalfi was not yet up high enough.

He looked up at the ceiling. One of the big stone slabs had a semicircular cup in it, not much bigger than a large coin. The flat edge was much worn.

Amalfi grinned and looked under the wooden table. Sure enough, there it was—a pole with a hooked bill at one end, rather like a halberd, slung in clips. He yanked it out, straightened, and fitted the bill into the opening in the stone.

The slab came down easily, hinged at one end as the block down below over the generator room had been. The ancestors of the Proctors had not been much given to varying their engineering principles. The free end of the slab almost touched the table top. Amalfi sprang onto the table and scrambled up the tilted face of the stone; as he neared the top, the translating center of gravity which he represented actuated a counterweighing mechanism somewhere, and the slab closed, bearing him the rest of the way.

This was the control cabin, all right. It was tiny and packed with panels, all of which were covered with dust. Bull's-eyes of thick glass looked out over the city at the four compass-points, and there was one set in overhead. A single green light was glowing on one of the panels. While he walked toward it, it went out.

That had been Karst, cutting the power. Amalfi hoped that the peasant would get out again. He had grown to like him. There was something in his weathered, unmovable, shockproof courage, and in the voracity of his starved intelligence, that reminded the mayor of someone he had once known. That that someone was Amalfi as he had been at the age of twenty-five, Amalfi did not know, and there was no one else who would be able to tell him.

Spindizzies in essence are simple; Amalfi had no difficulty in setting and locking the controls the way he wanted them, or in performing sundry small tasks of highly selective sabotage. How he was to conceal what he had done, when every move left huge smears in the heavy dust, was a tougher problem. He solved it at length in the only possible way; he took off his shirt and flailed it at all of the boards. The result made him sneeze until his eyes watered, but it worked.

Now all he had to do was get out.

There were already sounds below in Star Chamber, but he was not yet worried about a direct attack. He still had one of the black eggs, and the Proctors knew it. Furthermore, he also had the pole with the hooked bill, so that in order to open up the control room at all, the Proctors would have to climb on each other's shoulders. They weren't in good physical shape for gymnastics, and besides they would know that men indulging in such stunts could be defeated temporarily by nothing more complicated than a kick in the teeth.

Nevertheless, Amalfi had no intention of spending the rest of his life in the control room of IMT. He had only about six minutes to get out of the city altogether.

After thinking very rapidly for approximately four seconds, Amalfi stood on the stone slab, overbalanced it, and slid solemnly down onto the top of the table in Star Chamber.

After a stunned instant, half a dozen pairs of hands grabbed him at once. Heldon's face, completely unrecognizable with fury and fear, was thrust into his.

"What have you done? Answer, or I'll order you torn to pieces!"

"Don't be a lunkhead. Tell your men to let go of me. I still have your safe-conduct—and in case you're thinking of repudiating it, I still have the same weapon I had before. Cast off, or—"

Heldon's guards released him before he had finished speaking. Heldon lurched heavily up onto the table top and began to claw his way up the slab. Several other robed, bald-headed men jostled after him—evidently Heldon had been driven by a greater fear to tell some of the Great Nine what he had done. Amalfi walked backwards out of Star Chamber and down two steps. Then he bent, deposited his remaining black egg carefully on the threshold, and took off down the spiral stairs at a dead run.

It would take Heldon a while, perhaps as much as a minute, after he switched on the controls to discover that the generators had been cut out while he was chasing Amalfi; and another minute, at best, to get a flunky down into the basement to turn them on again. Then there would be a warm-up time of four minutes. After that—IMT would go aloft.

Amalfi shot out into the alleyway and thence into the public square, caroming off an astounded guard. A shout rose behind him. He doubled over and kept running.

The street was nearly dark in the twilight of the twin suns. He kept in the shadows and made for the nearest corner. The cornice of the building ahead of him abruptly turned lava-white, then began to dim through the red. He never did hear the accompanying scream of the mesotron rifle. He was concentrating on something else.

Then he was around the corner. The quickest route to the edge of the city, as well as he could recall, was down the street he had just quitted, but that was now out of the question; he had no desire to be burned down. Whether or not he could get out of IMT in time by any alternate route remained to be seen.

Doggedly, he kept running. He was fired on once more, by a man who did not really know on whom he was firing. Here, Amalfi was just a running man who failed to fit the categories; any first shot at him would be a reflex of disorientation, and consequently aimed badly.

The ground shuddered, ever so delicately, like the hide of a monster twitching at flies in its sleep. Somehow, Amalfi managed to run still faster.

The shudder came again, stronger this time. A long, protracted groan followed it, traveling in a heavy wave through the bedrock of the city. The sound brought Proctors and serfs alike boiling out of the buildings.

At the third shock, something toward the center of the city collapsed with a sullen roar. Amalfi was caught up in the aimless, terrified eddying of the crowd, and fought, with hands, teeth and bullet head—

The groaning grew louder. Abruptly, the ground bucked. Amalfi pitched forward. With him went the whole milling mob, falling in windrows like stacked grain. There was frantic screaming everywhere, but it was worse inside the buildings. Over Amalfi's head a window shattered explosively, and a woman's body came twisting and tumbling through the shuddering air.

* * *

Amalfi heaved himself up, spitting blood, and ran again. The pavement ahead was cracked in great, irregular shards, like a madman's mosaic. Just beyond, the blocks were tilted all awry, reminding Amalfi irrelevantly of a breakwater he had seen on some other planet, in some other century—

He was clambering over them before he realized that these could only mark the rim of the original city of IMT. There were still more buildings on the other side of the huge, rock-filled trench, but the trench itself showed where the perimeter of the ancient Okie had been sunk into the soil of the planet. Fighting for air with saw-edged rales, he threw himself from stone to stone toward the far edge of the trench. This was the most dangerous ground of all; if IMT were to lift now, he would be ground as fine as mincemeat in the tumbling rocks. If he could just reach the marches of the Barrens—

Behind him, the groaning rose steadily in pitch, until it sounded like the tearing of an endless sheet of metal. Ahead, across the Barrens to the east, his own city gleamed in the last rays of the twin suns. There was fighting around it; little bright flashes were sputtering at its edge. The rockets Amalfi had heard, four of them, were arrowing across the sky, and black things dropped from them. The Okie city responded with spouts of smoke.

Then there was an unbearably bright burst. After Amalfi could see again, there were only three rockets. In another few seconds there wouldn't be any: the City Fathers never missed.

Amalfi's lungs burned. He felt sod under his sandals. A twisted runner of furze lashed across his ankle and he fell again.

He tried to get up and could not. The seared turf, on which an ancient rebel city once had stood, rumbled threateningly. He rolled over. The squat towers of IMT were swaying, and all around the edge of the city, huge blocks and clods heaved and turned over, like surf. Impossibly, a thin line of light, intense and ruddy, appeared above the moiling rocks. The suns were shining *under the city*—

The line of light widened. The old city took the air with an immense bound, and the rending of the long-rooted foundations was ear-splitting. From the sides of the huge mass, human beings threw themselves desperately toward the Barrens; all those Amalfi saw were serfs. The Proctors, of course, were still trying to control the flight of IMT—

The city rose majestically. It was gaining speed. Amalfi's heart hammered. If Heldon and his crew could figure out in time what

Amalfi had done to the controls, Karst's old ballad would be re-enacted, and the crushing rule of the Proctors made safe forever.

But Amalfi had done his work well. The city of IMT did not stop rising. With a profound, visceral shock, Amalfi realized that it was already nearly a mile up, and still accelerating. The air would be thinning up there, and the Proctors had forgotten too much to know what to do—

A mile and a half.

Two miles.

It grew smaller. At five miles it was just a wavery ink-blot, lit on one side. At seven miles it was a point of dim light.

A bristle-topped head and a pair of enormous shoulders lifted cautiously from a nearby gully. It was Karst. He continued to look aloft for a moment, but IMT at ten miles was invisible. He looked down to Amalfi.

"Can . . . can it come back?" he said huskily.

"No," Amalfi said, his breathing gradually coming under control. "Keep watching, Karst. It isn't over yet. Remember that the Proctors had called the Earth cops—"

At that same moment, the city of IMT reappeared—in a way. A third sun flowered in the sky. It lasted for three or four seconds. Then it dimmed and died.

"The cops were warned," Amalfi said softly, "to watch for an Okie city trying to make a getaway. They found it, and they dealt with it. Of course they got the wrong city, but they don't know that. They'll go home now—and now we're home, and so are you and your people. Home on Earth, for good."

Around them, there was a murmuring of voices, hushed with disaster, and with something else, too—something so old, and so new, that it hardly had a name on the planet that IMT had ruled. It was called freedom.

"On Earth?" Karst repeated. He and the mayor climbed painfully to their feet. "What do you mean? This is not Earth—"

Across the Barrens, the Okie city glittered-the city that had pitched camp to mow some lawns. A cloud of stars was rising behind it.

"It is now," Amalfi said. "We're all Earthmen, Karst. Earth is more than just one little planet, buried in another galaxy than this. Earth is much more important than that.

"Earth isn't a place. It's an idea."

How Beautiful with Banners

Feeling as naked as a peppermint soldier in her transparent film wrap, Dr. Ulla Hillström watched a flying cloak swirl away towards the black horizon with a certain consequent irony. Although nearly transparent itself in the distant dim arc-light flame that was Titan's sun, the fluttering creature looked warmer than what she was wearing, for all that reason said it was at the same minus 316° F. as the thin methane it flew in. Despite the virus space-bubble's warranted and eerie efficiency, she found its vigilance—itself probably as close to alive as the flying cloak was—rather difficult to believe in, let alone to trust.

The machine—as Ulla much preferred to think of it—was inarguably an improvement on the old-fashioned pressure suit. Fashioned (or more accurately, cultured) of a single colossal protein molecule, the vanishingly thin sheet of life-stuff processed gases, maintained pressure, monitored radiation through almost the whole of the electromagnetic spectrum, and above all did not get in the way. Also, it could not be cut, punctured, or indeed sustain any damage short of total destruction; macroscopically, it was a single, primary unit, with all the physical integrity of a crystal of salt or steel.

If it did not actually think, Ulla was grateful; often it almost seemed to, which was sufficient. Its primary drawback for her was that much of the time it did not really seem to be there.

Still, it seemed to be functioning; otherwise, Ulla would in fact have been as solid as a stick of candy, toppled forever across the confectionery whiteness that frosted the knife-edge stones of this cruel moon, layer upon layer. Outside—only a perilous few inches from the lightly clothed warmth of her skin—the brief gust the cloak had been soaring on died, leaving behind a silence so cataleptic that she could hear the snow creaking in a mockery of motion. Impossible though it was to comprehend, it was getting still colder out there; Titan was swinging out across Saturn's orbit towards eclipse, and the apparently fixed sun was secretly going down, its descent sensed by the snows no matter what her Earthly eyes, accustomed to the nervousness of living skies, tried to tell her. In another two Earth days it would be gone, for an eternal week.

At the thought, Ulla turned to look back the way she had come that morning. The virus bubble flowed smoothly with the motion, and the stars became brighter as it compensated for the fact that the sun was now at her back. She still could not see the base camp, of course. She had come too far for that, and in any event it was wholly underground except for a few wiry palps, hollowed out of the bitter rock by the blunt-nosed ardor of prolapse drills; the repeated nannosecond birth and death of primordial ylem the drills had induced while that cavern was being imploded had seemed to convulse the whole demon womb of this world, but in the present silence the very memory of the noise seemed false.

Now there was no sound but the creaking of the methane snow; and nothing to see but a blunt, faint spearhead of hazy light, deceptively like an Earthly aurora or the corona of the sun, pushing its way from below the edge of the cold into the indifferent company of the stars. Saturn's rings were rising, very slightly awaver in the dark-blue air, like the banners of a spectral army. The idiot face of the giant gas planet itself, faintly striped with meaningless storms as though trying to remember a childhood passion, would be glaring down at her before she could get home if she didn't get herself in motion soon. Obscurely disturbed, Dr. Hillström faced front and began to unlimber her sled.

The touch and clink of the instruments cheered her a little, even in this ultimate loneliness. She was efficient—many years, and a good many suppressed impulses had seen to that; it was too late for temblors, especially so far out from the sun that had warmed her Stockholm streets and her silly friendships. All those null-adventures were gone now like a sickness. The phantom embrace of the virus suit was perhaps less satisfying—only perhaps—but it was much more reliable. Much more reliable; she could depend on that.

Then, as she bent to thrust the spike of a thermocouple into the wedding-cake soil, the second flying cloak (or was it that same one?) hit her in the small of the back and tumbled her into nightmare.

II

With the sudden darkness there came a profound, ambiguous emotional blow—ambiguous, yet with something shockingly familiar about it. Instantly exhausted, she felt herself go flaccid and unstrung, and her mind, adrift in nowhere, blurred and spun downward too into the swamps of trance.

The long fall slowed just short of unconsciousness, lodged precariously upon a shelf of a dream, a mental buttress founded four years in the past—a long distance, when one recalls that in a four-dimensional plenum every second of time is one hundred eighty-six thousand miles of space—and eight hundred millions of miles away. The memory was curiously inconsequential to have arrested her, let alone supported her: not of her home, of her few triumphs, or even of her aborted marriage, but of a sordid little encounter with a reporter that she had talked herself into at the Madrid genetics conference, when she herself had already been an associate professor, a Swedish Government delegate, a twenty-five-year-old divorcee, and altogether a woman who should have known better.

But better than what? The life of science even in those days had been almost by definition that life of the eternal campus exile; there was so much to learn—or, at least, to show competence in—that people who wanted to be involved in the ordinary, vivid concerns of human beings could not stay with it long, indeed often could not even be recruited; they turned aside from the prospect with a shudder, or even a snort of scorn. To prepare for the sciences had become a career in indefinitely protracted adolescence, from which one awakened fitfully to find one's self spending a one-night stand in the body of a stranger. It had given her no pride, no self-love, no defenses of any sort; only a queer kind of virgin numbness, highly dependent upon familiar surroundings and valueless habits, and easily breached by any normally confident siege in print, in person anywhere—and remaining just as numb as before when the seizure of fashion, politics, or romanticism had swept by and left her stranded, too easy a recruit to have been allowed into the center of things or even considered for it.

Curious—most curious—that in her present remote terror she should find even a moment's rest upon so wobbling a pivot. The Madrid incident had not been important; she had been through with it almost at once. Of course, as she had often told herself, she had never been promiscuous, and had often described the affair, defiantly, as that one (or at worst, second) test of the joys of impulse which any woman is entitled to have in her history. Nor had it really been that joyous: she could not now recall the boy's face, and remembered how he had felt primarily because he had been in so casual and contemptuous a hurry.

But now that she came to dream of it, she saw with a bloodless, lightless eye that all her life, in this way and in that, she had been repeatedly seduced by the inconsequential. She had nothing else to remember even in this hour of her presumptive death. Acts have consequences, a thought told her, but not ours; we have done, but never felt. We are no more alone on Titan, you and I, than we have ever been. *Basta, per carita!*—so much for Ulla.

Awakening in this same darkness as before, Ulla felt the virus bubble snuggling closer to her blind skin, and recognized the shock that had so regressed her: a shock of recognition, but recognition of something she had never felt herself. Alone in a Titanic snowfield, she had eavesdropped on an . . .

No. Not possible. Sniffling, and still blind, she pushed the cozy bubble away from her breasts and tried to stand up. Light flushed briefly around her, as though the bubble had cleared just above her forehead and then clouded again. She was still alive, but everything else was utterly problematical. What had happened to her? She simply did not know.

Therefore, she thought, begin with ignorance. No one begins anywhere else . . . but I didn't know even that, once upon a time.

Hence:

III

Though the virus bubble ordinarily regulated itself, there was a control box on her hip—actually an ultrashort-range microwave transmitter—by which it could be modulated, against more special environments than the bubble itself could cope with alone. She had never had to use it before, but she tried it now.

The fogged bubble cleared patchily, but it would not stay cleared. Crazy moires and herringbone patterns swept over it, changing direction repeatedly, and outside the snowy landscape kept changing color like a delirium. She found, however, that by continuously working the frequency knob on her box—at random, for the responses seemed to bear no relation to the Braille calibrations on the dial—she could maintain outside vision of a sort in pulses of two or three seconds each.

This was enough to show her, finally, what had happened. There was a flying cloak around her. This in itself was unprecedented; the cloaks had never attacked a man before, or indeed paid any of them the least attention during their brief previous forays. On the other hand, this was the first time anyone had ventured more than five or ten minutes outdoors in a virus suit.

It occurred to her suddenly that in so far as anything was known about the nature of the cloaks, they were in some respects much like the bubbles. It was almost as though the one were a wild species of the other.

It was an alarming notion and possibly only a trope, containing as little truth as most poetry. Annoyingly, she found herself wondering if, once she got out of this mess, the men at the base camp would take to referring to it as "the cloak and suit business."

The snowfield began to turn brighter; Saturn was rising. For a moment the drifts were a pale straw color, the normal hue of Saturn-light through an atmosphere; then it turned a raving Kelly green. Muttering, Ulla twisted the potentiometer dial, and was rewarded with a brief flash of normal illumination which was promptly over-ridden by a torrent of crimson lake, as though she were seeing everything in terms of a series of lithographer's color separations.

Since she could not help this, she clenched her teeth and ignored it. It was more important to find out what the flying cloak had done to her bubble, if she were to have any hope of shucking the thing.

There was no clear separation between the bubble and the Titanian creature. They seemed to have blended into a mélange which was neither one nor the other, but a sort of coarse burlesque of both. Yet the total surface area of the integument about her did not seem to be any greater—only more ill-fitting, less responsive to her own needs. Not *much* less; after all, she was still alive, and any really gross insensitivity to the demands and cues of her body would have been instantly fatal; but there was no way to guess how long the bubble would stay even that obedient. At the moment the wild thing that had enslaved it was perhaps most like a bear sark, dangerous to the wearer only if she panicked, but the change might well be progressive, pointed ultimately towards some Saturnine equivalent of the shirt of Nessus.

And that might be happening very rapidly. She might not be allowed the time to think her way out of this fix by herself. Little though she wanted any help from the men at the base camp, and useless though she was sure they would prove, she'd damn well better ask for it now, just in case.

But the bubble was not allowing any radio transmission through its roiling unicell wall today. The earphone was dead; not even the hiss of the stars came through it—only an occasional pop of noise that was born of entropy loss in the circuits themselves.

She was cut off. *Nun denn, allein!*

With the thought, the bubble cloak shifted again around her. A sudden pressure at her lower abdomen made her stumble forward over the crisp snow, four or five steps. Then it was motionless once more, except within itself.

That it should be able to do this was not surprising, for the cloaks had to be able to flex voluntarily at least a little in order the catch the thermals they rode, and the bubble had to be able to vary its dimensions, and surface tension over a wide range to withstand pressure changes, outside and in, and do it automatically. No, of course the combination would be able to move by itself; what was disquieting was that it should want to.

Another stir of movement in the middle distance caught her eye: a free cloak, seemingly riding an updraught over a fixed point. For a moment she wondered what on that ground could be warm enough to produce so localized a thermal. Then, abruptly, she realized that she was shaking with hatred, and fought furiously to drive the spasm down, her fingernails slicing into her naked palms.

A raster of jagged black lines, like a television interference pattern, broke across her view and brought her attention fully back to the minutely solipsistic confines of her dilemma. The wave of emotion, nevertheless, would not quite go away, and she had a vague but persistent impression that it was being imposed from outside, at least in part—a cold passion she was interpreting as fury because its real nature, whatever it was, had no necessary relevance to her own imprisoned soul. For all that it was her own life and no other that was in peril, she felt guilty, as though she was eavesdropping, and as angry with herself as with what she was overhearing; yet burning as helplessly as the forbidden lamp in the bedchamber of Psyche and Eros.

Another trope—but was it, after all, so far-fetched? She was a mortal present at the mating of inhuman essences; mountainously far from home; borne here like the invisible lovers upon the arms of the wind; empalaced by a whole virgin-white world, over which flew the banners of a high god and a father of gods; and, equally appropriately, Venus was very far away from whatever love was being celebrated here.

What ancient and coincidental nonsense! Next she would be thinking herself degraded at the foot of some cross.

Yet the impression, of an eerie tempest going on just slightly outside any possibility of understanding what it was, would not pass away. Still worse, it seemed to mean something, to be important, to mock her with subtle clues to matters of great moment, of which her own present trap was only the first and not necessarily the most significant.

And suppose that all these impressions were in fact not extraneous or irrelevant, but did have some import—not just as an abstract puzzle, but to that morsel of displaced life that was Ulla Hillström? She was certainly no Freudian—that farrago of poetry and tosh had been passé for so long that it was now hard to understand how anybody, let alone a whole era, had been bemused by it—but it was too late now to rule out the repulsive possibility. No matter how frozen her present world, she could not escape the fact that, from the moment the cloak had captured her, she had been equally ridden by a Sabbat of specifically erotic memories, images, notions, analogies, myths, symbols, and frank physical sensations, all the more obtrusive because they were both inappropriate and disconnected. It might well have to be faced that a season of love can fall due in the heaviest weather—and never mind the terrors that flow in with it, or what deep damnations. At the very least, it was possible that somewhere in all this was the clue that would help her to divorce herself at last even from this violent embrace.

But the concept was preposterous enough to defer consideration of it if there were any other avenues open, and at least one seemed to be: the source of the thermal. The virus bubble, like many of the Terrestrial microorganisms to which it was analogous, could survive temperatures well above boiling, but it seemed reasonable to assume that the flying cloaks, evolved on a world where even words congealed, might be sensitive to a relatively slight amount of heat.

Now, could she move inside this shroud of her own volition? She tried a step. The sensation was tacky, as though she were ploughing in thin honey, but it did not impede her except for a slight imposed clumsiness which experience ought to obviate. She was able to mount the sled with no trouble.

The cogs bit into the snow with a dry, almost inaudible squeaking, and the sled inched forward. Ulla held it to as slow a crawl as possible, because of her interrupted vision.

The free cloak was still in sight, approximately where it had been before, in so far as she could judge against this featureless snowscape—which was fortunate, since it might well be her only flag for the source of the thermal, whatever it was.

A peculiar fluttering in her surroundings—a whisper of sound, of motion, of flickering in the light—distracted her. It was as though her compound sheath were trembling slightly. The impression grew slowly more pronounced as the sled continued to lurch forward. As usual, there seemed to be nothing she could do about it except, possibly, to retreat; but she could not do that either, now; she was committed. Outside, she began to hear the soft soughing of a steady wind.

The cause of the thermal, when she finally reached it, was almost bathetic: a pool of liquid. Placid and deep blue, it lay inside a fissure in a low, heart-shaped hummock, rimmed with feathery snow. It looked like nothing more or less than a spring, though she did not for a moment suppose that the liquid could be water. She could not see the bottom of it; evidently, it was welling up from a fair depth. The spring analogy was probably completely false; the existence of anything in a liquid state on this world had to be thought of as a form of vulcanism. Certainly the column of heat rising from it was considerable; despite the thinness of the air, the wind here nearly howled. The free cloak floated up and down, about a hundred feet above her, like the last leaf of a long, cruel autumn. Nearer home, the bubble cloak shook with something comically like subdued fury.

Now, what to do? Should she push boldly into that cleft, hoping that the alien part of the bubble cloak would be unable to bear the heat? Close up, that course now seemed foolish, as long as she was ignorant of the real nature of the magma down there. And, besides, any effective immersion would probably have to surround at least half of the total surface area of the bubble, which wasn't practicable—the well wasn't big enough to accommodate it, even supposing that the compromised virus suit did not fight back, as in the pure state it had been obligated to do. On the whole, she was reluctantly glad that the experiment was impossible, for the mere notion of risking a new immolation in that problematical hole gave her the horrors.

Yet the time left for decision was obviously now very short, even supposing—as she had no right to do—that the environment-maintaining functions of the suit were still in perfect order. The quivering of the bubble was close to being explosive, and even were it to remain intact, it might shut her off from the outside world at any second.

The free cloak dipped lower, as if in curiosity. That only made the trembling worse. She wondered why.

Was it possible—was it possible that the thing embracing her companion was jealous?

IV

There was no time left to examine the notion, no time even to sneer at it. Act—act! Forcing her way off the sled, she stumbled to the mound and looked frantically for some way of stopping it up. If she could shut off the thermal, bring the free cloak still closer—but how?

Throw rocks. But were there any? Yes, there were two, not very big, but at least she could move them. She bent stiffly and tumbled them into the crater.

The liquid froze around them with soundless speed. In seconds, the snow rimming the pool had drawn completely over it, like lips closing, leaving behind only a faint dimpled streak of shadow on a white ground.

The wind moaned and died, and the free cloak, its hems outspread to the uttermost, sank down as if to wrap her in still another deadly swath. Shadow spread around her; the falling cloak, its color deepening, blotted Saturn from the sky, and then was sprawling over the beautiful banners of the rings—

The virus bubble convulsed and turned black, throwing her to the frozen ground beside the hummock like a bead doll. A blast of wind squalled over her.

Terrified, she tried to curl into a ball. The suit puffed up around her.

Then at last, with a searing, invisible wrench at its contained kernel of space-time, which burned out the control box instantly, the single creature that was the bubble cloak tore itself free of Ulla and rose to join its incomplete fellow.

In the single second before she froze forever into the livid backdrop of Titan, she failed even to find time to regret what she had never felt; for she had never known it, and only died as she had lived, an artifact of successful calculation. She never saw the cloaks go flapping away downwind—nor could it ever have occurred to her that she had brought heterosexuality to Titan, thus beginning that long evolution the end of which, sixty millions of years away, no human being would see.

No; her last thought was for the virus bubble, and it was only three words long:

You goddam philanderer—

Almost on the horizon, the two cloaks, the two Titanians, flailed and tore at each other, becoming smaller and smaller with distance. Bits and pieces of them flaked off and fell down the sky like ragged tears. Ungainly though the cloaks normally were, they courted even more clumsily.

Beside Ulla, the well was gone; it might never have existed. Overhead, the banners of the rings flew changelessly, as though they too had seen nothing—or perhaps, as though in the last six billion years they had seen everything, siftings upon siftings in oblivion, until nothing remained but the banners of their own mirrored beauty.

This Earth of Hours

The advance squadron was coming into line as Master Sergeant Oberholzer came onto the bridge of the *Novoe Washingtongrad,* saluted, and stood stiffly to the left of Lieutenant Campion, the exec, to wait for orders. The bridge was crowded and crackling with tension, but after twenty years in the Marines it was all old stuff to Oberholzer. The *Hobo* (as most of the enlisted men called her, out of earshot of the brass) was at the point of the formation, as befitted a virtually indestructible battleship already surfeited with these petty conquests. The rest of the cone was sweeping on ahead, in the swift enveloping maneuver which had reduced so many previous planets before they had been able to understand what was happening to them.

This time, the planet at the focus of all those shifting conic sections of raw naval power was a place called Callë. It was showing now on a screen that Oberholzer could see, turning as placidly as any planet turned when you were too far away from it to see what guns it might be pointing at you. Lieutenant Campion was watching it too, though he had to look out of the very corners of his eyes to see it at all.

If the exec were caught watching the screen instead of the meter board assigned to him, Captain Hammer would probably reduce him to an ensign. Nevertheless, Campion never took his eyes off the image of Callë, This one was going to be rough.

Captain Hammer was watching, too. After a moment he said, "Sound!" in a voice like sandpaper.

"By the pulse six, sir," Lieutenant Spring's voice murmured from the direction of the 'scope. His junior, very raw youngster named Rover, passed him a chit from the plotting table. "For that read: By the briefs five eight nine, sir," the invisible navigator corrected.

Oberholzer listened without moving while Captain Hammer muttered under his breath to Flo-Mar 12-Upjohn, the only civilian allowed on the bridge—and small wonder, since he was the Consort of State of the Matriarchy itself. Hammer had long ago become accustomed enough to his own bridge to be able to control who overheard him, but 12-Upjohn's answering whisper must have been audible to every man there.

"The briefing said nothing about a second inhabited planet," the Consort said, a little peevishly. "But then there's very little we *do* know about this system—that's part of our trouble. What makes you think it's a colony?"

"A colony from Callë, not one of ours," Hammer said, in more or less normal tones; evidently he had decided against trying to keep only half of the discussion private. "The electromagnetic 'noise' from both planets has the same spectrum—the energy level, the output, is higher on Callë, that's all. That means similar machines being used in similar ways. And let me point out, Your Excellency, that the outer planet is in opposition to Callë now, which will put it precisely in our rear if we complete this maneuver."

"*When* we complete this maneuver," 12-Upjohn said firmly. "Is there any evidence of communication between the two planets?"

Hammer frowned. "No," he admitted.

"Then we'll regard the colonization hypothesis as unproved—and stand ready to strike back hard if events prove us wrong. I think we have a sufficient force here to reduce *three* planets like Callë if we're driven to that pitch."

Hammer grunted and resigned the argument. Of course it was quite possible that 12-Upjohn was right; he did not lack for experience—in fact, he wore the Silver Earring, as the most-traveled Consort of State ever to ride the Standing Wave. Nevertheless Oberholzer repressed a sniff with difficulty. Like all the military, he was a colonial; he had never seen the Earth, and never expected to; and both as a colonial and as a Marine who had been fighting the Matriarchy's battles all his adult life, he was more than a little contemptuous of Earthmen, with their tandem names and all that they implied. Of course it was not the Consort of State's fault that he had been born on Earth, and so had been named only Marvin 12 out of the misfortune of being a male; nor that he had married into Florence Upjohn's cabinet, that being the only way one could become a cabinet member and Marvin 12 having been taught from birth to believe such a post the highest honor a man might covet. All the same, neither 12-Upjohn nor his entourage of drones filled Oberholzer with confidence.

Nobody, however, had asked MSgt. Richard Oberholzer what he

thought, and nobody was likely to. As the chief of all the non-Navy enlisted personnel on board the *Hobo,* he was expected to be on the bridge when matters were ripening toward criticality; but his duty there was to listen, not to proffer advice. He could not in fact remember any occasion when an officer had asked his opinion, though he had received—and executed—his fair share of near-suicidal orders from bridges long demolished.

"By the pulse five point five," Lieutenant Spring's voice sang.

"Sergeant Oberholzer," Hammer said.

"Aye, sir."

"We are proceeding as per orders. You may now brief your men and put them into full battle gear."

Oberholzer saluted and went below. There was little enough he could tell the squad—as 12-Upjohn had said, Callë's system was nearly unknown—but even that little would improve the total ignorance in which they had been kept till now. Luckily, they were not much given to asking questions of a strategic sort; like impressed spacehands everywhere, the huge mass of the Matriarchy's interstellar holdings meant nothing to them but endlessly riding the Standing Wave, with battle and death lurking at the end of every jump. Luckily also, they were inclined to trust Oberholzer, if only for the low cunning he had shown in keeping most of them alive, especially in the face of unusually Crimean orders from the bridge.

This time Oberholzer would need every ounce of trust and erg of obedience they would give him. Though he never expected anything but the worst, he had a queer cold feeling that this time he was going to get it. There were hardly any data to go on yet, but there had been something about Callë that looked persuasively like the end of the line.

Very few of the forty men in the wardroom even looked up as Oberholzer entered. They were checking their gear in the dismal light of the fluorescents, with the single-mindedness of men to whom a properly wound gun-tube coil, a properly set face-shield gasket, a properly fueled and focused vaulting jet, have come to mean more than parents, children, retirement pensions, the rule of law, or the logic of empire. The only man to show any flicker of interest was Sergeant Cassirir—as was normal, since he was Oberholzer's understudy—and he did no more than look up from over the straps of his antigas suit and say, "Well?"

"Well," Oberholzer said, "now hear this."

There was a sort of composite jingle and clank as the men lowered their gear to the deck or put it aside on their bunks.

"We're investing a planet called Callë in the Canes Venatici cluster," Oberholzer said, sitting down on an olive-drab canvas pack stuffed with lysurgic acid grenades. "A cruiser called the *Assam Dragon*—you were with her on her shakedown, weren't you, Himber?—touched down here ten years ago with a flock of tenders and got swallowed up. They got two or three quick yells for help out and that was that—nothing anybody could make much sense of, no weapons named or description of the enemy. So here we are, loaded for the kill."

"Wasn't any Calley in command of the *Assam Dragon* when I was aboard," Himber said doubtfully.

"Nah. Place was named for the astronomer who spotted her, from the rim of the cluster, a hundred years ago," Oberholzer said. "Nobody names planets for ship captains. Anybody got any sensible questions?"

"Just what kind of trouble are we looking for?" Cassirir said.

"That's just it—we don't know. This is closer to the center of the Galaxy than we've ever gotten before. It may be a population center too; could be that Callë is just one piece of a federation, at least inside its own cluster. That's why we've got the boys from Momma on board; this one could be damn important."

Somebody sniffed. "If this cluster is full of people, how come we never picked up signals from it?"

"How do you know we never did?" Oberholzer retorted. "For all I know, maybe that's why the *Assam Dragon* came here in the first place. Anyhow that's not our problem. All we're—"

The lights went out. Simultaneously, the whole mass of the *Novoe Washingtongrad* shuddered savagely, as though a boulder almost as big as she was had been dropped on her.

Seconds later, the gravity went out too.

II

Flo-Mar 12-Upjohn knew no more of the real nature of the disaster than did the wardroom squad, nor did anybody on the bridge, for that matter. The blow had been indetectable until it struck, and then most of the fleet was simply annihilated; only the *Hobo* was big enough to survive the blow, and she survived only partially—in fact, in five pieces. Nor did the Consort of State ever know by what miracle the section he was in hit Callë still partially under power; he was not privy to the self-salvaging engineering principles of battleships. All he knew—once he struggled back to consciousness—was that he was still alive, and that there was a broad shaft of sunlight coming through a top-to-bottom split in one wall of what had been his office aboard ship.

He held his ringing head for a while, then got up in search of water. Nothing came out of the dispenser, so he unstrapped his dispatch case from the underside of his desk and produced a pint palladium flask of vodka. He had screwed up his face to sample this—at the moment he would have preferred water—when a groan reminded him that there might be more than one room in his suddenly shrunken universe, as well as other survivors.

He was right on both counts. Though the ship section he was in consisted mostly of engines of whose function he had no notion, there were also three other staterooms. Two of these were deserted, but the third turned out to contain a battered member of his own staff, by name Robin One.

The young man was not yet conscious and 12-Upjohn regarded him with a faint touch of despair. Robin One was perhaps the last man in space that the Consort of State would have chosen to be shipwrecked with.

That he was utterly expendable almost went without saying; he was, after all, a drone. When the perfection of sperm electrophoresis had enabled parents for the first time to predetermine the sex of their children, the predictable result had been an enormous glut of males—which was directly accountable for the present regime on Earth. By the time the people and the lawmakers, thoroughly frightened by the crazy years of fashion upheavals, "beefcake," polyandry, male prostitution, and all the rest, had come to their senses, the Matriarchy was in to stay; a weak electric current had overturned civilized society as drastically as the steel knife had demoralized the Eskimos.

Though the tide of excess males had since receded somewhat, it had left behind a wrack, of which Robin One was a bubble. He was a drone, and hence superfluous by definition—fit only to be sent colonizing, on diplomatic missions or otherwise thrown away.

Superfluity alone, of course, could hardly account for his presence on 12-Upjohn's staff. Officially, Robin One was an interpreter; actually—since nobody could know the language the Consort of State might be called upon to understand on this mission—he was a poet, a class of unattached males with special privileges in the Matriarchy, particularly if what they wrote was of the middling-difficult or Hillyer Society sort. Robin One was an eminently typical member of this class, distractible, sulky, jealous, easily wounded, homosexual, lazy except when writing, and probably (to give him the benefit of the doubt, for 12-Upjohn had no ear whatever for poetry) the second-worst poet of his generation.

It had to be admitted that assigning 12-Upjohn a poet as an interpreter on this mission had not been a wholly bad idea, and that if Hildegard Muller of the Interstellar Understanding Commission had not thought of it, no mere male would have been likely to—least of all Bar-Rob 4-Agberg, Director of Assimilation. The nightmare of finding the whole of the center of the Galaxy organized into one vast federation, much older than Earth's, had been troubling the State Department for a long time, at first from purely theoretical considerations—all those heart-stars were much older than those in the spiral arms, and besides, where star density in space is so much higher, interstellar travel does not look like quite so insuperable an obstacle as it long had to Earthmen—and later from certain practical signs, of which the obliteration of the *Assam Dragon* and her tenders had been only the most provocative. Getting along with these people on the first contact would be vital, and yet the language barrier might well provoke a tragedy wanted by neither side, as the obliteration of Nagasaki in World War II had been provoked by the mistranslation of a single word. Under such circumstances, a man with a feeling for strange words in odd relationships might well prove to be useful, or even vital.

Nevertheless, it was with a certain grim enjoyment that 12-Upjohn poured into Robin One a good two-ounce jolt of vodka. Robin coughed convulsively and sat up, blinking

"Your Excellency—how—what's happened? I thought we were dead. But we've got lights again, and gravity "

He was observant, that had to be granted. "The lights are ours but the gravity is Callë's," 12-Upjohn explained tersely. "We're in a part of the ship that cracked up."

"Well, it's good that we've got power."

"We can't afford to be philosophical about it. Whatever shape it's in, this derelict is a thoroughly conspicuous object and we'd better get out of it in a hurry."

"Why?" Robin said. "We were supposed to make contact with these people. Why not just sit here until they notice and come to see us?"

"Suppose they just blast us to smaller bits instead? They didn't stop to parley with the fleet, you'll notice."

"This is a different situation," Robin said stubbornly, "I wouldn't have stopped to parley with that fleet myself, if I'd had the means of knocking it out first. It didn't look a bit like a diplomatic mission. But why should they be afraid of a piece of a wreck?"

The Consort of State stroked the back of his neck reflectively. The boy had a point. It was risky; on the other hand, how long would they survive foraging in completely unknown territory? And yet obviously they couldn't stay cooped up in here forever—especially if it was true that there was already no water.

He was spared having to make up his mind by a halloo from the direction of the office. After a startled stare at each other, the two hit the deck running.

Sergeant Oberholzer's face was peering grimly through the split in the bulkhead.

"Oho," he said. "So you did make it." He said some thing unintelligible to some invisible person outside, and then squirmed through the breach into the room, with considerable difficulty, since he was in full battle gear. "None of the officers did, so I guess that puts you in command."

"In command of what?" 12-Upjohn said dryly.

"Not very much," the Marine admitted. "I've got five men surviving, one of them with a broken hip, and a section of the ship with two drive units in it. It would lift, more or less, if we could jury-rig some controls, but I don't know where we'd go in it without supplies or a navigator—or an overdrive, for that matter." He looked about speculatively. "There was a Standing Wave transceiver in this section, I think, but it'd be a miracle if it still functioned."

"Would you know how to test it?" Robin asked.

"No. Anyhow we've got more immediate business than that. We've picked up a native. What's more, he speaks English—must have picked it up from the *Assam Dragon*. We started to ask him questions, but it turns out he's some sort of top official, so we brought him over here on the off chance that one of you was alive."

"What a break!" Robin One said explosively.

"A whole series of them," 12-Upjohn agreed, none too happily.

He had long ago learned to be at his most suspicious when the breaks seemed to be coming his way. "Well, better bring him in."

"Can't," Oberholzer said. "Apologies, Your Excellency, but he wouldn't fit. You'll have to come to him."

III

It was impossible to imagine what sort of stock the Callëan had evolved from. He seemed to be a thorough-going mixture of several different phyla. Most of him was a brown, segmented tube about the diameter of a barrel and perhaps twenty-five feet long, rather like a cross between a python and a worm. The front segments were carried upright, raising the head a good ten feet off the ground.

Properly speaking, 12-Upjohn thought, the Callëan really had no head, but only a front end, marked by two enormous faceted eyes and three upsetting simple eyes which were usually closed. Beneath these there was a collar of six short, squidlike tentacles, carried wrapped around the creature in a ropy ring. He was as impossible-looking as he was fearsome, and 12-Upjohn felt at a multiple disadvantage from the beginning.

"How did you learn our language?" he said, purely as a starter.

"I learned it from you," the Callëan said promptly. The voice was unexpectedly high, a quality which was accentuated by the creature's singsong intonation; 12-Upjohn could not see where it was coming from. "From your ship which I took apart, the dragon-of-war."

"Why did you do that?"

"It was evident that you meant me ill," the Callëan sang. "At that time I did not know that you were sick, but that became evident at the dissections."

"Dissection! You dissected the crew of the Dragon?"

"All but one."

There was a growl from Oberholzer. The Consort of State shot him a warning glance.

"You may have made a mistake," 12-Upjohn said. "A natural mistake, perhaps. But it was our purpose to offer you trade and peaceful relationships. Our weapons were only precautionary."

"I do not think so," the Callëan said, "and I never make mistakes. That you make mistakes is natural, but it is not natural to me."

12-Upjohn felt his jaw dropping. That the creature meant what he said could not be doubted: his command of the language was too complete to permit any more sensible interpretation. 12-Upjohn found himself at a loss; not only was the statement the most staggering he had ever heard from any sentient being, but while it was being made he had discovered how the Callëan spoke: the sounds issued at low volume from a multitude of spiracles or breath-holes all along the body, each hole producing only one pure tone, the words and intonations being formed in mid-air by intermodulation—a miracle of co-ordination among a multitude of organs obviously unsuitable for sound-forming at all. This thing was formidable—that would have been evident even without the lesson of the chunk of the *Novoe Washingtongrad* canted crazily in the sands behind them.

Sands? He looked about with a start. Until that moment the Callëan had so hypnotized his attention that he had forgotten to look at the landscape, but his unconscious had registered it. Sand, and nothing but sand. If there were better parts of Callë than this desert, they were not visible from here, all the way to the horizon.

"What do you propose to do with us?" he said at last. There was really nothing else to say; cut off in every possible sense from his home world, he no longer had any base from which to negotiate.

"Nothing," the Callëan said. "You are free to come and go as you please."

"You're no longer afraid of us?"

"No. When you came to kill me I prevented you, but you can no longer do that."

"There you've made a mistake, all right," Oberholzer said, lifting his rifle toward the multicolored, glittering jewels of the Callëan's eyes. "You know what this is—they must have had them on the Dragon."

"Don't be an idiot, Sergeant," 12-Upjohn said sharply. "We're in no position to make any threats." Nor, he added silently, should the Marine have called attention to his gun before the Callëan had taken any overt notice of it.

"I know what it is," the creature said. "You cannot kill me with that. You tried it often before and found you could not. You would remember this if you were not sick."

"I never saw anything that I couldn't kill with a Sussmann flamer," Oberholzer said between his teeth. "Let me try it on the bastard, Your Excellency."

"Wait a minute," Robin One said, to 12-Upjohn's astonishment. "I want to ask some questions—if you don't mind, Your Excellency?"

"I don't mind," 12-Upjohn said after an instant. Anything to get the Marine's crazy impulse toward slaughter sidetracked. "Go ahead."

"Did you dissect the crew of the *Assam Dragon* personally?" Robin asked the Callëan.

"Of course."

"Are you the ruler of this planet?"

"Yes."

"Are you the only person in this system?"

"No."

Robin paused and frowned. Then he said: "Are you the only person of your species in your system?"

"No. There is another on Xixobrax—the fourth planet."

Robin paused once more, but not, it seemed to 12-Upjohn, as though he were in any doubt; it was only as though he were gathering his courage for the key question of all. 12-Upjohn tried to imagine what it might be, and failed.

"How many of you are there?" Robin One said.

"I cannot answer that. As of the instant you asked me that question, there were eighty-three hundred thousand billion, one hundred and eighty-nine million, four hundred and sixty-five thousand, one hundred eighty; but now the number has changed, and it goes on changing."

"Impossible," 12-Upjohn said, stunned. "Not even two planets could support such a number—and you'd never allow a desert like this to go on existing if you had even a fraction of that population to support. I begin to think, sir, that you are a type normal to my business: the ordinary, unimaginative liar."

"He's not lying," Robin said, his voice quivering, "It all fits together. Just let me finish, sir, please. I'll explain, but I've got to go through to the end first."

"Well," 12-Upjohn said, helplessly, "all right, ahead." But he was instantly sorry, for what Robin One said was:

"Thank you. I have no more questions."

The Callëan turned in a great liquid wheel and poured away across the sand dunes at an incredible speed. 12-Upjohn shouted after him, without any clear idea of what it was that he was shouting—but no matter, for the Callëan took no notice. Within seconds, it seemed, he was only a threadworm in the middle distance, and then he was gone. They were all alone in the chill desert air.

Oberholzer lowered his rifle bewilderedly. "He's fast," he said to nobody in particular. "Cripes, but he's fast. I couldn't even keep him in the sights."

"That proves it," Robin said tightly. He was trembling, but whether with fright or elation, 12-Upjohn could not tell; possibly both.

"It had better prove something," the Consort of State said, trying hard not to sound portentous. There was something about this bright remote desert that made empty any possible pretense to dignity. "As far as I can see, you've just lost us what may have been our only chance to treat with these creatures . . . just as surely as the sergeant would have done it with his gun. Explain, please."

"I didn't really catch on until I realized that he was using the second person singular when he spoke to us," Robin said. If he had heard any threat implied in 12-Upjohn's charge, it was not visible; he seemed totally preoccupied. "There's no way to tell them apart in modern English. We thought he was referring to us as 'you' plural, but he wasn't, any more than his 'I' was a plural. He thinks we're all a part of the same personality—including the men from the Dragon, too—just as he is himself. That's why he left when I said I had no more questions. He can't comprehend that each of us has an independent ego. For him such a thing doesn't exist."

"Like ants?" 12-Upjohn said slowly. "I don't see how an advanced technology . . . but no, I do see. And if it's so, it means that any Calläan we run across could be their chief of state, but that no one of them actually is. The only other real individual is next door, on the fourth planet—another hive ego."

"Maybe not," Robin said. "Don't forget that he thinks we're part of one, too."

12-Upjohn dismissed that possibility at once. "He's sure to know his own system, after all. . . . What alarms me is the population figure he cited. It's got to be *at least* clusterwide—and from the exactness with which he was willing to cite it, for a given instant, he had to have immediate access to it. An instant, effortless census."

"Yes," Robin said. "Meaning mind-to-mind contact, from one to all, throughout the whole complex. That's what started me thinking about the funny way he used pronouns."

"If that's the case, Robin, we are *spurlos versenkt*. And my pronoun includes the Earth."

"They may have some limitations," Robin said, but it was clear that he was only whistling in the dark. "But at least it explains why they butchered the *Dragon*'s crew so readily—and why they're willing to let us wander around their planet as if we didn't even exist. We don't, for them. They can't have any respect for a single life. No wonder they didn't give a damn for the sergeant's gun!"

His initial flush had given way to a marble paleness; there were beads of sweat on his brow in the dry hot air, and he was trembling harder than ever. He looked as though he might faint in the next instant, though only the slightest of stutters disturbed his rush of words. But for once the Consort of State could not accuse him of agitation over trifles.

Oberholzer looked from one to the other, his expression betraying perhaps only disgust, or perhaps blank incomprehension—it was impossible to tell. Then, with a sudden sharp snick which made them both start, he shot closed the safety catch on the Sussmann.

"Well," he said in a smooth cold empty voice, "now we know what we'll eat."

IV

Their basic and dangerous division of plans and purposes began with that.

Sergeant Oberholzer was not a fool, as the hash marks on his sleeve and the battle stars on his ribbons attested plainly; he understood the implications of what the Callëan had said—at least after the Momma's boy had interpreted them; and he was shrewd enough not to undervalue the contribution the poor terrified fairy had made to their possible survival on this world. For the moment, however, it suited the Marine to play the role of the dumb sergeant to the hilt. If a full understanding of what the Callëans were like might reduce him to a like state of trembling impotence, he could do without it.

Not that he really believed that any such thing could happen to him; but it was not hard to see that Momma's boys were halfway there already—and if the party as a whole hoped to get anything done, they had to be jolted out of it as fast as possible.

At first he thought he had made it. "Certainly not!" the Consort of State said indignantly. "You're a man, sergeant, not a Callëan. Nothing the Callëans do is any excuse for your behaving otherwise than as a man."

"I'd rather eat an enemy than a friend," Oberholzer said cryptically. "Have you got any supplies inside there?"

"I—I don't know. But that has nothing to do with it."

"Depends on what you mean by 'it.' But maybe we can argue about that later. What are your orders, Your Excellency?"

"I haven't an order in my head," 12-Upjohn said with sudden, disarming frankness. "We'd better try to make some sensible plans first, and stop bickering. Robin, stop snuffling, too. The question is, what can we do besides trying to survive, and cherishing an idiot hope for a rescue mission?"

"For one thing, we can try to spring the man from the *Dragon*'s crew that these worms have still got alive," Oberholzer said. "If that's what he meant when he said they dissected all but one."

"That doesn't seem very feasible to me," 12-Upjohn said. "We have no idea where they're holding him—"

"Ask them. This one answered every question you asked him."

"—and even supposing that he's near by, we couldn't free him from a horde of Callëans, no matter how many dead bodies they let you pile up. At best, sooner or later you'd run out of ammunition."

"It's worth trying," Oberholzer said. "We could use the man-power."

"What for?" Robin One demanded. "He'd be just one more mouth to feed. At the moment, at least, they're feeding him."

"For raising ship," Oberholzer retorted. "*If* there's any damn chance of welding our two heaps of junk together and getting off this mudball. We ought to look into it, anyhow."

Robin One was looking more alarmed by the minute. If the prospect of getting into a fight with the Callëans had scared him, Oberholzer thought, the notion of hard physical labor evidently was producing something close to panic.

"Where could we go?" he said. "Supposing that we could fly such a shambles at all?"

"I don't know," Oberholzer said. "We don't know what's possible yet. But anything's better than sitting around here and starving. First off, I want that man from the *Dragon*."

"I'm opposed to it," 12-Upjohn said firmly. "The Callëans are leaving us to our own devices now. If we cause any real trouble they may well decide that we'd be safer locked up, or dead. I don't mind planning to lift ship if we can—but no military expeditions."

"Sir," Oberholzer said, "military action on this planet, is what I was sent here for. I reserve the right to use my own judgment. You can complain, if we ever get back—but I'm not going to let a man rot in a worm-burrow while I've got a gun on my back. You can come along or not, but we're going."

He signaled to Cassirir, who seemed to be grinning slightly. 12-Upjohn stared at him for a moment, and then shook his head.

"We'll stay," he said. "Since we have no water, Sergeant, I hope you'll do us the kindness of telling us where your part of the ship lies."

"That way, about two kilometers," Oberholzer said. "Help yourself. If you want to settle in there, you'll save us the trouble of toting Private Hannes with us on a stretcher."

"Of course," the Consort of State said. "We'll take care of him. But, Sergeant . . ."

"Yes, Your Excellency?"

"If this stunt of yours still leaves us all alive afterwards, and we do get back to any base of ours, I will *certainly* see to it that a complaint is lodged. I'm not disowning you now because it's obvious that we'll all have to work together to survive, and a certain amount of amity will be essential. But don't be deceived by that."

"I understand, sir," Oberholzer said levelly. "Cassirir, let's go. We'll backtrack to where we nabbed the worm, and then follow his trail to wherever he came from. Fall in."

The men shouldered their Sussmanns. 12-Upjohn and Robin One watched them go. At the last dune before the two would go out of sight altogether, Oberholzer turned and waved, but neither waved back. Shrugging, Oberholzer resumed plodding.

"Sarge?"

"Yeah?"

"How *do* you figure to spring this joker with only four guns?"

"Five guns if we spring him—I've got a side arm," Oberholzer reminded him. "We'll play it by ear, that's all. I want to see just how serious these worms are about leaving us alone, and letting us shoot them if we feel like it. I've got a hunch that they aren't very bright, one at a time, and don't react fast to strictly local situations. If this whole planet is like one huge body, and the worms are its brain cells, then we're germs—and maybe it'd take more than four germs to make the body do anything against us that counted, at least fast enough to do any good."

Cassirir was frowning absurdly; he did not seem to be taking the theory in without pain. Well, Cassirir had never been much of a man for tactics.

"Here's where we found the guy," one of the men said, pointing at the sand.

"That's not much of a trail," Cassirir said. "If there's any wind it'll be wiped out like a shot."

"Take a sight on it, that's all we need. You saw him run off—straight as a ruled line, no twists or turns around the dunes or anything. Like an army ant. If the trail sands over, we'll follow the sight. It's a cinch it leads someplace."

"All right," Cassirir said, getting out his compass. After a while the four of them resumed trudging.

There were only a few drops of hot, flat-tasting water left in the canteens, and their eyes were gritty and red from dryness and sand, when they topped the ridge that overlooked the nest. The word sprang instantly into Oberholzer's mind, though perhaps he had been expecting some such thing ever since Robin One had compared the Callëans to ants.

It was a collection of rough white spires, each perhaps fifty feet high, rising from a common doughlike mass which almost filled a small valley. There was no greenery around it and no visible source of water, but there were three roads, two of them leading into oval black entrances which Oberholzer could see from here. Occasionally—not often—a Callëan would scuttle out and vanish, or come speeding over the horizon and dart into the darkness. Some of the spires bore masts carrying what seemed to be antennae or more recondite electronic devices, but there were no windows to be seen; and the only sound in the valley, except for the dry dusty wind, was a subdued composite hum.

"Man!" Cassirir said, whispering without being aware of it. "It must be as black as the ace of spades in there. Anybody got a torch?"

Nobody had. "We won't need one anyhow," Oberholzer said confidently. "They've got eyes, and they can see in desert sunlight. That means they can't move around in total darkness. Let's go—I'm thirsty."

They stumbled down into the valley and approached the nearest black hole cautiously. Sure enough, it was not as black as it had appeared from the hill; there was a glow inside, which had been hidden from them against the contrast of the glaringly lit sands. Nevertheless, Oberholzer found himself hanging back.

While he hesitated, a Callëan came rocketing out of the entrance and pulled to a smooth, sudden stop.

"You are not to get in the way," he said, in exactly the same piping singsong voice the other had used.

"Tell me where to go and I'll stay out of your way," Oberholzer said. "Where is the man from the warship that you didn't dissect?"

"In Gnitonis, halfway around the world from here."

Oberholzer felt his shoulders sag, but the Callëan was not through. "You should have told me that you wanted him," he said. "I will have him brought to you. Is there else that you need?"

"Water," Oberholzer said hopefully.

"That will be brought. There is no water you can use here. Stay out of the cities; you will be in the way."

"How else can we eat?"

"Food will be brought. You should make your needs known; you are of low intelligence and helpless. I forbid nothing, I know you are harmless, and your life is short any case; but I do not want you to get in the way."

The repetition was beginning to tell on Oberholzer, and the frustration created by his having tried to use a battering ram against a freely swinging door was compounded by his mental picture of what the two Momma's boys would say when the squad got back.

"Thank you," he said, and bringing the Sussmann line, he trained it on the Callëan's squidlike head and squeezed the trigger.

It was at once established that the Callëans were as mortal to Sussmann flamers as is all other flesh and blood; this one made a very satisfactory corpse. Unsatisfied, the flamer bolt went on to burn a long slash in wall of the nest, not far above the entrance. Oberholzer grounded the rifle and waited to see what would happen next; his men hefted their weapons tensely.

For a few minutes there was no motion but the random twitching of the headless Callëan's legs. Evidently he was still not entirely dead, though he was a good four feet shorter than he had been before, and plainly was feeling the lack. Then, there was a stir inside the entrance.

A ten-legged animal about the size of a large rabbit emerged tentatively into the sunlight, followed by two more, and then by a whole series of them, perhaps as many as twenty. Though Oberholzer had been unabashed by the Callëans themselves, there was something about these things that made him feel sick. They were black and shiny, and they did not seem to have any eyes; their heavily armored heads bore nothing but a set of rudimentary palps and a pair of enormous pincers, like those of a June beetle.

Sightless or no, they were excellent surgeons. They cut the remains of the Callëan swiftly into sections, precisely one metamere to a section, and bore the carrion inside the nest. Filled with loathing, Oberholzer quickly forward and kicked one of the last in the procession. It toppled over like an unstable kitchen stool, but regained its footing as though nothing had happened. The kick had not hurt it visibly, though Oberholzer's toes felt as though he had kicked a Victorian iron dog. The creature, still holding its steak delicately in its living tongs, mushed implacably after the others back into the dubiety of the nest. Then all that was left in the broiling sunlight was a few pools of blackening blood seeping swiftly into the sand.

"Let's get out of here," Cassirir said raggedly.

"Stand fast," Oberholzer growled. "If they're mad at us, I want to know about it right now."

But the next Callëan to pass them, some twenty eternal minutes later, hardly even slowed down. "Keep out of the way," he said, and streaked away over the dunes. Snarling, Oberholzer caromed a bolt after him, but missed him clean.

"All right," he said. "Let's go back. No hitting the canteens till we're five kilometers past the mid-point cairn. March!"

The men were all on the verge of prostration by the time that point was passed, but Oberholzer never once had to enforce the order. Nobody, it appeared was eager to come to an end on Callë as a series of butcher's cuts in the tongs of a squad of huge black beetles.

V

"I know what they *think,*" the man from the *Assam Dragon* said. "I've heard them say it often enough."

He was a personable youngster, perhaps thirty, with blond wavy hair which had been turned almost white by the strong Callëan sunlight: his captors had walked him for three hours every day on the desert. He had once been the *Assam Dragon*'s radioman, a post which in interstellar flight is a branch of astronomy, not of communications; nevertheless, Oberholzer and the marine called him Sparks, in deference to a tradition which, 12-Upjohn suspected, the marines did not even know existed.

"Then why wouldn't there be a chance of our establishing better relations with the 'person' on the fourth planet?" 12-Upjohn said. "After all, there's never been an Earth landing there."

"Because the 'person' on Xixobrax is a colony of Callë, and knows everything that goes on here. It took two planets in co-operation to destroy the fleet. There's almost full telepathic communion between the two—in fact, all through the Central Empire. The only rapport that seems to weaken over short distances—interplanetary distances—is the sense of identity. That's why each planet has an 'I' of its own, its own ego. But it's not the kind of ego we know anything about. Xixobrax wouldn't give us any better deal than Callë has, any more than I'd give Callë a better deal than you would, Your Excellency. They have common purposes and allegiances. All the Central Empire seems to be like that."

12-Upjohn thought about it; but he did not like what he thought. It was a knotty problem, even in theory.

Telepathy among men had never amounted to anything. After the pioneer exploration of the microcosm in the Arpe Effect—the second of two unsuccessful attempts at an interstellar drive, long before the discovery of the Standing Wave—it had become easy to see this would be so. Psi forces in general were characteristic only of the subspace in which the primary particles of the atom had their being; their occasional manifestations in the macrocosm were statistical accidents, as weak and indirigible as spontaneous radioactive decay.

Up to now this had suited 12-Upjohn. It had always seemed to him that the whole notion of telepathy was a dodge—an attempt to bypass the plain duty of each to learn to know his brother, and, if possible, to learn to love him; the telepathy fanatics were out to short-circuit the task, to make easy the most difficult assignment a human being might undertake. He was well aware, too, of the bias against telepathy which was inherent in his profession of diplomat; yet he had always been certain of his case, hazy though it was around the edges. One of his proofs was that telepathy's main defenders invariably were incorrigibly lazy writers, from Upton Sinclair and Theodore Dreiser all the way down to . . .

All the same, it seemed inarguable that the whole center of the Galaxy, an enormously diverse collection of peoples and cultures, was being held together in a common and strife-free union by telepathy alone, or perhaps by telepathy and its even more dubious adjuncts: a whole galaxy held together by a force so unreliable that two human beings sitting across from each other at a card table had never been able to put it to an even vaguely practicable use.

Somewhere, there was a huge hole in the argument.

While he had sat helplessly thinking in these circles, even Robin One was busy, toting power packs to the welding crew which was working outside to braze together on the desert the implausible, misshapen lump of metal which the Marine sergeant was fanatically determined would become a ship again. Now the job was done, though no shipwright would admire it, and the question of where to go with it was being debated in full council. Sparks, for his part, was prepared to bet that the Calleans would not hinder their departure.

"Why would they have given us all this oxygen and stuff if they were going to prevent us from using it?" he said reasonably. "They know what it's for—even if they have no brains, collectively they're plenty smart enough."

"*No* brains?" 12-Upjohn said. "Or are you just exaggerating?"

"No brains," the man from the *Assam Dragon* insisted. "Just lots of ganglia. I gather that's the way all of the races of the Central Empire are organized, regardless of other physical differences. That's what they mean when they say we're all sick—hadn't you realized that?"

"No," 12-Upjohn said in slowly dawning horror. "You had better spell it out."

"Why, they say that's why we get cancer. They say that the brain is the ultimate source of all tumors, and is itself a tumor. They call it 'hostile symbiosis.'"

"Malignant?"

"In the long run. Races that develop them kill themselves off. Something to do with solar radiation; animals of planets of Population II stars develop them, Population I planets don't."

Robin One hummed an archaic twelve-tone series under his breath. There were no words to go with it, but the Consort of State recognized it; it was part of a chorale from a twentieth-century American opera, and the words went: *Weep, weep beyond time for this Earth of hours.*

"It fits," he said heavily. "So to receive and use a weak field like telepathy, you need a weak brain. Human beings will never make it."

"Earthworms of the galaxy, unite," Robin One said.

"They already have," Sergeant Oberholzer pointed out. "So where does all this leave us?"

"It means," 12-Upjohn said slowly, "that this Central Empire, where the stars are almost all Population I, is spreading out toward the spiral arms where the Earth lies. Any cluster civilizations they meet are natural allies—clusters are purely Population I—and probably have already been mentally assimilated. Any possible natural allies *we* meet, going around Population II stars, we may well pick a fight with instead."

"That's not what I meant," Sergeant Oberholzer said.

"I know what you meant; but this changes things. As I understand it, we have a chance of making a straight hop to the nearest Earth base, if we go on starvation rations—"

"—and if I don't make more than a point zero five percent error in plotting the course," Sparks put in.

"Yes. On the other hand, we can make *sure* of getting there by going in short leaps via planets known to be inhabited, but never colonized and possibly hostile. The only other possibility is Xixobrax, which I think we've ruled out. Correct?"

"Right as rain," Sergeant Oberholzer said. "Now I see what you're driving at, Your Excellency. The only thing is—you didn't mention that the stepping stone method will take us the rest of our lives."

"So I didn't," 12-Upjohn said bleakly. "But I hadn't forgotten it. The other side of *that* coin is that it will be even longer than that before the Matriarchy and the Central Empire collide."

"After which," Sergeant Oberholzer said with a certain relish, "I doubt that it'll be a Matriarchy, whichever wins. Are you calling for a vote, sir?"

"Well—yes, I seem to be."

"Then let's grasshopper," Sergeant Oberholzer said unhesitatingly. "The boys and I can't fight a point zero five percent error in navigation—but for hostile planets, we've got the flamers."

Robin One shuddered. "I don't mind the fighting part," he said unexpectedly. "But I *do* simply loathe the thought of being an old, old man when I get home. All the same, we do have to get the word back."

"You're agreeing with the sergeant?"

"Yes, that's what I said."

"I agree," Sparks said. "Either way we may not make it, but the odds are in favor of doing it the hard way."

"Very good," 12-Upjohn said. He was uncertain of his exact emotion at this moment; perhaps gloomy satisfaction was as close a description as any. "I make it unanimous. Let's get ready."

The sergeant saluted and prepared to leave the cabin; but suddenly he turned back.

"I didn't think very much of either of you, a while back," he said brutally. "But I'll tell you this: there must be something about brains that involves guts, too. I'll back 'em any time against any critter that lets itself be shot like a fish in a barrel—whatever the odds."

The Consort of State was still mulling that speech over as the madman's caricature of an interstellar ship groaned and lifted its lumps and angles from Callë. Who knows, he kept telling himself, who knows, it might even be true.

But he noticed that Robin One was still humming the chorale from *Psyche and Eros;* and ahead the galactic night was as black as death.

TESTAMENT OF ANDROS

Beside the hearth lie the ashes. There are voices in them. Listen:

My name is Theodor Andresson. I will write my story if you wish. I was at one time resident in astrophysics at Krajputnii, which I may safely describe as the greatest center of learning in the Middle East, perhaps of the entire Eastern Hemisphere. Later—until the chain of incidents which brought me to this *Zucht-Haus*—I was professor emeritus in radioastronomy at Calimyrna University, where I did the work leading to the discovery of the solar pulsation cycle.

I am sure that this work is not credited to me; that is of no importance. I would like it clearly understood that I am not making this record for your benefit, but for mine. Your request means nothing to me, and your pretense of interest in what I may write cannot deceive me. My erstwhile colleagues in the so-called sciences were masters of this kind of pretense. But they, too, were unable to prevent me from penetrating the masquerade at the end. How then does a simple doctor hope to succeed where the finest charlatanry has failed?

And what is allocation of credit—of what importance is priority of discovery before the inexorability of the pulsation cycle? It will work to its new conclusion without regard for your beliefs, my colleagues', or mine. Neither the pretended solicitude nor the real metal bars with which you have surrounded me will matter after that.

I proceed, therefore, to the matter at hand. My position at Calimyrna in that remote time before the cycle was discovered befitted my age (eighty-four years) and the reputation I had achieved in my specialty. I was in excellent health, though subject occasionally to depressions of spirit, readily ascribable to my being in a still-strange land and to those scars inflicted upon me in earlier times.

Despite these fits of moodiness, I had every reason to be happy. My eminence in my field afforded me the utmost satisfaction. Despite poverty and persecution in youth, I had won through to security. I had married Marguerita L—, in her youth and mine the toast of twelve continents, not only for her beauty but for her voice. I can still hear now the sound of her singing as I heard it for the first time—singing, on the stage of La Scala in Moscow, the rapturous quartet from the second act of Wagner's *Tristan et Messalina*.

It is quite true—I admit it immediately and calmly—that there were certain flaws in my world, even at Calimyrna. I do not mean the distractions which in old age replace, in the ordinary man, the furies of youth, but rather certain faults and fissures which I found in the world outside myself.

Even a man of my attainments expects at some time to grow old, and to find that process changing the way in which he looks at the world around him. There comes a time, however, when even the most rational of men must notice when these changes exceed the bounds of reason, when they begin to become extraordinary, even sinister. Shall I be specific? Consider, then—quite calmly—the fact that Marguerita did not herself grow old.

I passed into my eighth decade without taking more than perfunctory notice. I was deeply involved in the solar work we were then carrying on at Calimyrna. I had with me a young graduate student, a brilliant fellow of about thirty, who assisted me and who made certain original contributions of his own to the study. His name, and you will recognize it, was Mario di Ferruci. Calimyrna had completed its thousand-inch radiotelescope, the largest such antenna anywhere in the world, except for the 250-foot Manchester instrument. This was at once put to work in the search for so-called radio stars—those invisible bodies, many of them doubtless nearer to Earth than the nearest visible star, which can be detected only by their emission in the radio spectrum.

Completion of the thousand-inch freed the 600-inch paraboloid antenna for my use in solar work. The smaller instrument had insufficient beam width between half-power points for the critical stellar studies, but it was more suitable for my purpose.

I had in mind at that time a study of the disturbed sun. Hagen of the Naval Research Laboratory had already done the definitive study on the sun in its quiet state. I found myself more drawn to what goes on in the inferno of the sunspots—in the enormous, puzzling catastrophes of the solar flares—the ejection of immense radioactive clouds from the sun's interior high into its atmosphere.

It had already become clear that the radio-frequency emission from the disturbed sun was not, and could not be, thermal in origin, as is the RF emission of the quiet sun. The equivalent temperature of the disturbed sun in selected regions at times rises to billions of degrees, rendering the whole concept of thermal equivalency meaningless.

That the problem was not merely academic impressed me from the first. I have, if you will allow me the term, always had a sense of destiny, of *Schicksal,* an almost Spenglerian awareness of the pressure of fate against the retaining walls of human survival. It is not unique in me; I lay it to my Teutonic ancestry. And when I first encountered the problem of the disturbed sun, something within me felt that I had found destiny itself.

For here, just *here*, was the problem in which destiny was interested, in which some fateful answer awaited the asking of the omnipotent question. I felt this from the moment I first opened Hagen's famous paper—NRL Report 3504—and the more deeply I became interested in the sun as an RF radiator, the more the sensation grew.

Yet how to describe it? I was eighty-four, and this was early in 1956. In all those preceding years I had not known that the mortal frame could sustain such an emotion. Shall I call it a sensation of enormous, unresolvable dread? But I felt at the same time an ecstasy beyond joy, beyond love, beyond belief. And these transports of rapture and terror did not alternate as do the moods of an insane man, but occurred simultaneously—they were one and the same emotion.

Nor did the solar flares prove themselves unworthy of such deep responses. Flares have been observed in many stars. Some of them have been major outbursts, as indeed they would have to be to be visible to us at all. That such a flare could never occur on our own sun, furthermore, could not be said with certainty, for flares are local phenomena—they expend their energy only on one side of a star, not in all directions like a nova—and we had already seen the great detonation of July 29, 1948, on our own sun, which reached an energy level one hundred times the output of the quiet sun, which showed that we did not dare to set limits to what our own sun might yet do.

It was here, however, that I ran into trouble with young di Ferruci. He persistently and stubbornly refused to accept the analogy.

"It's penny-dreadful," he would say, as he had said dozens of times before. "You remind me of Dr. Richardson's stories—you know, the ones he writes for those magazines, about the sun going nova and all that. Whenever it's cloudy at Palomar he dreams up a new catastrophe."

"Richardson is no fool," I would point out. "Other suns have exploded. If he wants to postulate that it could happen to ours, he has every right to do so."

"Sure, Dr. Andresson, in a story," di Ferruci would object. "But as a serious proposition it doesn't hold water. Our sun just isn't the spectral type that goes nova; it hasn't ever even approached the critical instability percentage. It can't even produce a good flare of the Beta Centauri type."

"I don't expect it to go nova. But it's quite capable of producing a major flare, in my opinion. I expect to prove it."

Di Ferruci would shrug, as he always did. "I wouldn't ride any money on you, Dr. Andresson. But I'll be more than interested in what the telescope shows. Let's see what we have here right now. The thermocouple's been calibrated; shall I cut in the hot load?"

At this point—I am now reporting a particular incident, although it, too, was typical of many of these conversations—I became aware that Marguerita was in the observatory. I swung sharply around, considerably annoyed. My wife is innocent of astronomical knowledge, and her usually ill-timed obtrusions upon our routine—although I suppose they were born of the desire to "take an interest" in her husband's profession—were distracting.

Today, however, I was not only annoyed, but stunned. How had I failed to notice this before—I, who pride myself on the acuity of my observation? What stood before me was a young woman!

How shall I say how young? These things are relative. We had married when she was thirty-six and I was forty-four. A difference of eight years is virtually no difference during the middle decades, though it is enormous when both parties are young. Marguerita had been in no sense a child at the time of our marriage.

Yet now, as I was finding, a spread as small as eight years can again become enormous when the dividing line of old age insensibly approaches. And the difference was even greater than this, for now Marguerita, as she stood looking down at our day's three-dimensional graph of solar activity, seemed no older to me than on the day I had first met her; a woman tall, graceful, lithe, platinum-haired, and with the somber, smoldering, unreadable face of Eve—and yet, compared to me now, a child in truth.

"Good afternoon, Mrs. Andresson," di Ferruci said, smiling.

She looked up and smiled back. "Good afternoon," she said. "I see you're about to take another series of readings. Don't let me interrupt you."

"That's quite all right; thus far it's routine," di Ferruci said. I glanced sidewise at him and then back to my wife. "We'd just begun to take readings to break up the monotony of the old argument."

"That's true," I said. "But it would be just as well if you didn't drop in on us unexpectedly, Marguerita. If this had been a critical stage—"

"I'm sorry," she said contritely. "I should have phoned, but I'm always afraid that the telephone will interrupt you, too. When I'm here I can hope to see whether or not you're busy—and you can see who's calling. The telephone has no eyes."

She touched the graph delicately. This graph, I should explain, is made of fourteen curves cut out in cardboard, and assembled so that one set of seven curved pieces is at right angles to the other set. It expresses the variation in intensity of RF emanation across the surface of the sun at the ten-centimeter wave length, where our readings commonly are taken; we make a new such model each day. It shows at a glance, by valley or peak, any deviation from the sun's normal output, thus helping us greatly in interpreting our results.

"How strange it looks today," she said. "It's always in motion, like a comber racing toward the shore. I keep expecting it to begin to break at the top."

Di Ferruci stopped tinkering with the drive clock and sat down before the control desk, his blue-black helmet of hair—only a little peppered by his memories of the Inchon landing—swiveling sharply toward her. I could not see his face. "What an eerie notion," he said. "Mrs. Andresson, you and the doctor'll have me sharing your presentiments of doom any minute now."

"It isn't a question of presentiments," I said sharply. "You should be aware by now, Mario, that in the RF range the sun is a variable star. Does that mean nothing to you? Let me ask you another question. How do you explain Eta Carina?"

"What's Eta Carina?" Marguerita said.

I did not know quite how to begin answering her, but di Ferruci, who lacked my intimate knowledge of her limitations, had no such qualms.

"It's a freak—one of the worst freaks of the past ten years," he said eagerly. "It's a star that's gone nova three times. The last time was in 1952, about a hundred years before the previous explosion. Before that it had an outburst in the 1600s, and it may have blown up about 142 A.D., too. Each time it gains in brightness nearly one hundred thousand times—as violent a stellar catastrophe as you can find anywhere in the records." He offered the data to her like a bouquet, and before I could begin to take offense, swung back upon me again. "Surely, Doc, you don't maintain that Eta Carina is a flare star?"

"All stars are flare stars," I said, looking steadily at him. His eyes were in shadow. "More than that: all stars are novas, in the long run. Young stars like our sun are variable only in the radio spectrum, but gradually they become more and more unstable, and begin to produce small flares. Then come the big flares, like the Beta Centauri outburst; then they go nova; and then the cycle begins again."

"Evidence?"

"Everywhere. The process goes on in little in the short-term variables, the Cepheids. Eta Carina shows how it works in a smaller, noncluster star. The other novas we've observed simply have longer periods—they haven't had time to go nova again within recorded history. *But they will.*"

"Well," di Ferruci said, "if that's so, Richardson's visions of our sun exploding seem almost pleasant. You see us being roasted gradually instead, in a series of hotter and hotter flares. When does the first one hit us, by your figures?"

Mario was watching me steadily. Perhaps I looked strange, for I was once again in the grip of that anomalous emotion, so impossible to describe, in which terror and ecstasy blended and fused into some whole beyond any possibility of communication. As I stated for the first time what I saw, and saw so clearly, was ahead for us all, this deep radical emotion began to shake me as if I had stepped all unawares from the comfortable island of relative, weighable facts into some blastingly cold ocean of Absolute Truth.

"I don't know," I said. "It needs checking. But I give us six months."

Marguerita's and di Ferruci's eyes met. Then he said, "Let's check it then. We should be able to find the instability threshold for each stage, from RR Lyrae stars right through classical Cepheids, long-periods, and irregulars to radio-variables. We already know the figure for novas. Let's dot the i's and cross the t's—and then find out where our sun stands."

"Theodor," Marguerita said, "what—what will happen if you're right?"

"Then the next flare will be immensely greater than the 1948 one. The Earth will survive it; life on Earth probably will not, certainly not human life."

Marguerita remained standing beside the model a moment longer, nursing the hand which had been touching it. Then she looked at me out of eyes too young for me to read, and left the observatory.

With a hasty word to di Ferruci, I followed her, berating myself as I went. Suspecting as I did the shortness of the span left to us, I had planned not to utter a word about what was in store in her presence; that was one of the reasons why I had objected to her visits to the observatory. There had simply been no reason to cloud our last months together with the shadow of a fate she could not understand.

But when I reached the top of the granite steps leading down to the road, she was gone—nor could I see either her figure or any sign of a car on the road which led down the mountain. She had vanished as completely as if she had never existed.

Needless to say, I was disturbed. There are cabins in the woods, only a short distance from the observatory proper, which are used by staff members as temporary residences. We had never made use of them—radioastronomy being an art which can be carried on by day better than by night—but nevertheless I checked them systematically. It was inconceivable to me that she could be in the main observatory, but I searched that too, as well as the solar tower and the Schmidt shed.

She was nowhere. By the time I had finished searching, it was sunset and there was no longer any use in returning to my own instrument. I could only conclude that I had miscalculated the time lag between her exit and my pursuit, and that I would find her at home.

Yet somehow I did not go home. All during my search of the grounds another thought had been in my head! What if I was wrong? Suppose there was no solar pulsation cycle? Suppose my figures were meaningless? If this seems to be a strange thing for a man to be thinking, while searching for an inexplicably vanished wife. I can only say that the two subjects seemed to me to be somehow not unconnected.

And as it turned out, I was right. I have said that I have a sense of fate.

In the end, I went back to the observatory, now dark and, I supposed, deserted. But there was a light glowing softly inside, the evenly lit surface of the transparency viewer. Bent over it, his features floating eerily in nothingness, was Mario di Ferruci.

I groped for the switch, found it, and the fluorescents flashed on overhead. Mario straightened, blinking.

"Mario, what are you doing here? I thought you had left before sundown."

"I meant to," di Ferruci said slowly. "But I couldn't stop thinking about your theory. It isn't every day that one hears the end of the world announced by a man of your eminence. I decided I just had to run my own check, or else go nuts wondering."

"Why couldn't you have waited for me?" I said. "We could have done the work together much quicker and more easily."

"That's true," he said slowly. "But, Dr. Andresson, I'm just a graduate student, and you're a famous man, young as you are. I'm a little afraid of being overwhelmed—of missing an error because you've checked it already, or failing to check some point at all—that kind of thing. After all, we're all going to die if you're right, and that's hardly a minor matter. So I thought I'd try paddling my own canoe. Maybe I'll find the world just as far up the creek as you do. But I had to try."

It took me a while to digest this, distracted as I already was. After a while I said, as calmly as I could: "And what have you found?"

"Dr. Andresson—*you're wrong.*"

For an instant I could not see. All the red raw exploding universe of unstable stars went wheeling through my old head like maddened atoms. But I am a scientist. I conquered it.

"Wherein am I wrong?"

Di Ferruci took a deep breath. His face was white and set under the fluorescents. "Dr. Andresson, forgive me; this is a hard thing for me to say. But the error in your calcs is way the hell back in the beginning, in your thermodynamic assumptions. It lies in the step between the Chapman-Cowling expression and your derivation for the coefficient of mutual diffusion. Your derivation is perfectly sound in classical thermodynamics, but that isn't what we have to deal with here. We're dealing instead with a completely ionized binary gas, where your quantity D 12 becomes nothing more than a first approximation."

"I never called it anything else."

"Maybe not," di Ferruci said doggedly. "But your math handles it as an absolute. By the time your expanded equation fifty-eight is reached, you've lost a complete set of subscripts and your expressions for the electron of charge wind up all as odd powers! I'm not impugning your logic—it's fantastically brilliant—but insofar as it derives from the bracketed expression D 12 it doesn't represent a real situation."

He stared at me, half-defiantly, half in a kind of anxiety the source of which I could not fathom. It had been many years since I was young; now I was gravid with death—his, mine, yours, Marguerita's, everyone's. I said only: "Let's check it again."

But we never had the chance; at that moment the door opened soundlessly, and Marguerita came back.

"Theodor, Mario!" she said breathlessly. "Are you trying to work yourselves to death? Let's all live to our appointed times, whenever they come! Theodor, I was so frightened when you didn't come home—why didn't you call—"

"I'm not sure anyone would have answered," I said grimly. "Or if someone had, I would have suspected her of being an impostor—or a teleport."

She turned her strange look upon me. "I—don't understand you."

"I hope you don't, Marguerita. We'll take that matter up in private. Right now we're making a check. Dr. di Ferruci was about to knock the solar pulsation theory to flinders when you entered."

"Doc!" di Ferruci protested. "That wasn't the point at all. I just wanted to find—"

"Don't call me 'Doc'!"

"Very well," di Ferruci said. His face became whiter still. "But I insist on finishing my sentence. I'm not out to kick apart your theory; I think it's a brilliant theory and that it may still very well be right. There are holes in your math, that's all. They're big holes and they need filling; maybe, between us we could fill them. But if you don't care enough to want to do the job, why should I?"

"Why, indeed?"

He stared at me with fury for a moment. Then he put his hand distractedly to his forehead, stood up slowly, and began to pace. "Look, Doc—Dr. Andresson. Believe me, I'm not hostile to the idea. It scares me, but that's only because I'm human. There's still a good chance that it's basically sound. If we could go to work on it now, really intensively, we might be able to have it in shape for the triple-A-S meeting in Chicago two months from now. It'd set every physicist, every astronomer, every scientist of any stripe on his ear!"

And there was the clue for which, all unconsciously, I had been waiting. "Indeed it would," I said. "And for four months, old Dr. Andresson and young Dr. Ferruci would be famous, as perhaps no scientists had ever been famous before. Old Dr. Andresson has had his measure of fame and has lost his faith in it. But for young Dr.

Ferruci, even four months would be a deep draft. For that he is willing to impugn his senior's work, to force endless conferences, to call everything into question—all to get his own name added to the credits on the final paper."

"Theodor," Marguerita said. "Theodor, this isn't like you. If—"

"And there is even a touch of humor in this little playlet," I said. "The old man would have credited young Dr. Ferruci in the final paper in any case. The whole maneuver was for nothing."

"There was no maneuver," di Ferruci ground out, his fists clenched. The nervous movements of his hand across his forehead had turned his blue-black hair into a mare's nest. "I'm not an idiot. I know that if you're right, the whole world will be in ashes before the year is out—including any research papers which might carry my name, and any human eyes which might see them.

"What I want to do is to pin down this concept to the point where it's unassailable. The world will demand nothing less of it than that. *Then* it can be presented to the AAAS—and the world will have four months during which the best scientific brains on Earth can look for an out, a way to save at least a part of the race, even if only two people. What's fame to me, or anyone else, if this theory is right? Gas, just gas. But if we can make the world believe it, utterly and completely, then the world will find a loophole. Nothing less than the combined brains of the whole of science could do the job—and we won't get those brains to work unless we convince them!"

"Nonsense," I said calmly. "There is no 'out,' as you put it. But I'll agree that I looked deeper into you than I needed for a motive. Do you think that I have overlooked all these odd coincidences? Here is my wife, and here are you, both at improbable hours, neither of you expecting me; here is young Dr. di Ferruci interrupted at his task of stealing something more than just my work; here is Marguerita Andresson, emerged from wherever she has been hiding all evening, unable to believe that Earth's last picture is all but painted, but ready to help a young man with blue-black hair to steal the pretty notion and capitalize on it."

There was a faint sound from Marguerita. I did not look at her.

After a long while, di Ferruci said: "You are a great astronomer, Dr. Andresson. I owe you twenty years of inspiration from a distance, and five years of the finest training a master ever gave a tyro.

"You are also foul-minded, cruel-tongued, and very much mistaken. I resign from this University as of now; my obligation to you is wiped out by what you saw fit to say of me." He searched for his jacket, failed to find it, and gave up at once in trembling fury. "Good-bye, Mrs. Andresson, with my deepest sympathy. And Doc, good-bye—and God have mercy on you."

"Wait," I said. I moved then, after what seemed a century of standing frozen. The young man stopped, his hand halfway to the doorknob, and his back to me. Watching him, I found my way to a chart-viewer, and picked up the pair of six-inch dividers he had been using to check my charts.

"Well?" he said.

"It's not so easy as that, Mario. You don't walk out of a house with the stolen goods under your arm when the owner is present. A strong man armed keepeth his house. You may not leave. You may not take my hard-won theory to another university. You may not leave Hamelin with pipes in your hand. You may not carry both my heart and my brains out of this observatory as easily as you would carry a sack of potatoes. In short—*you may not leave!*"

I threw the points of the dividers high and launched myself soul and body at that hunched, broad back. Marguerita's sudden scream rang deafeningly as a siren in the observatory dome.

The rest you know.

I have been honest with you. Tell me, where have you hidden her now?

1. I, Andrew, a servant of the Sun, who also am your brother, he who was called and was sanctified, say unto you, blessed be he that readeth, and keepeth the word; for behold, the time is at hand; be thou content.

2. For behold, it was given to me, in the City of Angels, upon a high hill, to look upon His face; whereupon I fell down and wept.

3. And He said, I am the Be-All and End-All; I am the Being and the Becoming; except that they be pure, none shall look upon Me else they die, for the time is at hand. And when He had spoken thus, I was sore afraid.

4. And He said, Rise up, and go forth unto the peoples, and say thou, Unless thou repent, I will come to thee quickly, and shine My countenance upon thee. I shall loosen the seals, and sound the trumpets, and open the vials, and the deaths which shall come upon thee will be numbered as seven times seven.

5. The Sun shall become black as sackcloth of hair, and the moon

become as blood; and the stars of heaven shall fall onto the earth, and the heaven depart as a scroll when it is rolled together, and every mountain and island be moved out of its place. And all men shall hide themselves and say to the mountains and rocks, Fall on us, and hide us from the face of Him that sitteth on the throne.

6. There will be hail and fire mingled with blood, and these cast upon the earth; a great mountain burning with fire shall be cast into the sea; and there will fall a great star from heaven, burning as it were a lamp, upon the fountains of waters; and the third part of the Sun shall be smitten, and the third part of the moon; and there shall arise a smoke out of the pit, so that the air and the day be darkened.

7. And if there be any who worship not Me, and who heed not, I say unto you all, woe, woe, for ye shall all die; ye shall feast without sacraments, ye shall batten upon each other; ye shall be clouds without water, driven by dry winds; ye shall be dry sterile trees, twice dead, and withered; wandering stars, to whom is given the dark of the emptiness of eternity; verily, I say unto you:

8. Ye shall be tormented with fire and brimstone, the third part of trees shall be burnt up, and all green grass be burnt up, and the third part of creatures which were in the sea, and had life, shall die; and the waters shall become blood, and many men die of the waters, because they be bitter; and ever, and thou shalt have no rest, neither day nor night; for the hour of judgment is come.

9. And saying thus, He that spake to me departed, and His dread spirit, and I went down among the people, and spoke, and bade men beware; and none heeded.

10. Neither those who worshiped the stars, and consulted, one among the others; nor those who worshiped man and his image; nor those who made prayers to the invisible spirits of the air; nor those who worshiped any other thing; and the spirit of Him who had spoken was heavy upon me, so I went unto my chambers and lay me down in a swound.

11. And the angel of the Sun spoke to me as I lay, and spake with a voice like trombones, and said, Behold, all men are evil, but thou shalt redeem them, albeit thou remain a pure child of the Sun, and thou alone. Thou shalt have power; a two-edged sword shall go out of thy mouth, and thou shalt hold seven times seven stars in thy palm, and be puissant; this I shall give thee as thine own, if only thou remainest, and thou alone. And I said: Lord, I am Thine; do with me as Thou wilt.

Testament of Andros

12. And I went forth again, and spoke, and the nations of men harkened, and the kings of the world bent the knee, and the princes of the world brought tribute, seven times seven; and those who worshiped the stars, and the spirits of the air, and all other things, bowed down before Him; and it was well with them.

13. Now at this time there appeared a great wonder in heaven: a star clothed in a glory of hair, like a woman; and the people gathered and murmured of wonder, saying, Beware, for there is a god in the sky, clothed in hair like a woman, and with streaming of robes and bright garments; and, behold, it draws near in the night, and fears not the Sun; and the hem of this robe gathers about us.

14. And there arose a woman of the world, and came forward, preaching the gospel of the wild star, saying: Our god the Sun is a false god; his mate is this great star; they will devour us. There is no god but man.

15. And this woman, which was called Margo, summoned the people and made laughter with them, and derision, and scorned the Sun, and gave herself to the priests of the voices in the air, and to those who worshiped numbers, and to the kings and princes of the world; and there was whirling of tambourines in the high towers of the Sun.

16. And the angel of the Sun spoke to me with the sound of trombones, saying, Go with thy power which had been given to thee, and crush this woman, else thou shalt be given to the wild star, and to the flames of the wild star's hair, and with thee the world; I command thee, slay this woman, for thou hast been given the power, nor shall it be given thee again; I have spoken.

17. And I went, and the woman called Margo spoke unto me, saying: Thou art fair, and hath power. Give me of thy power, and I will give you of mine. Neither the wild star nor the Sun shall have such power as we have.

18. And I looked upon her, and she was fair, beyond all the daughters of the earth; and when she spoke, her voice was as the sounding of bells; and there was a spirit in her greater than the souls of men; and a star, clothed in a glory of hair, with streaming of robes and bright garments; and I kissed the hem of her robe.

19. And the voice of the angel of the Sun was heard like a sounding of trombones, saying: Thou hast yielded thy power to an harlot, and given the earth to the fire; thy power is riven from thee, and all shall die;

20. So be it.

My name is George Anders. I have no hope that anyone will read this record, which will probably be destroyed with me—I have no safer place to put it than on my person—but I write it anyhow, if only to show that man was a talkative animal to his last gasp. If the day of glory which has been foretold comes about, there may well be a new and better world which will cherish what I put down here—but I am desperately afraid that the terrible here-and-now is the day the voices promised, and that there will be nothing else for ever and ever.

This is not to say that the voices lied. But since that first night when they spoke to me, I have come to know that they speak for forces of tremendous power, forces to which human life is as nothing. A day of glory we have already had, truly—but such a day as no man could long for.

It was on the morning of March 18 that that day dawned, with a sun so huge as to dominate the entire eastern sky, a flaring monster which made the memory of our accustomed sun seem like a match flame. All the previous night had been as hot as high summer, although not four days before we had a blizzard. Now, with the rising of this colossal globe, we learned the real meaning of heat.

A day of glory, of glory incredible—and deadly. The heat grew and grew. By a little after noon the temperature in the shade was more than one hundred fifty degrees, and in the open—it is impossible to describe what an inferno it was under the direct rays of that sun. A bucket of water thrown into the street from a window boiled in midair before it could strike the pavement.

In some parts of the city, where there were wooden buildings and asphalt or tarred-black streets, everything was burning. In the country, the radio said, it was worse; forests were ablaze, grasslands, wheatfields, everything. Curiously, it was this that saved many of us, for before the afternoon could reach its full fury the sky was gray with smoke, cutting off at least a little of the rays of that solar horror. Flakes of ash fell everywhere.

Millions died that day. Only a few in refrigerated rooms—meatcoolers, cold-storage warehouses, the blast-tunnels for frozen-food firms, underground fur-storage vaults—survived, where the refrigeration apparatus itself survived. By a little after midnight, the outside temperature had dropped only to slightly above one hundred degrees, and the trembling and half-mad wraiths who still lived emerged to look silently at the ruined world.

I was one of these. I had planned that I would be. Months before, I had known that this day of doom was to come upon us, for the voices had said so. I can still remember—for as long as I live I will remember, whether it be a day or forty years—the onset of that strange feeling, that withdrawal from the world around me, as if everything familiar had suddenly become as unreal as a stage-setting. What had seemed commonplace became strange, sinister. What was that man doing with the bottles which contained the white fluid? Why was the uniform he wore also white? Why not blood in the bottles? And the man with the huge assemblage of paper; why was he watching it so intently as he sat in the subway? Did he expect it to make some sudden move if he looked away? Were the black marks with which the paper was covered the footprints of some minuscule horde?

And as the world underwent its slow transformation, the voices came. I cannot write here what they said, because paper would not bear such words. But the meaning was clear. The destruction of the world was at hand. And beyond it—

Beyond it, the day of glory. A turn toward something new, something before which all men's previous knowledge of grandeur would pale. A new Apocalypse and Resurrection? So it seemed, then. But the voices spoke in symbol and parable, and perhaps the rising of the hellish sun was the only "day of glory" we would ever see.

And so I hid in my shelter, and survived that day. When I first emerged into the boiling, choking midnight smoke I could see no one else, but after a while something white came out of the darkness toward me. It was a young girl, wearing what I took to be a nightgown—the lightest garment, at any event, she could have worn in this intolerable heat.

"What will happen to us?" she said, as soon as she saw me. "What will happen to us? Will it be the same tomorrow?"

"I don't know," I said. "What's your name?"

"Margaret." She coughed. "This must be the end of the world. If the sun is like this tomorrow—"

"It *is* the end of the world," I said. "But maybe it's the beginning of another. You and I will live to see it."

"How do you know?"

"By your name. The voices call you the mother of the new gods. Have you heard the voices?"

She moved away from me a little bit. There was a sudden, furious gust of wind, and a long line of sparks flew through the lurid sky overhead. "The voices?" she said.

"Yes. The voices of the powers which have done all this. They have promised to save us, you and I. Together we can recreate—"

Suddenly, she was running. She vanished almost instantly into darkness and the smoke. I ran after her, calling, but it was hopeless. Besides, my throat was already raw, and in the heat and the aftermath of the day I had no strength. I went back to my crypt. Tomorrow would tell the tale.

Sleep was impossible. I waited for dawn, and watched for it through my periscope from the buried vault of the bank where, a day before, I had been a kind of teller. This had been no ordinary bank, and I had never taken or issued any money; but otherwise the terms are just. Perhaps you have already guessed, for no ordinary vault is equipped with periscopes to watch the surrounding countryside. This was Fort Knox, a bed of gold to be seeded with promise of the Age of Gold under this golden fire.

And at last the sun came up. It was immense. But I waited a while, and watched the image of it which was cast from the periscope eyepiece onto the opposite wall of the vault. It was not as big as it had been yesterday. And where yesterday the direct rays from the periscope had instantly charred a thousand-dollar bill, today they made only a slowly growing brown spot which never found its kindling point.

The lesson was plain. Today most of what remained of mankind would be slain. But there would be survivors. Then I slept.

I awoke toward the end of the day and set about the quest which I knew I must make. I took nothing with me but water, which I knew I could not expect to find. Then I left the vault forever.

The world which greeted me as I came to the surface was a world transformed, blasted. Nearly everything had been leveled, and the rest lay in jumbled, smoking ruins. The sky was completely black. Near the western horizon the swollen sun sank, still monstrous, but now no hotter than the normal sun at the height of a tropic day. The great explosion, whatever it had been, was nearly over.

And now I had to find Margaret, and fulfill the millennium which the voices had promised. The tree of man had been blasted, but still it bore one flower. It was my great destiny to bring that flower to fruit.

Thus I bring this record to a close. I leave it here in the vault. Then I shall go forth into the desert of the world. If any find it, remember: I am your father and the father of your race. If not, you will all be smoke.

Testament of Andros

Now I go. My knife is in my hand.

My name is Andy Virchow, but probably you know me better as Admiral Universe. Nowhere in the pages of galactic history has there ever been a greater champion of justice. Who do you know that doesn't know Universe, ruler of the spaceways, hero of science, bringer of law and order in the age of the conquest of space? Not a planetary soul, that's who.

Of course not everybody knows that Andy Virchow is Admiral Universe. Sometimes I have to go in disguise and fool criminals. Then I am Andy Virchow, and they think I am only eight years old, until I have them where I want them and I whip out my Cosmic Smoke Gun and reveal my identification.

Sometimes I don't say who I am but just clean the crooks up and ride off in my rocket, the *Margy II*. Then afterwards the people I have saved say, "He didn't even stay to be thanked. I wonder who he was?" and somebody else says, "There's only one man on the frontiers of space like him. That's Admiral Universe."

My rocket is called the *Margy II* partly because my secret interstellar base is on Mars and the Mars people we call Martians call themselves Margies and I like to think of myself as a Margy *too*, because the people of Earth don't understand me and I do good for them because I am champion of justice, not because I like them. Then they're sorry, but it's too late. Me and the Margies understand each other. They ask me for advice before they do anything important, and I tell them what to do. Earth people are always trying to tell other people what to do. The Margies aren't like that, they ask what to do instead of always giving orders.

Also Admiral Universe calls his rocket *Margy II*, because my patron saint is St. Margaret who gets me out of trouble if I do anything wrong. Admiral Universe never does anything wrong because St. Margaret is on his side all the time. St. Margaret is the patron saint of clocks and is called the Mother of Galaxies, because she was a mother—not like my mother, who is always shouting and sending me to bed too early—and mothers have milk and *galaxy* is Greek for milk. If you didn't know I was Admiral Universe you'd ask how I know what's Greek for anything, but Admiral Universe is a great scientist and knows everything. Besides, my father was a teacher of Greek before he died and he was Admiral Universe's first teacher.

In all the other worlds in the universe everything is pretty perfect except for a few crooks that have to be shot. It's not like Earth at all. The planets are different from each other, but they are all happy and have lots of science and the people are kind and never raise their hands to each other or send each other to bed without their supper.

Sometimes there are terrible accidents in the spacelanes and Admiral Universe arrives on the scene in the nick of time and saves everybody, and all the men shake his hand and all the girls kiss him and say mushy things to him, but he refuses their thanks in a polite way and disappears into the trackless wastes of outer space because he carries a medal of St. Margaret's in his pocket over his heart. She is his only girl, but she can't ever be anybody's girl because she is a saint, and this is Admiral Universe's great tragedy which he never tells anybody because it's his private business that he has to suffer all by himself, and besides if anybody else knew it they would think he was mushy too and wouldn't be so afraid of him, like crooks I mean.

Admiral Universe is always being called from all over outer space to help people and sometimes he can't be one place because he has to be in some other place. Then he has to set his jaw and do the best he can and be tough about the people he can't help because he is helping somebody else. First he asks St. Margaret what he should do and she tells him. Then he goes and does it, and he is very sorry for the people who got left out, but he knows that he did what was right.

This is why I wasn't there when the sun blew up, because I was helping people somewhere else at the time. I didn't even know it was the sun, because I was so far away that it was just another star, and I didn't see it blow up, because stars blow up all the time and if you're Admiral Universe you get used to it and hardly notice. Margaret might have told me, but she's a saint, and doesn't care.

If I'd been there I would have helped. I would have saved my friends, and all the great scientists, and the girls who might be somebody's mothers some day, and everybody that was anybody except Dr. Ferguson, I would have left him behind to show him how wrong he was about me.

But I wasn't there at the time, and besides Admiral Universe never did like the Earth much. Nobody will really miss it.

My name is T. V. Andros. My father was an Athenian immigrant and a drunkard. After he came here he worked in the mines, but not very often because he was mostly soused.

Sometimes he beat my mother. She had TB but she took good

care of us until I was eight; early that year my father got killed in a brawl in a bar, and the doctor—his name I forget—sent her back to the little town in Pennsylvania where she was born. She died that March.

After that I worked in the mines. The law says a kid can't work in the mines but in company towns the law don't mean much. I got the cough too but the other miners took care of me and I grew up tough and could handle myself all right.

When I was fourteen, I killed a man with a pick-handle, one blow. I don't remember what we were fighting about.

Mostly I kept out of fights, though. I had a crazy idea I wanted to educate myself and I read a lot—all kinds of things. For a while I read those magazines that tell about going to other planets and stuff like that. I didn't learn anything, except that to learn good you need a teacher, and the last one of those had been run out by the company cops. They said he was a Red.

It was tough in the mines. It's dark down there and hot, and you can't breathe sometimes for the dust. And you can't never wash the dirt off, it gets right down into your skin and makes you feel black even at noon on Sundays when you've scrubbed till your skin's raw.

I had a sixteen-year-old girl but I was too dirty for her. I tried to go to the priest about it but he wasn't looking for nothing but sin, and kept asking me had I done anything wrong with the girl. When I said I hadn't he wasn't interested no more. I hadn't, either, but he made me so mad he made me wish I had. After that I sort of drifted away from going to church because I couldn't stand his face. Maybe that was bad but it had its good side, too; I missed it and I took to cracking the Bible now and then. I never got much of the Bible when I was going to church.

After a while, I took to drinking something now and then. It wasn't right for a kid but I wasn't a kid no more, I was eighteen and besides in a company town there ain't nothing else to do. It helped some but not enough. All the guys in the bar ever talk about are wages and women. You got to drink yourself blind and stupid to keep from hearing them, otherwise you go nuts. After a while I was blind and stupid a lot of the time and didn't no longer know what I did or didn't.

Once when I was drunk I mauled a girl younger than I was; I don't know why I did it. She was just the age I had been when my mother left me to go home and die. Then it was all up with me at the mines. I didn't mean her any harm but the judge gave me the works. Two years.

I got clean for once in my life while I was in the jug and I did some more reading but it just mixed me up more. Two years is a long time. When I got out I felt funny in my head. I couldn't stop thinking about the girl who thought I was too dirty for her. I was at the age when I needed girls.

But I wasn't going to mess with girls my age who could see the prison whiteness on the outside and all that ground-in coal dust underneath it. I couldn't forget Maggy, the girl that got me into the jam. That had been a hot night in summer, with a moon as big as the sun, as red as blood. I hadn't meant her any harm. She reminded me of myself when my mother had gone away.

I found another Maggy and when the cops caught me they worked me over. I can't hear in one ear now and my nose is skewed funny on my face. I had it coming because I hurt the girl. When they let me out again I got a job as a super, but there was another girl in the apartment above, and I went to fix a pipe there while her mother was away. It was a hot day with a big sun and no air moving, just like the day my mother left. I didn't really know nothing had happened until I saw that one of my hands was dark red. Then I tried to get her to talk to me but she wouldn't move. After a while I felt some woman's hands beating at my neck. She said, "Stop, you!"

This time they took me to a hospital and a Dr. Ferdinand talked to me. Write it all down, he said. It may help you. So I wrote it all down, like you see it here. Then they put me in a cell and said I would have to stay for a while. I don't talk to them much any more.

It is a real hot day. Outside the cell the sun is bigger. I don't breathe good any more but there's something wrong with the air. I pulled my mattress to pieces but I didn't find nothing.

Maybe something is going to happen. Something is going to happen.

My name is Man. I will write my story if you wish.
I was . . .
Here the ashes blow away. The voices die.

A Style in Treason

The *Karas,* a fragile transship—she was really little more than a ferry, just barely meriting a name—came fluttering out of the interstitium into the Flos Campi system a day late in a ball of rainbows, trailing behind her two gaudy contrails of fake photons, like a moth unable to free herself of her cocoon. The ship's calendar said it was Joni 23, 5914, which was probably wrong by at least ten years; however, nobody but a scholar of that style of dating could have been precise about the matter; the *Karas* was a day later than she should have been; just *what* day was at best only a local convention.

In the salon, Simon de Kuyl sighed and laid out the tarots again. Boadacea, the biggish fourth planet of the Flos Campi array and Simon's present port of call, was yet a week ahead in urspace, and he was already tired. He had reasons. His fellow passengers had been dull beyond belief, with the possible—because wholly unknown—exception of the entity who had spent the entire voyage in his cabin, with a diplomatic seal spidered over the palm plate on its door; and Simon suspected that they would have bored him even had he not had to present himself to them as a disillusioned Sagittarian mystic, embittered at himself for ever having believed that the Mystery that lay (or didn't lie) at the galactic center would someday emerge and set the rest of the universe to rights, and hence in too unpredictable a temper to be worth being polite to. Conceivably, indeed probably, some of the other passengers were trying to be as repellent to strangers as was Simon, but the probability did not make their surfaces any more diverting.

But of course none of these things—the ship, the delay, the passengers, the pose—was more than marginally to blame for his weariness. In these days of treason, politeness, easy travel, and indefinitely prolonged physical vigor, everyone was tired, just a little but all the time. After a while, it became difficult to remember who one was supposed to be—and to remember who one was, was virtually impossible. Even the Baptized, who had had their minds dipped and then rechannelled with only a century's worth of memories, betrayed to the experienced eye a vague, tortured puzzlement, as though still searching in the stilled waters for some salmon of ego they had been left no reason to suspect had ever been there. Suicide was unconcealedly common among the Baptized, and Simon did not think the reason (as the theoreticians and ministers insisted) was really only a minor imperfection in the process, to be worked out in time.

There was plenty of time; that was the trouble. People lived too damn long, that was all. Erasing the marks, on the face or in the mind, did not unwind the years; the arrow of entropy pointed forever in the same direction; virginity was a fact, not just a state of membrane or memory. Helen, reawakening in Aithra's Egyptian bed flensed of her history, might bemuse Menelaus for a while, but there will always be another Paris, and that without delay—time past is eternally in time present, as Ezra-Tse had said.

The ten-thousand-year-old analogy came easily to him. He was supposed to be, and in fact was, a native of High Earth; and in his *persona* as a Sagittarian (lapsed) would be expected to be a student of such myths, the more time-dimmed the better—hence, in fact, his interminable shipboard not-quite-game of tarot solitaire. Staying quite automatically in character was in his nature, as well as being one of his chiefest skills.

And certainly he had never allowed himself to be Baptized, though his mind had been put through not a few lesser changes in the service of High Earth, and might yet be forced into a greater one if his mission on Boadacea went awry. Many of his memories were painful, and all of them were painfully crowded together; but they were his, and that above all was what gave them their worth. Some professional traitors were valuable because they had never had, and never could have, a crisis of identity. Simon knew without vanity—it was too late for that—that High Earth had no more distinguished a traitor than he, precisely because he had such crises as often as once a year, and hadn't lost one yet.

"Your indulgence, reverend sir," said a voice at his back. A white hand, well-kept but almost aggressively masculine, came over his shoulder and moved the Fool onto the Falling Tower. "It is boorish of me to intervene, but it discomforts me to see an implication go a-begging. I fear I am somewhat compulsive."

The voice was a new one: therefore, belonging to the person who had been sequestered in the diplomatic cabin up to now. Simon turned, ready to be surly.

His next impulse was to arise and run. The question of *who* the creature was evaporated in recognition of just *what* it was.

Superficially, he saw a man with a yellow page-boy coiffure, wearing pale-violet hose, short russet breeches, and a tabard of deeper violet, as well as a kangaroo-shiv, a weapon usually affected only by ladies. A duplicate of the spider on the doorseal was emblazoned in gold on his left breast. Superficially; for Simon was fortunate—in no way he could explain—to be able to penetrate this seeming.

The "diplomat" was a vombis, or what in those same myths Simon had been thinking of earlier was called a Proteus: a creature which could imitate perfectly almost any life-form within its size range. Or nearly perfectly; for Simon, like one in perhaps five thousand of his colleagues, was sensitive to them, without ever being able to specify in what particular their imitations of humanity were deficient. Other people, even those of the sex opposite to the one the vombis had assumed, could find no flaw in them. In part because they did not revert when killed, no human had ever seen their "real" form—if they had one—though of course there were legends aplenty. The talent might have made them ideal double agents, had it been possible to trust them—but that was only an academic speculation, since the vombis were wholly creatures of the Green Exarch.

Simon's third impulse, like that of any other human being in like circumstances, was to kill this one instantly upon recognition, but that course had too many obvious drawbacks, of which the kangaroo-shiv was the least important. Instead, he said with only moderate ungraciousness: "No matter. I was blocked anyhow."

"You are most kind. May I be seated?"

"Since you're here."

"Thank you." The creature sat down gracefully, across the table from Simon. "Is this your first trip to Boadacea, reverend sir?"

Simon had not said he was going to Boadacea, but after all, it was written on the passenger list for anyone to see.

"Yes. And you?"

"Oh, that is not my destination; I am for deeper into the cluster. But you will find it an interesting world—especially the variations in the light; they make it seem quite dreamlike to a native of a planet with only a single, stable sun. And then, too, it is very old."

"What planet isn't?"

"I forget, you are from High Earth, to whom all other worlds must seem young indeed. Nevertheless, Boadacea is quite old enough to have many curious nations, all fiercely independent, and a cultural pattern which overrides all local variations. To this all the Boadaceans are intensely loyal."

"I commend them," Simon said; and then added sourly, "it is well for a man to have a belief he can cling to."

"The point is well taken," said the vombis. "Yet the pride of Boadacea springs from disloyalty, in the last analysis. The people believe it was the first colony to break with Old Earth, back in the first days of the Imaginary Drive. It is a breach they mean to see remains unhealed."

"Why not?" Simon said, shrugging. "I'm told also that Boadacea is very wealthy."

"Oh, excessively; it was once a great temptation to raiders, but the nations banded together against them with great success. Yet surely wealth does not interest you, reverend sir?"

"Marginally, yes. I am seeking some quiet country in which to settle and study. Naturally, I should prefer to find myself a patron."

"Naturally. I would suggest, then, that you try the domain of the Rood-Prince. It is small and stable, the climate is said to be clement, and he has a famous library." The creature arose. "For your purposes I would avoid Druidsfall; life there, as in most large cities, might prove rather turbulent for a scholar. I wish you success, reverend sir."

Placing its hand formally upon the jeweled shiv, the creature bowed slightly and left. Simon remained staring down at his cards, thinking icily but at speed.

What had all that meant? First of all, that his cover had been broken? Simon doubted that, but in any event it mattered little, since he would go almost into the open directly after landing. Assuming that it had, then, what had the creature been trying to convey? Surely not simply that life in Druidsfall would be even more turbulent for a traitor than for a lapsed divine. Naturally, it would expect Simon to know that; after all, Druidsfall was the center of the treason industry on Boadacea—that was why Simon was going there.

Or was it that Boadacea would be difficult for an ordinary traitor to buy, or was not for sale at all? But that might be said of any worthwhile planet, and no professional would let such a reputation pass without testing it, certainly not on the unsupported word of a stranger.

Besides, Simon was after all no ordinary traitor, nor even the usual kind of double agent. His task was to buy Boadacea while seeming to sell High Earth, but beyond that, there was a grander treason in the making for which the combined Traitors' Guilds of both planets might only barely be sufficient: the toppling of the Green Exarch, under whose subtle, nonhuman yoke half of humanity's worlds had not even the latter-day good sense to groan. For such a project, the wealth of Boadacea was a prerequisite, for the Green Exarch drew tithes from six fallen empires older than man—the wealth of Boadacea, and its reputation, which the vombis had invoked, as the first colony to have broken with Old Earth.

And such a project would necessarily be of prime interest to a creature of the Exarch. Yet security on it could not possibly have been broken. Simon knew well that men had died horribly for traveling under such assumptions in the past; nevertheless, he was sure of it. Then what—?

A steward walked slowly through the salon, beating a gong, and Simon put the problem aside for the moment and gathered up his cards.

"Druidsfall. One hour to Druidsfall. All passengers for the Flos Campi system please prepare for departure. Druidsfall in one hour; next port of call is Fleurety."

The Fool, he thought, has come to the Broken Tower. The next card to turn might well be the Hanged Man.

II

Boadacea proved indeed to be an interesting world, and despite all of Simon's preliminary reading and conditioning, quite as unsettling as the vombis had predicted.

Its sun, Flos Campi, was a ninety-minute microvariable, twinned at a distance of one light-year with a blue-white, Rigellike star which stood—or had stood throughout historical times—in high southern latitudes. This meant that every spot on the planet had a different cycle of day and night. Druidsfall, for example, had only four consecutive hours of quasi-darkness at a time, and even during this period the sky was indigo rather than black at its deepest—and more often than not flaring with auroras, thanks to the almost incessant solar storms.

Everything in the city, as everywhere on Boadacea, bespoke the crucial importance of fugitive light, and the fade-out-fade-in weather that went with it, all very strange after the desert glare of High Earth. The day after the *Karas* had fluttered down had dawned in mist, which cold gales had torn away into slowly pulsating sunlight; then had come clouds and needlelike rain which had turned to snow and then to sleet—more weather in a day than the minarets of Jiddah, Simon's registered home town, saw in a six-month. The fluctuating light and wetness was reflected most startlingly by its gardens, which sprang up when one's back was turned and did not need so much to be weeded as actually fought. They were constantly in motion to the ninety-minute solar cycle, battering their elaborate flowerheads against back walls which were everywhere crumbling after centuries of such soft, implacable impacts. Half the buildings in Druidsfall glistened with their leaves, which were scaled with so much soft gold that they stuck to anything they were blown against—the wealth of Boadacea was based anciently in the vast amounts of uranium and other power-metals in its soil, from which the plants extracted the inevitable associated gold as radiation shielding for their spuriously tender genes. Everyone one saw in the streets of Druidsfall, or any other such city, was a mutation of some sort—if he was not an outworlder—but after a few days in the winds they were all half yellow, for the gold scales smeared off the flying leaves like butter. Everyone was painted with meaningless riches—the very bedsheets glittered ineradicably with flakes of it; and brunettes—especially among the elaborate hair styles of the men—were at a premium.

Druidsfall proper was the usual low jumble of decayed masonry, slightly less ancient slums, and blank-faced offices, but the fact that it was also the home city of the Guild—hence wholly convenient, if not congenial, for Simon—gave it character. The traitors had an architectural style of their own, characterized by structures put together mostly of fragmented statues and petrified bodies fitted to each other like puzzle pieces or maps. Traitors on Boadacea had belonged to an honored social class for seven hundred years, and their edifices made it known.

So did their style of dealing. Simon attended upon the planet's Traitor-in-Chief with all due promptness, wearing the clasp which showed him to be a brother, though an outworlder, and made himself and his errand known with almost complete truthfulness—certainly much more than custom would have demanded. His opposite number, Valkol "the Polite," a portly, jowly man in a black abah decorated only with the clasp, with a kindly and humorous expression into which were set eyes like two bites of an iceberg, turned him out of the Guildhall with only as much courtesy as fraternal protocol strictly required—that is, twelve days to get off the planet.

Thus far, at least, the vombis had proven to be right about the Boadaceans, to the letter. The spirit remained to be tested.

Simon found an inn in which to lick his wounds and prepare for departure, as was permitted. Of course he had no intention of leaving; he was simply preparing to go to ground. Nevertheless, he had wounds to lick: After only four clockless days on Boadacea, he had already been driven into changing his residence, his methods, and his identity. It was a humiliating beginning.

III

Methods next. Listening automatically for the first sound of possible interruption, Simon emptied his little poisons into the catch basin in his new room, and ironically watched the wisps of wine-colored smoke rise from the corroded maw of the drain. He was sorry to see them go; they were old, though venomous, friends; but a man's methods can be as telltale as a thumbprint, and now it would have to be assumed that Valkol had sent for, and would soon receive, some sort of dossier on Simon. The dossier would be wrong, but there was no predicting *wherein* it would be wrong; hence, out with the poisons, and all their cousins among Simon's apparatus. When assuming a new identity, the very first rule is: *Strip!*

The almost worn-away maker's legend on the catch basin read: *Julius, Boadacea.* Things made on this planet were usually labeled that generally, as though any place in the world were like any other, but this was both true and not true. Druidsfall was unmistakably Boadacean, but as the central city of the traitors it was also distinctively itself. Those buildings with their curtain walls of petrified corpses, for instance . . .

Luckily, custom now allowed Simon to stay clear of those grim monuments, now that the first, disastrous formalities were over, and seek his own bed and breakfast. In the old, disinterestedly friendly inns of Druidsfall, the anonymous thumps and foreign outcries of the transients —in death, love, or trade—are said to make the regular lodgers start in their beds with their resident guilts. Of course all inns are like that, but nevertheless, that was why traitors liked to quarter there rather than in the Traitors' Halls run by the fraternity: It guaranteed them privacy, and at the same time helped them to feel alive. There is undoubtedly something inhibiting about trying to deal within walls pieced together of broken stone limbs, heads, and torsos, some of which had clearly been alive when the foundations were being dug and the scaffolding bolted together.

Thus, here in The Skopolamander, Simon could comfortably await his next contact, now that he had dumped his poisons. This—if there was to be one—would of course have to come about before the end of his immunity period. "Quarantine" was perhaps a more appropriate term.

No, the immunity was real, however limited, for as a traitor to High Earth he had special status. High Earth, the Boadaceans thought, was not necessarily Old Earth—but not necessarily *not*, either. For the rest of his twelve days, Simon would not be killed out of sheer conservatism, at least, though nobody official would attempt to deal with him, either.

He had eight of those days still to run—a dull prospect, since he had already completed every possible preliminary to going to ground, and spiced only by the fact that he had yet to figure out how long a day might officially be. The rhythms of Flos Campi offered no reliable clues his Sol-tuned diurnalism could read. At the moment there was nothing lighting the window of the room but an aurora, looking like a curtain of orange and hazy blue fire licking upward along a bone trestle. Radio around here, and probably even electrical power, must be knocked out as much as half the time, with so much stray magnetism washing back and forth. That might prove useful; he filed the thought.

In the meantime, there went the last of the poisons. Simon poured water from an amphora into the catch basin, which promptly hissed like a dragon just out of the egg and blurted a mushroom of cold blue steam which made him cough. *Careful!* he thought; acid after water, never water after acid—I am forgetting the most elementary lessons. I should have used wine. Time for a drink, in Gro's name!

He caught up his cloak and went out, not bothering to lock the door. He had nothing worth stealing but his honor, which was in his right hip pocket. Oh, and of course, High Earth—that was in his left. Besides, Boadacea was rich: One could hardly turn around without knocking over some heap of treasures, artifacts of a millennium which nobody had sorted for a century, or even wanted to be bothered to sort. Nobody would think to steal from a poor traitor any object smaller than a king, or, preferably, a planet.

In the tavern below, Simon was joined at once by a playwoman.

"Are you buying tonight, excellence?"

"Why not?" And in fact he was glad to see her. She was blond and ample, a relief from the sketchy women of the Respectables, whom fashion made look as though they suffered from some nervous disease that robbed them of appetite. Besides, she would exempt him from the normal sort of Boadacean polite conversation, which consisted chiefly of elaborately involuted jokes at which it was considered gauche to laugh. The whole style of Boadacean conversation, for that matter, was intended to be ignored; gambits were a high art, but end games were a lost one. Simon sighed and signalled for beakers.

"You wear the traitors' clasp," she said, sitting across from him, "but not much tree gold. Have you come to sell us High Earth?"

Simon did not even blink; he knew the query to be a standard opening with any outworlder of his profession.

"Perhaps. But I'm not on business at the moment."

"Of course not," the girl said gravely, her fingers playing continuously with a sort of rosary tasselled with two silver phalluses. "Yet I hope you prosper. My half-brother is a traitor, but he can find only small secrets to sell—how to make bombs, and the like. It's a thin life; I prefer mine."

"Perhaps he should swear by another country."

"Oh, his country is well worth selling, but his custom is poor. Neither buyer nor seller trusts him very far—a matter of style, I suppose. He'll probably wind up betraying some colony for a thousand beans and a fishball."

"You dislike the man—or is it the trade?" Simon said. "It seems not unlike your own, after all: One sells something one never really owned, and yet one still has it when the transaction is over, as long as both parties keep silent."

"You dislike women," the girl said, tranquilly, as a simple observation, not a challenge. "But all things are loans—not just chastity and trust. Why be miserly? To 'possess' wealth is as illusory as to 'possess' honor or a woman, and much less gratifying. Spending is better than saving."

"But there are rank orders in all things, too," Simon said, lighting a kief stick. He was intrigued in spite of himself. Hedonism was the commonest of philosophies in the civilized galaxy, but it was piquant to hear a playwoman trotting out the moldy clichés with such fierce solemnity. "Otherwise we should never know the good from the bad, or care."

"Do you like boys?"

"No, that's not one of my tastes. Ah, you will say that I don't condemn boy-lovers, and that values are in the end only preferences? I think not. In morals, empathy enters in, eventually."

"So, you wouldn't corrupt children, and torture revolts you. But you were made that way. Some men are not so handicapped. I meet them now and then." The hand holding the looped beads made a small, unconscious gesture of revulsion.

"I think *they* are the handicapped, not I—most planets hang their moral imbeciles, sooner or later. But what about treason? You didn't answer that question."

"My throat was dry . . . thank you. Treason, well—it's an art; hence, again, a domain of taste or preference. Style is everything; that's why my half-brother is so inept. If tastes changed he might prosper, as I might had I been born with blue hair."

"You could dye it."

"What, like the Respectables?" She laughed, briefly but unaffectedly. "I am what I am; disguises don't become me. Skills, yes—those are another matter. I'll show you, when you like. But no masks."

Skills can betray you too, Simon thought, remembering that moment at the Traitors' Guild when his proud sash of poison shells, offered in service, had lost him in an instant every inch of altitude over the local professionals that he had hoped to trade on. But he only said again, "Why not?" It would be as good a way as any to wile away the time; and once his immunity had expired, he could never again trust a playwoman on Boadacea.

She proved, indeed, very skillful, and the time passed . . . but the irregular pseudo-days—the clock in the tavern was on a different time than the one in his room, and neither even faintly agreed with his High Earth-based chronometer and metabolism—betrayed him. He awoke one morning/noon/night to find the girl turning slowly black beside him, in the last embrace of a fungal toxin he would have reserved for the Emperor of Canes Venatici, or the worst criminal in human history.

His immunity period was up, and war had been declared. He had been notified that if he still wanted to sell High Earth, he would first have to show his skill at staying alive against the whole cold malice of all the Traitors of Boadacea.

V

How the Exarchy or the prehuman interstellar empires were held together is unknown, but in human history, at least, the bureaucratic problems of managing large stellar holdings from a single center of government have proven to be insoluble. Neither the ultraphone nor the Imaginary Drive permitted the extension of human hegemony over a radius of more than ten light-years, a fact the colonies outside this sphere were not slow to appreciate and put to use. Luckily, a roughly uniform interstellar economy was maintained by tacit agreement after the political separations, since it was not widely recognized then —or now—that this much older invention can enforce a more thorough rule than can any personal or party autocracy.

In this connection, one often hears laymen ask, Why do the various worlds and nations employ professional traitors when it is known that they are traitors? Why would they confide to the traitors any secret valuable enough to be sold to a third party? The answer is the same, and the weapon is the same: money. The traitors act as brokers in a continuous interstellar bourse on which each planet seeks to gain a *financial* advantage over the other. Thus the novice should not imagine that any secret put into his hands is exactly what it is said to be, particularly when its primary value purports to be military. He should also be wary of the ruler who seeks to subvert him into personal loyalty, which tears the economic tissue and hence should be left in the domain of untrained persons. For the professional, loyalty is a tool, not a value. The typical layman's question cited above should of course never be answered.

—"Lord Gro": *The Discourses,* Bk. I, Ch. LVII

Simon holed up quickly and drastically, beginning with a shot of transduction serum—an almost insanely dangerous expedient, for the stuff not only altered his appearance but his very heredity, leaving his head humming with false memories and false traces of character, derived from the unknowable donors of the serum, which conflicted not only with his purposes but even with his tastes and motives.

Under interrogation, he would break down into a babbling crowd of random voices, as bafflingly scrambled as his karyotypes, blood groups, and retina- and fingerprints. To the eye, his gross physical appearance would be a vague, characterless blur of many roles—some of them derived from the DNA of persons who had died a hundred years ago and at least that many parsecs away in space.

But unless he got the antiserum within fifteen High Earth days, he would forget first his mission, then his skills, and at last his very identity. Nevertheless, he judged that the risk had to be taken; for effete though some of the local traitors (always excepting Valkol the Polite) seemed to be, they were obviously quite capable of penetrating any lesser cover—and equally obviously, they meant business.

The next problem was how to complete the mission itself—it would not be enough just to stay alive. High Earth did not petrify failed traitors and mortar them into walls, but it had its own ways of showing displeasure. Moreover, Simon felt to High Earth a certain obligation—not loyalty, Gro forbid, but, well, call it professional pride—which would not let him be retired from the field by a backwater like Boadacea. Besides, finally, he had old reasons for hating the Exarchy; and hatred, unaccountably, Gro had forgotten to forbid.

No: It was not up to Simon to escape the Boadaceans. He had come here to gull them, whatever they might currently think of such a project.

And therein lay the difficulty; for Boadacea, beyond all other colony worlds, had fallen into a kind of autumn cannibalism. In defiance of that saying of Ezra-Tse, the edge was attempting to eat the center. It was this worship of independence, or rather, of autonomy, which had not only made treason respectable, but had come nigh on to ennobling it . . . and was now imperceptibly emasculating it, like the statues one saw everywhere in Druidsfall which had been defaced and sexually mutilated by the grey disease of time and the weather.

Today, though all the Boadaceans proper were colonials in ancestry, they were snobs about their planet's prehuman history, as though they had not nearly exterminated the aborigines themselves but were their inheritors. The few shambling Charioteers who still lived stumbled through the streets of Druidsfall loaded with ritual honors, carefully shorn of real power but ostentatiously deferred to on be slightest occasion which might be noticed by anyone from High Earth. In the meantime, the Boadaceans sold each other out with delicate enthusiasm, but against High Earth—which was not necessarily Old Earth, but not necessarily *not*, either—all gates were formally locked.

Formally only, Simon and High Earth were sure, for the hunger of treason, like lechery, tends to grow with what it feeds on, and to lose discrimination in the process. Boadacea, like all forbidden fruits, should be ripe for the plucking, for the man with the proper key to its neglected garden.

The key that Simon had brought with him, that enormous bribe which should have unlocked Valkol the Polite like a child's bank, was temporarily useless. He would have to forge another, with whatever crude tools could be made to fall to hand. The only one accessible to Simon at the moment was the dead playwoman's gently despised half-brother.

His name, Simon had found out from her easily enough, was currently Da-Ud tam Altair, and he was Court Traitor to a small religious principate on the Gulf of the Rood, on the InContinent, half the world away from Druidsfall. Remembering what the vombis aboard the *Karas* had said about the library of the Rood-Prince, Simon again assumed the robes of a worn-out Sagittarian divine in search of a patron, confident that his face, voice, stance, and manner were otherwise utterly unlike his shipboard *persona,* and boarded the flyer to the InContinent prepared to enjoy the trip.

There was much to enjoy. Boadacea was a good-sized world, nearly ten thousand miles in diameter, and it was rich in more than money. Ages of weathering and vulcanism had broken it into many ecological enclaves, further diversified by the point-by-point uniqueness of climate contributed to each by the rhythmic inconstancies of Flos Campi and the fixity of Flos Campi's companion sun among the other fixed stars—and by the customs and colors of many waves of pioneers who had settled in those enclaves and sought to re-establish their private visions of the earthly paradise. It was an entirely beautiful world, could one but forget one's personal troubles long enough to really look at it; and the flyer flew low and slow, a procedure Simon approved despite the urgency the transduction serum was imposing upon the back of his mind.

Once landed by the Gulf, however, Simon again changed his plans and his outermost disguise; for inquiry revealed that one of the duties of the Court Traitor here was that of singing the Rood-Prince to sleep to the accompaniment of the sareh, a sort of gleeman's harp—actually a Charioteer instrument, ill-adapted to human fingers, which Da-Ud played worse than most of the Boadaceans who affected it. Simon therefore appeared at the vaguely bird-shaped palace of the Rood-Prince in the guise of a ballad merchant, and as such was enthusiastically received, and invited to catalogue the library; Da-Ud, the Rood-Prince said, would help him, at least with the music.

Simon was promptly able to sell Da-Ud twelve-and-a-tilly of ancient High Earth songs Simon had made up overnight—faking folk songs is not much of a talent—and had Da-Ud's confidence within an hour; it was as easy as giving Turkish Delight to a baby. He cinched the matter by throwing in free lessons on the traditional way to sing them.

After the last mangled chord had died, Simon asked Da-Ud quietly:

"By the way . . . (well sung, excellence) . . . did you know that the Guild has murdered your half-sister?"

Da-Ud dropped the imitation Charioteer harp with a noise like a spring-driven toy coming unwound.

"Jillith? But she was only a playwoman! Why, in Gro's name—"

Then Da-Ud caught himself and stared at Simon with sudden, belated suspicion. Simon looked back, waiting.

"Who told you that? Damn you—are you a Torturer? I'm not—I've done nothing to merit—"

"I'm not a Torturer, and nobody told me," Simon said. "She died in my bed, as a warning to me."

He removed his clasp from under the shoulder of his cloak and clicked it. The little machine flowered briefly into a dazzling actinic glare, and then closed again. While Da-Ud was still covering his streaming eyes, Simon said softly:

"I am the Traitor-in-Chief of High Earth."

It was not the flash of the badge that was dazzling Da-Ud now. He lowered his hands. His whole narrow body was trembling with hate and eagerness.

"What—what do you want of me, excellence? I have nothing to sell but the Rood-Prince . . . and a poor stick he is. Surely you would not sell me High Earth; I am a poor stick myself."

"I would sell you High Earth for twenty riyals."

"You mock me!"

"No, Da-Ud. I came here to deal with the Guild, but they killed Jillith—and that, as far as I'm concerned, disqualified them from being treated as civilized professionals, or as human beings at all. She was pleasant and intelligent, and I was fond of her—and besides, while I'm perfectly willing to kill under some conditions, I don't hold with throwing away an innocent life for some footling dramatic gesture."

"I wholly agree," Da-Ud said. His indignation seemed to be at least half real. "But what will you do? What *can* you do?"

"I have to fulfill my mission, any way short of my own death—if I die, nobody will be left to get it done. But I'd most dearly love to cheat, dismay, disgrace the Guild in the process, if it could possibly be managed. I'll need your help. If we live through it, I'll see to it that you'll turn a profit, too; money isn't my first goal here, or even my second now."

"I'll tackle it," Da-Ud said at once, though he was obviously apprehensive, as was only sensible. "What, precisely, do you propose?"

"First of all, I'll supply you with papers indicating that I've sold you a part—not all—of the major thing I have to sell, which gives any man who holds it a lever in the State Ministry of High Earth. They show that High Earth has been conspiring against several major powers, all human, for purposes of gaining altitude with the Green Exarch. They won't tell you precisely which worlds, but there will be sufficient information there so that the Exarchy would pay a heavy purse for them—and High Earth, an even heavier one to get them back. It will be your understanding that the missing information is also for sale, but you haven't got the price."

"Suppose the Guild doesn't believe that?"

"They'll never believe—excuse me, I must be blunt—that you could have afforded the whole thing; they'll know I sold you *this* much of it only because I have a grudge, and you can tell them so—though I wouldn't expose the nature of the grudge, if I were you. Were you unknown to them, they might assume that you were me in disguise, but luckily they know you, and, ah, probably tend rather to underestimate you."

"Kindly put," Da-Ud said with a grin. "But that won't prevent them from assuming that I know your whereabouts, or have some way of reaching you. They'll interrogate for that, and of course I'll tell them. I know them, too; it would be impossible not to, and I prefer to save myself needless pain."

"Of course—don't risk interrogation at all, tell them you want to sell me out, as well as the secret. That will make sense to them, and I think they must have rules against interrogating a member who offers to sell; most Traitors' Guilds do."

"True, but they'll observe them only so long as they believe me; that's standard, too."

Simon shrugged. "Be convincing, then," he said. "I have already said that this project will be dangerous; presumably, you didn't become a traitor solely for sweet safety's sake."

"No, but not for suicide's, either. But I'll abide the course. Where are the documents?"

"Give me access to your Prince's toposcope-scriber and I'll produce them. But first—twenty riyals, please."

"Minus two riyals for the use of the Prince's property. Bribes, you know."

"Your sister was wrong. You do have style, in a myopic sort of way. All right, eighteen riyals—and then let's get on to real business. My time is not my own—not by a century."

"But how do I reach you thereafter?"

"That information," Simon said blandly, "will cost you those other two riyals, and cheap at the price."

V

The Rood-Prince's brain-dictation laboratory was very far from being up to Guild standards, let alone High Earth's, but Simon was satisfied that the documents he generated there would pass muster. They were utterly authentic, and every experienced traitor had a feeling for that quality, regardless of such technical deficiencies as blurry image registration or irrelevant emotional overtones.

That done, he set himself in earnest to the task he had already been playing at, that of cataloguing the Rood-Prince's library. He could hardly run out on this without compromising Da-Ud, as well as drawing unwanted attention to himself. Happily, the chore was pleasant enough; in addition to the usual pornography, the Prince owned a number of books Simon had long wanted to see, including the complete text of Vilar's *The Apples of Idun,* and all two hundred cantos of Mordecai Drover's *The Drum Major and the Mask,* with the fabulous tipped-in Brock woodcuts, all hand-tinted. There were sculptures by Labuerre and Halvorsen; and among the music, there was the last sonata of Andrew Carr . . . all of this embedded, as was inevitable, in vast masses of junk; but of what library, large or small, might that *not* be said? Whether or not the Rood-Prince had taste, he certainly had money, and some of it, under some past librarian, had been well spent.

In the midst of all this, Simon had also to consider how he would meet Da-Ud when the game had that much furthered itself. The arrangement he had made with the playwoman's half-brother had of course been a blind, indeed a double blind; but it had to have the virtues of its imperfections—that is, to look as though it had been intended to work, and to work in fact up to a certain point—or nothing would be accomplished. And it would then have to be bailed out of its in-built fatalities. So—

But Simon was now beginning to find it hard to think. The transduction serum was increasingly taking hold, and there were treasons taking place inside his skull which had nothing at all to do with Da-Ud, the Rood-Prince, Druidsfall, Boadacea, the Green Exarch, or High Earth. Worse: They seemed to have nothing to do with Simon de Kuyl, either, but instead muttered away about silly little provincial intrigues nothing could have brought him to care about—yet which made him feel irritated, angry, even ill, like a man in the throes of jealousy toward some predecessor and unable to reason them away. Knowing their source, he fought them studiously, but he knew they would get steadily worse, however resolute he was; they were coming out of his genes and his blood stream, not his once finely honed, now dimming consciousness.

Under the circumstances, he was not going to be able to trust himself to see through very many highly elaborate schemes, so that it would be best to eliminate all but the most necessary. Hence it seemed better, after all, to meet Da-Ud in the Principate as arranged, and save the double dealing for more urgent occasions.

On the other hand, it would be foolish to hang around the Principate, waiting and risking some miscarriage—such as betrayal through a possible interrogation of Da-Ud—when there were things he might be accomplishing elsewhere. Besides, the unvarying foggy warmth and the fragmented, garish religiousness of the Principate both annoyed him and exercised pulls of conflicting enthusiasms and loyalties on several of his mask personalities, who had apparently been as unstable even when whole as their bits and pieces had now made him. He was particularly out of sympathy with the motto graven on the lintel of the Rood-Prince's palace: JUSTICE IS LOVE. The sentiment, obviously descended from some colonial Islamic sect, was excellent doctrine for a culture knit together by treason, for it allowed the prosecution of almost any kind of betrayal on the grounds that justice (disguised as that kind of love which says, "I'm doing this for your own good; it hurts me more than it does you") was being pursued. But Simon, whose dimly remembered parents had betrayed him often on just those grounds, found it entirely too pat. Besides, he was suspicious of all abstractions which took the form "A is B." In his opinion, neither justice nor mercy were very closely related to love, let alone being identical with it—otherwise, why have three words instead of one? A metaphor is not a tautology.

These bagatelles aside, it seemed likely to Simon that something might be gained by returning for a while to Druidsfall and haunting the vicinity of the Guildhall. At the worst, his address would then be unknown to Da-Ud, and his anonymity more complete in the larger city, the Guild less likely to identify him even were it to suspect him—as of course it would—of such boldness. At best, he might pick up some bit of useful information, particularly if Da-Ud's embassy were to create any unusual stir.

Very well. Presenting the Rood-Prince with a vast stack of punched cards and a promise to return, Simon took the flyer to Druidsfall, where he was careful to stay many miles away from The Skopolamander.

For a while he saw nothing unusual, which was in itself fractionally reassuring. Either the Guild was not alarmed by Da-Ud's clumsy proposals, or was not letting it show. On several days in succession, Simon saw the Boadacean Traitor-in-Chief enter and leave, sometimes with an entourage, more often with only a single slave. Everything seemed normal, although it gave Simon a small, ambiguous *frisson* which was all the more disturbing because he was unsure which of his *personae* he should assign it to. Certainly not to his fundamental self, for although Valkol was here the predestined enemy, he was no more formidable than others Simon had defeated (while, it was true, being in his whole and right mind).

Then Simon recognized the "slave"; and this time he did run. It was the vombis, the same one who had been travelling as a diplomat aboard the *Karas*. The creature had not even bothered to change its face to fit its new role.

This time he could have killed the creature easily from his point of vantage, and probably gotten away clean, but again, there were compelling reasons for not doing so. Just ridding the universe of one of the protean entities (if it did any good at all, for nobody knew how they reproduced) would be insufficient advantage for the hue and cry that would result. Besides, the presence of an agent of the Exarchy so close to the heart of this imbroglio was suggestive, and might be put to some use.

Of course, the vombis might be in Druidsfall on some other business entirely, or simply paying a courtesy call on its way back from "deeper into the cluster"; but Simon would be in no hurry to make so dangerous an assumption. No, it was altogether more likely that the Exarch, who could hardly have heard yet of Simon's arrival and disgrace, was simply aware in general of how crucial Boadacea would be to any scheme of High Earth's—he was above all an efficient tyrant—and had placed his creature here to keep an eye on things.

Yes, that situation might be used, if Simon could just keep his disquietingly percolating brains under control. Among his present advantages was the fact that his disguise was better than that of the vombis, a fact the creature had probably been made constitutionally incapable of suspecting by the whole thrust of its evolution.

With a grim chuckle which he hoped he would not later be forced to swallow, Simon flew back to the Gulf of the Rood.

VI

Da-Ud met Simon in the Singing Gardens, a huge formal maze not much frequented of late even by lovers, because the Rood-Prince in the throes of some new religious crotchet had let it run wild, so that one had constantly to be fending off the ardor of the flowers. At best, this made even simple conversations difficult, and it was rumored that deep in the heart of the maze the floral attentions to visitors were of a more sinister sort.

Da-Ud was exultant, indeed almost manic in his enthusiasm, which did not advance comprehension either, but Simon listened patiently.

"They bought it like lambs," Da-Ud said, naming a sacrificial animal of High Earth so casually as to make one of Simon's *personae* shudder inside him. "I had a little difficulty with the underlings, but not as much as I'd expected, and I got it all the way up to Valkol himself."

"No sign of any outside interest?"

"No, nothing. I didn't let out any more than I had to until I reached His Politeness, and after that he put the blue seal on everything—wouldn't discuss anything but the weather while anyone else was around. Listen, Simon, I don't want to seem to be telling you your business, but I think I may know the Guild better than you do, and it seems to me that you're underplaying your hand. This thing is worth *money.*"

"*I* said it was."

"Yes, but I don't think you've any conception how much. Old

Valkol took my asking price without a murmur—in fact, so fast that I wish I'd asked for twice as much. Just to show you I'm convinced of all this, I'm going to give it all to you."

"Don't want it," Simon said. "Money is of no use to me unless I can complete the mission. All I need now is operating expenses, and I've got enough for that."

This clearly had been what Da-Ud had hoped he would say, but Simon suspected that had matters gone otherwise, the younger man might indeed have given over as much as half the money. His enthusiasm mounted.

"All right, but that doesn't change the fact that we could be letting a fortune slip here."

"How much?"

"Oh, at least a couple of megariyals—and I mean *apiece,*" Da-Ud said grandly. "I can't imagine an opportunity like that comes around very often, even in the circles you're used to."

"What would we have to do to earn it?" Simon said, with carefully calculated doubt.

"Play straight with the Guild. They want the material badly, and if we don't trick them we'll be protected by their own rules. And with that much money, there are a hundred places in the galaxy where you'd be safe from High Earth for the rest of your life."

"And what about your half-sister?"

"Well, I'd be sorry to lose that chance, but cheating the Guild wouldn't bring her back, would it? And in a way, wouldn't it be *aesthetically* more satisfying to pay them back for Jillith by being scrupulously fair with them? 'Justice is Love,' you know, and all that."

"I don't know," Simon said fretfully. "The difficulty lies in defining justice, I suppose—you know as well as I do that it can excuse the most complicated treasons. And 'What do you mean by love?' isn't easily answerable either. In the end, one has to shuck it off as a woman's question, too private to be meaningful in a man's world —let alone in matters of polity. Hmmrnm."

This maundering served no purpose but to suggest that Simon was still trying to make up his mind; actually, he had reached a decision several minutes ago. Da-Ud had broken; he would have to be disposed of.

Da-Ud listened with an expression of polite bafflement which did not quite completely conceal a gleam of incipient triumph. Ducking a trumpet vine which appeared to be trying to crown him with thorns, Simon added at last: "You may well be right—but we'll have to be mortally careful. There may, after all, be another agent from High Earth here; in matters of this importance they wouldn't be likely to rest with only one charge in the chamber. That means you'll have to follow my instructions to the letter, or we'll never live to spend a riyal of the proceeds."

"You can count on me," Da-Ud said, tossing his hair out of his eyes. "I've handled everything well enough this time, haven't I? And, after all, it was my idea."

"Certainly. An expert production. Very well. What I want you to do now is go back to Valkol and tell him that I've betrayed you; and sold the other half of the secret to the Rood-Prince."

"Surely you wouldn't actually *do* such a thing!"

"Oh, but I *would,* and I *shall*—the deed will be done by the time you get back to Druidsfall, and for the same twenty riyals that you paid for your half."

"But the purpose—?"

"Simple. I cannot come to Druidsfall with my remaining half—if there's another Earthman there, I'd be shot before I got halfway up the steps of the Hall. I want the Guild to consolidate the two halves by what seems to be an unrelated act of aggression between local parties. You make this clear to them by telling them that I won't actually make the sale to the Rood-Prince until I hear from you that you have the rest of the money. To get the point across at once, when you tell His Politeness that I've 'betrayed' you—wink."

"And how do I get word to you this time?"

"You wear this ring. It communicates with a receiver in my clasp. I'll take matters from there."

The ring—which was actually *only* a ring, which would never communicate anything to anybody—changed hands. Then Da-Ud saluted Simon with solemn glee, and went away to whatever niche in history—and in the walls of the Guildhall of Boadacea—is reserved for traitors without style; and Simon, breaking the stalk of a lyre bush which had sprung up between his feet, went off to hold his muttering, nattering skull and do nothing at all.

VII

Valkol the Polite—or the Exarch's agent, it hardly mattered which—did not waste any time. From a vantage point high up on the Principate's only suitable mountain, Simon watched their style of warfare with appreciation and some wonder.

Actually, in the maneuvering itself the hand of the Exarchy did not show, and did not need to; for the whole campaign would have seemed a token display, like a tournament, had it not been for a few score of casualties which seemed inflicted almost inadvertently. Even among these there were not many deaths, as far as Simon could tell—at least, not by the standards of battle to which he was accustomed.

Clearly, nobody who mattered got killed, on either side. It all reminded Simon of medieval warfare, in which the nearly naked kerns and gallowglasses were thrust into the front ranks to slaughter one another, while the heavily armored knights kept their valuable persons well to the rear—except that here there was a good deal more trumpet blowing than there was slaughter. The Rood-Prince, in an exhibition of bravado more garish than sensible, deployed on the plain before his city several thousand pennon-bearing mounted troopers who had nobody to fight but a rabble of foot soldiers which Druidsfall obviously—at least, to Simon's eye—did not intend to be taken seriously; whereupon, the city was taken from the Gulf side, by a squadron of flying submarines which broke from the surface of the sea on four buzzing wings like so many dragonflies. The effect was like a raid by the twenty-fifth century upon the thirteenth, as imagined by someone in the twentieth—a truly dreamlike sensation.

The submarines particularly interested Simon. Some Boadaceous genius, unknown to the rest of the known galaxy, had solved the ornithopter problem—though the wings of the devices were membranous rather than feathered. Hovering, the machines thrummed their wings through a phase shift of a full hundred and eighty degrees, but when they swooped, the wings moved in a horizontal figure eight, lifting with a forward-and-down stroke, and propelling with the back stroke. A long, fish-like tail gave stability, and doubtless had other uses under water.

After the mock battle, the 'thopters landed and the troops withdrew; and then matters took a more sinister turn, manifested by thumping explosions and curls of smoke from inside the Rood palace. Evidently, a search was being made for the supposedly hidden documents Simon was thought to have sold, and it was not going well. The sounds of demolition, and the occasional public hangings, could only mean that a maximum interrogation of the Rood-Prince had failed to produce any papers, or any clues to them.

This Simon regretted, as he did the elimination of Da-Ud. He was not normally so ruthless—an outside expert would have called his workmanship in this affair perilously close to being sloppy—but the confusion caused by the transduction serum, now rapidly rising as it approached term, had prevented him from manipulating every factor as subtly as he had originally hoped to do. Only the grand design was still intact now: It would now be assumed that Boadacea had clumsily betrayed the Exarchy, leaving the Guild no way out but to capitulate utterly to Simon, with whatever additional humiliations he judged might not jeopardize the mission, for Jillith's sake—

Something abruptly cut off his view of the palace. He snatched his binoculars away from his eyes in alarm.

The object that had come between him and the Gulf was a mounted man—or rather, the idiot-headed apteryx the man was sitting on. Simon was surrounded by a ring of them, their lance points aimed at his chest, pennons trailing in the dusty viol grass. Some one of Simon's *personae* remembered that the function of a pennon is to prevent the lance from running all the way through the body, so that the weapon can be pulled out easily and used again, but Simon had more immediate terrors to engross him.

The pennons bore the device of the Rood-Prince; but every lancer in the force was a vombis.

Simon arose resignedly, with a token snarl intended more for himself than for the impassive protean creatures and their fat birds. He wondered why it had never occurred to him before that the vombis might be as sensitive to him as he was to them.

But the answer to that no longer mattered. Sloppiness was about to win its long-postponed reward.

VIII

They put him naked into a wet cell: a narrow closet completely clad in yellowed alabaster, down the sides of which water oozed and beaded all day long, running out into gutters at the edges. He was able to judge when it was day, because there were clouded bull's-eye lenses in each of the four walls which waxed and waned at him with any outside light. By the pattern of its fluctuation he could have figured out to a nicety just where on Boadacea he was, had he been in the least doubt that he was in Druidsfall. The wet cell was a sort of inverted oubliette, thrust high up into Boadacea's air, probably a hypertrophied merlon on one of the towers of the Traitors' Hall. At night, a fifth lens, backed by a sodium vapor lamp, glared down from the ceiling, surrounded by a faint haze of steam where the dew tried to condense on it.

Escape was a useless fantasy. Erected into the sky as it was, the wet cell did not even partake of the usual character of the building's walls, except for one stain in the alabaster which might have been the underside of a child's footprint; otherwise, the veinings were mockingly meaningless. The only exit was down, an orifice through which they had inserted him as though he were being born, and now plugged like the bottom of a stopped toilet. Could he have broken through one of the lenses with his bare hands, he would have found himself naked and torn on the highest point in Druidsfall, with no place to go.

Naked he was. Not only had they pulled all his teeth in search of more poisons, but of course they had also taken his clasp. He hoped they would fool with the clasp—it would make a clean death for everybody—but doubtless they had better sense. As for the teeth, they would regrow if he lived, that was one of the few positive advantages of the transduction serum, but in the meantime his bare jaws ached abominably.

They had missed the antidote, which was in a tiny gel capsule in his left earlobe, masquerading as a sebaceous cyst—left, because it is automatic to neglect that side of a man, as though it were only a mirror image of the examiner's right—and that was some comfort. In a few more days now, the gel would dissolve, he would lose his multiple disguise, and then he would have to confess, but in the meantime he could manage to be content despite the slimy, glaring cold of the cell.

And in the meantime, he practiced making virtues of deficiencies: in this instance, calling upon his only inner resources—the diverting mutterings of his other personalities—and trying to guess what they might once have meant.

Some said:
"But I mean, like, you know—"
"Wheah they goin'?"
"Yeah."
"Led's gehdahda heah—he-he-he!"
"Wheah?"
"So anyway, so uh."
Others:

"It's hard not to recognize a pigeon."
"But Mother's birthday is July 20."
"So he knew that the inevitable might happen—"
"It made my scalp creak and my blood curl."
"Where do you get those crazy ideas?"
And others:
"Acquit Socrates."
"Back when she was sane she was married to a window washer."
"I don't know what you've got under your skirt, but it's wearing white socks."
"And then she made a noise like a spindizzy going sour."
And others:
"Pepe Satan, pepe Satan aleppe."
"Why, so might any man."
"EVACUATE MARS!"
"And then she sez to me, she sez—"
". . . if he would abandon his mind to it."
"With all of love."

And . . . but at that point the plug began to unscrew, and from the spargers above him which formerly had kept the dampness running, a heavy gas began to curl. They had tired of waiting for him to weary of himself, and the second phase of his questioning was about to begin.

IX

They questioned him, dressed in a hospital gown so worn that it was more starch than fabric, in the Traitor-in-Chief's private office to begin with—a deceptively bluff, hearty, leather-and-piperacks sort of room, which might have been reassuring to a novice. There were only two of them: Valkol in his usual abah, and the "slave," now dressed as a Charioteer of the high blood. It was a curious choice of costume, since Charioteers were supposed to be free, leaving it uncertain which was truly master and which slave; Simon did not think it could have been Valkol's idea. The vombis, he also noticed, still had not bothered to change its face from the one it had been wearing aboard the *Karas,* implying an utter confidence which Simon could only hope would prove to be unjustified.

Noting the direction of his glance, Valkol said, "I asked this gentleman to join me to assure you, should you be in any doubt, that this interview is serious. I presume you know who he is."

"I don't know who 'he' is," Simon said, with the faintest of emphasis. "But it must be representing the Green Exarch, since it's a vombis."

The Traitor-in-Chiefs lips whitened slightly. Aha, then he hadn't known that! "Prove it," he said.

"My dear Valkol," the creature interposed. "Pray don't let him distract us over trifles. Such a thing could not be proved without the most elaborate of laboratory tests, as we all know. And the accusation shows what we wish to know, i.e., that he is aware of who I am—otherwise, why try to make such an inflammatory charge?"

"Your master's voice," Simon said. "Let us by all means proceed—this gown is chilly."

"This gentleman," Valkol said, exactly as if he had not heard any of the four preceding speeches, "is Chag Sharanee of the Exarchy. Not from the Embassy, but directly from the Court—he is His Majesty's Deputy Fomentor."

"Appropriate," Simon murmured.

"We know you now style yourself 'Simon de Kuyl,' but what is more to the point, that you claim yourself the Traitor-in-chief of High Earth. Documents now in my possession persuade me that if you are not in fact that officer, you are so close to being he as makes no difference. Possibly the man you replaced, the amateur with the absurd belt of poison shells, was actually he. In any event, you are the man we want."

"Flattering of you."

"Not at all," said Valkol the Polite. "We simply want the remainder of those documents, for which we paid. Where are they?"

"I sold them to the Rood-Prince."

"He had them not, nor could he be persuaded to remember any such transaction."

"Of course not," Simon said with a smile. "I sold them for twenty riyals; do you think the Rood-Prince would recall any such piddling exchange? I appeared as a bookseller, and sold them to his librarian. I suppose you burned the library—barbarians always do."

Valkol looked at the vombis. "The price agrees with the, uh, testimony of Da-Ud tarn Altair. Do you think—?"

"It is possible. But we should take no chances; e.g., such a search would be time consuming."

The glitter in Valkol's eyes grew brighter and colder. "True. Perhaps the quickest course would be to give him over to the Sodality."

Simon snorted. The Sodality was a lay organization to which Guilds classically entrusted certain functions the Guild lacked time and manpower to undertake, chiefly crude physical torture.

"If I'm really who you think I am," he said, "such a course would win you nothing but an unattractive cadaver—not even suitable for masonry repair."

"True," Valkol said reluctantly. "I don't suppose you could be induced—politely—to deal fairly with us at this late date? After all, we did pay for the documents in question, and not any mere twenty riyals."

"I haven't the money yet."

"Naturally not, since the unfortunate Da-Ud was held here with it until we decided he no longer had any use for it. However, if upon the proper oaths—"

"High Earth is the oldest oath-breaker of them all," the Fomentor said. "We—viz., the Exarchy—have no more time for such trials. The question must be put."

"So it would seem. Though I hate to handle a colleague thus—"

"You fear High Earth," the vombis said. "My dear Valkol, may I remind you—"

"Yes, yes, the Exarch's guarantee—I know all that," Valkol snapped, to Simon's surprise. "Nevertheless—Mr. De Kuyl, are you sure we have no recourse but to send you to the Babble Room?"

"Why not?" Simon said. "I rather enjoy hearing myself think. In fact, that's what I was doing when your guards interrupted me."

X

Simon was, naturally, far from feeling all the bravado he had voiced, but he had no choice left but to trust to the transduction serum, which now had his mind on the shuddering, giddy verge of depriving all three of them of what they each most wanted. Only Simon, of course, could know this; and only he could also know something much worse—that insofar as his increasingly distorted time sense could calculate, the antidote was due to be released into his blood stream at best in another six hours, at worst within only a few minutes. After that, the Exarchy's creature would be the only victor—and the only survivor.

And when he saw the Guild's toposcope laboratory, he wondered if even the serum would be enough to protect him. There was nothing in the least outmoded about it; Simon had never encountered its like even on High Earth. Exarchy equipment, all too probably.

Nor did the apparatus disappoint him. It drove directly down into his subconscious with the resistless unconcern of a spike penetrating a toy balloon. Immediately, a set of loudspeakers above his supine body burst into multi-voiced life:

"Is this some trick? No one but Berentz had a translation permit—"

"Now the overdrive my-other must woo and win me—"

"*Wie schafen Sie es, solche Entfernungen bei Unter-lichtgeschwindigkeit zurueckzulegen?*"

"REMEMBER THOR FIVE!"

"Pok. Pok. Pok."

"We're so tired of wading in blood, so tired of drinking blood, so tired of dreaming about blood—"

The last voice rose to a scream, and all the loudspeakers cut off abruptly. Valkol's face, baffled but not yet worried, hovered over Simon's, peering into his eyes.

"We're not going to get anything out of that," he told some invisible technician. "You must have gone too deep; those are the archetypes you're getting, obviously."

"Nonsense." The voice was the Fomentor's. "The archetypes sound nothing like that—for which you should be grateful. In any event, we have barely gone beneath the surface of the cortex; see for yourself."

Valkol's face withdrew. "Hmm. Well, something's wrong. Maybe your probe is too broad. Try it again."

The spike drove home, and the loudspeakers resumed their mixed chorus.

"*Nausentampen. Eddettompic. Berobsilom. Aimkaksetchoc. Sanbetogmow—*"

"*Dites-lui que nous lui ordonnons de revenir, en vertu de la Loi du Grand Tout.*"

"Perhaps he should swear by another country."

"Can't Mommy ladder spaceship think for bye-bye-see-you two windy Daddy bottle seconds straight—"

"*Nansima macamba yonso cakosilisa.*"

"Stars don't have points. They're round, like balls."

The sound clicked off again. Valkol said fretfully: "He can't be resisting. You've got to be doing something wrong, that's all."

Though the operative part of his statement was untrue, it was apparently also inarguable to the Fomentor. There was quite a long silence, broken only occasionally by small hums and clinks.

While he waited, Simon suddenly felt the beginnings of a slow sense of relief in his left earlobe, as though a tiny but unnatural pressure he had long learned to live with had decided to give way—precisely, in fact, like the opening of a cyst.

That was the end. Now he had but fifteen minutes more in which the toposcope would continue to vomit forth its confusion—its steadily diminishing confusion—and only an hour before even his physical appearance would reorganize, though that would no longer matter in the least.

It was time to exercise the last option—now, before the probe could bypass his cortex and again prevent him from speaking his own, fully conscious mind. He said:

"Never mind, Valkol. I'll give you what you want."

"What? By Gro, I'm not going to give you—"

"You don't have to give me anything; I'm not selling anything. You see for yourself that you can't get to the material with that machine. Nor with any other like it, I may add. But I exercise my option to turn my coat, under Guild laws; that gives me safe conduct, and that's sufficient."

"No," the Fomentor's voice said. "It is incredible—he is in no pain and has frustrated the machine; why should he yield? Besides, the secret of his resistance—"

"Hush," Valkol said. "I am moved to ask if you *are* a vombis; doubtless, the machine would tell us that much. Mr. De Kuyl, I respect the option, but I am not convinced yet. The motive, please?"

"High Earth is not enough," Simon said. "Remember Ezra-Tse? 'The last temptation is the final treason . . . to do the right thing for the wrong reason.' I would rather deal fairly with you, and then begin the long task of becoming honest with myself. But with you only, Valkol—not the Exarchy. I sold the Green Exarch nothing."

"I see. A most interesting arrangement, I agree. What will you require?"

"Perhaps three hours to get myself unscrambled from the effects of fighting your examination. Then I'll dictate the missing material. At the moment it's quite inaccessible."

"I believe that, too," Valkol said ruefully. "Very well—"

"It is not very well," the vombis said, almost squalling. "The arrangement is a complete violation of—"

Valkol turned and looked at the creature so hard that it stopped talking of its own accord. Suddenly Simon was sure Valkol no longer needed tests to make up his mind what the Fomentor was.

"I would not expect you to understand it," Valkol said in a very soft voice indeed. "It is a matter of style."

XI

Simon was moved to a comfortable apartment and left alone, for well more than the three hours he had asked for. By that time, his bodily reorganization was complete, though it would take at least a day for all the residual mental effects of the serum to vanish. When the Traitor-in-Chief finally admitted himself to the apartment, he made no attempt to disguise either his amazement or his admiration.

"The poison man! High Earth is still a world of miracles. Would it be fair to ask what you did with your, uh, over-populated associate?"

"I disposed of him," Simon said. "We have traitors enough already. There is your document; I wrote it out by hand, but you can have toposcope confirmation whenever you like now."

"As soon as my technicians master the new equipment —we shot the monster, of course, though I don't doubt the Exarch will resent it."

"When you see the rest of the material, you may not care what the Exarch thinks," Simon said. "You will find that I've brought you a high alliance—though it was Gro's own horns getting it to you."

"I had begun to suspect as much. Mr. De Kuyl—I must assume you are still he, for sanity's sake—that act of surrender was the most elegant gesture I have ever seen. That alone convinced me that you were indeed the Traitor-in-Chief of High Earth, and no other."

"Why, so I was," Simon said. "But if you will excuse me now, I think I am about to become somebody else."

With a mixture of politeness and alarm, Valkol left him. It was none too soon. He had a bad taste in his mouth which had nothing to do with his ordeals . . . and, though nobody knew better than he how empty all vengeance is, an inexpungeable memory of Jillith.

Maybe, he thought, "Justice is Love," after all—not a matter of style but of spirit. He had expected all these questions to vanish when the antidote took full hold, wiped into the past with the personalities who had done what they had done, but they would not vanish; they were himself.

He had won, but obviously he would never be of use to High Earth again.

In a way, this suited him. A man did not need the transduction serum to be divided against himself; he still had many guilts to accept, and not much left of a lifetime to do it in.

While he was waiting, perhaps he could learn to play the sareh.

A Case of Conscience

The stone door slammed. It was Cleaver's trademark: there had never been a door too heavy, complex or cleverly tracked to prevent him from closing it with a sound like a clap of doom. And no planet in the universe could possess an air sufficiently thick and curtained with damp to muffle that sound. Not even Lithia.

Ruiz-Sanchez continued to read. It would take Cleaver's impatient fingers quite a while to free him from his jungle suit, and in the meantime the problem remained. It was a century-old problem, first propounded in 1939, but the Church had never cracked it. And it was diabolically complex (that adverb was official, precisely chosen and literally intended). Even the novel which proposed the Case was on the Index, and Father Ramon Ruiz-Sanchez, S.J., had access to it only by virtue of his Order.

He turned the page, scarcely hearing the stamping and muttering in the hall. On and on the text ran, becoming more tangled, more evil, more insoluble with every word:

"... and Magravius knows from spies that Anita has formerly committed double sacrilege with Michael, *vulgo* Cerularius, a perpetual curate, who wishes to seduce Eugenius. Magravius threatens to have Anita molested by Sulla, an orthodox savage (and leader of a band of twelve mercenaries, the Sullivani), who desires to procure Felicia for Gregorius, Leo, Viteilius and Macdugalius, four excavators, if she will not yield to him and also deceive Honuphrius by rendering conjugal duty when demanded. Anita, who claims to have discovered incestuous temptations from Jeremias and Eugenius—"

There now, he was lost again. He backtracked resignedly. Jeremias and Eugenius were—? Oh, yes, the "brotherly lovers" at the beginning of the case, consanguineous to the lowest degree with both Felicia and Honuphrius—the latter the apparent prime villain and the husband of Anita. It was Magravius, who seemed to admire Honuphrius, who had been urged by the slave Mauritius to solicit Anita, seemingly under the urging of Honuphrius himself. This, however, had come to Anita through her tirewoman Fortissa, who was or at one time had been the common-law wife of Mauritius himself and had borne him children—so that the whole story had to be weighed with the utmost caution. And that entire initial confession of Honuphrius had come out under torture—voluntarily consented to, to be sure, but still torture. The Fortissa-Mauritius relationship was even more dubious, really only a supposition of Father Ware's, though certainly a plausible one considering the public repentance of Sulla after the death of Canicula, who was—yes, that was correct, Mauritius's second wife. No, his first wife; he had never been legally married to Fortissa. It was Magravius's desire for Felicia after the death of Gillia that had confused him there.

"Ramon, give me a hand, will you?" Cleaver shouted suddenly. "I'm stuck and—and I don't feel well."

The Jesuit biologist arose in alarm. Such an admission from Cleaver was unprecedented.

The physicist was sitting on a pouf of woven rushes, stuffed with a sphagnumlike moss, which was bulging at the equator under his weight. He was halfway out of his glass-fiber jungle suit, and his face was white and beaded with sweat, although his helmet was already off. His uncertain fingers tore at a jammed zipper.

"Paul! Why didn't you say you were ill in the first place? Here, let go of that; you're only making things worse. What happened?"

"Don't know exactly," Cleaver said, breathing heavily but relinquishing the zipper. Ruiz-Sanchez knelt beside him and began to work it carefully back onto its tracks. "Went a ways into the jungle to see if I could spot more pegmatite lies; it's been in the back of my mind that a pilot-plant for turning out tritium might locate here eventually—ought to be able to produce on a prodigious scale."

"God forbid," Ruiz-Sanchez said under his breath.

"Hm? Anyhow, I didn't see anything. Few lizards, hoppers, the usual thing. Then I ran up against a plant that looked a little like a pineapple, and one of the spines jabbed right through my suit and nicked me. Didn't seem serious, but—"

"But we don't have the suits for nothing. Let's look at it. Here, put up your feet and we'll haul those boots off. Where did you get—oh. Well, it's angry-looking, I'll give it that. Any other symptoms?"

"My mouth feels raw," Cleaver complained.

"Open up," the Jesuit commanded. When Cleaver complied, it became evident that his complaint had been the understatement of the year. The mucosa inside his mouth was nearly covered with ugly and undoubtedly painful ulcers, their edges as sharply defined as if cut with a cookiepunch.

Ruiz-Sanchez made no comment, however, and deliberately changed his expression to one of carefully calculated dismissal. If the physicist needed to minimize his ailments, it was all right with Ruiz-Sanchez. An alien planet is not a good place to strip a man of his inner defenses. "Come into the lab," he said. "You've got some inflammation in there."

Cleaver arose, a little unsteadily, and followed the Jesuit into the laboratory. There Ruiz-Sanchez took smears from several of the ulcers onto microscope slides and Gram-stained them. He filled the time consumed by the staining process with the ritual of aiming the microscope's substage mirror out the window at a brilliant white cloud. When the timer's alarm went off, he rinsed and flame-dried the first slide and slipped it under the clips.

As he had half-feared, he saw few of the mixed bacilli and spirochaetes which would have indicated a case of ordinary, Earthly, Vincent's angina—which the clinical picture certainly suggested. Cleaver's oral flora were normal, though on the increase because of all the exposed tissue.

"I'm going to give you a shot," Ruiz-Sanchez said gently. "And then I think you'd better go to bed."

"The hell with that," Cleaver said. "I've got nine times as much work to do as I can hope to clean up, without any additional handicaps."

"Illness is never convenient," Ruiz-Sanchez agreed. "But why worry about losing a day or so, since you're in over your head anyhow?"

"What have I got?" Cleaver asked suspiciously.

"You haven't *got* anything," Ruiz-Sanchez said, almost regretfully. "That is, you aren't infected. But your 'pineapple' did you a bad turn. Most plants of that family on Lithia bear thorns or leaves coated with polysaccharides that are poisonous to us. The particular glucoside you got today was evidently squill, or something closely related to it. It produces symptoms like those of trench-mouth, but a lot harder to clear up."

"How long will that take?" Cleaver said. He was still balking, but he was on the defensive now.

"Several days at least—until you've built up an immunity. The shot I'm going to give you is a gamma globulin specific against squill, and it ought to moderate the symptoms until you've developed a high antibody titer of your own. But in the process you're going to run quite a fever, Paul; and I'll have to keep you well-stuffed with antipyretics, because even a little fever is dangerous in this climate."

"I know it," Cleaver said, mollified. "The more I learn about this place, the less disposed I am to vote 'aye' when the time comes. Well, bring on your shot—and your aspirin. I suppose I ought to be glad it isn't a bacterial infection, or the Snakes would be jabbing me full of antibiotics."

"Small chance of that," Ruiz-Sanchez said. "I don't doubt that the Lithians have at least a hundred different antibiotics we'll be able to use eventually, but—there, that's all there is to it; you can relax now—but we'll have to study their pharmacology from the ground up, first. All right, Paul, hit the hammock. In about ten minutes you're going to wish you were born dead, that I promise you."

Cleaver grinned. His sweaty face under its thatch of dirty blonde hair was craggy and powerful even in illness. He stood up and deliberately rolled down his sleeve. "Not much doubt about how you'll vote, either," he said. "You like this planet, don't you, Ramon? It's a biologist's paradise, as far as I can see."

"I do like it," the priest said, smiling back. He followed Cleaver into the small room which served them both as sleeping quarters. Except for the window, it strongly resembled the inside of a jug. The walls were curving and continuous, and were made of some ceramic material which never beaded or felt wet, but never seemed to be quite dry, either. The hammocks were slung from hooks which projected smoothly from the walls. "But don't forget that Lithia's my first extrasolar planet. I think I'd find any new habitable world fascinating. The infinite mutability of life forms, and the cunning inherent in each of them . . . it's all amazing and very delightful."

Cleaver sprawled heavily in his hammock. After a decent interval, Ruiz-Sanchez took the liberty of heaving up after him the foot he seemed to have forgotten. Cleaver didn't notice. The reaction was setting in.

"Read me no tracts, father," Cleaver said. Then: "I didn't mean that. I'm sorry . . . but for a physicist, this place is hell. . . . You'd better get me that aspirin. I'm cold."

"Surely." Ruiz-Sanchez went quickly back into the lab, made up a salicylate-barbiturate paste in one of the Lithians' superb mortars, and pressed it into a set of pills. He wished he could stamp each pill

"Bayer" before it dried—if Cleaver's personal cure-all was aspirin, it would be just as well to let him think he was taking aspirin—but he had no dies for the purpose. He took two of the pills back to Cleaver with a mug and a carafe of Berkefield-filtered water.

The big man was already asleep; Ruiz-Sanchez woke him. Cleaver would sleep longer and awake farther along the road to recovery if he were done that small unkindness now. As it was, be hardly noticed when the pills were put down him, and soon resumed his heavy, troubled breathing.

That done, Ruiz-Sanchez returned to the front room of the house, sat down and began to inspect the jungle suit. The tear which the plant spine had made was not difficult to find, and would be easy to repair. It would be much harder to repair Cleaver's notion that their defenses were invulnerable, and that plants could be blundered against with impunity. Ruiz-Sanchez wondered if one or both of the other members of the commission still shared that notion.

Cleaver had called the thing which had brought him low a "pineapple." Any biologist could have told Cleaver that even on Earth the pineapple is a prolific and dangerous weed, edible only by a happy and irrelevant accident. In Hawaii, as Ruiz-Sanchez remembered, the tropical forest was quite impassable to anyone not wearing heavy boots and tough trousers. The close-packed, irrepressible pineapples outside of the plantations could tear unprotected legs to ribbons.

The Jesuit turned the suit over. The zipper that Cleaver had jammed was made of a plastic into the molecule of which had been incorporated radicals from various terrestrial anti-fungal substances, chiefly thiolutin. The fungi of Lithia respected these, all right, but the elaborate molecule of the plastic itself had a tendency, under Lithian humidities and heats, to undergo polymerization more or less spontaneously. That was what had happened here. One of the teeth of the zipper had changed into something resembling a piece of popcorn.

It grew slowly dark as Ruiz-Sanchez worked. There was a muted puff of sound, and the room was illuminated with small, soft yellow flames from recesses in every wall. The burning substance was natural gas, of which Lithia had an inexhaustible and constantly renewed supply. The flames were lit by adsorption against a catalyst, as soon as the gas came on. A lime mantle, which worked on a rack and pinion of heatproof glass, could be moved into the flame to provide a brighter light; but the priest liked the yellow light the Lithians themselves preferred, and used the limelight only in the laboratory.

For some things, of course, the Earthmen had to have electricity, for which they had been forced to supply their own generators. The Lithians had a far more advanced science of electrostatics than Earth had, but of electrodynamics they knew comparatively little. They had discovered magnetism only a few years before, since natural magnets were unknown on the planet. They had first observed the phenomenon, not in iron, of which they had next to none, but in liquid oxygen—a difficult substance from which to make generator coil cores!

The results in terms of Lithian civilization were peculiar to an Earthman. The tall, reptilian people had built several huge electrostatic generators and scores of little ones, but had nothing even vaguely resembling telephones. They knew a great deal on the practical level about electrolysis, but carrying a current over a long distance—say one kilometer—was regarded by them as impossible. They had no electric motors as an Earthman would understand the term, but made fast intercontinental flights in jet aircraft powered by *static* electricity. Cleaver said he understood this feat, but Ruiz-Sanchez certainly did not.

They had a completely marvelous radio network, which among other things provided a "live" navigational grid for the whole planet, zeroed on (and here perhaps was the epitome of the Lithian genius for paradox) a tree. Yet they had never produced a commercial vacuum tube and their atomic theory was not much more sophisticated than Democritus's had been!

These paradoxes, of course, could be explained in part by the things that Lithia lacked. Like any large rotating mass, Lithia had a magnetic field of its own, but a planet which almost entirely lacks iron provides its people with no easy way to discover magnetism. Radioactivity, at least until the Earthmen had arrived, had been entirely unknown on the surface of Lithia, which explained the hazy atomic theory. Like the Greeks, the Lithians had discovered that friction between silk and glass produces one kind of charge, and between silk and amber another. They had gone on from there to Widmanstatten generators, electrochemistry and the static jet—but without suitable metals they were unable to make batteries or do more than begin to study electricity in motion.

In the fields where they had been given fair clues, they had made enormous progress. Despite the constant cloudiness and endemic drizzle, their descriptive astronomy was excellent, thanks to the fortunate presence of a small moon which had drawn their attention outward early. This in turn made for basic advances in optics. Their chemistry took full advantage of both the seas and the jungles. From the one they took such vital and diversified products as agar, iodine, salt, trace metals and foods of many kinds. The other provided nearly everything else that they needed: resins, rubbers, woods of all degrees of hardness, edible and essential oils, vegetable "butters," rope and other fibers, fruits and nuts, tannins, dyes, drugs, cork, paper. Indeed, the sole forest product which they did *not* take was game, and the reason for this oversight was hard to find. It seemed to the Jesuit to be religious—yet the Lithians had no religion, and they certainly ate many of the creatures of the sea without qualms of conscience.

He dropped the jungle suit into his lap with a sigh, though the pop-corned tooth still was not completely trimmed back into shape. Outside, in the humid darkness, Lithia was in full concert. It was a vital, somehow fresh, new-sounding drone, covering most of the sound spectrum audible to an Earthman. It came from the myriad insects of Lithia. Many of these had wiry, ululating songs, almost like birds, in addition to the scrapes and chirrups and wing-buzzes of the insects of Earth.

Had Eden sounded like that, before evil had come into the world? Ruiz-Sanchez wondered. Certainly his native Peru sang no such song. Qualms of conscience—these were, in the long run, his essential business, rather than the taxonomical jungles of biology, which had already become tangled into near-hopelessness on Earth before spaceflight had come along to add whole new volumes of puzzles. It was only interesting that the Lithians were bipedal reptiles with marsupial-like pouches and pteropsid circulatory systems. But it was vital that they had qualms of conscience—if they did.

He and the other three men were on Lithia to decide whether or not Lithia would be suitable as a port of call for Earth, without risk of damage to either Earthmen or Lithians. The other three men were primarily scientists, but Ruiz-Sanchez's own recommendation would in the long run depend upon conscience, not upon taxonomy.

He looked down at the still-imperfect suit with a troubled face until he heard Cleaver moan. Then he arose and left the room to the softly hissing flames.

II

From the oval front window of the house to which Cleaver and Ruiz-Sanchez had been assigned, the land slanted away with insidious gentleness toward the ill-defined south edge of Lower Bay, a part of the Gulf of Sfath. Most of the area was salt marsh, as was the seaside nearly everywhere on Lithia. When the tide was in, the flats were covered to a depth of a meter or so almost half the way to the house. When it was out, as it was tonight, the jungle symphony was augmented by the agonized barking of a score of species of lungfish. Occasionally, when the small moon was unoccluded and the light from the city was unusually bright, one could see the leaping shadow of some amphibian, or the sinuously advancing sigmoid track of the Lithian crocodile, in pursuit of some prey faster than itself but which it would nonetheless capture in its own geological good time.

Still farther—and usually invisible even in daytime because of the pervasive mists—was the opposite shore of Lower Bay, beginning with tidal flats again, and then more jungle, which ran unbroken thereafter for hundreds of kilometers to the equatorial sea.

Behind the house, visible from the sleeping room, was the rest of the city, Xoredeshch Sfath, capital of the great southern continent. Like all the cities the Lithians built, its most striking characteristic to an Earthman was that it hardly seemed to be there at all. The Lithian houses were low, and made of the earth which had been dug from their foundations, so that they tended to fade into the soil even to a trained observer.

Most of the older buildings were rectangular, put together without mortar, of rammed-earth blocks. Over the course of decades the blocks continued to pack and settle themselves until it became easier to abandon an unwanted building than to tear it down. One of the first setbacks the Earthmen had suffered on Lithia had come through an ill-advised offer to raze one such structure with TDX, a gravity-polarized explosive unknown to the Lithians. The warehouse in question was large, thick-walled and three Lithian centuries old. The explosive created an uproar which greatly distressed the Lithians, but when it was over, the storehouse still stood, unshaken.

Newer structures were more conspicuous when the sun was out, for just during the past half-century the Lithians had begun to apply their enormous knowledge of ceramics to house construction. The new houses assumed thousands of fantastic, quasi-biological shapes, not quite amorphous but not quite resembling any form in experience either. Each one was unique and to the choice of its owner, yet all markedly shared the character of the community and the earth from which it sprang. These houses, too, would have blended well with the background of soil and jungle, except that most of them were glazed and so shone blindingly for brief moments on sunny days when the light and the angle of the observer was just right. These shifting coruscations, seen from the air, had been the Earthmen's first intimation that there was intelligent life in the ubiquitous Lithian jungle.

Ruiz-Sanchez looked out the sleeping-room window at the city for at least the ten thousandth time on his way to Cleaver's hammock. Xoredeshch Sfath was alive to him; it never looked the same twice. He found it singularly beautiful.

He checked Cleaver's pulse and respiration. Both were fast, even for Lithia, where a high carbon dioxide partial pressure raised the pH of the blood of Earthmen to an abnormal level and stimulated the breathing reflex. The priest judged, however, that Cleaver was in little danger as long as his actual oxygen utilization was not increased. At the moment he was certainly sleeping deeply—if not very restfully—and it would do no harm to leave him alone for a little while.

Of course, if a wild allosaur should blunder into the city . . . but that was about as likely as the blundering of an untended elephant into the heart of New Delhi. It could happen, but almost never did. And no other dangerous Lithian animal could break into the house if it were sealed.

Ruiz-Sanchez checked the carafe of fresh water in the niche beside the hammock, went into the hall, and donned boots, macintosh and waterproof hat. The night sounds of Lithia burst in upon him as he opened the stone door, along with a gust of sea air and the characteristic halogen odor most people call "salty." There was a thin drizzle falling, making haloes around the lights of Xoredeshch Sfath. Far out, on the water, another light moved. That was probably the coastal side wheeler to Yllith, the enormous island which stood athwart the Upper Bay, barring the Gulf of Sfath as a whole from the equatorial sea.

Outside, Ruiz-Sanchez turned the wheel which extended bolts on every margin of the door. Drawing from his macintosh a piece of soft chalk, he marked on the sheltered tablet designed for such uses the Lithian symbols which meant "Illness is here." That would be sufficient. Anybody who chose to could open the door simply by turning the wheel, but the Lithians were overridingly social beings, who respected their own conventions as they would respect natural law.

That done, Ruiz-Sanchez set out for the center of the city and the Message Tree. The asphalt streets shone in the yellow lights cast from windows, and in the white light of the mantled, wide-spaced street lanterns. Occasionally he passed the eight-foot, kangaroolike shape of a Lithian, and the two exchanged glances of frank curiosity, but there were not many Lithians abroad now. They kept to their houses at night, doing Ruiz-Sanchez knew not what. He could see them frequently, alone or by twos or threes, moving behind the oval windows of the houses he passed. Sometimes they seemed to be talking.

What about?

It was a nice question. The Lithians had no crime, no newspapers, no household communications systems, no arts that could be differentiated clearly from their crafts, no political parties, no public amusements, no nations, no games, no religions, no sports, no celebrations. Surely they didn't spend every waking minute of their lives exchanging knowledge, discussing philosophy or history? Or did they? Perhaps, Ruiz-Sanchez thought suddenly, they simply went inert once they were inside their jugs, like so many pickles! But even as the thought came, the priest passed another house, and saw their silhouettes moving to and fro . . .

A puff of wind scattered cool droplets in his face. Automatically, he quickened his step. If the night were to turn out especially windy, there would doubtless be many voices coming and going in the Message Tree. It loomed ahead of him now, a sequoialike giant, standing at the mouth of the valley of the River Sfath—the valley which led in great serpentine folds into the heart of the continent, where Gleshchetk Sfath, or Blood Lake in English, poured out its massive torrents.

As the winds came and went along the valley, the tree nodded and swayed. With every movement, the tree's root system, which underlay the entire city, tugged and distorted the buried crystalline cliff upon which the city had been founded as long ago in Lithian prehistory as was the founding of Rome on Earth. At every such pressure, the buried cliff responded with a vast heart-pulse of radio waves—a pulse detectable not only all over Lithia, but far out in space as well.

These bursts, of course, were sheer noise. How the Lithians modified them to carry information—not only messages, but the amazing navigational grid, the planetwide time-signal system, and much more—was something Ruiz-Sanchez never expected to learn, although Cleaver said it was all perfectly simple once you understood it. It had something to do with semi-conduction and solid-state physics, which—again according to Cleaver—the Lithians understood better than any Earthman.

Almost all knowledge, Ruiz-Sanchez reflected with amusement, fell into that category. It was either perfectly simple once you understood it, or else it fell apart into fiction. As a Jesuit—even here, forty light-years from Rome—Ruiz-Sanchez knew something about knowledge that Cleaver would never learn: that all knowledge goes through *both* stages, the annunciation out of noise into fact and the disintegration back into noise again. The process involved was the making of increasingly finer distinctions. The outcome was an endless series of theoretical catastrophes. The residuum was faith.

The high, sharply vaulted chamber, like an egg stood on its large end, which had been burned out in the base of the Message Tree, was droning with life as Ruiz-Sanchez entered it. It would have been difficult to imagine anything less like an Earthly telegraph office or other message center, however.

Around the circumference of the lower end of the egg there was a continual whirling of tall figures, Lithians entering and leaving through the many doorless entrances and changing places in the swirl of movement like so many electrons passing from orbit to orbit. Despite their numbers, their voices were pitched so low that Ruiz-Sanchez could hear blended in with their murmuring the soughing of the wind through the enormous branches far aloft.

The inner side of this band of moving figures was bounded by a high railing of black, polished wood, evidently cut from the phloëm of the tree itself. On the other side of this Encke's Division a thin circlet of Lithians took and passed out messages steadily and without a moment's break, handling the total load faultlessly—if one were to judge by the way the outer band was kept in motion—and without apparent effort by memory alone. Occasionally one of these specialists would leave the circlet and go to one of the desks which were scattered over most of the rest of the sloping floor, increasingly thinly, like a Crepe Ring, to confer there with the desk's occupant. Then he went back to the black rail, or, sometimes, he took the desk and its previous occupant went to the rail.

The bowl deepened, the desks thinned, and at the very center stood a single, aged Lithian, his hands clapped to the ear-whorls behind his heavy jaws, his eyes covered by their nictitating membrane, only his nasal fossae and heat-receptive postnasal pits uncovered. He spoke to no one, and no one consulted him—but the absolute stasis in which he stood was obviously the reason, the sole reason, for the torrents and countertorrents of people which poured along the outermost ring.

Ruiz-Sanchez stopped, astonished. He had never himself been to the Message Tree before—communicating with the other two Earthmen on Lithia had been, until now, one of Cleaver's tasks—and the priest found that he had no idea what to do. The scene before him was more suggestive of a bourse than of a message center in any ordinary sense. It seemed unlikely that so many Lithians could have urgent personal messages to send each time the winds were active; yet it seemed equally uncharacteristic that the Lithians, with their stable, abundance-based economy, should have any equivalent of stock or commodity brokerage.

There seemed to be no choice, however, but to plunge in, try to reach the polished black rail, and ask one of those who stood on the other side to try and raise Agronski or Michelis again. At worst, he supposed, he could only be refused, or fail to get a hearing at all. He took a deep breath.

Simultaneously, his left elbow was caught in a firm four-fingered grip. Letting the stored breath out again in a snort of surprise, the priest looked around and up at the solicitously bent head of a Lithian. Under the long, traplike mouth, the being's wattles were a delicate, curious aquamarine, in contrast to its vestigial comb, which was a permanent and silvery sapphire, shot through with veins of fuchsia.

"You are Ruiz-Sanchez," the Lithian said in his own language. The priest's name, unlike that of most of the other Earthmen, fell easily in that tongue. "I know you by your robe."

This was pure chance; any Earthman out in the rain in a macintosh would have been identified as Ruiz-Sanchez, because he was the only Earthman who seemed to the Lithians to wear the same garment indoors. "I am Chtexa, the metallist, who consulted with you earlier on medicine and on your mission and other matters. We have not seen you here before. Do you wish to talk with the Tree?"

"I do," Ruiz-Sanchez said gratefully. "It is so that I am new here. Can you explain to me what to do?"

"Yes, but not to any profit," Chtexa said, tilting his head so that his completely inky pupils shone down into Ruiz-Sanchez's eyes. "One must have observed the ritual, which is very complex, until it is habit. We have grown up with it, but you I think lack the coordination to follow it on the first attempt. If I may hear your message instead . . ."

"I would be most indebted. It is for our colleagues Agronski and Michelis. They are at Xoredeshch Gton on the northeast continent, at about thirty-two degrees east, thirty-two degrees north—"

"Yes, the second benchmark, at the outlet of the Lesser Lakes; the city of the potters. And you will say?"

"That they are to join us now, here, at Xoredeshch Sfath. And that our time on Lithia is almost up."

"That me regards. But I will bear it."

Chtexa leapt into the whirling crowd, and Ruiz-Sanchez was left behind, considering again his thankfulness at the pains he had taken to learn the Lithian language. Several members of the terrestrial commission had shown a regrettable lack of interest in that tongue: "Let 'em learn English," had been Cleaver's classic formulation. Ruiz-Sanchez was all the less likely to view this idea sympathetically considering that his own native language was Spanish and his preferred foreign language German.

Agronski had taken a slightly more sophisticated stand: it was not, he said, that Lithian was too difficult to pronounce—certainly it wasn't any harder than Arabic or Russian on the soft palate—but, after all, "it's hopeless to attempt to grasp the concepts that lie behind a really alien language in the time we have to spend here, isn't it?"

To both views, Michelis had said nothing; he had simply set out to learn to read the language first, and if he found his way from there into speaking it, he would not be surprised, and neither would his confreres. That was Michelis's way of doing things, thorough and untheoretical at the same time. As for the other two approaches, Ruiz-Sanchez thought privately that it was close to criminal to allow any contact-man for a new planet ever to leave Earth with such parochial notions. Of Cleaver's tendency to refer to the Lithians themselves as "the Snakes," Ruiz-Sanchez's opinion was such as to be admissible only to his remote confessor.

And in view of what lay before him now in this egg-shaped hollow, what was Ruiz-Sanchez to think of Cleaver's conduct as communications officer for the group? Surely he could never have transmitted or received a single message through the Tree, as he had claimed to have done. Probably he had never been nearer to the Tree than the priest had been.

Of course, it went without saying that he had been in contact with Agronski and Michelis by *some* method, but that method evidently had been a private transmitter concealed in his luggage. . . Yet, physicist though he most definitely was not, Ruiz-Sanchez rejected that solution on the spot; he had some idea of the practical difficulties of ham radio on a world like Lithia, swamped as it was on all wavelengths by the tremendous pulses which the Tree wrung from the buried crystalline cliff. The problem was beginning to make him feel decidedly uncomfortable.

Then Chtexa was back, recognizable not so much by any physical detail—for his wattles were now the same ambiguous royal purple as those of most of the other Lithians in the crowd—as by the fact that he was obviously bearing down upon the Earthman.

"I have sent your message," he said at once. "It is recorded at Xoredeshch Gton. But the other Earthmen are not there. They have not been in the city for some days."

That was impossible. Cleaver had said he had spoken to Agronski only a day ago. "Are you sure?" Ruiz-Sanchez said cautiously.

"It admits of no uncertainty. The house which we gave them stands empty. The many things which they had with them are gone." The tall shape raised its small hands in a gesture which might have been solicitous. "I think this is an ill word. I dislike to bring it you. The words which you brought me when we first met were full of good."

"Thank you. Don't worry," Ruiz-Sanchez said distractedly. "No man could hold the bearer responsible for the word, surely."

"Whom else would he hold responsible for it? At least that is our custom," Chtexa said. "And under it, you have lost by our exchange. Your words on iron have been shown to contain great good. I would take pleasure in showing you how we have used them, especially so since I have brought you in return an ill message. If you would share my house tonight, without prejudice to your work . . ."

Sternly Ruiz-Sanchez stifled his sudden excitement. Here was the first chance, at long last, to see something of the private life of Lithia! And through that, perhaps, gain some inkling of the moral life, the role in which God had cast the Lithians in the ancient drama of good and evil in the past and in the times to come. Until that was known, the Lithians in their Eden were only spuriously good: all reason, all organic thinking machines, ULTIMACs with tails and without souls.

But there was the hard fact that he had left behind a sick man. There was not much chance that Cleaver would awaken before morning; he had been given nearly fifteen milligrams of sedative per kilogram of body weight. But if his burly frame should somehow throw it off, driven perhaps by some anaphylactic crisis impossible to rule out this early, he would need prompt attention. At the very least, he would want badly for the sound of a human voice on this planet which he hated and which had struck him down.

Still, the danger to Cleaver was not great. He most certainly did not require a minute-by-minute vigil. There was, after all, such a thing as an excess of devotion, a form of pride among the pious which the Church had long found peculiarly difficult to stifle. At its worst, it produced a St. Simon Stylites, who though undoubtedly acceptable to God had for centuries been very bad public relations for the Church. And had Cleaver really earned the kind of devotion Ruiz-Sanchez had been proposing, up to now, to tender him as a creature of God? And with whole planet at stake, a whole people—

A lifetime of meditation over just such problems of conscience had made Ruiz-Sanchez, like any other gifted member of his Order, quick to find his way through all but the most complex ethical labyrinths to a decision. An unsympathetic observer might almost have called him "agile."

"Thank you," he said, a little shakily. "I will share your house very gladly."

III

"Cleaver! Cleaver! Wake up, you big slob. Where the hell have you been?"

Cleaver groaned and tried to turn over. At his first motion, the world began to rock gently, sickeningly. His mouth was filled with burning pitch.

"Cleaver, turn out. It's me—Agronski. Where's the father? What's wrong? Why didn't we hear from you? Look *out,* you'll—"

The warning came too late and Cleaver could not have understood it anyhow; he had been profoundly asleep and had no notion of his situation in space or time. At his convulsive twist away from the nagging voice, the hammock rotated on its hooks and dumped him.

He struck the floor stunningly, taking the main blow across his right shoulder, though he hardly felt it as yet. His feet, not yet part of him at all, still remained afloat far aloft, twisted in the hammock webbing.

"Good Lord!" There was a brief chain of footsteps, like chestnuts dropping on a roof, and then an overstated crash. "Cleaver, are you sick? Here, lie still a minute and let me get your feet free. Mike—Mike, can't you turn the gas up in this jug? Something's wrong back here."

After a moment, yellow light began to pour from the glistening walls. Cleaver dragged an arm across his eyes, but it did him no good; it tired too quickly. Agronski's mild face, plump and anxious, floated directly above him like a captive balloon. He could not see Michelis anywhere, and at the moment he was just as glad. Agronski's presence was hard enough to understand.

"How . . . the hell . . . he said. At the words, his lips split painfully at both corners. He realized for the first time that they had become gummed together, somehow, while he was asleep. He bad no idea how long he had been out of the picture.

Agronski seemed to understand the aborted question. "We came in from the lakes in the 'copter," he said. "We didn't like the silence down here and we figured that we'd better come in under our own power, instead of registering in on the regular jet-liner and tipping the Lithians off—just in case there'd been any dirty work afloat."

"Stop jawing him," Michelis said, appearing suddenly, magically in the doorway. "He's got a bug, that's obvious. I don't like to feel pleased about misery, but I'm glad it's that instead of the Lithians."

The rangy, long-jawed chemist helped Agronski lift Cleaver to his feet. Tentatively, despite the pain, Cleaver got his mouth open again. Nothing came out but a hoarse croak.

"Shut up," Michelis said, not unkindly. "Let's get him back into the hammock. Where's the father? He's the only one capable of dealing with sickness here."

"I'll bet he's dead," Agronski burst out suddenly, his face glistening with alarm. "He'd be here if he could. It must be catching, Mike."

"I didn't bring my mitt," Michelis said dryly. "Cleaver, lie still or I'll have to clobber you. Agronski, you seem to have dumped his water carafe; better go get him some more, he needs it. And see if the father left anything in the lab that looks like medicine."

Agronski went out, and, maddeningly, so did Michelis—at least out of Cleaver's field of vision. Setting his every muscle against the pain, Cleaver pulled his lips apart once more.

"Mike."

Instantly, Michelis was there. He had a pad of cotton between two fingers, wet with some solution, with which he gently cleaned Cleaver's lips and chin.

"Easy. Agronski's getting you a drink. We'll let you talk in a little while, Paul. Don't rush it."

Cleaver relaxed a little. He could trust Michelis. Nevertheless, the vivid and absurd insult of having to be swabbed like a baby was more than he could bear; he felt tears of helpless rage swelling on either side of his nose. With two deft, noncommittal swipes, Michelis removed them.

Agronski came back, holding out one hand tentatively, palm up. "I found these," he said. "There's more in the lab, and the father's pillpress is still out. So's his mortar and pestle, though they've been cleaned."

"All right, let's have 'em," Michelis said. "Anything else?"

"No. There's a syringe cooking in the sterilizer, if that means anything."

Michelis swore briefly and to the point. "It means that there's a pertinent antitoxin in the shop someplace," he added. "But unless Ramon left notes, we'll not have a prayer of figuring out which one it is."

As he spoke, he lifted Cleaver's head and tipped the pills into his mouth. The water which followed was cold at the first contact, but a split second later it was liquid fire. Cleaver choked, and at that precise moment Michelis pinched his nostrils shut. The pills went down.

"There's no sign of the father?" Michelis said.

"Not a one, Mike. Everything's in good order, and his gear's still here. Both jungle suits are in the locker."

"Maybe he went visiting," Michelis said thoughtfully. "He must have gotten to know quite a few of the Lithians by now."

"With a sick man on his hands? That's not like him, Mike. Not unless there was some kind of emergency. Or maybe he went on a routine errand, expected to be back in just a few moments, and—"

"And was set upon by trolls for forgetting to stamp his foot three times before crossing the bridge."

"All right, laugh."

"I'm not laughing, believe me."

"Mike . . ."

Michelis took a step back and looked down at Cleaver, his face floating as if detached through a haze of tears. He said: "All right, Paul. Tell us what it is. We're listening."

But it was too late. The doubled barbiturate dose had gotten to Cleaver first. He could only shake his head, and with the motion Michelis seemed to go reeling away into a whirlpool of fuzzy rainbows.

Curiously, he did not quite go to sleep. He had had nearly a normal night's sleep, and he had started out the enormously long day a powerful and healthy man. The conversation of the two Earthmen and an obsessive consciousness of his need to speak to them before Ruiz-Sanchez returned helped to keep him, if not totally awake, at least not far below a state of light trance—and the presence in his system of thirty grains of acetylsalicylic acid had seriously raised his oxygen consumption, bringing with it not only dizziness but a precarious, emotionally untethered alertness. That the fuel which was being burned to maintain it was largely the protein substrate of his own cells he did not know, and it could not have alarmed him had he known it.

The voices continued to reach him, and to convey a little meaning. With them were mixed fleeting, fragmentary dreams, so slightly removed from the surface of his waking life as to seem peculiarly real, yet at the same time peculiarly pointless and depressing. In the semiconscious intervals there came plans, a whole succession of them, all simple and grandiose at once, for taking command of the expedition, for communicating with the authorities on Earth, for bringing forward secret papers proving that Lithia was uninhabitable, for digging a tunnel under Mexico to Peru, for detonating Lithia in one single mighty fusion of all its lightweight atoms into an atom of cleaverium, the element whose cardinal number was aleph-null . . .

AGRONSKI: Mike, come here and look at this; you read Lithian. There's a mark on the front door, on the message tablet.

(Footsteps.)

MICHELIS: It says "Sickness inside." The strokes aren't casual or deft enough to be the work of the natives. Ideographs are hard to write rapidly. Ramon must have written it there.

AGRONSKI: I wish I knew where he went afterwards.

(Footsteps. Door shutting, not loudly. Footsteps. Hassock creaking.)

AGRONSKI: Well, we'd better be thinking about getting up a report. Unless this damn twenty-hour day has me thrown completely off, our time's just about up. Are you still set on opening up the planet?

MICHELIS: Yes. I've seen nothing to convince me that there's anything on Lithia that's dangerous to us. Except maybe Cleaver in there, and I'm not prepared to say that the father would have left him if he were in any serious danger. And I do not see how Earthmen could harm this society: it's too stable emotionally, economically, in every other way.

(*Danger, danger,* said somebody in Cleaver's dream. *It will explode. It's all a popish plot.* Then he was marginally awake again and conscious of how his mouth hurt.)

AGRONSKI: Why do you suppose these two jokers never called us after we went north?

MICHELIS: I don't have any answer. I won't even guess until I talk to Ramon. Or until Paul's able to sit up and take notice.

AGRONSKI: I don't like it, Mike. It smells bad to me. This town's right at the heart of the communications system of the planet. And yet—no messages, Cleaver sick, the father not here . . . there's a hell of a lot we don't know about Lithia.

MICHELIS: There's a hell of a lot we don't know about central Brazil.

AGRONSKI: Nothing essential, Mike. What we know about the periphery gives us all the clues we need about the interior—even to those fish that eat people, the what-are-they, the piranhas. That's not true on Lithia. We don't know whether our peripheral clues about Lithia are germane or just incidental. Something enormous could be hidden under the surface without our being able to detect it.

MICHELIS: Agronski, stop sounding like a Sunday supplement. You underestimate your own intelligence. What kind of enormous secret could that be? That the Lithians eat people? That they're cattle for unknown gods that live in the jungle? That they're actually mind-wrenching, soul-twisting, heart-stopping, bowel-moving intelligences in disguise? The moment you see any such proposition, you'll deflate it yourself. I would not even need to take the trouble of examining it, or discussing how we might meet it if it were true.

AGRONSKI: All right, all right. I'll reserve judgment for the time being, anyhow. If everything turns out to be all right here, with the father and Cleaver, I mean, I'll probably go along with you. I don't have any reason I could defend for voting against the planet, I admit.

MICHELIS: Good for you. I'm sure Ramon is for opening it up, so that should make it unanimous. I can't see why Cleaver would object.

(Cleaver was testifying before a packed court convened in the UN General Assembly chambers in New York, with one finger pointed dramatically, but less in triumph than in sorrow, at Ramon Ruiz-Sanchez, S.J. At the sound of his name the dream collapsed and he realized that the room had grown a little lighter, Dawn—or the dripping, wool-gray travesty of it which prevailed on Lithia—was on its way. He wondered what he had just said to the court. It had been conclusive, damning, good enough to be used when he awoke; but he could not remember a word of it. All that remained of it was a sensation, almost the taste of the words, but with nothing of their substance.)

AGRONSKI: It's getting light. I suppose we'd better knock off.

MICHELIS: Did you stake down the 'copter? The winds here are higher than they are up north, I seem to remember.

AGRONSKI: Yes. And covered it with the tarp. Nothing left to do but sling our hammocks—

MICHELIS: *Shh.* What's that?

(Footsteps. Faint ones, but Cleaver knew them. He forced his eyes to open a little, but there was nothing to see but the ceiling. Its even color, and its smooth, ever-changing slope into a dome of nothingness, drew him almost immediately upward into the mists of trance once more.)

AGRONSKI: Somebody's coming. It's the father, Mike—look out here. He seems to be all right. Dragging his feet a bit, but who wouldn't after being out helling all night?

MICHELIS: Maybe you'd better meet him at the door. It'd probably be better than our springing out at him after he gets inside. After all he doesn't expect us. I'll get to unpacking the hammocks.

AGRONSKI: Sure, Mike.

(Footsteps going away from Cleaver. A grating sound of stone on stone: the door-wheel being turned.)

AGRONSKI: Welcome home, father! We got in just a little while ago and—what's wrong? Are you ill? Is there something that—Mike! *Mike!*

(Somebody was running. Cleaver willed his neck muscles to turn his head, but they refused to obey. Instead, the back of his head seemed to force itself deeper into the stiff pillow of the hammock. After a momentary and endless agony he cried out.)

CLEAVER: Mike!

AGRONSKI: Mike!

(With a gasp, Cleaver lost the long battle at last. He was asleep.)

IV

As the door of Chtexa's house closed behind him, Ruiz-Sanchez looked about the gently glowing foyer with a feeling of almost unbearable anticipation, although he could hardly have said what it was that he hoped to see. Actually, it looked exactly like his own quarters, which was all he could in justice have expected—all the furniture at "home" was Lithian except the lab equipment.

"We have cut up several of the metal meteors from our museums, and hammered them as you suggested," Chtexa said behind him, while he struggled out of his raincoat and boots. "They show very definite, very strong magnetism, just as you predicted. We now have the whole planet alerted to pick up meteorites and send them to our electrical laboratory here, regardless of where found. The staff of the observatory is attempting to predict possible falls. Unhappily, meteors are rare here. Our astronomers say that we have never had a 'shower' such as you described as frequent on your native planet."

"No; I should have thought of that," Ruiz-Sanchez said, following the Lithian into the front room. This, too, was quite ordinary, and empty except for the two of them. "In our system we have a sort of giant grinding-wheel—a whole ring of little planets, many thousands of them, distributed around an orbit where we had expected to find only one normal-sized world. Collisions between these bodies are incessant, and our plague of meteors is the result. Here I suppose you have only the usual few strays from comets."

"It is hard to understand how so unstable an arrangement could have come about," Chtexa said, sitting down and pointing out another hassock to his guest. "Have you an explanation?"

"Not a good one," Ruiz-Sanchez said. "Some of us think that there was a respectable planet in that orbit ages ago, which exploded somehow. A similar accident happened to a satellite in our system— at least one of our planets has a similar ring. Others think that at the formation of our solar system the raw materials of what might have been a planet just never succeeded in coalescing. Both ideas have many flaws, but each satisfies certain objections to the other, so perhaps there is some truth in both."

Chtexa's eyes filmed with the mildly disquieting "inner blink" characteristic of Lithians at their most thoughtful. "There would seem to be no way to test either answer," he said at length. "By our logic, lack of such tests makes the original question meaningless."

"That rule of logic has many adherents on Earth. My colleague Dr. Cleaver would certainly agree with it." Ruiz-Sanchez smiled suddenly. He had labored long and hard to master the Lithian language, and to have understood and recognized so completely abstract a point as the one just made by Chtexa was a bigger victory than any quantitative gains in vocabulary alone could ever have been. "But I can see that we are going to have difficulties in collecting these meteorites. Have you offered incentives?"

"Oh, certainly. Everyone understands the importance of the program. We are all eager to advance it."

This was not quite what the priest had meant by his question. He searched his memory for some Lithian equivalent of *reward,* but found nothing but the word he had already used, *incentive.* He realized that he knew no word for *greed,* either. Evidently offering Lithians a hundred dollars a meteorite would simply baffle them. Instead he said, "Since the potential meteor-fall is so small, you're not likely to get anything like the supply of metal that you need for a real study, no matter how thoroughly you cooperate on it. You need a supplementary iron-finding program: some way of concentrating the traces of the metal you have on the planet. Our smelting methods would be useless to you, since you have no ore-beds. Hmm. What about the iron-fixing bacteria?"

"Are there such?" Chtexa said, cocking his head dubiously.

"I don't know. Ask your bacteriologists. If you have any bacteria here that belong to the genus we call *Leptothrix,* one of them should be an iron-fixing species. In all the millions of years that this planet has had life on it, that mutation must have occurred, and probably very early."

"But why have we never seen it before? We have done perhaps more research in bacteriology than we have in any other field."

"Because," Ruiz-Sanchez said earnestly, "you didn't know what to look for, and because such a species would be as rare as iron itself. On Earth, because we have iron in abundance, our *Leptothrix ochracea* has found plenty of opportunity to grow. We find their fossil sheaths by uncountable millions in our great ore-beds. It used to be thought, as a matter of fact, that the bacteria *produced* the ore-beds, but I've never believed that. While they do obtain their energy by oxidizing ferrous iron, such salts in solution change spontaneously to ferric salts if the oxidation-reduction potential and the pH of the water are right—and those are conditions that are affected by ordinary decay bacteria. On our planet the bacteria grew in the ore-beds because the iron was there, not the other way around. In your case, you just don't have the iron to make them numerous, but I'm sure there must be a few."

"We will start a soil-sampling program at once," Chtexa said, his wattles flaring a subdued orchid. "Our antibiotics research centers screen soil samples by the thousands every month, in search of new microflora of therapeutic importance. If these iron-fixing bacteria exist, we are certain to find them eventually."

"They must exist," Ruiz-Sanchez repeated. "Do you have a bacterium that is a sulphur-concentrating obligate anaerobe?"

"Yes—yes, certainly!"

"There you are," the Jesuit said, leaning back contentedly and clasping his hands across one knee. "You have plenty of sulphur and so you have the bacterium. Please let me know when you find the iron-fixing species. I'd like to make a sub culture and take it home with me when I leave. There are two Earthmen whose noses I'd like to rub in it."

The Lithian stiffened and thrust his head forward a little, as if baffled. Ruiz-Sanchez said hastily, "Pardon me. I was translating literally an aggressive idiom of my own tongue. It was not meant to describe an actual plan of action."

"I think I understand," Chtexa said. Ruiz-Sanchez wondered if he did. In the rich storehouse of the Lithian language he had yet to discover any metaphors, either living or dead. Neither did the Lithians have any poetry or other creative arts. "You are of course welcome to any of the results of this program which you would honor us by accepting. One problem in the social sciences which has long puzzled us is just how one may adequately honor the innovator. When we consider how new ideas change our lives, we despair of giving in kind, and it is helpful when the innovator himself has wishes which society can gratify."

Ruiz-Sanchez was at first not quite sure he had understood the proposition. After he had gone over it once more in his mind, he was not sure that he could bring himself to like it, although it was admirable enough. From an Earthman it would have sounded intolerably pompous, but it was evident that Chtexa meant it.

It was probably just as well that the commission's report on Lithia was about to fall due. Ruiz-Sanchez had begun to think that he could absorb only a little more of this kind of calm sanity. And all of it—a disquieting thought from somewhere near his heart reminded him—all of it derived from reason, none from precept, none from faith. The Lithians did not know God. They did things rightly, and thought righteously, because it was reasonable and efficient and natural to do and to think that way. They seemed to need nothing else.

Or could it be that they thought and acted as they did because, not being born of man, and never in effect having left the Garden in which they lived, they did not share the terrible burden of original sin? The fact that Lithia had never once had a glacial epoch, that its climate had been left unchanged for seven hundred million years, was a geological fact that an alert geologist could scarcely afford to ignore. Could it be that, free from the burden, they were also free from the curse of Adam?

And if they were—could men bear to live among them?

"I have some questions to ask you, Chtexa," the priest said after a moment. "You owe me no debt whatsoever, but we four Earthmen have a hard decision to make shortly. You know what it is. And I don't believe that we know enough yet about your planet to make that decision properly."

"Then of course you must ask questions," Chtexa said immediately. "I will answer, wherever I can."

"Well, then—do your people die? I see you have the word, but perhaps it isn't the same as our word in meaning."

"It means to stop changing and to go back to existing," Chtexa said. "A machine exists, but only a living thing, like a tree, progresses along a line of changing equilibriums. When that progress stops, the entity is dead."

"And that happens to you?"

"It always happens. Even the great trees, like the Message Tree, die sooner or later. Is that not true on Earth?"

"Yes," Ruiz-Sanchez said, "yes, it is. For reasons it would take me a long time to explain, it occurred to me that you might have escaped this evil."

"It is not evil as we look at it," Chtexa said. "Lithia lives because of death. The death of leaves supplies our oil and gas. The death of some creatures is always necessary for the life of others. Bacteria must die, and viruses be prevented from living, if illness is to be cured. We ourselves must die simply to make room for others, at least until we can slow the rate at which our people arrive in the world—a thing impossible to us at present."

"But desirable, in your eyes?"

"Surely desirable," Chtexa said. "Our world is rich, but not inexhaustible. And other planets, you have taught us, have peoples of their own. Thus we cannot hope to spread to other planets when we have overpopulated this one."

"No real thing is ever inexhaustible," Ruiz-Sanchez said abruptly, frowning at the iridescent floor. "That we have found to be true over many thousands of years of our history."

"But inexhaustible in what way?" said Chtexa. "I grant you that any small object, any stone, any drop of water, any bit of soil can be explored without end. The amount of information which can be gotten from it is quite literally infinite. But a given soil can be exhausted of nitrates. It is difficult, but with bad cultivation it can be done. Or take iron, about which we have already been talking. Our planet's supply of iron has limits which we already know, at least approximately. To allow our economy to develop a demand for iron which exceeds the total known supply of Lithia—and exceeds it beyond any possibility of supplementation by meteors or by import—would be folly. This is not a question of information. It is a question of whether or not the information can be used. If it cannot, then limitless information is of no help."

"You could certainly get along without more iron if you had to," Ruiz-Sanchez admitted. "Your wooden machinery is precise enough to satisfy any engineer. Most of them, I think, don't remember that we used to have something similar: I've a sample in my own home. It's a kind of timer called a cuckoo clock, nearly two of our centuries old, made entirely of wood, and still nearly 100 percent accurate. For that matter, long after we began to build seagoing vessels of metal, we continued to use lignum vitae for ships' bearings."

"Wood is an excellent material for most uses," Chtexa agreed. "Its only deficiency, compared to ceramic materials or perhaps metal, is that it is variable. One must know it well to be able to assess its qualities from one tree to the next. And of course complicated parts can always be grown inside suitable ceramic molds; the growth pressure inside the mold rises so high that the resulting part is very dense. Larger parts can be ground direct from the plank with soft sandstone and polished with slate. It is a gratifying material to work, we find."

Ruiz-Sanchez felt, for some reason, a little ashamed. It was a magnified version of the same shame he had always felt at home toward that old Black Forest cuckoo clock. The electric clocks elsewhere in his villa back home all should have been capable of performing silently, accurately and in less space—but the considerations which had gone into the making of them had been commercial as well as purely technical. As a result, most of them operated with a thin, asthmatic whir, or groaned softly but dismally at irregular hours. All of them were "streamlined," over-sized and ugly. None of them kept good time, and several of them, since they were powered by constant-speed motors operating very simple gearboxes, could not be adjusted, but had been sent out from the factory with built-in, ineluctable inaccuracies.

The wooden cuckoo clock, meanwhile, ticked evenly away. A quail emerged from one of two wooden doors every quarter of an hour and let you know about it, and on the hour first the quail came out, then the cuckoo, and there was a soft bell that rang just ahead of the cuckoo's call. It was accurate to a minute a week, all for the price of running up the three weights which drove it, each night before bedtime.

The maker had been dead before Ruiz-Sanchez had been born. In contrast, the priest would probably buy and jettison at least a dozen cheap electric clocks in the course of one lifetime, as their makers had intended he should.

"I'm sure it is," he said humbly. "I have one more question, if I may. It is really part of the same question: I have asked if you die; now I should like to ask how you are born. I see many adults on your streets and sometimes in your houses—though I gather you yourself are alone—but never any children. Can you explain this to me? Or if the subject is not allowed to be discussed.

"But why should it not be? There can never be any closed subjects," Chtexa said. "You know, of course, that our mates have abdominal pouches where the eggs are carried. It was a lucky mutation for us, for there are a number of nest-robbing species on this planet."

"Yes, we have a few animals with a somewhat similar arrangement on Earth, although they are live-bearers."

"Our eggs are laid into these pouches once a year," Chtexa said.

"It is then that the women leave their own houses and seek out the male of their choice to fertilize the eggs. I am alone because, thus far, I am no woman's first choice this season. In contrast you may see men's house at this time of year which shelter three or four women who favor him."

"I see," Ruiz-Sanchez said carefully. "And how is the choice determined? Is it by emotion, or by reason alone?"

"The two are in the long run the same," Chtexa said. "Our ancestors did not leave our genetic needs to chance. Emotion with us no longer runs counter to our eugenic knowledge. It cannot, since it was itself modified to follow that knowledge by selective breeding for such behavior.

"At the end of the season, then, comes Migration Day. At that time all the eggs are fertilized, and ready to hatch. On that day—you will not be here to see it, I am afraid, for your announced date of departure precedes it by a short time—our whole nation goes to the seashores. There, with the men to protect them from predators, the women wade out to swimming depth, and the children are born."

"In the sea?" Ruiz-Sanchez said faintly.

"Yes, in the sea. Then we all return, and resume our other affairs until the next mating season."

"But—but what happens to the children?"

"Why, they take care of themselves, if they can. Of course many perish, particularly to our voracious brother the great fish-lizard, whom for that reason we kill when we can. But a majority return when the time comes."

"Return? Chtexa, I don't understand. Why don't they drown when they are born? And if they return, why have we never seen one?"

"But you have," Chtexa said. "And you have heard them often. Here, come with me." He arose and led the way out into the foyer. Ruiz-Sanchez followed, his head whirling with conjecture.

Chtexa opened the door. The night, the priest saw with a subdued shock, was on the wane; there was the faintest of pearly glimmers on the cloudy sky to the east. The multifarious humming and singing of the jungle continued unabated. There was a high, hissing whistle, and the shadow of a pterodon drifted over the city toward the sea. From the mudflats came a hoarse barking.

"There," Chtexa said softly. "Did you hear it?"

The stranded creature, or another of his kind—it was impossible to tell which—croaked protestingly again.

"It is hard for them at first," Chtexa said. "But actually the worst of their dangers are over. They have come ashore."

"Chtexa," Ruiz-Sanchez said. "Your children—the *lungfish*?"

"Yes," Chtexa said. "Those are our children."

V

In the last analysis it was the incessant barking of the lungfish which caused Ruiz-Sanchez to faint when Agronski opened the door for him. The late hour, and the dual strains of Cleaver's illness and the subsequent discovery of Cleaver's direct lying, contributed. So did the increasing sense of guilt toward Cleaver which the priest had felt while walking home under the gradually brightening, weeping sky; and so, of course, did the shock of discovering that Agronski and Michelis had arrived sometime during the night while he had been neglecting his charge.

But primarily it was the diminishing, gasping clamor of the children of Lithia, battering at his every mental citadel, all the way from Chtexa's house to his own.

The sudden fugue only lasted a few moments. He fought his way back to consciousness to find that Agronski and Michelis had propped him up on a stool in the lab and were trying to remove his macintosh without unbalancing him or awakening him—as difficult a problem in topology as removing a man's vest without taking off his jacket. Wearily, the priest pulled his own arm out of a macintosh sleeve and looked up at Michelis.

"Good morning, Mike. Please excuse my bad manners."

"Don't be an idiot," Michelis said evenly. "You don't have to talk now, anyhow. I've already spent much of tonight trying to keep Cleaver quiet until he's better. Don't put me through it again, Ramon, please."

"I won't. I'm not ill; I'm just very tired and a little overwrought."

"What's the matter with Cleaver?" Agronski demanded. Michelis made as if to shoo him off.

"No, no, Mike. I'm all right, I assure you. As for Paul, he got a dose of glucoside poisoning when a plant-spine stabbed him this afternoon. No, it's yesterday afternoon now. How has he been since you arrived?"

"He's sick," Michelis said. "Since you weren't here, we did not know what to do. We settled for two of the pills you'd left out."

"You did?" Ruiz-Sanchez slid his feet heavily to the floor and tried to stand up. "As you say, you couldn't have known what else to do, but I think I'd better look in on him—"

"Sit down, please, Ramon." Michelis spoke gently, but his tone showed that he meant the request to be honored. Obscurely glad to be forced to yield to the big man's well-meant implacability, the priest let himself be propped back on the stool. His boots fell off his feet to the floor.

"Mike, who's the father here?" he said tiredly. "Still, I'm sure you've done a good job. He's in no apparent danger?"

"Well, he seems very sick. But he had energy enough to keep himself half-awake most of the night. He only passed out a short while ago."

"Good. Let him stay out. Tomorrow we'll probably have to begin intravenous feeding, though. In this atmosphere one doesn't give a salicylate overdose without penalties." He sighed. "Can we put off further questions?"

"If there's nothing else wrong here, of course we can."

"Oh," Ruiz-Sanchez said, "there's a great deal wrong, I'm afraid."

"I knew it," Agronski said. "I knew damn well there was. I told you so, Mike, didn't I?"

"Is it urgent?"

"No, Mike—there's no danger to us, of that I'm positive. It's nothing that won't keep until we have all had a rest. You two look as though you need one as badly as I."

"We're tired," Michelis agreed.

"But why didn't you ever call us?" Agronski burst in aggrievedly. "You had us scared half to death, father. If there's really something wrong here, you should have—"

"There's no immediate danger," Ruiz-Sanchez repeated patiently. "As for why we didn't call you, I don't understand that any more than you do. Up to tonight, I thought we were in regular contact with you both. That was Paul's job and he seemed to be carrying it out. I didn't discover that he wasn't doing it until after he became ill."

"Then obviously we'll have to wait," Michelis said. "Let's hit the hammock, in God's name. Flying that 'copter through twenty-five hundred miles of fog-bank wasn't exactly restful, either; I'll be glad to turn in. . . . But, Ramon—"

"Yes, Mike?"

"I have to say that I don't like this any better than Agronski does.

Tomorrow we've got to clear it up, and get our commission business done. We've only a day or so to make our decision before the ship comes and takes us off for good, and by that time we *must* know everything there is to know, and just what we're going to tell the Earth about it."

"Yes," Ruiz-Sanchez said. "Just as you say, Mike—in God's name."

The Peruvian priest-biologist awoke before the others: actually, he had undergone far less purely physical strain than had the other three. It was just beginning to be cloudy dusk when he rolled out of his hammock and padded over to look at Cleaver.

The physicist was in a coma. His face was dirty gray and looked oddly shrunken. It was high time that the neglect and inadvertent abuse to which he had been subjected was rectified. Happily, his pulse and respiration were close to normal now.

Ruiz-Sanchez went quietly into the lab and made up a fructose IV feeding. At the same time he reconstituted a can of powdered egg into a sort of soufflé, setting it in a covered crucible to bake at the back of the little oven; that was for the rest of them.

In the sleeping-chamber, the priest set up his IV stand. Cleaver did not stir when the needle entered the big vein just above the inside of his elbow. Ruiz-Sanchez taped the tubing in place, checked the drip from the inverted bottle and went back into the lab.

There he sat, on the stool before the microscope, in a sort of suspension of feeling while the new night drew on. He was still poisoned-tired, but at least now he could stay awake without constantly fighting himself. The slowly rising soufflé in the oven went *plup-plup, plup-plup,* and after a while a thin tendril of aroma suggested that it was beginning to brown on top, or at least thinking about it.

Outside, it abruptly rained buckets. Just as abruptly, it stopped.

"Is that breakfast I smell, Ramon?"

"Yes, Mike, in the oven. In a few minutes now."

"Right."

Michelis went away again. On the back of the workbench, Ruiz-Sanchez saw the dark blue book with the gold stamping which he had brought with him all the way from Earth. Almost automatically he pulled it to him and opened it to page 573. It would at least give him something to think about with which he was not personally involved.

He had quitted the text last with Anita, who "would yield to the lewdness of Honuphrius to appease the savagery of Sulla and the mercenariness of the twelve Sullivani, and (as Gilbert first suggested), to save the virginity of Felicia for Magravius"—now hold on a moment, how could Felicia be considered still a virgin at this point? Ah: ". . . when converted by Michael after the death of Gillia"; that covered it, since Felicia had been guilty only of simple infidelities in the first place. ". . . but she fears that, by allowing his marital rights, she may cause reprehensible conduct between Eugenius and Jeremias. Michael, who has formerly debauched Anita, dispenses her from yielding to Honuphrius"—yes, that figured, since Michael also had had designs on Eugenius. "Anita is disturbed, but Michael comminates that he will reserve her case tomorrow for the ordinary Guglielmus even if she should practice a pious fraud during affriction which, from experience, she knows (according to Wadding) to be leading to nullity."

Well. This was all very well. It even seemed to be shaping up, for the first time. Still, Ruiz-Sanchez reflected, he would not like to have known the family hidden behind the conventional Latin aliases, or to have been the confessor to any one of them. Now then:

"Fortissa, however, is encouraged by Gregorius, Leo, Viteilius and Macdugalius, reunitedly, to warn Anita by describing the strong chastisements of Honuphrius and the depravities *(turpissimas)* of Canicula, the deceased wife of Mauritius, with Sulla, the simoniac, who is abnegand and repents."

Yes, it added up, when one tried to view it without outrage either at the persons involved—and there was every assurance that these were fictitious—or at the author, who for all his mighty intellect, the greatest perhaps of the preceding century among novelists, had still to be pitied as much as the meanest victim of the Evil One. To view it, as it were, in a sort of gray twilight of emotion, wherein everything, even the barnaclelike commentaries which the text had accumulated, could be seen in the same light.

"Is it done, father?"

"Smells like it, Agronski. Take it out and help yourself, why don't you?"

"Thanks. Can I bring Cleaver—"

"No, he's getting an IV."

Unless his impression that he understood the problem at last was once more going to turn out to be an illusion, he was now ready for the basic question, the stumper that had deeply disturbed both the

Order and the Church for so many years now. He reread it carefully. It asked:

"Has he hegemony and shall she submit?"

To his astonishment, he saw as if for the first time that it was two questions, despite the omission of a comma between the two. And so it demanded two answers. Did Honuphrius have hegemony? Yes, he did, for Michael, the only member of the whole complex who had been gifted from the beginning with the power of grace, had been egregiously compromised. Therefore, Honuphrius regardless of whether his sins were all to be laid at his door or were real only in rumor could not be divested of his privileges by anyone. But should Anita submit? No, she should not. Michael had forfeited his right to dispense or to reserve her in any way, and so she could not be guided by the curate or by anyone else in the long run but her own conscience—which in view of the grave accusations against Honuphrius could lead her to no recourse but to deny him. As for Sulla's repentance, and Felicia's conversion, they meant nothing, since the defection of Michael had deprived both of them, and everyone else, of spiritual guidance.

The answer, then, had been obvious all the time. It was: yes, and no.

He closed the book and looked up across the bench, feeling neither more nor less dazed than he had before, but with a small stirring of elation deep inside him which he could not suppress. As he looked out of the window into the dripping darkness, a familiar, sculpturesque head and shoulders moved into the truncated tetrahedron of yellow light being cast out through the fine glass into the rain.

It was Chtexa, moving away from the house.

Suddenly Ruiz-Sanchez realized that nobody had bothered to rub away the sickness ideograms on the door tablet. If Chtexa had come here on some errand, he had been turned back unnecessarily. The priest leaned forward, snatched up an empty slidebox and rapped with a corner of it against the inside of the window.

Chtexa turned and looked in through the steaming curtains of rain, his eyes completely filmed. Ruiz-Sanchez beckoned to him, and got stiffly off the stool to open the door. In the oven his share of breakfast dried slowly and began to burn.

The rapping had summoned forth Agronski and Michelis as well. Chtexa looked down at the three of them with easy gravity, while drops of water ran like oil down the minute, prismatic scales of his supple skin.

"I did not know that there was sickness here," the Lithian said. "I called because your brother Ruiz-Sanchez left my house this morning without the gift I had hoped to give him. I will leave if I am invading your privacy in any way."

"You are not," Ruiz-Sanchez assured him. "And the sickness is only a poisoning, not communicable and we think not likely to end badly for our colleague. These are my friends from the north, Agronski and Michelis."

"I am happy to see them. The message was not in vain, then?"

"What message is this?" Michelis said, in his pure but hesitant Lithian.

"I sent a message, as your colleague Ruiz-Sanchez asked me to do, last night. I was told by Xoredeshch Gton that you had already departed."

"As we had," Michelis said. "Ramon, what's this? I thought you told us that sending messages was Paul's job. And you certainly implied that you didn't know how to do it after Paul took sick."

"I didn't. I don't. I asked Chtexa to send it for me."

Michelis looked up at the Lithian. "What did the message say?" he asked.

"That you were to join them now, here, in Xoredeshch Sfath. And that your time on our world was almost up."

"What does that mean?" Agronski said. He had been trying to follow the conversation, but he was not much of a linguist, and evidently the few words he had been able to pick up had served only to inflame his ready fears. "Mike, translate, please."

Michelis did so, briefly. Then he said: "Ramon, was that really all you had to say to us, especially after what you had found out? We knew that departure time was coming, too, after all. We can keep a calendar as well as you, I hope."

"I know that, Mike. But I had no idea what previous messages you'd received, if indeed you'd received any. For all I knew, Cleaver might have been in touch with you some other way, privately. I thought at first of a transmitter in his personal luggage, but later it occurred to me that he might have been sending dispatches over the regular jet-liners. Or he might have told you that we were going to stay on beyond the official time. He might have told you I was dead. He might have told you anything. I had to be sure you'd arrive here *regardless* of what he had or had not said.

"And when I got to the local message center, I had to revise my message again, because I found that I couldn't communicate with you directly, or send anything at all detailed. Everything that goes out from Xoredeshch Sfath by radio goes out through the Tree, and until you have seen it you haven't any idea what an Earthman is up against there in sending even the simplest message."

"Is that true?" Michelis asked Chtexa.

"True?" Chtexa repeated. "It is accurate, yes."

"Well, then," Ruiz-Sanchez said, a little nettled, "you can see why, when Chtexa appeared providentially, recognized me and offered to act as an intermediary, I had to give him only the gist of what I had to say. I couldn't hope to explain all the details to him, and I couldn't hope that any of those details would get to you undistorted after passing through at least two Lithian intermediaries. All I could do was yell at the top of my voice for you two to get down here on the proper date—and hope that you heard me."

"This is a time of trouble, which is like a sickness in the house," Chtexa said. "I must not remain. I will wish to be left alone when I am troubled, and I cannot ask that, if I now force my presence on others who are troubled. I will bring my gift at a better time."

He ducked out through the door, without any formal gesture of farewell, but nevertheless leaving behind an overwhelming impression of graciousness. Ruiz-Sanchez watched him go helplessly, and a little forlornly. The Lithians always seemed to understand the essences of situations; they were never, like even the most cocksure of Earthmen, beset by the least apparent doubt.

And why should they be? They were backed—if Ruiz-Sanchez was right—by the second-best Authority in the universe, and backed directly, without intermediaries or conflicting interpretations. The very fact that they were never tormented by indecision identified them as creatures of that Authority. Only the children of God had been given free choice, and hence were often doubtful.

Nevertheless, Ruiz-Sanchez would have delayed Chtexa's departure had he been able. In a short-term argument it is helpful to have pure reason on your side—even though such an ally could be depended upon to stab you to the heart if you depended upon him too long.

"Let's go inside and thrash this thing out," Michelis said, shutting the door and turning back toward the front room. "It's a good thing we got some sleep, but we have so little time left now that it's going to be touch and go to have a formal decision ready when the ship comes."

"We can't go ahead yet," Agronski objected, although, along with Ruiz-Sanchez, he followed Michelis obediently enough. "How can we do anything sensible without having heard what Cleaver has to say? Every man's voice counts on a job of this sort."

"That's very true," Michelis said. "And I don't like the present situation any better than you do—I've already said that. But I don't see that we have any choice. What do you think, Ramon?"

"I'd like to hold out for waiting," Ruiz-Sanchez said frankly. "Anything I may say now is, to put it realistically, somewhat compromised with you two. And don't tell me that you have every confidence in my integrity, because we had every confidence in Cleaver's, too. Right now, trying to maintain both confidences just cancels out both."

"You have a nasty way, Ramon, of saying aloud what everybody else is thinking," Michelis said, grinning bleakly. "What alternatives do you see, then?"

"None," Ruiz-Sanchez admitted. "Time is against us, as you said. We'll just have to go ahead without Cleaver."

"No, you won't." The voice, from the doorway to the sleeping-chamber, was at once both uncertain and much harshened by weakness.

The others sprang up. Cleaver, clad only in his shorts, stood in the doorway, clinging to both sides of it. On one forearm Ruiz-Sanchez could see the marks where the adhesive tape which had held the IV tubing had been ripped off.

VI

"Paul, you must he crazy," Michelis said, almost angrily. "Get back into your hammock before you make things twice as bad for yourself. You're a sick man, can't you realize that?"

"Not as sick as I look," Cleaver said, with a ghastly grin. "Actually I feel pretty fair. My mouth is almost all cleared up and I don't think I've got any fever. And I'll he damned if this commission is going to proceed an inch without me. It isn't empowered to do it, and I'll appeal against any decision—any decision, I hope you guys are listening—that it makes without me."

The other two turned helplessly to Ruiz-Sanchez.

"How about it, Ramon?" Michelis said, frowning. "Is it safe for him to be up like this?"

Ruiz-Sanchez was already at the physicist's side, peering into his mouth. The ulcers were indeed almost gone, with granulation tissue forming nicely over the few that still remained. Cleaver's eyes were still slightly suffused, indicating that the toxemia was not completely defeated, but except for these two signs the effect of the accidental squill inoculation was no longer visible. It was true that Cleaver looked awful, but that was inevitable in a man recently quite sick, and in one who had been burning his own body proteins for fuel to boot.

"If he wants to kill himself, I guess he's got a right to do so, at least by indirection," Ruiz-Sanchez said. "Paul, the first thing you'll have to do is get off your feet, and get into a robe, and get a blanket around your legs. Then you'll have to eat something; I'll fix it for you. You have staged a wonderful recovery, but you're a sitting duck for a real infection if you abuse yourself during convalescence."

"I'll compromise," Cleaver said immediately. "I don't want to be a hero, I just want to be heard. Give me a hand over to that hassock. I still don't walk very straight."

It took the better part of half an hour to get Cleaver settled to Ruiz-Sanchez's satisfaction. The physicist seemed in a wry way to be enjoying every minute of it. At last he had a mug of *gchteka*, the local equivalent of tea, in his hand, and Michelis said:

"All right, Paul, you've gone out of your way to put yourself on the spot. Evidently that's where you want to be. So let's have the answer. Why didn't you communicate with us?"

"I didn't want to."

"Now wait a minute," Agronski said. "Paul, don't break your neck to say the first damn thing that comes into your head. Your judgment may not be well yet, even if your talking apparatus is. Wasn't your silence just a matter of your being unable to work the local message system—the Tree or whatever it is?"

"No, it wasn't," Cleaver insisted. "Thanks, Agronski, but I don't need to be shepherded down the safe and easy road, or have any alibis set up for me. I know exactly what I did that was ticklish, and I know that it's going to be impossible to set up consistent alibis for it now. My chances for keeping anything under my hat depended on my staying in complete control of everything I did. Naturally those chances went out the window when I got stuck by that damned pineapple. I realized that last night, when I fought like a demon to get through to you before the father could get back, and found that I couldn't make it."

"You seem to take it calmly enough now," Michelis observed.

"Well, I'm feeling a little washed out. But I'm a realist. And I also know, Mike, that I had damned good reasons for what I did. I'm counting on the chance that you'll agree with me wholeheartedly when I tell you why I did it."

"All right," Michelis said, "begin."

Cleaver sat back, folding his hands quietly in the lap of his robe. He was obviously still enjoying the situation. He said:

"First of all, I didn't call you because I didn't want to, as I said. I could have mastered the problem of the Tree easily enough by doing what the father did—that is by getting a Snake to ferry my messages. Of course I don't speak Snake, but the father does, so all I had to do was to take him into my confidence. Barring that, I could have mastered the Tree itself. I already know all the technical principles involved. Mike, you should see that Tree, it's the biggest single junction transistor anywhere in this galaxy, and I'll bet that it's the biggest one anywhere.

"But I wanted a gap to spring up between our party and yours. I wanted both of you to be completely in the dark about what was going on, down here on this continent. I wanted you to imagine the worst, and blame it on the Snakes, too, if that could be managed. After you got here—if you did—I was going to be able to show you that I hadn't sent any messages because the Snakes wouldn't let me. I've got more plans to that effect squirrelled away around here than I'll bother to list now; there'd be no point in it, since it's all come to nothing. But I'm sure it would have looked conclusive, regardless of anything the father would have been able to offer to the contrary.

"It was just a damned shame, from my point of view, that I had to run up against a pineapple at the last minute. It gave the father a chance to find out something about what was up. I'll swear that if that hadn't happened, he wouldn't have smelled anything until you actually got here—and then it would have been too late."

"I probably wouldn't have, that's true," Ruiz-Sanchez said, watching Cleaver steadily. "But your running up against that 'pineapple' was no accident. If you'd been observing Lithia as you were sent here to do, instead of spending all your time building up a fictitious Lithia for purposes of your own, you'd have known enough about the planet to have been more careful about 'pineapples.' You'd also have spoken at least as much Lithian as Agronski by this time."

"That," Cleaver said, "is probably true, and again it doesn't make any difference to me. I observed the one fact about Lithia that overrides all other facts, and that is going to turn out to be sufficient.

Unlike you, father, I have no respect for petty niceties in extreme situations, and I'm not the kind of man who thinks anyone learns anything from analysis after the fact."

"Let's not get to bickering," Michelis said. "You've told us your story without any visible decoration, and it's evident that you have a reason for confessing. You expect us to excuse you, or at least not to blame you too heavily, when you tell us what that reason is. Let's hear it."

"It's this," Cleaver said, and for the first time he seemed to become a little more animated. He leaned forward, the glowing gaslight bringing the bones of his face into sharp contrast with the sagging hollows of his cheeks, and pointed a not-quite-steady finger at Michelis.

"Do you know, Mike, what it is that we're sitting on here? Do you know, just to begin with, how much rutile there is here?"

"Of course I know. If we decide to vote for opening the planet up, our titanium problem will be solved for a century, maybe even longer. I'm saying as much in my personal report. But we figured that that would be true even before we first landed here, as soon as we got accurate figures on the mass of the planet."

"And what about the pegmatite?" Cleaver demanded softly.

"What about it?" Michelis said, looking puzzled. "I suppose it's abundant; I really didn't bother to look. Titanium's important to us, but I don't quite see why lithium should be; the days when the metal was used as a rocket fuel are fifty years behind us."

"And yet the stuff's still worth about twenty thousand dollars an English ton back home, Mike, and that's exactly the same price it was drawing in the 1960's, allowing for currency changes since then. Doesn't that mean anything to you?"

"I'm more interested in what it means to you," Michelis said. "None of us can make a nickel out of this trip, even if we find the planet solid platinum inside—which is hardly likely. And if price is the only consideration, surely the fact that lithium is common here will break the market for it? What's it good for, after all, on a large scale?"

"It's good for bombs," Cleaver said. "Fusion bombs. And, of course, controlled fusion power, if we ever lick that problem."

Ruiz-Sanchez suddenly felt sick and tired all over again. It was exactly what he had feared had been on Cleaver's mind, and he had not wanted to find himself right.

"Cleaver," he said, "I've changed my mind. I would have sought you out, even if you had never blundered against your 'pineapple.'

That same day you mentioned to me that you were checking for pegmatite when you had your accident, and that you thought Lithia might be a good place for tritium production on large scale. Evidently you thought that I wouldn't know what you were talking about. If you hadn't hit the 'pineapple,' you would have given yourself away to me before now by talk like that; your estimate of me was based on as little observation as is your estimate of Lithia."

"It's easy," Cleaver observed indulgently, "to say 'I knew it all the time'"

"Of course it's easy, when the other man is helping you," Ruiz-Sanchez said. "But I think that your view of Lithia as a cornucopia of potential hydrogen bombs is only the beginning of what you have in mind. I don't believe that it's even your real objective. What you would like most is to see Lithia removed from the universe as far as you're concerned. You hate the place, it's injured you, you'd like to think that it really doesn't exist. Hence the emphasis on Lithia as a source of tritium, to the exclusion of every other fact about the planet; for if that emphasis wins out, Lithia will be placed under security seal. Isn't that right?"

"Of course it's right, except for the phony mind-reading," Cleaver said contemptuously. "When even a priest can see it, it's got to be obvious. Mike, this is the most tremendous opportunity that man's ever had. This planet is made to order to be converted, root and branch, into a thermonuclear laboratory and production center. It has indefinitely large supplies of the most important raw materials. What's even more important, it has no nuclear knowledge of its own for us to worry about. All the clue materials, the radioactive elements and so on which you need to work out real knowledge of the atom, we'll have to import; the Snakes don't know a thing about them. Furthermore, the instruments involved, the counters and particle-accelerators and so on, all depend on materials like iron that the Snakes don't have, and on principles they do not know, like magnetism to begin with, and quantum theory. We'll be able to stock our plant here with an immense reservoir of cheap labor which doesn't know and—if we take proper precautions—never will have a prayer of learning enough to snitch classified techniques.

"All we need to do is to turn in a triple-E Unfavorable on the planet to shut off for a whole century any use of Lithia as a way-station or any other kind of general base. At the same time, we can report separately to the UN Review Committee exactly what we do have in Lithia: a triple-A arsenal for the whole of Earth, for the whole commonwealth of planets we control!"

"Against whom?" Ruiz-Sanchez said.

"What do you mean?"

"Against whom are you stocking this arsenal? Why do we need a whole planet devoted to making tritium bombs?"

"The UN itself can use weapons," Cleaver said dryly. "The time isn't very far gone since there were still a few restive nations on Earth, and it could come around again. Don't forget also that thermonuclear weapons only last a few years—they can't be stockpiled indefinitely, like fission bombs. The half-life of tritium is very short. I suppose you wouldn't know anything about that. But take my word for it, the UN's police would be glad to know that they could have access to a virtually inexhaustible stock of tritium bombs, and to hell with the shelf-life problem!

"Besides, if you've thought about it at all, you know as well as I do that this endless consolidation of peaceful planets can't go on forever. Sooner or later—well, what happens if the next planet we touch on is a place like Earth? If it is, its inhabitants may fight, and fight like a planetful of madmen, to stay out of our frame of influence. Or what happens if the next planet we hit is an outpost for a whole federation, maybe bigger than ours? When that day comes—and it will, it's in the cards—we'll be damned glad if we're able to plaster the enemy from pole to pole with fusion bombs, and clean up the matter with as little loss of life as possible."

"On our side," Ruiz-Sanchez added.

"Is there any other side?"

"By golly, it makes sense to me," Agronski said. "Mike, what do you think?"

"I'm not sure yet," Michelis said. "Paul, I still don't understand why you thought it necessary to go through all the cloak-and-dagger maneuvers. You tell your story fairly enough now, and it has its merits, but you also admit you were going to trick the three of us into going along with you, if you could. Why? Could not you trust the force of your argument alone?"

"No," Cleaver said bluntly. "I've never been on a commission like this before, where there was no single, definite chairman, where there was deliberately an even number of members so that a split opinion couldn't be settled if it occurred—and where the voice of a man whose head is full of pecksniffian, irrelevant moral distinctions and two-thousand-year-old metaphysics carries exactly the same weight as the voice of a scientist."

"That's mighty loaded language," Michelis said.

"I know it. If it comes to that, I'll say here or anywhere that I think the father is a hell of a fine biologist, and that that makes him a scientist like the rest of us—insofar as biology's science.

"But I remember once visiting the labs at Notre Dame, where they have a complete little world of germ-free animals and plants and have pulled I don't know how many physiological miracles out of the hat. I wondered then how one goes about being as good a scientist as that, and a churchman at the same time. I wondered in which compartment in their brains they filed their religion, and in which their science. I'm still wondering.

"I didn't propose to take chances on the compartments getting interconnected on Lithia. I had every intention of cutting the father down to a point where his voice would be nearly ignored by the rest of you. That's why I undertook the cloak-and-dagger stuff. Maybe it was stupid of me—I suppose that it takes training to be a successful *agent provocateur* and that I should have realized it. But I'm not sorry I tried. *I'm only sorry I failed.*"

VII

There was a short, painful silence.

"Is that it, then?" Michelis said.

"That's it, Mike. Oh—one more thing. My vote, if anybody is in doubt about it, is to keep the planet closed. Take it from there."

"Ramon," Michelis said, "do you want to speak next? You're certainly entitled to it—the air's a mite murky at the moment."

"No, Mike; let's hear from you."

"I'm not ready to speak yet either, unless the majority wants me to. Agronski, how about you?"

"Sure," Agronski said. "Speaking as a geologist and also as an ordinary slob that doesn't follow rarefied reasoning very well, I'm on Cleaver's side. I don't see anything either for or against the planet on any other grounds but Cleaver's. It's a fair planet as planets go, very quiet, not very rich in anything else we need, not subject to any kind of trouble that I've been able to detect. It'd make a good way-station, but so would lots of other worlds hereabouts. It'd also make a good arsenal, the way Cleaver defined the term. In every other category it's as dull as ditch-water, and it's got plenty of that. The only other thing it can have to offer is titanium, which isn't quite as scarce back home these days as Mike seems to think, and gem-stones, particularly the semi-precious ones, which we can make at home without traveling forty light-years. I'd say, either set up a way-station here and forget about the planet otherwise, or else handle the place as Cleaver suggested."

"But which?" Ruiz-Sanchez asked.

"Well, which is more important, father? Aren't way-stations a dime a dozen? Planets that can be used as thermonuclear labs, on the other hand, are rare—Lithia is the *first* one that can be used that way, at least in my experience. Why use a planet for a routine purpose if it can be used for a unique purpose? Why not apply Occam's Razor—the law of parsimony? It works in all other scientific problems. It's my bet that it's the best tool to use on this one."

"*You* vote to close the planet, then," Michelis said.

"Sure. That's what I was saying, wasn't it?"

"I wanted to be certain," Michelis said. "Ramon, I guess it's up to us. Shall I speak first?"

"Of course, Mike."

"Then," Michelis said evenly, and without changing in the slightest his accustomed tone of grave impartiality, "I'll say that I think both of these gentlemen are fools, and calamitous fools at that because they're supposed to be scientists. Paul, your maneuvers to set up a phony situation are perfectly beneath contempt, and I shan't mention them again. I shan't even bother to record them, so you needn't feel that you have to mend any fences as far as I'm concerned. I'm looking solely at the purpose those maneuvers were supposed to serve, just as you asked me to do."

Cleaver's obvious self-satisfaction began to dim a little around the edges. He said, "Go ahead," and wound the blanket a little bit tighter around his legs.

"Lithia is not even the beginning of an arsenal," Michelis said. "Every piece of evidence you offered to prove that it might be is either a half-truth or the purest trash. Cheap labor, for instance: with what will you pay the Lithians? They have no money, and they can't be rewarded with goods. They have everything they need, and they like the way they're living right now—God knows they're not even slightly jealous of the achievements we think make Earth great." He looked around the gently rounded room, shining softly in the gaslight. "I don't seem to see any place in here where a vacuum cleaner would find much use. How will you pay the Lithians to work in your thermonuclear plants?"

"With knowledge," Cleaver said gruffly. "There's a lot they'd like to know."

"But what knowledge? The things they'd like to know are specifically the things you can't tell them if they're to be valuable to you as a labor force. Are you going to teach them quantum theory? You can't; that would be dangerous. Are you going to teach them electrodynamics? Again, that would enable them to learn other things you think dangerous. Are you going to teach them how to get titanium from ore, or how to accumulate enough iron to enable them to leave their present Stone Age? Of course you aren't. As a matter of fact, we haven't a thing to offer them in that sense. They just won't work for us under those terms."

"Offer them other terms," Cleaver said shortly. "If necessary, tell them what they're going to do, like it or lump it. It'd be easy enough to introduce a money system on this planet: you give a Snake a piece of paper that says it's worth a dollar, and if he asks you just what makes it worth a dollar—well, the answer is, We say it is."

"And we put a machine-pistol to his belly to emphasize the point," Ruiz-Sanchez interjected.

"Do we make machine-pistols for nothing? I never figured out what else they were good for. Either you point them at someone or you throw them away."

"Item: slavery," Michelis said. "That disposes, I think, of the argument for cheap labor. I won't vote for slavery. Ramon won't. Agronski?"

"No," Agronski said uneasily. "But it's a minor point."

"The hell it is. It's the reason that we're here. We're supposed to think of the welfare of the Lithians as well as of ourselves—otherwise this commission procedure would be a waste of time, of thought, of money. If we want cheap labor, we can enslave any planet."

Agronski was silent.

"Speak up," Michelis said stonily. "Is that true, or isn't it?"

Agronski said, "I guess it is."

"Cleaver?"

"Slavery's a swear word," Cleaver said sullenly. "You're deliberately clouding the issue."

"Say that again."

"Oh, hell. All right, Mike, I know you wouldn't. But you're wrong."

"I'll admit that the instant that you can demonstrate it to me," Michelis said. He got up abruptly from his hassock, walked over to the sloping window-sill and sat down again, looking out into the rain-stippled darkness. He seemed to be more deeply troubled than Ruiz-Sanchez had ever before thought possible for him.

"In the meantime," he resumed, "I'll go on with my own demonstration. Now what's to be said about this theory of automatic security that you've propounded, Paul? You think that the Lithians can't learn the techniques they would need to be able to understand secret information and pass it on, and so they won't have to be screened. There again, you're wrong, as you'd have known if you'd bothered to study the Lithians even perfunctorily. The Lithians are highly intelligent, and they already have many of the clues they need. I've given them a hand toward pinning down magnetism, and they absorbed the material like magic and put it to work with enormous ingenuity."

"So did I," Ruiz-Sanchez said. "And I've suggested to them a technique for accumulating iron that should prove to be pretty powerful. I had only to suggest it, and they were already halfway down to the bottom of it and traveling fast. They can make the most of the smallest of clues."

"If I were the UN I'd regard both actions as the plainest kind of treason," Cleaver said harshly. "Since that may be exactly the way Earth will regard them, I think it'd be just as well if you told the folks at home that the Snakes found out both items by themselves."

"I don't plan to do any falsifying of the report," Michelis said, "but thanks anyhow—I appreciate the intent behind what you say, if not the ethics. I'm not through, however. So far as the actual, practical objective that you want to achieve is concerned, Paul, I think it's just as useless as it is impossible. The fact that you have here a planet that's especially rich in lithium doesn't mean that you're sitting on a bonanza, no matter what price per ton the metal is commanding back home. The fact of the matter is that you can't ship lithium home.

"Its density is so low that you couldn't send away more than a ton of it per shipload; by the time you got it to Earth the shipping charges on it would more than outweigh the price you'd get for it on arrival. As you ought to know, there's lots of lithium on Earth's own moon, too, and it isn't economical to fly it back to Earth even over that short distance. No more would it be economical to ship from Earth to Lithia all the heavy equipment that would be needed to make use of lithium here. By the time you got your cyclotron and the rest of your needs to Lithia, you'd have cost the UN so much money that no amount of locally available pegmatite could compensate for it."

"Just extracting the metal would cost a fair sum," Agronski said, frowning slightly. "Lithium would burn like gasoline in this atmosphere."

Michelis looked from Agronski to Cleaver and back again. "Of course it would," he said. "The whole plan's just a chimera. It seems to me, also, that we have a lot to learn from the Lithians, as well as they from us. Their social system works like the most perfect of our physical mechanisms, and it does so without any apparent repression of the individual. It's a thoroughly liberal society, that nevertheless never even begins to tip over toward the other side, toward the kind of Gandhiism that keeps a people tied to the momma-and-poppa-farm and the roving-brigand economy. It's in balance, and not precarious balance, either, but perfect chemical equilibrium.

"The notion of using Lithia as a tritium bomb plant is easily the strangest anachronism I've ever encountered—it's as crude as proposing to equip a spaceship with canvas sails. Right here on Lithia is the real secret, the secret that's going to make bombs of all kinds, and all the rest of the antisocial armamentarium, as useless, unnecessary, obsolete as the Iron Boot!

"And on top of all that—no, please, I'm not quite finished, Paul—on top of all that, the Lithians are centuries ahead of us in some purely technical matters, just as we're ahead of them in others. You should see what they can do with ceramics, with semiconductors, with static electricity, with mixed disciplines like histochemistry, immunochemistry, biophysics, teratology, electrogenetics, limnology and half a hundred more. If you'd been looking, you *would* have seen.

"We have much more to do, it seems to me, than just vote to open the planet. That's a passive move. We have to realize that being able to use Lithia is only the beginning. The fact of the matter is that we actively *need* Lithia. We should say so in our recommendation."

He unfolded himself from the window-sill and stood up, looking down on them all, but most especially at Ruiz-Sanchez. The priest smiled at him, but as much in anguish as in admiration, and then had to look back at his shoes.

"Well, Agronski?" Cleaver said, spitting the words out like bullets on which he had been clenching his teeth during an amputation without anesthetics. "What do you say now? Do you like the pretty picture?"

"Sure, I like it," Agronski said, slowly but forthrightly. It was a virtue in him, as well as it was often a source of exasperation, that he always said exactly what he was thinking, the moment he was asked to do so. "Mike makes sense; I wouldn't expect him not to, if you see what I mean. Also he's got another advantage: he told us what he thought *without* trying first to trick us into his way of thinking."

"Oh, don't be a thumphead!" Cleaver exclaimed. "Are we scientists or Boy Rangers? Any rational man up against a majority of do-gooders would have taken the same precautions that I did."

"Maybe," Agronski said. "I don't know. They still smell to me like a confession of weakness somewhere in the argument. I don't like to be finessed. And I don't much like to be called a thumphead, either. But before you call me any more names, I'm going to say that I think you're more right than Mike is. I don't like your methods, but your aim seems sensible to me. Mike's shot some of your major arguments full of holes, that I'll admit; but as far as I'm concerned, you're still leading—by a nose."

He paused, breathing heavily and glaring at the physicist. Then he said:

"But *don't push,* Paul. I don't like being pushed."

Michelis remained standing for a moment longer. Then he shrugged, walked back to his hassock and sat down, locking his hands between his knees.

"I did my best, Ramon," he said. "But so far it looks like a draw. See what you can do."

Ruiz-Sanchez took a deep breath. What he was about to do would without any doubt hurt him for the rest of his life, regardless of the goodness of his reasons, or the way time had of turning any knife. The decision had already cost him many hours of concentrated, agonized doubt. But he believed that it had to he done.

"I disagree with all of you," he said. "I believe that Lithia should be reported triple-E unfavorable, as Cleaver does. But I think it should also be given a special classification: X-1."

"X-1 —but that's a quarantine label," Michelis said. "As a matter of fact—"

"*Yes,* Mike. I vote to seal Lithia off from *all* contact with the human race. Not only now, or for the next century, but forever."

VIII

The words did not produce the consternation that he had been dreading—or, perhaps, had been hoping for, somewhere in the back of his mind. Evidently they were all too tired for that. They took his announcement with a kind of stunned emptiness, as though it were so far out of the expected order of events as to be quite meaningless. It was hard to say whether Cleaver or Michelis had been hit the harder. All that could be seen for certain was that Agronski recovered first, and was now ostentatiously cleaning his ears, as if he were ready to listen again when Ruiz-Sanchez changed his mind.

"Well," Cleaver began. And then again, shaking his head amazedly, like an old man: "Well . . ."

"Tell us why, Ramon," Michelis said, clenching and unclenching his fists. His voice was quite flat, but Ruiz-Sanchez thought he could feel the pain under it.

"Of course. But I warn you, I'm going to be very roundabout. What I have to say seems to me to be of the utmost importance, and I don't want to see it rejected out of hand as just the product of my peculiar training and prejudices—interesting perhaps as a study in aberration, but not germane to the problem. The evidence for my view of Lithia is overwhelming. It overwhelmed me quite against my natural hopes and inclinations. I want you to hear that evidence."

"He wants us also to understand," Cleaver said, recovering a little of his natural impatience, "that his reasons are religious and won't hold water if he states them right out."

"Hush," Michelis said. "Listen."

"Thank you, Mike. All right, here we go. This planet is what I think is called in English a 'setup.' Let me describe it for you briefly as I see it, or rather as I've come to see it.

"Lithia is a paradise. It resembles most closely the Earth in its pre-Adamic period just before the coming of the great glaciers. The resemblance ends just there, because on Lithia the glaciers never came, and life continued to be spent in the paradise, as it was not allowed to do on Earth. We find a completely mixed forest, with plants which fall from one end of the creative spectrum to the other living side by side in perfect amity. To a great extent that's also true of the animals. The lion doesn't lie down with the lamb here because Lithia has neither animal, but as an analogy the phrase is apt. Parasitism occurs far less often on Lithia than it does on Earth, and there are very few carnivores of any sort. Almost all the surviving land animals eat plants only, and by a neat arrangement which is typically Lithian, the plants are admirably set up to attack animals rather than each other.

"It's an unusual ecology, and one of the strangest things about it is its rationality, its extreme, almost single-minded insistence on one-for-one relationships. In one respect it looks almost as though someone had arranged the whole planet to demonstrate the theory of sets.

"In this paradise we have a dominant creature, the Lithian, the man of Lithia. This creature is rational. It conforms as if naturally and without constraint or guidance to the highest ethical code we have evolved on Earth. It needs no laws to enforce this code; somehow, everyone obeys it as a matter of course, although it has never even been written down. There are no criminals, no deviants, no aberrations of any kind. The people are not standardized—our own very bad and partial answer to the ethical dilemma—but instead are highly individual. Yet somehow no antisocial act of any kind is ever committed.

"Mike, let me stop here and ask: what does this suggest to you?"

"Why, just what I've said before that it suggested," Michelis said. "An enormously superior social science, evidently founded in a precise psychological science."

"Very well, I'll go on. I felt as you did at first. Then I came to ask myself: how does it happen that the Lithians not only have no deviants—think of that, *no* deviants—but it just happens, by the uttermost of all coincidences, that the code by which they live so perfectly is point for point the code we strive to obey. Consider, please, the imponderables involved in such a coincidence. Even on Earth we never have found a society which evolved independently *exactly* the same precepts as the Christian precepts. Oh, there were some duplications, enough to encourage the twentieth century's partiality toward synthetic religions like Theosophism and Hollywood Vedanta, but no ethical system on Earth that grew up independently of Christianity agreed with it point for point.

"And yet here, forty light-years from Earth, what do we find? A Christian people, lacking nothing but the specific proper names and the symbolic appurtenances of Christianity. I don't know how you three react to this, but I found it extraordinary and indeed completely impossible—mathematically impossible—under any assumption but one. I'll get to that assumption in a moment."

"You can't get there too soon for me," Cleaver said morosely.

"How a man can stand forty light-years from home in deep space and talk such parochial nonsense is beyond my comprehension."

"Parochial?" Ruiz-Sanchez said, more angrily than he had intended. "Do you mean that what we think true on Earth is automatically made suspect just by the fact of its removal into deep space? I beg to remind you, Cleaver, that quantum mechanics seems to hold good on Lithia, and that you see nothing parochial about behaving as if it did. If I believe in Peru that God created the universe, I see nothing parochial about believing it on Lithia.

"A while back I thought I had been provided an escape hatch, incidentally. Chtexa told me that the Lithians would like to modify the growth of their population, and he implied that they would welcome some form of birth control. But, as it turned out, birth control in the sense that my Church interdicts it is impossible to Lithia, and what Chtexa had in mind was obviously some form of conception control, a proposition to which my Church has already given its qualified assent. So there I was, even on this small point, forced again to realize that we had found on Lithia the most colossal rebuke to our aspirations that we had ever encountered: a people that seemed to live with ease the kind of life which we associate with saints alone.

"Bear in mind that a Muslim who visited Lithia would find no such thing. Neither would a Taoist. Neither would a Zoroastrian, presuming that there were still such, or a classical Greek. But for the four of us—and I include you, Cleaver, for despite your tricks and your agnosticism you still subscribe to the Christian ethical doctrines enough to be put on the defensive when you flout them—what we have here on Lithia is a coincidence which beggars description. It is more than an astronomical coincidence—that tired old phrase for numbers that do not seem very large any more—it is a transfinite coincidence. It would take Cantor himself to do justice to the odds against it."

"Wait a minute," Agronski said. "Holy smoke. Mike, I don't know any anthropology, I'm lost here. I was with the father up to the part about the mixed forest, but I don't have any standards to judge the rest. Is it so, what he says?"

"Yes, I think it's so," Michelis said slowly. "But there could be differences of opinion as to what it means, if anything. Ramon, go on."

"I've scarcely begun. I'm still describing the planet, and more particularly the Lithians. The Lithians take a lot of explaining; what

I've said about them thus far states only the most obvious fact. I could go on to point out many more equally obvious facts that they have no nations and no national rivalries (and if you'll look at the map of Lithia you'll see every reason why they should have developed such rivalries), that they have emotions and passions but are never moved by them to irrational acts, that they have only one language, that they exist in complete harmony with everything, large and small, that they find in their world. In short, they are a people that couldn't exist, and yet do.

"Mike, I'd go beyond your view to say that the Lithians are the most perfect example of how human beings *ought* to behave than we're ever likely to find, for the very simple reason that they behave now the way human beings once did before a series of things happened of which we have record. I'd go even farther beyond it, far enough to say that as an example the Lithians are useless to us, because until the coming of the Kingdom of God no substantial number of human beings will ever be able to imitate Lithian conduct. Human beings seem to have built-in imperfections that the Lithians lack, so that after thousands of years of trying we are farther away than ever from our original emblems of conduct, while the Lithians have never departed from theirs.

"And don't allow yourselves to forget for an instant that these emblems of conduct are the same on both planets. That couldn't ever have happened, either. But it did.

"I'm now going to describe another interesting fact about Lithian civilization. It is a fact, whatever you may think of its merits as evidence. It is this: that your Lithian is a creature of logic. Unlike Earthmen of all stripes, he has no gods, no myths, no legends. He has no belief in the supernatural, or, as we're calling it in our barbarous jargon these days, the 'paranormal.' He has no traditions. He has no taboos. He has no faiths, blind or otherwise. He is as rational as a machine. Indeed, the only way in which we can distinguish the Lithian from an organic computer is his possession and use of a moral code.

"And that, I beg you to observe, is completely irrational. It is based upon a set of axioms, of propositions which were 'given' from the beginning—though your Lithian will not allow that there was ever any Giver. The Lithian, for instance Chtexa, believes in the sanctity of the individual. Why? Not by reason, surely, for there is no way to reason to that proposition. It is an axiom. Chtexa believes in juridical defense, in the equality of all before the code. Why? It's possible to behave reasonably from the proposition but not to reason one's way to it.

"If you assume that the responsibility to the code varies with age, or with the nature of one's work, or with what family you happen to belong to, logical behavior can follow from one of those assumptions, but there again one can't arrive at the principle by reason alone. One begins with belief: 'I think that all people ought to be equal before the law.' That is a statement of faith. Nothing more. Yet Lithian civilization is so set up as to suggest that one can arrive at such basic axioms of Christianity, and of Western civilization on Earth as a whole, by reason alone, in the plain face of the fact that one cannot."

"Those are axioms," Cleaver growled. "You don't arrive at them by faith, either. You don't arrive at them at all. They're self-evident."

"Like the axiom that only one parallel can be drawn to a given line? Go on, Cleaver, you are a physicist; kick a stone for me and tell me it's self-evident that the thing is solid."

"It's peculiar," Michelis said in a low voice, "that Lithian culture should be so axiom-ridden without the Lithians being aware of it. I hadn't formulated it in quite this way before, Ramon, but I've been disturbed myself at the bottomless assumptions that lie behind Lithian reasoning. Look at what they've done in solid-state physics, for instance. It's a structure of the purest kind of reason, and yet when you get down to its fundamental assumptions you discover the axiom that matter is real. How can they know that? How did logic lead them to it? If I say that the atom is just a hole-inside-a-hole-through-a-hole, where can reason intervene?"

"But it works," Cleaver said.

"So does our solid-state physics—but we work on opposite axioms," Michelis said. "That's not the issue. I don't myself see how this immense structure of reason which the Lithians have evolved can stand for an instant. It does not seem to rest on anything."

"I'm going to tell you," Ruiz-Sanchez said. "You won't believe me, but I'm going to tell you anyhow, because I have to. *It stands because it's being propped up.* That's the simple answer and the whole answer. But first I want to add one more fact about the Lithians.

"They have complete physical recapitulation outside the body."

"What does that mean?" Agronski said.

"Do you know how a human child grows inside its mother's body? It is a one-cell animal to begin with, and then a simple metazoan resembling the freshwater hydra or the simplest jellyfish. Then, very rapidly, it goes through many other animal forms, including the fish, the amphibian, the reptile, the lower mammal, and finally becomes enough like a man to be born. This process biologists call recapitulation.

"They assume that the embryo is passing through the various stages of evolution which brought life from the single-celled organism to man, on a contracted time scale. There is a point, for instance, in the development of the fetus when it has gills. It has a tail almost to the very end of its time in the womb, and sometimes still has it when it is born. Its circulatory system at one point is reptilian, and if it fails to pass successfully through that stage, it is born as a 'blue baby' with patent ductus arteriosus, the tetralogy of Fallot or a similar heart defect. And so on."

"I see," Agronski said. "I've encountered the idea before, of course, but I didn't recognize the term."

"Well, the Lithians, too, go through this series of metamorphoses as they grow up, but they go through it *outside* the bodies of their mothers. This whole planet is one huge womb. The Lithian female lays her eggs in her abdominal pouch, and then goes to the sea to give birth to her children. What she bears is not a reptile, but a fish. The fish lives in the sea a while, and then develops rudimentary lungs and comes ashore. Stranded by the tides on the flats, the lungfish develops rudimentary legs and squirms in the mud, becoming an amphibian and learning to endure the rigors of living away from the sea. Gradually their limbs become stronger, and better set on their bodies, and they become the big froglike things we sometimes see leaping in the moonlight, trying to get away from the crocodiles.

"Many of them do get away. They carry their habit of leaping with them into the jungle, and there they change once again to become the small, kangaroolike reptiles we've all seen, at one time or another, fleeing from us among the trees. Eventually, they emerge, fully grown, from the jungles and take their places among the folk of the cities as young Lithians, ready for education. But they have already learned every trick of every environment that their world has to offer except those of their own civilization."

Michelis locked his hands together again and looked up at Ruiz-Sanchez. "But that's a discovery beyond price!" he said with quiet excitement. "Ramon, that alone is worth our trip to Lithia. I can't imagine why it would lead you to ask that the planet be closed! Surely your Church can't object to it in any way—after all, your theorists did accept recapitulation in the human embryo, and also the geological record that showed the same process in action over longer spans of time."

"Not," Ruiz-Sanchez said, "in the way that you think we did. The Church accepted the facts, as it always accepts facts. But—as you yourself suggested not ten minutes ago—facts have a way of pointing in several different directions at once. The Church is as hostile to the doctrine of evolution—particularly in respect to man—as it ever was, and with good reason."

"Or with obdurate stupidity," Cleaver said.

"All right, Paul, look at it very simply with the original premises of the Bible in mind. If we assume just for the sake of argument that God created man, did he create him perfect? I should suppose that he did. Is a man perfect without a navel? I don't know, but I'd be inclined to say that he isn't. Yet the first man—Adam, again for the sake of argument—wasn't born of woman, and so didn't really *need* to have a navel. Nevertheless he would have been imperfect without it, and I'll bet that he had one."

"What does that prove?"

"That the geological record, and recapitulation too, do not prove the doctrine of evolution. Given *my* initial axiom, which is that God created everything from scratch, it's perfectly logical that he should have given Adam a navel, Earth a geological record and the embryo the process of recapitulation. None of these indicate a real past; all are there because the creations involved would have been imperfect otherwise."

"Wow," Cleaver said. "And I used to think that Milne relativity was abstruse."

"Oh, any coherent system of thought becomes abstruse if it's examined long enough. I don't see why my belief in a God you can't accept is any more rarefied than Mike's vision of the atom as a hole-inside-a-hole-through-a-hole. I expect that in the long run, when we get right down to the fundamental particles of the universe, we'll find that there's nothing there at all—just nothings moving no-place through no-time. On the day that that happens, I'll have God and you will not—otherwise there'll be no difference between us.

"But in the meantime, what we have here on Lithia is very clear indeed. We have—and now I'm prepared to be blunt—a planet and a people propped up by the Ultimate Enemy. It is a gigantic trap prepared for all of us. We can do nothing with it but reject it, nothing but say to it, *Retro me, Sathanas.* If we compromise with it in any way, we are damned."

"Why, father?" Michelis said quietly.

"Look at the premises, Mike. One: reason is always a sufficient guide. Two: the self-evident is always the real. Three: good works are an end in themselves. Four: faith is irrelevant to right action. Five: right action can exist without love. Six: peace need not pass understanding. Seven: ethics can exist without evil alternatives. Eight: morals can exist without conscience. Nine—but do I really need to go on? We have heard all these propositions before, and we know who proposes them.

"And we have seen these demonstrations before—the demonstration, for instance, in the rocks which was supposed to show how the horse evolved from Eohippus, but which somehow never managed to convince the whole of mankind. Then the discovery of intra-uterine recapitulation, which was to have clinched the case for the so-called descent of man—and yet, somehow, failed again to produce general agreement. These were both very subtle arguments, but the Church is not easily swayed; it is founded on a rock.

"Now we have, on Lithia, a new demonstration, both the subtlest and at the same time the crudest of all. It will sway many people who could have been swayed in no other way, and who lack the intelligence or the background to understand that it is a rigged demonstration. It seems to show us evolution in action on an inarguable scale. It is supposed to settle the question once and for all, to rule God out of the picture, to snap the chains that have held Peter's rock together all these many centuries. Henceforth there is to be no more question; there is to he no more God, but only phenomenology—and, of course, behind the scenes, within the hole that's inside the hole that's through a hole, the Great Nothing itself, the thing that has never learned any word but *no:* it has many other names, but we know the name that counts. That's left us.

"Paul, Mike, Agronski, I have nothing more to say than this: we are all of us standing on the brink of hell. By the grace of God, we may still turn back. We must turn back—for I at least think that this is our last chance."

IX

The vote was cast, and that was that. The commission was tied, and the question would be thrown open again in higher echelons on Earth which would mean tying Lithia up for years to come. The planet was now, in effect, on the Index.

The ship arrived the next day. The crew was not much surprised to find that the two opposing factions of the commission were hardly speaking to each other. It often happened that way.

The four commission members cleaned up the house the Lithians had given them in almost complete silence. Ruiz-Sanchez packed the blue book with the gold stamping without being able to look at it except out of the corner of his eye, but even obliquely he could not help seeing its title:

FINNEGANS WAKE
James Joyce

He felt as though he himself had been collated, bound and stamped, a tortured human text for future generations of Jesuits to explicate and argue.

He had rendered the verdict he had found it necessary for him to render. But he knew that it was not a final verdict, even for himself, and certainly not for the UN, let alone the Church. Instead, the verdict itself would be the knotty question for members of his Order yet unborn:

Did Father Ruiz-Sanchez correctly interpret the divine case, and did his ruling, if so, follow from it?

"Let's go, father. It'll be take-off time in a few minutes."

"All ready, Mike."

It was only a short journey to the clearing, where the mighty spindle of the ship stood ready to weave its way back through the geodesics of deep space to the sun that shone on Peru. The baggage went on board smoothly and without fuss. So did the specimens, the films, the special reports, the recordings, the sample cases, the vivariums, the aquariums, the type-cultures, the pressed plants, the tubes of soil, the chunks of ore, the Lithian manuscripts in their atmosphere of neon; everything was lifted decorously by the cranes and swung inside.

Agronski went up the cleats to the airlock first, with Michelis following him. Cleaver was stowing some last-minute bit of gear, something that seemed to require delicate, almost reverent care before the cranes could be allowed to take it in their indifferent grip. Ruiz-Sanchez took advantage of the slight delay to look around once more at the near margins of the forest.

At once, he saw Chtexa. The Lithian was standing at the entrance to the path the Earthmen themselves had taken away from the city to reach the ship. He was carrying something.

Cleaver swore under his breath and undid something he had just done to do it in another way. Ruiz-Sanchez raised his hand. Immediately Chtexa walked toward the ship.

"I wish you a good journey," the Lithian said, "wherever you may go. I wish also that your road may lead back to this world at some future time. I have brought you the gift that I sought before to give you, if the moment is appropriate."

Cleaver had straightened up and was now glaring suspiciously at the Lithian. Since he did not understand the language, he was unable to find anything to which he could object; he simply stood and radiated unwelcomeness.

"Thank you," Ruiz-Sanchez said. This creature of Satan made him miserable, made him feel intolerably in the wrong. How could Chtexa know—?

The Lithian was holding out to him a small vase, sealed at the top and provided with two gently looping handles. The gleaming porcelain of which it had been made still carried inside it, under the glaze, the fire which had formed it; it was iridescent, alive with long quivering festoons and plumes of rainbows, and the form as a whole would have made any potter of Greece abandon his trade in shame. It was so beautiful that one could imagine no use for it at all. Certainly one could not fill it with left-over beets and put it in the refrigerator. Besides, it would take up too much space.

"This is my gift," Chtexa said. "It is the finest container yet to come from Xoredeshch Gton; the material of which it is made contains traces of every element to be found on Lithia, even including iron, and thus, as you see, it shows the colors of every shade of emotion and of thought. On Earth, it will tell Earthmen much of Lithia."

"We will be unable to analyze it," Ruiz-Sanchez said. "It is too perfect to destroy, too perfect even to open."

"Ah, but we wish you to open it," Chtexa said. "For it contains our other gift."

"Another gift?"

"Yes, a more important one. A fertilized, living egg of our species. Take it with you. By the time you reach Earth, it will be ready to hatch, and to grow up with you in your strange and marvelous world. The container is the gift of all of us; but the child inside is my gift, for it is my child."

Ruiz-Sanchez took the vase in trembling hands, as though he expected it to explode. It shook with subdued flame in his grip.

"Goodbye," Chtexa said. He turned and walked away, back toward the entrance to the path. Cleaver watched him go, shading his eyes.

"Now what was that all about?" the physicist said. "The Snake couldn't have made a bigger thing of it if he'd been handing you his own head on a platter. And all the time it was only a pot!"

Ruiz-Sanchez did not answer. He could not have spoken even to himself. He turned away and began to ascend the cleats, cradling the vase carefully under one elbow. While he was still climbing, a shadow passed rapidly over the hull—Cleaver's last crate, being borne aloft into the hold by a crane.

Then he was in the airlock, with the rising whine of the ship's generators around him. A long shaft of light outside was cast ahead of him, picking out his shadow on the deck. After a moment, a second shadow overlaid his own: Cleaver's. Then the light dimmed and went out.

The airlock door slammed.

Making Waves: The Good, the Bad, the Indifferent

From a talk presented at a conference in Birmingham, UK in 1970.

The use of the word "speculative" to denote science fiction and the fringe areas around it seems to have been begun by Robert A. Heinlein back in 1947; but it has only recently caught on. There seem to be two reasons for this: first, some people are now embarrassed by what they think to be the pulp connotations of "science fiction," and want a name that sounds more respectable, and perhaps more acceptable to the academic community; and second, there is a small but highly vocal group of editors and writers in the field who are innocent of any knowledge of science, and want a label that will cover what they do.

It seems to me that the new term is not much of an improvement. Those who promulgate it seem not to have noticed that all fiction is speculative, and that science fiction differs from other types of fiction only in its subject-matter. Surely a good label ought to tell us what that subject-matter is, as do the terms "historical novel" or "Western story." Nor can we call it "future fiction," since that leaves out a lot of the territory for example, the parallel-worlds story, or time travel into the past. No, I am afraid that if there is any single subject which dominates this genre, it is science and technology, and that Mr. Gernsback's term is therefore still the best we have. It has a virtue, also, which has gone relatively unnoticed: Its grammatical form, cognate with terms like "detective story," also distinguishes it from a recognizably different class of work, of which *Arrowsmith* and the novels of C. P. Snow are examples. These are not science-fiction novels, but novels of science.

I end, as I started, with this question of terminology because before we undertake to shoot down bad science fiction, we ought to know what kind of animal we are gunning for. I therefore propose to rule out of my consideration any story which does not contain any trace of any science, on the grounds that on the contrary, good science fiction must not only contain some science but depend upon it; as Theodore Sturgeon points out, the story ought to be impossible without it.

A further qualification is also important. It is a matter of fact that science fiction today is one form of commercialized category fiction. Once one examines the implications of this statement, much that is wrong about modern science fiction is instantly explicable, though perhaps no less regrettable. For this fact we owe that same Mr. Gernsback a blow to the chops. Prior to 1926, science fiction could be published anywhere, and was; and it was judged by the same standards as other fiction. Some of the pre-1926 work looks naïve to us now, but unredeemably dreadful work almost never got past the editors' desks. Today it does so regularly, because there are magazines with deadlines which cannot appear with blank pages, and there is also a firm and ever-widening audience which will devour any kind of science fiction and rarely reads anything else. This is a situation already quite familiar to us in the field of the detective story. Once Gernsback created a periodical ghetto for science fiction, the gate was opened to the regular publication of bad work; in fact, this became inevitable.

I can easily use myself as a horrible example. Of the first thirteen stories that I sold, all in the very early 1940's, only two had any recognizable shred of merit. The other eleven nevertheless saw print, because there were many magazines then and I came cheap. The fact that I knew absolutely nothing about the craft of fiction, and indeed I didn't even begin to learn until after the war, had no bearing on the situation, which was governed solely by deadlines, money and a whole lot of white space.

Editorial standards rose sharply in that decade, but this did not, of course, abolish the production of execrable work as anyone can testify who has the misfortune to remember the collaborations of Randall Garrett with Lou Tabakow, Robert Silverberg and Larry Janifer. Under present conditions, such trash is the inevitable and perhaps necessary ooze in which the gems will continue to be embedded.

We must not allow this to put us off, or allow the outsider to use it to put us down. Perhaps some of you saw the item in *The Sunday Times* [London] last January in which a British scientist who apparently had something to do with the *Doctor Who* show was quoted as having decided to go in for science fiction on a bigger scale. He added in the next breath, "Of course most science fiction is utter rot," thus establishing his purity and, I suppose, indirectly proclaiming his intentions to improve us. (Judging by *Doctor Who*, he is not leading from strength.) This is a very familiar attitude; again to quote Ted Sturgeon, "Never before in the history of literature has a field been judged so exclusively by its bad examples."*

I have a counter-ploy which I use on such people which is sometimes effective: I ask them, "How many good novels of any kind have you read lately?" Occasionally, you can trap your opponent into admitting that he hasn't in fact read anything in the past twelve months but *Valley of the Dolls,* or that the only modern science fiction he has ever opened was *The Andromeda Strain,* and then you've got him by the scruff; but you have to know your man fairly well to bring this one off.

In criticism, as in teaching, there is no substitute for knowing the subject-matter thoroughly and also, knowing as much of the surrounding, larger ground as you can possibly cover. People who read nothing but science fiction and fantasy—the Moskowitz syndrome—are fundamentally non-readers, just as people who read nothing but detective stories are non-readers; their gaping jaws signal not wonder, but the utter absence of any thought or sensation at all. They are easy to spot by their reactions when a fifty-year-old storytelling innovation finally reaches science fiction: They are either utterly bowled over by it and proclaim it the wave of the future, or they find it incomprehensible and demand the return of E. E. Smith, who, unfortunately, is dead.

In other words, the subject-matter of science-fiction *criticism* is not science fiction, but literature as a whole, with particular emphasis upon philosophy and craftsmanship. I stress philosophy not only because science is a branch of it, but because all fiction is influenced by the main currents of thought of its time, and to be unaware of these is like having no windows on the east side of the house; you don't get to see the sun until the day is half over. Craftsmanship should be an obvious item, but I am perpetually startled by how many science-fiction readers, editors and writers try to get by on intuition instead; as for the critics in science fiction, the only ones whose published work shows any awareness of writing as a craft are Damon Knight and Sour Bill Atheling—and before you conclude

---

*From that same seminal speech cast before the Little Monsters.

that I am blowing my own horn, let me add that it is profoundly dissatisfying for a creative writer to find that half the informed technical criticism he can find in his chosen field has been written by himself under a pen name.

This point emphasizes, also, that criticism, like creative writing, is essentially a lonely art quite unrelated to sales figures or annual popularity contests. Cohn Wilson, in his first and best book *[The Outsider]*, remarked that the plots of Dostoevsky novels resemble sofa pillows stuffed with lumps of concrete. God knows what he would have said of the plot, if that's the word I'm groping for, of the typical A. Merritt novel, but it is a lovely image and quite just, no matter what one thinks of Dostoevsky's strengths in most other departments; bad construction is bad construction, and the fact that millions of readers have failed to detect it means nothing more than does the fact that millions of people have bought defective automobiles, or believed every word that came out of the mouth of Senator Joe McCarthy.

The awards are equally unreliable guides, and for the same reason. The list of the Hugo winners in the science fiction novel is not quite as depressing as a summary of Pulitzer prizes, but give us an equivalent amount of time and we may well beat the Pulitzer jury by miles. Is there a soul who is now alive who remembers *They'd Rather Be Right*, by Mark Clifton and Frank Riley, which in 1955 drew the second Hugo ever awarded a piece of fiction? Unfortunately, I do, and I wish I didn't. And lest you accuse me of shooting sitting ducks, let me add that of the four Heinlein novels which won Hugos, only one is a work of genuine merit, and one is a borderline case; while one took the award away from Kurt Vonnegut's *The Sirens of Titan,* which was not only the best science-fiction novel of its year, but one of the best ever written. The split 1968 novella award to Philip José Farmer is a plain case of the bowling-over of non-readers by daring innovations taken lock, stock and barrel out of the "Cave of the Winds" chapter of Joyce's *Ulysses,* which first saw print in *The Little Review* in 1919. As for the Nebula awards, some of these can be explained only as the product (in the arithmetical sense) of indefatigable log-rolling and pathological faddism. No matter how fair the balloting, small groups are inherently vulnerable to such pressures, since the winning margin can be tiny. (My 1959 Hugo, I was told, was swung only by a last-minute influx of British votes.)

Why should we expect otherwise? Literature, as Richard Rovere has remarked, is not a horse-race; there are no winners and not even any final posts to pass. I am even prepared to entertain the notion that my own Hugo was undeserved, though if I do not hear cries of "No, no," I shall stomp off the platform in a huff. [Solitary cry of "No, no."] Well, it's a good thing I brought my wife. Literary merit is built into the work regardless of who sees it, or how soon he sees it; there is no absolutely reliable guide but the judgment of time, as Matthew Arnold said. No individual critic has the lifespan to wait time out—observe, for instance, the fluctuating reputations of Chaucer, Shakespeare, Johann Sebastian Bach—and his only recourse is to make himself the master of his subject as best he can, and defend his perceptions of the good, the bad and the indifferent against juries, shifts in taste, ignorance, popularity contests and all other forms of mob action, including other critics who are trying to create or mount bandwagons.

And there is one other defense the critic has, if he has the heart for it. If he does, it will save him a lot of acrimony, and vastly enlarge his own appreciation of the work he is criticizing. Unhappily, it is the rarest of all critical attributes, as well as the most admirable:

He should not be afraid to change his mind.

Entertaining a change of mind appears to be extraordinarily difficult for a segment of s-f fandom, for all the fans' claims to wider mental horizons than the mainstream reader. As I have noted above, and had earlier at the Pittcon *(The Issue at Hand,* p. 128), science fiction is now old enough so that there are now some readers who have been reading it since childhood and regard it as comfortable and safe—and do not want it to change. It is for them a sort of pastoral, in which spacemen take the place of shepherds (apparently they are opposed to shepherdesses) and space becomes the meadow of refuge from the more complex affairs of the world around them.

But of course it *will* change all the same, and in recent years the change has come to be called the New Wave. This is now old enough so that it is possible to attempt a characterization of it. It has consisted mainly of the following elements: (1) Heavy emphasis upon the problems of the present, such as overpopulation, racism, pollution and the Vietnam war, sometimes only slightly disguised by s-f trappings; (2) Heavy emphasis upon the manner in which a story is told, sometimes almost to the exclusion of its matter, and with an accompanying borrowing of devices old in the mainstream but new to science fiction, such as stream of consciousness, dadaism, typographical tricks, on-stage sex, Yellow Book horror and naughty words; (3) Loud claims that this is the direction in which science fiction must go, and all other forms of practice in the field are fossilized; (4) Some genuinely new and worthy experiments embedded in the mud.

Let's look closer—and try to keep our heads.

Like most movements in the arts (in music there are the examples of the French Six and the Russian Five). the New Wave in science fiction includes a number of people whose aims and approaches are quite different. Hence at the outset the critic who wants to discuss it is confronted with the problem of just what it is lie is talking about; furthermore, each critic may have a separate cast of characters, so I had best start by identifying my own.

The chiefest advocate of the New Wave or the most vocal, at least up to 1967, when a contender surfaced was Judith Merril. Though she is the author of a small number of short stories, including one good one and one very well known one (not identical), and two sentimental novels, Miss Merril is mainly an editor and book reviewer whose reputation rests upon a series of annual anthologies of "Best S-F" stories.

These anthologies had an enormous influence on the New Wave, quite apart from Miss Merril's subsequent championing of it. They were originally fairly conventional productions, quite well edited but otherwise distinguished only by the impressiveness of their publisher, Simon and Schuster. The conventionality was in part a by-product of the publisher, in fact. In the early years of the project, Miss Merril was required to submit for each volume many more stories than could actually be used, and the final selection was made in the publisher's office; the rejects ended up as "honorable mentions." To the best of my knowledge, no public acknowledgement of this procedure was ever made; but as Miss Merril's reputation grew and her choices became more idiosyncratic, it led to a break and a search for another publisher which wound up at Delacorte.

The change in emphasis which led to the break may most succinctly be described as an outcome of education. As can be seen in her early fan magazine writings, particularly for the Vanguard Amateur Press Association, Miss Merril at the beginning of her career resembled most other young fans of the day in having read almost nothing but science fiction and fantasy; her knowledge of literature at large was bounded on one side by Walt Whitman and on the other by Thomas Wolfe. Unlike the standard model of such fans, however, her reading widened, at first apparently out of a desire (perhaps the publisher's, rather than her own) to make science fiction look respectable by cramming into the anthologies as many famous names as possible. Whatever the motive, the actual process inevitably involved a whole series of belated literary discoveries in Miss Merril's middle years, and these in turn were reflected in the anthologies; the most recent books in the series have in fact been described as fundamentally autobiographical by several critics (particularly, Algis Budrys and Brian W. Aldiss).

There is, however, another contributing factor, upon which only Budrys has previously commented and that only glancingly: In the beginning, Miss Merril knew as little about the sciences as she did about the arts, and indeed never has felt comfortable with them. These two traits belated discovery of mainstream literature, and continuing non-comprehension of the scientific enterprise and spirit— seem to have been catalyzed by a proposal Damon Knight took from Heinlein that science is not absolutely essential to science fiction, and that the genre might equally well be called "speculative" fiction.*

Miss Merril seized this proposal as avidly as though it were a life preserver, and promptly announced (in the 11th anthology, 1966) that henceforth the "S" in the "S-F" of her anthology title meant "speculative." This rubric has since been used to justify the inclusion in the annuals of fantasies, surrealist pastiches, bad verse, comic strips, political satire, pseudo-scientific articles, old jokes, macabre cartoons, how-to-write-it pieces, ancient reprints, perfectly ordinary mainstream stories, and in fact anything at all that Miss Merril discovered that she liked.

Except for the implicit deception involved, such catholicity is very far from being a bad thing. It is certainly more broadening for all concerned than trying to become the Greatest Living Authority on science fiction alone, which is about as rewarding as being the Greatest Living Authority upon the fishes of Penobscot Bay. Miss Merril was tempted, as her 1962 dog-in-the-manger attack upon Kingsley Amis painfully revealed; but it is entirely to her credit that she did not fall.

The choice, furthermore, paid off. There turned out to be a large number of writers and fans waiting in the wings who were as uncom-

*In Search of Wonder, revised edition, pp.1, 5; The Issue at Hand, p. 33.

fortable with, or actively distrustful of, the sciences as Miss Merril, and for whom the "speculative" formulation was equally liberating and self-justifying. They had always been there (*e.g.*, Bradbury) but they had never before had a critical banner. Perhaps the Heinlein-Knight pioneer proposal had been too tentative for them; Miss Merril's had the all-out fervor of a mystical experience.

The proclamation also was issued at a peculiarly favorable time. Though modern science fiction had earlier spawned some highly literate and/or self-consciously experimental writers like Theodore Sturgeon and Philip José Farmer, it happened that there was a high concentration of them in the field in this particular period. Accidentally, most of them were English, but even that accident proved timely and fruitful.

At the head of this group must stand J. G. Ballard; though he is a totally solitary man impossible to imagine in a group, impossible to imitate, and not the best writer of the New Wave, he was already well known to the science fiction audience as an explosively original writer, and even today most arguments about the meaning and value of the movement whirl around his head, a situation exacerbated by the fact that, as a reviewer for a newspaper, he has taken the position that he has made all of his predecessors and most of his contemporaries old hat.

Ballard is the author of four book-length novels to date, all of which belong to that peculiar British type which might be dubbed the one-lung catastrophe, pioneered by, of all people, Conan Doyle. In stories of this type, the world is drowned, parched, hit by a comet, smothered by volcanic gas, sterilized by the Van Allen belts, or otherwise revisited by some version of Noah's Fludde; and the rest of the story deals either with the Ark or with Adam and Eve. (In Ballard's versions, everybody gives up and nobody survives.) Ballard is not especially good at this kind of thing, partly because of the almost pathological helplessness of his characters, and partly because his rationales either make little sense or are not revealed at all (though it must be admitted that *The Crystal World* is lovely nevertheless). His real radicalism shows in his short stories.

For about ten years, Ballard has been engaged in putting together a myth. Those short stories which do not belong to an identifiable, conventional series such as the Vermilion Sands stories are pieces of a mosaic, the central subject of which is not yet visible, rather as though a painter were to go about making a portrait by filling in the background in minute detail and leaving a silhouetted hole where the sitter should be. The nature of this attempt has been somewhat masked by the fact that the minor characters—of which there are not very many—sometimes appear in the stories under different names; but there can be little doubt that these fragments (which are the Ballard works which most exacerbate his detractors) are going somewhere, by the most unusual method of trying to surround it, or work into it from the edges of the frame. The difficulty of seeing it whole is further compounded by the equally odd choices Ballard makes of narrative method for example, presenting one fragment in the form of the notes of a psychotic, another as articles excerpted from some mad encyclopedia. He calls these pieces "condensed novels," and has published them as a collection, but clearly the enterprise is far from being finished.

The outcome may be a failure, or it may be a seminal masterpiece. Nobody at this point in the attempt's history could possibly predict which; the plain, blunt fact is that we do not yet know what it is Ballard is talking about (and, of course, there is always the possibility that he doesn't either; we shall just have to wait and see). That Ballard is not very good as a conventional science-fiction novelist is quite beside the point, since Ballard's mosaic myth is not a convention novel and has no antecedents. (Confronted by anything out of the ordinary in science fiction, even friendly critics like Miss Merril are all too ready to compare it to something they call Finnegan's Wake; but in Ballard's case, as in all the others but one, there turns out to be no such relationship. Michael Moorcock has said that Ballard is the originator of his form; I think this is true.) Ballard has a most imperfect grasp of the sciences—he uses "quasars" like authors of the 1920's used "radium," as a magic word—and his discipline is dubious, but he also has a great deal of raw creativity and is a poet; and these, I take it, are the four qualities which characterize almost all the New Wave writers.

Almost; but I will immediately have to except Brian W. Aldiss, who is not ignorant of the sciences (though he sometimes scamps them) and is perhaps the most thorough, disciplined professional ever to concentrate his gifts upon science fiction. As a man who loves the English language with profound and contagious passion, and knows it far too well to be showy about it, Aldiss was from the beginning almost in himself a New Wave in science fiction, and almost for that reason alone got lumped in with the group (and seems to be much in sympathy with it); but he differs from almost everybody else in it not only by being almost always in control of what he writes, but by being convinced of the desirability of being in control. In consequence, he is virtually the only New Wave writer who never offers aborted experiments in disguise of finished work. It sometimes seems, indeed, that only Aldiss' receptivity, and his willingness to try any drink once, tie him to the New Wave at all; but as a poet and an experimentalist he belongs with them, however more easy to take his professionalism makes his work for the ordinary reader. For example, his *Report on Probability A*, though it is the first attempt to adapt the French anti-novel to a science-fictional end, and does not succeed at it, is so cunningly carpentered that even its failure is definitive; while *Barefoot in the Head*, which actually does derive heavily and directly from late Joyce, brings JJ's "Eurish" as close to accessibility by the ordinary reader as it is ever likely to come. (More about *Barefoot* later.)

John Brunner is also a poet and an experimentalist with a thoroughly professional approach, and has appeared in *New Worlds;* two of his books, including the dinosaurian, Hugo-winning *Stand on Zanzibar,* confessedly borrow techniques wholesale from Dos Passos, for example. Yet I find myself hesitating to think of him as a New Wave writer, for reasons so unclear to me that they are probably invalid. Always staggeringly prolific, Brunner has in his past a good many completely conventional s-f books (as has Aldiss, although on a considerably smaller scale) and even his experimental work shows many of the conventional stigmata, such as a predominance of wheeler-dealer characters and the imposition of mechanically pat endings. He is, however, clearly a perfectionist by nature and one may confidently expect these blemishes to disappear sooner or later; in the meantime, so much that was conventional has already been eliminated from his work that to rule him out of the New Wave would in logic force one to conclude that there was no such thing as a New Wave at all.

Another important figure is Michael Moorcock, for whose reconstructed magazine *New Worlds* Aldiss finagled an Arts grant of £1,800 ($4,320), and whom Aldiss has called an editorial genius. This judgment is perhaps a little excessive. Rather like Miss Merril, Moorcock was a fan who until assuming this editorship had exhibited no signs of talent for writing (his major productions were the worst kind of sword-and-sorcery hackwork, carefully hidden under a pen name until it was revealed by one of *his* editors, Ted White). When he was put in charge of *New Worlds,* he turned it physically into a semi-slick, thin magazine resembling the *New Scientist* (a British version of *Scientific American,* but much less expensively produced), and engaged for it the worst distributor in England (in three weeks of looking for the current issue all over London in 1967, I found only one copy, in Paddington Station, and Britain's two major newsstand chains, Smith and Menzies, stock and display the magazine even today both seldom and erratically). He filled a large part of his limited space with non-illustrative artwork, mostly surrealism and collages, plus art-nouveau and psychedelic designs, together with articles about these pictures written in a pastiche of the mindless jargon of the American *Art News.*

The purpose of this format, as was (perhaps apocryphally) explained in 1969 by an interim editor, James Sallis, was to provide a home for a wide range of manifestations of the modern age, including but not confined to science fiction. Nevertheless, quite a lot of science fiction did appear there, including *Report on Probability A,* much of *Barefoot in the Head* and all of Disch's *Camp Concentration,* and in making up a first selection of such pieces for a book, Moorcock led from strength and chose well. The non-science fiction in the magazine has been predictably obsessed with drugs and the Vietnam war, and Moorcock's own chief fictional contribution has been an interminable series about an imitation James Bond named Jerry Cornelius. A Moorcock story in *New Worlds,* called "Behold the Man," later became a novel which won a Nebula in 1968.

Harlan Ellison is not only the most audible but possibly the most gifted of the American members of the New Wave. When he first hove into sight in 1956, spinning around lampposts and bragging of imaginary adventures and achievements, I thought him all noise and no talent, and told him so. In the succeeding decade he proved me dead wrong about this, and very few acts as a writer have given me so much pleasure as acknowledging this (in a 1967 book dedication). Personally, Harlan can be very engaging, but he can also be the most annoying man in the world; this blinded me. He is in fact a born writer, almost entirely without taste or control but with so much fire, originality and drive, as well as compassion, that he makes the conventional virtues of the artist seem almost irrelevant; his work strongly resembles that of Louis-Ferdinand Céline (of whom he has probably never heard[*]), even to its black, wild humor. (He can also be a superb technician if somebody else is in a position to force him to be, as a television script of his I have seen attests; but he is almost the embodiment of the old saying that it takes two men to make a masterpiece one man to hold the brush, and one man standing behind the first with a hammer to hit him on the head with when it's finished.) He is as ignorant of the sciences as a polliwog, and just as happy in that state; what he writes are fantasies of violence and love, every one an experiment and seldom the same experiment twice. Of course these do not always work, but when they do the results are explosive. (He is both a Hugo and a Nebula winner.)

His grandest experiment to date is *Dangerous Visions* and its successor. Without throwing around terms like "editorial genius," it might be noted that selling, organizing, collecting and promoting this collection of 33 original stories (xxix + 520 pp.), much of the advance money for which came out of Ellison's own pocket, required editorial control and persistence of no mean order; and as for editorial acumen, the prizes collected by the stories included, and the sales record of the collection, do not suggest that Ellison did not know what he was doing. The sequel, *Again, Dangerous Visions,* hasn't appeared at this writing, but as of January 1970 the fiction content alone (as will be noted below. the editorial gristle in an Ellison anthology tends to be extensive) had reached 436,000 words, or seven times the length of the average novel.

In one of the introductions to the parent volume, Ellison says: "By the very nature of what they write, many authors were excluded because they had said what they had to say years ago. Others found that they had nothing controversial or daring to contribute. Some expressed lack of interest in the project." Still another reason for non-inclusion is suggested by Poul Anderson, who *is* represented but who "insists [his story] is not 'dangerous' and could have sold to any magazine." Ellison ducks this point by invoking now impossible outlets for it *(McCall's* and *Boys' Life),* but the fact remains that Anderson is right—and furthermore, there is *no* story in this collection that would have been rejected *for thematic reasons* by any of the current science-fiction magazines. At least some unrepresented writers probably doubted, with reason, that anything is inherently unpublishable in these Grove Press days simply because of its subject-matter.

But it should be noted that there is a substantial hole in this argument, and the truly revolutionary nature of *Dangerous Visions*

---

*I was wrong about this, too.

is concealed in it. While almost any one of these stories *could* have appeared in, say, *If* or *Analog,* it would have been surrounded there by more conventional pieces. This book consists of *nothing but* experiments. As such, it is indeed a monument, and will be a gold mine of new techniques and influences for writers for many years to come. It may also, eventually, drastically change readers' tastes, and perhaps even the whole direction of the field.

It is hard reading on several different counts. One of its problems, which could have been avoided, is that it is overloaded with apparatus: there are three prefaces, and each story is both preceded by an introduction in which the editor explains the author, and followed by an afterword in which the author explains himself. This is too much, and tends to suggest an air of distrust in the whole project which is heightened by the shrilly aggressive tone of much of the editor's copy. Good wine needs no bush.

Another minor drawback, quite unavoidable, is that in a collection in which all the stories are determinedly peculiar, none of them shines as brightly as it might have, had it been embedded in more conventional work. They tend to pull each other's teeth. However, the reader can remedy this for himself, simply by sampling, and giving each individual story ample time to sink in.

Finally—and again, unavoidably—well more than half of these experimental stories are failures, as any reasonable man would expect of any body of experiments. Some are simply assemblages of typographical tricks; some are wearisomely portentous; some are one-punchers which are not as shocking as they were intended to be, or are even quite predictable; some are incoherent, and a few exhibit a distressingly small acquaintance with the English language, or even a positive distaste for it. The Farmer story, the longest in the book, shows almost all of these faults at once (and, it is the story mentioned in the opening of this chapter which split the Hugo Award for the novella for 1968).

Except for the excessive editorial matter (some of which, to he sure, is delightfully witty), these drawbacks are intrinsic to the nature of the project, and nobody should allow himself to be put off by them. There has never been a collection like this before, and both Ellison and Doubleday deserve well or us for it.

Two American members of the group whom Ellison has published, and both of whom are both Nebula and Hugo winners, are Roger Zelazny and Samuel R. Delany, whose work resembles Ellison's in many respects particularly in exuberance, efflorescent vocabulary, and very little control over either internal detail or major form; however, they resemble each other more than they do anyone else, as both seem well aware.* Though Zelazny made his first mark as a short-story writer and Delany his as a novelist, both are primarily retellers of myths in science-fictional terms, with complex cross-references to literary systems derived from myth which show a scholar's bent for which Ellison lacks patience, and probably inclination too. Of the two, I find Delany harder to read, because his imagery is so constantly to the fore, and so consistently foggy, that I often suspect that he himself does not know what he means by it—and his explanations (in the fan press and on the academic lecture platform) seem to fog the matter still further. Here I am very much out of step. His novel *Babel 17* won a Nebula as the best of 1966, but I thought it pretty close to being the worst, and when his *The Einstein Intersection* won the same award in 1968, I stepped quietly out into the kitchen and bit my cat. That Delany has drive, insight, and a certain music I cannot doubt, but neither his clotted style nor his zigzag way of organizing a story strike me as being much better than self-indulgent and misdirected. If I am right about this—and my experience with Ellison suggests that I am more than likely to be wrong about it—Delany's early popularity, laid on well before he was either in control or was convinced of the necessity of being in control of his manner or his matter, may well turn out to be destructive. He would not be the first writer whom immoderate early praise (though every writer longs for it) put out of business, at least for a damagingly long period; see my remarks on Sturgeon.

But there is hope for the Nebula voters yet. In 1969 they gave a Nebula to Richard Wilson, whose high, clean, and heart-breakingly precise narrative prose I recommended as a corrective to Chip

---

*There can be few science-fiction fans who have not met both men, but for those who have not, the assonance of their names is a complete accident and neither is a pen name for the other. Delany is a merry and handsome young Negro who travels in hippie dress and has educated himself as a composer as well as a writer; Zelazny is a courtly young white of Polish ancestry who looks like the business end of a hatchet and works for the Social Security Administration in Baltimore (as of 1969). The similarities in their approaches to science fiction would pose a major puzzle to any purely biographical critic.

Delany on our first meeting in 1965, much to the embarrassment of both men. I am still dead sure that Wilson's way, which would be classified as "uptight" by Delany's admirers, is the better of the two, and likely to last the longer.

I am somewhat more in sympathy with Zelazny's work, mainly because he pays closer attention to the sciences (though intermittently, like Aldiss) and his attitude toward language is not so anarchistic (quite unlike Aldiss, who started as a formalist and is now a terrorist). But both Delany and Zelazny share with each other first of all, and secondarily with all the major New Wave writers except John Brunner, a dangerously ill-considered attitude (it is now very close to being a fad). There is no standard critical term for it, since it appears to be obsessive only in modern science fiction, though it was around before. I have therefore invented my own term: *mytholatry.* It is a term which I may never use again, but just in case I must, I offer an extended definition, with clay feetnote. The definitive example is *Creatures of Light and Darkness,* by Roger Zelazny.

The publication of Joyce's *Ulysses* in 1924 prompted T. S. Eliot to suggest that for the modern novel in general, myth might prove an acceptable replacement for poetic structure or plot. In our field, we saw a lot of use of myth in the *Unknown* era—Pratt/de Camp come to mind at once—but these stories were games. It has remained for the New Wave writers, some 45 years later, to catch up with Eliot's proposal. Lately we have seen Chip Delany (to whom the present novel is dedicated, not, I think, "Just Because") and Michael Moorcock take on the Christ myth; Zelazny in *Lord of Light* adopted Hindu mythology, and Greek in *This Immortal;* and Emil Petaja has been hashing his way through the Finnish *Kalevala* . . . all in dead earnest.

Zelazny's *Creatures of Light and Darkness* tries to turn Egyptian mythology into a serious science-fiction novel. Despite some good passages, I think it is a flat failure.

It is a failure in conception. No excuse at all is offered for its primary assumption that the Egyptian gods were real creatures with real power to control the universe of experience, for the lack of any evidence for this in thousands of years of real Egyptian writings about them, or for their survival as creatures of power into the very far future. The notion is utterly arbitrary; a cute notion is all it is.

It is ignorant and inconsistent. The personifications of the gods in Zelazny's hands are undignified, stupid, uncharacteristic and antihistorical. Creatures from other mythologies (*e.g.*, the Norns, Cerberus, the Minotaur) are shoved in at random, as are several which are apparently Zelazny inventions. One of the inventions is an ineducable immortal called the Steel General with a fix on lost causes, who owns a mechanical horse which dances senselessly up and down and pulverizes the landscape whenever his master gets into a fight.

Stylistically, it is a hash. Some parts are evocative in the authentic and unique Zelazny manner, but he cannot sustain the tone; the gods call each other "Dad," and a speech that starts out with thee's and thou's winds up with "ambulance-chaser;" a 411-word sentence describing a dead city, intended to be hypnotic, is killed before it starts by the arch instruction, "Color it dust." There are moments of authentic comedy, such as the tentative prayers of Madrak ("Thank you, Dad") to Whomever may or may not be listening, but most of the putative humor is at the Batman level and seems just as dated.

Moreover, this is another of those recently multiplying novels of apparatus, told in bits and scraps, zigzagging among viewpoints and tenses, and dropping into quotations or verse for no reason beyond an apparent desire to seem experimental or impressive. The book ends in dramatic form—that is, as a section from a play—with a scene which absolutely demands straightforward, standard narrative and for which the playscript is the worst possible choice.

Beyond these blemishes, there is an important theoretical misconception here. As Darko Suvin has noted, the displacements from the world of experience involved in myth attempt to explain that world in terms of eternal forces which are changeless; the attempt is antithetical to the suppositions of science fiction, which center around the potentialities of continuous change. Once one invokes such great names as Anubis, Osiris and Thoth, one willy-nilly also invokes the whole complex of associations which goes with them, the static assumptions of a fixed cosmos about which everything important is already known. You are writing an allegory whether you want to or not, and if you don't even realize that this is the problem, the end product is bound to ring false.

This is the third time Zelazny has fallen into this trap, and this time around it seems to have put his self-critical sense completely to sleep. One more like this, and the late Leroy Tanner will have justified his existence after all.

There is, however, a way out of the trap, entirely viable for science fiction and mostly lacking—though not entirely devoid of—the dangers of producing what is chiefly a tricksy repainting of a stalled machine. This is the difficult path of creating one's own myth, or showing one in the process of formation. Here no specific historical instance needs to be aped; after all, the general process is shown clearly in Frazer's *The Golden Bough* (Graves' *The White Goddess* had better be avoided unless the writer is knowledgeable enough to use it highly selectively), and it has the advantage of *being* a process, with an open end, rather than a rigidly boxed universe tied with the ribbons of some particular sect.

Aldiss has done this in *Barefoot in the Head,* and the result is so spectacular—and so complex—that it merits close study.

In the *Sunday Times* [London] early in 1970, a very well-known reviewer awarded almost awed praise to a novel which—as his highly detailed plot summary made clear—was only another worn retread of the post-World War III barbarism story. The present text is also set in a post-World War III barbarism, although a mint-original one; and on the immediately preceding Sunday, a *Times* reviewer unknown to me gave it about three paragraphs so uninformative about the book and so abusive in tone as to suggest some sort of personal vendetta.

If jealousy or enmity is not the answer, then what did make the difference? For clearly the Aldiss—to a disinterested eye, however unfriendly—could not possibly be all that bad, and its successor in the same pages merited virtually no attention, let alone praise. One reason might be found in the fact that the blurb on the jacket of *Barefoot* twice mentions science fiction, while the other book was published "straight;" many readers, and almost all publishers, still have compartments in their heads stuffed with broken dolls, like the striking Erró jacket illustration for Aldiss' novel.

But I think the difficulty reaches more deeply than that. Aldiss' war, like that in Franz Werfel's *Star of the Unborn,* was fought with psychedelic agents (now a much more likely proposition than it was in Werfel's day) and in consequence almost everyone in the novel is mad and the language reflects this. They are the "new autorace, born and bred on motorways; on these great one-dimensional roads rolling they mobius-stripped themselves naked to all sensation, beaded, bearded, belted, busted, bepileptic, tearing across the synthetic twen-cen landskip, seaming all the way across Urp, Aish, Chine, leaving them under their reefer-smoke, to the Archangels, godding it across the skidways in creasingack selleration bitch you'm in us all in catagusts of living."

It is not all like this, but there are enough such passages to baffle—and thereby give offense—to the lazy. Clearly the kind of mind that greeted the denser chapters of *Ulysses,* and all of *Finnegans Wake,* with snarls of ignorant scorn is with us yet.

Although *Barefoot* includes one highly explicit bow to *Ulysses* (a hideously effective pun on page 93, "Agenbite of Auschwitz") and resembles it in both structure and narrative (though only in the most fundamental sense in each case), its texture is much more like that of *FW,* even to the echoing of some of *FW's* most easily recognizable mannerisms (puns that cross over word breaks, chains of long words ending in "-ation," catalogue sentences) and its unique grammar (which, to the best of my knowledge, no other imitator has ever even recognized, let alone captured). Like *Ulysses,* it includes many of the popular songs of its time (in this case, of course, the future); like *FW,* it also includes original verse (some of it the "visual chiromancy," or magic-square arrangement of words so that pictures are also formed, which so fascinated the American scholastic realist, Charles Peirce of Milford; some of it concrete poetry, consisting of repeated letters, or sometimes syllables of words, in what are supposed to be significant arrangements—happily, Aldiss' samples make surface sense, which is rare in this kind of thing).

Okay. It has been observed before by friends of the *New Worlds* school—not often by its enemies, who seldom seem to have read anything but old science fiction—that the techniques it has been exploiting are all thirty to fifty years old: dada. surrealism, vorticism, Dos Passos, and now late Joyce.

The only new aspect of all this is the application of these techniques to science fiction. Though I have expressed in print my disturbance that a genre focused on Tomorrow should become so fascinated by the idioms and fads of Yesterday, John Brunner has correctly reminded me that Yesterday is just as much a part of the Past as are such techniques as the sonnet. Under this rubric I have no more right to judge a writer harshly for imitating Dos Passos than I would for his faithfully following Fowler's *English Usage.* What counts is a) How appropriate is the device in the individual example at hand, and b) how well assimilated is it. ditto?

Obviously, the smashed and reassembled fragments of language ("the abnihilization of the etym") Joyce invented to tell a dream are equally appropriate for the conveying of the thoughts of madmen bombed (both literally and in the slang sense) "back into the Stone Age" with shattered memories of their old cultures still sticking to them. I am less sanguine about the problem of assimilation. Certainly Aldiss has come closer to making the language of *FW* his own than has anybody but Anthony Burgess; but unlike Burgess' similar passages, Aldiss' are often more Joyce than they are Aldiss, to no visible purpose. Take, for example, the above-mentioned chains of long words ending in "-ation." In *FW*, these chains invariably announce the pub-keeper hero's twelve customers, who in the dream are also the jurymen who are to pass upon his shadowy crimes, and also Joyce's pompously hostile critics; the device is therefore both funny and functional. I can find no such function for it in *Barefoot,* and though echolalia is indeed one of the symptoms of a toppling mind, the borrowing is what strikes the eye first, sending me, at least, on a vain search for Joyce's twelve Doyles. (Or does Brian mean to suggest that Charteris' disciples are analogous figures? An allusion that subtle would be hard to find outside *FW*, too.)

The question may be a relatively minor one, but it further raises a critical problem which *Barefoot* also shares with *FW*. In the Joyce novel, though it includes chapters told from several different points of view, all these seem to be filtered through the unconscious mind of the dreaming pub-keeper—but there is a fairly substantial section toward the end where he appears to be awake and observed from the outside, though the dream *language* continues. Is it now Joyce's dream? Is it *all* Joyce's dream? Similarly, *Barefoot* shifts viewpoints fairly frequently; but although the language does show that some of the characters are less stoned than others, or stoned in different ways, they all seem to share the same *specific* culture, including details of education. (For the most obvious example, they all have to have read *FW.*) The only way around this is to assume that the language is the author's throughout, and that while the characters are thinking these thoughts and making these speeches, they are not doing so in this way Melville's illiterate sailors spouting high Elizabethan blank verse; Joyce's lower-middle-class barman dreaming in a mixture of thirty languages, including classical Greek and Sanskrit. It's a convention the reader simply must accept for the sake of its poetic effectiveness; should he stop to examine its implications, as though this were a realistic novel, the whole structure will come apart in his hands.

It is somewhat easier to accept the novel's philosophical underpinning. As *FW* leans on Vico and Bruno, so *Barefoot* leans on Ouspenski and Gurdjieff, whom even the walk-ons seem to have read. As mystics go, Ouspenski was a remarkably rational and certainly difficult thinker and it is impossible to imagine a world of acid-heads following him for more than three pages; but his teacher was the more usual kind of nut, a shell of impressive phrases connected any old which way and completely hollow inside, the perfect guru for the world Aldiss describes.

I think I have said enough to show that *Barefoot in the Head* is a long way indeed from being any sort of naturalistic novel, conventional or otherwise. It is a poetic construct, highly artificial, allusive, multi-leveled, symbolic; and built around the skeleton of a convention, the post-Bomb science-fiction novel. *(Gernsbacks Wake?* Oh God.) It is also very difficult to read, unless you actively enjoy an almost continuous stream of puns and portmanteau words; if you do, you will find wit, gusto, and some genuine poetry (I except the imitation pop stuff, whose pretentious emptiness Aldiss has captured all too faithfully) in *Barefoot . . .* and, as an incidental dividend, you will have been nicely trained to take on *FW* itself.

Beneath all the wordplay, and quite frequently on top of it, is a rather simple, straightforward story. Its hero, like the central figures of most recent Aldiss, is a lonely man on a physical odyssey which is also a search for himself, crippled by being ninety percent a product of the madness of his time, and surrounded or assaulted by figures who are totally immersed in and victimised by it. He is a Serb whose *Drang nach Albion* has led him to adopt a literary English name, Cohn Charteris, after Leslie Charteris, author of the Saint; and in the Midlands takes over a messiah racket from a fading guru, killing his manager in a semi-accident and also taking over the manager's wife. He is highly successful at the racket, which doesn't entirely surprise him, for from the beginning of the novel he has felt that he has had a new insight into reality, though it remains uncaptured. He leads a motorcade into Europe which ends in a multi-car smashup which, in turn, is restaged as part of a documentary film being made about him; and in an immense premiere in which the film is *not* shown but Brussels is burned down instead, he becomes briefly convinced of his own divinity; and by the end, having become unconvinced, he is en route to becoming a sort of divinity after all, that is, a myth.

Even after allowing for the fact that this plot summary has left out all but one of the important secondary characters, it is no better an account of the book than would be a summary of *Othello* which told you the play is about a Negro who murdered his white wife because she had lost her handkerchief. The story could have come from any hand; some elements of the treatment are distinctly second-hand; but the whole is unique, moving and almost completely successful.

Be warned, however, that it demands study. Any work of art, of course, requires study for its understanding; but *Barefoot in the Head* belongs to the more specialized category of works which without study are incomprehensible even on the surface. It does begin in a fairly straightforward prose, and leads only gradually into the multi-level language, but the farther reaches are complex indeed. Nevertheless, do persist; the rewards are considerable.

One of them is that this novel, unlike most modern science fiction, can be mined; it is not simply a diagram or a Tale, but a world, with rich veins beneath the surface. Among these is the biological hypothesis that modern man is stuck with equipment (particularly mental equipment) which served well enough in the Neolithic Age but is of increasingly less use as man's world multiplies in complexity. Aldiss never once says this directly, but instead makes it active in the fiction: the characters find themselves trapped in a series of repetitive actual and spiritual experiences, and thanks to the dazzlement created by the language, neither they nor the reader can ever be sure that a given event really is a repetition, or instead a totally new happening being thought about in an inadequate, inappropriate old way.

Here Aldiss departs decisively from Joyce, for in *FW* the Viconian cyclical view of history is intended to be taken as a fact of nature: history does repeat itself, endlessly, in various guises, and therefore it is appropriate to tell the story of one such cycle as if it were all of them happening together. Aldiss, on the other hand, has distorted Ouspenski's mystical experience of "the eternal return" to a completely subjective end; history may not in fact repeat itself, but we are going to go on, suicidally, thinking and behaving as if it did.

Almost every aspect of the book, large and small, reinforces and enriches this view of what H. G. Wells, in his last book, called "mind at the end of its tether." The epigraph from General LeMay, and the title of the novel itself, sound the first warnings. The crux of the novel is Charteris' realisation that he has allowed himself to be kidded into sainthood, and the next step is probably crucifixion. He breaks away from his escalating success to seek a new pattern, but since he's stuck with the old equipment, the best he can do is to stop seeking patterns at all, to retreat into ambiguity. He cannot, of course, have it both ways. In a reflective passage, we are told that Charteris was originally named Dušan (a Serbian emperor who fell while he was on his way to conquer Byzantium). By rejecting him and his name, Charteris has committed the repetitive event of not winning himself glory before the story even begins. Angeline, the only loving character, is what that idiot Dr. Edmund Bergler would have called a psychic masochist: she repeatedly, helplessly falls in love with suicidal false messiahs. By the time Charteris is in love with her, she is out of love (and patience) with him, and he in turn hasn't the equipment to tell her he loves her, he has literally forgotten both the fact itself and how to say it. The repetitive car crash sequences are the product of stone-age brains unable to cope with modern speeds, and in addition are symbolic of the awful speeding up of all events as the book proceeds. The very town of Dover, where an important part of the action takes place, is in living fact just as repetitive an experience as Aldiss paints it as being. People who should be acting remain mired instead in nostalgia (*e.g.,* for Glenn Miller, a childhood memory for some of the characters, a pseudo-memory for the others) or Wordsworthian nature mysticism. Even the imagery is repetitive.

Some of this technique was foreshadowed in *Report on Probability A,* but *Barefoot* is not an anti-novel; it is evolutionary. Although the hippies who are its people (none of them hippies by their own choice, but the parallels are clear) are incapable of building any new order, the artist can; that is, he can take a situation which is inexorably emptying itself of all meaning, and by re-ordering it, create a structure which in itself has meaning. That is what Aldiss has done.

I should note, finally, that some of these insights came to me from the author directly, not filtered through the book. Ordinarily I would regard this as cheating—after all, how many potential readers could have such an advantage? —but here it is primarily another measure of the novel's complexity. I have been reading the book for less than a year; all these levels of meaning and technique are indubitably there, but I cannot even begin to guess how long it would have taken me to see them all, by myself. I have been reading *FW* since 1939, as well as the immense critical apparatus that continues to build around it, and may now understand perhaps ten percent of it; *Barefoot* is not so formidable, but were it not at least comparable, I shouldn't have raised the issue at all.

It should now be easy to see—at least as easy as it was to predict—that the New Wave has from the beginning been in the process of pulling itself apart. Each of these writers and editors is going in a different and unique direction. One important figure whom I have not discussed, Thomas M. Disch, appears to be headed out of science fiction altogether, insofar as one can judge by his published remarks about "children's literature" and "greener pastures," and the fact that he withdrew his novel *Camp Concentration* from the 1969 Nebula competition. Aldiss is now in an ideal position to do this, too, for he has just published a mainstream novel *The Hand-Reared Boy)* which was an instant best-seller in Britain, and it is announced as the first volume of a tetralogy; however, at the Birmingham conference referred to at the beginning of this chapter, he reported that he has another science-fiction novel cooking. At the 1969 convention of the British Science Fiction Association at Oxford, Miss Merril announced formally that she was leaving science fiction; but I am inclined to suspect that she did so in about the same spirit that Richard Nixon left politics after his California defeat—and Mr. Nixon had his law practice to fall back upon while he was catching his breath, while science fiction is the only subject Miss Merril knows anything at all about.

That this disintegrative process has reached an advanced stage was visible at the 1970 BSFA Convention, where it was noisily evident that there was nothing formally left of any New Wave group but a dying magazine and a tiny group of drunks and hangers-on, bent chiefly on calling attention to themselves by disrupting the proceedings. It may also be seen in the 1970 Nebula voting, for while both Ellison and Delany won prizes, Norman Spinrad's novel *Bug Jack Barron,* which was aggressively and second-handedly trendy in all the ways that *New Worlds* (where it first appeared) holds dear, did not.

The major figures of the New Wave have quite outgrown the need for such a group, if indeed they ever did need it for moral support or anything else; writers of substance learn early that they have to be their own moral support. Nevertheless, it was a lively old thing while it lasted, filling the local air with shrieks, boasts, counter-crusades, slander, flying glassware, wet firecrackers, propaganda, dead horses, sitting ducks, non-issues, straw men, tin gods, and millions of words of unreadable prose. It also fertilized the production of a surprisingly large number of works of genuine merit, plus a lot of experimentation which even at its worst jarred many people into rethinking their critical stances.

Willy-nilly, we have had a revolution, and it cannot be undone. In retrospect, I can even manage to be grateful for it—a critical stance which might be defined as crockery recollected in tranquility.

Two Poems

Scenario:
The Edefice

    No doubt it is a prison. At its base
(we see depicted here in coloured clays)
stands the hill called Chokotien, whose caves,
a litter of *coups de poing*, seeds, and crude quartz flakes,
are like the scooped-out skulls of men whose brains
were eaten. Outside is the grinding, groaning ice,
and at the door burns the Red Flower.
                              Abris
ring it, before which hides are strung from posts
to serve as windbreaks; also piled stone walls.
    On its sides, earthworks, ringing a fortress
and labyrinth, threaded by a monster
horned like a bull. This is the bellowing cellar
    of a temple (as may be seen carved on this frieze)
from which go forth at noon grim-robed men
to strike off the heads of the tallest stalks of grain.
    Its upper reaches, though served by good roads
(the poet says) and aqueducts, are quite obscured
by clinging tenements, in which deposed
kings (here are statues of them, although much
defaced) and freed slaves starve, six to a room.
This part is blackened by fire,
                              and topped
by many layers of chantries (shown in the tapestry)
humming with Glorias to the flatness of the earth.
    Robed scholars (see the borders of the manuscript)
sit on their shoulders, each in his static cell

(the woodcut, which has been somewhat dubiously attributed
to a fifteen-year-old boy, shows that their belfries
were latterly much distracted by witches) attempting
to prove by logic the existence of God, but women
are forbidden to learn the language.
                    And there is
no doubt that the palace above this is glorious (see
the rendering by Ucello, the largest oil cartoon in the world);
though the tiles are slimy with blood, and the galleries
reek of gunpowder, they know there the world is round.
        But silence now, O Muse, for just above
A shepherdess reclines, and dreams of Love.
Oblivious of th'Eternetie on which she stands,
Box'd like a Universe within her silken Bands,
the fair *Phyllida* rises from the Wrack,
And locks of hair distributes to the treacherous Pack,
(Immortalized, it may be for a Week,
by some dumb Poet and his hunchback'd Book).
        O larks! and now, from the sweet sleep of Earth, arise
on plumes of steam, and borne by slapping belts
(though these are not well shown in the daguerrotypes)
soot-smeared glassy palaces with plush-lined drawing rooms
haunted by phthisic ladies, foot by well-turned foot,
pure as the Innsbruck snow, and longing passionately
only to vote. They have good servants.
        The story next, a noisy one, is much bedaubed
with mud and poppies, in which the barbed wire's embedded
(the photographs are all too clear for comfort; turn
the page) and fragile triple-winged beetles snarl about it.
        And at the very top (these X-ray plates are hard to read)
intolerable light.
                    Yes, no doubt it is a prison,
but from here on up, one cannot see the walls;
they may be stars. (May we have the next slide, please?)
Ah.
        Embedded in this hand-axe is a tiny shell.
It is perhaps a hundred million years old.

Two Brands for the Burning

To be kind is a movement of thought, not a coin to buy kindness.
The kind are kind, the cruel cruel because it gives them pleasure;
The thoughtless tap at the tree and let the heart rot,
Not because they know pain, though they do, and would give or take it away.

But if the brook winds wastefully down to the river and is not eternal,
The great heat-clock, half unwound already, cools in the dark,
Little by little, like music, each thing that we have goes out from us:
To be brave, to be kind, to be heard; to be silent; to be what we are.

Acknowledgments

This book, like all NESFA Press books, was created with the help of many volunteers. Laurie Mann, Sarah Prince, and Rick Katze scanned many of the stories. Mary Tabasko, Mark Olson, Leslie Mann, Dave Grubbs, Chip Hitchcock, Laurie Mann, Joe Ross, and Sharon Sbarsky helped with proofing. Kevin Riley did another marvelous job in designing and laying out the dust jacket. And Mark Olson and Dave Grubbs provided advice and guidance in a number of areas. Thanks to you all.

                                                        Jim Mann
                                                        Editor

This book was set in Adobe Garamond using Adobe InDesign CS2 on a Dell XPS running Windows Vista. The dust jacket was created on a Macintosh Powerbook G4 using Adobe Photoshop CS3 and InDesign CS3.

The New England Science Fiction Association (NESFA) and NESFA Press

Other Books from NESFA Press:

A New Dawn: The Don A. Stuart Stories of John W. Campbell, Jr. $26
Immodest Proposals:
   the Complete Science Fiction of William Tenn, Vol. 1 .... $29
The Mathematics of Magic
   by L. Sprague de Camp and Fletcher Pratt $26
From These Ashes: The Complete Short SF of Fredric Brown $29
Ingathering: the Complete People Stories by Zenna Henderson $25
Norstrilia by Cordwainer Smith $22
The Rediscovery of Man:
   The Complete Short Science Fiction of Cordwainer Smith $25
Transfinite: The Essential A. E. van Vogt $29

Details on these and many more books are online at: www.nesfa.org/press. Books may be ordered online or by writing to:

NESFA Press
PO Box 809
Framingham, MA 01701

We accept checks (in US$), Visa, or MasterCard. Add $5 postage and handling for one book, $10 for two or more. ($6/$12 for locations outside the U.S.) Please allow 3–4 weeks for delivery. (Overseas, allow 2 months or more.)

NESFA

NESFA is an all-volunteer, non-profit organization of science fiction and fantasy fans. Besides publishing, our activities include running Boskone (New England's oldest SF convention) in February each year, producing a semi-monthly newsletter, holding discussion groups on topics related to the field, and hosting a variety of social events. If you are interested in learning more about us, we'd like to hear from you. We can be contacted at info@nesfa.org or at the address above. Visit our web site at www.nesfa.org.